Kingdoms & Empires

Dark Rage

D.J. DARCEY

Copyright © 2023 by D.J. Darcey

ISBN: 978-1-77883-177-5 (Paperback)

All rights reserved. No part of this publication may be reproduced, distributed, or transmitted in any form or by any means, including photocopying, recording, or other electronic or mechanical methods, without the prior written permission of the publisher, except in the case brief quotations embodied in critical reviews and other noncommercial uses permitted by copyright law.

The views expressed in this book are solely those of the author and do not necessarily reflect the views of the publisher, and the publisher hereby disclaims any responsibility for them. Some names and identifying details in this book have been changed to protect the privacy of individuals.

BookSide Press
877-741-8091
www.booksidepress.com
orders@booksidepress.com

Contents

Part 1—The Phoenix and the Dragon

Chapter 1: Enter Queen Laxur 9
Chapter 2: An Odd Treasure 21
Chapter 3: The After Effects 38
Chapter 4: Princess Training 56
Chapter 5: Dreadnought 69
Chapter 6: Darkcon Research 79
Chapter 7: Asora's Science Fair 91
Chapter 8: The Fires of Terror 104
Chapter 9: The Renegade 116
Chapter 10: The Scullery Maid 127
Chapter 11: Diplomacy 150
Chapter 12: In Queen Laxur's Court 171
Chapter 13: The World of the Humans 184
Chapter 14: Havaina's Underworld 195
Chapter 15: Bars and Brawls 206
Chapter 16: Madimoy's Vacation 222
Chapter 17: Jeia's New Plant 243
Chapter 18: T'a's Lesson 257
Chapter 19: A Secret Meeting 270
Chapter 20: Combat Training 282
Chapter 21: Wrath of the Dark Queen 295
Chapter 22: The Legend of Rowaton 306
Chapter 23: Into the Mountains 317
Chapter 24: The Princess's Quest 330

Chapter 25: Attack on the Palace 342
Chapter 26: The Temple Mount 353
Chapter 27: The Rule of the Dark Queen 363
Chapter 28: Asora, the Dragon Dancer 376
Chapter 29: Rebuild 388
Chapter 30: The True Plot 399

Part 2—The Swaye Family

Chapter 31: Laxur's Costume Party 413
Chapter 32: Asora's Holiday Mystery 430
Chapter 33: The House of Countess Marien 449
Chapter 34: Shadows of the Vanguard 461
Chapter 35: Father Dear 472
Chapter 36: The Wrath of Laxur 485
Chapter 37: Inside Asora's Storybook—Ela 496
Chapter 38: Inside Asora's Storybook—A Pirates Life 506
Chapter 39: Inside Asora's Storybook—The Games Afoot 517
Chapter 40: A Glimpse of the Future 528
Chapter 41: The Coins of Power 539
Chapter 42: For Laxur's Heart 552
Chapter 43: The Wraith 563
Chapter 44: Other Voices 577
Chapter 45: Clash of the War Machines 590
Chapter 46: In Her Torment 601

Part 3—The Dark Goddess

Chapter 47: The Legend of Z'yon and Tera 613
Chapter 48: The Chase 624
Chapter 49 : The Challenges 634
Chapter 50: Rise of the Malicious Goddess 644
Chapter 51: The Other Laxur's 665
Chapter 52: Revenge of the Empire 679
Chapter 53: The Shadows of Tera 704
Chapter 54: The Vault 717

Chapter 55: The Historian 727
Chapter 56: Asora's Nuclear Firestorm 741
Chapter 57: The Second Battle of Z'yon 752
Chapter 58: Escape from Z'yon 762
Chapter 59: The Price of Vengeance 773
Chapter 60: Before the Storm 786

Appendix
Factions

Part One

The Phoenix and the Dragon

Chapter One

Enter Queen Laxur

The void was tranquil and calm. Hiding the approaching storm. In a planetary system in which the clam void enveloped was at a crossroads between two great powers that ruled the realm of the known universe. This place was between the Utopian Kingdom and the Darkcon Empire. This place had seen many battles across the millions of years of known history.

The star at the center was an average sized yellow main sequence star nearing the later stages of its stable life. In its orbit were seven worlds. Two gas giants, an ice giant, and four rocky worlds. Only one had life on its surface naturally.

The peaceful world of Carlon was a planet not of great oceans but of massive lakes surrounded by green, then shifting to the browns and beiges of desert. It was a human world with a colony of elves. Peace was only recently seen between the two species on Carlon's surface.

It was dusk at the largest settlement. The planet quite suddenly, became surrounded by an armada of ships floating above. The skies and inner orbit were being filled with uncountable numbers of ships. They all carried the seal of the Darkcon Imperial Navy. A black anchor with chains with crossed harpoons with stars surrounding them. The stars showed that they were space worthy as well.

The symbol of the Darkcon Empire was one of three swords, and a spear in between each one. Below this formation of weapons was a crown that represented the monarch in power. Above all this were several four-pointed stars. Each representing the various great lords and houses of the empire.

The Darkcon's ships were vessels of wood and steel, surrounded by enchanted bubbles for space travel, were high above the planet. These bubbles had in a breathable atmosphere and gravity to keep the crews alive and able to work.

They had just come from the magical gates, or divine paths, as they are known. These paths linked the worlds of the known universe together. The realm as it is also called depended on these gates. They required very skilled and powerful navigator witches and warlocks to make use of them.

The first thousand ships were made exclusively of a wood and crystal-like substance. They were ships with masts and sails that sprouted from the hulls. The second fleet of ships was forged from iron and steel, and they left a trail of black dust in their wake, billowing from their funnels. They used fire and pressure to force themselves forward like rockets.

The last few ships were of all manner of materials. These were not just sailing vessels; they were flying machines and enchanted boats. They were meant to fly in the skies of enemy worlds, terrorizing the inhabitants with a rain of fire, cannons, and bullets.

The largest of the ships was the flagship and the one carrying the Darkcon queen herself. The IDS Searasen was shaped like a large think disk with spikes and sails as well as towers and doors. It also had a massive observation deck from where the queen could watch the attack from a very safe distance. But the queen was not content on staying up in orbit.

The immediate order, when they were all surrounding Carlon, was to go forward and secure the planet. It was issued by the dark Queen, Laxur, who was already on the planet.

On the surface of Carlon upon a mountain side overlooking the biggest city. The Darkcon soldiers were amassing. They came down and out of their ships, or they came through portals. With her personal

Enter Queen Laxur

guard of werewolves and other creatures, headed by another wolf, General Obsidian. In pale human form, he was two and half meters tall with tufts of gray fur and deep black eyes.

Laxur's personal bodyguard was a fallen angel by the name of Dari. She was immense at three meters, golden skinned, and large powerful muscular form with short white hair and green eyes.

The two of them were dressed in the Darkcon uniform of a double-breasted black leather jacket with black pants and boots. Underneath the jackets was a thin layer of steel to protect the wearer. Dari had a large sword in its sheath on her hip. Obsidian preferred to use his claws and had armored and bladed gauntlets on his arms.

A new portal appeared in front of the Darkcon forces. It was in between Obsidian and Dari. It formed into the figure of a very beautiful and young woman. Once it vanished the queen herself was fully present. Everyone around her stood at attention and all went silent.

The Darkcon Queen was dressed in the same uniform but had a cape and a large circlet of gold with black diamonds. She looked down and around at the landscape with her glittering eyes. She was terrifyingly gorgeous with her hourglass figure inherited from her human mother, along with her full lips and emerald-green eyes. Her thick blue-black hair, height of more than two meters, and wings that tucked, unseen, into her body came from her angelic father. She was called a dark siren because she could lure any male to do her bidding. There were a great many that fought for her favor at court. She was a terrifying enemy with her beauty, deadly purpose, and magical powers.

Laxur's generals arrived minutes before the fleet, using the queen's ability to create a portal. The supreme war master, General Sysu, a female vampire with long black hair streaked with white and braided out of the way of her face. She walked over the world, seeing the planet with cold pale-blue eyes. She was speaking to the other generals to coordinate the attack. She spoke in a harsh voice as she walked slightly behind her queen. She was ancient yet looked like she was a young woman. She was arrogant with most beings except with her queen, whom she cared for since Laxur came to the Darkcon worlds at a young age. Sysu raised her to be the mighty woman she had become. The general was known for her bravery on the battlefield and her odd sense of humor.

A nondescript ten-story building enthralled the bold human-angel beauty that was the queen. It was located outside of the main town. This world was good to have, being on the border between her Darkcon Empire and the Grand Utopian Kingdom, but what was in the building was the true prize. Or many prizes as the queen wished to have.

It was the site of a weapons manufacturing plant with an emphasis on laser weaponry. It was also scientific research laboratory as well. Unlike the village around it, this building stood out. The village was mostly a collection of medieval like buildings, but the main structure looked more like a large and futuristic aircraft hangar. Better built and able to withstand most conventional attacks. But the queen was not one to give up based on looks. She honestly loved a challenge.

The building was mainly of human design. What was made within its structure was far superior to what she had. It was the work of the humans and not the Grand Utopian Kingdom's other beings. The human that owned it hoped to sell the technology to the Utopians to bring them into the modern world. *Ha! Like that would happen, not with that backward kingdom.* The Queen had a twisted smile of derision. She knew that her foe, the Utopian Kingdom was set in its ways. Technology was something they saw as a waste. But it was the future.

The humans were a very dangerous problem for the empire; alone, they could devastate her nation with great ease. A first strike offense could provoke the humans to counterattack. What she knew was that human, being part of the Utopian Kingdom, might be prevented from striking back by the royal court. The elves, dwarves, or centaurs were not up for a fight; they would restrain the humans, at least long enough for her people to develop the weaponry. And deploy these new inventions thus giving Laxur the edge in war she needed.

Laxur moved forward with Sysu and her personal brigade of soldiers, which was filled with all the races of the Darkcon realm demons: trolls,

Enter Queen Laxur

fallen angels, werewolves, corrupt humans, goblins, pixies, sirens, succubuses, incubuses, dark elves, and vampires—Sysu's 'family.' They were a vicious bunch and had absolute loyalty to her, soldiers who were the best of the best.

Laxur was surprised to see that the royal honor guard of the kingdom had surrounded the facility. They were also milling about in the village. That meant one thing: Princess Asora, the reigning monarch of the Utopians, was inside. *Well, well, well. That is interesting.* She then noticed that only a few royal guardsmen could be seen. The rest were preparing a defense. It was time to test her troops.

"Take that building! But I want prisoners taken! No one dead. Do you understand me?" Laxur glared at the troops.

Together they called back, "We understand, Your Majesty."

"Good! Now move!" Laxur roared.

No one dared to go against her. Everyone wanted to keep their heads. Sysu raised her black-leathered fist and sent them forward. The vast numbers of Darkcon's surged past their leaders. Like an avalanche coming down a mountain, the Darkcon warriors ran down the cliffs and begun their raid.

The guards fought the soldiers, but they were outnumbered. The Darkcons had superior weapons, such as guns; the Utopians fought with only swords, arrows, and lances. It was a disaster for the Utopians.

Queen Laxur, Dame Dari, General's Obsidian and Sysu watched their forces attack. Laxur took a dark joy in watching the Utopians cry in terror as the Darkens unleashed themselves upon them. She smiled when she heard the clashing between her troops and the royal guard.

Obsidian then charged down he mountain in his wolf form. Sysu transformed into a large black bat and flew down.

"Come Dari, let us introduce ourselves," Laxur said to her taller guardian.

Dari smiled down at the queen. Queen Laxur unfurled her large black feathery wings. Both she and Dari jumped into the air and glided down.

In the town square Laxur landed by herself and looked around to see the town in ruins. She sent Dari to scout the main building. Fires, dirt, debris, and trash were all over the place. People were running from the flames or from Laxur's soldiers. She saw dead royal guardsmen, that was fine to her. Soldiers only fought and died as she was told to expect. She did not want large scale casualties, but that did not apply to the guardsmen as she wanted them dead.

A few of her troops saw her and came up to her to listen to her. They looked up at the queen at attention. Laxur commanded their respect, and she was like a hero to them. They loved and respected her. And she showed it to them too.

Laxur turned to her guards, "Search the wreckage for survivors. They will be useful." Then she added. "You do not need to show the same kindness to the guardsmen."

Her troops did as they were told. They fanned out into the various roads, back roads, and into buildings. Laxur stood alone in the center of the town. It felt exhilarating to be here now. She was now the conqueror, the one who will be their ruin. Just as they tried to ruin her. But this was merely the beginning. She did need to test them first, like any wise leader should.

As Queen Laxur walked around the burning wreckage of a building. She heard the crying of a small child. That drew her attention. She used her magic to lift a large pillar and there was a small boy who looked to have a broken leg. Laxur's rage and anger melted as she saw this innocent human/elf boy crying.

Laxur kneeled to him and was gentle. "Do not fear me. I can help you."

"Who are you?" The boy struggled to say in between sobs.

"I am Queen Laxur. And I want to help you." Laxur said. "What is your name?"

"Vam," the boy said weakly.

She used a spell to take away the pain. She then closed the wound and mended the bone. "Feel better?" The boy nodded. "Do you have parents?"

"No one here had parents," the boy said.

"That confused Laxur at first. Then she spotted the remains of a sign that said that this building was once and orphanage.

"Oh, I see," Laxur said. "Would you like to come with me? My people can take better care of you." Laxur then hugged the boy. The boy nodded. Laxur then snapped her fingers. A male siren with legs and plated skin came up to her. He bowed to the queen. "Take young Vam here to my flagship and see to his needs."

"Yes, your majesty," the man said.

Queen Laxur gently gave Vam to the soldier, and he ran back to the landing ships. Laxur did not want any child hurt. She loved children and wanted to care for them. They were innocent of any crime that the adults around them commit. And orphans held Laxur sorrow.

The queen then got up and walked out of the crumbling building. Several other troops gathered to see if she needed help. "Search this building for any other survivors. Only render aid to children. Leave the guards to rot."

The Darkcons did as Laxur commanded. Nearly a hundred small Darkcon soldiers began to dig. Laxur felt that her troops could care for the rest. So, she walked off to explore the battlefield.

An arrow flew past her face and disappeared into the fires and smoke. Laxur turned around to see a Utopian Guardsmen in thin silver armor. He was an elf and looked young, possibly a young adult. And a recruit. He looked so nervous that his bow was shaking.

"So very close, boy. But You cannot hurt me," Laxur smirked.

"I had it at our head you foul witch!" the guardsman said.

"Oh," Laxur mocked. "I have a fun little hex upon myself that prevents anything magical from hurting me. So, you may have been on target, but you will never be able to land a blow on me with that." Laxur pointed at the guardsman's bow and arrows.

The guardsman dropped his bow and unsheathed his sword. "We shall see about that."

Laxur cocked an eyebrow and was still smirking and chuckling. She was amused by this young man's boldness. But he was still a stupid teenage boy as far as Laxur was concerned. The guardsman charged at Laxur, but she merely stepped to the side and let him fall forward. He stopped and turned around and growled in anger. He swung his sword as hard as he could in Laxur's general direction. Again, Laxur just side stepped, bent, and dodged the attacks.

"This is getting very boring," Laxur teased.

"Hold still and I will fix that," the guardsman said.

"As you wish," Laxur said. The queen stood her ground and let the blade come at her. Once the sword hit Laxur's uniform the blade dissolved. "I guess memory retention and basic intelligence is not in the Utopian Royal Guardsmen job description?" Laxur grabbed the guardsman by his arm.

She then pulled him forward and flipped him over her head and slammed him on the ground flat on his back. The guardsman puked up blood and was in terrible pain and could barely move. Laxur put her foot on his chest and leaned in putting much of her weight on that leg. Laxur did not look heavy, but she was very heavy at least to the guardsman anyway. The pressure from Laxur made it hard to breath.

"Count our blessings that I will allow you to live this day," Laxur said. "Your kind deserve to be where you are now. At the bottom of my boot."

The guardsman had another sword, but Laxur grabbed it from him and snapped the steel blade in two like a twig. She then drooped both sword parts on the ground. Her strength was also great enough to bend the guardsmen's armor. She could break it and rip it like paper.

"You were quite amusing and brave to stand up to me. But there is a fine line between bravery and out right stupidity. Remember that the next time you try to fight a superior power," Laxur said.

She removed her foot from his chest. When the guardsman tried to breathe easier, he was kicked on the side of his head by the queen. He fell unconscious as Laxur walked away.

"Have fun?" Obsidian asked.

The werewolf came up next to the queen. He was in his wolf form. Also, several other wolves and man-wolves gathered around them.

"Indeed I did. Just too bad he did not last all that long," Laxur said.

"You expected that puny little boy to stand up to you?" Obsidian asked amused.

"I suppose not. But it was a good teaching moment, and I got a small workout too," Laxur laughed. The man-wolves also laughed. Laxur was their alpha and acted like one. "Where are the other Utopians?"

"Many are scattered across town," Obsidian said. "We have managed to flush out most of them."

Several long arrows then landed and planted themselves in front of the queen and her man-wolf guards. Obsidian growled in anger.

"Get too cover!" Obsidian ordered.

All except Laxur got to cover as more long arrows came down. The arrows dissolved into water and dust as they came near the queen. Laxur waved her hand. A spell that both she and the werewolves could see where they were coming from.

Sysu reformed from her giant black bat form to her humanoid form. She was in front of a wood shop. Hundreds of black cats, and bats assembled around her. Sysu could hear that several people inside. Guardsmen in heavy armor in fact.

Then came the explosion. Sysu ducked out of the way. She saw that they had launched a cannon ball at her and her 'family.'

"They have a cannon in there!" A small male cat said.

"Yeah, I noticed," Sysu said. "Take who ever you need and get into the building by the smallest ways."

The cat ran off with several others following him. Sysu got back up to make sure that they kept their attention on her.

"Hey, utopian pigs!" Sysu yelled. "You missed!"

"Let's change that," someone inside yelled.

Another blast came from inside. Sysu again was able to dodge it, but just barely. She felt the heat and powerful wind rush by her. It was enough to throw her to her back.

"Bastards," Sysu said.

Then she heard the guardsmen scream in panic as they were being attacked by wild black cats, bats, and other terrified animals inside. Sysu smiled wickedly as she looked in to see the smoke coming out. Then the animals came running out. The male cat that Sysu spoke to before came up to her.

"Three, two, one," he counted down.

Then the whole shop exploded. Sysu used her cape as a shield to protect herself from the blast and debris. Once everything calmed down the male cat was laughing.

"Like badgers to an annoying porcupine!" The cat was rolling on the ground laughing.

"Nice job," Sysu said. She looked at the nearby large human building. "Now we get to that."

Dame Dari was soaring above an inn near the facility. She was struck by a bullet from a more powerful human weapon. Dari was hit in her left shoulder. The large woman then landed next to several Darkcon troops that were wandering the streets looking for a fight.

"Dame Dari? Are you hurt?" a small gremlin in armor asked.

"Yeah, give me a moment," Dari said as she ripped the bullet out of her shoulder. "We have human snipers up there."

Dari pointed to a security tower that guarded the property of the building. The human facility had a large security zone that was fenced off and had guard towers everyone hundred meters. As far as Dari could tell there were three in the tower that was closest to her. The other towers started to use machine guns on the Darkcon invaders.

"We need to take this tower down," Dari said. "This is the best spot to enter."

Dari then jumped into the air and up to the top of the tower and landed on the only machine gun the tower had. Her landing destroyed it and sent the three guards back.

"Howdy boys and girls," Dari said evilly. "I did not appreciate you shooting me."

"Well, what did you except you oversized gorilla?" The woman guard with her sniper snapped. "You are attacking us!"

"It is still rude," Dari said as she grabbed the woman guard.

She also yanked the sniper rifle from her grasp and crushed it. One of the male guards was able to stab Dari in her thigh. It was enough for Dari to throw the female guard down as she screamed in pain. In a fit of rage and pain Dari punched the man with the knife so hard that his head was torn from his neck. Dari then ripped the knife from her thigh and planted it in the other guard's chest as he was calling for help. The female guard then tried to knock Dari down with the only weapon she had left, a shock baton. Walking Dari as hard as she could but the giant fallen angel was able to grab the baton and break it and she punched the female guard off the side of the tower, and she fell to her death.

Dari used her magic to heal herself and she landed back on the ground. More Darkcon troops gathered near her. Dari then braced herself against the tower. She used her unnatural strength to topple the tower. As it fell it took out power and communications with the other towers. It was even able to take down the two other flanking towers that were a hundred meters away.

Queen Laxur then came up next to Dari.

"Nice work," Laxur commented.

"Thank you, your majesty," Dari said.

"The way is clear!" Laxur said. "Into the security zone!"

The Darkcons cheered as they charged past the facility defenses. The main doors to the facility were barricaded and locked down hard. Laxur, and Dari were in front of the main entrance. It said, "Fusion Corp Carlos Research and Development Building."

Next Sysu and Obsidian came up to the two black winged angels. Obsidian sent his forces to roam the building but to also keep the remains of the Royal Guard outside of the security zone. Sysu had her forces explore the building's outer structure for any way in.

"I do not suppose that you could make us a door?" Sysu asked Dari.

"I am strong but not that strong," Dari pointed out. "This building is a combination of three-meter-thick cement, carbon steel, and only the architect knows what else."

"Then it is the front door then," Obsidian said as he looked at it. "It is mostly glass and thin aluminum."

"You are forgetting the blast shield," Laxur pointed at the think metal plates that were behind the glass. "Got to get past those first."

A combination of long arrows and sniper rounds impacted the ground in front of Queen Laxur. This caused her to take a few steps back. Dari looked up and saw that a balcony had popped out of the building's fifth level. It had several people in it, and they were able to shoot through machicolations like holes built into the concrete balcony.

"Dari, take them out!" Laxur commanded.

Dari got up close to the walls of the building. She then jumped into the air and flew up and nearly broke the sound barrier the second her feet left the ground. This speed allowed her to burst through the concrete and destroy the balcony. This sent debris and the seven people on the balcony crashing down.

Laxur then fired bolts of powerful magical lightening at the massive whole Dari just made and this cause a massive crack to form. The crack grew into a massive hole at the ground level. Laxur was then able to blast the massive metal plates away. The glass was shattered, and everything fell into place.

"Their outer defenses are broken! Storm them!" Laxur roared.

The Darkcon's cheered as they ran past their queen. Laxur then followed her forces inside with her privy council of Dari, Sysu, and Obsidian following close behind her.

Chapter Two

An Odd Treasure

The vampire leader Sysu advised her generals that she was going inside the targeted building to secure it for her monarch. She warned them that they were only too subdue the inhabitants and that killing should be held to a minimum. This planet was to be made part of the empire, and you could not tax inhabitants or get them to work for you if they were dead.

The tall queen walked over the bodies of elves, dwarves, centaurs, and a few humans as she approached the coveted building. She waited for the general to take the building from the inside. It took some time, and she could hear screams and pistols.

"Damn it, Sysu! I told her that I wanted prisoners." She marched forward, and instantly Dari, the proto-typically tall and muscular angel, along with Obsidian, the werewolf with a pack at his heels, surrounded the queen to protect her.

"It could not be helped your majesty," Sysu said. "Humans are as stubborn as dwarves."

"There are still a lot of people still alive," Obsidian said.

"That is not the point!" Laxur snapped. "I need experts and to show that they are better off under the Darkcon flag."

Sysu jumped behind the secretary's desk and tossed a body off its chair. Then she saw something that she really hated. It was a computer. More specifically a computer monitor. Sysu like most Darkcons did not like computers.

"Well?" Laxur asked. "Where is the main lab?"

Sysu grunted as she tried to figure out how to make the computer show her what she wanted. The monitor kept telling Sysu to enter passwords or Access Denied. The vampire was about to smash the monitor when Laxur rolled her eyes and then stepped behind the desk and gently pushed Sysu aside. Queen Laxur then typed in a series of commands into the keyboard. The monitor showed access granted to the queen.

"Okay, when we get back, I am going to hold lessons of how to use computers," Laxur said. She had the computer bring up a map of the facility. "There it is."

"You got it to show you to the main labs?" Obsidian asked.

"Yes, it is down that hallway," Laxur pointed down a very large and machine-like passageway that had dozens of smaller doors along the sides, but one massive steel door at the far end. "Cover the doors and break into them. They are all single rooms. According to the floor plan here. But my prizes are behind that big one at the end."

Dari snapped her fingers and dozens of Darkcon soldiers ran to the smaller doors. Obsidian then barked to get his pack's attention. He then took off towards the main large steel blast doors.

Queen Laxur looked at Sysu and saw that she was about ready to rip apart the computer monitor. Laxur really did not understand her people's frustration with computers. They embraced all the other things that she gave them. It was computers that seemed to be where they drew the line.

"Sysu, leave the computer alone. I will take it. You get your family to break down the door," Laxur commanded.

"Yes, your majesty," Sysu bowed then morphed into a bat and flew off screeching.

Laxur had the computers powered down and had the machines dismantle themselves using her magic. Several Darkcon soldiers brought in large boxes and crates. The computers and data files as well as documents danced their way into these crates and boxes. The queen ordered that those be taken to the ships and taken back to Dorien for processing.

They did as Laxur commanded. Queen Laxur was pondering if she needed to slow down her advancements of her people to allow them to catch up. But if her true plans are to come to fruiting, she needed them to keep up.

She heard that the rooms that lined the sides of the hall were mostly empty. Some had useful items that she would need some time to look at later. But from what Laxur was able to understand from the floor plan, many of these were storage bays for failed projects or display items. They could be useful later.

Queen Laxur made her way down the hall where Dari and her dames were trying to bash down the door. Only that this door was far more durable than the outer defense doors.

"What kind of steel did these humans make this out of?" One of the soldiers asked.

"It looks like a combination of materials," Obsidian said. "Humans say that there are almost five hundred different kinds of steel."

"Why can they not use the same steel as everyone else?" Sysu complained.

"Because we can break it," Laxur pointed out. "That looks like carbon steel with some tungsten in there."

"So how do we break it?" Dari asked.

Queen Laxur thought for a moment. "This is a place of science. So, we use a method of science here."

"In what science can we use to break carbon steel?" Dari asked.

"Plasma," Laxur answered.

"Fire?" Obsidian asked. "Steel is known for being able to handle fire."

"Plasma is not ordinary fire, my dear general. A few million degrees will melt any metal," Laxur pointed out. "That should work here."

"Can you do that?" Sysu asked.

"My flames can be as hot as I desire," Laxur said smugly.

"I have never seen you make a flame that is millions of degrees.

That is star level heat," Obsidian pointed out.

"Well," Laxur started. "Time to test my fire."

A small circle hidden under the queen's coat glowed red then blue. Laxur breathed heavily as if she was trying to lift something heavy. She held both her hands out and each handheld a flame. In her right hand a red flame formed. In her left hand a blue flame formed. Everyone could feel the increasing heat coming from Laxur's hands. She then brought her hands together and a powerful and very hot flame shot from Laxur's, and the plasma flame started to melt the door. It took almost a minute before the door dissolved. Laxur stopped the flame the moment there was a hole large enough for her and her troops to pour in.

The room beyond the door was a vast cavern like room that stretched far. The platform that the Darkcons came into was nearly ten stories above the ground of this vast room, and there were an additional twenty stories of vast room above them. On the ground level was a vast maze-like complex of desks, workshops, robot welders, container, and hundreds of other industrial and scientific equipment. Along the walls were another series of rooms that appeared to be offices. From the tall ceilings there were robotic cranes, and lifts.

Queen Laxur looked down towards the center where there was movement. There was then a tall column of light, an angelic magical protective barrier. What the queen saw as she arrived deep inside the building were the employees; the rest of the royal honor guards stood before the dark-haired Princess Asora, who was fluttering high above them using her angelic wings of virginal white, which matched her long, flowing gown. The young human- angel woman had cast the enchanted shield to protect them.

Queen Laxur flew down to the bottom level. She came just outside of the column of light. It was powerful to be sure, but Laxur was more then capable of getting through it. But she wanted to toy with the princess. This also would double as a distraction as the Darkcons raided the offices.

Laxur smiled up at her. "Asora. So good to see you. It has been ages. How is Mother?"

The princess looked down at her foe, and keeping the shield up, she shouted back, "Laxur! What in the name of the Maker do you think you are doing? This world is under the protection of the Grand Utopian Kingdom!"

Near the shield, a dark-skinned man of middle years with a scar reaching from his ear to his chin, wearing a uniform of a much-decorated red wool jacket and blue trousers, sneered. "Supreme War Master General Sysu! Why am I not surprised?" He was holding a big handgun pointed at the vampire.

The harshness left the general's face, and she said in a seductively humorous tone, "Hello, buttercup! I am surprised to see you. What are you doing here?"

The man smiled back with bright white teeth that looked like he could take a bite out of the vampire. He replied, "Charmed, as always. And it is Supreme Commander Admiral Yane."

The vampire clapped slowly. "Supreme Commander Admiral Yane? You mean a human is allowed to be in a place of power? Amazing. So, things have changed with the new Princess. Congratulations. Last time we met was on the world of Irison when we had that little dustup between the colonists. You were a simple Admiral with little prospects, not being an elf and all."

The man frowned. "Your people had no rights to that continent, and you knew that! As usual, you are overstepping your bounds, General Sysu. Take your troops and get out!"

"Oh, buttercup—oops . . . that is *Supreme Admiral* Buttercup. You have missed me. I am touched," Sysu purred cruelly.

"You are touched—in the head." He looked at Laxur. "As always, you are in over your head and in violation of the peace treaties."

Sysu looked annoyed. "You have to know that you are surrounded and outnumbered. You may carry a gun, but you are the only one. I suggest, before you get hurt, buttercup, that you surrender."

Yane immediately snapped back. "We will not surrender! You have no rights to this planet. Get out!" Laxur walked up to the shield and raised her head to look at the Princess. "No, this world is mine. As the treaty I am operating under states, per the last King of your kingdom, I got rid of the raiders around this area of the border. I did what the treaty wanted me to do. This was one of their strongholds, and I intend to keep it out of their hands."

"What are you talking about? I heard nothing of this! This world is under my protection as well!" Duke Jeia, a determined young man, marched up to Laxur, almost to Asora's shields. He wore a long coat and pants of brown wool. He was tall for a human at two meters. He was leanly muscular with curly black hair and deep brown eyes.

"And Jeia is here! Good. I heard that this factory was yours. Giving our sister a tour? As I am your new landlord, perhaps you would like to give me a tour too," Laxur greeted wickedly to Jeia.

"Laxur—" Jeia started to say. "*Queen* Laxur!" Obsidian growled. The laser that was on a table beside her distracted the dark beauty. "Enough!" Laxur tapped it.

"This is a pretty toy. That is my property, *Queen* Laxur." Jeia dragged his hands through his black hair and stared into her eyes.

"Of course, it is not, at least not anymore. It is now property of the Darkcon Empire, and I am the empire, so it belongs to me." She ran her finger over the laser.

"Ah! You cannot do this!" The duke turned to his monarch. "Princess!"

The blue-black-haired queen called up to the princess. "Yes, Asora, what are you doing up there? Come down and we will talk."

The dark-haired Princess shook her head. "You still have weapons trained at my people. I am not a fool."

"I see. You do not trust me." Laxur looked around and nodded. The soldiers put their weapons down at their sides. She turned to look up at Asora and sighed. The Princess was so young and earnest, only seventeen. It was too bad. Laxur was five years older, but she felt a hundred and was a more powerful witch. She was going to have to use that power against the young woman, no doubt about that, but she regretted having to do it.

"You may have had them put them down, but they are not holstered. I want safe passage for my people, Laxur." Asora could feel tears burning the back of her cerulean eyes, but she refused to let them show, and she was starting to feel the strain of keeping the enchanted shield up. "Back them off."

The queen shook her head. "They will not go. They are my personal guard. They would die first, just like yours have."

The princess swallowed. "You did not have to do that."

"Yes, I did. I wanted this facility, and your people fought us and died honorably. They were protecting you." Laxur sighed. "I did not know you would be here. It was unfortunate. You may leave but leave the employees. They will work for me now."

"I cannot do that. They are Utopians. They leave with me," Asora retorted harshly, her melodic voice hardened.

"Come down from there, and I will think about it." Laxur smiled supremely, confidently, yet inside she had her doubts. It was one thing to take the planet and another to hold the ruler of the Grand Utopian Kingdom. This was a tricky situation. Neither the humans nor the angels would look kindly to her hurting the part-human ruler angel. She knew that she needed Asora off the world as soon as possible. She was getting nervous, and her guards were feeling it.

A blond-haired woman with flashing gray eyes and a lance bristled. She was Asora's bodyguard and a knight of the realm. "Your Highness." She stared at Dari, her opposite number, with malice. She did not like that Dari's hand was twitching near her handgun. Dari smiled insolently.

Asora saw the look. "It is all right, Dame Sarea." She turned back to the Queen. "I do not think so, Laxur. I want to leave with the rest of my people. You do not want to keep me here. I promise that there will be retribution if you do, and you know this is true." With a ring of truth, Asora continued to float and hold up the shield.

"I want to talk with you, not to go to war," the queen insisted.

That was something that the Princess believed. The empire and the kingdom had not been to war for a very long time, and last time it had cost both sides dearly; yet her sister had invaded the planet. Asora felt her spirits drop. Darkcons were pushing at the border to see how many planets they could get before the kingdom would respond. Asora wondered that herself, so she had to shove back now before the Darkcons got too bold.

Dari was paying attention to Sarea and fingered her handgun again. Sarea pushed forward to the shield. She did not like the angel fallen angel threatening her Princess. The female knight was a powerful witch, and she was able to pass through the shield.

She walked up to Dari, who was surprised at the aggressive human, and did not have time to react when Sarea slashed at her hard with her lance, opening a wound in her face. The angel fallen angel pulled her gun, but Sarea reacted again, knocking Dari's arm, and the shot went wild.

Asora was distracted by what her bodyguard was doing, and in her inexperience, she let her guard down and dropped the shield. This was a costly mistake, and the bullet hit her hard in the shoulder.

Laxur immediately reacted by thrusting her hands out at Dari and Sarea. A powerful spell hit them, and they flew apart. The dark queen called out, "Asora!" Jeia caught his adopted sister as she fell and turned on Laxur. "Open a portal so we can get her home before she bleeds to death."

"Yes. I will open a portal for you—for your people, not for Asora. She needs immediate attention by someone who has knowledge of bullet wounds. Your people have no experience."

Yane was furious with the situation. He knew Laxur was right about the healer. He hesitated to send his troops away and allow Sysu access to Asora. He doubted that the Queen would allow her younger sister to die or take her prisoner, but you never really knew Laxur.

Asora opened her eyes and struggled to look at the Admiral. "Yane. Take the people home. Get them out of danger."

He came to her as Jeia cradled her in his arms. "Princess Asora, you cannot ask me to leave you at her mercy. I cannot do it."

"That was an order, Yane. Only you can tell the others what has happened." She took a raw breath, ragged and tortured. "Get my people to safety."

He bowed to her. "I will get them to safety, but I will not leave you alone, nor will the rest of your honor guards."

The princess then turned to Laxur, whispering, "Please let the people leave. They are nothing to you."

The dark queen nodded. "I want no war with you. So that this horrible accident does not turn into a greater crisis, I will open a portal for your people. You may stay, Yane, to be sure that I do nothing to endanger my sister. I will take the bullet out and make her comfortable and able to travel. When I am finished, I will open another portal to take you home, as Asora is not capable of it."

Asora closed her eyes, passing out from the shock of the bullet.

Laxur closed her eyes briefly and stretched out her hands. A whirlpool of color, then a hole appeared, showing that it was night on the Evorn palace grounds, the home world of the Grand Utopian Kingdom. The torches were lit, and the humongous stone front doors of the great palace could be seen.

Laxur turned her head toward Jeia. "This should not have happened. I will punish Dari. Tell your people to go, but I will see to Asora. The bullet must be taken out."

"Maybe it would be better to take her to her own healers—" Jeia was cut off.

"Your healers will not know how to fix the damage. They have never seen bullet wounds before!" The dark Queen walked up to the young Duke. "We need room so that we can lay her on the floor or a table."

Jeia hesitated. He turned to the mass of beings, elves, dwarves, and humans that had been protected and called out, "Go! Now! We will be behind you." They milled about, all staring at the Princess in her long white gown with a red stain growing ever wider. "I said go! Do as I say! Damn you, go! I cannot do anything for Her Highness until you do. You are in the way!"

Sarea woke up, got up off the floor, and ran over to Jeia. "My Duke! What has happened?"

"You messed up! That is what! Now help me get the people out of here! Make them leave!" He clutched his sister closer, spreading her blood onto his brown coat.

The bodyguard was horrified. It was her life to give to her Princess, not the other way around. She looked at Asora and Jeia with fear.

"I said do it, or we will lose her!" the dark Queen shouted at the Duke. Yane took command. "All employees leave now. Bodyguards, you wait here. Sarea?"

"Yes, sir!" She turned to the people. "You heard the Admiral. All employees, you need to go. Queen Laxur cannot keep this portal open forever!" When only a few moved, she urged, "You are endangering the Princess! Move!" She gestured with her lance, and they broke out of their stupor and walked quickly through the portal, pushing each other to move faster.

The royal guards stood their ground, surrounding the Duke, the Admiral, and Sarea in a semicircle. They faced Laxur's better armed forces with their lances.

Laxur collapsed the portal as the last of the employees left. "Put her on the table."

Jeia threw the laser onto the floor, missing Laxur's wince at her toy being broken, and laid her down with Sarea standing right beside her. "Any false moves and I will kill you, Queen or no Queen."

Jeia smiled slightly at the hiss of the bodyguard, and Laxur raised her eyebrows.

"I believe you would try. Now, hold her gently but firmly. This will not be easy for her." The dark Queen put her right hand over the hole. It shimmered, and Asora cried out and suddenly opened her eyes to stare at the four above her.

"Be calm. I am removing the bullet and cauterizing the wound,

Asora. I will attempt to knit some of the muscle together. It will hurt," the Darkcon Queen informed the Utopian Princess.

"I will anesthetize the wound and spell your pain, Highness." Sarea added her hand over Laxur's to help with the magical surgery.

Laxur suddenly snatched up her hand as the bullet flew up. She threw it down and quickly put her hands back as the blood spurted out. Asora moaned as she fell into the sleeping spell Sarea put on her.

Jeia, terrified, was turning as ashen as his sister. "For the Maker's sake, hurry!"

"I am going carefully, knitting as fast as I can. You need to understand, this is only an emergency patch. Asora will need a lot more care, and she will need a lot of blood when you get her home. I am doing what I can so that your healers will have an easier time. If they do their jobs right, she should not have a scar." Laxur looked up at Jeia for a split second.

Laxur looked deep into the wound with her magic and saw that she had stopped the bleeding. She could have wept, seeing Asora like this. She was such a strong and passionate young woman. The Princess was still young, and Laxur was glad that she would live to see another day.

The Admiral watched the Queen working furiously with her magic and her mind. He admired her quick action and dexterous motions. She was fantastic to watch. The healers on Evorn could learn a lot from her. She was an exceptional woman, but he could not forget that she was also dangerous.

"All right." Laxur was sweating from the efforts of using so much of her magic on such an intricately delicate procedure. "Pick her up, and I will open a portal. Remember, she needs blood and still needs healers to continue my work."

Jeia picked up the sleeping Princess, with the battered Sarea and Yane watching. They waited for Laxur to open the portal. The honor guard came to attention and moved to either side of the duke.

The dark Queen raised her hand to brush Asora's cheek gently. Laxur then turned slightly and raised both hands, opening the portal.

Jeia walked forward, stopped, and turned, saying, "Thank you, Laxur. You are a true healer, but I damn you for the taking of Carlon. This will not end well, and you must know that."

Laxur gave him a twisted smile. "She means a great deal to many humans. But I think that others, including your elf-filled government, would rather she die a martyr's death."

Jeia swallowed. In his heart, he felt that Laxur cared more than the people Asora led. He knew that the dark Queen did what she did for practicality; after all, the death of Asora by Laxur's people would cause immediate retaliation from the humans and angels, even though not everyone was happy with the human-angel Princess. The inner workings and interspecies relationships of the Utopian Kingdom where unfriendly at best, especially among humans and elves, mostly due to differing opinions on almost everything.

Jeia was not an idiot. He saw the new weapons that the Darkcons had, and he saw disaster brewing.

"What you say may be true, but I think that you still want war even though you helped the Princess. By the Hananaka, I hope I am wrong."

Laxur smiled again, insolently. "You run along now, Duke Jeia, before our sister begins bleeding again. I will be looking over your factory and deciding how to best use your new designs. Thank you for the new toy. Hurry now, before Asora slips into a coma."

Yane knew that Laxur, the sexy woman, was the single most dangerous enemy that the Grand Utopian Kingdom had to face. Her sister, Princess Asora, was only six months into her reign and had hard decisions to make. The Utopian court could decide to go to war over this insignificant planet, but they were ill prepared. The Princess was untried, which was probably why Laxur felt comfortable testing their resolve.

The Darkcons had not lashed out at the Utopians for generations, and their development was decades ahead of the kingdom. Laxur had been nibbling at the Utopians for a while now, testing them, probing for weaknesses to exploit.

The Admiral, now on Utopian soil, felt in more control. He turned to watch Laxur's face as the portal collapsed. It was a mask of contradictions. He saw her concern for Asora and her hand picking up the discarded laser, her prize. The portal closed. Damn, he wanted that weapon for the Utopians. Now, he was even less sure he could beat back the Darkcons.

"Take Her Highness to her rooms. I will inform the court and have Lady T'a meet you there." Yane slammed open the doors, forcing everyone to back away.

Jeia walked behind Yane. No one touched them, and T'a led the way inside. "Yes, Admiral. I will see to it at once." She touched Jeia, and she spelled them to Asora's suite of rooms.

They appeared inside the white sitting room. "Quickly, Your Grace, bring her into her bedroom. Lady T'a has been called."

They walked briskly into the huge bedroom. The soft white satin bed dominated it. The twenty-four-year-old man placed his younger sister on the bed. It was immediately stained with blood.

Sarea went back to the doorway to await the elder elf, who was the Princess's healer and friend, Lady T'a.

It did not take long before there was a knock on the door; a maid went to answer it. "Yes?"

"It is Lady T'a here for the Princess." The head of the royal guard, the knight Joes, a centaur, told her in his deep voice.

"She may enter." The doors opened, letting in a six-foot one-inch elf with gray-streaked brown hair. She had blue almond-shaped eyes and carried a leather bag.

"Come quickly. She was shot. Queen Laxur took the bullet out, but she lost a lot of blood. Can you do anything for her?" Jeia informed T'a.

"I got a report from the others that came through the first portal. I brought her blood with me.

She has a rare blood type, being one of the only human-angel hybrids alive. Only she can supply her own blood. We can hang it from the bed," Lady T'a instructed. "I have never seen a bullet wound, so let us hurry."

They walked quickly through Asora's rooms, finding Jeia bent over the unconscious Princess and talking softly to her. He looked up with relief upon finding T'a rushing in.

The elf put her bag on the bed, saying, "We will need to undress her. You will need to leave, Duke Jeia."

Without warning, in whizzed four blobs of light—Asora's fairy maids and ladies-in-waiting. "What has happened?" the head fairy, Gourani, asked.

"Princess Asora has been shot. We have need of your assistance to undress her so Lady T'a may treat her," Sarea answered.

They took off for the bedroom. They quickly undressed her using their magic and put her under the covers. Lady T'a went to work. It took hours to repair the damage and give her blood, but she was healed.

Back on Carlon, Queen Laxur and her minions were preparing to loot the lab. Laxur herself was wandering around looking at all the new inventions and equipment that was now hers.

Queen Laxur was in a manager's office looking through the papers in the desk. The office was industrial, but it was nice enough. She then saw it. A book of notes that Fusion Corp had gathered on the Coins of Power. Laxur took out the coin that she wore around her neck. It showed what little Fusion Corp knew of these coins. For a corporate entity, Fusion Corp was showing a surprising interest in these powerful and divine magic.

Most of the notes were mostly scientific nonsense that did not appeal to Laxur. However, it did point out that there were once thirteen. But only nine were needed to open the doors to Z'yon and unlock its great power. That got the queen's attention. This was what she was looking for. And this would be most helpful in her quest.

Several Darkcon soldiers started to shout. Then there was an explosion. Laxur quickly packed up the papers and research materials into an armored briefcase. Then she ran out of the room and into the main research lab. Then she heard gun fire from human weapons.

A bullet struck Laxur in the shoulder. She when spiraling the other direction and then to the floor with a thud. More gun shots ripped out from the dark corners of the lab. Many bounced off metal, crashed through glass, tore through flesh, and impacted plastic.

"Get down!" Obsidian bellowed.

Laxur held her shoulder. She still had some of that magic she used on Asora earlier. With much less gentle force, Laxur ripped the bullet out from her shoulder. "I guess it is my day for healing bullet wounds?" She tossed the bullet away and looked around.

Three of Asora's elite troops lead by Sarea now was setting up explosives. They had orders to destroy the lab and everything in it. Sarea and a human/elf hybrid with a large shotgun were behind an overturned table using it as cover.

"Cover me," Sarea said to her companion.

He nodded to Sarea. The silent shooter blasted a vampire that was nearby. Sarea got onto her stomach and crawled along the floor. She took plastique explosives, industrial tape, and wireless transmitters and planted them on the underside of desks, chairs, and tanks.

Two Darkcon soldiers using flame magic set fire to a section of the lab.

"Come out, come out where ever you are," one of the Darkcons sang.

Another one of Sarea's allies responded by planting a dagger into the Darkcon's leg and yanked on him. The Darkcon disappeared into the fire he made. The other Darkcon soldier found a human gun and started to shoot.

Dari jumped into the air and used her enormous wings to remain aloft. She looked down and around to see if she could spot the Utopian saboteurs. Dari is hit with several shotgun shells. Because of her super dense muscle mass and powerful combat magic Dari was able to withstand the attack without protection. But they were annoying, so Dari landed with force at the silent Utopian shooter. Dari ran him through the shoulder with her large glowing sword.

Laxur spotted something moving in the fire and dirt. Laxur unfurled her wings and sent a gust of wind to make herself a path. She grabbed Sarea by the back of her armor plate and tossed her onto a table.

"You little brat! You have just destroyed months of planning!" Laxur spat.

"That was the general idea you bimbo," Sarea replied.

Laxur then noticed an arming switch in Sarea's hand. "You set charges!"

"To keep you from achieving victory," Sarea then looked to a particularly large tank with red and black writing on it.

Laxur looked at it and she turned pale. The Queen looked around, "Everyone out! The room is filling with Hydrogen gas!" Laxur knew how dangerous hydrogen was, she was an expert alchemist and chemist. She looked to see Obsidian, "Find the fire suppression system! The Halon controls have to be there!"

"Too late," Sarea punched Laxur in the jaw and she rolled off the table and onto the floor.

Obsidian ran to Laxur's side and helped her up. Laxur got back up onto her feet and told Obsidian to get everyone outside. Sarea saw that she was the only one of the group of Utopians still alive. She found the gunmen that was giving her cover. Dari's sword left an enormous hole on his shoulder and practically ripped off his arm. He was breathing hard and irregular as he struggled. He also had a remote detonator.

"Go," he said to Sarea. "I will finish up here."

Sarea looked sad but it was his duty, and she had her own to attend to. Sarea vanished into a portal that took her to Evorn.

The gunman raised the detonator with his other arm and squeezed.

The laboratory building exploded violently. The shockwave sent vibrations into the ground. Debris, trash, dirt, bodies, fireballs, and chemicals rain down from the sky. Obsidian, Sysu, and Dari looked around to see where their queen was.

Before the panic could set in, another small explosion forced tons of debris away from a buried passageway. Queen Laxur emerged from the darkened passageway. Her uniform was burned and torn away. Most of her body was exposed but undamaged, only her clothing was damaged or destroyed. She knew that she was almost half naked and she did not care. Laxur had in her hand the armored brief case full of the most valuable technology, and research papers that was in the building.

Dari, Sysu, and Obsidian ran up to Laxur and bowed.

"How hurt are you?" Sysu asked.

"Actually, I will need a change of clothes, but other than that, I feel fine," Laxur said. "Being the most powerful being in the realm has nothing but advantages, as you can see." Laxur walked forward to her forces. "Now, back to Dorien!"

Chapter Three

The After Effects

At dawn, in a small assembly room in the palace on Evorn, the tall Veartis waited. He was elegant in a black wool suit with a long coat and tall boots. A vampire with long black hair, he was the Darkcon Ambassador to the Utopian Kingdom. The door opened, and Archduke Frenzen walked in with the princess.

Frenzen was an older, deeply tanned elf with short graying brown hair, deep brown eyes, and a goatee. He wore a long-coated suit of dark-blue wool with a gold sash, which displayed his rank of Prime Minister. He waited while Asora sat and arranged her long white skirts. He took another plush red high-backed chair and motioned for the vampire to sit around a small table set with coffee.

The archduke began. "Ambassador Veartis, please explain why your queen has taken Carlon and what you have done with the inhabitants."

The vampire took a breath and raised his chin arrogantly. "We have taken nothing. Carlon is ours by right. As for the people, they are now part of the Darkcon Empire. I would not worry about them."

"We do worry about *our* people. Carlon is yours only by force, and what made you believe we would give it up?" Frenzen motioned for a footman to pour a cup of coffee.

"Do you have blood? I came early, as you requested, and did not have my breakfast." The ambassador looked, unblinkingly, with red eyes at Frenzen.

The elfish prime minister gave Veartis an odd look, cocking one eyebrow. He then snapped his fingers, and servants hustled to retrieve what the Ambassador ordered.

One servant went to the door to meet another. He brought in a tray and offered it to Veartis, who smiled graciously while picking up the goblet.

"You always remember. It is very kind of you. How do you keep it warm?" Veartis asked coolly.

Frenzen kept the revulsion to himself, as did his princess. "We have people volunteer in the kitchens. You have not told us about what you intend to do or why, ambassador."

Veartis smacked his lips, smiling. "I have told you. We obtained it through diplomacy with your last monarch—the same as Ceti-Delphi, Lord Jeia's home world. Pity, that. His kin should not have fought back, or he and the rest of his family would be here today."

The archduke saw Asora tense up but said nothing, having agreed that Frenzen would conduct the meeting. He knew that Veartis wanted to take control of the meeting, and this was his way.

"You speak of diplomacy in Ceti-Delphi and Carlon. What do you mean?" The elf needed to hear the words that would condemn Asora's predecessor.

"That is right." He smiled wolfishly. "You were not at court when the treaty was signed. You were at home. Well, it was the same. The Darkcons kept the skies clear of dwarf raiders, elf pirates, and human terrorists. To do this, we had to take the planet from the Utopians and will keep it from ever being used as a base of operations again by pirates and raiders. Funny how they were both human worlds."

"I have never heard of this." The archduke had an ugly feeling that this was exactly what had happened.

The military had always thought that fighting the pirates was beneath them, even though the pirates interfered with shipping and caused many deaths. The last monarch had done it while Archduke Frenzen was gone from court so that there would be no one to say nay against it. Damn the court! Frenzen had been kept out of the politics of the court for years and was usually caught off guard when their policies came up to him.

Veartis shrugged indifferently. "It is the truth that what we plan to do is catalogue the planet's mineral wealth and put the people to work."

"You mean put them to work in the shipyards." Asora said.

The vampire narrowed his red eyes. He did not like where the young lady was taking this conversation.

"What do you mean?" Frenzen asked.

"Queen Laxur has spent most of her money on new metal ships, land battleships, and generally upgrading her military, as did her now-deceased husband. However, she is enjoying her unmarried life for the moment." Veartis explained.

The prime minister watched the ambassador closely. He was looking for any hint of true possible motive. Or any other hint of what this vampire was saying.

"Ah, yes. She needs to stimulate the economy, as did the old prince regent. It has worked well." He smiled a cold smile and put his glass down.

"Stimulate the economy? Queen Laxur has overloaded it with military hardware." Frenzen smiled equally as cold, while Asora continued to stare unblinkingly at the vampire.

"Do you insult us? Suggesting that our queen is more interested in conquest than peace? You cannot afford to fight us. Only the humans can beat us, and even though you now have a human on the throne, I doubt Countess Marien, the ruler of humanity, will fight a battle for your kingdom." The ambassador stood up.

Asora stood, saying, "We will confirm this treaty and let you know." The two men bowed as she left the room.

Asora awaited the head of the delegation for the consortium, Bremmer Arton, in her private sitting room. It was a white room with white furnishings, suitable for the virgin princess. Asora would not be allowed colors until she was married in three years' time, when they would then change to the red and gold of the Utopian Kingdom.

"Bremmer is here, Your Highness," Gourani announced as she fluttered in with the forty- eight-year-old gentleman.

Arton was a pleasant man with a sunny disposition. He had short blond hair and sharp blue eyes. He was plain faced with a medium build. He was dressed in the fashion of court, which was a long coat with a vest and long pants. He wore gray. He was known for his poker games, which were a highlight for the other races. He would often win but was gracious—that was how he did business. He was no one's fool, and if you thought his witty remarks and careful dressing were signs that he was, then you were the fool.

"Princess Asora." He went to her and kissed her hand as she lifted it up. "It is just after dawn, yet I hear such things. How are you? I heard that Laxur's bodyguard shot you?" He sat down on a comfortable chair across her.

"It is true, but I am recovering. I am sure Jeia has told you and Countess Marien that Carlon has been invaded." Asora nodded to Gourani to pour coffee for them.

Bremmer, smiling slightly, took his cup from the fairy. "Thank you, Gourani." He put it down in front of him and looked hard at Asora. "Are we at war?"

"Are you suggesting we should be?" the princess countered. "Is that what you and the countess believes is proper? War? I have seen the new weapons the Darkcons have. They are far superior to what the Utopian army has. They have grenades, guns, rifles, and the Maker knows what else. We are no match for them. They killed my royal guards within minutes. We will be annihilated."

"They have attacked us, and we will do nothing!" Bremmer longed to stand up and pace the room, but royal etiquette decreed he sit there and wait for Asora to stand before he could.

"Laxur stated that there had been an agreement with the past monarch to clear the shipping lanes of pirates in that sector. They have used that as an excuse to take Carlon. I have the prime minister looking into it." Asora picked up her coffee and then set it down again, waiting for the explosion from the ambassador. She did not have long to wait.

"Just like Ceti-Delphi. I see." Bremmer got up and walked to the window to stare at the calm sea. "If it is like Ceti-Delphi, will the court allow us to get our people out? We have grenades, guns, and rifles more advanced than the Darkcons'. You know that. We, as you know, do have an army. We could get our people back."

"Our people? You mean humans?" Asora calmly watched Bremmer. "Will you sit, please?"

He jerked away from the window and bowed low to Asora. "I disrespected you, like the court does. Please accept my apologies."

She raised her hand to raise him up. As he stood, she said, "Of course. You are distraught. I am distraught. I have not heard of the treaty that Laxur and Veartis talked about, and I am not sure that it is true, to be honest."

"You are young and were not born when, twenty-four years ago, the Darkcons invaded Ceti- Delphi, your brother's home world, but it was the same. Countess Marien sent in a force to help liberate people, including your brother. Again, it is happening to Jeia, and the countess has great affection for him. I believe she would be willing to send in another force." Bremmer smiled. "We will even get the elves off. They will want them removed. The elves will never become dark and pray to the Architect."

Asora laughed ruefully. "That would help, but I do not see the court allowing the humans to arm themselves for battle. The Great War is still fresh in their minds."

"That was five hundred years ago, and we ended up under the Utopian Kingdom." He sighed heavily.

"Those that lived, and are still part of the court, know that we humans won that war at a great cost. So great that we could no longer function and had to be taken into the kingdom," Asora reminded him.

"We had to be a part of the kingdom because the kingdom could no longer function either. The angels made this treaty that we all must live under," Bremmer remarked. "There will come a time when it will no longer be necessary."

"It is talk like that which makes the other Utopians nervous and causes them to refuse to allow military action," Asora advised.

"You could demand that we go in there and get as many people out as possible," Bremmer said, knowing it was unlikely.

"You know I can only suggest such things. I will not be queen for another nineteen and a half years, and until then, my power is limited. We can request that it be done." Asora stood up and gave him her hand. "You will convey this to Countess Marien, and I will see you at court later this morning."

Arton stood and kissed her hand. "Of course, Princess Asora. I will see you later this morning."

Gourani fluttered up and led him out. Sarea walked in. "It is time for services."

"Yes, thank you. Let us go to my private temple. Nona should be there to give the thanksgiving for the morning." Asora said.

She was joined by her bodyguard Sarea at the door, and they went down the stairs to the small temple. Before walking in, they covered their heads in sheer white scarves.

It was a bright large oval room of white marble with many windows and a tall one of stained glass with a depiction of the Great Maker near the entrance. The picture was of a beautiful woman with white hair and pale skin and eyes wearing a long, flowing white gown surrounded by flowers, vines, and trees. It spilled a kaleidoscope of colors onto the walls and floor.

There were several pews for the small number of people and a white-covered altar brimming with roses and holding a golden goblet of wine. Standing behind the altar was a young elf with long blond hair and blue eyes. She wore her long hair down and wore a yellow underdress with a red overcoat.

"Good morning, Nona, the Maker be with you." Asora approached, her steps echoing on the white marble, while Sarea walked a step behind her.

"The Maker be with you, Nona," Sarea called out.

Nona came from behind the altar to stand in front. She bowed deeply to Asora before returning the greetings in a pleasant voice, "The Maker bless you this day, Princess Asora, and you too, Dame Sarea."

The door burst open, and four fluttering fairies came whizzing in. It was Gourani, B'nei, Friea, and Rayne, Asora's ladies-in-waiting.

"Good. We are all here now, and we apologize for being late," Princess Asora said. "I am sure you have heard of what happened on Carlon yesterday. I feel a great need to say my prayers of thanksgiving to the Maker for my recovery. But we must be quick, for I have yet to have my meetings with the prime minister."

"As you say, your highness. Let us begin." Nona turned and faced the larger-than-life marble statue of the Maker, which stood in front of the stained glass. Asora and her entourage bowed their heads and folded their hands in prayer.

"We give thanks to you for your creations and our destinies. We marvel in your works and wonders. It is said that one day your power will return. We wait for that day and ask, as we wait, for your continuing guidance and love. With this we say glory be unto you," Nona chanted.

"Glory be to you," the women chanted.

"You created life and light," Nona chanted.

"Glory be to you," the women chanted.

"You give us love and magic," Nona chanted.

"Glory be to you," the women chanted.

Nona turned around, picked up the golden goblet, and held it up. "With your blessing, we begin our day." She took a sip and then came around to the kneeling women.

She went first to Asora, who took the cup, saying, "With your blessing, I begin my day." She sipped and handed it back.

This was repeated until they had all drunk, stood, and placed their left hands on their hearts in supplication. The prayers were over, and Asora and her friends rushed out, thanking Nona.

She met with Archduke Frenzen for a late breakfast in her private dining room. As was custom for them.

"I met with Bremmer. He wants to send a contingent of soldiers into Carlon to rescue as many people as they can."

The prime minister sat forward and looked urgently into Asora's eyes. "It will be seen as an attack of the Utopian Kingdom, and if there was a treaty, we will be in violation of it. Last time this happened, on Ceti-Delphi, the humans had to beat back the entire Darkcon army, and the Darkcons killed Lord Jeia's family." Frenzen sat back. "Finally, I do not see the rest of the court, with the exception of the fairies, allowing it."

"I have not forgotten that my brother's family was killed. I also told Bremmer as much, that the court would not want the humans to be armed." Asora pushed her half-eaten plate away and sighed.

"The elves, centaurs, dwarves, and mer-people will never forget that they lost the Great War, with humans having the dragons' and jewel elves helped, five centuries ago. The fairies have forgiven us, and now side with them almost every time, which will not help with only two-fifths vote." Frenzen poured himself coffee.

"Do you think that the angels will get involved?" Asora asked tentatively. "Do you think Dominus will help if things go badly?"

"You know as well as I do that the angels will make their own decision. They prefer that we and the Darkcons work out our own problems unless the Maker and Architect call upon them as they did during the Great War." Frenzen picked up his coffee cup and took a sip.

"I will still offer the help of the humans, but I do not want to go to war. We are so ill-prepared. The Darkcons are more powerful than they have ever been. I do not see a positive outcome from this. My people, humans, could easily overcome them. They have steel ships and armaments far superior to the Darkcon's, and yet they will not be allowed to fight to regain Carlon." Asora fiddled with her coffee cup, sighing as she did.

"We can only put forward Bremmer's suggestion. I do not see it passing. The court may want to go to war because of the elves on

Carlon," Frenzen stated.

"And let the humans rot? That sounds like the court, but if they want the elves evacuated, then they need to get the humans out as well. There will be no compromise on this," the princess demanded.

"The elves know this. Not all elves are that prejudiced. The court is just leery of humans arming themselves. They still remember the Great War." Frenzen reminded her.

"That war was started by the Utopians," Asora reminded him.

"Granted, but elves are an old race. They are arrogant, but they are not cruel. They would not leave the humans to the Darkcons," Frenzen said.

"It does not seem like that, at times. You are correct on one thing though: not all elves are prejudiced. The jewel elves come to mind," Asora pointed out.

Frenzen groaned at the mention of the jewel elves. "They are an odd race of elf."

"We humans do not think so. They were very helpful and were the only ones that helped us during the Great War," the princess said.

"They are too curious and reckless," the archduke said.

"Agreed. However, that recklessness and curiosity helped us," Asora said in return.

"So we will tell the court of Bremmer's suggestion and investigate the treaty that allowed Laxur to take Carlon. The treaty against the pirates and raiders, unfortunately, does not say how the Darkcons could get rid of them. That will be what Laxur is counting on," Frenzen said dully.

The throne room seemed to be a kilometer long and wide. It was made of white marble, shining brightly in the morning sun, which streamed through tall windows. The windows brought in the scent of pine and sea, for the enormous palace was set between the forested mountains and the wondrous ocean.

Asora subtly rotated her shoulder that still pained her, though it had been a day since her injury. T'a had said that Laxur had done a marvelous job, but it would still take a week, even with the magic, for the muscles and nerves to heal completely. She grimaced and took a breath when she realized her fairies, who had dressed her earlier, had cinched her corset too tight. It was their way of showing their displeasure with her for getting up to speak to the court when she should have been in bed recovering. She shook out her white silk skirts.

"We cannot go to war. We are ill-prepared. My sister's empire has far superior numbers, weapons, and battleships. That is just to name a few problems." She sat back into her throne to wait for the fight from the arrogant courtiers. "We could send in the humans to get our people out, the elves included."

An older elf, dressed in purple wool, grunted in disdain. "The royal guard has always triumphed over the Darkcons. Why should this be any different? We do not need the humans."

"I agree with Lord Turkin!" another male elf, wearing blue wool, shouted over the arguing court.

"Thank you, Yoser," Turkin replied loudly.

They bowed to each other, and Asora's head began to ache. The elves were supremely confident in the outdated military, but she had noticed that the Darkcons carried guns. The Utopians did not. Guns were a human invention; therefore, they were ignored by the kingdom. Swords, bow and arrows, spears, lances, maces, and axes had won in past wars, so the elves, who made up most of the court, could not see the danger that confronted them all: a Darkcon Empire that was not fighting by the old rules.

"My company's property is in the hands of that crazy sister of ours! I want it back. There is important research in her hands. We cannot afford to have her developing the projects." Jeia came forward, pushing aside all the courtiers, until he stood in front of Asora.

There was an upsurge of cries for war, and the Princess's eyes rolled back into her head. She did not need her brother's cry inflaming the nobles. "Jeia, we cannot go to war over your company being taken by the Darkcons, not if the treaty is real. No one is answering that question."

"It is more than my company's property! Think of the people left on

Carlon. They are in danger." He ran a hand over his curly black head.

"There is a colony of elves as well. Think of them!" Lord Turkin commanded.

"The Darkcons do not attack innocent citizens. They merely incorporate them into the empire." She tried to take another deep breath to relax herself but failed and cursed the fairies. "And if that treaty is real, we have no grievance."

A male angel named Dominus, who had long, flowing golden hair and deep blue eyes came forward. He wore a long robe of soft gray cotton with a hood that hung down, as was his custom unless fighting, when he wore his golden angelic armor. He was the known cousin to the Princess, and he stepped forward to Asora. He was over three and a half meters tall but appeared in court at more then two meters. "Princess, with Queen Laxur, we do not even know if that is true anymore. They may not be caring for the people at all. There have been rumors about what she orders and does."

Princess Asora looked at her cousin with a look of concern. "Can this be true?" Asora questioned Dominus. All he did in response was shrug.

"It is a corrupt empire which does not worship as we do, and they tax them to death and work them to death—or so they say. Why would we give up an elvish world?" Turkin pointed out.

Admiral Yane stepped out of the shadows and walked to the throne, standing beside Jeia. "I am concerned about what Lord Jeia has said about military hardware and software being in Darkcon control. This is dangerous. They have already had a day to study the material."

He had a point, though the technology that her sister had was human and, therefore, above the level of Utopian comprehension. It was worth a surgical strike to get the materials back.

She gripped the arms of her chair. The difficulty was that the Grand Utopian Kingdom would be devastated. If Laxur had handguns and rifles, they may have more impressive weapons in their arsenal. They were still hundreds of years behind the humans, but decades ahead of the Kingdom.

The After Effects

Yane pushed the issue, knowing what Asora was thinking and understanding the danger. "The more time they have, the further the Utopians fall behind. We cannot send in the Utopian Army to fight with what we have. If we cannot have the humans fight, give me the chance to negotiate with the humans for more useful weapons. Then we can attempt to retake Carlon."

The puro, or the oldest religious leader, an old, wrinkled elf dressed in a black robe decorated with gold, was quick to protest. "What you say is blasphemy. We do not require assistance from the humans."

Yane, who was the first human admiral, took offense. "Then you condemn us because of nothing more than prejudice and the old way of thinking. The humans are not the enemy. It is time to think of the future." He looked around the great hall. "Will you go to war with one hand tied behind your back because of the ridiculous notions of your old ways?"

Asora knew the Admiral was right, and she spoke up. "Admiral Yane is correct. The army and navy, as it is, will not be able to withstand a confrontation. The Darkcons have projectile weapons decades ahead of our military. I have decided. I only pray that the humans will be persuaded to help."

"If you, Yane, and I go to Countess Marien, I am sure that she will," Jeia excitedly said. "This will not be like Ceti-Delphi, where the Grand Utopian Kingdom did nothing to intervene. I know the countess will see reason as she did with Ceti-Delphi. It will prove that you are being on the throne will be different for our people."

"It is worth a try." Asora nodded. "And before you protest again, Puro Aga, remember your place," she hissed.

The court gasped at the young human-angel asserting herself. Asora trembled, knowing she was in danger, knowing that if the puro dissented, she could be in trouble; but then again, so would Aga. She could replace him. It would cause unrest in the kingdom, but if she must, she must.

Her determination must have gotten through to the puro, and

he bowed his head with his arms outstretched. The nobles sighed and bowed their heads with arms outstretched.

The prime minister, who stood beside Asora's throne, stepped forward to speak to the court. "It is decided. We will not declare anything until Admiral Yane speaks to Countess Marien regarding purchasing weapons. We can ill afford our military to go against the Darkcon Empire. I have read the reports of the surviving soldiers assigned to our Princess. They nearly died too. If our monarch had not been as powerful as she is, it would have been so. We *need* the help of the humans."

Bremmer now spoke. "Agreed. Now what about the Darkcons? They still have their ambassador here on Evorn."

Frenzen approached the throne and leaned down to speak softly. "They will know what we are doing. We may not be declaring war, but Laxur will believe it has already happened. These nobles are gossipers. I suggest that we close this meeting and talk more privately with Admiral Yane."

She nodded softly. "The court is dismissed. Any business left over will wait until tomorrow." Frenzen tapped down with his large staff on the mirror-like marble floor.

The nobles looked like they wanted to protest, but once the prime minister made a statement, it was not to be questioned. They bowed, arms outstretched, walked backward a few paces, and retreated from the cavernous great hall.

"Let us go to the small throne room." Asora arose, and the hundred twirling stars circling above her throne, which represented the one hundred home worlds of the kingdom, dimmed. Yane and Frenzen bowed before her as she passed them to walk to a door behind the dais, and followed her. Joes, the centaur, and head of her personal guard, stood at attention before the door. The elf opened it.

Puro Aga, his black eyes blazing, walked quickly out of the throne room and magically transported himself to the palace temple where his priests and priestesses, all elves, were waiting for him. It was in the middle of the palace grounds, and it soared upward in gothic sweeps. It was made of white marble and limestone. The windows were stained glass of the different species and prophets of the Maker.

"Damn her! That heretic! How dare she speak to me in that manner!" The puro ranted.

A young priest, dressed in white, added, "Or at all. She should not even be on the throne. A human! It is sacrilege."

An older priestess, or videc, wearing royal purple, sighed. "We hear this every day, puro. She is the monarch, and you cannot change that. So why are you so fixated on her?"

"She is an idealist, Videc Shison," Aga spat. "She thinks that she can better the peasants' lives that they should be able to vote! She wants a constitutional monarchy!"

Shison, who was graying-haired and blue-eyed, smiled grimly. "The nobles will fight her all the way, but the people love her."

Aga smiled a terrible smile. "Then that is where we must strike—the people."

The priests and priestess smiled, except for Shison, who replied, "That will be a hard sell. The people—"

"Will do as I say or they will be branded as heretics. We will vilify her in the temples—" Aga said.

"You have already done so without anyone caring. The people continue to love her, and she has only been a princess for six months. In those six months, she has made jobs for the poor, new road systems, building projects, and introduced electricity. She forced those things through despite the nobles' objections," Shison countered.

"And do the nobles not hate her for it!" T'lon, a young priest in white who had brown hair with hazel eyes, exclaimed. "They have confessed to me that they are sick of her already, and she will rule for a hundred years, her children after that, perhaps. They hate her. In twenty years, she will become the queen, and then nothing can be done."

Another priest, in royal purple, Arch Videc U'agon, a middle-aged elf with black hair, rolled his brown eyes. "It does not matter what they think. It is what must be done! We must break her."

This intrigued Aga. "How?"

Nona, an ambitious young priestess with platinum blonde hair and blue eyes, sidled up to Shison and whispered, "This could be dangerous. Asora has reprimanded Aga already. We should tread lightly."

The elder elf looked at the young elf coolly. "Do you think that you should be the princess's personal priestess? You are still in training. You are only there for a short time until another can take your place."

"I was thinking it would be you," Nona answered with a sugary smile.

Shison shrugged. "Perhaps."

"What are you two whispering about?" Aga demanded.

The older priestess calmly said, "We were discussing the fact that Nona could be more aggressive in getting the princess's confidences. The more she trusts Nona, the more personal her confessions will be."

Aga smiled nastily. "You think she would trust you?"

"I have not given her reason not to trust me. I have been deferential and respectful of her. I only give her daily mass. I could try to become more intimate with her," the blonde suggested.

"An excellent idea. Become her friend and get her to tell you, her secrets. Guide her to our cause, Priestess Nona," the Arch Videc agreed enthusiastically.

Aga shouted, "No! I want to destroy her! That freak is an affront to the Maker! She is disgusting. She is a mutant animal, not fit as royalty. I do not care how impeccable her lineage is! They only put her on throne because of her angelic heritage. Those cretins that chose her to rule this Grand Utopian Kingdom should be punished. We should take them to the inquisitors, who will show them the errors of their ways. I doubt it would take long before they recanted their choice," he harrumphed.

Videc Shison frowned. "The choice was made. The angels are pleased, and the nobles wanted to please the angels—or more precisely, no one wanted to displease the angels. No one in their right mind would deliberately antagonize them. They are too close to the Maker. I do not want to be cursed or damned by them for harming the princess. Asora is the royal princess. That cannot be undone, for now. We must win her over to our side. Or we can ruin her."

"Very well. We will proceed with your plan, Videc." Aga turned to Nona with a wicked smile. "And you, my dear. Learn Asora, become intimate with her, and turn her decisions to our will."

"Yes, my puro. I will not fail you." Nona bowed.

It was a relief to be out of the oppressive great hall, but Asora needed one more person, General Hurak, a dwarf with curly black hair and black eyes, the head of the army, to discuss the situation with Yane, Dominus, and Frenzen.

Before the door closed, she called to Joes, "Bring me Hurak."

Joes bowed and closed the door. Sarea stood inside near the princess. These were friends and they were dedicated to Asora.

Asora turned to face the other two. "This will be a war. No surgical strike. Once Laxur sees Utopian soldiers, it is all over. She will retaliate. I have read the reports on the buildup of the Darkcons. I mentioned only the guns, but they have iron ships, and we only have—"

"Wooden ships?" Admiral Yane sighed. "We will be decimated."

"We need new ideas. I think we need to have a science fair and invite anyone with innovations or any good idea that can help. We need to bring this kingdom into the future," Asora declared.

The next day, the discussion continued in the throne room between the court and Asora's military commanders. A dwarf general was there, dressed in his formal uniform: a red jacket, braids, and blue pants falling to shiny black shoes.

"General Hurak can you review for us the current standings of our and the Darkcons' military strengths," a female courtier, Lady Teralay, a centaur, demanded of the general.

"It is hard to know for sure, but our estimates are as follows: The Darkcon army may have a standing force of eight hundred billion strong.

Our estimates for their navy are twelve hundred mystical spaceships, two thousand aquatic ships with roughly three billion sailors. As for how long? Well, that would really depend," Hurak stated.

"Depend on what, general?" Lady Teralay asked again.

"The willingness of our people to fight an overwhelming foe. We also need experienced and knowledgeable commanders," Hurak mentioned.

"I see, well, we will rely on your abilities to rectify the situation," the courtier said to the already-angry general.

The dwarf was flabbergasted, but he repressed his rage and walked in front of Princess Asora to stand before the court.

"Queen Laxur was interested in something that was at the Fusion Corp facility. It was many technological wonders, and I believe that is why she took the planet," Asora stated with trepidation.

"And what was this something?" Lord Turkin demanded.

"Jeia, would you like to explain since these were your creation?" The princess smiled nervously.

"And what exactly is this worthless technological weapon system?" Lord Turkin sneered at Jeia.

Jeia pressed his lips together, trying to repress his rage at the comment. "One of the technologies was for a laser cannon!" Jeia yelled.

"What is a laser?" a mermaid known as the duchess asked. She was there in her humanoid form to represent her people at court.

"A laser is a device that focuses a narrow beam of photons with extreme energy on a single target point," Jeia explained.

The whole court looked completely lost at Jeia's simple explanation. This was to be expected as human technology was something that the average Utopian were mostly ignorant of.

"Lord Jeia, perhaps you should dumb it down to the lowest possible level for these people," Admiral Yane pointed out.

"How dare you, admiral!" Baron Yoser exclaimed.

There was laughter in the human delegation. "Did you understand what the hell he just said?" Bremmer asked. Everyone looked at each other and then back to Jeia. "The admiral's comment can stand."

"A laser narrows the flow of light into a single, straight, and powerful beam that is invisible. It will burn through almost anything. You can only see the beam if you can see infrared," Jeia finished.

"Basically, this laser is an overly expensive flashlight that cooks things and melts metal? How ridiculous!" Count Runik, a dwarf, laughed.

"Well, it does not seem ridiculous if it drew Queen Laxur's attention," Princess Asora pointed out. "I have seen the potential that this laser has, and it would be a great equalizer. And that is what we need if we cannot muster the numbers needed to battle the Darkcon Empire. And, in light of this, I am hosting a science fair."

"What? We do not need such an event. We are at war now." Lord Turkin complained.

"I think it is a wonderful idea." Bremmer bowed with a smile at Asora.

"You would, Arton." Lord Turkin glowered.

"Well, it is my prerogative, and I am well within my rights to host such an event. If you all wish to attend to see these new, wondrous devices, then I *highly encourage* every one of you to come," Asora stated. "We may see something new that the military could use."

"By encourage, you mean we do not have a choice?" an older courtier, Marquis Tyles, a centaur, asked.

"Pretty much. I need new ideas, and who knows, maybe someone will come up with an idea to counter a potential Darkcon laser weapon," Asora said, ending all discussion.

Chapter Four
Princess Training

"My Princess, the fine china and the tea that the other princesses have demanded," a maid told Asora. "Fine, whatever, just make sure it is already." Asora rushed out the maid.

She had to get out of the main rooms. She wanted some privacy. So Asora made her way through the halls and to her chambers. She had a small parade of maids, and servants follow her. Princess Asora was so annoyed and was mad at herself for agreeing to this.

Asora really did not like any of the other minor princesses that were coming. She had met them before, and it was not a pleasant encounter, to say the least. Asora was still acting like a human instead of the Utopian royal that she now was.

She was doing this because the Royal Court had pulled a fast one on her. For her to have her science fair she had to agree to this 'Princess Training.' If she passed, then her science fair would be unopposed. If not, the court could suspend the fair and force Asora to be their spokes person instead of the leader of the kingdom.

Princess Asora made it to her chambers. The guards opened the doors to her chambers and closed them behind her. Asora went to her desk and sat down and laid back and let out a sigh.

The door opened again, and Lady Madimoy stepped through. She looked at Asora with mock disappointment.

"You should really remember your princess manners if you are to be successful with the other ladies," Madimoy said.

Madimoy ignored Asora's frustrating sighs and went to the walk-in closet. She picked out a dress for Asora to wear. She wanted her best friend to be as successful as possible. But she also knew that her friend was as stubborn and in some cases as violent as an angry dwarf.

Asora, meanwhile, was playing with her military game board. She found this game pleasantly distracting. "Planning for war is so much easier than being diplomatic with a bunch of spoiled brats."

The next day, three of the nineteen expected Princesses arrived at the palace. Princess Yala of Habos, Princess Aratica of Canva Prime, and Princess T'isa of Wea. Princess Asora put on as good a face as she could to hide her contempt.

"Princess Asora," Yala a short, young-looking centaur woman greeted properly.

"Lady Yala," Asora responded as she was supposed to.

A lady with sparkly skin that smelled of the ocean stood in front of Asora, staring at her directly, trying to intimidate her. Asora did not back down and stood there with stiff military posture. "You have not changed much."

"Nor have you, Lady Aratica," Asora responded.

"I see we have much work to do with you, human," a very tall and regal elf lady stated.

"As you wish, Lady T'isa," Asora, again, responded duly.

The fairy maids—Gourni, Friea, B'nei, and Rayne—escorted the guests to their rooms to settle in. They would see to the guests' accommodations as was their duty.

The following day, the rest of the princesses showed up—Lady Manidai, who was also from Canva Prime; Ladies Hana, Urasa, Luoa, and Kisa from the fairy kingdoms; Ladies T'dia, T'siral, and T'yisa from Geldreon; a little sprite princess, who looked like a child, named Amina. Two were dwarves, and they looked like the males of their race,

Ladies Drk, and Fryga. Five of the princesses were, in fact, animals from throughout the kingdom. A tiger by the name of Serka, a bear called Basra, a wolf known as Halasa, a very tiny queen bee, whose name no one outside her hive knew, and a cat named Serila.

Every princess was given a room to prepare for their long stay to further train and help Asora. The utopian princess herself sat in the lounge room with an electronic tablet, reading the news from home. Asora heard someone step into the doorway. She saw the little sprite princess, Amina.

"Hello," Amina said, smiling and friendly.

"Hello. What can I do for you?" Asora asked.

"I'm hungry," the little girl said.

"Well, let's see what the butlers have." Asora turned off her tablet, got up, and took Amina to the kitchen, where they were surrounded by the usual happenings of a busy kitchen. Asora saw a tray full of chocolate muffins. "Do you like chocolate muffins?"

"Yes!" Amina smiled.

Asora grabbed one and handed it to the little girl. They walked out without the chefs even noticing. Clearly, Princess Asora showed kindness, and what she did not know was that this was the first test, and she had passed.

The next morning, Asora awoke to her fairy maids opening curtains and running water for her bath. Rayne drew the bath, Gourani opened the curtains for sunlight, Friea picked out today's clothes, and B'nei prepared the makeup set for the princess. They rushed Asora out of bed and into the bathroom. Rayne left for a moment to grab soaps. They did their best to prepare Asora as fast but as gentle as they could.

Within an hour, Asora was ready to greet the day. She wore the dress that Friea had picked out. It was white like all her other dresses. But all her white dresses all had different and unique designs and patterns on them. This was allowed for her.

She walked to the royal court room and saw the other nineteen princesses in different places throughout the room. They looked bored mostly. Then Asora saw T'siral sat upon the throne, looking bored.

"You do realize that you are sitting on my throne?" Asora said cynically.

"Are you aware that you have the power to shape this throne to show your power over all people?" T'siral asked. "Why have you chosen such a small utilitarian style?" She moved around on it. "But I will give you this, the seat cushion is very comfortable."

It was obvious that T'siral was highly critical of Asora. The elf lady was one of those who were trying to become the supreme princess of the Utopian Kingdom. Last year all twenty of them were in the Royal Academy to be trained to be the next monarch. There were two hundred students, but in the end Asora prevailed. Much to the dismay of everyone around. Asora herself included.

"You know, I do not have to explain myself to you. I feel that my throne is just fine," Asora said.

T'siral could not make the throne change because it was Asora's. It was also obvious that the elf princess was trying to antagonize Asora and put her human-angel hybrid emotions on display. This had proven to be a dangerous process back during their academy days. Asora was known for violent outbursts when angered too far.

"There is more to being a leader than sitting there and looking pretty," Asora started. "How do you pay for grains to keep the supply going?"

T'siral looked at Asora oddly. This was an odd question. But it was a familiar one. This was a question that was asked many times in class last year.

"Usually, the prime minister deals with such things," T'siral responded.

"But you also realize that the head of the royal house has to make policies on the economy, defense, diplomacy, and other things, right?" Asora pointed out. "I seem to remember that you said in class that it was the minister's responsibilities and all the royalty does is show off." Asora continued. "That was wrong, but the instructor allowed the answer, which was also wrong."

T'siral tried to maintain her cool. Asora was now playing this game with her too. "Very well, then. How would you pay for the grain to help maintain the supply?"

"Well, you will need money to pay for the transport of the grain, and that means taxes. Before starting to tax, a calculation is needed to know what to spend. Transport is the first, then preservation for long routes. Also, if the government provides the transport, that knocks down the price of bread and other grain-based staples," Asora explained.

"You obviously gave some thought to this. So, who would you tax?" T'siral demanded.

"You would say the commoners, but that is a limited pool of income. So, I would have to tax the wealthier, such as the aristocrats and landowners," Asora responded.

"That is begging for trouble. You need allies in court, and you have next to none." T'siral smirked.

"Well, I have one advantage, I am the owner of Evorn and a few other Utopian worlds, thanks to my family and the Great War," Asora said. "They do not pay taxes, but they will pay the fees and rent for the worlds I own. Utopians are traditionalists and nostalgic. That plays into my hands."

"You would not!" T'dia stated, worried.

"Pay taxes and I will not," Asora warned. "It would be better to pay taxes as that is fairer and even, then paying rent and fees. I can target more precisely."

"You would make a better prime minister," T'siral said.

"Here is another question. How would you combat a foe with superior firepower?" Asora asked, knowing the answer, thanks to history.

"I remember you asking that very same question in class," Manidai said.

"You are right. I asked that because that was something that actually happened and is playing out now!" Asora stated.

"You are referring to the Great War and our current situation with the Darkcons? The Darkcon problem will be resolved, as was the Great War," Aratica said.

She was a child when the war broke out, and she watched her warrior mother get killed by a human submarine with their sonar weapons.

"You humans killed nearly forty percent of the entire population of the kingdom," T'siral said.

"And your kind killed sixty percent of the Consortium's population," Asora quoted.

"Now, would any of you care to answer my question?" The other princesses said nothing as their answers would feed Asora's ego. War was not for ladies in their class and stature. Yet Asora seemed well attuned to this. "Nothing? I know, but I feel that all of you would disagree, as you do with everything else."

"Arrogance is not very becoming for a lady," T'siral pointed out.

"Strange, I thought arrogance was part of the job description, at least that is what I have gathered from most of you," Asora said. "Or is it only you elves?"

"Humans are so pathetic. You creatures know nothing and mutilate the nature around you," T'siral sounded like she was losing her patience.

"You elves are so primitive that single-celled organisms are more intelligent. Every human zoo should have a pair of elves." Asora smirked, hoping to infuriate the arrogant woman.

T'siral turned red, got off the throne, and marched up to Asora. Like most elves, she towered over Asora by several centimeters. Asora folded her arms in defiance. T'siral slapped Asora on her face with great strength. Asora lost balance but quickly rebalanced herself. She smiled and kicked T'siral's knee and punched her in the face like a man would. This sent T'siral backward to the floor. The elf lady cried in pain.

"Anyone else?" Asora spat. "I am going to my room."

After that, Asora marched out of the throne room. She needed to get out before she became more violent with them. She once fought all nineteen of them back in the academy. And she won those fights. Bloodied messes all of them as the nurses and doctors were kept busy because of Asora. She was the toughest lady, but she was also respected by many.

Asora had remained in her room for hours, distracting herself with strategic war games on her computer when her door burst open to reveal the other princesses. "What are you doing here?" Asora demanded in a very high-pitched voice.

"I see your human toy there is a very propaganda-oriented machine," T'siral said as she saw that the war game on the table and used elves as the enemy and targets.

"After dealing with you, I needed to unwind!" Asora said.

"You are a violent person," the sprite princess said, looking like she was going to cry.

"I can be," Asora admitted. "If provoked."

One of the princesses saw a military uniform on a display manikin. It was curious to see. As a noble lady of their standing had never seen combat. The only noble ladies that went into war were the dames. But knights and dames were the lowest of the noble ranks. These ladies, Asora included were among the highest. So, war and combat were foreign to them.

One of the princess's took off the coat from the manikin to look at it. Manidai was curious about it and the pretty colors on it. That got Asora's attention, and she stormed up to her.

"And, that is none of your concern!" Asora swiped her old uniform from the mermaid's hands.

"Well, this answers why you are so violent. You were a soldier," T'yisa said.

"Seriously? You had not picked up on that?" Asora asked dumbfounded as she put the coat back up.

"How did you become a soldier while you were in school with us?" Aratica asked.

"Remember the year that we had before the big announcement? I went through a crash course in the Red Guard Military Academy,"

Asora explained. "I hold the rank of colonel."

"What is a colonel?" the sprite princess asked.

"A commander of the various armies on the field. And it is a step below any of the general ranks," Asora explained.

Halasa sniffed the uniform and noticed something. "This smells as if it was in a battle."

"I was in one actual battle. That is how I got the rank of colonel," Asora admitted. "I was a trainee student, but I got a battlefield commission for it."

"Why were you in the military?" T'siral asked.

"In the human realm, everyone must serve the military in some fashion regardless of status. So, I had to serve, but I received a sped-up version of the training," Asora explained.

"What was the battle?" T'siral asked, now curious, secretly searching for something to use against her.

Asora began, *"On Havaina, inside the capital of Aunsborg, there was a massive military academy. At that time, I was being trained in both physical and intellectual needs. I then joined the Red Guard's Army and was automatically made a trainee captain and lead a company called Delta.*

One day there were a series of explosions following a message in the newspapers. The terrorists behind the attacks, known as the Freedom First Movement, targeted the financial district, residential apartments, playgrounds, military bases, and schools. Most of the military forces were away on training missions, and only the army trainees were available. The police were ambushed, and most were killed. The general in charge of the trainees ordered that they arm themselves. The enemy targeted Countess Marien's home as well, wanting to get rid of the royal family.

There were about three hundred trainees that were heavily armed and buried in armor. A firefight erupted in a grade-school field. The general was then shot in the head. Before he died, he gave me command since I was the closest thing to an actual officer still alive and there.

One of my classmates had a grenade launcher, another a machine gun. I only possessed an automatic rifle. However, I also had command of the field. The master HUD controls were at my disposal. I saw a man in the ruble of an apartment building spraying rifle bullets at people evacuating the building. I ordered a sniper to take the lunatic out. With one shot, he killed him and cleared the area for the trainee force. I had a plan and codenamed it Operation Dreadnought.

A trainee who was very good with drone warfare had discovered that several tactical and spy drones survived the bombings. I had him ready the drones for combat so I could command the battle space.

Dozens of drones flew overhead, and they relayed their information to my HUD systems. The extremists tried to target the drones but failed mostly. I commanded the drones to attack anyone who engaged them. This left them in an automatic attack mode.

The drones now knew that there were eight remaining terrorists and that they were gathering in a business building. A woman was listening to the enemy's communications, and this allowed for me to plan an attack.

The sun had gone down, but the fires throughout the city lit up the damage. I took the building and ordered them to surrender. They simply laughed at me. However, at the edges of a crater and in the ruble, I had hundreds of heavily armed young soldiers training their weapons on them. I, however, revealed that the image they were all seeing of me was a complex hologram and disappeared. I was outside of the building in front of a holo-camera.

The maniacs opened fire, but I ordered that they remain alive so the trainees could cripple them. In five minutes, the villains were taken down, but still alive.

The next day, the Freedom First Movement was charged with mass murder, terrorism, possession of deadly materials, false propaganda, rape, intimidation, and several other crimes. Countess Marien was one of thirteen judges that condemned them to the death penalty. The death penalty had not been used for the last five hundred years.

I was allowed to keep my battlefield-commissioned rank of colonel for my leadership in stopping the terrorists. The following month, I had to return to Evorn for the big decision."

"Well, that was quite a story. However, it is hard to believe," T'siral said. "I believe that you are making it up."

"Believe what you want, bimbo. That is how I got those medals and ropes," Asora spat.

"Well, be ready, for tomorrow is all manners," T'isa now spoke.

The nineteen princesses finally left the chamber.

"Ugh," Asora said to herself.

Princess Asora went to the palace library to get some peace and quiet. There, however, she saw Marevin, her betrothed. Marevin was a very nice human and a childhood friend. They even went through the trainee program together. And went through the Royal Academy together. As well as being betrothed.

"Ah, Asora, come sit," Marevin warmly greeted.

"Thanks," Asora said in the human language. "Ugh, what a day." Asora held her head in frustration.

"I heard that those she merks have been giving you a hard time," Marevin said.

"I wish you could snipe them the same way you took out those extremists last year," Asora said casually.

"I would if I could. But I did not apply for your position, and you knew that this was coming," Marevin pointed out. "Imagine if Jeia had gotten this job. He would be chasing them across the lawn with an elephant gun." Asora and Marevin laughed together.

"Could you be there tomorrow for me?" Asora asked.

"Of course I will, colonel or princess or both." Marevin tried to make Asora smile. "Princess will do," Asora said back softly.

The following day ensued, as promised, as the nineteen princesses sat Asora at a dining table to evaluate her manners. But, also as promised, Marevin was there, to the dismay of T'siral. But this also showed that Asora was willing to adhere to some of the traditions of a princess.

"Now, Asora. Organize the silverware for us," T'siral ordered.

"There are five forks, and Maker knows how many spoons and knives," Marevin said.

"Well, uh, Marevin, is it? This is civility," T'isa said.

"As is being patient," Marevin said.

"Why are you here? You are not a prince," Queen Bee buzzed.

"I was requested," Marevin said.

"So, Asora, you have the need for a prince part down, but this man is not a prince," T'siral said.

Marevin and Asora looked at each other with cocked eyebrows. To them this was absurd. In their culture love crossed social lines all the time. It was normal for the upper classes and commoners to intermingle. For nobles of different stations to love was also normal. This prevented inbreeding in their culture.

Then they turned to the elf lady as if she was nuts. "You do realize that he is my betrothed and it is his duty to be by my side?" Asora asked.

"The fact that he is not a prince is unusual," T'isa said.

"His family is one of the most powerful, and his father runs the second-largest defense company in the consortium," Asora said. "He is wealthier than your betrothed, if that is what you are getting at?"

"He is still below your setting," T'isa said.

"And you are below my tolerance," Marevin said to the female elf.

"That is it!" T'siral complained. "You creatures are of the most insufferable apes I have come across."

"What is the matter? Cannot take the insults? I can be more vulgar with the taunts," Marevin threatened.

"Enough! Let's get this task over with so we can move on!" Asora stated angrily.

Asora quickly assembled the silverware and dinnerware in the way that a skilled butler would. She also did this as fast as she could. She also wanted to make the others stop.

"Very good, and no magic either," T'siral noted, unimpressed.

"What else do you have for me?" Asora asked.

"Set the rest of the table," T'siral ordered.

"Usually, dozens of people set the table, because of the size," another voice said.

From the pantry came another regal lady elf. She was so elegant and beautiful that she made the other women envious. This was by design for this sub race of elves, the jewel elves. The sub race of elves that preferred the human lifestyle over the traditional elf lifestyle.

"Lady T'ula? Why are you here?" T'isa asked, shocked.

Lady T'ula was one of the most powerful elves in the entire kingdom. Not just in wealth and beauty, but also in magical power. T'ula in theory rivaled Asora's powers.

"I am here to make sure that you do not bully Princess Asora," T'ula said.

"Bully her, we are teaching her to be a proper princess," T'siral stated.

"Teaching and bullying can get blurred. And I remember what you are capable of. Also, Princess Asora is entitled to a defense," T'ula said. She turned to Asora. "Use the table setting spell to make up the whole table. It would take you over a week to set this table by hand."

Asora enchanted the plates, silverware, centerpieces, glasses, and napkins. They came up, as if on legs, and jumped to their positions. Asora whistled a tune to keep the spell going.

"How is that for a magical princess?" Asora asked triumphantly.

The next day, Admiral Yane, Asora's war minister, and her brother, who was also Asora's representative from the consortium and the Fusion Corp CEO, arrived.

"Ma'am," Yane said.

"Hey, sister," Jeia greeted as he hugged her.

"Hey, brother," Asora replied. "Admiral."

"You are not to show such affection to anyone except to your mate!" T'siral said, walking up to them.

"Who the fuck are you?" Jeia demanded, knowing that his comment was offensive, as he wanted it to be.

Jeia knew who she was, but he wanted to make her mad. He got a kick out of it.

"How dare you, you puny human!" T'isa spat, defending T'siral.

"You really want to tango with me? You are certainly welcome to try, pointy ears!" Jeia said with a threatening undertone.

"Jeia, you know better than to tease the animals," Yane said.

"You call us animals?" Questioned the she elf, but she never got the chance to finish.

"No, that is an insult to animals. I would say parasites, but those are above you as well," Yane said.

T'isa tried to slap Yane, but the old human admiral grabbed the elf's hand, rolled it along his arm, and forced T'isa to the ground and kicked her in the butt, making the elf eat dirt. "If you witches think you are so tough, then how did this old guy make you eat dirt? And I know that you have been harassing Asora for the last few days. My friend here and I are going to return the favor," Yane said.

"Asora! Call off your attack dogs!" T'siral demanded.

"These happen to be my friends and family. Now you are going to be fair, or I will allow them all have their way with you," Asora said, now in a position to challenge T'siral.

Now, Asora had allies and backup. She felt that it was time to make her side known to these lower princesses. Also, Asora was enjoying seeing T'siral get what she deserved.

Fearing that Princess Asora would call upon her brother and allies, the other princesses were kinder and stopped being difficult following T'siral's embarrassing ordeal.

Chapter Five

Dreadnought

It was day twelve of Asora's princess training, and she was being further lectured on Utopian manners. However, Asora was able to handle the training with more ease as her allies had returned to her side and the bullying had, for the most part, ceased.

The only Royal Guardsman that helped Princess Asora was a large centaur who also happened to be the captain of the guard named Joes. He was present to assist in one of the challenges. A test annoyed both Joes and Asora. But they did it none the less.

"A princess is to know what a guardsmen can and cannot do," Manidai said.

"The guardsmen are soldiers that take orders from a higher authority," Aratica added.

"They do not require an order form a mere prince or princess," T'sial said. "They will answer to the prime minister and the royal court. This is something that you have a hard time understanding that."

"The Royal Guard of the Utopian Kingdom are the kingdom's main line of defense. They need someone in high enough power to help cut through the bureaucracy," Asora replied.

"A girl has no place on the battlefield or telling generals what to do," T'yisa said.

"So says the dicks in power," Asora commented off handedly.

"Such vulgar language is not well received in the royal court," Aratica said. "It may be acceptable on Havaina, but not here."

"In the consortium we do not care if our leaders are men or women. We only care about competence. Something the kingdom has a serious lack of," Asora added.

"Humans do not seem to mind putting their women on the battlefield," T'sial said.

"We are a more equal society," Asora pointed out. "Being a colonel is far less of a headache then dealing with you."

"I thought that being colonel meant dealing with arrogant commanders?" Joes asked.

"True, but I was allowed to put them in their place," Asora said looking at T'sial and Aratica.

"Beast," T'sial said too Asora.

"A beast is a wild animal. I like to think I am more like a cyber," Asora said to T'sial.

"A cyber?" Amina asked.

"A terrible killing machine from the Great War five hundred years ago," T'yisa answered. "The humans and jewel elves created an army of metal automatons and used them to slaughter all life."

"The cybers were a race of intelligent machines. Originally made to help us. They were no enemy of life as these pointed eared brats claim," Asora said.

"Fortunately, your people were forced to destroy them," T'sial commented.

"No thanks to your people's lack of understanding," Asora replied.

Archduke Frenzen, the prime minister of the Utopian Kingdom, had also arrived, interrupting the training. He looked worried as he had a yellowish envelop in his hands. The type of envelop that humans normally used.

"Prime Minister, why are you here?" Manidai demanded.

"I have a letter for the princess," Frenzen said, annoyed. "I do have the authority to interrupt if it is important."

He gave Asora the letter. She opened it, looking confused as she read it.

"What does it say?" Yane asked.

"Boom!" was all the princess said.

An explosion erupted from a tower near the throne room. The smoke and flames broke out and damaged other nearby towers and palace structures. Glass was shattered all as well across the palace grounds.

Asora made the stained glass vanish from the hall so they could all see the damage. One of the towers was on fire. Another tower was in the middle of collapsing. Another explosion erupted in a room below the throne room. The floor opened near the window. Aratica cast a spell to keep everyone from falling into the hole. The water then turned to ice to keep everyone from falling in. Then a fourth explosion blasted through the auxiliary armory at the far end of the palace. That was where the guardsmen maintained their weapons. It was now a fire and smoke-filled ruin.

"Boom indeed!" the Queen Bee said.

"We have to get out of here!" Madimoy screamed.

T'siral transported everyone out of the room. Another explosion erupted from the kitchen. The past hour was filled with more explosions from multiple locations. They had no idea what or who was causing it.

Yane and T'ula were running to catch up to the princesses. T'ula stopped for a moment as something odd caught her eye. Jane stopped just a few paces in front of her.

"What is it?" Jane asked.

"What is this?" T'ula said.

T'ula looked down at something that was small but out of place. They found a black box behind a potted plant. Yane recognized the box as a remote-controlled bomb. Yane gently took off the face plate and disarmed it.

"We have to get to Princess Asora now," Yane said.

Yane and T'ula brought the black box to Asora. The princesses were in another room. T'ula could hear the princesses yelling and screaming.

"Admiral!" Madimoy yelle din a panic. "What is happening?"

"These," Yane said as he showed the black box.

Princess Asora recognized it. She took the dismantled black box from Yane and examined it.

"There are more than likely a few more of these," Yane pointed out.

"What is this?" asked Manidai.

"A type forty-three remote explosive device," Yane answered.

"A human weapon? But how did these get in?" T'isa asked.

"Admiral. Was there not a massive robbery of the Hagal Armory recently?" Asora asked Yane.

"Yes, there was, in fact. Just last month. They think that the Freedom First Movement was responsible," Yane said.

"The Freedom First Movement?" Queen Bee asked.

"They are a right-wing radical extremist terrorist organization," Asora said.

"Oh joy, human terrorists," T'isa said mockingly. "The most unhinged kind of rogues."

"Unfortunately, I agree with you," Asora said.

That shocked everyone, Asora herself included.

"That has to be a first," T'siral commented.

Another explosion tore through the halls, sending shrapnel flying. Amina was badly hurt, but she vanished as the dust settled. The screaming from everyone around them also distracted Asora.

The destruction stopped, and this allowed the guards to clean up the dead bodies and debris. Asora found another letter that told her to go to the entry to the palace wine cellar. The guards gathered around the door to the cellar. An explosion ripped through the air, injuring everyone who had not fully evacuated the premises. The guards were all badly injured and had to be pulled out.

"Asora, you will be the only one to go down the stairs, and only you. I will know if anyone follows you," a voice on a speaker ordered to the princess. "Oh, leave all your weapons."

"You cannot be serious!" Jeia spat.

"He wants me. Just keep everyone out here," Asora ordered to her brother. "Besides, I can take care of myself. If I do not come back, then you and T'ula can have my crown."

T'siral and the rest looked shocked as Asora walked down the dark stairs. This was brave of her to do this.

Princess Asora finally reached the bottom and saw several doors around her. "Where are you?"

"The third door to your left," the voice said.

Slowly she walked up to the door. However, she did not need to open the door; the man behind it did. A gun was now in Asora's face. The man was holding a squeeze handle with an antenna. He made enough room to make Asora walk inside slowly. But he did not close the door.

Asora recognized the badly shaved man who walked with a limp. "I know you."

"Yeah, I'm the one whose leg you blew off!" the man shouted, shaking nervously.

He lifted one of his pant legs to show a prosthetic leg that went all the way up to his hip. His whole left leg was completely gone, leaving him with an eternal limp.

"What did you expect? You and your friends were mass-murdering innocent people!" Asora stated.

"There is no such thing as innocents! Anyone who obeys the oppressive government that takes away more and more deserve to die, along with the overlords that run everything!" the man shouted in Asora's ear as he moved around her, still pointing his gun at her head.

"You do realize that you will not be getting out of here in one piece, right?" Asora pointed out.

"Shut up!" the man screamed nervously. "Sit down!" Asora refused to move.

In response the man punched Asora in the face. It was not hard as he needed to keep the device in his hand still. But the intent was clear. He was fighting Asora for control of the situation.

"That hand of yours must be getting really tired." Asora commented as she rubbed the area he hit on her face.

Both then heard the creaking from the floor. The crazy man vanished into the dark, still pointing the gun at Asora. On the floor, Asora saw footprints in the dust. The crazy man grabbed a bottle of wine and slammed it into what turned out to be an invisible person. While the invisible person staggered around the man then slammed his full fist into the person's head harder then he hit Asora with. The whack and the wine forced T'siral to become visible.

"I told you to come alone!" the man screamed.

"I did, I do not know why she is here!" Asora sounded frustrated.

Princess Asora then helped T'siral up to her feet. She also attempted to clean off some of the wine that stained the elf princess.

"Well, you two can watch," The man said.

He clicked a switch using his one free finger, and a floodlight showed the littlest princess. Amina tied to a chair with a thick vest strapped to her.

"Amina!" T'siral cried.

"Help me!" the little princess cried, frightened.

"Make any stupid moves and her brains will redecorate the walls," the man said.

"Who is this sick psycho?" T'siral asked Asora.

"His name is Thasis Arave, one of the Freedom First Movement's tactical advisers and one of the few that escaped our justice system," Asora answered.

"That's right, tell her what you did!" Thasis ordered.

"She did? Now I believe her," T'siral said. She turned to Asora and whispered, "What is that device in his hand?"

"It is a dead man's switch. If he lets go, then all the explosives he has planted will go off," Asora whispered back.

"We have to get Amina out of here," the lady elf said.

"That vest worries me. I want Amina out of here too, but that vest. It might be a suicide bomber vest," Asora said.

"A what?" T'siral looked horrified.

"Hey, you two wenches, quit whispering!" Thasis screamed.

"I have an idea," Asora said. The princess folded her arms and walked up to Thasis. "Thasis, why bother with her? I am the greater prize. I am the overbearing government, or embody it, as you say. It is me that you should be targeting."

Asora's logic confounded Thasis for a moment. He giggled insanely. "Nice try, colonel. But these Utopian vermin need to have a message sent to them as well."

"I command the Utopian Kingdom, and the destiny of the Human Consortium. Come at me," Asora stated.

"I want that elf out of here," Thasis pointed his gun at T'siral's head.

"Go, T'siral, I can deal with him," Asora ordered.

"As you wish," T'siral said as she slowly backed away and up the stairs.

"As for you, colonel or princess or whatever. It's time to punish you." Thasis slammed the butt of his gun at Asora's forehead, knocking her down. "You will watch this." Thasis shot the little princess in the head.

T'siral ran up the stairs, sweating. She looked like she was carrying a sack, and it was wiggling. She ran up to the other princesses, Jeia, T'ula, and the newly arrived guardsmen. She took off the magical sack to reveal the little Princess Amina.

"We have to help, Princess Asora." Amina cried.

"And we will," T'siral said. She summoned every fairy in the palace. "Find every little black box and throw them into space, now!" She turned to the others and explained what was happening. "Asora is going to distract him while we find all the bombs."

They then heard a gunshot, and the worst was thought. However, the other princesses knew that Asora was still alive. They could feel her strong life force. They also heard fighting.

In less than five minutes, tens of thousands of fairies swarmed the palace like a swarm of bees. They ripped many black boxes, casting spells on them to prevent premature detonation.

Jeia had several missiles brought to the outer court yards of the palace. They were delivered by large Fusion Corp hover craft. The missiles could reach space. The fairies loaded the black boxes, and the missiles went into space as soon as they were full.

Rayne buzzed her wings at a frequency that Asora could hear. A fairy buzz could only be heard by certain magical peoples. Asora was certainly capable of hearing her fairy maid's buzz. Each was unique, and each held a special meaning. Rayne's buzz was a low sound that was carried on the air that only Asora could hear. This was the signal for Asora to fight back.

Princess Asora and Thasis had been trading blows. But she allowed Thasis to bloody her to give him the illusion of winning. Asora was holding back just long enough. This was a standard Red Guard Strategic Defense Command close quarters combat tactic when dealing with terrorists. Asora was on the floor in a corner breathing hard. Then she heard Rayne's signal.

She got back up and charged the madman. They wrestle, punch, kick, and bite. Asora was trying to get the gun out of Thasis's hand. She was no longer concerned about him releasing the deadman's switch. She was now showing her true strength to him. Asora broken his other leg and slammed him into the wall. Asora then picked him up by his shirt with one arm showing that she was easily ten times stronger than he was. Her angelic heritage gave her many gifts, super strength came standard as she thought of it. Asora then tossed him into a shelf.

"You're just as mad!" Thasis said.

"So says the expert," Asora said.

Asora made the magical fake body of Amina disappear. "You tricked me!"

"Of course I did." Asora snapped.

Thasis got back up and charged at the princess. Asora slammed her foot into Thasis's chest, sending him back into several wooden boxes. Next, the princess went for Thasis's hand that held the dead man's switch. She took out a knife that was hidden under her dress. She and was about to cut off Thasis hand. Thasis then shot Asora in her stomach three times, causing her to fall back in pain.

"See you in hell." Thasis released the switch and dropped it. But nothing happened. "No, it's not fair, it's not fair!"

Asora punched him in the face so hard that Thasis lost consciousness. "What can I tell you? Life is never fair."

Asora grunted in pain as she held her bleeding belly. She wanted to scream but she knew not to. Her old military training kicked in and she had to stay still. She held her belly as it bled out. Asora then fell slowly to the floor and lost consciousness.

Princess Asora woke up with her belly in bandages and feeling as if she would throw up at any moment. The pain from the healing muscles in her abdomen also did not help her mood. Asora's eyes were still adjusting to the light from the room. She looked around and saw that she was in the palace hospital. She had her own private recovery room that was decorated and designed to make her feel comfortable. There was no technology that she was used to in human hospitals. The Utopians used all magical means of healing. Asora thought that this was stupid and tried to get her doctors to upgrade with technology. But why listen to a princess? Their job is to keep her healthy not listen to her.

The door opened and several people came in. They were the other minor princesses. Behind them were also T'ula, and Jeia. Prime Minister Frenzen was the last to step in.

"You are awake!" Amina squealed with joy.

"How do you feel?" the prime minister asked.

"Like I want to vomit violently," Asora said, looking ill. "So, no food please."

"I am not surprised. I have been shot and impaled in my gut a few times myself. So, I know you feel," Frenzen said. "Congratulations on your new battle scare."

"Thanks," Asora said.

"Battle scares?" T'sal asked.

"She was and still is a soldier," was all Frenzen said.

Archduke Frenzen was a fell officer in the military, and he knew what Asora went through. She also knew the Code of the Soldier that was present in all cultures. So Asora understood the comment.

"Asora!" Jeia yelled, bringing in a massive vase of flowers. "Glad you are still here with us."

"I think you over did the flowers?" Asora asked.

"To show how important you are to me." Jeia smiled as he put down the vase.

"You were very brave. We will not challenge you with that. You were far braver than any of us," T'siral said as she walked up.

"She saved us, and that is a true leader. I say she is worthy." Amina smiled.

"I am glad that I have earned your approval." Asora smiled.

"Drink some Arals Leaf Tea. It will get rid of the vomiting feeling that you are having," T'siral suggested.

"What happened to Thasis?" Asora asked.

"The prime minister here took care of him," Jeia said.

"What did you do?" the princess asked.

"I used a special Forgotten Spell on him. I erased his mind and created a new personality. He will now work here in the palace as part of the cleaning crew and will enjoy his new job," Frenzen said. "Better than condemning him to death. Plus, he now has some new friends."

"I suppose that works. But cleaning crew is justice enough," Asora said. "He can live out his final days here in peace."

"Well, we are going back home. You are worthy of being the princess of the Utopian Kingdom," T'siral said.

"Wow, she paid you a compliment," Jeia said.

"When you are well, my princess, the kingdom needs you. The new queen of the Darkcon Empire has begun making incursions into the kingdom again," Frenzen said.

Chapter Six

Darkcon Research

Dorien was the capital planet of the Darkcon Empire. It was a world that was covered entirely in thick black clouds, which obscured the sky. This gave it a permanent night across the planet. There were also powerful and violent storms that plague the coastlines and flatlands on a regular basis. This world had a strange beauty to it, as the clouds had caused plants to develop their own light—photoluminescence. They covered the entire world in a radiant loveliness. The landscape caused visitors to gasp in awe at the unnatural shimmering plants and flowers against the natural black earth and stone mountains.

A fortress dominated a region in the northern continent, made of black opal marble and with a large, dark city at its base, stood tall over a vast expanse of flat land. This place was called the Onyx Palace. It was the Darkcon Empire's equivalent to the Utopian Kingdom's Royal Palace. The Onyx Palace was smaller but far more efficient and easier to upgrade and defend.

Coming toward the medieval styled complex was a convoy; at its center was an automobile that carried Queen Laxur and some of her privy council. In the backseat was the dark beauty herself, reading the technical journals of the engineers and scientists from Carlon. With her was Dari, who was studying the remains of the circuit card that was destroyed when the laser was thrown to the floor. Dari like most Darkcon's knew of these sorts of technology but did not quite understand it.

They bounced along on the newly built street, which was constructed for the use of the new automobiles that were the current rage for the Darkcons. Roads were under construction all over the world. Also, across many Darkcon worlds across the empire. Everyone was to enjoy them, from the richest of the rich to the commoners. The roads were most useful to the military. Queen Laxur was having a special road system built to allow her new machines to move across Dorien to the portals with ease. This was also to be a common feature of Laxur's new highway system for her people to enjoy and her forces to use.

Thus far, the roads were several lanes wide in both directions, but in some areas, there was nothing but dirt. In cities and villages, there were fueling stations for the automobiles, signs for road rules, and even advertisements for nobilities' products. Everything that was associated with the road systems was being built up with incredible speed, with soldiers, contractors, ordinary citizens, and even prisoners working on the project.

What also came up where Highway, or railroad cities started to pop up across the empire. These pop-up cities had mostly business establishments and tourist attractions. Queen Laxur used her knowledge of human urban design and taught the Darkcon how to take advantage of it. One of the endless gifts that Laxur gave her people. Their love and loyalty to her was mostly from this. It guaranteed her power and the more she gave them, the more power they gave her.

New wealth had emerged from the commoner ranks in recent years because the young queen had allowed a limited form of capitalism. Because of that, the empire was able to rise from the seemingly eternal poverty they had always suffered to a booming economy. Queen Laxur used the humans' economic system and adopted it for the empire. There were even a few cases of commoners becoming richer than most of the nobility. With these successes, the monarch had earned the love of most of her people, and she used it to her advantage. They loved her, though they knew she was dangerous. But that made her exciting. This also gave her a new source of income. Under Queen Laxur's reign taxes famously went from a life-or-death event to a mere mild annoyance for all.

As the convey approached the Onyx Palace Laxur had to look out to admire her work. The Darkcon were now a great economic power that now outdid the Utopian Kingdom for the first time.

The Onyx Palace outwardly looked as it always had. But all the modernizations and changes were inside its walls. The limousine pulled up to the guard point. The guards were nasty and wild looking gremlins that looked to be permanently hyperactive psychos. But they were in fact some of the best guards anyone could ever ask for. Laxur herself preferred them to protect her and her people and property.

The guards demanded identifications. They did not care if they delayed the queen's return. Laxur had the window rolled down and she showed the small gremlin in a professional looking guard uniform. The gremlin spat out some grunts in their language that most could not understand. The guard point allowed them to enter.

Queen Laxur entered her fortress, and sat upon her throne of metal and flesh, still reading. Or as it appeared to be flesh. Like Princess Asora's throne, Laxur's throne changed depending on Laxur's personality and mood. She was feeling evil and triumphant, so her throne took this form to show all that her mission was a success.

Laxur was still reading the massive tech manual. It was not unusual for a Darkcon woman to be passionate readers. Laxur seemed to embody this trait. Several servants were struggling to hold all the other tech manuals as they followed Laxur to her throne.

"I must say, this is actually quite brilliant," Laxur commented.

"What is brilliant, my queen?" Dari asked.

"These journals mention far more than the laser weapon systems that the humans were developing. It also mentions where they have been getting all their ideas." The queen smiled wickedly.

"Really? So, the humans did not come up with this stuff? Someone else gave them these ideas?" said a black cat, which was next to Laxur.

"Not exactly, Sysu. No one handed them this knowledge. It looks like they reverse engineered some spacecraft of unknown origin," Laxur explained.

"An unknown technology? Do they say who built it or where it came from?" Dari asked.

"No, the journals do not. All they say is that they found it decades, if not hundreds of years, ago in the Goalan deserts on Havaina," Laxur informed her. "But what they got from it was everything that they now have—from electricity to flying machines to an understanding of modern and quantum sciences."

One of Laxur's servants increased the power to the lights, which brightened the room. Laxur had electric lights and other electric devices installed throughout the Onyx Palace. This was something new to their part of the realm. At least until Laxur became their queen. The Utopians had yet to embrace this new science, except for the humans, though Asora was trying, or so the queen's spies had informed her.

"Much better. Now then, where was I? Oh yes, the use of internal combustion engines and gas turbines." The dark beauty ran her scarlet fingernail down the page.

"My queen, our scientists have determined that the circuit card is not repairable," a werewolf growled, bringing the remains of the card to his monarch.

He was Obsidian in his human form. He was a handsome, pale, long-haired man. Very muscular and wore pants with light armor.

"That thing is of no consequence to me, Obsidian. These journals describe how to build them," Laxur said, pointing to a book. "They describe the theories needed to build circuit cards."

An ugly big troll in a studded leather military-like uniform scrunched up his face in concentration. Like most people throughout the empire, he had a hard time wrapping his head around the idea of a circuit. But he did like what his queen said about them and how they could help them.

"What do those journals say about other new weapons that the Utopians may be working on?" the troll general rumbled.

"The humans have been busy on many projects, and not many are meant for the Utopians, if you catch my meaning, Urax," Laxur replied. She looked over the heads of the court members, thinking.

"Sysu, I want our scientists and engineers to learn this science and make these devices," Laxur ordered.

She held out the books. Sysu ordered her servants to take them from the queen. Sysu was not a fan of this advanced technology. She still hated the idea of a computer. She understood its benefits and why the queen wanted them. But Sysu really did not care for this technology.

"Yes, your majesty, it will be done." Sysu hissed at a vampire standing close by. "Take the journal and follow me, Lucius."

The male vampire was starstruck with the queen, so he bowed deeply to Laxur and took the journals with a shaky hand. Sysu hissed again at the youngster and swatted at his ankle, drawing blood. Lucius moved quickly toward the cat. Sysu then blended into the darkness surrounding the throne, with the man following close on her paws.

"Obsidian, I want you to bring to me my most notable corrupt humans. I want to know if they are aware of any of this," Laxur demanded.

Obsidian bowed and walked off. He was followed by several other werewolves in their wolf forms.

The queen called him back. "Wait. Bring me the priest, Illumin. He was a scientist for the humans before he was called to serve the Architect."

"As you command, Majesty." Obsidian bowed again and quickly left.

In an hour, Illumin's long silver-and-black cloak swept behind him as he approached the throne. Beneath the cloak, he wore the slim black cossack shirt of his order. He was two meters tall with an athletic build. He had a solemn expression in his chocolate-brown eyes, framed by long black hair. He bowed to the queen.

Laxur was standing and had dressed her voluptuous form in her customary black. Her dress had a low neckline, showing a great deal of her breasts. A less prideful woman might cover up for a religious man, but the queen simply smiled and took to her throne. She enjoyed flaunting her assets. She enjoyed the lust that she could inspire in others.

"Illumin. Good. Has Obsidian told you why I called for you?" Laxur asked gently.

"He has not, majesty. I assumed you wanted a religious discussion. I am pleased to pray with you," he said in a deep, gracious voice.

"I thank you for your concern over the state of my soul, but that is not what I want to speak with you about. I wish to have discourse about the humans." The queen smiled.

"Majesty? I do not understand," Illumin questioned.

"Prior to your conversion to the gods or the Architect, you were an amateur scientist with the countess's people, were you not?" Laxur demanded.

"Yes, majesty." He looked leery.

"What did you work on?" the queen asked.

"Perhaps you would like to tell me what you really need," Illumin calmly said.

The queen stood up and walked to the priest, overshadowing him by many centimeters. She wanted to watch his face. She also wanted to intimidate him and show him that she was the one in charge.

"All right. I want to know about the alien spacecraft that was unearthed in Havaina." Illumin nodded. "Ah. I have heard these stories."

"Stories or truths?" Her voice turned dark and lowered in tone.

"Truths." He looked her in the eyes. "I had many people tell me many things when I was studying to become a priest and warlock."

"A warlock, which is forbidden by Utopian law. You are human. Therefore, you are prohibited to perform magic unless by special dispensation under unique conditions. It is by religious law, as is praying to the Architect." She smiled mockingly. "Barring special situations."

He bowed his head slightly. "Which is why I am here, majesty."

She turned and sauntered back to her throne. "Ratted out by your own flock, if I remember correctly. But before that, you were a theoretical physicist. Did you work on any project that had to do with reverse engineering?"

The priest sighed. "I worked on force fields—not the magical barriers that we use on our flying vessels, but scientific ones, using plasma and electromagnetic devices."

Laxur gripped the armrests. "These things are possible?"

"Very much so. It was highly classified. If your people had not broken me out of prison, I would be dead," Illumin said softly.

"For being a warlock. Now you are corrupt. Obsidian brought you to my attention for your religious calling. Anyone who tells the puro to think of humans as precious as elves has my admiration. You dared to go against the elite." The queen smiled, but her eyes were hard and probing.

"I had nothing else to lose, Majesty. I had already been called a heretic and blasphemous for using magic." He smiled slightly.

The queen sighed. "Considering your work, I think the military would have stood by you."

"I worked for the human government, and they had little say, as always. This, of course, was before your sister came to the throne. It may be different now," Illumin stated.

Laxur shifted in her throne. "Asora is a figurehead. The court only made her Princess to appease the humans and the angels. They needed to do something. It is rumored that the humans, and even the fairies, are getting cranky about their treatment by the rest of the Utopian Kingdom, the so-called Kingdom of Light. It is doubtful that they take her seriously. She is only seventeen, after all. They figured that they could run the government as the court saw fit."

He bowed to her. "As you say, majesty."

"I do say. They also did it to spite me. They think by having her as their leader, I will behave myself. As if her being on the throne will stop me." She laughed.

The priest gave a small smile. "Who can stop the wind?"

The black-haired beauty grinned back, sliding back in her throne. "Exactly. You understand very well, Priest. I can see that you are an intelligent man."

He bowed again. "Thank you, Majesty. Is there anything else that I can do for you?"

Laxur slid off the throne and swayed toward him. "Yes, Illumin, there is. I want to know if you still have contacts within the Utopian science community. Do you?"

"What you want to know is if I am still in contact with any scientists who worked on the Havaina projects." Illumin stared at his queen.

Laxur walked around the priest. "Yes, that is exactly what I want. Are you?"

He waited until the queen stood before him again. "I have spoken with them since I came to the Darkcon Empire. I go through the underground to get messages in and out. They have spoken of working with the alien technology, but I must stress that they are loyal to the countess."

The queen frowned. "This was the same countess that allowed you to be tried for heresy?"

"She has no power over the puro. Only the king did," Illumin reminded Laxur.

"And you were saved by the underground and sent here. I expect your loyalty is now to me and not the countess. She may be the monarch of the humans, but she is still part of the Grand Utopian Kingdom. Do I have your loyalty?" The Queen purred as she stared at the man.

The priest felt his next words could be his last if he spoke the wrong ones. "Your Majesty, I am your servant."

She smiled again. "Good. Now get in touch with your friends and see what they are up to. I want to know more about these aliens." Laxur sat on her throne.

The priest looked dubious. "Um, I do not think it will be that easy. Those secrets are strictly guarded by the Hananaka. The countess would find out," he pleaded.

The queen stared at the uncomfortable Illumin and suddenly stood up. "My mother believed in the Hananaka, and I believe that is where I will find the answer."

Illumin looked with wonder at Laxur. "Your mother? She believed the stories were real?"

"Yes. When I was a child, she told me that they, the gods, had often come to our worlds and left part of themselves behind. I thought she meant our culture and religion, but they must have left spacecraft and artifacts. That is why the humans have advanced more quickly than any other species. They are willing to risk being called heretics than to denounce the ones whom humanity pray's too, the Hananaka gods to the puro, but the humans walk the line by also praying to the Maker," Laxur postulated. "There are no temples for the Hananaka gods, neither for their heroes."

"If that is so, then Countess Marien will be even more protective of the information and artifacts. She will not help you become more powerful," Illumin advised.

"Who said that I want to become more powerful with this technology? I want to help my people grow strong, as strong as the humans are. I believe in the cause of the humans. Was I not brought up to honor those values, as a human?" Laxur said.

"True, Majesty." He shifted slightly, looking down then up at his Queen. "I could speak to the others, use those words. I may be able to convince them, but could you not speak to Countess Marien?"

Laxur sat down. "That is not your concern, priest. You may go."

Illumin bowed low and walked out backward until he slipped away into the shadows. As he turned to walk out of the hall, he ran into General Sysu. The vampire, dressed in her black leather uniform, grabbed his shoulder with her leather-clad hand.

"I would suggest that you do as the queen says. I like you, Priest. I would hate to be the one to issue your death order for failure to comply," Sysu said with a hint of malice.

Illumin smiled briefly. "Do not worry, general. I do not fail when I give my word. I believe that we humans will be served best by linking our future with the Darkcon Empire."

Sysu gave him a searching look. "Why?"

Illumin gave her the truth. "We are persecuted in the Kingdom of Light," he sneered. "Where can our people go but here, to the Empire of Darkness? We find more freedom here than we ever had in the Utopian Kingdom. We can hold high positions of power, do any job we are qualified for, or even go to a university to learn whatever we want. We are not limited, and we can pray to whom we want. We can even practice magic. It may be a more militaristic society, but it needs a tough ruler to keep the demon warlords in check."

The vampire smiled wide and clapped him on the shoulder. "I liked you before, but now I can call you friend. Good. You will go far. I may even come to your sermons."

"I believe in the Darkcons. I believe in their future. If you will excuse me, I have work to do." Illumin pushed past Sysu and let out a slow breath.

The vampire watched him go then heard Obsidian tell Laxur about the raiders.

"They *were* on Carlon, as we suspected, but the pirates were gone by the time we landed. The information we got from talking to the people proves that they had prior notice of our taking of Carlon. We have a leak, as you have speculated." The werewolf was conciliatory.

"Hmm." Laxur tapped her armrest. "Whom do you suspect, General Obsidian?"

He shook his head. "I have no idea. But my pack is working on it."

"Never mind then. Just tell me you have an idea of where to find them." The dark queen waved a hand.

"Barnell, Your Majesty. As you know, it is a nonaligned world with both Darkcon and Utopian presence." The general shrugged.

"Let me guess—they are on the Utopian side?" Laxur sighed heavily. "There is no other way to get to them except to go in there and take their new base. We will inform Veartis so that he can tell Asora. It will probably escalate the situation with the Utopians, and I have no problem with that. They are a paper tiger. They still fight with spears and bow and arrows, for the Maker's sake. We only need to fear the angels and the humans, and I doubt either one will interfere," Laxur said.

"I agree. We will prevail over the pitiful attacks of the Utopians." Sysu laughed. "Majesty, they are pathetic. If you command me to take Barnell, I will go immediately. It should take a month to ready my troops, and even if the raiders run, we will have destroyed a bolthole for them to run to in the future."

"I command you to take Barnell, general. Now, go prepare." Laxur smiled.

The queen and her bodyguard went to the top of the fortress's tower. The room was her private laboratory, where she created her potions and spells. It was made of smooth black stone and had two stories, one overlooking the other. Against one wall on the first floor was a bookcase filled with ancient manuscripts. On the opposite wall, there were magical herbs and crystals in a wooden floor-to-ceiling cabinet. A large workbench was in the center, and bottles of potions in varied colors floated around the room. Laxur opened the door, and flames burst into the fireplace and onto the wicks of candles. There was no electricity in this lab because of the violent nature of the magic performed by Laxur. The dark-haired Queen walked to the wooden bench and peered through a magnifying glass at a chemical substance.

"Dari, give me the black ulipsis herbs from the other table," Laxur ordered her bodyguard. The fallen angel brought the herbs as her sovereign asked.

"What are you making now, if you do not mind me asking?" Dari questioned the queen.

"I am making more of the illicit potions," the queen responded as she mixed the ingredients together.

"Would you let me try it sometime? I have always wanted to try," the female bodyguard asked.

Laxur held the bottle up to the light, and the florescent green fluid glowed. It was her favorite potion. She turned to Dari. "Another day, perhaps."

Chapter Seven

Asora's Science Fair

It had been eight weeks since Princess Asora announced her great science fair. She was excited to see the new ideas that her people might bring to the table. As she and Archduke Frenzen predicted, it was mostly humans that were present, but there were a few other species presenting projects as well. Which gave Frenzen some sense of pride in his people.

The Utopian princess was in her chambers in the early hours, preparing for the first day of the first ever Utopian Kingdom Science Fair. Asora planned to have the fair last for three days. That was not if she endured from the other princesses. But Asora ordered that the Royal Court attend and learn. She was going to exercise all the power she had now over them.

The princess's four fairy ladies-in-waiting dressed the princess in her white and gold courtier dress. It was a long silk gown with a small neckline: the dress of the virgin princess. She also had a light amount of jewelry in the shape and form of leaves, flowers, flames, and water waves.

"Thank you. I would like the little circlet crown for today's science fair." Asora tilted her head. "Do you not think? It should be something modest."

"Oh yes, your highness. Do you know if any fairies are presenting anything?" B'nei, the snow fairy, asked out of curiosity. She fluttered over her head to comb a strand of the princess's hair into an intricate curl.

"Actually, yes. There are a few fairies presenting. And one thing that I am extremely interested in is a new form of electricity for Evorn, called alternating current. It is known on the fairies' worlds and on the humans', but not in the Utopian Kingdom," Asora said.

"What is alternating current?" Rayne, the purple dressed storm fairy, asked.

"It is a way of conducting electricity," Asora explained. "One of two in fact."

Her comments made the fairies flutter with excitement. Friea, the red dressed fire fairy, placed the circlet crown upon Asora's head and adjusted it for the princess's comfort.

"Thank you, Friea. So, are you four going to the science fair?" Asora asked.

"We will go with you, your highness. We would like to see these new ideas too!" Gourani exclaimed.

Asora, with her four fairies fluttering about her, walked out of her chambers and into the sitting room, where Sarea stood at attention. The mighty dame was Asora most loyal guard.

"You wish to go now, highness?" Sarea asked.

The princess nodded. "Yes, Sarea. Open the door."

They stepped out, and the honor guards snapped to attention. In the middle of the hallway stood Lady Madimoy, a human. She was a delicate redhead who was wearing a long dress of moss green. With her was her fairy friend and servant Rentha, another fiery redhead lady. She wore a dress of yellow. They were talking to Lady T'a. They were debating on the differing opinions of other races regarding technology and knowledge.

"I am pleased to see that you three have gotten into the spirit of things today." Asora smiled.

"Well, I am, my princess, but Lady Death over here has reservations about this science fair of yours." Madimoy pointed to T'a.

"I do not have reservations about the science fair, Lady Madimoy. Personally, I fancy the idea. However, many people have come to me with concerns," T'a started. "I am merely bringing them to the princess's attention."

"Concerns that are more like complaints. Those arrogant, backward animals!" Madimoy exclaimed exasperatedly.

"Please, Madimoy! I am simply relaying messages, and you, my dear lady, are acting as arrogantly as we 'animals' as you see us," T'a returned the insult.

"Why you little piece of—" Madimoy spat.

"Madimoy! Please, not here and not now," Asora interrupted Madimoy's rant. "You two can hash it out later behind closed doors," Asora warned the two feuding women. "And as for you, T'a, tell those that have reservations that they had better enjoy these next few days, or I will see to it that there will be more of these fairs to come. That I promise."

"Yes, your highness. As I said, I am looking forward to seeing the new ideas," T'a said.

"Yes, I bet, because you still feel sorry for the Great War. Am I right, witch queen?" Madimoy sneered. T'a looked as if she was guilty of a crime. She lowered her head and walked off.

"Madimoy, that was out of line!" Asora snarled.

"How was that out of line? Have you forgotten what that elf witch did to our people?" Madimoy yelled back.

"She did great harm to Lady Madimoy's family." Rentha, the little fairy woman, fluttered close to her mistress.

"That was five hundred years ago," Asora said.

"We humans are known for our long-term collective memories. You should know that princess," Madimoy answered back.

"Yes, but still she continues to make amends for it," Asora reminded her friend.

"Not to all of us. She is still a monster, as far as I am concerned—she and the rest of her kind. For the Maker's sake, your sister and the Darkcons do not even come close to that level of evil," Madimoy stated angrily.

Asora knew Madimoy's anger all too well, and she was not the only human that felt this way. Asora's mother's family harbored such hatred, but the princess did not see the reason behind it. What was past was past, and the kingdom must move forward. She did once, but Asora believed that the only way to heal these old wounds was to move forward. Asora saw herself as the Utopian Kingdom's redemption and she would lead them on that path.

"But, Madimoy, is not your stepmother an elf?" Asora reminded her.

"Do not mention that slave driver to me. She took my daddy from me, and I was forced to be a little puppet girl for all her shows and balls." Madimoy vented her anger.

"Very well, my friend. Far be it from me to change your perspective on the world." Asora sighed sadly.

"Oh, my princess before I forget there is a Mr. Anco waiting for you in your private study," B'nei said floating next to Asora's face.

"Yes, I had better take that," Asora said.

"Anco?" Madimoy blurted out in a fright. "Why is he here?"

"I asked for him," Asora said.

Madimoy looked anxious as the name Anco along struck fear in almost everyone. Only Asora seemed unafraid of him. The princess then vanished in a cloud of gray mist.

Asora reappeared in her study in her chair at her desk. There was a man in a green military uniform from the Human Consortium Red Guard. He was average height battle scared and had a demeanor that made him appear hostile.

"I was wondering when you would get here," Asora said.

"These palace guards are very inefficient at their security practices. Besides I am not a merk," Anco said.

He smiled at Asora and the two hugged. They were friends in fact and Asora saw him as a mentor not as a terror.

"Yes general," Asora said. "But I am glad you came."

"I would not miss an opportunity to help one of my best students and best colonel," Anco smiled and then sat down. "I feels strange being on this side of a desk."

"Especially to a subordinate," Asora pointed out.

"Well, you are not a subordinate anymore. You lead this sham of a kingdom," Anco said.

"I am trying to change it. To make it better for everyone," Asora pointed out.

"I understand. But I am assuming that you are finding that to be a task better said then done?" Anco said.

"You have no idea," Asora replied with sarcasm.

"I am also assuming that you did not call me all the way out here to have a one on one chat," Anco said.

"You are correct. I suspect that there will be attempts to sabotage this fair and all of my other black project plans," Asora said.

"A reasonable assumption, but the Utopians are not intelligent enough to pull off such levels of obstructionism," Anco said.

"Legally yes they can. Militarily you are right," Asora pointed out. "But I think that the Freedom First Movement and other right wing nut jobs from the consortium will also be an issue."

"You could be right," Anco said.

"I need a specialized police force that can deal with these sorts of things," Asora said.

"You want me to establish an enforcement and investigation organization? Like the old Husad?" Anco asked.

"I was thinking of having the Husad expand their role to include the whole Utopian Kingdom," Asora said.

"Colonel," Anco stopped himself. "My apologizes, princess. The Husad are a special operations unit and for all intents and purposes secret police, and officially do not exist. I do not think the Utopians will stand for it?"

"I know. That is why I need a reason for it," Asora said with a wicked grin. Anco nodded in approval.

"You have always been good at games and theory," Anco said.

"I learned from the best," Asora replied.

An hour later, the princess was escorted by her fairies through the display/audience chambers of the palace to where the science fair was being held. By her side was her personal assistant, an elf woman known as Lady T'ula. Lady T'ula was the one responsible for setting up the fair.

She was a tall woman with a bright smile and long blue-black hair. She wore deep blue, her family's color. T'ula also bore a nearly identical shape, form, and appearance to the queen of the Darkcon Empire, Queen Laxur. This earned her the nickname of the 'Good Laxur.' T'ula was loved by all other elves but supposedly had no love for science and technology. Despite this, she did her task and did it well. Asora was very impressed with the elf's work. Which made sense since she was a jewel elf.

Jewel elves were closer to humans in personality. Jewel elves preferred science and technology. When a jewel elf says they do not. They are merely being diplomatic. So, they can use this as a political maneuver. So T'ula's opinion of science was merely for show as far as Asora could tell. She knew T'ula well and trusted her dearly.

"I must say, Lady T'ula, you have done a magnificent job setting up this fair. I thank you for it," Asora said gratefully.

"I always do the best at whatever I am tasked to do, my princess," T'ula responded dutifully.

Asora thought that T'ula's response was rather arrogant, but she had no room to complain. She had done her job admirably. Jewel elves do have a very high opinion themselves. So, this response was to be expected.

"Lady T'ula, who and what is first?" Asora asked.

"This is, my princess." They stood before a large, decorated cubicle. "This is Sir Galia of Evorn, and he has what looks like a giant balloon?" T'ula questioned as she looked at the odd device that the elf man had.

"It is called a dirigible: a flying ship that has bladders of helium to hold it aloft. Imagine flying through the skies, seeing the world as a bird would, the wonder and beauty," Sir Galia excitedly chatted. "The actual size will be a hundred times larger. I have one, but it was too big to bring with me, hence the model."

"A luxury liner would be more practical than a flying one, not to mention a lot safer," Asora pointed out.

The princess wanted this fair, but she was going to be tough and not allow crackpots to make things worse. She did have standards and wanted to enforce them. However, she knew that some of the best ideas did come from out of the box ideas.

The man looked let down. He was the only elf at the fair, and he was ridiculed for coming. If he could not make this work, he was finished. He really wanted to make something that could be useful and fun.

"However, Sir Galia, I see another potential for this dirigible. Evorn has a real problem with fires in the deep forest, away from any major water source, especially during the long summer months. Could this thing be reconfigured to carry large quantities of water and dump it over a blazing fire?" Asora asked, hoping to help. "Like an artificial cloud."

"Yes, yes, it could, but I would need to make a lot of modifications. But yes, my sovereign, it can be done!" Sir Galia said, rather pleased.

"Well then, draw up some new schematics by the end of the fair and present them to me. I would love to see it," Asora commanded with a smile. "We really need to stop those fires."

The elf looked extremely happy and proud as he went to a back room. His fun vehicle may have been a bust, however, the idea of his device saving lives and land was a far better alternative. He was mad that he did not think of that first.

"Well, that was fun. Shall we continue, my princess?" T'ula insisted.

"Yes, we shall. Who is next?" Asora asked.

The two walked to the next stand. This one had dozens of little fairies, both male and female wearing different colors and wing types. They buzzed around like excited children. This got Asora's four fairy maids excited, and their joy seem to float around Asora and T'ula.

"This is the only stand to have fairies, my Princess. They are displaying . . . AC?" T'ula questioned. Both she and Asora sat down and awaited the presentation. "As in the electricity type?"

"Welcome, my princess, Lady T'ula, and my fellow fair folk. We are from Alsiea, home of the fair folk. We are here to introduce a new form of electricity, AC, or alternating current to the Utopian Kingdom. There is DC, or direct current, but it has some severe limitations. For DC to work, you need to build a repeater station every few miles from the power plant to the city. AC, on the other hand, alternates between positive and negative charges and does not have as great a power loss over the transmission wires. No need for repeater stations," a small male fairy explained.

"All right, so they created this alternating current to eliminate those ugly repeater stations. Am I correct?" T'ula questioned Asora.

"That's one reason behind this, but what I find fascinating is the method of generating the power and the lesser amount of wire needed," Asora pointed out to her assistant. "The Consortium has been using AC for centuries, which we got from the fairies in recent times, but the Utopians still use DC in the very few things that need it. We hope that the Utopians will see this demonstration and agree to the change on Evorn and the other worlds. Plus, it will look better if it came from a fellow Utopian race."

'Fascinating," T'ula said. "This could be useful."

"Thank you very much, all of you. This is a great improvement to the electrical system, and I would love to implement it as soon as possible," Asora said. "I pray you will have many people come to your exhibit." Asora paused for a moment. "It would look better if it came from a fellow magical race."

T'ula looked at her pad of paper, which had a list that she generated for this event. "The next exhibit is with a human woman named Dr. Ielula, and she has researched something called nanotechnology."

"*This* should be interesting. I have never heard of such a thing," Asora commented.

Both she and T'ula sat down in the chairs provided. The fairies fluttered about Asora, and Sarea looked on with interest. Asora had heard of nano machine tech, but not nano biotech.

"Welcome, my princess. My project is a new form of medical science. I have here two versions of nanoprobes," the doctor started. She handed T'ula, Sarea and Asora a set of containers and put up a graph to show the technical specification of the two types of nanoprobes. "The first type is a biologically enhanced cell that is designed to attack viruses and deadly bacteria inside a complex organism. The second is a completely technological machine meant to repair technology quickly."

"Impressive. I like the first one. It seems that it could stop disease and alleviate plagues. How close are you to making this?" Asora asked, sitting forward.

"It is only theory right now, but the idea came from our nano scaffolding technology," the doctor informed Asora.

"Nano scaffolding?" T'ula questioned.

"Nano scaffolding is a relatively new medical practice that involves rebuilding organs or body parts using specially made organic mass and stem cells," the doctor explained to T'ula. The princess had no problem explaining these things to T'ula. Asora rather enjoyed it.

"Rebuilding organs? Sounds like a freak creation of nature, but it works, right?" T'ula asked.

"It does actually," Sarea mentioned. "Admiral yang has had several nano scaffolding procedures done to him."

"Really?" T'ula asked. "He does not look like he has."

"That is how good it is," Area added.

"Thank you. Shall we, T'ula, Sarea?" Asora offered.

The three ladies moved to the next exhibit.

"And we have here?" Asora started, rather intrigued.

"This is Mr. Dracak from Havaina, and he is presenting a theory on antimatter?" T'ula looked confused as she read her notes.

"Antimatter is the opposite of normal matter. All normal matter has a positive energy charge, whereas antimatter is negatively charged," Dracak explained calmly with a smile. He was an interesting-looking man with a slick haircut and smooth clothing.

"What is the point of this antimatter?" T'ula questioned.

"Well, antimatter could be the next generation of power creation and could even power FTLs, if we can make them work right," Dracak answered.

"FTL?" T'ula asked this time.

"Faster-than-light drive engines," Dracak said. "Also, antimatter could become a devastating weapon, if used correctly."

"How devastating a weapon are we talking about?" Asora asked.

"Well, that all depends on the amount of antimatter. A golf ball size of the stuff is enough to blow a hole the size of a small continent on a world," Dracak said. That shocked both Asora, Sarea, and T'ula. "But antimatter has a better and more practical future as a starship fuel."

"Is antimatter natural, or does it need to be made artificially?" T'ula asked.

"It does exist in nature, but not enough of it to be effective. In theory, antimatter can be made in a factory," Dracak mentioned.

"Generating antimatter sounds extremely difficult and expensive, so if you can figure out how to do it economically, I would love to see it power my ships one day." Asora thanked Dracak and stood up with T'ula. "Next?" she asked.

"Lord Jeia, my princess. He is presenting something called a rail guns," T'ula checked her clipboard. They went outside into the massive gardens.

"A rail gun? This should be interesting," Asora said. Both she and T'ula saw Jeia directing several personnel on control consoles. Others were readying a massive machine. "Jeia, are you ready to present your machine?"

"Uh, actually, yes, we are, but I want to make sure everything will work before we show it off," Jeia explained.

"All right, well then, maybe you should tell us what this rail gun is," Lady T'ula pushed.

"Very well." He strode closer to them. "Basically, a rail gun is the beginning of a kinetic energy weapon. This does not operate the same way as a normal gun would. Normal guns use controlled chemical explosions to push an object. Instead, this railgun uses ultra-powerful magnets, and a projectile made of magnetic material is blown out at speeds beyond Mach ten. There is also no explosive needed. The power comes from the release of the projectile," the duke explained.

"No explosives, and yet this packs a heavier punch than a normal gun? Fascinating," Asora commented. "This looks like a scaled down version of a battleship cannon?"

"Not only that, but the power these things have is greater than a laser weapon," Jeia put out.

"A rail gun is more powerful than a laser. Do you believe that this competes with the laser that the Darkcons may build from the stolen journals?" Asora questioned Jeia.

"Oh yes. I believe that this high-tech gun will outdo the laser." Jeia smiled confidently.

"But I thought that a laser had limitless ammunition, as long as you had power. With a rail gun, you still need ammo to make it work. So, it seems that this thing will be useless without the magnetized bullets," T'ula hypothesized.

"True, to a degree. But a laser is vulnerable to electromagnetic radiation, while a rail gun is immune to it. If you have a laser nearby this behemoth, the laser will short out from the magnets inside the gun," Jeia reassured T'ula.

"The electromagnetic energies generated by the rail gun would, as a side effect, disable all other electronic devices. Will the rail gun be shielded to prevent it from shorting out friendly technologies?" Asora asked.

"Of course, unless you are at the business end of this thing," Jeia responded. An assistant told Jeia that the rail gun was ready for test firing. The duke told them to move it farther out in order to show off the device. Asora and T'ula followed Jeia to a testing range that he had his people set up earlier. One of his assistants gave Princess Asora and Lady T'ula a pair of earmuffs, and they were warned that the machine was very loud.

"Ready, ladies?" Jeia asked excitedly. Both Asora and T'ula gave him a look, and Asora signaled that they were ready. Standing behind an armored wall, the rail gun could be heard powering up. Then, in an instant, it released its projectile at a speed so fast that no one could see anything except the trail of the nonexplosive shell. The target exploded so violently and so rapidly that it took a moment for the event to register in everyone's minds.

"Wow! Now that is powerful, Jeia! How long does it take to reload and rearm this thing?" Asora grinned.

"You can fire nine shots at once before it overheats, and reload time is about four seconds, but that depends mainly on the person loading it," Jeia explained to Asora.

"Uh, Lord Jeia? We are having a problem with the power level regulator. Could you help me, sir?" a male assistant asked his boss.

Jeia jumped up to the platform to help. He was annoyed and embarrassed. But his technicians had been encountering issues for weeks on this machine.

"It looks as if the whole power regulator unit is malfunctioning. I will open the console to see for sure," Jeia said to his technician.

Once he opened the console, a massive bolt of electricity surged through his body and sent him flying off the platform, and he crashed onto the ground, not moving.

"JEIA!" Asora screamed, and she and Sarea ran toward him. However, this time her royal guardsmen stopped Asora from running. "Damn it! That is my brother! He needs help!" Asora screamed.

Lady T'ula put a freezing spell on the guards to prevent them from restraining the anxious princess. The guards had the knowledge to break the spell, but it held them long enough for Asora to run to Jeia's side. Sarea had gotten to his side and was doing chest compressions to keep his heart going.

She knelt to Jeia, and she put her right hand over his stopped heart. Using her angelic powers, the princess was able to inject soothing magical energies into Jeia's injured heart. The young man's heart started beating again, and he coughed violently.

"Oh maker! Dear brother, I thought I lost you!" Asora yelled and hugged her big brother tightly.

"You will again, if you squeeze any harder!" Jeia said, out of breath. Then two of Asora's bodyguards took Jeia to the royal hospital, and the redheaded Madimoy was summoned to go with him. Sarea then followed them out with Madimoy crying in her arms.

CHAPTER EIGHT

THE FIRES OF TERROR

An hour had passed since the incident at the Fusion Corp booth. Princess Asora was talking with the other attendance. The Royal Court nobility had vanished, leaving Asora with her Privy Council. Princess Asora was not happy about that. She was screaming in rage at the Royal Guardsmen who seem to be ignoring her. All except for one centaur guardsmen named Joes.

The Captain of the Guard was the only Royal Guardsmen that Asora trusted and that happened to be Joes. He watched as Princess Asora tore into his troops and their obvious disrespect for her.

"May I?" Joes asked Asora.

"Sure," Asora said out of breath.

Joes stomped on the foot of the lower ranking officer. He screamed in pain as Joes picked him up and stared him down. "Did you understand what her highness has demanded of you? Because if you have not, it will be ten lashes for all of you!"

Princess Asora folded her arms and watched as her Captain of the Guard threatened to horse whip them if they did not understand what Asora was so mad at them about. While she appreciated Joes and his efforts to help her, she was angry that none of the guardsmen seem to take Asora seriously.

This had been a recurring issue between Princess Asora and the Utopian Kingdom's primary military force. Asora herself was once a soldier too, she did not understand why the Royal Guard had such a hard time with her. The Consortium Red Guard had no issue with her and was vastly superior to the Royal Guard in virtually every manner.

"Now get the hell out of here and do your jobs. There will no time off for the rest of the month new!" Joes finished yelling at his subordinates.

The guardsmen walked away very angry and depressed. The officer whose foot Joes stepped on had to be carried out and to the palace infirmary. Joes politely approached Asora.

"I am sorry about that," Joes said. "It was extremely disrespectful of them."

"What is their problem with me?" Asora asked Joes. "You are the only one that does not have any issue with me."

Joes took a moment to formulate his response. He knew the reasons why. There were several reasons, and he knew that his answers would make the princess even more infuriated. Joes had nothing respect for her as she was a fellow soldier, and he liked the fact that the kingdom finally had a fighting lady who could benefit the military greatly.

"I am not sure if you will like the answers to that question," Joes said.

"I, see?" Asora said. "Tell me anyway."

"The biggest reason is that you are a princess, a young teenage girl and women as far as they are all concerned has no place giving them orders," Joes said. "Even though you are the smartest strategist we have had in power in a very long time."

"Why is me being a girl have any bearing on this?" Asora was genuinely confused.

"You come from a culture were both genders are equal and expected to do what the other can do," Joes said. "That is very unusual for the rest of the Realm."

"The Darkcon do that too?" Asora pointed out.

"They are more liberal about because of necessity. Not from culture," Joes said. "For the Consortium it is culture that demands that women be able to do what a man can do. To ensure the continuation of your society."

Princess Asora understood what Captain Joes was saying to her.

The answer did irritate her as she was in fact use to a different culture then the one, she was now leading. She sighed in annoyance.

"Is there anything I can do to make them listen to me, other then having them sacked?" Asora asked.

"Nothing that I can think of at the moment," Joes said. Then he thought of something as a joke to help lighten Asora's mood. "You could always make a brand-new military force and replace the Royal Guard?"

Princess Asora looked at him and she looked to have been thinking about it. She hummed to herself as she thought about it.

"That is an idea," Asora said.

Joes did not know if he had just sealed his fate or if Asora was joking with him in response. It would be an impossible feat for her to pull off. Asora had to know that too. But from what he knew of this young lady, she had a a unique ability to make the impossible, possible.

"See to it that the guardsmen help the attendees. I have some bad news to deliver," Asora said as she walked towards Lady T'ula.

Asora approached T'ula and the tall elf noticed her. "Your highness, I am so sorry."

"Thank you, this is not your fault," Asora said.

"I can have this fixed, and" T'ula was cut off by Asora.

"I am sorry, Lady T'ula, I have no choice but to cancel the science fair for today. Please do try to enjoy the rest of the day," Asora advised sadly and with a pensive dark edge. That was no accident; Jeia had been receiving death threats, and her intuition said that was an attempt on his life.

"Yes, Your Highness." T'ula sighed, watching Asora walk away quickly to the hospital.

"Damn it! I spent the last month setting this all up, and with one accident, it all goes up in smoke. Oh maker, damn it!" T'ula cursed and turned to look around. "Well, the rest of the day can go on," she said to herself.

A team of investigators from Jeia's company showed up. Only that

Jeia said that he did not ask for any investigators. This made Asora nervous and she summoned Admiral Yane. The old man arrived so quickly that Asora was impressed at this old man's speed.

"Get General Anco," Asora ordered to Yane.

Yane pulled out a smartphone from his pocket and hit the speed dial for Anco's top aid. While Yane was arguing over the phone Asora saw the team of investigators head towards the railgun. Once Yane was finished, he put the phone away and demanded that Asora stay away while he investigated.

"Admiral! I am your sovereign, and I am the one that gives orders!" Asora reminded him.

"I know that. I do not want you getting hurt. It is my job to help keep you from harm," Yane pointed out.

"That is also Sarea's job," Asora said pointed to Sarea who was now behind Yane.

"The three of us will go and talk to them then," Asora said. "We cannot afford for more state secrets to be taken from us."

Yane sighed, "As you wish."

"I do agree with the admiral," Sarea said.

"We will discuss this later," Asora reminded the two of them.

Yane walked ahead of Asora and Sarea towards the team. He wanted to secure the scene as fast as he could so that Asora would not be in danger. She was the most stubborn person that Yane knew, but he admired her for it. She was also the one who saved his life once during a vicious fire fight a few years ago. She was Colonel Asora then and she was tougher than she appeared. Yane owed her his life and he intended to keep her safe even if it was against her wishes.

"Hey! Where are your papers?" Yane demanded of the five-man team.

"Who are you?" one of them asked.

"I am he one who will stick you in cells if you do not do as I instruct!" Yane stated.

"Do as he says," Asora ordered.

Her dress had transformed into an elegantly designed armor of angelic design. The designs were etched in the metal and some of the lines glowed. Her wings were still in her back. Asora did not have her helmet on since this was not a magical fight, and the helmet will only work against magical opponents. The metal on the armor was thin but it was tough and lightweight. It was able to stop handgun sized bullets like nine millimeters.

"You got it," the leader of the team said.

He reached into his backpack and pulled out a gun. He shot at Asora, but this time she blocked it with a fast protection spell. Both Yane and Sarea ducked. The admiral pulled out his point forty-four caliber revolver and shot one of the now terrorist team members in the head. The guy's head exploded violently and the rest of him dropped.

"No explosives!" Asora ordered. "We do not know what gasses are here!"

"Right," Yane replied.

The leader shot at Asora again, but the bullets merely bounced off her armor. However, the impacts were enough to force her back. She crashed into a set of empty chemical tank cylinders. Sarea grabbed a flash bang grenade that she had on and pulled the pin. She counted to three and tossed it.

"Princess, Admiral! Cover your eyes and ears!" Sarea warned.

The flash bang went off temporarily blinding the terrorists. Asora then high kicked one of the terrorists in the chest. Yane tackled another to the ground and pounded him with the butt of his gun. Sarea punched a female terrorist so hard that she dislocated the jaw of the smaller human woman.

The leader of the group ran to the stairwell that led up to the control system of the giant railgun. Asora ran after him. Yane and Sarea were about to follow when they discover that there were more than five in the team of terrorists.

"You have got to be kidding me!" Sarea spat.

"More targets for us to knock down," Yane said.

Climbing up the stairwell as fast as he could, the leader occasionally looked back to see Asora catching up to him. He would then shoot at her only to have the bullets bounce off her armor or magical barrier that she managed to get up in time. But the kinetic forces slowed her down. Every time she got shot; she was blown back a bit. Asora grabbed a gun from Yane before she gave chase. It was a nine-millimeter hand, but it was enough. Asora occasionally returned fire when she had enough of a chance. She would have used her magical powers, but she did not want the railgun destroyed so small arms fire was the only other option. Some of the gasses and chemicals used in the railgun did not work well with magic. The metal that the railgun was made from was tough enough to deflect bullets anyway.

However, the leader was too far ahead of her and the only way to get to the controls at the top was to fly up. But that would expose her to his weapons fire. Unless she was quick. So Asora unfurled her wings and created a gray fog that moved up. The fog covered the whole railgun complex, and this gave Asora the cover she needed to fly up. She jumped into the air and zoomed up. Asora landed on the control platform and accessed the computer. She was preparing a counter insurgency program.

"Stop!" a loud voice bellowed from behind her.

Asora turned around and saw the leader on another platform that was three meters away from her. He had his gun pointed right at her. He was panting as he was exhausted from climbing the several stories worth of ladders and stairwells.

"You seriously think that you can harm me with that pea shooter?" Asora asked sarcastically. "I have been shot enough already."

"Maybe not. But the punches from the bullets will force you back, you witch!" the leader said. "Don't think I haven't noticed."

"And you risk destroying your prize," Asora pointed out. The terrorist leader realized what Asora was talking about. "You right wing terrorist gun nuts never think things through and always wonder why your plans never go according to plan."

"We are also fighting for the freedom of our way of life," the leader said.

"Your way of life is gone and has been gone for centuries now. Your ideals are relics. You are better off investing into new things," Asora said.

"It is people like you that traditions are being destroyed. You subvert it into some progressive plot," the leader said now sounding a bit crazy.

"Do you understand what you just said?" Asora asked. "Anything new and beneficial is dangerous? But I think that it is only part of it."

"Oh and what is the real reason?" the leader demanded.

"Power, anything that is new often takes away from the old. Your kind are afraid of losing power and control that you have enjoyed for so long. But instead of embracing and adapting, you lash out in such a primitive attempt to maintain the status quo. Then tradition becomes a threat to society if it refuses to change," Asora said.

"What a load of crap!" the leader spat.

"That load of crap is fact. And you are too simple minded to understand that" Asora said.

The terrorist leader shoots at Asora in a rage. The bullets bounce off her and deflect onto the controls. The control system arcs and sparks. A power builds up inside told Asora that it was going to explode.

"You idiot! You have killed us all!" Asora said. She turned to the destroyed console with the leader still shooting her but with no effect. Asora sent a bolt of lightning at him and knocked him out. Asora then ripped off a panel covering the inner mechanism of the control system. She was looking for the emergency shutdown switch. "Uh Jeia, why can you not just put these things on the outside where it can be easily accessed?"

The access port was large enough for Asora to get her torso through so she could see inside. Her tiara started glowing to give her light. But it was weak as something was in here interfering with the magic in her tiara or her body.

"Covered in metal in an electrified enclosed space. Not smart," Asora said to herself. She turned her metal armor into rubber and leather. She hoped that was all she needed. "Hopefully there is nothing radioactive in here?"

Asora looked around and saw a large circuit breaker colored red with the words 'Emergency Disconnect' written on it. The breaker was as large as her head and the breaker was on a spring load. Asora was not strong enough to force the flip of the switch on the breaker down. So Asora crawled all the way inside and held on to the switch. She used all her bodyweight and finally forced the switch down. She opened the breaker and cut all power to the system. She relaxed inside the conduit.

"Okay Jeia. You and I are going to have a little talk about designing your control systems," Asora said to herself.

Asora crawled out of the access hole only to be grabbed by the terrorist leader and pulled to her feet.

"You stupid little freak! I am going to kill you slowly," the terrorist leader said with venom in his voice.

"You are certainly welcome to try," Asora then head butted the man in the face.

The resulting shock released Asora, and she bent down. She then did an uppercut into the man's stomach. Then Asora punched him in the side of his head. The man went flying backwards and crashed into a chair. He vomited up blood from Asora's powerful punch.

The terrorist tried to point his gun at Asora again, but this time she grabbed his hand and forced up off the chair and slammed him to the deck. She then started to punch and stomp on his wrist in an effort to release his grip on the weapon. He grabbed her and forced her on top of him and held Asora in a bear hug. Asora then dug her teeth into his arm. He screamed and released her and as she got up, Asora elbowed him in the ribs. Asora then kicked the gun away and it fell off the platform.

The terrorist pulled out a knife and took several swipes at Asora. He managed to figure out that her spells only worked with fast moving objects and not slow-moving objects. A blade can be just as effective. He sliced into Asora's arm and drew blood. Asora now had to dodge the knife. Asora grabbed a bar of steel and swung it at the terrorist leader.

He grabbed it with his only good hand which was with his knife in it. Asora then swung the bar and caused him to crash into a wall face first. He fell to the floor and dropped his knife. Asora kicked the knife away.

Asora then stood over the terrorist leader. She put one foot on his chest and grabbed both arms. And with one powerful pull she yanked up and dislocated both arms from their sockets and dropped them. The man screamed in pain and could not move.

The Royal Guard finally got up to the platform to see what Asora did to the terrorist leader. They looked both annoyed and nervous. Also, there were a few Red Guardsmen in black jumpsuits.

"I see you have not lost it," Anco commented. He came up from behind the guardsmen.

"Put that trash to the dungeon. Heal him there," Asora said. "What about the others?"

"The rest have been arrested. You did it," Anco said.

"Thank you," Asora said. "I need to wash up."

"And another visit to the infirmary," Anco pointed out to all Asora's injuries. "Damn you are a badass as I remember."

Princess Asora smiled and chuckled at General Anco's comment. She was helped up by the general and he took her to the palace hospital.

Hours later, the vendors packed up their displays and left, all as disappointed as their princess was. T'ula walked through the remains of the displays, and she spotted something that fascinated her—a horseless carriage, but the humans call it an automobile or a car.

"What device is this, sir?" T'ula asked the human in a gray business suit who was displaying the car.

"Oh, Lady T'ula! I thought that we had to leave?" the humble man asked.

"At your own pace, good sir," T'ula responded kindly.

"Well, this is the Herald, made by Odyssey Automotive. This one is classified as a sports car," the man told T'ula.

"What makes the sports car different from other cars?" T'ula asked.

"A sports car has speed and power, so they are the fastest of all. They do lack storage capabilities, but that's not what they are meant for. This thing is designed for style. It has that sexy look to it. For a woman, this is a nice item to have," the human explained. "A sort of status symbol."

"Sexy indeed. I like the red painting on it. Can I look inside it, sir?" T'ula asked hopefully.

"Of course, my lady," the human man said.

He opened the driver's door for T'ula, and she put her head inside to look around. The seats and steering wheel were made of leather. The dashboard, as the man called it, had a rather large array of gauges that displayed readings from the engine. There was a single passenger's seat and a variety of other devices. T'ula was truly intrigued by this machine.

"May I try this car?" T'ula asked.

"I do not see why not. Here are the keys, and I will show you how to operate it, my lady." The man gave T'ula the keys to the car, and she got into the driver's seat.

The man sat in the passenger's seat to give her a tutorial. He told her about the ignition, the braking system, the gas, and the other controls. T'ula was a very fast learner, and within minutes, she was able to control the car outside the hall. She was enjoying every minute in this machine; she had never had anything like it.

After an hour of driving, T'ula stopped, and the man took it back. "Thank you, Mr. Eran. I really enjoyed the car."

He began taking it back to his ship, and T'ula walked back inside to see Asora staring at her with a smile. She knew that the princess did not mind the little joyride. To her at least something good came out of this.

"Did you enjoy the car?" Asora asked.

"Yes, I did, Your Highness. And I must confess, I thought that this fair was a waste of time, but as I put this together, I started to see why you wanted this. I have learned a lot today, and that automobile was very fun to drive," T'ula confessed.

The princess laughed softly. "I know. I am looking at getting a car myself, but Evorn lacks the roads to support it. Only the human worlds have them. If I can get infrastructure bills passed, then I could build them so that ladies like you and I can have cars here," Asora said happily.

"Maybe if you are a good girl, my Princess, someone will give one to you for your birthday." T'ula laughed playfully.

"Maybe, but what about you?" Asora asked.

"Who would want to give me such a lavish gift? My adopted family forbids it, and none of my so-called friends will bother," T'ula said sadly.

Asora saw in T'ula's eyes a girl that had everything in her family and had nothing for herself. She was a true elvish aristocrat—how typical. It must hurt her to see everyone else with so much freedom and herself with so little. Her adopted family were elves, but her origins were that of a jewel elf. Elf families liked to adopt jewel elves as their beauty and abilities often brought them great fortunes and appeal.

"Well, my dear T'ula, if you do as good a job as you did today, I could see to it that your next bonus is an automobile. Maybe not as good as the Odyssey's Herald, but maybe close. Or I might be able to call in a few favors and get the Herald for you," Asora said.

T'ula's eyes lit up like a small child's. "You would really do that for me, your highness?"

"Of course I would, for anyone that helps me. I will do all in my power to help them," Asora said. "Also, I need all the friends that I can get, and I can tell you do too."

A tear of joy came down T'ula's cheek. "Thank you, My Sovereign." Then T'ula hugged Asora, and the princess returned the embrace.

"T'ULA!" a feminine voice roared over the empty exhibition hall.

"Oh no!" T'ula sighed in disappointment and fear. She released Asora.

"You stupid little child!" the woman charged up to T'ula and slapped her across the face.

The woman had pointed ears, just like T'ula's, and Asora assumed they were related.

"How dare you attack my assistant! GUARDS!" Asora yelled in anger.

"Do not get involved in our family's affairs, princess! This does not concern you," the woman said back to Asora.

"I do not think so. You have attacked my assistant and insulted me. Therefore, you are going to be arrested," Asora said threateningly with five royal guardsmen standing behind her.

"Princess, please, it is all right. This is my stepmother. Please, do not arrest her. I have been disobedient," T'ula said almost robotically. She looked scared and defeated. But Asora would not have this.

"I do not care if you have a problem. You can take it up with me behind closed doors, not in front of the whole kingdom. Now get out or you will spend the night in the dungeon!" Asora ordered.

"Very well, princess! And as for you, T'ula. If it was not for her, I would have you on your knees crying for this embarrassment," T'ula's stepmother threatened her daughter, all for driving the car. She glared at them, and then the angry elf woman stormed off.

"How dare she do that to you! Come on," Asora ordered T'ula.

That display of family abuse was common from what Asora could tell between the different species of elves. Especially between jewel elves and mountain elves.

"Thank you, my princess. No one has ever done anything like that for me before," T'ula said sheepishly.

"I will defend all my subjects and, more importantly, my friends, from anyone," Asora said kindly to T'ula.

The two young women walked back inside the palace as the sun set behind them. Asora will find some way to end this. And she was motivated because she wanted to protect those that she loved and treasured.

Chapter Nine

The Renegade

Queen Laxur was known for her great alchemy knowledge. She was in another lab, making several different potions; most were of a green color. It was a creation of fairy origin adopted by many magical peoples. But she did make other colored potions too. Each color had a different and unique effect on the person taking them. In all there were nine different colors for these potions.

Also, the potions each had a unique and very sweet taste. They also tended to be addictive. If one was not careful, they would become dependent on them. Queen Laxur however did not care. She enjoyed them and making them was therapeutic in a way. And they were also slightly altered to fit her needs.

Her workstation was big and full of flasks, tubes, burners, and several deep shelves full of all sorts of things, ingredients, supplies, and more. She also had books, scrolls, and single sheets of paper all marked with notes, words, and pictures. All made by the queen herself. She was trying to create the ultimate power potion that would give her a permanent advantage at anything she did. Laxur desired to be the most powerful being and hoped one day she can achieve this.

Behind her was an army of workers and technicians who were busy building a massive device. When Laxur had finished her potions, she put most in a rack on the desk and a few others into pockets in her dress. The queen then turned around to see them all working. She loved seeing progress and her people made her proud. And her visibility also added to her appeal to the Darkcon as she was a working queen and was in the dirt with them. And she was giving them things to make their lives easier. Laxur then walked over to one of her technicians.

"Yukina, how goes the construction of my newest weapon?" Laxur demanded.

"The laser is a very complex system, but we should be ready to test it within a few months; however, we are not sure if we have the technology or the technical know-how to fully develop this device," Yukina, a corrupt human man, informed Laxur timidly.

"I see," Laxur said. "What issues are you encountering?"

"Well, the main control circuits keep overloading when we power it up," Yukina said. "And the chemical vats do not seem to be good enough."

"The chemical vats? What is wrong with them?" Laxur asked.

"I think they are not the right type of chemicals," Yukina said. "I think the manuals said something about using carbon dioxide or neon. None of which we have in abundance."

"Damn it," Laxur said slowly. She breathed slowly. "What about using Ydritium? We have that."

"That would need a lot of remodeling and reconfiguration according to the manuals," Yukina warned.

"Very well then, make the changes, and continue on. I am going to my chambers, and I will return in a few hours," Laxur informed forcefully.

In truth, she did not care how quickly the development took, if they were working on it. It also kept the Utopians leery about attacking them. She strode out of the lab with Dari in tow. After a few minutes, the two women reached Laxur's private chambers.

"Dari, you may wait outside with the other guards. I am going to take a bath," Laxur ordered.

"Yes, Your Majesty," Dari responded, and she took her place in front of Laxur's doors.

Four hours later, Queen Laxur reemerged from her chambers,

refreshed and dressed in a traditional queen's gown designed by the finest Darkcon artisans, which were pixies, gremlins, and succubus. It was black and purple, off the shoulder with a long, flowing skirt and a waist cinched. She walked to the throne room with Dari by her side. Laxur sat upon her large and changing throne. It made itself more imposing to show the queen's power.

Once upon the throne, Laxur was bored, and she wanted to do something to pass the time. Golcon, a hellspawn demon, and her prime minister, walked over to her. He was leathery dark, smooth-skinned, bald, and almost two meters of muscle. His eyes were red, as most demons were. He wore black leather with crimson piping. He was a feared and respected man, but Laxur did not think much of him.

"We have a problem," Golcon said.

"What is it?" Laxur demanded.

"The issue is with Shia Rakon," Golcon said.

"Again? What is it this time?" Laxur complained.

Golcon cleared his throat. "He, ah, has been inciting the lords, warlords, and other nobles."

The queen stood up and walked slowly to the hell-spawn in a very intimidating manner. She towered over the prime minister, and this did make her intimidating. She was not happy to hear this. She had worked for years to fashion herself into an all-powerful monarch and a master of magic and modernization.

"Inciting them how?" Laxur demanded.

"Saying that you are wasting the empires' money on your ship building and armies instead of tending to the people. He is also commenting on your many lovers," Golcon informed weakly.

"My lovers? And what else? I am not spending money on the people. Since I have become queen, I have built hospitals and universities, I have built roads and bridges, I have created railroads, I have done all these things on all our worlds." She cast her large emerald eyes upward, sighing. "I need to talk to him."

"Dari, bring me Shia Rakon. I think that a fencing match will allow me to talk to him," Laxur ordered.

"Uh, Your Majesty, Rakon may not be in the mood to play with you." Golcon cleared his throat.

"WHAT! Where the hell is he!" Laxur bellowed angrily.

"I think that he is in the Chamber of Lords? Getting inebriated," Golcon added.

"I will go get him and teach him some manners, my queen," Dari offered.

"No. I will go and teach him a lesson myself!" Laxur blasted.

"My queen, you might want to wait for us to call Obsidian to deal with this. The Chamber of Lords is not a place for a great queen like you." Golcon warned.

Laxur stared at Golcon and then laughed. The dark queen stormed out of the throne room and headed for the Chamber of Lords, which was on the other side of the massive Onyx Palace. The Chamber of Lords was the Darkcon's version of the Royal Court. The Lords had been her greatest allies and gave her all she wanted. She made them rich and powerful and expanded the chamber to include hundreds of new members. Laxur found that getting them to do what she wanted was quite easy. She suspected that most of the lords and ladies of the chamber had a romantic opinion of her. And that was fine to her if they gave her what she wanted.

Instead of walking to the chamber, which would have taken an hour. Laxur opened a portal, and all three jumped to the outside doors of the Chamber of Lords. Once outside the doors, Laxur could hear cheers, yelling, boos, which suggested to Laxur that there was a celebration going on inside. The doors were huge and made of black stone with metal bracing.

"Dari, Golcon, open the doors," Laxur ordered.

Golcon and Dari did as they were instructed. The doors were too heavy for either Dari or Golcon could move. It would take the strength of thousands to move them. That was the point. They could only be moved by those in power. Dari and Golcon were ones in power. So, they used a magical enchantment. Golcon had a key, and Dari sang an ancient poem. The giant doors slowly opened to allow the three to enter.

Once inside, Queen Laxur was rather disgusted by what she saw. The lords and ladies were celebrating the Darkcon Empires' recent victory over the Utopian Kingdom. They were all very drunk and belligerent, and none noticed that Queen Laxur had entered. Right now, the queen spared them little thought; she wanted to find Rakon and put him in his place.

She was not opposed to celebrating a victory. But she preferred that it was civil. This was not what she had in mind. Dari pulled Laxur back as a wave of beer washed across where she once stood.

"Thank you," Laxur said to Dari.

"Of course, my queen," Dari bowed.

"Damn it is warm in here," Laxur said. "This place has devolved into a tavern."

"There are thousands of people in here," Dari pointed out.

Then a heavily armored dark elf woman suddenly hugged Laxur and picked her up. She was obviously drunk and did not see that the woman she was attempted to feel up was the queen. Laxur grunted in rage. She freed herself and punched the armored woman into a barrel of wine. That got a lot of cheers from the others in the room. They all did not realize that it was Laxur. They thought that she was just as drunk and in a happy mood as they were.

The smell of alcohol and the heat made Laxur even more unfriendly. She did not actually mind the smell of alcohol; it was the unclean that it was that made her mad. She worked hard to make the Darkcons a respected and feared nation. This did not help.

A drunken troll made the unfortunate mistake of barging in front of Laxur, and to prevent himself from losing his balance, he accidentally grabbed hold of Laxur's body, mainly her upper torso area. Laxur growled with anger, and using her magic to magnify her strength, she slammed her fist into the troll's head, and he went crashing down at the queen's feet, where Dari hissed.

She took out her pistol and pointed it at him. "Be gone from here before I shoot you for touching your queen."

The troll peed on himself and crawled away into the drunken lords, who laughed at him. It was known that Queen Laxur was tough and that added to her allure for them. But right now, was not the best time.

"Drunken pig! How dare he touch me in such a manner? I am no whore!" Laxur hissed at the retreating troll.

Then she spotted Rakon in a corner by himself with a large mug of ale. The dark queen made her way toward the sword master. He had seen her come in and was enjoying the queen's attempts to navigate the drunken orgy.

Shia (meaning "teacher") Rakon was an elemental demon, a metal wielder. He could create metal and magnetism. He was one of the Darkcon Empire's best swordsmen and military strategists. Many believed that he was the best and deadliest warrior, and he was held in great respect and awe. He was dark and leathery, with hard ridges on his head, red eyes, and long black hair. He was tall, at two meters, and had a solid, muscular build of two hundred and thirty pounds. He wore deep-red leather with gold piping and encrusted steel.

The demon had seen Queen Laxur's little offense that she just suffered. He thought it was amusing, yet he would not show it until she was in range of him. Laxur, Dari, and Golcon were standing next to the booth that Rakon was sitting at. He belched loudly before drunkenly rumbling. He knew that this would make her mad.

"Well, if it is not our almighty queen and her two loyal lap dogs. What is it that I can do for you today?" Rakon asked in a mocking tone to Laxur. The queen smirked lightly, and she sat in the seat across Rakon. Dari and Golcon remained standing. Dari and Golcon then surrounded Rakon. "And do not you two horses' asses have something better to do than to piss me off, because you two are going to get hurt," Rakon threatened Dari and Golcon in a slurred tone.

"These two are here because they have to go where I go, for I am the sovereign of the empire, and it is their duty to protect me," Laxur started.

Rakon laughed lightly—yet another insult to her. "Protect you from what? All your boy toys that you sleep with every night?" Rakon laughed again. "And all the broken-hearted women that you leave in your wake?"

That offended Dari and Laxur immensely. Rakon stopped laughing so he could take a swig of his ale. Laxur punched Rakon in the face as he was drinking his ale. His mug was broken, and he was drenched with ale. His cheek was beginning to swell. But that did not really concern him.

"How dare you speak to me in such a fashion? I am the queen, not a prostitute, as much as you may think otherwise. My title demands respect from all, and you would do well to remember that!" Laxur stated threateningly.

"You have not changed much. You get the crown, your ego inflates to planetary size, and you think that the empire is your personnel playground. What a waste." Rakon picked up a napkin to wipe his face. "And pissing away our wealth for meaningless things."

"They are not meaningless!" Laxur snapped. "I am advancing our people to become a powerful civilization!"

"You were not born a Darkcon. You were the little girl that we found in the trash on Evorn," Rakon reminded her. "We showed you kindness and mercy and here you are now, being a tyrant, just like all the rest of the Utopian noble ladies."

"Is this the reason why you do not care for me anymore? I hear that you are going behind my back and spreading rather undignified rumors about me. You know that, even if you do not like me, you must respect my crown. So, what is your problem?" Laxur preached.

Rakon blew a raspberry at Laxur. "Oh please, you stupid wench! I knew training you was a mistake. You have squandered our resources with your war machines and declared war for no good reason, other than to get even with your little sister." Rakon took a breath. "Those are no rumors. As for the undignified, it is a well-known fact that you flirt with almost every man, even the occasional woman, to get your way. The fact that your bed is never without a lover waiting for you is disrespectful to your dead husband," Rakon said. "Oh, and you know my respect is for the empire, not for some whore with a tiara."

"I have respect for you, Rakon, even if you have none for me, but you have become a liability, and I hate liabilities. So I am going to either beat this into your worthless head—that I am your Queen and your master," Laxur calmly explained.

Rakon belched again in her face again. He was not going to be convinced. Laxur knew that her old teacher and rescuer was a stubborn old man. He was one of the Darkcons that did rescue her from Evorn when she was abandoned. Rakon did not think much of her then, and what little respect he did have for her was no longer present. He saw her private life as an insult to tradition that all nobility and monarchies followed. Laxur was too open minded for his taste.

"Really? Well then, your worthless majesty, a fight to the death it is." Rakon said.

Rakon blasted Laxur with a powerful bolt of lightning, and then he sent the pieces of his metal mug crashing into Laxur's stomach. The pieces did nothing to her as she wore a thin layer of armor under her dress. The queen flew through the booth's wall and into the next booth.

Fortunately, Queen Laxur had on her body armor and was ready for a clash. She knew that this encounter was going to be violent. Rakon unsheathed the sword at his side and swung at Dari and Golcon. He managed to hit Golcon in the chest with a swipe. The prime minister was sent to the floor, bleeding, and Rakon used his electrical magic to blast Dari, who was sent flying across the chamber. Dari was stunned as she flew and was unable to move. But that did help her as she crashed into a table. Dari's crash also took down five others and sent food, beer, and condiments flying.

The clash got everyone's attention, and they were cheering and chanting, "Fight, fight, fight!" This irritated Laxur more as now this was more of a bar fight then an actual duel.

"Come on, you oversized bitch! Get up so I can knock you down again!" Rakon demanded as he jumped onto the table.

Laxur sat back up, growling with anger, her face red with rage. The queen had her large black wings out now, and her demonic sword appeared in her left hand with black smoke. Purple electric arcs sparked across Laxur's body as she was charging herself up. The queen towered over Rakon, but her size never truly gave Rakon pause. More like she was challenge as he was use to taking on opponents who tended to out class him in size and strength. Both of which Queen Laxur had.

"You will pay for that, you wretched demon!" Laxur fumed.

Then with her own magic, Laxur blasted Rakon with a powerful wave of black energy. The wave threw Rakon fifteen meters into the air, and he crashed into a bricked wall. With a wave of her sword, the queen sent another wave of purple electrical energy surging through the room, destroying everything in front of her, as the wave headed toward Rakon. The wave hit the sword master with incredible force, and he nearly passed out from the pressure.

He was repeatedly being struck by wave after wave. Laxur loved overwhelming power and it was her more preferred attack form. Rakon was reminded of a lesson he gave her once. Laxur said that power was the greatest weapon and that the more that she could unleash the more she can force a surrender.

Laxur then charged toward Rakon, using her wings to fly. She landed in front of Rakon's face as he crawled on the floor. The angry woman picked Rakon up by his throat. Her grip was surprisingly strong. It was also impressive that she could lift him up with only one arm. Both of them were breathing very heavily.

"Any more insults, funny guy, huh!" Laxur screamed into Rakon's face. "Never forget that I am the queen."

"You are no queen. Hell, I do not even know what you are. You're not human or an angel. You're closer to a succubus—the only thing that you really are is a freak," Rakon responded weakly, choking out the words.

Hearing the word *freak* made Laxur think back to her childhood, when everyone called her a freak because she was different. Images from her youth when other children taunted her for being different. Freak was the choice of words that everyone called her. Not just children, but adults too. She was beaten because of her wings and divine glow. Things did not get better when she was a teenager. Only her family protected her. She was weak and a freak. It never felt her mind. But the 'Weak Freak' now was master of an empire.

Well, Rakon would soon learn that was the wrong word to say to Laxur. Growling in a fit of rage. Than she let out a roar of pure anger. Laxur put her sword to her side. She stomped over to the fallen elemental demon and proceeded to beat Rakon with her dark magic fist. She lost all sense of her surroundings and just wanted to beat him. With powerful strikes, she slammed her bloody fist into Rakon's blood soaked face. All while still holding him by his neck. The chamber went uncomfortably quite as everyone watched the queen beat the living daylights out of Rakon.

Laxur then threw Rakon across the room again, and while he was in the air, she jumped up and gave him a powerful kick in the back. The demon crashed onto a table, and it collapsed. He was unconscious and badly hurt. Blood trickled down his face, and chest. She landed next to him, picked him up by the back of his head, and was about to beat him again.

"My queen, he is down, and he will not trouble you," Dari said as she came to Laxur's side.

Dari had grabbed Laxur's arm to get her attention. Laxur looked to Dari then back to the unconscious Rakon. The queen breathed heavily and sighed as she came back to her sense. She let Rakon go and he fell to the floor with a thud.

The Chamber of Lords was very quiet as everyone managed to sober up. Golcon had managed to get back to his feet. He tossed people in front of him aside as he made his way to Laxur's side. He saw the mess that Rakon was in and it made Golcon smile.

"About fucking time someone kicked your ass," Golcon said.

"Agreed," Laxur replied with a heavy breath.

Golcon snapped his fingers and started to bark orders at the guards that were now coming in. He also was cursing out the other nobles for their disrespect towards the queen. The guards came up to Laxur with Golcon behind them.

"Your majesty?" A guard asked.

"I have decided his fate. Remove him from my empire. Seize his property and titles, destroy it all, and throw him out like the trash he is," Laxur ordered, and she started to walk away.

"My queen, why not simply kill him?" Golcon asked. "I can do it for you."

She stopped. "He is too popular to the people, and he did teach me. To kill him outright would be a mistake, and the people would start to unite against me. They might think some of the things he said were true. I will simply get rid of him and leave him to his own devices," Laxur explained. "Send him somewhere where he would be unwelcome."

The dark queen walked away from Rakon. The guards picked up the body of Rakon. She stopped and spotted a goblet full of ale. She drank it and had a disgusted look on her face.

"Fogo Ale? Weaklings! Where is the hard liquor, you babies?" Laxur said confidently.

The dark beauty was also known for her legendary drinking habits with powerful liquors. She could drink more hard liquor than anyone. After such a fight she needed a drink. She learned not too long ago she learned that powerful alcohol could take away much of her pain, and memories.

Chapter Ten
The Scullery Maid

The daily meetings of the Royal Court continued. Even after the events of the science fair. Life quickly returned to normal. Normally the Royal Court would see this as a triumph over Princess Asora. But that quickly fell apart as the princess's science fair was popular. They feared that Asora could make it an annual event. Even a terrorist attack did not stop the popularity of the fair. So, in their victory they were defeated.

However, Princess Asora did not seem to realize this. If she did, then the princess did not show it. She sat upon her throne listening to the daily meeting points. Asora normally tuned out the endless talk until something important came up. But she listened today.

Archduke Frenzen started to take notice of both the Royal Court nobles and Princess Asora's depression. This was not good as war with the Darkcon Empire was inevitable. This was abad situation that he had to find a way to fix. And hopefully get both eh court and the princess on the same side.

A small plump woman in the official maids uniform came in with the obligatory refreshments and snacks for the court, princess, and other officials in the meeting. The woman was a dwarf/elf mixed girl with a short height. She had brown hair, light skin and she had a friendly personality.

"Oh excuse me my lord," the sweet maid said to Frenzen.

"Of course," Frenzen said politely. "Do what you need to Kika."

KINGDOMS AND EMPIRES—DARK RAGE

Archduke Frenzen stood to the side. This allowed the maid Kika to have the cart she had with her to be pushed in. She hummed a happy tune as she walked by. Several other carts magically followed Kika in.

The site of Kika made everyone cheer up. Princess Asora mostly as she loved Kiki's chocolate cake. The royal announcer stopped talking as Kika came forward.

"Did I come in at a bad time?" Kika asked.

"Oh thank the maker you are here," Puro Aga said with a sigh. "We need a break."

"I second that," Asora added. "Please take orders."

"Of course your highness," Kika said happily.

The popular maid made her way around the Royal Court taking snack, refreshment, and lunch orders. Normally she should not be in their presence when they were in high level meetings. But no one, not even Princess Asora cared. Kika was known for being able to keep secrets. As she listened and felt the depression in the room, Kika came up with an idea.

"May I make a suggestion?" Kika spoke up.

"Please," Nona called out.

"The Science Fair was popular, but there is something that has always been popular with every state in the kingdom, including the consortium," kick pointed out.

"That is?" Frenzen asked.

"Theater," Kika said happily.

That got everyone's attention. Princess Asora sat up a little straighter as she thought about it. Nona and several lady nobles smiled at the idea. Frenzen and the male nobles where in as deep a thought as Asora was.

"That is a divine idea," Nona said. "What do you have in mind?"

"I was thinking of a theater fair," Kika said. "It is an art that all we utopians treasure. Why not use it?"

"Hmm," Asora said. "I never thought about that."

"Nor have we," Aga added.

"What kind of theater?" Asora asked. "Theater means something different to me as did does to them," Asora ushered to the court.

"Why not both?" Kika asked.

"Human theater is a screen with lights and speakers," Asora said trying to simplify the idea to Kika.

"I know," Kika said. "I have seen human movies. And I think that there is a way to combine both on stage and movie screening."

"I am not sure if that is possible?" Asora said.

"It might be," Frenzen said.

"Well, we should have experts in these two fields of theater come and see if it could be done?" Madimoy suggested from Asora's side.

"Oh, this will be so much fun!" A courtier cheered with excitement.

"I agree," Asora said with a smile. "Prime Minister, summon our best stage director, and movie director."

"Yes, your highness," Frenzen bowed and walked away.

Weeks later Dorien the capital world of the Darkcon Empire, Queen Laxur was meeting with her marshals. War has not broken out yet, but it was seen as inevitable. The queen wanted her empire to be ready. A sentiment shared by her marshals. She was almost idolized by the military as powerful strongwoman that was on the verge of restoring the empire's prestige. Unlike the Utopians, Queen Laxur promoted based on merit. So, most of her marshal, generals, and admirals were once peasants until they showed an impressive military aptitude. And this had paid off for Laxur greatly. This also gave her the near absolute loyalty of the military and the newly formed defense industry that she created.

"So, our numbers are at a level where we can take and hold territory," one of the marshals said.

"Our fleet is also substantially more powerful than the Utopians ships," the only female admiral said. "But I still am not sure if they will be able to handle Consortium forces. They are a part of the Utopian Kingdom after all."

"Agreed," an older work general spoke. "Is there a way we can break the Utopians down?"

"There is," Laxur said. "And it may not be as hard as you think."

"This war will be easier without the Consortium in it," one of the younger marshals added.

"Maybe we should try a propaganda blitz on Havaina?" Another general suggested. "IF we can convince the Consortium leadership to be more resistant to Evorn's demands when war comes, it makes things easier on us."

"There is a problem with that," Obsidian spoke who was next to Laxur. "Princess Asora."

One Laxur's other side was Sysu, and she spoke next. "Asora is very popular with the Consortium, and she is the first one of their kind to sit on the throne."

"Princess Asora is off limits," Laxur said. "She is mine."

"Of course, your majesty," another admiral said.

A magical message popped up in front of Queen Laxur. These came up when ever a royal message was sent out across the realm. It worked for all the monarchies, so Laxur got them constantly. It was very annoying.

"Damn it, now what?" Laxur sighed.

She opened the message, and it was a call for talent for a new form of experimental theater. This annoyed the queen greatly. She was about to toss it out, but Dari entered the room and her lit up.

"An invite to a theater talent?" Dari asked.

Queen Laxur gave Dame Dari the message. "Knock yourself out."

Dari read the message and she seemed excited by it. That got everyones attention.

"Dame Dari?" Sysu asked. "Are you well?"

"I love theater," Dari answered. "This could also be a great way to get our message through."

Queen Laxur, and her military leaders looked at Dari oddly. They were confused at first. Obsidian and Sysu looked at each other and sighed. Dari was a big fan and lover of all thing's theater. She loved plays, movies, and stage performance, and annoyed the werewolf and vampire as she tended to drag them into it.

"Uh, Dame Dari," the female admiral started. She was a female corrupt human with a lot of scars on her face. "This does not help our mission."

"It can in a way," Dari said. "I can give the realm our message and it can chaos the Utopians to become more amenable to our wishes."

Queen Laxur had her doubts. She did use propaganda to maintain control of the empire. But all of that was calibrated for the Darkcons and to convince them to allow Laxur to do what she needed and wanted. The was aware that propaganda was a powerful tool if done right. But the Utopians were far too varied to have most forms of propaganda to work correctly.

"Hmm, this could be a good experiment to run," Laxur suggested to her military leaders.

"How so?" A general demanded. "Theater is entertainment, not a weapon."

"Theater can also be a powerful tool to communicate our message," Laxur said. She turned to Dari. "Take Obsidian and Sysu with you. Attend this talent recruitment. Make me proud."

Dari looked like an excited child. Obsidian and Sysu looked at each other with wide scared eyes. Dari dragged both with her as they left the room.

"Are you sure about this?" A general asked the queen.

"This is merely an experiment. Plus, I love seeing my people happy," Laxur explained.

Two weeks later on Evorn, a dwarf and his entourage were welcomed in to the palace throne room. He was a famous Utopian theater play director and writer. He was very popular with the nobility and was seen as the father of the modern Utopian stage.

"Sir Saranine, welcome," Puro Aga.

The puro held out his hand to shake Saranine's hand. The stage director shook the Puro's hand. Nona then came up to him and gave the director a bouquet of flowers.

"Lovely welcome," Saranine said friendly.

"You are welcome," Nona said in a very polite tone.

Saranine then looked at the throne to see Princess Asora. She looked pleasant enough to the dwarf. The stage director and his group then approached the princess. Saranine bowed to Asora.

"Your highness, thank you for inviting me here personally. It is not every day that the supreme monarch of the kingdom gives you an invite," Saranine said. "Though I am curious about why."

"We need a form of art that can revitalize the Utopian artistic spirit. Especially in story telling," Asora started. "And since you are the founder of modern stage theater, we felt that you and one other will be perfect for this."

"Who is the other?" Saranine asked.

"He will be here in an hour," Lady Madimoy answered.

"Again, who?" Saranine asked.

"Mister Karaix Nolib," Asora said.

"Who?" Saranine asked.

"He is the Consortium's movie producer and director," Asora answered.

"Movies? As in giant silver screen and moving images?" Saranine asked dumbfounded.

"Yes, those," Asora said.

"I think it would be an interesting experiment," Nona said. "Can we meld the two."

"I do not see how?" Saranine said.

"Movies are a Utopian art now. And the Darkcons are going to take it from us, just like they did with stage performances," Nona said.

"Very well, I will see what I can do," Saranine said.

An hour later a jewel elf wearing a black suit and tie and black shiny shoes walked into the throne room with several people behind him. Princess Asora was happy to see him.

"Well Colonel, oh I am sorry Princess Asora. You look stunning," the jewel elf said happily to Asora.

Asora giggled like a fan girl. "Thank you, Mister Nolib, I am just glad that you managed to get here so fast."

"Of course, I owe you a lot, it is the least I can do," Nolib said.

"Do you two know each other?" Aga asked.

"During the attack on Aunsborg a few years back, the princess here was a young colonel and fought off some terrorists. She saved my life and my team too," Nolib said.

"And I happen to be a fan of your work," Asora said.

"Ah and a lady of higher taste," Nolib complemented.

"I also have seen some of your works too," Nona said. "I found the film Lost Cloud to be of particular fascination."

"I see you have surrounded yourself with equally greatly knowledgeable people too," Nolib said.

The director then kissed Nona's hand. That made the blonde female elf blush. She looked at Asora who was grinning at her.

"I see why you two are friends. I would be too," Nona added.

"Oh, we also put out a call for auditions to start," a courtier said.

This took Asora by surprise, but she did not see any problem with this. This was one area where Asora and the royal court had in common. They all believe that this was needed, and the court even understood the power this had. What took Asora by surprise was that film or movies were gaining in popularity across the kingdom. This was perfect, even Puro Aga was on board with this.

Sir Saranine walked in to see Nolib talking to Asora and Nona. The dwarf stopped and looked Nolib up and down.

"Who is this?" Nolib asked.

"I am Sir Saranine, the father and founder of modern Utopian Stage Theater!" Saranine introduced.

"Ah, the old way of acting," Nolib said.

"What?" Saranine blasted in an offended tone.

The dwarf shoved past both Asora and Nona and the two directors faced off. They started to use each other out. Nona created a thunder to quiet the two men.

Then Asora roared, "Stop it the both of you!"

All was quiet until they heard someone clapping from the doorway. Everyone looked to see Dame Dari and behind her were Obsidian and Sysu.

"Now that was entertaining," Dari said.

"How the hell did you get here?" Aga demanded.

"We were invited," Dari said. The giant fallen angel woman took out the invitation that was sent to Queen Laxur. "Her majesty sent me in her stead."

Princess Asora sighed in annoyance. Nona looked confused.

"That was meant for Utopians only," Nona pointed out. "And we are on the verge of war with your people. It does not make sense for you to be here."

"Actually, it does," Dari said. "It will show everyone who and what we all are. Besides this was a royal invitation. I am allowed by your own law to be here."

"And what is it that you hope to do?" Asora asked.

"I came to audition of course," Dari said.

Both directors looked at each other and then between Asora, Nona, and Dari and her companions. They were at a loss as to what was going on. Both directors felt that this whole project was about to go out of control.

In the palace library both Saranine and Nolib were rummaging through all their notes and books to get some ideas of what to write and portray. Both Princess Asora and Priestess Nona were observing the two men as they occasionally flew into a rage and started yelling at each other or no one in particular.

"I am starting to think that we have created a mess," Nona said.

"For once I completely agree with you," Asora replied.

The Scullery Maid

Maid Kika came into the library to serve the princess and the priestess.

"Your highness, my lady," Kika said happily. "What would you two like to have?"

"Coffee," Asora said. "And do not skip on the sugar."

"Red leaf tea, with extra honey," Nona said.

Kika wrote down the orders and went to her magical trolly cart. She heard the directors yelling at each other as they ripped up notes and threw books at each other. Kika wanted to show what she had.

Princess Asora then noticed Kika's movements," Did you want to ask me something?"

It is silly," Kika said trying to wave it off.

"Tell me anyway," Asora said.

Kika then took out a thick stack of papers in a note binder. She haded it to Nona who opened it up to read it.

"This is a stage play?" Nona asked.

"It had been a secret passion of mine," Kika said sheepishly.

Nona gave the binder to Asora who started reading it. Nona looked impressed by it. Asora looked at Kika and smiled. She ushered both women to follow her.

Princess Asora threw Kiki's script on the table in front of the two directors, "Here is your new work."

Nolib read the title, "The Scullery Maid?"

Saranine then yanked it out of Nolibs hands, "What is this?"

"It is a romance story," Kika said sheepishly from behind Asora.

"You wrote this?" Nolib asked the maid.

"Yes," Kika said in a small peep.

Nolib sighed. He wanted to throw it out, but Princess Asora gave it to him and told him to adapt it. He was not sure if Asora read it. It was not really that good. But he got an idea.

"Can we make some modifications to the story?" Nolib asked Kika.

"What kind of modifications?" Nona asked.

Nolib tossed the binder to Saranine, and he read more into it,

"I agree. If we can make a few modifications, this could be a more interesting story."

Asora looked to Kika, "Would you be all right with that?"

"Of course, as long as the main idea of the story is the same," Kika said.

"I think I can merge an old passion project of mine into this," Nolib said.

"I have one too that can work here," Saranine said.

"It would make sense as the Scullery Maid story is a passion project," Nona said.

Nolib started to write notes. He looked to be brainstorming quickly. Saranine read what the crazy jewel elf was writing.

"What is an AI?" Saranine asked.

"Artificial Intelligence," Nolib replied.

"You are going to put in science fiction elements?" Saranine complained.

"There are science fiction elements in the core story, so why not?" Nolib defended.

"AI?" Kika asked Asora.

"The Consortium once used them to control the cybers," Asora said.

"Those were scary, I remember those from the Great War," Nona added.

"Why add the cybers into the story?" Kika asked.

"I do not know. Maybe to fill it out more," Asora thought out loud.

"One thing is for certain," Nona started. "This will be getting more interesting."

The following day talent and tryouts were being held int he public gardens. As promised, this was open to all who could make the journey. Dame Dari was the only Darkcon talent present. She was next to Lady T'a and a few other Utopian noble ladies hoping to get the part of the main lead lady. The lowly scullery maid who is the main character.

Dari was imposing to nearly every lady around her except for Lady

T'a who seemed comfortable around the giant of a warrior woman. Also, Dari was not rude or mean to T'a either. Many were speculating that Dari may fancy T'a. T'a was aware of the rumors and while flattering, T'a was not interested. What was not known was that both T'a and Dari's relationship went far back in time.

"Are you hoping to get the role?" Dari asked T'a.

"Oh, no I do not want the role of the maid. I am hoping to get the role of the main villainess," T'a said.

Dari raised an eyebrow at her. "Really? You want to be the villainess? The cruel witch that torments the maid?"

"Why not? Villains in stories tend have fun," T'a said.

At the main judges table Nona and Madimoy were placed in charge of tryouts. T'ula and Jeia were to assist the two directors. They were all bored but did not appear to be. There were so many people lined up hoping to get the main roles.

"Okay, I have the final draft done, and we can have more characters," Nolib said.

"How many more?" Saranine asked.

"Four," Nolib replied.

"That may not be enough," Saranine pointed to the line of people.

Nolib turned to Princess Asora, "You know you would be perfect to play the part of the maid."

"Oh no, I love plays, movies, and theater. I do not act well," Asora said.

"Shame, you are perfect for it," Saranine said.

Princess Asora was what these two directors would consider the perfect actress. She was more then just beautiful, she was smart, and can be tough. Nona also fell into this category for them. Just like Asora, Nona also refused any role. But Nona's reasons were different. A priestess has no place on the stage, as per the faith of the kingdom's main religion. Unless it is to spread the word of the Great Maker only.

Jeia came up to Asora, "This is going to be a disaster."

"Why do you say that?" Asora asked.

Jeia pointed to a corner where a bunch of noble women were arguing and even hitting each other. The competition for the roles were as competitive in the rest of the kingdom as it was in the Consortium.

"How many are jockeying for the main lead role?" Asora asked.

"Two hundred and forty," Jeia said with a sigh.

Asora thought for a moment. Then she saw Kika who was looking around. She was also in the line to try out for the main led role. That gave Asora an idea on solving this powder keg. She called Kika over to her.

"Here is your leading lady," Asora showed Kika to Nolib and Saranine.

"The one who made the script?" Saranine asked.

"She knows the role perfectly and knows what to do more easily than anyone else," Asora added.

"Me?" Kika looked up at Asora. "I am not pretty enough."

"That is a load of crap," Asora said. "You are pretty, and you deserve it!"

"You want to make that maid into the main lead?" A noble woman cried in anger.

Kika lowered her head in shame. She wanted to cry, but this made Asora mad. The princess snapped her fingers. The noble lady floated to Asora and then the princess had the lady dropped to her knees in front of Kika.

"Apologize!" Asora ordered.

"Never!" The woman snapped.

"May I?" Saranine offered to Asora.

"What?" Asora asked annoyed.

"Kika is actually the best choice, and she requires no time to train for the role as it was her creation. As for everyone else, there are other big roles," Saranine offered.

"The main role is the one everyone wants!" The lady on her knees said.

"Not me," T'a said walking up to them. "I want to be the villain in the play."

"Well, there are two villains now," Saranine admitted. "Which one were you after?"

"The witch," T'a said. "Who is the other?"

"I forget what Nolib called it, but it was something that humans often use in their action and horror movies," Saranine said.

"It was a time traveling cyber!" Nolib yelled in annoyance. "And she fits the bill perfectly." Nolib pointed at Dari who was in the line too.

Dari raised an eyebrow at Nolib, "A cyber? Really? There are cybers in this story?"

"There are now," Nolib said.

Princess Asora knew that Nloib and Saranine made heavy modifications to Kick's script. They also foresaw this problem and added new characters to help stop this competition for the led role. They created new led roles. They also made the original villain the powerful monarch witch into another led role instead of a major minor role. The addition of cybers was completely new.

"So, we have our three main female leads," Saranine said.

"Let me see that," Dari ripped the script from Nolib's hands and read it. She was mad that she was not going to be the maid. But when she read the cyber's role, lines, and purpose in the script. "Oh, never mind. I like this one." She then tossed the script at Nolib's head.

Princess Asora was dumbfounded. As were Obsidian and Sysu who were nearby. Obsidian growled in annoyance. He lowered his head and turned into a large silver-grey wolf. Sysu then turned into a small black short haired cat.

"Ugh, we are stuck on this glow blue for longer!" Sysu complained.

"Why do you two not try out?" Asora asked the two Darkcons.

"Screw that," Obsidian said. "I prefer radio shows."

"Theater is not something I am into," Sysu said.

"We are only here to protect Dame Dari and assist her," Obsidian said.

"And spy on me for your queen I am assuming," Asora added folding her arms.

"Maybe," Sysu meowed. "To be honest I think there is not much for us to spy on. This waste of time beauty contest."

"This was originally meant for us Utopians. Your three are the only Darkcons here," Asora pointed out. "I am surprised that Queen Laxur is not here."

"Queen Laxur wants those who follow her to be happy. Theater is a passion of Dari's," Sysu said.

"If it will help stop the war that is to come, I will allow it. I have in hopes of that," Asora said.

Obsidian barked that sounded more like a snort, "Do not count on it."

"I know," Asora told the wolf. "But it is worth a try."

"Why are you leading these monsters?" Sysu asked. "You are obviously overqualified and too good for them." Sysu pointed her paw at the line of complaining noble women. "You and your sister are the two most powerful beings, and monarchs that have ever lived."

"The Utopian Kingdom needs change. And redemption," was Asora's official answer as she walked away.

"What was that for?" Obsidian asked Sysu.

"I just planted a seed in her mind," Sysu purred.

After much debate, threats, and more the cast was selected. In another attempt to stop the coming war the Royal Court invited Queen Laxur to view the new form of theater. Dame Dari was able to get a role, though not the one she originally wanted. But the one she got was good enough to her. The Darkcon Imperial delegation had arrived earlier in the day.

Princess Asora was overseeing the finishing construction of the palace theater. The theater already existed; it was in the middle of a remodel. The workers did know the the princess was in their presence, but they seem to ignore her. But she told them to ignore her. They however could not ignore the mighty Darkcon queen as she came in.

"So, this is where you are hiding," Laxur teased.

"I was not hiding," Asora said as she looked at the queen. "I am supervising."

Laxur chuckled, "Of course. Must make sure that these people do their jobs right."

"No, I was actually interested in how they do their job," Asora said. "Also, whatever it is that you are planning. Do not!"

"Why baby sister? Whatever do you mean?" Laxur asked with mock innocence.

"You are one of the most cunning people leaders I have ever known. You have managed to stay within the bounds of agreements while venting your rage. And you are an absolute monarch with total power. So, there is no way to check you. Except here," Asora explained.

Queen Laxur smiled down at Asora. "Nice to know that you think so highly of me." Laxur blew Asora a kiss. "You are the best baby sister." Then Queen Laxur walked off.

Princess Asora looked at her elder sister with suspicion. Then someone else came up to Asora. Someone that she was not expecting. General Anco approached her, and she was not aware that he was on Evorn.

"Colonel," Anco said.

He refused to call her princess as he felt that it was an insult to Asora. She was better then that, and she was like a daughter to him. Asora understood this and allowed just in between them.

"What are you doing here?" Asora asked worried. "When you show up like this, it is never good."

"Well, you are completely right about that," Anco said. He looked around to make sure that only Asora was within earshot. "We need a place to talk."

"Follow me," Asora said as she walked to a small room in the theater. She closed the door and used her magic to make the room soundproof. "What is it?"

"Do you remember Velinus?" Acno asked.

"What about him?" Asora asked. "I thought he was in isolation at Camabor Prison?"

"Some of the more radical members of the FFM managed to break in and free him three days ago," Anco said. "And we all know your history with him."

"Damn it," Asora sand in annoyance. "I thought me breaking his legs would have gotten the point across."

"He is most likely after you again," Anco warned. "Should I have Marevin permanently sent here?"

"I am no helpless damsel," Asora snapped.

"I know that. Hell, you have kick my ass before and you are one of a hand full of people in the realm that is not afraid of me," Anco said. "But I do not trust the Royal Guard to protect you. I am still surprised that you have not gotten an element of the Red Guard to be your personal protectors."

"Countess Marien expressed a similar concern," Asora said. "But I would like to have Marevin with me. He and Sarea would be good to have."

"I fully trust Sarea," Anco said. "One of a few humans allowed to practice magic and is a tough woman. But she may need help."

"Agreed," Asora said. "Send Marevin to me when he is able to come."

"In the meantime, I will be here with a contingent of Red Shadow Guards. I just need you to tell the few trusting Royal Guardsmen about it," Anco said.

"I will let Captian Joes know," Asora said.

Days later the theater was finished, and the premier was to be viewed by all the nobility and monarchies of the realm. Queen Laxur and her privy council were given a fancy box to sit in and had a perfect view of the stage. This box was also for Princess Asora and her privy council. The 'Monarch Box' as it was nicknamed was the most heavily guarded part of the theater.

To Laxur's surprise Asora and Jeia came into the box with bags of popcorn and drinks. The other monarchs were confused. Laxur however was amused. She made a bag of popcorn and a drink appear in her hands.

"I remember this when we were small," Laxur said.

"Me too," Jeia said. "Those were good days."

"We can have more of those," Asora added.

Laxur looked at her siblings Asora and Jeia. "Nice try you two."

Down near the entryway to the stage, and dressing room, three unknown individuals made their way through the theater. They were putting up devices underneath the stage and doors.

Kika was in her dressing room crying as she just endured another round of bullying from the noble women who were still jealous of her. Only Dari did not bully her. Then she heard someone moving around on the other side of the door. She went to open the door just a crack and saw three shadows in the dark doing something. She stayed quiet and slowly followed them.

The Royal Orchestra started up and Lady T'a began the introductions. Kika stopped following and got to the curtain. Dari noticed Kiki's perplexed expression.

"Is something the matter?" Dari asked Kika.

"The only thing that is the matter is that she's short and fat," some girl said from behind them.

Kika lowered her head in shame. Dari looked furious but she figured that she would get even for Kika later.

"Why do you take that?" Dari asked. "You are the led and should be proud."

"I am nowhere close to being beautiful," Kika sobbed gently. "I am short and fat."

"I do not think that you are ugly," Dari said.

"Yes, for you to say. You are a mountain of a goddess," Kick sobbed.

"And you are more normal than I am," Dari said. "Queen Laxur felt just like you once."

"Queen Laxur is the most beautiful and attractive woman to ever live. I have no chance with or any other lady here," Kika said.

"Beauty is subjective my dear," Dari mentioned.

Kika then saw a human moving around in the shadows. She remembered this man talking to Princess Asora a few days ago. He appeared to be looking around for something, or someone. Kika then walked to him.

"Are you lost?" Kika asked.

The man looked at Kika with an odd expression. He was not expecting Kika to come up to him. She thought the man was cute, but she did not know that this human was General Anco the most feared human alive.

"Actually, I am tracking three individuals that should not be here," Anco said.

"Are we in danger?" Kika asked worried.

"Possibly," Anco said.

"The Darkcons?" Kika asked.

"No, the FFM," Anco replied.

"The FFM?" Kika had not heard of these people before.

"The Freedom First Movement. It is a right-wing terrorist organization hell bent on causing mayhem and chaos," Anco said.

"Can I help?" Kika asked.

Anco thought for a moment, "Actually you can." He looked at the line up of actors and actresses. "Do any of those people look out of place to you?"

Kika looked at the line of actors and actresses. She looked closely. But they all were familiar.

"They are who they appear to be," Kika said. "But I did see three people moving around in the corridor where the actors' rooms are."

"Where is that?" Anco asked.

"Down there," Kika pointed back to the rooms.

"I will be back," Anco said as he went down to the rooms.

Anco made his way into the darkened area. He used the music and loud noises of the play to hide his presence. In a beam support Anco saw a small black box. He did not touch as he noticed a small blinking red light on it. It was a bomb. Then he saw another one on a nearby beam, and another, and another. The whole stage was rigged to blow. Then he saw someone climbing to the top of the stage. He had a rocket launcher strapped to his back.

"Oh shit!" Anco spat as he gave chase.

On stage Kika was speaking her part and acting in a stage set of a scullery. Her tears and emotions were so well acted that she seemed to be the best actress. Little did anyone know what that her tears were real. Even on stage she was still bullied.

The scene changed to Dari as she played something else. She was to a next generation cyber as Nolib called it. Disguised as an organic. Dari had the build and might to pull it off. Dari had nearly no lines, but her role was all action. Her first action was to kill a nearby noble woman and take her identity. She was to merely knock her out. But Dari was feeling vindictive and wanted Kika to see that she had one friend. The actress that Dari came at poorly pretended to die. But Dari corrected this by punching her unconscious.

Meanwhile the FFM operative could not get a lock on Princess Asora. But he could get a lock on the actors and actresses on stage. He was told to either assassinate Asora or ensure that a war between the Utopian Kingdom and the Darkcon Empire became a reality. And since Dari was a high-ranking member of the empire, killing her would guarantee this.

Before the assassin could open fire, Anco tackled him to the floor of the tall catwalk. Dari and Kika did look up to see that the catwalk above the stage was moving. A grenade from the terrorist's belt fell and exploded in the middle of the stage. The catwalk collapsed and both eh terrorist and Anco fell onto the stage. The audience had no idea what was happening and many screamed. Everyone on it was buried in debris.

Kika managed to unbury herself to see a human in black body armor and a broken rocket launcher on his back. He took out a knife and charged at Dari. Dame Dari managed to get up and saw the man coming at her. Dari did not have the chance to defend herself. But she did not need to. Kika stood in front of him, and she took the knife strike. The terrorist stabbed Kika in the chest and he tossed her aside. Then Anco came at him with a stick and whacked the man in the head.

Anco ran to Kick's side and puled the knife out of Kiki's chest. Dari got up and ran to Kick's fallen body. Anco was holding Kika. The audience then realized what was happening.

The other two terrorists come out in an attempt to hold the theater patron's hostage. They had radioactive elements in their armor to protect them from the magical people.

"Where is only three of them?" Laxur asked Asora.

"The FFM are not known for thinking things through," Asora pointed out.

"The FFM? I thought that they were all gone?" Laxur asked. "Those idiots are like roaches."

The two men were then attacked by the theater patrons, and they ripped their guns from them as the Royal Guards took them down.

Asora was looking at the stage and saw Kika dying. Asora had a look of rage, and Laxur saw her protector Dari helping Anco comfort the small dying woman.

Back on the stage Kika felt cold and was being held in Ancho's arms. Dari looked at the terrorist that stabbed kick with anger. She charged at the man and knocked he's weapons out of his hands. Dari picked him up by his neck.

"Why?" Dari hissed her demand.

"She got in the way," the man whizzed. "You were supposed to die."

Dari chuckled. "The Utopians are right. You FFM types are surprisingly idiotic."

"Dari!" Anco called. The tall dame turned and looked down at Anco. "Give him to me."

"Why? He deserves to die for what he did to Kika," Dari snapped.

"Yes, he does, but not by your hand," Anco pointed out. "Killing someone by Darkcon hands is grounds for war. This is an internal matter."

"He admitted to attempting to assassinate me," Dari pointed out.

"I know that. But I will see to it that he and these friends have a violent end. Outside the views of everyone here," Anco said.

Kika saw that her two new friends were fighting over how to punish the ones that harmed her. The pain was incredible as she got up and limped her way to Dari and Anco. The two saw Kika coming to them, and they both looked worried.

"Sit down," Dari said to Kika. "You are injured."

"Thank you for caring," Kika smiled up at Dari. "Let Anco take him."

"But he tried to kill you," Dari said in a soft tone.

"He wanted to kill you. I did not want you hurt. You were the only one in this production that had been nothing but kind to me," Kika said. "You are my friend. I did not want you hurt."

Dari looked surprised. The whole exchange was heard by the whole theater. Both Saranine and Nolib recorded the whole thing.

Dari then turned to Anco. "What will you do to him?" Dari demanded still holding the man by his throat.

"Trust me, you are being gentle compared to what I have in mind," Anco said.

"No," Kika said to both Dari and Anco. "Rehabilitate him."

"This parasite is a right-wing nut job. It is better to put them to death then waste our resources on them," Anco said.

"I agree," Dari added.

"That is why they still exist. The FFM will never fully be destroyed if you keep that mentality towards them," Kika said.

Kika then felt lightheaded, and she fell to the floor.

Kika then woke up in the palace infirmary. She saw that her chest had been bandaged. The wound had been repaired as the magical healing spells did their work on her. She saw on a nightstand a large vase full of beautiful glowing purple flowers fresh from Dorien. Then she saw what looked like a medal from the Consortium's SDC. The medal was inscribed with 'honor and bravery to the small and tough.'

"Finally," a friendly voice said.

It was Princess Asora. She was smiling and had the magical trolley cart behind her.

"These are all for you," Asora said.

"Where did these come from?" Kika pointed to the flowers and medal.

"Dame Dari said that you were her best friend and she moved heaven and earth to get these flowers for you. Even Queen Laxur herself was impressed with you," Asora said. "So much so that she was willing to cool things down with the war matra."

"I stopped a war?" Kika sounded impressed.

"More like you put it on hold," Asora said. "That medal we in the SDC only give to civilians who show incredible courage. You are one on elf seven people in history to get that one and the only Utopian to have one. I am jealous." Asora giggled. "General Anco was impressed by you."

"What happened to the three men?" Kika asked.

"Both Anco and Dari wanted to rip their heads off to see which on of them could avenge you," Asora explained. "But they knew that you would have been horrified so they did something else."

The door opened again, and the three men came in dressed as doctor's assistances. Kika was worried until she saw them check her vitals. They also looked happier too.

"She will be ready to return to normal in a day or two. But I recommend at the very least a week to fully recover," the former terrorist turned doctor's assistant said to Asora.

"Thank you. I will make sure it happens," Asora smiled.

"What did you do to them?" Kika asked.

"Actually, Lady T'a took care of them," Asora said. Then Asora snapped her finger. "Oh, before I forget. General Anco asked me to give this to you."

Princess Asora gave Kika a letter. It was from Anco, and he told her that he was impressed by her bravery. Also, he told her to respect herself and know that she has friends. He even with much difficulty said that Dari is also a good friend. And he thought Kika was cute too.

"He is such a charmer," Kika giggled with a blush.

"You are the first girl that I known of that he likes and is willing to admit too," Asora said. "That is impressive to me."

"What about Dari?" Kika asked.

"Queen Laxur was so taken by your bravery that she was willing to tone down the war mongering. She also wanted to personally thank you for saving Dame Dari too," Asora said. "But she had to go back to Dorien. But I was told to convey her thanks to you."

"Thank you," Kika said.

"Now do as your nurses said and get some rest," Asora said.

Princess Asora then walked out of the room with the three reformed men following behind her. Kika then rested her head on the pillow and saw her flowers glow lovingly. It spelled out 'Thank You.'

"You are welcome," Kika said in reply.

Chapter Eleven

Diplomacy

On the Utopian capital world of Evorn, Princess Asora had forced early retirement of her minister of state for failing to come up with an effective peace solution for the Darkcon Empire. Even after the actions of Kika, the overall dilemma remained. Queen Laxur made sure that was known to all.

The top three of the government where Princess Asora, Prime Minister Frenzen, and Master of War Yane agreed on one thing: who the next minister of state should be. Asora hoped that her new minister would be more successful. She knew this man well and believed he would bring new respect to the kingdom's government.

"Maybe we should give up Carlon. It is a lost cause, and they are attacking other worlds as well," Yane said. "The humans are not going to fight for that."

"Not to mention the loss of life and money," Frenzen added.

"I agree, but the court here does not want to hear that, as you know," Asora reminded them.

"And who will replace Sir Hierant as your minister of state?" asked Lady Teralay, a woman centaur. She was a white mare with long yellowish-white hair, and she wore a long vest over her upper torso that splayed over her back.

"We have recommended Prince S'tie of Galeron to fill the role of minister of state," Archduke Frenzen responded.

As he said that, a tall, handsome, dark brown-haired man with twinkling light- blue eyes walked in toward Asora's throne. He was twenty-five years of age. His thin yet muscular body was dressed in the Galeron royal uniform: a long, heavy green jacket and pants of the same color with a deep-blue stripe on the outside of each leg. The court seemed to agree with Frenzen's choice; there were nods and smiles as S'tie approached.

He was the grandson of a past high noble of the kingdom, the great elf lord W'arren, who married the human beauty, Grace. He was a war hero and a decorated soldier of Carlon, where he battled as a frontline officer. He was a participant in the process that decided the next ruler of the Utopian Kingdom. Through the Royal Academy not too long ago. Asora won that contest, but S'tie had no ambition for the throne or crown, and he was known to be a friend to the princess.

"My princess, I thank you for the responsibilities that you have bestowed upon me, and I will not fail you," the new minister of state declared as he bowed to Asora.

The princess stood up from her throne and approached S'tie. She held out her right hand. S'tie gently took her hand and kissed it to show his loyalty to her. Then S'tie whispered to her, "You know, your highness, I would rather fight the Darkcon imperial forces than do this political bull."

The princess smiled slightly, trying not to laugh outright.

He was standing before the princess. Even though S'tie was seven inches taller than Asora, she was standing on the steps leading up to her throne, making her appear taller.

"As my new minister of state, are you aware of the current situation?" Asora asked.

"Yes, I am, your highness, and I am currently working on a solution to the problem," S'tie responded efficiently. "I already have a few ideas."

"I look forward to hearing them. Now, the admiral is going to tell us about the situation on Carlon," Asora stated. She motioned for S'tie to stand beside her chair, as she sat down to listen to Yane.

"Thank you, my princess. The Carlon conflict has cost us too much in both lives and money. The Darkcons are simply too many and too advanced in terms of their weaponry. Simple arrows, swords, and light magic are not enough anymore. And the limits of special mages and other advanced magic users make for even greater difficulty when fighting the empire," Yane summed up.

"So what are our options, admiral?" S'tie asked Yane.

"We can increase the human numbers in our military. They are allowed to use their own weapons, which are more powerful than the Darkcons' weapons. We also could equip the royal guard with guns, rifles, pistols, and grenades instead of swords and arrows. Then we can expect a major turnaround in battlefields where we still have a strong presence," Admiral Yane announced to the Royal Utopian Court.

"That's ludicrous! We cannot do that! We can understand adding humans to the royal guard, that can be done, but arming our men with such weapons would be an even bigger folly than arming them with rocks," Lady Teralay pronounced.

"The Darkcons have made great use of more advanced weapons and just look at the results!" Prime Minister Frenzen stated in response.

"Princess, if I may?" S'tie asked.

Asora gestured to proceed, "Be my guest."

"Ladies and gentlemen of the Grand Utopian Royal Court! It is common knowledge in all militaries that the force with the greatest advantage wins. Long ago, that advantage was magic, and the kingdom excelled in it. But now the winds of advantage have changed, and technology is the new weapon on the battlefield. If we do not accept that, then we will go into the sands of history, and it will be the Darkcons that will emerge victorious for the next age," S'tie preached.

"Very stirring, Prince S'tie, but it is our tradition, since the founding of the kingdom in the ancient times, that magic is our weapon," a male dwarf said.

"Were you morons paying attention? He is right! Either embrace the new or perish into oblivion!" Yane exploded.

Asora put her hand on her face in both frustration and embarrassment.

"Admiral, stop. You and I will have words later about this," Asora stated threateningly.

"Yes, my princess," Yane said quietly.

"However, both Admiral Yane and Prince S'tie is right. I will order that the royal guard start accepting human recruits and start using more advanced weapons," Asora said, and the court began to complain.

"Only the human troops will carry guns and grenades. The rest can still use their swords and arrows. The humans are the most qualified to use these new weapons, and this way there will be no accidents with those that know little of these weapons." The various courtiers complained.

S'tie laughed abruptly. "At least the humans will live. It will please them to have shown up the other Utopians."

There were low grumbles, but none of the nobles spoke out against him. It was a loaded statement to them. But they did know of its advantages. But in the end Utopian pride won the day. Much to the dismay of Asora and the kingdom.

"We appreciate the advantage." Bremmer laughed.

"The Darkcons are also known to have metal ships. They are primitive by human standards but more powerful than any wooden Utopian vessel," Yane mentioned. "Plus, Queen Laxur has moved from Carlon to neighboring worlds. She is beginning her conquest of the Realm using more powerful weapons. War is here."

"Is she using the weapon that was stolen from Lord Jeia's factory?" a dwarf named Count Runik asked.

"No, there has not been time for them to fully develop one," Yane reassured the court.

"Have these metal ships been used against us?" the count pressed, concern written on his face. "Other then on Carlon?"

"Yes, they have. The humans have more advanced ships, both aquatic and space, but you have yet to approve the funds needed to purchase them so that we can fight back." Asora stepped in.

"Those human toys may not be effective against the Darkcon ships," a centaur said.

"Not true. They have been very effective against raiders and pirates," Yane added. "Plus, there was the history element here."

"But they have not been proven against Queen Laxur's metal ships," Yoser insisted.

"Metal against metal is more effective than wood against metal. A metal ship is needed to utilize a new weapon that was presented at my science fair. Since you were at my science fair, you would have seen it," Asora said.

"And what is this new weapon?" a female elf asked demandingly. Asora gestured to Lady T'ula to come forward.

"It is referred to as a rail gun. It is more powerful than a laser or a normal cannon that the Royal Guard use. It has the power of a meteor impact. Only a metal ship can be equipped with it and a powerful onboard generator can wield it. If it were on a wooden ship, the rail gun would destroy both the target and the firing ship," T'ula explained.

"Lady T'ula, as a respected member of the court and privy council and of the elvish race, do you believe that all this is necessary to prevail?" Count Runik asked.

"In my opinion, yes. If we want to survive, we must do this. The rail gun would be an effective weapon, as would the aircraft, metal ships, and drones," T'ula said honestly. "After all, Queen Laxur has been victorious so far because she is using new technology. She will win if we do nothing."

"Thank you, Lady T'ula. We will deliberate on your words," the dwarf count said, and the courtiers left.

Asora was stunned and a little mad that they asked T'ula for her opinion and did not listen to her or the admiral or Frenzen; however, Asora hoped that T'ula's words had an effect. She said what the princess wanted. The court was hoping that T'ula would say something that would affirm their position, but she had reinforced Asora's point. T'ula was one of the best choices to be in the privy council. T'ula continued to impress Asora more and more.

"So, do you think it will work?" Lady Madimoy asked.

She had been in the audience, quietly listening to the events. She now came closer to the throne, and Rentha flew over to join them. Rent was a small sixteen-centimeter-tall red haired fairy that mirrored her friend Madimoy quite well.

"I hope so, Lady Madimoy," T'ula said to her friend.

Madimoy did not like elves, but T'ula was an exception because she had the characteristics of a jewel elf. Jewel elves were a sub race of elves that preferred the human way of living and liked technology. T'ula said that she was not a fan of technology. But that was a lie, and jewel elves only say that when they are trying to get into positions of authority in the Utopian Kingdom. It worked too and humans loved it.

"Those primitive cave dwellers better approve all of this, or we are all doomed," the redhead prophesied.

"Lady Madimoy, they are used to winning. Elves are old and only remember the wars fought against a more arcane Darkcon Empire. The Darkcons have been preparing for this for a long time. The last king, Laxur's dead husband, knew the prophecies and believed himself to be the great leader who would unite the empire and kingdom. Tylus married an angel, who was to be by the conqueror's side. He had already begun the modernization twenty years before marrying Laxur, and when she appeared, he believed it was the prophecy," S'tie reminded her. "The elves, centaurs, and dwarves have closed their eyes to this threat for all that time, refusing to acknowledge the threat because the king died. The fairy spies have been warning us for decades. And the humans do not care."

S'tie turned to Asora. "My father and grandfather agree with you, princess, which is why they encouraged me to take this position. They will continue to work behind the scenes, but that will not be able to help us now." He turned back to the redheaded Madimoy. "And neither will antagonizing the nobles. You have the fairies and humans, who are ferocious fighters. Be glad, because the rest are just fodder for Laxur until they change the way they fight."

"They are killing their own people." Madimoy smiled nastily. "No great loss." She turned to Asora. "I do not see the downside."

"Not all of my people deserve to die." T'ula faced them all with her chin in the air. "They will come to understand the need to be more progressive. They will!" She pleaded with them.

"The universe does not work in the ways that we wish. It does what it wants, and we only react to it," Asora pointed out.

"And how is Jeia?" Frenzen asked, judging it was time to change the charged atmosphere.

"He is well now, but he needs time to recover from such a powerful shock," Madimoy said.

"So when is your wedding?" T'ula asked.

"It was going to be in the next few months, but he may not be well for it, so I think it may get pushed back further," Madimoy said sadly.

Rentha spoke up. "My lady has rarely left his side, but she thought this was an important event. Lord Jeia will want to know what Prince S'tie has said."

"Oh, I am sorry, Madimoy. I know that you have been planning your marriage to Jeia for months, and it went up in smoke." Asora was saddened.

"Princess, do you want to tell her what the investigators found out?" Frenzen asked Asora.

"Yes, I will," Asora responded.

"Tell me what?" Madimoy asked, worried.

"An investigation team looking over the rail gun prototype has found that the wiring was tampered with. Someone may have tried to assassinate Jeia," Asora said. "The attack afterwards was for me and everyone else."

Madimoy had a look of horror on her face, and she was now very worried about her future husband. Also, for Asora who was going to be her sister in law one day.

"What! Why? Who?" Madimoy flew into a frenzy.

"We do not know, but I have a team looking after him. We may want to have them look after you as well," Asora said. "But we think it was elements of the FFM."

Madimoy was in tears, and T'ula held her. The tall jewel elf tried her best to keep Madimoy from becoming a hysterical mess.

"What am I going to do? I cannot have people with me everywhere, and I cannot go through life looking over my shoulder every day. No one should live like that!" Madimoy cried.

"No one should live like that, but you have Rentha. She is a powerful fairy and can call for help if needed." T'ula put her hand on Madimoy's shoulder.

"I will ever be your friend and protector, Madimoy." The fairy landed softly on the floor and grew to two meters. She towered over the redhead and had a sword in her hand. "I need to get a gun."

"I am sure we can fine one for you," Yane added.

Several hours later, the court approved Asora's plan to allow humans into the royal guard. Asora could then order nine metal spaceships and twelve metal aquatic ships. The princess wanted more ships than that, but it was a start. Now she had to convince Countess Marien, the ruler of the Consortium to have a detachment of Red Guard soldiers. Asora hoped that a series of joint military operations. However, Asora was under no illusion that such a peace co-existence between the two military's would not happen.

The Royal Guard and the Red Guard had a long and violent history. Asora knew this history well as she was once an officer in the Red Guard. The Great War was something that the Royal Guard seemed to be unable to get over. The Consortium's various colored guard forces routinely destroyed during that conflict.

Princess Asora's ancestor was the leader of the Consortium at the time. Emperor Jurano was a great hero to humans, jewel elves, and daemons alike. But he was a terror to the majority of the Utopian Kingdom. Her shared bloodline with the old emperor was also part of the reason why the royal court and much of the Utopian Kingdom was so resistant to her. Asora loved her ancestor and often looked to his legend of inspiration.

A week later, Prince S'tie went to Princess Asora in the library with his plan to deal with the Darkcon Empire. He wanted to discuss his plan with her first before anyone else was to hear of it.

"Prince S'tie, what do you think?" Asora demanded.

"I have found that the Darkcons were given carte blanche in methods for getting rid of the pirates and raiders. Veartis says that taking the planet from them and putting it in Darkcon control is justified," S'tie said. "Much to my dismay."

"This is devastating." Asora put a hand to her throat, where she could almost feel her sister's hand. "She had no right to take the planet. But she was right. We should have done this diplomatically. We should have had time to get the people moved or told them of their choices. Why was I not told of this before?"

"I am not sure," S'tie replied.

"I will tell you! The court conspires to make me look weak and like a fool so that they can rule. I may have to wait twenty years to be made Queen, but if they think that I will be made a joke at the expense of the kingdom during that time, they are wrong. They made this war." Asora said. "Plus, I do not think they appreciate my bloodline to add to it."

"Also, I believe that Queen Laxur wanted this war, but I think that we can stop it before it gets any worse," S'tie pointed out.

"How? Laxur wanted a war, and she got it. Convincing her to stop is damn near impossible." Asora said.

"Nothing is impossible, kiddo—oh, I mean, princess. Sorry, I am not used to that yet, I guess," S'tie apologized.

"It is fine between you and me. We have been friends forever, S'tie. I cannot believe that the court thinks that we should marry. I mean, do not get me wrong, you are a good guy, but I am not . . ." Asora could not finish.

"I'm not your type. I understand. And no offense, Asora, you are a wonderful friend, but you would not be a good wife for me, and I would not be a good husband for you." S'tie smiled.

"Though, the court thinking we might marry has benefits for me. I do not have every female trying to corner me in the hallways. I just say that I am not available, and they think it is because we will be married. The reality is that I simply do not find any of them attractive, not after Asaria, but they do not need to know that." Asora added.

Both Asora and S'tie chuckled lightly at each other, and both think of Asaria. What an exquisite and gentle girl she had been; what a horrific tragedy it was.

Swallowing the sadness, she smiled. "And I do not think that Marevin would like that," Asora reminded him.

"No, I do not think he would," S'tie replied.

"What have you decided to do about the Darkcons?" Asora asked.

"Since our diplomats on shared worlds have worked very slowly, I and a team of diplomats will go to Dorien and talk with Queen Laxur herself," S'tie announced.

"I hope that my sister can be reminded of the love and friendship that once existed between you and her. You are my secret weapon against Laxur," Asora pointed out.

"I hope she remembers me. Maybe love will convince her to stop this madness." S'tie added.

"I hope so too. Have you seen what she looks like?" Asora asked.

"I know she changed her name. Why Laxur? Her original name was so beautiful and fit her well," S'tie said.

"Forget your love for Asaria. I will warn you now. She can put a spell on you by simply looking at you. She is that beautiful," Asora warned. "I can only image what she would be like when alone with you."

"She has always been beautiful," S'tie said.

"No, you do not understand. Any man, or women, that looks at her fall for her," Asora said. "It is a dark spell of infatuation."

"Okay, princess, I get it. I will be careful," S'tie promised.

"All right. Do what you feel is needed to be done," Asora pronounced.

Days later, Madimoy and Jeia were outside the palace walls on a hike. Madimoy got Jeia out of the palace to enjoy the day. He had been out of the hospital for two days, and Jeia felt like a new man. Instead of going to the seashore, they decided to go into the Cold Mountains, which were pungent with pine and full of ferns and flowers.

"You know, today would have been our wedding, darling. Now we need to find another perfect day to have it on," Madimoy gently reminded Jeia.

"I know, and I so wanted a red-haired wife today too," Jeia teased.

"Well, you will get one, eventually. You only must be a good boy and wait little while longer," Madimoy teased back.

She loved teasing back and forth with him. They had been in love for two years and wanted to marry for over a year, but things kept coming up.

"This spot will do. It is next to the lake," Jeia pointed out.

"Oh, wonderful," Madimoy expressed happily.

Both sat down on a flat rock overlooking a lake far from the palace grounds. What the two lovers did not know was that Dame Sarea and Captain Joes were watching them, by Princess Asora's order, and they were accompanied by Rentha. Madimoy had a basket with food in it; she had spent all morning making the sandwiches and snacks for them. Jeia laid his head on Madimoy's lap, and she smiled and held him.

"You know, Madimoy, you are a really fine lady, especially from down here," Jeia teased.

"Well, of course I am, Jeia. No matter how you look at me," Madimoy teased back. She lowered her head and kissed Jeia on the lips.

"You're lucky I love you, or you would be in the lake right now." Jeia laughed at Madimoy's comment. Both Madimoy and Jeia dozed off to sleep.

Hours later, Jeia woke up to a change in the ever-constant gentle splash of the waves on the shore. Madimoy also woke to the slight scratching on the beach. They looked toward the banks of the lake and saw a body on the beach. The young couple splashed along the beach, running up to see if the person needed help. Madimoy turned over the body, and it was an elemental demon. He was a bony-headed, leathery, muscular brute; his hair was long and black; he wore deep-red studded leather.

"What the hell! What is a demon doing here?" Jeia demanded.

"He could be a spy," Madimoy thought out loud.

"I'm no spy, you idiot!" the demon roared as he regained consciousness.

"How dare you call me an idiot?" Madimoy fired back.

"Because you are an idiot, you stupid girl!" the demon restated, holding his head. Then, without warning, the demon got a fist in his face from Jeia.

"You are the stupid one. Now, who the hell are you?" Jeia demanded.

"First off, where am I? It is too bright!" the demon complained.

"You are on Evorn, the Utopian capital world. Who are you?" Madimoy demanded.

"My name is Rakon. How the hell did I end up here?" Rakon cried out in pain from all his injuries.

"What happened to you?" Jeia asked.

"What does it look like, troll bait? I was beat to a pulp by Laxur and thrown out of my home.

Everything of mine is gone. I am a demon with no home, title, or purpose," Rakon mourned.

"Wow. So, your beloved Queen repaid you with beatings and banishment. What a sovereign," Jeia commented sarcastically.

"I did not want that whore on the throne. I trained her to be a warrior, not a royal!" Rakon yelled.

"You trained Laxur to be a warrior? Why?" Madimoy asked in horror.

Then, as Rakon was about to answer, thunder rocked the skies and clouds formed above. "Perhaps we should talk about this under shelter," Rakon recommended. Jeia, Madimoy, and Rakon ventured to a nearby house where T'a lived, despite Madimoy's feelings toward her. The house was a small one-story building standing alone in the mountainside with a view of the palace and coastline. T'a welcomed them in, and she treated Rakon's wounds with magical herbs and spells.

"My, Queen Laxur really pounded you to the bone. Now hold still. This is going to hurt a little," T'a warned, and she pressed a warm cloth on an open wound on Rakon's right arm. He screamed loudly at it.

"That hurt, you COW!" Rakon yelled.

T'a pressed a little harder than necessary to make Rakon regret his words. He screamed yet again. She was not going to take such rude words or behavior from this old man.

"It sounds like you are torturing him, T'a. Like all those humans you murdered so long ago," Madimoy said flatly.

T'a stopped what she was doing and dropped her head in shame. She left the room to get some more bandages and water.

"Wow! That was cold," Rakon said. "Even by my standards."

"It is what she deserves for what she did to us," Madimoy said begrudgingly.

"I assume you are referring to the Great War between the old kingdom and the human consortium, right?" Rakon asked the angry redheaded woman.

"Their war, young lady, not yours. You would do well to remember that. Has that elf witch done anything to you personally?" Rakon demanded. "I was there and if anything, I can make such clams and yet I do not."

Madimoy did not answer back, for she knew what Rakon was doing. "So why are you here, Rakon?" Madimoy asked.

"I was dumped here. You would have to ask the whore queen herself," Rakon pointed out.

"Then tomorrow we will introduce you to Princess Asora, and she can decide your fate," Jeia declared.

"Why wait?" Sarea stepped into the house, with Joes standing in the doorway.

"We can take him to see her now. He will not give us much trouble the way he is." Rentha buzzed in and flew immediately to Madimoy.

Diplomacy

"Can you carry him?" T'a asked. "He can barely walk, and it is a long way, several hours."

Joes ducked his head to stomp into the room. "I can help him walk, and it will give me a chance to interrogate him on the way."

"Where did you three come from anyway? Were you expecting Rakon?" Jeia walked up to Sarea, who was now standing in front of Rakon and T'a.

He was surprised to see that Sarea was dressed casually in brown canvas pants and shirt, the same as an elf peasant man. Her blond hair was pulled back in a braid. Joes also was out of his red-and-blue uniform.

Sarea flipped her hair back. "We were watching over the two of you on the princess's orders. She was worried that there might be trouble but did not want to alarm you."

"Hmm. You have a magic eye on you, do you not? I think you should call the princess and advise her that the sword master is here and see what she wants to do." T'a added another bandage to Rakon's face.

Sarea opened a pouch on her belt and pulled out a foot-wide glass ball. She swiped her hand over the surface, and it began to cloud, then an image of Asora came into view. "My princess, the duke and the lady are fine, but they have come across a demon, Sword Master Rakon. He has been badly beaten and thrown into the lake by Lady T'a's home, which is where we are. He claims that Laxur has done this."

The features of the princess's face became tight. "Is he requesting asylum? How do we know that his injuries are really from a fight with my sister? What does Lady T'a think?"

Sarea handed the eye to the elf. T'a took it and lifted it up to Rakon so Asora could see the demon. "Princess, I have examined him, and he has a concussion, multiple bruises and abrasions, four broken ribs, broken fingers, and a dislocated kneecap. I have healed most of his injuries, but he will not be able to walk all the way to the palace."

"I have had intel that says that Rakon has been thrown out of the empire, but do you believe it is true?" Asora interjected.

"I have a truth stone," T'a began.

"So do I. I want him at the palace. Portal him here to my privy council room. I will see you in few moments." They saw Asora's hand wave over the eye, and it went clear.

Joes stepped up to Rakon. "Sword Master, you will stand now. Lady T'a will open a portal, and we will walk through so that Princess Asora can interrogate you."

"Just a moment. We want to be there too. We will all go," Jeia said, tugging Madimoy to him.

"All right. Everyone stand still." T'a raised her hand.

T'a with a slashing action, a tear opened to the privy council room, where they saw Asora waiting. The room was square with very tall, narrow windows. The princess stood before a small throne, which was behind a large round table with eight chairs around it.

Jeia, Madimoy, Rentha, and T'a entered first, followed by Sarea walking in front of Joes and Rakon. They all bowed to Asora, including Rakon. Joes took the demon forward, with Sarea holding her gun to this Rakon's head.

"I had heard that you have been disgraced in the empire. What say you?" Asora sat calmly.

Joes punched Rakon in the head. "Answer her!"

Rakon growled at his captor and then turned to Asora. Rakon rubbed the back of his head as he did all this.

"I am not the one disgraced. It is that whore sister of yours. I simply said so, and for my opinion, I was beaten and sent here. I was beaten by her until I was unconscious, and I woke up in that lake."

"Why do you think Queen Laxur sent you here?" Asora asked quietly, watching the truth stone and his face.

"She probably believes you will kill me for her," Rakon retorted. "Or she has a sick sense of humor."

She saw the truth in that, and it made sense. She knew that the sword master was highly respected, and if it came to be known that the kingdom had killed or imprisoned Rakon, then that would make the empire's people even more unforgiving in battle. Even being banished or exiled, Raking as still popular. Very clever of the queen.

"What do you think I should do with you?" Asora asked.

The demon stared at the princess for a moment before answering. "Laxur has put us in a unique position. I am no traitor, but I do not believe in her wars—I see them as the tantrums of a spoiled girl. The worst thing is that she is winning, but as I told her, she will begin to lose. It will not take much more time before the humans decide to side with you. Some how you will make it worth their while."

Asora gave a small smile, sitting up slightly. "I will?"

"What I know of the humans, and I know quite a few—" Rakon was then interrupted.

"Corrupt humans," Joes interjected.

Rakon gave the centaur a disgusted look. "Humans are humans, whether they practice dark magic, pray to the architect or the maker, they are fundamentally the same: Utopian."

Asora raised a hand to calm the room. "You are quite right, sword master. Continue, please."

The demon smiled and pointed to her. "There! That is the reason that the humans will side with you. You see them as you should, and being one of them, you can make life better for them, except—"

Dominus, T'ula, Yane, and Frenzen came into the room quietly, but Rakon heard them and looked over. Joes punched him in the head again. "Turn around and address the princess!"

Rakon bared his teeth at Joes and turned back to Asora. "As I was saying, except your court will not let you, not yet. That is what the humans are waiting for—for the court to become desperate." The demon smiled cannily. "Are they desperate yet?"

Frenzen moved to his chair, and the others followed, except for Joes and Sarea, who stood next to the prisoner. The prime minister adjusted his chair, placed his hands on the table, looked Rakon in the face, and shook his head. "No. They are not. They should be, but they are not. The humans will send us some troops, but not enough to stop the empire from taking more worlds. Does Queen Laxur plan to attack any elf worlds? That will make the difference. So far, she has only moved against Carlon and another world that is only partly human. Queen Laxur is smart to keep from the highly populated human worlds."

Rakon nodded. "She will be moving against another world soon, and it will be of a dwarf, centaur, or elf population. I doubt she wants a mer-peoples world, but then again, she does like sushi. She will want to show her strength against the kingdom without the humans showing up. She must keep winning, or her hold on the empire will slip."

"What are her strengths?" Yane sat forward.

"I know less than you. I am a shia, a teacher, not a general or war master." Rakon pointed out.

"You know enough. Do not make Joes hit you in the head again." Yane sighed.

"Do you think that would make me talk if I chose not to?" Rakon laughed and then laughed harder when Joes punched him. Dominus waved his hand, and Joes stepped back.

"No, I do not believe anything we do to you would make you say anything you do not wish to say." Yane slammed his fist down on the table. "I want to know the numbers of ships and soldiers! Weapons!"

The demon lunged forward, striking his palm on the table. "I am no dock whore here to tell you these things! You have spies for that! Do not look to me! I am not here by my choosing!" Rakon shouted at the group.

The sound of a gun being cocked cut through the room, and Rakon felt the muzzle at the back of his head. He raised his hands, and Sarea led him back from the table.

Asora sat forward. "What will you tell us?"

Rakon shrugged. "I do not want to tell you anything that will hurt my people."

The angel stood up and walked to the demon. "If you tell us nothing, it will be as if you had. You see, I am going to recommend that the princess allow you to stay here, sequestered of course, but word will get out that you have come here. The question will be if the people believe

Diplomacy

Queen Laxur sent you here or you came here freely because you were fed up with her. It will not be easy for you. There really is no way for us to send you back either. I know that you will not harm Princess Asora or any of us. We are not your enemy, and you know that." Dominus turned to the group. "I will take responsibility for the sword master. He can stay in my rooms until something better can be arranged."

"Lord Dominus, you cannot be serious! He is probably here as an assassin!" T'ula cried.

The demon grunted, and the angel smiled. Rakon was at some level enjoying the Utopian's confusion.

"Are you an assassin? Are you here to kill us?" someone demanded.

"To what end? There is no honor in assassinations. Queen Laxur has others for that. I am here because it amused her majesty to send me here so that I would appear to be a traitor, so that everything I have said against her will be nullified. She is a freaky whore, but she can be clever." Rakon explained.

"But you do not want to be here. He could cause trouble for us." T'ula looked anxiously around the room and saw grim faces, except for Dominus, who looked unconcerned. "Lord Dominus, you must see that this will not go well!"

The angel smiled at the elf and turned to Rakon. "Would you cause problems? Spy on us?" He turned back to T'ula. "And whom would he tell? The ones who dropped him off? Perhaps Veartis, the Darkcon Ambassador? No, he left too. Of course, there could be a spy here in the palace, but then why would they need the sword master here? Lady T'ula, I have been alive longer than Archduke Frenzen or any other person you can think of, and there are several things I know. One is the honor of an elemental demon."

He turned to Rakon. "I do have spies, and they tell me that the sword master has been causing trouble for Queen Laxur and her cronies. He has gotten even the most warmongering Lords to question the war. They are happy now that they are winning, and they are ready to back the queen, but they are not seeing their fair share. It is all going back into the war and her military budget—her bank accounts. They want conquest with benefits, but they are not seeing any benefits. They are seeing the war costs. Queen Laxur is only able to keep the demons from her throat because she is winning, but she cannot rely on winning alone."

"Rakon has harped on her many lovers. She is supposed to be the grieving widow of their great king. The merry-go-round in her bedchamber is an embarrassment and an insult to the man and the people." Dominus laughed. "That is what really got him sent here. As I said, Laxur wants us to either imprison or execute him so that she can inflame her people or say that he became a traitor. Either way, she wins. We only win if we keep him alive and out of jail. He will not spy on us. He will give us his word, which to a demon is his honor."

"Why should I?" the sword master growled.

"Yes, why should he?" Jeia asked.

"My spies in the empire can also make sure that the circumstances of his hasty departure are known—that it was Queen Laxur that sent him here to be killed or imprisoned. The people will start to look elsewhere for a leader when she begins to lose, or if her perfidy becomes known. The people may turn to Rakon when he is returned."

Rakon snorted. "I do not want to lead! If I wanted to lead, I would be on the council."

"You *were* on the council, the king's council." Dominus laughed. "You are a leader of men. You are a sword master, Shia Rakon. That made you a powerful member of the House of Lords."

The angel turned to his ruler. "If you did not know, Your highness, he is the champion of the empire. Queen Laxur needed us to take him out. I doubt many would believe that he turned traitor. It will be easy for my spies to tell the truth."

"You want me to stop the war, *after* I get rid of the queen?" The demon shook his head. "She is the rightful ruler. I cannot take the throne or put someone else on it. It will cause a civil war, and I will not put my people through that for you."

"Yet you do not believe in the war, Sword Master," Frenzen stated.

"No, I do not. I believe she is doing this because she detests her family. Oh, she might love you, your highness, but she has a need to punish her family for what she calls their abandonment of her. And she kept referring to the Utopian crown and throne needed to be destroyed."

"Abandonment of her? She ran away when she was a child!" Asora spat out. "She ran to the Darkcons and left us!"

"She never explained to me while I trained her. It was simply her reason for becoming a soldier, a sword master, which she had." Rakon shook his head. "I regret that, but she was young, and I saw only the beautifully tragic child that she was. She told me of the beatings and humiliations that she had endured here in the kingdom. I could understand not wanting to be victim any longer. I assumed that none of her family helped her."

"That is not true! Our mother often came to the school, and Lady T'a also intervened!" Asora exclaimed.

The demon shrugged. "Whatever. She is getting back at you for past injuries, making you pay for your cruelty to her. And it helps that her views align quite well with the Darkcon as well." As Asora began to protest again, he raised a hand. "Real or imagined, it does not matter. The main point is that we do not need the war. We are self-sufficient. We have not gone to war in centuries, and we were not invaded. She says that the kingdom declared war on her after she had cleaned up the astral shipping lanes and took Carlon to get rid of the pirates and raiders."

He looked around the table at the Utopians. "You gave her a reason! Idiots! Now she will not stop until she has injured and humiliated you."

"I realize the court erred, but are you willing to be sequestered in my quarters? Queen Laxur cannot say that you are dead or alive, or even a traitor, if you are not heard from. Give her a new pain and disappear until we can send you home."

Yane stood up. "I still want more information. We should interrogate him some more."

Frenzen stood up. "He will say no more admiral. I agree with

Dominus. We should hide him. Queen Laxur will spit nails, and I like that we are able to give something back to her. Plus, she may wonder what he has told us. She will be more cautious, and that will give us an edge, if only for a short while."

"Sword Master Shia Rakon, will you agree to this?" the princess asked. Rakon looked around and slowly nodded.

Chapter Twelve

In Queen Laxur's Court

It was early morning, and Prince S'tie was in final preparations for his trip to Dorien. His assistants were already, and he was in final talks with Princess Asora about his orders. He would bring with him a full diplomatic staff, which was about a hundred people, and a small contingent of guards to protect him.

"Now, S'tie, do whatever you feel is necessary to awaken the goodness in my sister's heart and get her to stop this fighting before it gets worse," Asora ordered.

"I understand, my princess. I will do all that is possible to get Queen Laxur to stop." S'tie nodded. "And hopefully awaken Asaria within her."

The tall prince bowed to the lovely Utopian princess, and he walked off. S'tie boarded a magical wooden Utopian spacecraft. The ship softly took off into the skies and caught the winds of the universe.

The journey from Evorn to Dorien took roughly three months. They made the trip using the divine gateways, which were in every solar system that had habitable worlds. They were enormous magical pathways to the different worlds built by the angels and their masters eons ago. It took many slides through the different gateways to reach their destination. And it required a powerful mage from any race to open and navigate the gateways.

The magical wooden vessel was quite large, but after a few months, it could get rather crazy being cooped up inside. The three massive sails were used to propel the vessel across space and the gateway pathways.

"How much longer, captain? I really need to have my feet on the ground, or I will go crazy," S'tie complained to the dwarfish captain.

"Not much longer my prince. Another day and we will be on Dorien. You know the best way to cure cabin fever, sir, is to swab my deck," the short redheaded dwarf remarked.

"Very funny, captain. I have not done any real chores since I was young," S'tie shot back.

"I would never have guessed." The captain snickered.

S'tie went back below deck to his quarters to read his book, which he had already read twice. This was not enough. He was so mind numbingly bored. You could only stare at the flashing stars for so long.

"Maker damn! How much more bored can I get?" S'tie yelled out to himself.

Absentmindedly, the prince reached into his coat and pulled out a small glass star. This glass star was S'tie's most precious possession. It was a gift to him from his childhood friend and love, now known as Queen Laxur. He remembered giving her a magical rose that always bloomed and stayed fresh.

"Asaria, what happened to you?" S'tie whispered to himself.

Two days later, the Utopian diplomatic staff arrived on Dorien, near the Onyx Palace that housed the Darkcon royalty and government. S'tie had his servants and assistants unload the supplies. But he was to exit first and greet the Darkcon meeting and greeting party.

When the prince stepped off the ship, Queen Laxur herself greeted him with a large contingent of guards. She was wearing the most elegant dress that was befitting a queen of any nation. The dress was all black with gold bordering, and the golden eagle of the empire was embroidered across her voluptuous chest; the image used her curves to shape its design. The only skin that was showing was her head and hands. Laxur was the greatest beauty that S'tie had ever seen. The rumors turned out to be very true. He hoped that Asaria was still there inside her.

"Greetings, Prince S'tie. I, Queen Laxur, great monarch of the Darkcon Empire, bid you welcome to Dorien," the dark Queen greeted.

The prince as she held out her hand to him. Her smile alone was enough to make S'tie fall in love with her all over again. If he was not careful, he could forget why he was there. Asaria was once just as beautiful. But Laxur was much deadlier and more seductive.

"Thank you, Queen Laxur, for welcoming me and my staff to your world." S'tie gently grasped the queen's palm and kissed her hand.

He was holding her hand longer than he was supposed to, but it seemed that the dark beauty not only did not mind but also wanted to hold on to him longer too. S'tie let go of Laxur's hand and stood back up. S'tie was a few centimeters taller than the queen. To S'tie, this woman was perfect, but he had to subdue his feelings to complete his mission.

"Shall we, my dear prince?" Queen Laxur ushered S'tie and his staff to a series of coaches that were waiting for them.

The Utopian diplomats, assistants, and guards boarded the coaches and were taken to the castle. Queen Laxur escorted the prince to her private coach. It was just the two of them inside, while Dari was outside, driving.

"Rather impressive, your majesty," S'tie commented, trying to break the ice.

"When we are alone, S'tie, you do not need to be so proper. We are, after all, the best of friends and so much more," Laxur said sensuously.

The young queen was so close and with a genuine smile. She enveloped his hands in hers, and they intertwined their fingers. Her touch was so gentle and warm.

"Are you sure you wish this?" S'tie asked, unsure.

"Only if it is the two of us." Laxur answered.

She slowly kissed S'tie as if she had been waiting for this her whole life. The queen pulled away very slowly with a gentle smile upon her exquisite face. Her eyes were a green that reminded S'tie of beautifully cut jade.

"S'tie, you are on my world now, so shut up and do as I say." She giggled playfully, just like the little girl he knew so many years ago. "Oh, my prince, I am so glad that you are here with me now."

Laxur sat next to S'tie and held him in her arms. The prince returned the gesture by putting his arms around the queen and holding her tightly to his body. For the first time in a long time, she felt both loved and safe. How she dreamed of this day—to be in S'tie's arms once more.

The prince looked out the window and noticed that they were not heading for the castle. "Uh, my beauty, where are we going?" the prince asked, a little alarmed.

She liltingly laughed. "Oh, do not worry, my love. I had the driver take us on a little detour. I want to give you a tour of my empire." Laxur smiled supremely.

The carriage stopped at a large, flat area that seemed remarkably like a human airfield. When S'tie stepped out, he saw many things. Laxur walked around the carriage to his side. It was an airfield like the ones he had seen on human dominated worlds. Only the Darkcon versions were smaller. Newly built aircraft were being moved about across the field. The airport had hangers, terminals, and other stations that S'tie did not know what they were for.

"I see you are intrigued by the new airfield I had constructed. I call it Yeocor. Named after the famous air battle between the empire and the Utopians in the early days," Laxur said.

"Are those airplanes?" S'tie pointed to a series of flying machines being worked on by goblins and pixies.

"Of course. They are nowhere near as advanced as the humans' warplanes, but we have capabilities that can bring ruin to a less advanced opponent, like the Utopian Royal Guard," Laxur explained.

"How far in development are your aircraft? If you do not mind my asking, Majesty?" S'tie asked.

He had never seen a real plane before, not even the human jets. His mind was numbed by the damage that the Darkcons could do to the kingdom, which had no aircraft other than magical flying ships.

"All our aircraft are of propeller engines, though we have begun to experiment in creation of our own gas turbine engines. I know that humans have had gas turbine technology for years, and now they have replaced them with . . . uh, what are they called?" Laxur thought out loud.

"Breather engines, better known as scram jet engines," S'tie corrected Laxur.

S'tie was familiar with the concepts, designs, and capabilities of these machines. His human mother kept science magazines for him to look at when he was young. He always loved the idea of flying. So, by natural means or artificial were all the same to him. The human concepts were interesting as he learned about the physics behind flight.

"Oh yes, breather engines. Thank you, my love." Laxur smiled. "We have not been able to understand the engineering needed to create them."

S'tie now had a better idea of the Darkcons' technical development. He was surprised that Laxur was not aware of how to have her own advanced engines built. But he knew that as Asaria she was not too interested in them. So that could be a factor in this. But eventually the Darkcon would develop it.

"Did you have as much trouble convincing your people to develop all this technology as Princess Asora has?" S'tie asked.

"Of course not. We Darkcons love new things, and, for me especially, getting things done is very easy," Laxur remarked, the last part rather sensually. "Especially since I am the queen now. I always get what I want."

"I can see that, if you would forgive my words." The prince smiled.

Laxur held his hand. "I thought that you would, and I have nothing to forgive you for—you are merely stating fact."

The queen chuckled lightly, then she gently pulled S'tie around with her. They walked to a hangar, and a set of trolls opened the doors to reveal what was inside. It was a vast laboratory for aircraft. Inside were many species of the Darkcon Empire working on many things—from engines to new fuels to new alloys.

"As you can see, we are a very productive people, unlike the Utopian Kingdom." She smiled widely.

"The kingdom can be as productive and prosperous as you are," S'tie pointed out.

Queen Laxur burst out laughing at S'tie's comment. "Right! Maybe once, long ago, but now they are decadent and incompetent. What hope do those arrogant bastards have to match me? And now I hear that they are pushing their pride and stupidity on the humans. It is a wonder that the humans have not rebelled yet."

"It seems you have thought of everything, except one thing," S'tie stated.

"Oh? And what would that be?" Laxur asked.

"The age-old proverb: 'Never underestimate your opponent.' Remember the Darkcons' history with the angels?" S'tie pointed out.

"What is to underestimate? I should be, and I am, concerned about the humans and angels. I admit that the angel-Darkcon conflict was a serious miscalculation on our part, though I was not queen then. After all, it happened centuries ago." Laxur laughed.

"Seven days and nights of mayhem and havoc, not to mention all the plagues and death. I would not call that a miscalculation," S'tie pointed out.

"We are not going to bother the angels this time. They may be part of the kingdom, but they have made no effort to stop me in any way. I do not think that they will try to do anything to me," Laxur retorted with a raised chin.

S'tie looked back at the outside, deep in thought.

"Why do we not retire to a more comfortable place—my private chambers? There we can talk and play," she suggested sexually.

An automobile drove up to S'tie and Laxur. It was big and black with large wheels. It bore the seal of the queen on it to show that this was Queen Laxur's personal transportation.

"I see that you are impressed. I thought that Galeron had automobiles and roads?" the dark beauty asked.

"We do have roads and automobiles, but by tradition, my family cannot use them. We must keep with tradition, but I have always wondered what it would be like to ride in one," S'tie said.

"You see what I mean? You Utopians are so wrapped up in your traditions, and you frown on innovation," Laxur pointed out. "I will take you to the Onyx Palace in this automobile."

Dari opened a door for Queen Laxur, while another servant opened one for S'tie. Both entered, and Dari sat up front next to the driver, who was a male dark elf. In a flash, the car took off, surrounded by several other automobiles and motorcycles. S'tie assumed that they were Laxur's security detail.

The trip lasted no more than thirty minutes from the airfield to the palace; on the way, S'tie saw the huge hydroelectric dam and the geothermal processing plant, both of which fed the insatiable need for electricity on Dorien. As well as the heat and light of the growing cities on the dark world that was Dorien. A lot of this reminded S'tie of the time he visited the human capital world of Havaina a few years back. Only Aunsborg was far more impressive. The Darkcon were in the early stages of city building.

Once at the vast fortress like palace, Queen Laxur's servants opened the doors for their monarch and S'tie. The prince followed the Darkcon queen inside, with rows of guards surrounding them. There were also servants that ran all over the palace. The more senior servants soon in a line behind the guards.

"Would you like a tour of my castle, Prince S'tie?" Laxur asked generously.

"I would, if you agree to a peace meeting." S'tie demanded.

"Are you still on that? We can do that tomorrow. I think that today you and your staff should be orientated on how things are done on my world," Laxur insisted firmly.

"As you wish, your majesty." S'tie sighed in defeat. He knew that she would not change her mind.

Later, Queen Laxur gave S'tie a private tour of her home. She had already shown him the dining hall, the throne room, the chapel, which was recently put in. She seemed happy in S'tie's presence.

"Most impressive, my queen, I see that you run a tight ship," S'tie complimented Laxur.

"Thank you, Prince S'tie. We have one other place that I would love to show you." Laxur laughed softly.

She led S'tie up a large stairwell that led to the bedrooms of all the high officials of the empire. The queen's private chamber was on the top floor of the wing, and S'tie knew that was where they were going. The doors of her bedroom were large and made of what looked like black marble. With her powers, Laxur magically opened the doors. The queen walked in, and she ushered S'tie to follow. S'tie saw that Dari was also in the room. The doors closed, and the dark beauty vanished into another room with her bodyguard. S'tie was left alone, and he looked around Queen Laxur's bedroom. Against the far wall crackled a very large fireplace, making the room smell of applewood.

A large black leather couch sat in front of the fireplace, with an artful black coffee table in front of it. Ankle-deep rugs adorned the floor, and black drapes flowed over all the walls. Jeweled throw pillows were scattered around.

S'tie saw Laxur's very large bed situated away from the fireplace and doors. It looked very hard, but when he placed his hand on it, the bed felt very soft. The material seemed to mold around his hand. He found his thoughts wandering to Laxur and everything they had never done since she had disappeared at twelve years old.

On the walls there were paintings of two people: two men that were apparently very important to Laxur. S'tie noticed many photoluminescence flowers around the room. They were beautiful and had a pleasing scent; however, by the bed on a lonely nightstand was a vase with a single rose that did not belong on this world. It was the rose that he gave her when they were children. She kept it; she loved it. S'tie smiled, thinking maybe Laxur—no, *Asaria*—had not forgotten their love after all. He went to it and noticed that she had taken care of it. The vase was the most lavish that he had ever seen; it was fluted and tastefully made of gold, platinum, and diamonds.

The dark beauty and Dari appeared in the queen's dressing room. Laxur began to remove the regal dress one layer at a time. Dari started to massage Laxur's shoulders. Dari decided to make conversation.

"The war seems to be going well, my queen, but I do worry about the humans and our angel brethren," Dari started.

"Those two races we should be careful, but neither of them has made any hostile moves against me. Without them, the elves, fairies, dwarves, mer-people, centaurs, and all the rest do not stand a chance against us," Laxur reassured Dari.

The queen removed her long, flowing skirt to reveal her stockings and shoes. She started to remove them as well. Dari could not help but massage Laxur's legs. Laxur enjoyed Dari's touch and lust that she can feel from her protector.

"Besides, the humans have far too much resentment towards all the other magical people anyway. If anything, they may even help me defeat the kingdom. I do, after all, want them. Plus, Dari, the angels historically have other races fight their wars for them. So, there should not be anything to worry about."

"As you say, my queen" was all Dari said in response. She believed her people would, more than likely, not interfere now.

"Dari, tell the maid to have the chef bring up our dinner," Laxur ordered.

"Yes, my queen. It shall be done." Dari bowed and walked out.

Laxur continued to undress herself, and she put on more comfortable clothing. She put on another corset of purple and black with gold trimming. Over the flexible corset, she put on a black nightgown that hung off her shoulders.

Once Laxur was satisfied with the way she looked, she decided to go out and impress S'tie with her body. She was used to this and she could it easy to seduce anyone she desired. She enjoyed the power her curvy body gave her. She liked the way she looked, but she wanted more. She may be the peak of feminine power, but she could go further. And she planned to go further.

The prince heard the doors to the dressing chamber open, and he turned to look. His dark beauty stepped out, dressed in the most seductive nightgown of purple, blue, and gold—her favorite colors. It was tight-fitting and had tiny straps. Her hair reached to her back in a lightly curling fall.

Her hair brought out her emerald eyes and luscious red lips. From head to toe, the queen was so stunning that he could not think of anything else. The war and his promise to Asora were nothing compared to his lust for her.

"Do you like what you see, my love?" Laxur smiled.

She was barefoot and walking to him across her thick rugs. All S'tie could do was stare at her, and she smiled wider.

"I will take your love-struck silence as a yes. That is very good, my love." Laxur extended her hand.

S'tie took it, and the queen guided him to a dinner table near a window. Outside there was a storm raging with lightning and rain. The weather increased the mood. Laxur loved storms for this reason.

"It looks like another storm. That is the fourth one in a week." She laughed lightly. "I am not complaining. I happen to love storms."

Dari opened the doors to allow the servants to enter with trays of food, and then they all left to stand outside. Laxur had both her and S'tie's favorite dishes made. She was eating a Darkcon delicacy known as mertian. It has the appearance of black steak, and it was poisonous if not prepared properly.

S'tie had been given his favorite beef stew. It is made with the mertian beef and many familiar vegetables.

"This is delicious," S'tie complimented.

"Yes, it is. One of the advantages of having the best cooks working for me." Laxur chuckled lightly. "Do you have any questions for me? And please do not ask me for diplomatic solutions tonight. Save them for tomorrow."

"Uh, yes, I do. Who are those two men in the paintings over there?" S'tie asked.

"Those two? They are others that loved me, but they are not here anymore," Laxur started.

"The one on the right is my father, Serafus, of the highest of the angel's order. The other was the Prince Regent Tylus. He was the last ruler of the Darkcon Empire before me, and as you know," Laxur removed the chemise to reveal her custom-made black leather corset.

"What happened to him?" he asked. "There are many stories."

"Of course there are. Everyone likes to tell stories." She licked her lips. "To start, he fell for me after my first mission as part of his guard. He was my mentor at first, then a friend, and then love blossomed between us. He healed me, made me strong, and even made me beautiful at my request. He asked me to marry him, and I accepted. When we were married, he became king, and I became queen. We were married for less than a year. He was a good man. He did not deserve what happened to him," Laxur explained, now depressed.

"How did he die, if you do not mind me asking?" S'tie asked, concerned.

"No, I do not mind you asking. We were in his chambers, in bed together. You must understand, he was a physically weak man. When he suddenly choked on his own blood . . ." She sighed heavily, placing her fork onto the table carefully.

"I tried to help him, but he died in my arms. All my magic was not enough. I was in tears, inconsolable. Another man that truly loved me was dead. First, my father, then Tylus, and I am afraid that you could suffer the same fate as they did. That is why I am advancing on you so quickly. I will not lose this opportunity, and I do not want to lose another loving man," Laxur stated firmly.

"I am very flattered, Your Majesty, but you must realize that the only reason I am here is to find a diplomatic solution for the war. I see the good that you are trying to do for your people, but you must realize that war is not the answer," S'tie pleaded.

"I was not the one that declared war. It was those damn fat courtiers of the Utopian court. My sister did not even have a say in it," Laxur stated.

"Princess Asora is trying to correct the kingdom's ways, but this conflict does not help," S'tie pointed out.

"Please! According to my spies, Asora is trying, yes, but she cannot do a damned thing. They will turn her into a puppet, and she will get the blame if things go wrong," Laxur said. "I love my little sister with all my heart, but I hate what she represents, and I hate the people she governs and protects. They are all troll bait."

"If you would give her a chance and help her, Asora could turn things around. As queen of the Darkcons, you have incredible influence and power over realm politics," S'tie said.

"Right! I will give them a chance, under my boot." Laxur laughed. "Any other questions? Because that last part lightened my mood a little."

"Why do you hate us so much? I do not understand," S'tie questioned, greatly worried.

"I do not hate you or Asora. It is everyone else." Laxur fumed at the last part.

"You do realize that I am part elf, right? And a Utopian too?" S'tie pointed out.

"Unfortunately, yes, I am aware of that, but I do not think of you with elvish blood," the dark queen said, regretting her choice of words.

"Laxur, I do not know how you are going to deal with that. I happen to enjoy my elf heritage," S'tie said.

"Regrettable, but that is your prerogative, and that shall not stop me from loving you," Laxur commented.

She cleaned her lips with a black linen napkin. She was finished with her dinner, and she watched S'tie eat the remainder of his stew. The prince noticed Laxur's attention to him as he ate. The queen took a breadstick and dipped it into S'tie's stew. She then ate it in a very erotic way. She repeated the process many times and each time she moaned with pleasure each time.

"I see that you are still hungry," S'tie commented.

"I am always hungry—not just for food." Laxur smiled sensuously.

"I see, Your majesty. Maybe I should finish this stew later," S'tie stated, accepting the Queen's latest advance.

"I thought you might. You were always a smart man," the dark beauty purred.

She got up and sat in his lap. Despite her size, Laxur was surprisingly light. She made herself comfortable on his lap and wrapped her arms around him, embracing tightly. He put his arms around the queen as well, holding her to him.

"I have always loved the way you held me. Especially now." Laxur sighed as she came closer to the prince's face.

Once she was close enough, Laxur kissed S'tie on the lips, and the two embraced each other further. The dark queen removed the prince's clothes with her magic, and they disappeared in a cloud of purple smoke.

At the same time, S'tie removed the outer layer of Laxur's nightgown, revealing her lacy corset. That was all that she had on now—a corset that covered her large breasts.

"What are you waiting for, S'tie? I know you want to. I want you to do it." Laxur moaned as she held S'tie's head to her breast. She slid her hands all over him and kissed his neck.

S'tie stood up with Laxur still firmly in his grip. They both fell onto the queen's bed, and Laxur forced S'tie on top of her.

"Just where I want you," the dark beauty teased as she kissed him again. With her powers, she made her corset disappear, leaving both of them naked. They looked into each other's eyes and saw their sexual desires. A cloud of black smoke rolled around them, and Laxur's spell wove deeply into S'tie's blood.

Chapter Thirteen
The World of the Humans

Days later, a man came to see Queen Laxur. He was a dark elf dressed in black and brown, easily blending into the background. He had short black hair and gleaming brown eyes. He was tall, about two meters, with a rangy body and sleek muscles.

He saw Dame Dari standing in front of the door. He smiled and walked up to the tall muscular fallen angel woman.

"I am here to see the queen at her request," the elf said.

Dari looked down at him with a mischievous smile, "She is not in her chambers. But I can help you."

"Oh, I know you can," the elf man laughed. "We can do our thing later tonight as usual."

"Oh, I need it," Dari said. "The queen took her new pet to the library."

"The Utopian prince?" The elf asked.

"Yes, he is cute I will admit, but he really is not what I would desire," Dari pointed out.

"I thought you desired our queen?" The man asked.

"I do, and I have other too," Dari admitted.

"Oh, I know you do," the elf man said. "Anyway. Thank you for telling me. And I will see you tonight."

Dari smiled as she watched her friend walk off.

The World of the Humans

The dark beauty that was Queen Laxur and Prince S'tie were in the imperial library, reading a tome together. Laxur spend much of her time flirting with the prince. She knew that he was here as a means by her little sister, Princess Asora of the Utopian Kingdom as a reminder of her past. Laxur knew that Asora hoped that by having S'tie here, that she would become distracted and stop the war. Laxur thought it was clever of her little sister. But the queen knew how to turn a situation to her advantage.

Slowly Queen Laxur turned Prince S'tie to her side. Powerful spells and good old fashion sexual pleasure. Laxur did find that men under spells tend to be boring. So, She opted to keep him semi free minded. She enjoyed having him last night and he was more into her then any other woman. This was what she was normally used to hearing from her lovers. But S'tie was different. He was her first love, and they never lost their passion for one another. Even after what happened years ago in the Utopian Kingdom's Royal Academy.

In those days Laxur was called Lady Asaria. She was the most beautiful woman in the academy. Her powers were great, and growing. This caused incredible envy, jealously, and out right hatred towards her from anyone outside her family. S'tie had been her best friend since they were both five years old. He was always kind to her and thought her a goddess. He never betrayed her, and other women tried to force him away from her. One managed to but only after attempting to murder Asaria and dumping her in the trash on a snowy night. That jealous woman then took S'tie from her.

It was there that Laxur was born. All of Asaria's anger, sorrow, and need to survive took hold. The Darkcon's found her and healed her. She was rescued by these people, her people. The ruler of the empire at the time Prince Tylus fell for her and after a contest she became his queen. His love for her was true and the Darkcon adored her. When he died the Darkcon turned to her for leadership, and they were as angry as she was.

The Utopians hated her, the Darkcon loved her. Laxur would make the Utopians fear her, and the Darkcon's her children. But all of that, she never lost her love for the young man that shared his cupcakes and flowers with her. S'tie was hers once more, and she will not let him go.

S'tie then sat down at a comfortable couch. Laxur then sat not he arm rest next to him. She showed off her legs to him to playfully distract him. He put his arm around her waist and held her close. Laxur enjoyed his touch on her.

The dark elf entered the library saw them and was enraged at Prince S'tie touching the Queen. Laxur noticed the dark elf. She smiled and beckoned him to come to her.

"Oh, Heranian! Please come in. I have an assignment for you." The queen said sweetly.

"And who is this man?" Heranian asked, visibly upset, in a powerful yet soft voice.

"Oh, Heranian, do not tell me that you are jealous of my dear S'tie?" She sighed at the angry dark elf. Then she noticed the prince's confusion. "Oh, S'tie, this is Heranian, my personal spy and assassin."

"Your personal assassin?" S'tie was shocked, and the man looked very unhappy with him.

The assassin reminded him of Asora's warning that his lover was a dangerous woman now. What was she doing with a *personal* killer? He felt as if she had tricked him, or maybe it was he who fooled himself. This woman was at war with his kingdom, and he had forgotten that. He felt a coldness seep into his heart. His mind was racing at all these thoughts.

He asked the dark elf, "Why are you angry with me?"

"He is mad at you because he was my companion in bed before you came," Laxur mentioned casually with a shrug of her elegant shoulder. "I told you that."

"I see," S'tie said in return.

He was not sure how he should feel. He was still thinking about Heranian being her personal assassin. He was suddenly scared. His man could murder him in his sleep for stealing his woman.

Heranian looked at her with a look of embarrassment. Laxur enjoyed embarrassing him and making it up to him later, the bitch, but she was his bitch. *Damn this prince.* He comforted himself with the thought that she would get bored with the Utopian and return to him. Of course, he would never say that to her. Herenian liked Laxur for her intense sexual prowess, but he found Dari more attractive in the end.

"My dear Heranian, I have a special task for you—one that is very important, and it requires your special skills," Laxur said.

Piqued, Heranian smiled at her. "And that would be, my queen?"

"I want you to venture to Havaina and discover the secrets of the human's technological revolutions," Laxur commanded.

"To Havaina? But those inventions came about over the last thousand years. Maybe the humans are simply more intelligent than the other races?" Heranian suggested.

"No, Heranian! These ideas are coming from somewhere, and I want to know from where or what or whom!" Laxur demanded.

"As you wish, my queen." Heranian bowed to Queen Laxur and gave an angry look to her prince.

Laxur looked back to S'tie and saw that he looked worried.

Laxur laughed, "Oh relax. Herenian will not hurt you."

"Is he the type that likes to get revenge?" S'tie asked.

Laxur sat on his lap. "He will not harm you. I will not allow it."

Laxur then kissed him passionately and forced herself on St'ie even more. She wanted another round with him and she did not care that they were in the library at the moment. Her sexual appetites were well known and it in a way gave her more power. And more power was always a good thing. She could never have enough. She wanted all the power that there was in the universe. And then she would find more.

As Herenian stalked off, he shook his head in anger and pity. That prince did not realize that he was falling under a love spell. It would not be long before he was completely under her control. He would do anything for her. The prince would willingly spy for her; more importantly, he would kill for her. He would give up his nation's secrets, all for a smile from her. He pitied him for the day that the spell wore off; the prince would find that everything he loved was gone, and any respect that others had for him had evaporated. Heranian knew this from experience. He was not an assassin before he met Laxur.

The assassin looked for the Priest Illumin. He knew he still had connections to the Utopian Kingdom, so Illumin went into the old city. He walked in the shadows through the black stone buildings, keeping away from the street-lamps. He wanted as few of the people to see him as possible, and he kept his black hooded cape down low. It was a lifetime habit for a spy and assassin.

Heranian found Illumin in the old temple. It was magnificent, made of soaring-high shiny black stone with many arches and stained glass depicting the two gods of the Darkcons. It was strange to Heranian, who had grown up in the kingdom and prayed to the Maker. Here they prayed to the Architect, the male god Hasatan, the god of prophecy and dark magic, not the female god, Quintessa, the Maker, whom the Utopians prayed to.

Herenian walked through the large oak and iron doors to look inside. He found whom he was looking for by the altar at the far end of the temple. The priest was walking around the stage seemingly looking at things. Herenian was not sure what, but Illumin was a wonderful ma nd an organizer that the dark elf could respect.

"Illumin." Keeping to the shadows, he walked quickly up to him.

The priest turned around and smiled as he pulled him into a bear hug. "Herenian, how are you? I have not seen you since you were here for the celebration of Theo, the founding of the empire. Always an exciting day. The day that the great god Hasatan helped create the Darkcon Empire. It was a wondrous day many eons ago."

"It was a wondrous day. I owe the Darkcons my life. To answer your question, I am well, but I have something to discuss with you." Herenian looked around at others scattered praying around the chapel. "In private."

Illumin nodded. He looked around and motioned for Heranian

to follow him. "Come with me, my friend."

They walked quickly out and began navigating through private areas of the temple, ending up in Illumin's study. The priest closed the door and motioned for Heranian to sit in front of the fire burning in the stone fireplace.

"What troubles you, my friend?" Illumin asked.

"I know that the queen has questioned you about the humans," Heranian began.

Illumin stared at the fire then back at the assassin. He got up and went to a table where there was a decanter of wine and several glasses. He brought the wine and two glasses back to the small table between them. He poured the wine for each and sat down. "She has. She believes that the humans are using the magic of the Hananaka."

The dark elf halted the glass he had raised to his lips. "That is not possible."

"I believe that she is correct. This is for your ears only. I have told the queen some of this, but not all. When I was still in theoretical physics with the kingdom, I saw a spacecraft that was thousands of years more advanced than anything we or anyone in the realm has. It had writing on it that was in the language of the Hananaka." Illumin said.

Heranian stared at Illumin and then got up and paced back and forth behind the chairs while the priest watched, saying nothing. He always did this as he went into deep thought.

Finally, the dark elf stopped and spoke. "She wants me to go in and get that kind of information. The queen wants proof. What can I do to get that kind of proof? How can I get to the ship? I cannot bring back a spacecraft."

"Sit down, Heranian. I may be able to help," Illumin ordered.

He sat down. "Help? How?"

"Before I was labeled a heretic and smuggled into the empire, I was friends with a group of scientists. We had all worked on the ship. I did not tell Laxur that. Through the years, I have been able to keep in touch with those friends." Illumin sat down, turning to face Heranian.

"Why would they help a dark elf?" Heranian questioned.

"They believe, along with myself, that the technology should be shared, especially if the humans decide to seek freedom from the kingdom. They will need the friendship of the Darkcons to keep their independence," Illumin informed.

"Queen Laxur would welcome the humans' revolution. She has made it clear she has no love for the kingdom," Heranian stated.

"The war is going well," Illumin commented wryly. "But wars tend to be very fluid. I imagine that Queen Laxur knows that and wants to make sure that she comes out on top."

Heranian sighed. "She did not declare war on the kingdom. The kingdom declared war on us. And yes, we are winning on all counts. The humans and angels are the only ones who could hurt us. If the humans decide to rebel, it would end this war. The Utopians would have to surrender."

"Then it is important that you do not get caught on Havaina." He took a sip of wine.

"Is that where the ship is?" Heranian poured himself some more wine.

Illumin nodded. "It is in the Goalan desert on the North Togan continent."

"If I remember right, that is the hottest place on Havaina. A few thousand kilometers away from Aunsborg," Herenian said.

"Correct," Illumin replied.

"Can you get me there? I need to see it for myself." He looked deeply into his friend's eyes urgency.

Illumin stared back. "I do know of some people, but I will need some time to talk to my friends. Oh, and you will need surgery."

"Surgery? I am not ill," Heranian insisted.

"No, but you are a dark elf, which means there is no way that you will get on Havaina without being questioned. The humans do not, in general, like elves. Jewel elves are the only exception."

"True but—ah! I need my ears bobbed." He fingered the points of his ears. He then got up, saying, "I better get that done while you talk to your friends."

Illumin stood. "Good idea. I will contact you in a few days."

Heranian shook hands with the priest and walked swiftly out. Illumin stared thoughtfully at the closed doors before sighing heavily and taking the wine back to the table.

Three days later, Heranian, dressed in ordinary jeans, a human-made brown T-shirt, and a hooded brown sweatshirt, used a powerful portal-making jewel to send him to Havaina. He appeared outside a small forest village at dawn. A large road was lined with several small buildings, and a couple of automobiles were going up and down the street. The spy walked to a store to meet his informant. A step inside and Heranian was overcome with the smell of animals of all kinds.

"I take it that you have not been to a farm supply store before?" an older woman asked, chuckling at his hand that covered his mouth.

"Not for a long time, no. I am just looking around," Heranian said flatly.

A tall, brunette human man came out of the shadows and grinned at him. "Heranian? Illumin said I should look for a man who was uncomfortable. I am Garvin."

The assassin was uncomfortable at the blatant use of his name and the easy way that he had been picked out—he must be slipping—but he smiled. "Good to meet you. Shall we?"

"Go?" Garvin looked confused, and then it dawned on him to be more circumspect. "Oh! Right." Illumin's friend cleared his throat. "This way." He walked out of the feed store to a car parked out front. He and Heranian got in.

Before starting the car, Garvin handed the dark elf a fat envelope. "Open it. It contains identification papers. Your name will be Tinean. You are an administrator for the Red Dawn Project, the reverse engineering operation that we are working on. These papers will help you fit in. There is also the keycard, which will unlock most of the doors." Garvin started the car and pulled out of the parking lot. Heranian looked over each piece before looking up. "Where are we going?"

"The train station. The train will take us to the desert where the base is," the human informant said.

"Base? You mean like a military base?" the assassin questioned, astonished.

"Yes. That is where we are studying," Garvin answered.

"Studying what?" Herenian asked.

"It will be easier to show you." Garvin replied.

"All right, I suppose that is best. I am not a scientist, and I doubt I could fake it. What exactly is my position?" Heranian asked.

"We made you an oversight manager. Those people oversee the projects in the financial department. It gives you the authority to go to the sites. You should get a good idea of what kind of scientific information we are getting." The scientist whipped a smile at the Heranian. "That should assure your queen that we are capable of standing alone from the kingdom. She would acknowledge us as separate worlds from the Utopians, right?"

Heranian nodded. "Queen Laxur, I know will be very happy if what you are telling me is true."

Garvin sighed in relief. "I am putting myself in danger. My friends and I could be caught and hung for treason, so you need to take a look and get out of there as soon as possible. Illumin said that you have a way off this world. Is that correct?"

"Do not worry. I have no desire to die either. I have a crystal that will take me back to Dorien," the dark elf assured the human.

Garvin reached behind him and took out a sack. "We should be on the road for another hour. I packed some lunch, if you are hungry."

Heranian reached in and grabbed a sandwich. "Thank you. Will I need to do anything when we get to the station?"

Driving one-handed while eating with the other, the scientist answered, "All you need to do is show them your identification card. I have already scanned you in. Do not worry. Act normal and it will go well. Illumin said that you were a professional and you will not fail us."

Heranian laughed. "That I am. This is actually going better than I hoped. I thank you and your friends. And do not worry. You are doing a great thing. I am sure Queen Laxur will find my report to be very useful to her decision regarding the freedom of you humans."

"I have put myself into a precarious position, but I believe that this is for the good of the human race." He reached behind him and pulled up a heavy bag. "I have some clothes for you. You should get them on while I drive."

The assassin put on the new clothes. They were only slightly different from his usual attire, but those slight differences could mean his life. He changed into gray pants, a white collared shirt, a suit jacket that matched his pants, and a long overcoat. There was also a tie. He noted the way that Garvin had tied his in a knot around his neck and quickly did the same.

He was ready for the train ride, or so he thought. It was unlike any train he had ever seen. This train did not use steam or coal to run, but electricity, and he had to fight the look of awe at how fast it moved. The locals referred to it as a bullet train or hyper train. That meant it was able to break the sound barrier at ground level. This one was one of a few allowed to go that fast.

The train took them quickly away from the population zones and into the wilderness, which changed from wooded areas to desolate wastelands. Garvin pulled Heranian into an empty compartment. "We will be stopping soon."

"Why?" Heranian questioned.

"We will be disembarking at an airfield. The next leg of the journey will be by air. The aircraft we will be using is what we call a jet. Have you heard of such things? Because you cannot act surprised or overwhelmed, or they will know that you are not a human or a jewel elf," Garvin said.

"I have not seen one before, except in pictures." Herenian pointed out. "Also Queen Laxur talked about them before."

"They are incredibly noisy, so do not be surprised, *Tinean*," Garvin warned again as the train began to slow.

"I am prepared. How far are we to fly?" The dark elf peered out of the window at high fences that enclosed the airport. "You neglected to say that the airplane was so large. It is five times as large as a plane with a propeller."

"Quickly, we need to get with the rest to disembark. Follow me and be ready with your identification card. And remember that your name is Tinean." The scientist pulled his own ID card from his pocket and opened the door to the compartment, joining the rest of the scientists and technicians.

Chapter Fourteen
Havaina's Underworld

The flight took an hour, and they landed on a strip of land near a mountain range. They walked across the tarmac to the base of the mountains, where there was a large cave opening. On either side of the opening were two huge blast doors. A large guard complex was present at the mouth of the doors. Herenian and Garvin walked up to one of the guards. They were asked for their IDs before hopping on a monorail going deeper into the cave.

It traveled for fifteen minutes before it stopped, and several people got off. The scientist motioned silently for the dark elf to remain where he was, and the monorail moved on. It stopped several more times before Garvin got up. Heranian followed, when suddenly the human turned to him.

"So you will be going over our team's developments today, Tinean?" Garvin asked.

"Yes. I need to see your progress so that I can do my reports on Red Dawn. My supervisors are asking for more information," Heranian informed.

"I hope I will be able to accommodate you," Garvin responded.

"Hope? You need to reassure me and my supervisors. They want progress, not vague assurances." Heranian grumbled.

Garvin smothered his smile of approval. "Of course. Come with me, and I will introduce you to my team."

Everyone ignored them, going about their own business, as the two conspirators went deeper into the mountain. As far as they were all concerned Herenian was just another supervisor, and Garvin was yet another worker showing his progress.

Suddenly, as they rounded a curve, the cave opened into huge cavern. It was at least a hundred stories high, with the alien aircraft dug out into mountain. It looked like the craft had been in the mountain for many thousands of years, or the humans had hollowed out the mountain to hide what they had been doing. Either way, Heranian was impressed, but he kept a controlled, blank face and followed Garvin closer to the ship.

It was shaped like a giant brown winged bird with a sphere-like structure at its center. It had two engines on each wing. IF that was what they were. Herenian was no expert on alien starship designs. He also heard that these were the parts that were still intact and what remained of them.

As the scientist showed him around, he found that it had four giant cargo holds. Garvin told him that only a select few knew what had been in them, and Garvin was not one of the select. But the rumors said it was more parts for the various systems that the ships had.

After several hours, it was break time, and Heranian decided it was time to look further than the ship. But first he had to get his bearings as the complex was just huge. The Onyx Palace could fit in the mountain complex. That amazed him, and that was only the start of the secrets that were in this mountain fortress.

"What else is there to see?" the dark elf asked.

The scientist looked around. "There is the power source. You may want to see it. Take the elevator marked in red. Your ID will allow you to use it, we made sure."

Herenian smiled slightly. "More surprises that will astound me?"

The scientist smiled widely. "Oh yes."

Herenian went to the elevator painted in red. He pushed a button on the control panel and the door opened to allow him in. He saw the level marked power plant and pushed that button. The Elevator jolted and moved quickly down the shaft. The elevator stopped at the bottom, and the door opened. What Heranian saw bewildered him. A vast machine stood many stories tall and seemed to stretch for kilometers in every direction.

Heranian heard a big commotion from the other side of the facility. He moved over to see what was going on. A crowd had gathered around a set of people. Mostly workers and a few security guards. But Herenian heard over the intercom about a very important state visit.

"And here, King Adium, is the Large Particle Collider. Think of it as the largest tool ever made," a beautiful human woman explained.

She was a beautiful blond-haired royal woman with large green eyes. She was about average height for a human and wore a blue business suit. She also looked young to middle aged. In fact she reminded Herenian a lot of Queen Laxur, as those two seem to share a lot of features.

She was standing next to a small male fairy, king of the fair folk. He was sixteen centimeters tall with black hair and gleaming eyes, and he wore black business suit. Fairies do not generally like suits but he wore it because it provided him with some form of protection from eh high energy experiments.

"Countess Marien, what is it meant for?" King Adium asked.

"Originally, it was designed to be a particle accelerator to study the behavior and anatomy of atoms, but we reconverted it to be used to mass produce antimatter," Marien explained.

"What is antimatter?" the king asked curiously.

"In layman's terms, it is the opposite of normal matter. Normal matter has protons with positive electrical charges, neutrons with no charge, and electrons with negative charges. Antimatter is the opposite—it still has neutrons with no charge, but there are positrons, which are the opposite of electrons," Marien explained. "When matter and antimatter collide, they destroy each other, and the energy created from it is one hundred percent energy conversion."

"Very well. I believe that I understand what this antimatter is, but why in this Great Maker's universe would anyone create such a thing?"

Adium asked.

"To answer that, it would be best to show you, your majesty," Marien replied.

Heranian climbed up to a catwalk above the collider to get to an elevator on the other side. Looking down at the collider below. Heranian felt puny next to all this machinary. The spy discovered a guard standing watch over the elevator.

He calmly handed him his identification, and the guard gave it a look, smiled vaguely at him, and handed it back. "Have a good day, Tinean."

"Thank you. You, as well." Herenian said as good natured as he could.

Heranian pushed the button for the bottom most level. The elevator was quick in its descent through the levels. It stopped at the bottom floor, and the doors opened. It was dark, but he could hear people talking and working. He saw Countess Marien and King Adium, with their guards, gathered in front of a metal loading dock door.

"You were going to show me what uses there are for antimatter. You are being far more cryptic than usual, countess." King Adium looked around.

"Your answer is beyond these blast doors." Marien turned to a guard.

The guard opened the blast doors for the countess. They rumbled open slowly to reveal the countess's secret. A massive cavern, which had to be the size of an entire mountain, held five strange objects. The broken hulls looked like wings of ships that may have resembled birds. Two were enormous; one was almost the size of a city. The city-size one, however, was not like the other four. It had a star like shape to it, but its points were in several pieces, exposing the inner working. The top section had stubs that seemed to once have been parts of towers.

"Are these the things that you were talking about?" King Adium asked in awe.

"They belonged to the Hananaka, our sky gods. They left their technology behind, and we have been studying and using the technology that they gave us," Marien said. "Long ago, the Hananaka came to the human worlds, gave us knowledge, and taught us to survive. They even protected us from our enemies. In fact, there are legends of the Hananaka. Many are favorites of my people, much to the disgust of the Maker's priests."

"Yes. Our Visitors did similar things for us. I think that we agree that they are fairly similar to the Hananaka that you humans worship," Adium said.

"I agree, the Hananaka and the Visitors are one and the same. Our people certainly agree about that. The ships that you have brought here have confirmed that," Marien said. "And I have a surprise for you."

"You do?" Adium asked.

"We have bodies," Marien casually mentioned.

She walked off with everyone behind her. Heranian followed the detail of people, for he was curious about the bodies. The countess led everyone to another dark room with a hidden door. Marien placed her hand on a panel. The panel was a hand scanner that controlled the locking system. The door opened up to a room filled with red light.

Heranian went inside with the rest of the people, and he did not understand what he saw next. There were at least four dozen tubes with bodies in a strange fluid, but these bodies were unlike anything that he had ever seen. Some were skeletal remains; others were in a state of decay; but these creatures, Heranian could not even describe. He thought that they must be the Hananaka or the Visitors that Countess Marien and King Adium described. But they are very alien.

"How many are there?" Adium asked.

"So far, we know of nearly fifty different species, including the machines over there." Marien pointed to a corner with beds full of machines in the shape of bodies. "Some were even rumored to live inside their machines."

"That is impossible!" Adium was astounded, then he thought, *But then again, anything is possible if you are a god or an alien.*

"They are the Hananaka, but we now know that they are aliens. Still, most humans, jewel elves, and daemons believe in the Hananaka, so we make sure that they continue to think that the Hananaka are gods. It gives them something to believe in. Just like the fairies believe in the kindly Visitors," Marien explained, waving an elegant hand toward the tubes.

"Yes. Once, long ago, when the Utopian Kingdom was young, we fair folk were new to it. Our worlds were overcome with a terrible plague. No cure worked for us; even elfish medicine was not effective. But one day, many centuries ago, beings from the sky came down to us, and they brought us a cure. They also taught us how to live properly to prevent the plague from coming back. They saved us," King Adium explained passionately.

The fairies loved the Visitors for teaching them how to live. King Adium knew, as well as Marien, that these gods were in fact aliens, but to their people, they were gods. Both leaders wanted their people to have something to believe in.

Heranian believed that he could not learn anymore, so he left the room. What he did not realize was that Countess Marien had noticed him. She made a quick hand motion to her troops.

So the humans and fairies were planning a rebellion against the kingdom using the alien technology. I never thought I would see them rebel outright. They really hate the kingdom. This should please Laxur. If these two races pull it off, the Utopians would be in ruins and this would make the Darkcons' war easier. Herenian slipped out of the room and out to the remains of the huge alien ships. He needed to leave, and now was the time to find an empty room to use the enchanted gem and get back to Dorien.

The dark elf could not find any more doors near him. He thought the next best option would be to get on the elevator and stop it long enough for the gem to work. That would mean going back into the room, but he was not sure that was a good idea. The countess would wonder what he was doing, and he would be showing his face again, which for any good assassin or spy knew was never a good idea. It made no difference—the door opened, with both Marien and Adium coming out with their entourages. They had their heads together when they suddenly looked at him. Heranian casually turned and walked toward the ships. He was hoping to get lost in the crowd of workers.

He heard a crack, and fire flew past his face. He spun around and saw another ball of lightning fly toward him. It was King Adium in human size, and he looked angry.

"Halt!" Countess Marien pointed, and her guards ran toward him.

He decided it was time to act. If he could freeze them and then use the gem, he could get out of there. He breathed in and let the spell fly. A few guards and onlookers froze. Heranian reached into his pocket, but he was hit in the chest by a fireball. He jumped back and cursed, knowing he would have to take out the king.

"Get on the ground, everyone! Now!" Countess Marien called out.

Heranian let fly a shot of electricity straight at her and the king. Their guards immediately jumped in front of them and took the blast, freezing instantly.

The onlookers flung themselves to the ground. Heranian felt exposed and dove out of the way of another fireball. He tried again to hit Adium with a freeze spell, but the king managed to avoid it, taking Marien with him. He struggled to get the gem out as he was lying on the ground, but he was hit hard with a snowball, almost knocking him out. He rolled away, maneuvering behind the guards that stood frozen, using them as shields. As he stood, a hand dropped onto his shoulder. He looked, and the countess punched him in his face.

Marien now stood above him. She kicked him in the head, and his arms suddenly became tight against his sides, while his legs locked. Adium had used a tie spell. The dark elf could not move. He did not struggle. He waited to see what they would do.

Adium walked up to stand alongside the countess. They both looked down on him, but she was the first to speak. "Who are you?"

Herenian kept silent.

"I know you." Marien used her foot to push his face this way and that. "I cannot figure out where I know you from, but I do." She looked at the fairy king. "Do you recognize him?"

"No, he is not familiar, but he is obviously a magic user—a dark elf, perhaps?" the fairy king postulated.

"Who sent you here?" The countess suddenly became agitated.

"Perhaps we should get him to a secluded room where we can interrogate him," the fairy king calmly suggested as he looked around the great cavern.

"You are right. Could you get your guards to take him? Mine are frozen," Marien asked.

"Of course," Adium replied.

He snapped his fingers, and fairies swarmed around Heranian and lifted him up. The dark elf felt himself swiftly borne up. He was carried, immobile, for fifteen minutes before he hit a wall hard. He looked around and saw he was in a medium-size room with a desk and several chairs. They dropped him to the floor. He was left unable to move, waiting for the interrogation to begin. He had never felt so helpless. He knew that he had to keep his wits about him; now was not the time to give in to fear.

"Who sent you? Was it the Puro? Are you working for him?" Countess Marien angrily motioned, and he was put into a sitting position so she could see his face.

Adium looked at the guards and nodded his approval. "You may leave us now. He is immobile. We will be fine. Wait outside the door."

The fairies grinned wickedly at the spy and zipped out the door. Their human and jewel elf counterparts closing it behind them.

Heranian decided that his best defense was silence. He noted that the countess seemed to be upset at the thought that her religious leader was somehow involved. That was interesting.

The fairy looked at the dark elf. "What was your mission?"

The countess kept staring at him. Marien walked up to Heranian and punched him in his stomach. The countess had the strength and terror of a professional. Military interrogator. That surprised Herenian, and Marien did not look the part either.

"I know you from somewhere, and I will remember." She growled.

Adium straightened suddenly. "This is ridiculous. We should have him killed. We cannot afford to have him report to Puro Aga."

Heranian decided that now was the time to speak, and he did it painfully. "If I was sent by the Puro and I did not report, then he would assume, rightly so, that you were hiding something."

"If? Are you saying you are not?" Marien leaned down to stare into his brown eyes.

"I could be from a corporation that wants new technology but are not willing to wait for you to hand over the goods," Heranian joked.

The countess and the king looked at each other. Marien huffed, "Not again. Can you people never wait?"

Heranian breathed an invisible sigh of relief. Perhaps he could still get out of this. But he could tell that Marien and Adium did not believe him. But they were putting on a show for him as much as he was. So, this was going to require a considerable amount of mental gymnastics. These two were not the standard Utopian morons that Herenian was used to.

Adium shook his head. "How do we know? Countess, it could be either one. He is a dark elf—a dark elf, for the Maker's sake!"

She sighed. "We do not know that. He could be anything, being used by one of the corporations to do their dirty work, or else they turn him in to Puro Aga. That would not be the first time."

"Could we test him? You have a vast laboratory here. Could we check his blood?" The king leaned down, grabbed Heranian's chin, and stared in the dark elf's face.

The countess cocked her head to the side. "It is possible. It would help to know what he is, and who he really works for."

"Would it? Both a dark elf and a corrupt human are in the same danger from the Puro," Heranian pointed out.

Knowing that it was true. Many people who had come from the kingdom had spoken of hiding from Puro Aga. And from his more fanatical priests and priestesses.

"He has a point." She sighed in frustration.

"We need to talk about this. Let us leave him here, and we will go talk privately." The fairy king let go of his face.

"If you could just let me move around?" Herenian twisted his body with his limbs still clamped tightly.

"I do not think so." The king laughed.

"Give him his hands. We will have guards outside." Marien moved toward the door. The fairy moved his finger, and Heranian could move his arms again. "Thank you, and I am not from the Puro, I assure you."

"Of course not," the countess said in a flat voice.

They left the room, and immediately he reached into his pants. He grabbed the gem and smashed it under his boot. The room became a white light. He felt his reality wavering around him, and suddenly he was in his rooms at the Dorien castle. He sat down, shaking, in the nearest chair and sighed in relief. "Thank the Architect. I made it."

The door opened. "Has he left?" the countess asked.

"Yes." The king smiled.

"Good." Adium raised an eyebrow. "You know that was Heranian, Queen Laxur's lover."

"Yes. I am betting she used this assignment to get rid of him while she dallies with Prince S'tie." The Countess's smile turned derisive.

Adium shook his head. "Seems more likely that she was hoping for a permanent solution. He may find his homecoming less than jovial."

"It matters not. We showed him what we needed him to see." Countess Marien shifted her weight on her high heels. "Thank you for playing your part. We could not have done this without you and the fair folks' help."

"Anything for the cause," Adium commented.

"And thank you for being so convincing, Colonel Garvin," Marien said to the same man that lead Heranian into the facility.

"My pleasure, my countess. And you too, King Adium." Garvin bowed.

"Now, down to business," Marien stated.

She walked into another room with a very long table. It had many people sitting at either end, both humans and fairies. At the table were scientists, engineers, politicians, and military leadership from both sides. Garvin sat down, and Adium sat in the only empty seat on the fairies' side; Marien did the same on the human's side.

"Now that we have our message to the Darkcons on its way, we can make the final arrangements for the trade deals and alliances between our people," Adium opened.

"Yes. In exchange for your newly developed nanotechnology, humans will provide you with advanced starship construction plans and techniques," Marien started.

"In addition, I believe that everyone would benefit if we were to become one great force instead of two allies, as we have been," a male fairy general added.

"You are right, General Heo. My generals and yours, Marien, have been discussing a possible united force. SEALS and Rangers are the most powerful warriors in the known universe. Combined, they could overwhelm any enemy," Adium stated.

"And the Naval Forces would benefit as well," a female human admiral said.

"Admiral Ewan, do we not have a deficiency in our Navy, both aquatic and space?" Marien asked.

"Yes, we have a bad tendency to build oversized, overly powerful warships. We need smaller support vessels, like destroyers, frigates, corvettes, and other support ships," the Admiral pointed out.

"Well, our best ships are submarines, but if we had access to human technology, we could make the ships you need, and we could build the bigger ships we need to engage large foes," Heo added in.

"It is agreed then. We shall unite as one. We will work in secret to build our forces and combine our resources so that one day we can all be free," Countess Marien pronounced. She and the fairy king signed several documents, making the alliance official.

Chapter Fifteen

Bars and Brawls

The Utopian/Darkcon War was in full swing. The Utopian Royal Guard was on the back foot. Queen Laxur's forces were led by very intelligent generals, admirals, and marshals. They are also better armed and trained then the Utopian forces were. The Utopian Royal Guard relied on an army of knights and even more conscripts. The only exception was the Consortium's Red Guard which was an all-volunteer force. They were more advanced then the Darkcon's new and improved military force.

The Human Consortium's leader Countess Marien had refused to allow her forces to assist the Utopian Royal Guard in the war. Princess Asora did convince the countess to allow the purchase of military equipment and other resources.

To get further assistance and possible military assistance, Princess Asora had asked for a meeting with Countess Marien and the representatives of the Red Guard. The Red Guard loved Princess Asora as she still held the rank of colonel in their service. She had a good relationship with them, and she hoped that Countess Marien could be persuaded to render help.

Princess Asora's Royal Guard generals Asora concluded had to be idiots. As they did everything wrong in both strategy and execution. They also refused to listen to her. They told her that a princess has no place to tell the military on how to run a war. Even though Asora was a special forces officer and a top-level strategist. There was not much she could do because a princess had limited authority. But Asora was cunning if anything else. So, she plotted alternatives to get around the nobility.

On Evorn in the Royal Palace, Princess Asora stormed out of yet another waste of time meeting between the her, the court, and the military high command. She punched a statue and it shattered in front of the servants and the Royal Guard forces around.

Captain Joes quickly made his way to Princess Asora. He was the only Royal Guard officer that Princess Asora trusted. He even listened to her and used his authority to put the princess's strategies forward. It got him praise for coming up with such clever strategies. He never took credit for them. He was an honorable centaur man.

"Your highness," Joes asked coming up to Asora.

"Damn them all," Asora hissed.

"Let me guess," Joes started. "Because you are a princess, no one needs to listen to you?"

"You know that so well," Asora calmed down.

Captain Joes and Princess Asora walked through the palace to the library. Asora usually went to the library to relax as she loved the atmosphere it gave to her. She wanted to use the magical garden, but she needed to be available for meetings.

"I just do not understand," Asora started. "Just because I am a princess should not mean that my input is worthless?"

"Ancient habits die hard," Joes replied.

"I am an officer in the Red Guard, one of my areas of expertise was strategy!" Asora snapped.

"I know and that makes you the most bearable noble to me," Joes said. "You understand."

"Thank you," Asora said. "It is just so damned frustrating!" Asora then thought. "You know, they listen to you. And you put one of my strategies into practice. Maybe you can do that again?"

"I am not comfortable with doing that. It is wrong to me," Joes said.

Asora could not help but smile. "And that is why I trust you more then anyone else in the Royal Guard."

"I hope you can convince Countess Marien or her Red Guard commanders to render aid. We need it," Joes said sadly. "I cannot stand seeing so many dead broken bodies of the conscripts coming back."

Asora was silent as she knew how Joes felt. She could not stand it either. But her military flag officers seem to use the high casualty numbers as a twisted form of pride. The conscripts were trash and cannon fodder as far as the Royal Guard knights were concerned. It made Joes sick, and Asora noticed. She trusted him and allowed him to make the recommendations to his leadership and even take credit. But his high honor did not allow for it.

"I will find away to stop the unneeded slaughter," Asora said.

"We will," Joes said as they both stopped. "You re not the only one that has a stake in this."

Princess Asora smiled as she felt that at least someone in the Royal Guard listened to her and believed in her. The two walked into the library. There they saw someone who was not normally present except at Asora's request. Joes froze in terror at the man.

"General Anco?" Asora asked in surprise.

The human military general was looking at a book. It was a chronicle of Utopian battle strategies. He seemed to treat it like it was a comedy.

"Wow, these people are dumb. Not to mention the thickness of the book is only this big for stats," Anco laughed.

"Why are you here?" Joes demanded.

"I am here to be one of the Red Guard and Consortium Representatives. Countess Marien will not be able to make it. But she is sending someone to represent her," Anco explained.

"You are here on behalf of the SDC?" Asora asked.

"I am. And as your former commander, I have a vested interest in helping you," Anco said.

"So, you are on Princess Asora's side?" Joes asked.

"I am on Colonel Asora's side," Anco said.

"She is a princess," Joes reminded the smaller human man.

"I will not insult my best officer by demeaning her like the Royal Guard does on a regular basis," Anco said.

He had nothing but respect for Asora and was on her side, even if it did not look like it. She was his prodigy and best student. She was the daughter he wished to have had. Anco did have many children and a wife. But his children were not very impressive, his daughters were spoiled, and his sons were lazy. His wife was always overworked as he was. Asora had met them, and she had the same opinion of them as Anco did. Anco's eldest son found Asora attractive, but she wanted nothing to do with him. Anco allowed Asora to beat and break his son for his inappropriate behavior towards her. Asora was Ancho's ideal child and the daughter he always wanted. He had planned one day that Asora would take over for him as leader of the SDC. But that was unlikely now.

"That book you have is old. It is not the updated version," Joes pointed to another book near the SDC general.

"I know," Anco said. "I was just comparing them. Not much has changed," Anco said.

"Treat Captain Joes right. He is my only Royal Guard ally," Asora said.

"I know. And I just do not understand why a knight of his caliber is stuck in such a cesspit of a military?" Anco said.

"Someone needs to show them what honor is," Joes said.

"If you say so," Anco sighed.

The following day came the biggest meeting of the Utopian Kingdom's military flag officers from every corner of the kingdom. The Royal Guard was the primary force that protected all but two of the states within Asora's realm. The Human Consortium, and the Angelic Empire both have their own private militaries to protect them instead of the Royal Guard. The Angelic Empire's Guardians of Light, and the Human Consortium's Red Guard were independent of the Royal Guard.

This meeting happened once every ten years. They are held on Evorn and in the Royal Palace. It was the responsibility of the reigning monarch to host this meeting. These meetings also generated a lot of gossip and news about the rather lively interactions. Often the village played host to the thousands of soldiers that drank and brawled. This made the villagers and the monarchy nervous every time.

The mayor of the village was giving Princess Asora and Prime Minister Frenzen a tour. The downtown area was the most beautiful and artistic part of the village. Shops, bars, restaurants, services, and tourist points made up the village's famous and beautiful downtown district.

"So, your highness, what do you think?" The merman mayor asked.

"You have done well," Asora replied.

"Were you able to get extra police and constables this time?" Frenzen asked as he read from his clipboard.

"I hope so," the mayor said with a nervous laugh. "The last time the constables got rolled over. Too many troops come here."

"How badly do they damage the village?" Asora asked. "And I am not just talking about physical damage, but also economic?"

"Honestly," the mayor started. "It is a disaster. Almost on par with a tornado strike on a human city."

"That bad?" Asora gasped in surprise. "I had no idea."

"Of course not. The nobility never cared," the mayor complained.

"Well, I am here. Tell me and I will do what I can," Asora offered.

Before the merman mayor with the glittery skin could say anything. A battalion of Royal Guardsmen marched down the Main Street. That made Frenzen frown as he looked at his pocket watch. The time was correct. The Royal Guard should not be on the march yet, so what were they doing? The prime minister went up to the commander of the battalion who was a fellow elf.

"What are you doing here, commander?" Frenzen demanded.

"We are practicing," the commander bowed to Frenzen.

"The villagers also need the street to carry out their daily tasks," Frenzen said.

"The villagers can wait," the commander replied.

The traffic jam of carriages, walkers, and cyclists gathered at the on coming streets. Princess Asora waved down a dwarf constable. She asked him to have his police and constable ward to redirect traffic. The dwarf constable sighed with exasperation as he saw that Asora was right. The constable nodded and he had his fairy messenger tell the other constables to redirect traffic of annoyed villagers. The villagers noticed Princess Asora's annoyance who they shared. She could not do anything, and her people seemed to feel as helpless as she was.

A few moments later the roar of fighter jets and powerful aircraft soared above. Asora knew this roar well as she flew them before. Some of the aircraft had VTOL abilities. A large aircraft landed in an empty field. It bore the symbols of the Red Guard and the Consortium. A whole company of humans, jewel elves, and daemons came out in a mad rush.

Then a single stocky person jumped out of the aircraft. A human woman with dark skin, old scares, and a prosthetic left arm approached Princess Asora. The woman had a head of grey hair and was shorter then Asora, but she was better built. The old woman marched up to the princess and stopped a mere meter from Asora. The woman saluted Asora sharply.

"Colonel Lardana, welcome," Asora greeted.

"That's it?" Lardana asked.

Asora could not hide her smile and laughter. The colonel grinned and then hugged Asora like a sister.

"So, they finally managed to force you into a white dress after all?" Lardana laughed.

"Yes," Asora replied. "Where are the others?"

"They will be along shortly. We had a race and a bet going," Lardana said. "I've got a lot of collecting to do."

"How many are coming?" Asora asked.

"Fifteen colonels, captains, field commanders, generals, admirals, marshals, and your brother along with four other corporate CEO's,"

Lardana said.

"Oh great," Asora said. "Well, the Angelic Empire are sending one representative, and the fairies have three coming."

"What about the Royal Guard?" Lardana asked.

"Too many. It is a time when they have medal measuring contests," Asora paused. "If you know what I mean?"

Lardana laughed, "Oh this will be fun."

Hours later the rest of the consortium's representatives had arrived. There were more representatives from the consortium this time around, because of Princess Asora. Asora met the representatives as they arrived. One was her elder brother Jeia, and one of his top scientist's a beautiful and intelligent woman who's was Doctor Amana.

"Well, your highness," Jeia started kindly. "This is going to be one hell of a meeting."

"Sir," Amana called. "The proposals?"

"Oh yes," Jeia laughed. "We have new updated methods of procurement and manufacturing. It should help you sell Fusion Corp's proposal to the Royal Court more easily."

"That is good to hear," Asora said.

"Don't say anything until you hear mine!" A woman dressed as well as Jeia barked as she came up to them.

"Miss Walabara, welcome," Asora smiled.

"Princess Asora, my company, The Unigoarn Conglomerate has what you require," Walabara said confidently. "We all know Fusion Corp is expensive and their tech is beyond the average Utopian's intelligence."

"I am a Utopian and I understand both of your corporations technology just fine," Frenzen said from Asora's side. "Even during the Great War itself."

"How do you know that?" Walabara asked the elf.

"I was the one who came up with the plan to hijack the Leviathan," Frenzen said. "It was a massive battleship that took the resources of all of the consortium's corporations, and the state to build."

"You were the architect of that operation?" Walabara asked astounded. "Damn, I like you already!"

The CEO of the Unigoarn Conglomerate walked away with her assistance in tow. Frenzen was perplexed by the old woman's reaction. Frenzen was familiar with the consortium's politics and how its power structure worked. It was his mission during the Great War to know this. And even five hundred years later he still kept up with it. It also helped that Princess Asora helped him with that.

"She likes you. I am impressed," Asora said.

"I would have thought that she would have been angry?" Frenzen said.

"The destruction of the Leviathan actually saved her conglomeration form bankruptcy," Asora explained. "So in a twisted way, you saved The Unigoarn Conglomerate from the brink."

"I see, I was not aware of that," Frenzen said. "I need to update my knowledge of them."

"That would be a good idea, but the fact that she likes you, helps me," Asora said.

"I understand," Frenzen replied.

"We have four corporations in attendance for once. The first two are here. Where are the others?" Asora asked.

Lady T'ula then came running up to Asora and Frenzen. She stopped and was breathing heavily. She had been running around all day.

"My apologizes," T'ula said out of breath. "I got the constabulary the needed equipment and access to the Royal Guard's internal policemen."

Asora put her hand on T'ula's shoulder. "You did well, relax."

Captain Joes then joined them as he directed the guardsmen and servants to assist the guests. He then approached Asora, Frenzen, and T'ula.

"Here come the other two," Asora pointed out to the next two aircraft coming down.

An imposing daemon wearing a black business suit. He had small drones hovering around him and his team of assistance. Princess Asora knew him as Mister Jarakan of the Halaburus Company. A company that was famous for its automation, drones, robots, and AI research and development for commercial and military use. He also happened to be a childhood friend to Asora.

The towering and imposing Mister Jarakan stopped in front of Princess, Asora, Joes, Frenzen, and T'ula. The nearly a dozen tiny drones hovered around them.

"Thank you for coming," Asora said.

"I would not miss this, and I could never say no to you," Jarakan said. "No matter how hard I try."

Both Jarakan and Asora laughed at that. It was an inside joke between them. Jarakan was an old friend of Asora's and the two often got into trouble when they were children. Much to Jarakan's dismay.

"What are these things?" Joes demanded as several of the tiny drones hovered around him.

"Those are our latest in surveillance and intelligence drones. Almost fully autonomous," Jarakan explained.

"I have no idea what any of that means?" Joes looked very worried.

"Relax horse man, they are harmless," Jarakan laughed. "These are the unarmed demo versions."

"They remind me of giant flies," Joes complained.

Jarakan looked at one of his human assistance. The young human male had an electronic tablet. He typed in a series of commands and the drone moved away from Joes. They instead floated around Princess Asora. Unlike the centaur, Asora did not mind the drones. She in fact grabbed one in mid air and examined it.

"This is a unique model," Asora said.

"That one in particular is the short-range surveillance unit," Jarakan said.

"I look forward to your presentation," Asora said as she let the drone go and it flew away.

The Halaburus Company representatives then were escorted by hand-picked guardsmen that Joes brought.

"Those things creeped me out," Joes complained.

"Drones are something you have to get use to," Asora said.

"I remember older models during the Great War," Frenzen said. "They were bigger and had a tendency to attack with chain guns and missiles."

"The Halaburus Company has been the consortium's primer drone and automation manufacturer for millennia," Asora pointed out.

"I thought Fusion Corp built everything?" Joes asked.

"Fusion Corp is the largest corporation, but there are others, and some do things better," T'ula pointed out.

The commander of the Royal Guard then came up to Prime Minister Frenzen. As he did a female jewel elf in a grey tight business suit approached. She was new to Asora, but she did recognize the corporate symbol that was on her assistant's blazers. They were from the Cophen Shipyard.

"Princess Asora," the jewel elf woman greeted with a smile. "I am Mrs. T'ilra of the Cophen Shipyard and Space Docks."

"Welcome," Asora shook T'ilra's hand. "I look forward to your presentation."

"The Cophen Shipyards?" The commander asked Frenzen.

"They are one of the biggest manufacturers of the consortium's ships and spacecraft. As well as one of the top tier research and development for new technology," Frenzen explained.

"How do you know that?" The commander asked.

"Simple. I travel and attend seminars," Frenzen answered. "You would be surprised what you can learn."

"We need nothing from these corporations," the commander complained.

"Really?" Asora looked at the commander. "All of your equipment, weapons, supplies, and tactics are horribly outdated. The consortium even showed you that five hundred years ago. And you still have not learned. I am trying to fix that."

The sun in Evorn's sky was going down and night fell upon the continent. The palace was in the glow of lamp light and the village was seeing its main streets flooded with patrons, shoppers, and entertainers.

The biggest group of guests were of course the soldiers, troops, and security forces from across the kingdom. Thousands of them and that made many of the villagers nervous. This gathering always led to violence no matter what.

The violence mostly came from the Royal Guard and the Red Guard mostly. The rivalry between the two Utopian forces were epic and terrifying. The villagers hoped for the dawn when the thousands of troops will be in the palace attending the military conferences.

The head constable was out with the hundreds of other constables to keep the peace. As Princess Asora had promised she gave him, and his constables help. That help came from one source that the head constable did not expect. The dreaded SDC was instructed to assist the village constabulary by all legal and possible means. General Anco said that he deployed at least three dozen of his agents into the village in various ways.

In a popular pub near the port of the village a large gathering of Royal Guardsmen Knights and Red Guard Officers gathered. As a result most of the constabulary and SDC forces had also gathered there. The pub was a fairly large establishment as it was also a restaurant that specialized in sea food.

Inside the pub the Red Guard officers sat at tables and the Royal Guard knights were at the bar counters. On one wall was the symbol and seal of the Royal Guard. The seal was that of a knight's helmet with crossed swords behind it, on a purple background. On the other side was the Red Guard's seal. The Red Guard seal was of what looked like a planetary system with smaller simple symbols orbiting a star. Each symbol represented the different branches of the Red Guard military.

Princess Asora was with her privy council on a palace balcony that looked out at the coast and village beyond the palace walls. With the princess was Prime Minister Frenzen, Lady's Madimoy, T'ula, and

T'a. Also with them was Priestess Nona, and the four fairies Gourni, Rayne, Friea, and B'nei. Jeia and Amana were also present along with Puro Aga, Captain Joes, Admiral Yane and General Anco.

Princess Asora had invested them all to the balcony for her monthly dinner gathering. General Anco and Miss Amana were new and welcomed guests. The four fairy sisters were told to be guests this time and not serve them. This was Asora's way of thanking them for their service.

Princess Asora and her fifteen guests were enjoying the warm night sky and a feast prepared by the palace's chefs. They were deep into the feast when someone started a conversation.

"What the hell are you talking about?" Anco bellowed at Puro Aga.

"You heard me!" Aga barked back.

"Uh oh," Madimoy said.

Before Princess Asora could intervene. A low noise from the village in the distance could be heard. T'a got up and used her sharp elfin eye sight to see what was happening.

"Looks like the troops have started early this year," T'a commented.

"What?" Jeia complained.

"I have to stop it," Asora said.

"Wait!" T'ula called. "That is the job of the constabulary. Not you."

Princess Asora knew that T'ula was right. This need to take charge has been an issue with Asora. Her closest friends, and allies have been trying to help her with these flaws.

Back in the village the fighting broke out between two neighbors near the downtown markets. Not by the different troops present. However, that did not stop the armed forces and the local law enforcement forces to intervene and carry the fighting forward.

In the dock bar and grill, the atmosphere was already tense. The top Royal Guard Knights and the higher-ranking Red Guard Officer corp were trying to not attack each other. However, that will not last.

One major difference between the Royal Guard and the Red Guard was the fact that the Red Guard had women in their ranks at every level and in every part of the force. The men of the Red Guard do not care about such things, but to the Royal Guard having women in their ranks was obscene to them. To the knights a woman has no place on the battlefield. Most of the female officers in the Red Guard tended to be jewel elves. The only offshoot of elves that embraced science and technology. There were human women in the ranks like normal as well, and daemon's too.

Drunk military men tend to not see women in uniform as equals. And two female Red Guard Officers were about to find out.

A dark skinned human woman and her jewel elf friend and colleague where heading back to their table with several of their fellow officers. They were stopped by two knights who were both drunk and did not see that these two women were professional soldiers.

After being drawn into his arms, the human woman dropped the tray of food. It got the attention of her fellow Red Guard Officers. The female jewel elf put the knight into a headlock and forced him to let her friend go. Next thing that came was a fist to her face. Both women went to the floor. Before the knights could get at them, some of the male Red Guard Officers flipped a table and tackled the knights to the floor.

Bottles, plates, trays, tables, silverware, and chairs suddenly went flying throughout the bar and grill. The dwarf constable heard the commotion and went to the docks. What he saw were several people being thrown from the windows and doors. They crashed to the streets, and some even fell into the waters in between the massive boats and ships that were docked. The dwarf fired off a signal flare from his fingers to get reinforcements.

A sword went flying and almost hit the dwarf constable. Fortunately, he was able to dodge it. He rolled into a corner as knights and officers threw each other around.

Then a shotgun blast from the corner nearest the constable rang out. A daemon woman in a black and green SDC uniform came out of the shadows. Her presence made everyone in the area stop.

"The next dip stick that moves without me saying so it going to have their face blown off!" The SDC officer said. "Now sober up and get the hell out of here!" A chair went flying at her and she was able to punch it to pieces. "Bad move!"

The SDC officer then fired her shotgun again. The rounds this time were taser shells. Two Red Guard Officers went down, as well as four Royal Guard Knights. The constable used a paralyzing spell to help the SDC operative immobilize the rest.

"Thanks," the constable told the SDC operative.

"This crap is happening all over town," the SDC operative said.

"Too many," the dwarf said.

"No kidding. We need to knock them all down," the daemon replied.

"At least the ones that will not listen to us," the constable said.

A thunderstorm had gathered above the village. There was a single figure flying in the middle of it. An angel of incredible power. The angel landed and it was none other then Princess Asora herself. She wore a scowl so mean that she could kill with it. She saw all her forces, her forces fighting each other. Enough was enough. Asora commanded many lightning bolts to shoot down and strike the ground and lightly hit the fighting troops.

"ENOUGH!" Asora's voice boomed.

Her anger even acted her voice to the level of a hyper sonic blast. She even managed to shatter some building. But mostly she shattered glass and windows.

This made everyone stop. It was though everyone was holding their breath. All eyes were on Asora now.

"I do not care who or what started this, but you will all go to your barrack and stay there for the rest of your visit!" Asora commanded.

"Why should we take orders from a little girl like you?" A knight with such audacity.

Asora looked at him with such anger. It was obvious that the man was drunk. This challenge could not go unanswered. And she had enough of this. The Royal Guard had been nothing but a problem and was slowly becoming a liability to Asora's plans.

"You have a problem with me?" Asora demanded.

"The realm has a problem with you," the knight laughed.

The next thing he knew Princess Asora was in his face like an angry drill sergeant from a boot camp, or a very angry officer.

"All your problems are irrelevant. Just as you are irrelevant. I very highly suggest that you sober up and stay out of things beyond you," Asora snarled menacingly.

In response the knight grabbed her like a bar maid. This made Asora snap. She twisted his arm and got out of his grasp. Then she spun him around and broke his arm and then dislocated his whole arm from its socket. She then kicked him at the base of his spine. The knight crashed face first into the ground. Asora flipped him over and stomped on his stomach. His armor was unable to stop Asora's brutal attack. She hen stomped again on his private area. The knight puked blood and cried in pain. Asora then pinned him by his other arm and then proceeded to pummel him in the face repeatedly.

On the fifth punch Asora's fist was grabbed. In a fit of rage Asora turned to see Admiral Yane. He had stopped her from going any further. It took her a few moments, but Asora calmed down. She looked back to see that she had broken the knight. Several broken bones, bruised ribs, maybe some internal bleeding, and who knew what else.

"I think you have made your point," Yane said.

Captain Joes then ran up to them and saw the site. Everyone was looking at Asora in shock and horror. Joes looked down as he knew who the knight was. He also saw that Asora was covered in his blood as if she was reveling in it.

"Take this," Asora pointed at the now unconscious knight. "Get him fixed up and put in a drunk tank for a few days. Then have him dishonorably discharged."

"Yes, your highness," Joes bowed.

Admiral Yane escorted Princess Asora back to the palace. And the night became calm once more. Yane knew that this was going to be a constant problem.

"The Royal Guard is useless," Asora said.

"Not much cane be done about it," Yane pointed out.

Asora sighed as she knew that he was right. The Royal Guard represented all that was wrong with the Utopian Kingdom. If it was going to survive, the Royal Guard would need to change. But that was not possible for a princess to do. Then an idea struck her.

"The Royal Guard is useless, and they refuse to adapt," Asora started.

"And nether you nor anyone on the Privy Council can change that," Yane added.

A small smile crept onto Asora lips. She had an idea. "Then let us go around them."

"What do you have in mind?" Yane asked.

"I think it is time for a new military force to rise," Asora replied.

"This will be interesting," Yane added.

The two made their way to a waiting carriage to take them back to the palace. The carriage then drove off once Asora and Yane were inside. Here Asora explained her idea to her top military commander.

Chapter Sixteen
Madimoy's Vacation

It was a warm day on Evorn. Princess Asora was wandering through her gardens. She was picking flowers in peace with her four fairies. She had had a very bad week with all the politics, and this was one of the things that helped her calm down. The fairies, T'ula, Madimoy, and Rentha were walking with Asora. These regal women worked hard, and even they needed stress relief. Asora smiled as she worked her hands over a flower. The Princess put a rose into a basket containing a myriad of flowers and carried it inside the palace. She placed the basket on a desk next to a waiting crystal vase and arranged the lush bouquet.

"Oh no! I did not get any water for the flowers," Asora thought out loud. "Wait! I have the water coin." Asora pulled out a locket on her necklace that held a golden coin with a design that resembled waves on it. She dangled the coin over the vase, and water poured from it into the crystal.

This coin was ancient and extremely powerful. It gave Asora the ability to control water itself— from rivers, ponds, lakes, even the great oceans of any world—as well as the power to create it from nothing.

She was not the only one with a coin of power. Queen Laxur had one of her own, the coin of fire.

If she was going to defeat Queen Laxur, Asora was going to need the other coins. The other six coins controlled the other elements of nature. The time coin was rumored to have been either destroyed or lost.

Asora realized that it would take more than speeches and new weaponry to defeat Laxur. It would take powerful magic and advanced technology to do the job. Finding these coins would be a good first step. She had heard a rumor that one of the nine coins was on a world named Canva Prime, Madimoy's home world. The Princess needed the coin, but she could not leave Evorn. However, Madimoy might be able to retrieve it. She could also send T'ula to assist.

"B'nei, Friea, can you two bring Lady Madimoy and Lady T'ula to me, please?" Asora kindly asked the two fairies.

Both bowed while floating in the air, then they zipped off so fast that they appeared to be red and green blurs.

Minutes later, Ladies Madimoy and T'ula walked into Princess Asora's private study.

"Good, you two are here. I have a mission for you both," Asora proclaimed.

"What mission would that be, Your Highness?" Lady T'ula asked.

"Are you two aware of the coins of power?" Asora asked.

"Those are merely legends. They are not real!" Lady Madimoy stated firmly.

"Oh, and what would you call this, Madimoy?" Asora pulled out her coin of water.

"So they do exist. Which one is that?" T'ula asked.

"I will show you!" She gave a demonstration with the water in another vase. Asora made the liquid rose and make loops and circles, and then she dropped the water back into the vase.

"I take it that you have the coin of water, then?" T'ula postulated with a smile.

"You are correct, Lady T'ula. I have one. Unfortunately, Queen Laxur has one of her own— the coin of fire." Asora said.

"That is not good! How many coins are there?" Madimoy asked with a concerned look.

"There are a total of nine, but one of them is thought to have been destroyed. Our Princess has the water coin, and she said that Laxur has the fire coin. As for the rest, they are scattered across the universe. What are left are the coins of lightning, earth, wind, light, life, and darkness. The one that was destroyed was the coin of time," Lady T'ula said. "There is another one that was forgotten as well."

"I am impressed with your knowledge of these coins, Lady T'ula. You will assist Lady Madimoy on the mission that I have given her," Asora stated. "I believe that one of the coins has turned up on Canva Prime. I need you two to go and get it for me, before Queen Laxur knows it is there and gets it herself."

"One of these coins is on my home world? I will do as you ask of me, my Princess." Madimoy and T'ula both bowed and left Asora to her floral arrangements.

"Come on, T'ula! We are going to be late!" Madimoy yelled.

"I am coming, Madimoy! I am coming!" T'ula yelled back.

"Princess Asora made all of our arrangements a week ago, and I am not going to be late,"

Madimoy complained. "I thought that you did not want to go home after that fight you had with your mother?" T'ula asked.

"She is not my mother. She is my stepmother. And never mind that! I do want to see my daddy again," Madimoy retorted.

The two women walked outside to the courtyard and saw Asora conjuring a spell that would allow them to travel to Canva Prime. They would simply walk to her world without needing a ship. Madimoy and T'ula walked through the portal, and in an instant, they were on another Utopian world.

Canva Prime was mostly water—roughly ninety percent—and home to the mer-people. The many islands were occupied by mostly humans and dwarves, along with a few noble elvish families. "Ah, home sweet home. Oh, how I missed the smell of the ocean." Madimoy breathed in heavily. "It is much heavier here than at the palace."

"Ugh, that smell! I never really liked fish, or anything that swims in its own toilet, for that matter." T'ula complained as she held her nose.

"Oh, get over it, because seafood is pretty much the only thing to eat here," Madimoy said.

"You know there is an old elvish joke about seafood," T'ula casually mentioned.

"Oh, and that is?" Madimoy asked.

"I see food, and I eat it." T'ula giggled.

Madimoy thought the joke was lame, but she humored T'ula and laughed with her. "So where do you suppose this coin of power could be? This is a big world."

"We could look through the temples, even the ones underwater," T'ula suggested.

"That will take too long, and we cannot ask anyone. Asora wants this to be kept secret so that Laxur does not catch on," Madimoy reminded T'ula.

"Yes, I know. But just the two of us? Is Asora mad, thinking that just the two of us can find this blasted coin on this huge world?" T'ula complained.

"We are the only ones that the Princess can trust. We will just have to work with what we have got," Madimoy reiterated.

T'ula blew out a breath and walked along side Madimoy. They were in front of Madimoy's home.

It was a dark-brown multistoried mansion. It had wooden colonnades with red brick and breathtaking stained glass. Servants opened the heavy large doors for the ladies to enter. There, in the grand golden marble foyer, was an older man that Madimoy recognized.

"Daddy! Oh, Daddy! I am so happy to see you!" The redhead squeaked as she ran into her father's arms.

The red-and-gray-haired man laughed. He was much taller than his diminutive daughter and wore a Utopian-style suit—long wool pants and a long coat—of navy blue.

"Oh, my baby girl! How have you been?" her father asked, hugging her tightly.

"A little tired, Daddy, but nothing that I am not used to. Oh, this is a friend of mine. She is Lady T'ula of Taliano."

"Welcome to Canva Prime, Lady T'ula of Taliano. My name is Jeranci, and as you have probably figured out, I am Madimoy's father," Jeranci said.

"A pleasure, sir." T'ula shook his hand. If she were higher in the Utopian court, he would have to kiss her hand.

Later, Madimoy was in her old childhood bedroom, and T'ula was in the guest quarters. The women decided that the best thing to do was ask Madimoy's parents first. Madimoy did not want to be pleasant to her stepmother at dinner, but she also did not want to make T'ula uncomfortable. They might be able to discover some information because her stepmother was a member of one of the ruling families of Canva Prime.

The dining room was a light, airy room overlooking the ocean at the back of the house. The sun was setting on the water when they began to eat.

Madimoy turned to the elf who was married to her father. "T'mil, have you ever heard of the coins of power? I heard there may be one on Canva Prime."

T'ula dropped her fork and glared at Madimoy.

T'mil and Jeranci looked at each other sharply. Her father cleared his throat, and her stepmother put her fork down to answer.

"That is a dangerous question. The coins are quite powerful and not to be played with. Why do you ask such a question?"

"It is necessary and why I am here. I do not wish to play with it," Madimoy answered irritably.

T'ula spoke up. "We are here to be sure that it is locked away, before someone else comes to claim it. We mean no disrespect, but it is urgent. We believe that Laxur may be looking for it. That would be disastrous. We were sent by the government to look for it quietly. If Laxur is not aware of the coin being here, then it should remain so, we do not want her to become interested in your world."

T'mil smiled at Madimoy and T'ula. "I understand. There is a legend that a coin could be here. It is kept in a temple. Whether it is in one below or above the waves is not clear. Does that help? I could talk to others, but you said that you wanted no one else involved."

"Thank you, T'mil. I appreciate your help." Madimoy choked the words out. She wished her stepmother would not be so accommodating; she knew that was not her nature. "We will begin looking tomorrow. I will act as a guide to T'ula. It will not seem strange, as she is here on vacation."

"Good." Jeranci smiled at the women, glad that they were all getting along. He turned to his wife. "This is a delicious dinner, darling."

The next day, T'ula and Madimoy began their quest. They traveled to several island temples first. They were mostly made of white marble with tall outer columns all around the buildings. Slanted roofs wrapped around the buildings, and under them were painted reliefs depicting the many beings of the kingdom in heroic poses.

They took the tours and gently poked around. At each temple, T'ula cast a spell to look for strong magic. Each time, the spell pointed to the staffs that the priests and priestesses used. They asked about any special items that the temples had. A few showed them some gems that were enchanted.

On the twenty-first day, the women came to a temple on the water's edge. It was different from the others; it was made of the local limestone and was a simple round tower. It was also a wreck; it was situated on a stormy shoreline in an earthquake zone. There were no priests in attendance.

T'ula, wearing a becoming light-blue gown, looked around the altar, and Madimoy, dressed in soft green, headed for the stairs. Madimoy stopped at a window on the fourth floor that looked out over the ocean and beach. She looked out at the sunset and was in awe at its majesty. On the beach she spied a mermaid sitting on a rock, without a care in the world.

She had something shiny in her hands. Mermaids were known for being attracted to shiny objects, even human junk; however, the object fascinated Madimoy. Through a telescope, which she once used as a toy, Madimoy could see that the mermaid had a coin in her hand and was trying to figure out how it worked. The coin bared a striking resemblance to Asora's coin of water.

"That is it! She has it. I need to get it from her," Madimoy spoke to herself.

The redhead quickly went down to the beach. She had to be able to sneak up on the mermaid, but suddenly Madimoy slipped off a rock and plunged into the ocean.

"HELP! PLEASE, SOMEONE HELP ME!" Madimoy's head started to submerge.

Her heavy skirts caught in the undertow, until someone grabbed her by the waist and swam back to shore. She crawled onto the beach, coughing, and choking on seawater. She saw that her rescuer was the mermaid that she was trying to sneak up on.

"Are you well, human?" the mermaid asked with genuine concern. This was unusual, since humans and mer-people had a very bad history.

"Yes, I am all right, thank you." Madimoy smiled at the mermaid.

"Why were you on the rocks at this late hour?" the mermaid asked.

"Ironically enough, I was looking for you. That coin you have—I need to have a look at it," Madimoy explained.

"My new shiny thing? Why?" the mermaid said nervously.

Madimoy looked at the mermaid. She had multicolored hair with red, white, green, brown, blue, and orange streaks. This was common for mermaids, as were long life spans; they were typical traits for mystical beings. The tradeoffs for long lives were fewer children; humans were more prolific but lived shorter lives.

"That coin looks like something that my sovereign wants." Madimoy pushed wet red hair out of her face.

"But this shiny thing is mine! I found it!" the mermaid yelled.

"Do you even know what that is?" Madimoy asked.

"It is shiny! What else is there to know?" The mermaid said.

"There are more to shiny things than being shiny. Some things that are shiny can be very dangerous." Madimoy pointed out.

"Like your people's metal ships?" The mermaid questioned.

"Well, machinery gray paint does not exactly make it shine, but in a sense, yes," Madimoy replied. "That coin is special to my princess. Is there anything that you would accept in return for that coin?"

"What would I take in return? Well, do you have a conjeral seashell?" the mermaid asked with a teasing smile.

"A conjeral seashell? They are as rare as diamonds. I do not know where to find one," Madimoy complained.

"Well, then I am keeping this shiny thing, unless you can find me a conjeral seashell," the mermaid stated.

"Very well then. I will take it!" a powerful female voice proclaimed.

Madimoy and the mermaid turned to see Queen Laxur, dressed in her black armor, with her bodyguard, Dari, standing behind them.

"You! Where did you come from!?" Madimoy demanded.

"From the sky, where else, you idiot?" Laxur said. She turned her attention to Manidai.

"Mermaid, surrender that coin to me, NOW!" Laxur ordered.

"Make me, you human wench!" the mermaid blasted Laxur. In response, Laxur unfurled her black angelic wings, which frightened the mermaid. The mermaid tried to swim away, but Laxur cast a spell that made her float in midair. "Let me go, you witch!"

"Dari, take care of the Utopian runt. I will get the coin," Laxur ordered.

Dari unsheathed her sword and readied to strike down Madimoy. The redheaded girl forgot to bring her own weapons; she was unarmed. As Dari got ready to land a fatal blow to Madimoy, another sword intercepted hers.

"I think not!" T'ula threatened.

"You worthless, pointy-eared mouse! I will slit your throat!" Dari blasted.

T'ula was overwhelmed by Dari's enormous strength. The fallen angel was well over three meters with powerful muscles. Then Madimoy landed a powerful kick to Dari's stomach. The fallen angel tumbled backward, slipping on the wet surface. T'ula helped the redhead up and gave her a sword.

"Thank you, T'ula. We have got to stop Laxur from getting that coin!" Madimoy warned.

"Very well, Madimoy. I will deal with Dari. You keep Laxur from getting the coin," T'ula said as she charged at Dari.

Madimoy ran toward Laxur, as the Queen was forcing the coin from the mermaid. She suddenly noticed, as she got close, that a small being was attacking Queen Laxur with glittery magic.

"Rentha? Are you crazy?" Madimoy said, recognizing the fairy.

The little fairy was keeping her distance, so her magic was only getting Laxur's attention and not hurting her.

"You worthless little bug!" Laxur yelled. The mad queen unleashed a wave of black magic that struck Rentha. The little fairy went down; however, before she hit the ground, Madimoy grabbed her. "How noble of you, little girl, but it shall help you not!"

The redhead pointed her sword at Laxur, warning her not to come close.

"Back away, witch! Leave Rentha and the mermaid alone!" Madimoy ordered.

"Who are you to give me orders? You are nothing but a worthless Utopian brat!" Laxur boomed.

"Ha! Takes one to know one." Madimoy ran right at Laxur and rammed her with all her might; however, Laxur withstood Madimoy's hit, unfazed. The redhead landed flat on her butt with a headache.

"So are there any other stupid Utopian tricks that you wish to try?" Laxur teased cruelly and laughed.

"Give me a moment, and I am sure I will come up with something," Madimoy replied.

"Oh, take your time, human. While you do, I shall claim my prize."

Madimoy got back up.

She readied her sword and charged at Laxur again. The Darkcon queen was aware of Madimoy's advance and was ready, but both were stopped when another being came out of the waves.

An odd-looking mermaid came out of the water. She looked like a cross between a normal, blue-finned mermaid and a squid. There were twelve tentacles in her gray hair, and she had the tail of a fish.

"Oh, no! Valar!" Manidai, the first mermaid, cried.

"You, you hideous sea cucumber! How dare you show your face to me again?" Laxur yelled in fury.

"Nice to see you too, Laxur," Valar teased evilly.

"Bad move, Valar," Manidai mentioned. "That woman leads the empire."

"Why should I be afraid of this wench, Manidai? She is a sea slug herself," Valar insulted.

"You worthless parasite! I knew I should have killed you when I had the chance!" Laxur fumed.

"Yes, you should have, because now I have the coin that you and that redheaded fish bait want, hashanah." Valar showed the coin to Laxur and Madimoy, and then she disappeared back into the ocean.

"Did you hear what she called me? How dare she call me that hideous, bottom-feeder name? I really hate that hideous sea witch!" Laxur blasted.

Dari and T'ula came up, both looking badly hurt from their fight.

"It looks as if we will need to get that coin back from Valar," T'ula huffed, still out of breath. "Well, if you can hold your breath for a few hours, go ahead and try," Dari said.

"Enough! All of you! We need to get that coin before Valar can make anything from it!"

Madimoy screamed. "Agreed. For now, we need to work together to get that coin away from Valar," Laxur said. Her words shocked everyone, and she released Manidai back into the water.

"Queen Laxur, do you have some magic trick to allow us to breathe underwater?" T'ula demanded.

"I do have a number of spells that can help—this one in particular." She pulled a set of red vials from a pocket in her armor and handed them to the others.

"Drink this and get ready to swim," Madimoy, Laxur, T'ula, and Dari drank the red liquid.

The four women transformed into mermaids. Madimoy had a green tail, T'ula had a red tail, Dari formed a black tail, and Laxur's legs turned into ten tentacles and purple in color. The four crawled into the water, and they followed Manidai into the ocean. The water pressure and temperature seemed to have no effect on them; they could even breathe and speak, and gills had grown on the sides of their necks.

"Where does this Valar live?" Dari asked Manidai.

"In the Kembo trench," Manidai answered.

"The Kembo trench? That is one of the deepest places on Canva Prime!" Madimoy said, deeply concerned that they wouldn't be able to reach the great depth.

"Relax, redhead. The potion you drank makes you immune to the pressure and the cold of the deep water. But only for a short time," Laxur explained, rather annoyed. "I used blue squid blood as the main ingredient in this potion."

"Blue squid blood? Yuck!" T'ula spat.

"Actually, it makes sense," Madimoy said.

"How so, Madimoy?" T'ula asked.

"Squids can dive to great depths and are unaffected by the temperatures or the pressure. It must be why Valar can go so deep," Madimoy explained.

"Madimoy, you are not as dumb as I thought. Maybe you should consider coming over to my side. I could use more intelligent people in my new science divisions," Laxur offered with an ingratiating smile.

"No, thanks. Princess Asora needs all the help that she can get," Madimoy countered, rather shocked by the offer.

"Yeah, that is true." Dari laughed.

"How dare you!" T'ula yelled.

"Quiet, all of you, or Valar will hear us coming," Manidai hissed loudly.

Eventually, the group of five came across a deep pitch-black underwater canyon. The five women descended into the darkness. All their hair glowed, so they were able to keep track of one another. Madimoy's hair glowed red, T'ula's glowed a bluish-black and silver, Dari's hair glowed brown, Laxur's hair glowed purple, and Manidai's was gold.

"Keep up, everyone! It is right up ahead!" Manidai said.

The five swam deeper into the canyon, and their surroundings became darker and darker. In the blackness they could see a slight glowing coming from a small cave entrance.

"There! That is where Valar lives." Manidai pointed.

They swam to the entrance, and they heard singing and wailing.

Then, a large amount of seaweed and urchin spikes sprang to life and ensnared the women. They were held, unable to move.

"Well, well, well. It looks as if you have found me, and you have fallen into my trap." Valar laughed.

"What do you want with us?" T'ula demanded.

"What do I want? I want all of you. Look at me! I am an old woman, but I have a plan to reverse the clock, and all of you are going to help me become young, beautiful, and powerful again," Valar explained, chuckling.

"Since when were you beautiful?" Laxur said insultingly.

"Four hundred years ago I was the most beautiful creature in the universe, but the ages have done their worst to me. But now, with two of the coins of power, I can restore my beauty and increase my powers," Valar crowed.

"You are mad to think that you can reverse time!" Dari yelled.

"Oh, I can, and I will do more than restore my beauty. When I am done, not only will I be the most beautiful creature in the universe, but I will also be the most powerful. I will have your eternal youth, T'ula;

your strength, Dari; your grace, Manidai; and your curves, Laxur. And I will take all your powers as well," Valar explained. She saw Madimoy struggling to break herself free. "However, human trash is of no use to me, so you will be shark bait." Valar had the seaweed restraints move Madimoy to an area outside crawling with sharks.

Madimoy screamed when she was released and left at the mercy of the bloodthirsty sea monsters.

In Valar's underwater cave, she had the four other women tied together above a cauldron while she worked on a spell. She did, in fact, have two coins of power: the one that she stole from Manidai and another that she found long ago on a different water-filled world.

"The coins of wind and earth will make me great once more. I will have the strength to leave this world once again, and then I will find the rest and be able to control all the elements of nature." Valar rubbed the coins together. "Most of all, I cannot wait to be young and strong again. It will be fabulous to have Laxur's curves. I have always wanted to look the way she does."

"I bet you would, but you have always been an ugly hag, and you never will have great power. And what makes you think that you can handle my curves?" Laxur blasted.

"Consider that my spells have negated your powers and you are helpless in my domain. You never should have gotten rid of me, Your worthless Majesty."

"I knew I was right to get rid of you. You were always scheming. You even tried to kill Tylus eight times before I came in!" Laxur yelled.

"Only because he would not have me—he wanted you!" Valar spat.

"You were old, ugly, and power-hungry. Besides, if a male is on the throne, only a female fallen angel may marry him. Last I checked, you were an old, mutant mermaid," Laxur pointed out rudely.

"Like I said, in another hour, that will change." Madimoy had been swimming for her life, trying to outrun the sharks. She was looking for an underwater submarine base that was rumored to be nearby.

"I'm not bleeding, so why are they after me?" Madimoy yelled.

"You are food, mermaid!" one of the sharks said.

"You can talk?" Madimoy asked, baffled.

"Mermaids and mermen can understand any creature of the ocean," the shark answered.

"But I am not a mermaid! I am a human!" Madimoy screamed.

"Liar! Humans do not have fins. They ride the oceans in boats," the shark said.

At last, a manmade structure appeared in the distance, and the sharks became afraid. It was a massive human naval submarine. At first, Madimoy was thankful, but then she realized that if they fired the sonar, she would be dead. If she could get close enough and yell as loud as possible, they might not activate their sonar.

"Please do not fire your sonar! I need your help! Please help me!" Madimoy screamed.

The sub stopped, and one of the torpedo tubes opened for Madimoy to enter. She swam inside, and the hatch closed behind her. Madimoy was alone in the dark inside a very small space; she was deeply frightened. Another hatch opened, the water flooded out, and Madimoy crawled out of the tube. Four human officers, one female and three males, greeted her. Her gills were not needed, and she was able to breathe air—a byproduct of the magic.

"Well, mermaid, what do you want?" one of the male officers demanded.

"I am not a mermaid. I am very much a human, like you. I took a potion to become a mermaid to retrieve something in the water. My name is Lady Madimoy," she explained.

One of the male officers tested Madimoy's blood—it was a simple test for humans—and confirmed that she was indeed human.

"Our apologies, my lady. As you are aware, we have had problems with the mer-people, especially in this area," the female officer said.

"I know. I was born and raised on this world. Uh, you will need to carry me. I cannot exactly walk right now. I have no idea how long it will take for this spell to wear off," Madimoy explained. The third male officer scooped up Madimoy in his arms after the female officer put a coat on Madimoy's nearly bare top.

Queen Laxur and Dari tried to escape with their brute strength, but despite these Darkcon women being the strongest of their people, they could not break Valar's restraining seaweeds. Manidai and T'ula, on the other hand, had been trying to cut the seaweed with no success.

"We have to keep trying. We cannot let this demented witch take our powers," Dari said. "I need my sword or my dagger, but Valar took them from me." T'ula breathed out.

"Are you little wenches looking for these?" Valar pointed to a giant open clamshell, upon which were all their weapons and Laxur's potions.

"So many pointy objects. You are all very violent. And Laxur, you have a great deal of potions. I take it you like these green ones. You have so many of them." Valar chuckled.

"More like fat-headed," T'ula said. Both Laxur and Dari chuckled.

"Nice one, pointy ears," Dari complimented. Valar slapped T'ula across her face, leaving behind a red mark.

"It is time for me to become young again, this time forever!" Valar laughed evilly.

The four women were dumped into the cauldron of boiling pink liquid. They felt as if they were melting away, and all four screamed in agony. The energy and youth of the four women began to bleed off them, and Valar allowed the steam to wash over her, smiling as she did. As it flowed over her, the wrinkles on her skin vanished. Her whole body began to grow. Her tentacle hair was becoming longer and fuller. Her curves now mirrored Laxur's perfectly—her hips, stomach, breasts, face, and shoulders. The transformation only took a minute, but Valar was now a new being. In fact, none of the four women could recognize her. She had become as young as they, and she was bigger than both Laxur and Dari. Her hair was as blue-black as Laxur's and just as long and thick. Her body had Laxur's perfect hourglass figure, but she had

T'ula's beautiful facial features. Valar now appeared as youthful as Manidai, and she had Dari's immense strength.

The witch laughed hysterically. "Oh yes, this is it! This power, this youth, is now eternal. I am forever young and powerful!" Valar laughed with joy.

Laxur realized that the seaweed restraints were now gone, and they were free, but there was no point in trying to fight. Valar had all their strengths and powers; however, Laxur had been restored to normal because of her own coin, which was on a chain around her neck.

"I forgot that I had this thing," Laxur said out loud.

"You forgot what?" Valar demanded.

"This!!" Laxur threw a plasma fireball at Valar.

Valar was burned, and this gave Laxur a chance to get out. The Darkcon Queen realized that she was going to need help.

"Get up, you idiots, before she recovers," Laxur ordered.

She used what limited powers she had to restore Dari and the two Utopian women, knocking over the pot they were in. As they changed back, Laxur grabbed what she could from the seashell table and swam out with the others behind her.

What Laxur did not realize was that she left one of her green potions behind, and Valar grabbed it and went after them.

"Where is Madimoy?" Manidai asked, worried.

"Forget her. We need those coins!" Dari stated.

"But first we need to get rid of Valar," Laxur pointed out.

"And how do we do that?" T'ula demanded.

"You cannot be rid of me, for I am now eternal!" Valar bellowed as she appeared in front of them.

Laxur would normally attack with her powers, but Valar stole them. The only powers that she had were her potions and her coin of fire, which she used to restore her fellow prisoners.

"None of you has the power to defeat me, so what will you do when I drink this?" Valar took out Laxur's the green vial.

"Uh-oh," Manidai blurted out.

"What does it do?" T'ula asked Laxur.

"It makes you grow tall and amplifies your powers a thousand fold," Laxur explained. "Do not let her drink it!"

Manidai and Dari swam at full speed toward Valar, but they were not fast enough.

Valar drank the whole potion and laughed as she did. The ocean began trembling, and Valar's body started to expand in all directions. Laxur, Manidai, T'ula, and Dari swam for the surface, as Valar's expanding form consumed the ocean below them. The four women broke the surface, were thrown out of the water, and were caught in Valar's tentacles. They freed themselves and dove back into the ocean. Valar's laughter now sounded like booming thunder.

"My, look at all the tasty plankton specks," Valar boomed.

Manidai heard an odd noise coming from the other direction.

"What is that noise?" the mermaid asked. Laxur heard it and turned to see.

"TORPEDOES! SWIM!" Laxur screamed.

She and the others swam away. A powerful explosion erupted in front of Valar. The giant mutant mermaid screamed in agony.

"Where did those come from?" Dari asked.

"That!" T'ula pointed to a huge black military submarine coming to the surface. "Oh, I hate those things!" Manidai complained.

"Be thankful for small favors, you idiot," Laxur said.

"Captain, torpedoes have hit the target. The target is damaged but is still combat effective," a female naval officer said.

"Very well! Lady Madimoy, what are your recommendations for explosive yield?" the captain asked.

"Are you equipped with Mark 8 warheads?" Madimoy asked.

"Yes, we are," the captain answered.

"Torpedo room, load tubes 3 and 4 with Mark 8s," the female officer ordered.

"Aye, XO. Loading Mark 8 torpedoes," the torpedo room operator responded through the COMM.

The submarine fired with the Mark 8s. The explosive yield was three times more powerful and covered Valar in water and shrapnel.

"You pathetic humans will pay!" Valar cried in rage.

She grabbed the two coins that were on a necklace around her neck. The wind coin gave Valar control of the wind, and she blew as hard as she could. The submarine submerged fast to avoid the turbulence.

"The Imperium missiles will finish this thing off. Missile room, prepare for underwater launch of Imperium missiles. Ready tubes five, eight, thirteen, and twenty-one!" the captain ordered over the COMM system.

"Imperium missiles will set the whole area ablaze, making the water like petroleum," Madimoy said.

"Plasma-based fire will burn that sea witch to cinders!" the captain replied.

"We had an agreement with the mer-people that we would not use those!" Madimoy cried.

"Considering the circumstances, I am sure that they will understand. Valar is a bigger problem for them than us, but we will put her down ourselves," the captain stated.

Valar used her tentacles to capture the submarine; however, the submarine had its hull electrified, and Valar got a nasty shock. Laxur used her fire coin to burn Valar's skin, and the sea hag was now after Laxur.

"That is the disadvantage to being huge: you cannot get small things so easily," Manidai taunted the oversized Valar.

Madimoy jumped into the ocean to warn the others to clear out.

"We have to get as far away as possible! They are going to fire the Imperium missiles!" Madimoy shouted.

"What? But you humans promised to not use those horrible weapons!" Manidai complained.

"Would you rather have a giant Valar running around?" Laxur yelled in Manidai's face.

"Good point. Let's get out of here!" Manidai yelled out.

The five quickly swam as far as they could, while the submarine kept Valar occupied, and were soon miles away from Valar and the sub. Maneuvering around as fast as the sub's engines could push. The hatch to one of the missile tubes popped out. Fire belched out, and a gray missile flew out at a speed that Valar could not see. The weapon flew into the sky and arched down directly on top of Valar. A flash of light and a large fire could be seen in the distance, along with a powerful and agonizing scream. A heavy sonic boom was heard. Next was the air burst shock wave blowing everything away. Valar was burned by the intense energy. The sub had submerged before the explosion happened. T'ula saw the two coins of power flying toward the shores. Their race was on to get to the coins.

Madimoy got to shore first and only saw one coin. She used her fins to crawl toward it.

"The wind coin! I need to get it and the other one before that witch does," Madimoy thought out loud.

Laxur was the next one to reach shore, but unlike Madimoy, the Queen was able to break her own spell, and her legs reformed on her naked body. She walked up to Madimoy. The redhead was sitting on a rock with her fin dangling in front, and in her hand was the coin of wind.

"Put some clothes on, Laxur. You are too unbecoming to be looking like that," Madimoy said rudely.

Laxur could hear a hint of jealously in Madimoy's voice.

"My dear Madimoy, you sound so very jealous," the Queen teased as she flaunted her full breasts. "Though, my dear Madimoy, if you were to give me that coin, I could make you the most attractive human woman ever seen. What possible use could you have for it? Humans in the Utopian Kingdom are forbidden from practicing magic, so you cannot use that coin. You would be branded a heretic, and you would have to come to me anyway."

"I do not want this. Someone else does, and I will deliver!" Madimoy yelled.

"I assume that someone else is Princess Asora. So, she is after the coins too. That will make for more entertainment." She smiled derisively at the redhead. "I assume that Asora will just pat you on the back and tell you good job," Laxur started. "However, if you give it to me, I will reward you greatly. By the way you look at me, I think you would like to be a grander woman. I can make that happen, my dear Madimoy."

"And become like Valar? I do not think so. Besides, Jeia would not appreciate it."

"Jeia? Why him?" Laxur asked. "Oh yes, I forgot you and he are to marry soon. Do you not think that he would want a beautiful and strong wife with incredible curves, who is very fertile?" Laxur cooed sexually to Madimoy.

Madimoy considered what Laxur was saying. If she did, and if Laxur kept her word, Madimoy would become so beautiful that Jeia would want her even more, but then again, she would be betraying Asora.

"No, I cannot! Plus, Jeia loves me the way I am, and he is very special to me. I will never betray my best friend to get some extra curves!" Madimoy fired back.

"Really? Men fall for the woman with the most curves. I am willing to share my form with you, and all I want is that coin," Laxur said.

"You're wrong. Not every man is that shallow, and Jeia is proof of that!" Madimoy yelled out.

"Then he is not a real man," Laxur said cruelly.

Madimoy, now upset, used the wind coin on Laxur. The Darkcon Queen was blown back into the water nearly a mile away.

T'ula and Manidai came up to shore. Like Madimoy, T'ula still had a tail, and she crawled up to shore.

"Did you find the coin, Madimoy?" T'ula asked.

"Yes, I did. It is right here." Madimoy showed the coin to T'ula and Manidai.

"You can keep it, Madimoy, as a thank-you for helping me," Manidai said gently.

"Thank you. Let us go home. Maybe Asora can break this spell and give us our legs back." "Yes, I have had enough water to last me awhile," T'ula complained.

Dari carried Laxur to shore. The wind had caused her to land hard in the ocean, bruising her ribs.

"I cannot believe that brat did this to me!" Laxur fumed. Dari set her Queen down on her own feet.

"Well, Your Majesty, we do have a consolation prize." The bodyguard held up the other coin.

"Oh, Dari! You are delicious." Laxur cooed at her guard, and the fallen angel gave her the coin of earth. "Now I have two coins."

"But your sister has two of her own?" Dari asked with concern.

"For now," Laxur chuckled with malice.

Chapter Seventeen
Jeia's New Plant

Instead of clear skies, gray rainy clouds had claimed the day. Princess Asora was in the throne room, in session with the royal court. Today's subject was the Utopian Kingdom's budget for the year. It was customary for the monarch and the heads of court to each submit a budget, while the rest of the members debated which one was more suitable. This was Princess Asora's first time submitting a budget, and she put money where she felt was needed. She had the help of Archduke Frenzen, Dominus, and Marevin, but they were having trouble getting their version passed.

The princess sat silently upon her throne, drumming her fingers on the armrest. She was bored out of her mind, waiting for a verdict.

"You know, my kitty, maybe you should try to help their decision?" Marevin said softly to Asora. He was almost two meters tall, slender, and sinewy. He wore a gray Utopian suit and white shirt. He had dark-blond hair, cut stylishly short, and greenish-blue eyes.

Asora hated it when he called her by that pet name. Marevin and Asora were betrothed, but most of the time, Marevin unintentionally embarrassed her. Asora liked him and thought that he was sweet, but he was also overprotective and seemed desperate to please her.

"Marevin? Do not call me kitty here in front of the court!" Asora grinned through her teeth. "I know that you want to cheer me up, my dear friend, but now is not a good time!"

"Princess Asora, we were not able to decide upon which budget is best for the kingdom. We will continue next week," Lord Turkin announced.

"But the budget is nine weeks past due! I worked so hard on it, and all you can do is say we will try again next week?" Asora looked as if her rage was getting ready to boil over.

"Know your place, princess. We will continue to deliberate next week. You must be patient," the elf stated.

Asora looked as if she was getting ready to strike down her own courtiers. "My Princess, compose yourself," Frenzen ordered quietly.

The court began to break up and leave. Bremmer walked up to the throne and said, "I will try for a compromise during my, um . . . during the after-hours."

"You mean the poker game. Sounds like a good idea." Dominus laughed. Bremmer shook his hand and left. The court finished walking out, leaving Asora, Frenzen, Dominus, and Marevin.

"I cannot believe those arrogant bastards would do this to me," Asora grumbled.

"Just relax, kitty." He snapped his fingers, and a servant walked up with a cloth-covered tray. "I have a cup of chocolate ice cream for you—your favorite." Marevin whipped off the cloth and offered Asora a big cup.

"You're lucky I love anything chocolate." Asora took the ice cream. "And stop calling me kitty!"

Marevin looked upset, and he walked out of the throne room. Dominus could not help but laugh at his cousin.

"And what is so funny, Dominus?" Asora demanded.

"You have not changed at all, and you two are acting ridiculously. Marevin is just trying to make you happy," Dominus explained, smiling.

Asora looked frustrated, and she turned to her cup of ice cream.

"And he is your betrothed. You should try to get to know him better—learn to like him and love him. You are going to be married to him in three years' time," Dominus pointed out.

"I know, I know. I like Marevin, I really do. He is a sweetheart, but he embarrasses me, and it needs to stop," Asora asserted. "When I was a child, and we were first betrothed, calling me kitten or kitty was acceptable, and I liked it, but not now that I am the Princess. He should realize this is no longer proper."

Jeia walked in, reading a stack of papers on a clipboard. Without realizing it, Jeia walked right into a pillar and crashed to the floor. The sight was funny enough to make everyone laugh.

"Yeah, laugh it up!" Jeia blasted.

"Oh, I am sorry, big brother. Forgive me." Asora tried to stifle her laugh, and Jeia looked annoyed with his little sister.

"If you stop, I might," Jeia stated. Asora stopped laughing, but she still had a smile on her face. "So what do you have to report?" Asora asked Jeia.

"My new facility on Dergo is finished and is in full operation." Jeia said.

"What does your facility do?" Dominus asked.

"It is a research lab, a manufacturing plant, and a power plant," Jeia answered.

"Great. Do you require help, my brother?" Asora asked.

"Actually, now that you mention it, I do."

"Well, then I have the perfect candidates for you," Asora said.

"Just make sure that they can fight, because the Clan has been known to operate in the area," Jeia reminded the Princess.

Marevin was wandering the grand halls of the palace, downcast. All he wanted to do was make Asora smile, but all he seemed to do was embarrassed her. If only there was something that he could do to make it up to her. He loved to see his Princess smile. Marevin truly loved Asora, but did she love him? With everything else, he was intelligent, but with her, he was a complete fool.

As he was ruminating on this, one of Princess Asora's ladies-in-waiting, the fairy Gourani, came up to him.

"Lord Marevin? Our princess requests your presence in the throne room immediately," the fairy stated and flew off.

Marevin ran back to the throne room excitedly. Maybe Asora wanted him to do something for her. Well, whatever it was, he was determined to do the best job that he could, just to see her smile.

The young lord ran into the throne room, but he did not stop soon enough; like Jeia, he crashed into the pillar next to the door.

"Marevin! Are you well?" Asora cried out in concern and came to his side.

"Yes, I am fine," Marevin said weakly as he staggered back to his feet. "I was told you wanted to see me, my Princess?"

"Yes, I did. How do you feel about going to Dergo?" Asora asked kindly.

She asked Marevin to go not to get rid of him but because he was one of the bestanti-terrorist specialists in the kingdom.

"Dergo? There is nothing out there except those damn terrorists, the Clan, and deserts," Marevin said.

"Jeia built a new plant on Dergo, and he is worried about the Clan raiding his new facility. You are the only one in my court who has any real experience in dealing with terrorists. I want you to go with Jeia and Frenzen to Dergo. There, you are to train his security forces to handle the Clan. After that, you can come back to Evorn," Asora ordered.

Marevin thought that this was his best chance to make Asora happy, and he felt useful. It was true that he had experience in dealing with the Clan. He fought them many times when he was younger. His planet had been the target of the Clan because it was a small planet with small villages, and they mined gold, platinum, silver, and precious gemstones. As a younger man, he had been an officer in a special unit that handled the Clan. The terrorists were all humans using the human weapons, and Marevin survived a raid that killed his mother. He violently detested them.

"I will do as you ask of me, my fair Princess Asora," Marevin said.

He was trying to charm Asora. It did get Asora's attention, but not in the way he intended. Asora turned a little red, but she smiled weakly and thanked him for his compliment.

Jeia's New Plant

Jeia clapped Marevin on the shoulder. "Come on, love dove, you and I and pointy ears over there have a job to do." Then, in a lower tone, he said, "Stop trying to coo my sister!"

Arriving by a portal, which Asora had opened, Jeia, Frenzen, and Marevin, accompanied by twenty armed elves, arrived right outside the plant on Dergo. The facility was enormous. It seemed to be as large as the Utopian royal palace. The mountainous structure spanned an area the size of a large city. There were several smaller structures surrounding the central structure. Jeia advised them that there were also underground networks and facilities.

"That is one big plant, Jeia. And by the looks of it, I would say that it does more than what you and Asora have told the court," Frenzen said.

"Sorry, PM, but that is classified—only I, Asora, and Admiral Yane know the details. Now, as for you, Marevin, quit thinking about my sister and concentrate on the task she gave you. Those terrorists have already begun to put out feelers for my plant's defenses," Jeia explained.

"I cannot help but think of the beauty that is Princess Asora, the shining star in my sky," Marevin said in a daydream.

"That was the sorriest speech you have told me thus far. So drop it and do your damn job!" Jeia almost yelled.

Marevin stayed silent and followed Jeia and Frenzen into the facility. Inside were hundreds of security guards and scientists. "Let's get to work, everyone!"

Three days passed; Frenzen had finished getting clearance to see the facility, and Marevin had been set up with a training area for Jeia's security troops. The duke, in his dark-gray business suit, was in his corporate boardroom, meeting with the board members.

"Your Grace, are you sure that we can trust the prime minister? He is, after all, an elf, and they will do anything to prevent us from advancing our agenda," a male board member said with concern. He was gray haired and wore a black business suit.

"This is the only way to get the court off our backs. Marevin can train the security detail. He is the best when it comes to dealing with the Clan," Jeia pointed out to the twelve board members.

"The Clan is another concern to us. We have intelligence that suggests they may attack our Dergo facility," a female board member declared. She was blond, blue eyed, and wore a blue business suit.

"Fusion Corp has weathered worse than the Clan and the elves, so we can get through this. If we can make more warships, then we can adequately defend this place," Jeia reassured the skeptical board. "We can do this. We must."

"Now, begin!" Marevin, wearing combat fatigues, blew a whistle and started a stopwatch. Fifty humans and giant fairies hit the dirt and crawled under barbed wire and walls; they busted down fake doors and shot at practice targets. Another set of eighty engaged in other military-like exercises and drills, while the rest of the fifteen thousand security people were training elsewhere.

On another world, a small habitable moon near Dergo, the Clan had built up a base.

"Fusion Corp's facility has been finished and is in full operation. There is a report that the idiot Jeia is having his security detail trained to handle us." An agent laughed.

He was a pale muscular man dressed in worn brown leather.

"Do not underestimate Jeia. He knew that he was building his base in our territory. But the headmaster said that he has something deep inside his new building that can give us an advantage against both the kingdom and the empire," the leader proclaimed. "I do not know how he survived the rail gun electrocution."

"Who is training Jeia's security detail?" another agent asked.

"Some human called Marevin. He is Princess Asora's representative from her privy council. We have had dealings with him before," another agent informed the others.

"Marevin? That insolent fangut? I look forward to finally ridding myself of that foolish little man," the leader said as he rubbed a huge scar on his right cheek.

"Laxur is still having trouble with her new laser toy, thanks to us. She will have to be dealt with one day, but for now, she is a good distraction for Jeia."

Fifteen more days passed. Marevin was in Jeia's office; they were both dressed casually in worn jeans and business shirts with their sleeves rolled up.

"Well, bubbles, how are troops coming along?" Jeia asked, teasing Marevin.

"Do not call me bubbles! As for your troops, not as well as I would like, but if they stay with the training that I have outlined, then they will get better over time," Marevin stated with a shrug.

"They better be more prepared than that, because one of our satellites has detected a fleet of Clan ships heading this way. They had better be ready." Jeia showed Marevin a satellite picture of the approaching ships.

"What about your fleet?" Marevin asked with an intense look in his eye.

"Still under construction." Jeia thumped his fist on the desk in frustration.

"Oh, Great Maker!" Marevin was appalled. "What about defenses?"

"Antiair defenses, but they are untested except for the manned guns and the ground troops that you trained," Jeia said.

"How long until they arrive?" Marevin demanded.

"One hundred twenty-five hours," Jeia answered.

"This will be a ground war. We will see how much of my training sunk in." Marevin turned and walked back to the practice area.

One hundred twenty-five hours passed, and Marevin was pushing the troops hard, reminding them that the assault would happen soon. The men practiced with intensity; they knew that their lives, as well as others', were on the line.

The Clan had landed just outside of the anti-air defense range. As

Marevin said, they were coming in by foot. Marevin, Jeia, and Frenzen were watching the battle at the front gates of the base. The raiders had come in massive numbers; Jeia's security forces were outnumbered nine to one. Jeia could only speculate that they knew that he had something of enormous value in this plant. He would not lose this one like he lost Carlon. They were eight hours into the battle.

"Bring the automated defenses online. We trained for this. Let's go. Have the security details retreat to the underground structures," Jeia ordered. "We cannot let them take what is in there."

"And what exactly is underground?" Frenzen demanded.

"Ever hear of the Hananaka?" Jeia asked.

"The who?" Frenzen demanded.

"The Hananaka! The gods. But that would mean? That is why you built this place here. You and Asora found an ancient ship here?" Marevin postulated.

"It took you long enough to figure that out," Jeia said rudely.

"But there is something else that you found, is there not?" Frenzen demanded.

"You could say that, and it is something that I do not want let out," Jeia stated firmly.

He walked away with Marevin and Frenzen in tow. They entered an elevator, and Jeia commanded it to take them to the lower underground levels.

Outside, the troops were screaming and retreating. Explosions rocked the terrain, as the security troops evacuated inside. They closed all the doors behind them, as the last of them got inside. It had been twenty-nine hours since the attack began.

"Sir, they have sealed the main entrance," a Clan agent told his leader.

The leader had a talon for a left hand. He was a bald elf-and-human hybrid, and he ordered, "Break it down and kill anyone in your way."

"Yes, sir," the agent replied as he tried to burn through the entrance using a fire spell.

"Do not bother! Blow it up!" the leader ordered.

As he commanded, one of his female agents recited a powerful explosion spell. It did nothing. The explosives team moved in with a massive amount of force. The door disappeared in a violent shock wave of fire and metal.

"Take the base!" the leader ordered. "But I want Marevin Aranto alive."

Jeia, Frenzen, and Marevin were at the lowest level of the underground chambers. They looked like bunkers with cemented walls and ceilings. Frenzen looked and saw a room that was sealed away.

"Jeia, what is in that room?" Frenzen asked.

"Believe me, Frenzen, you really do not want to know," Jeia responded. Then, fighting could be heard above them. "Oh crap! If they get down here, we are all dead!"

"You do not have enough troops to protect this place, let alone the troops experienced enough to deal with them," Marevin pointed out harshly.

"Enough, both of you! Jeia, do you believe that this Hananaka ship can help?" Frenzen asked.

"Since when do you believe in the Hananaka, Frenzen?" Marevin asked.

"If it helps, I will believe in them. Jeia, can it?" Frenzen demanded.

"I do not know. We cannot read all of their language, let alone figure out how anything works on that ship," Jeia answered.

"You may want to figure it out *fast*, because the Clan has just blasted their way past the upper-level defenses," Marevin pointed out.

An explosion rocked through the ceiling, and three Clan agents landed in front of the trio.

"Finally, the human in charge of this facility! Take him alive!" the leader ordered.

"I think not!" Frenzen roared. The elfish guards drew swords, while Jeia and Marevin pulled handguns from their coats.

"Well, Marevin, I was wondering if you were here," the Clan leader growled evilly.

"I was wondering if you were coming down here, Ranckor, so I could cut you up again." Marevin taunted the Clan leader with a twisted smile.

"Ranckor? The 'poison fist' of the Clan?" Frenzen questioned, astonished.

"More like claw bait now." Marevin pointed to Ranckor's left hand.

"No thanks to you, you little fangut!" Ranckor slashed at them.

"You bastards are trespassing. Get out before I kick your sorry ass!" Jeia threatened, pointing his gun at Ranckor.

"You are in no position to threaten me, Utopian scum," Ranckor threatened back. "I want that door opened!"

"No, you idiot! Do not breach that containment wall!" Jeia cried.

He was too late. The door was blown away, and an alarm sounded.

"Warning. Containment breach, med-lab 9!" an automated voice boomed over the intercom system.

"Oh crap! You idiots! Do you have any idea what you have done"? Jeia thundered.

A strange sound came from the breached room. It sounded like a frightening animal, and it was glowing.

"What was in that room, Jeia? Tell me now!" Frenzen demanded.

"We found living organisms inside the ship," Jeia answered. He nervously kept his eyes on the breached doorway.

"What kind of organisms?" Marevin demanded.

"We do not know. I have never seen such life forms before," Jeia said weakly.

"Is it possibly a Hananaka?" Frenzen asked.

"No. We know that for sure. It is more like a macro-virus," Jeia explained.

"What is a macro-virus?" Ranckor demanded.

"A disease that is as big as a small animal!" Jeia explained as best he could.

What came out was not what Jeia expected. A horde of small particle-like things came flying out of the hole.

"RUN!" The nine men did as Jeia ordered and ran from the research lab.

Two of Frenzen's elvish guards were overcome by the alien macro-virus particles. Their skin was melting off, and their bodies twisted into unrecognizable masses of muscles, tentacles, teeth, and jellied blood. After eating their way through the bodies, the virus multiplied and attacked.

"Great Maker! What horror is this?" Frenzen said in shock as he watched his guards become gnarled.

"Into the hangar bays! GO!" Jeia ordered.

Jeia's security forces opened fire with guns and flamethrowers. They worked for a short while, until the alien simply overwhelmed them and then moved on. The macro-virus kept coming, and more of Jeia's people, as well as Clan agents, were mutated into biomass-infected creatures.

The survivors reached the hangar bay.

"Quickly! Seal the doors!" Jeia ordered.

Marevin, Ranckor, and Frenzen forced the giant hangar doors closed just before the macro-virus and infected people got to them.

"So what now, boy?" Ranckor demanded of Jeia.

"What am I, Jasil Maranto? I am making this up as I go along!" Jeia declared, terrified.

Jasil Maranto was a famous character from a human novel that Jeia used to read.

"Oh, that's very reassuring," Ranckor said sarcastically, the fear carefully masked. "Jeia, is that the Hananaka ship?" Marevin asked.

He pointed to a spacecraft made of a non-metalic material. It was shaped like a bird and smaller than a Utopian ship.

"Yes, that is it," Jeia said briefly.

"We cannot allow that macro-virus to get out. If it does and gets off this world, then the Utopian Kingdom, Darkcon Empire, the unaligned worlds, and even the Clan will end up like those poor bastards in the corridors," Jeia warned.

"And you were the one that found that damned virus in the first place!" Ranckor yelled.

"If you idiots did not blow up the containment units, it would not be loose!" Jeia countered angrily, coming face-to-face with Ranckor.

"Knock it off! Jeia, can we rig that ship's power plant to explode?" Marevin asked.

"I do not know. We have not had much time to study this thing. We do not know what controls the power source," Jeia said.

"You had better figure it out fast, because I do not think that the doors will hold them for long." Frenzen pointed to the very strained doors.

They were beginning to deform and weaken from the pounding.

Jeia grunted, and he ran to the alien ship and went inside. The duke seemed to know where he was going. Frenzen cautiously followed Jeia inside. The old elf was amazed by what surrounded him: metal walls, black panels, and red lights. A light was emitted from an open room, and Frenzen could hear Jeia talking to his assistant.

"But, sir! I have not figured out which one is the power control panel yet," the male assistant complained. He was a young brunette man in a business shirt with rolled-up sleeves, jeans, and sneakers. "I cannot believe that the Clan were stupid enough to let the monsters free."

"What about the weapons!" Jeia yelled angrily.

"I think it is that one, but then again, that could control the plumbing," the assistant answered weakly.

"Cute. Have you discovered anything useful? What the hell do I pay you for!" Jeia yelled.

"I did figure out where the self-destruct mechanism is controlled from," the assistant replied. "It looks like they deliberately set up a system. Probably due to the cargo they carried, sir."

"Very well. We shall use that then," Frenzen ordered as he walked in.

"What? We cannot blow this up! It is a valuable find, and the Princess wants it," Jeia said.

"Under the circumstances, I am sure that Princess Asora would understand," Frenzen stated.

"Young man, make preparations to activate the self-destruct system."

"No! This is my facility, and you have no right to—"

"I am the Prime Minister! We are still in the Utopian Kingdom, and I have higher authority. My word is law. If the princess has a problem with that, I will do the explaining!" Frenzen ordered.

"Maker damns you, you pointy-eared freak! Do it, Qerac. Activate the self-destruct system," Jeia stated angrily.

"Yes, sir." Qerac went to a panel and pushed a few buttons. In a few seconds, the ships' alarms blared, and an alien number system appeared on a large screen—a countdown.

"We should get out of here. The blast will be equivalent to thirty megatons!" Qerac said loudly.

Jeia, Frenzen, and Qerac ran out of the ship. "Quickly, everyone! To the rail cars!" Jeia ordered. "They are fast enough to get us to safety!" A set of small train-like rail cars were at the other end of the hangar bay. Qerac activated the rail cars, as he and the others got in. The cars moved at lightning-fast speed, while at the same time, the macrovirus horde finally broke down the doors and surrounded the alien ship.

Inside the ship, the countdown ended, and in a blinding flash of light, the ship exploded. The shock wave destroyed Jeia's new plant and everything within fifty miles.

The rail cars were derailed and sent flying into the mountains. Jeia climbed out from the dirt and debris. He looked back at his new plant, and all he saw was a gigantic mushroom cloud. But Frenzen was right—it did destroy the macro-virus.

Marevin, Frenzen, and Qerac dug themselves out and helped Jeia to his feet. Ranckor was gone.

"My plant!" Jeia cried.

"You can build a new one," Frenzen reminded him in an annoyed tone.

"Let us go home. I need some sleep and a counselor," Marevin complained.

Chapter Eighteen

T'A'S LESSON

Asora had just sent Madimoy on her way to Canva Prime, and Lady T'ula accompanied her. She had also sent Jeia, Frenzen, and Marevin to Dergo to see to Jeia's new facility. It was now the weekend, and the court would not debate until the start of the new session. That meant that Asora had at least three weeks to herself. With everyone gone, the princess could get some private time; however, her adviser and former teacher, Mistress T'a, was still in the palace. Asora liked T'a, but her lessons could be a bit annoying. Even though it was T'a's job and Asora personally asked T'a to be on her council.

"My princess, what are you going to do with three whole days to yourself?" T'a asked sweetly, almost mother-like. She wore a wool dress of ice blue, which matched her eyes.

"To be honest, I am not too sure. I have not had a day to myself in years. This will be a first. Perhaps I will sleep or catch up on some reading, or maybe—" Asora was interrupted.

"Or maybe you should try to practice your spells and exercises," T'a cut in. "And practice your manners."

"You really know how to ruin a fun time, you know that, T'a?" Asora complained.

"It is in your best interest, and I will not have you slacking on the throne. You are the grand monarch of the Utopian Kingdom, and the kingdom needs its leaders to be strong and wise," T'a explained. "And your actions and manners leave something to be desired.

"It does not help when you are surrounded by greedy, corrupt, and stupid courtiers. And that evil puro, uh, I shudder thinking of him. They want a war when we cannot adequately fight back, and the budget is a joke. They live in a fantasy. Foolish old idiots. I would be better off declaring war on the court and ridding myself of those responsible for this!" Asora stated in a momentary fit of rage. "I am sure that Queen Laxur would pause the war and pull up a chair to watch such a thing."

"Princess Asora Darcshia Serafus! How could you think or say of such things?" T'a scolded Asora.

"It is true! They are forcing me to do everything that I do not want to do! Do you have any idea what that is like?" Asora yelled.

"Actually, my princess, I do know what it is like," T'a responded in a lower tone.

"How so?" Asora demanded.

"Five hundred years ago, I was the Queen of the Utopian Kingdom, as you are aware," T'a explained.

"Yes, and you started the Great War and killed billions of people," Asora pointed out rather rudely.

T'a expected that response, and she had always felt guilty for it. She wanted to tell Asora what really happened. Asora also knew better to blame T'a for that as Asora was not alive at the time. Also, Asora's view of the Great War was very skewed. The princess was the rightful descendant of the old emperor of the Consortium himself. Asora was proud of that and T'a understood and wanted Asora to be proud. T'a did have memories of that man. Asora was so like him.

"Could you meet me in the library in an hour? I shall explain what truly happened, not what the history texts recorded, if you are willing to keep an open mind, my Princess," T'a asked. "And what Emperor Jurano was like as well."

"Very well then. I will see you in one hour." Asora sighed and walked off.

T'a wanted to do this. She loved Asora, and the elf did not want her to make the same mistake that she did so long ago. What happened then still haunted her, and she still had nightmares about it. The humans, jewel elves, and daemons still cursed her name. Even though many had forgotten, some refused to forget. But a growing number of the current population has found it to forgive her. Also, she made a promise to Jurano that she intended to carry out.

One hour later the pretty, dark-haired princess met T'a in the library. She was sitting in a chair next to a cheerfully burning fire. T'a had prepared the mood to tell her story. T'a loved this method as she found it was the best way to tell stories or give a personal lesson.

"Glad you decided to come and hear me talk," T'a greeted Asora.

She poured the young woman a glass of red wine. T'a also had a tray of cookies and small snacks for the two of them to enjoy.

"Yes. You have piqued my interest. I want to hear your side of the story." Asora sat down in the opposite chair, arranging her white skirts. "And what my ancestor Emperor Jurano was like to you."

"Very well then. Here it goes," T'a began.

She cast a spell to show Asora what happened. She did this by spreading a magical dust into the fireplace. This caused the flames to flare up and form images. These images were controlled by T'a's words.

The fire changed into many colors and grew as it showed the story. Over one hundred thousand years of peace had befallen the Utopian Kingdom, a time of progress and expansion. Their main adversary, the Darkcon Empire, was in ruins and unable to challenge them. King Tarminan had died of disease and ancient age. Queen Aethinea was gone after her crimes were revealed. They left the kingdom to their only child, their daughter Princess T'a, who not only was to be crowned queen but also was to marry: a noble man whom she loved dearly by the name of Haravan. He would be crowned king alongside her. They both had great plans and wished for a family. The whole kingdom celebrated the marriage, as is Utopian tradition. The celebration was to last a year. However, the party was short-lived as Haravan became ill with the same illness that had fallen on many across the kingdom. She was terrified and did not want to lose him. The whole kingdom seemed to freeze up and hold its breath. The disease had no cure, and the king would die after years of agony. The angelic ambassador had mentioned that the Human Consortium had a possible cure.

The Utopians had encountered the humans a couple of times, and each time, the humans seemed to have more powerful toys. The Utopians thought very little of them and saw the humans as a parasitic nuisance. Nevertheless, Queen T'a wanted to save her husband and was willing to open a dialogue with their mysterious neighbors. Most of the royal court hated the humans and did not want a diplomatic relation with them. They feared the economic costs and another religious intrusion. Another rebellion would be disastrous. The kingdom started to become unstable as a result.

During the time of the Hananaka, the Human Consortium experienced an explosion of technology and knowledge. They added the jewel elves, as they called themselves, and a race of Daemons, or Dragons, to their population. And now a new race created by the hands of the Consortium, the cybers, a race of artificially intelligent machines. A new emperor and his wife had come to power: Jurano of Havaina. He appointed the daughter of the legendary Lord Jewel to be the new supreme commander of the Consortium's forces, lady, or in this case, Supreme Commander T'eama. The Consortium spanned countless worlds and harnessed technology so advanced that they had begun experimenting with star formations and, only recently, the creation of faster-than-light flight. Giant spaceships and heavy weapons were new industries. New technology creation was the norm and was needed for the economy.

The Consortium boasted a massive and technologically advanced armed force that dwarfed the Utopians and Darkcons combined. The jewel elves taught magic and defense against magic to their human loves to ready them for an eventual showdown.

T'A'S LESSON

Jurano saw T'a as a typical spoiled Utopian child, and T'eama dealt with her as well. T'eama denied T'a the cure, claiming that the Consortium cared nothing for another dead elf. The jewel elves saw their kin as the enemy and deserved whatever punishment came their way. There was still a lot of bad blood as the humans say between the jewel elves and the rest of their race and sub races. The jewel elves preferred the human way of life. Science and technology was something that was wondrous to them. Even the dark side of science and technology.

In pure anger, T'a ordered a general attack on Havaina to take the cure by force. This, however, did not work out the way the Utopians had originally planned. T'eama and her forces laid a trap and ambushed the royal guard and laid waste to them. The humans were simply too technologically advanced for the Utopians. Emperor Jurano declared war against the Utopian Kingdom for its aggression. He demanded revenge for the innocent that lost their lives when the Utopians sacked Havaina long ago. The jewel elves rallied to the call to arms. In one month, the Consortium mustered an army of trillions of soldiers and fleets of ships that numbered in the millions. Emperor Jurano proclaimed that the foolish Utopians had awakened an angry giant.

The human forces retaliated by striking the closest world, Dala first and conquered it in days by blasting it away from orbit, a tactic called orbital bombardment. Thousands of human warships surrounded the various Utopian worlds and burned their way across the kingdom. Unlike the Darkcons, who were more of a rebellion, the humans were a fully functioning nation and, apparently, a vicious superpower. At first, the Utopian news downplayed the defeats and massive human forces that were rampaging across the kingdom almost unchallenged. One world after another was laid low by the Consortium led by Lady T'eama.

They would start by isolating the targeted world in every manner possible. Then giant MAC cannon batteries would bomb the surface from orbit, destroying major settlements. Then the ground forces would descend and fight the local Defense Forces. Human guns proved devastating to the royal guard, and both the Consortium's Vanguard and Red Guards destroyed all remaining defenses. Canva Prime saw some of the most brutal fighting. The humans pounded away with sonar weapons to force the mer-people away from the aquatic fleets. When the mer-people did manage to sink a few of the human ships, all life became violently ill and died in agony from cancers. The Utopians called it the Techno Blight; the humans called it radiation poisoning. Most human aquatic warships were powered by nuclear fission reactors designed to breach if the ship was destroyed in battle. The mer-people did not figure this out until they managed to capture a human alive. There was no way for the radiation to be cured; it had to be waited out.

A dwarf world became the first world to be slammed by constant nuclear strikes. From orbit, the Consortium fleets fired wave after wave of one hundred megatons of nuclear explosives, practically glassing the surface. The dwarves refused to surrender, but they were oblivious to the fact that the humans did not care and would just simply stay in orbit and continue the nuclear attack.

On the sprite's main world, a playful childlike race was forced into service against the approaching human forces, a Vanguard Special Forces Unit meant to cause terror and create chaos. The sprites did not believe in fighting but were forced to combat the more powerful human forces. The humans came with cybers and massive numbers of drones. The humans burned the forests to the ground and turned the sprite world into a cinder. The Vanguard made no distinction between a friendly and a harmless Utopian and the more aggressive types; to the Vanguard, they were all the same. The sprites refused to adhere to the kingdom's monarchy after this fight and threatened to leave and join the Darkcon Empire.

Not wanting any defectors, T'a gave the sprites a new home, far away from the current fighting. The king finally died in complete agony and unaware of the war that was besieging the kingdom. T'a fell into total sadness, and the kingdom seemed to stop, unless they were at the front. Queen T'a then went to Prince

Tylus of the Darkcon Empire, and, in front of his people, asked him for help. The Darkcons outright refused to help; they saw this war as a divine punishment against the Utopians. Most wanted the Utopians to burn; others wanted to open diplomatic ties with the Consortium. The more radical elements wanted the Darkcon Empire to side openly with the humans and help them. T'a had removed all the sanctions and isolation measures against the Darkcons, but it was too little, too late. Most of the Utopian Kingdom's allies either were too afraid of the humans or were already conquered. The Darkcons were the last hope, and they openly refused. Now it was the Utopians who were alone, isolated, and under attack from a more powerful foe.

On the sixth year of the Great War, a gigantic human force assaulted Evorn. A fleet of ten thousand massive warships surrounded the planet and began a limited bombardment. They landed up to nine hundred million troops and ten thousand aquatic warships. Drones, fighter jets, bombers, missiles all darkened the skies and set the ground ablaze in white phosphorous and nuclear fire. The human forces penetrated the palace defenses and broke down the guard—their mission, capture the queen and terminate the royal court. The Red Guard was in charge of this operation. This massive shock-and-awe campaign was a sudden surprise that worked very well. Now, the fear of the Consortium struck the Utopians as the average citizen now knew the level of which they were fighting the foe. Defeatist rumors and thoughts plagued the Utopian Kingdom as the humans claimed to have conquered Evorn.

The queen and most of the royal court were able to escape, but the average peasants were left at the mercy of the Red Guard. And the Consortium was not kind to the inhabitance of Evorn. Team's most feared commander General Romcarr lead the attack and conquest of Evorn. His hatred for the Utopian Kingdom was so great that Team purposely allowed the daemon general to do as he pleased on Evorn.

As an act of spite and insult, the humans gutted the palace and turned it into a military bunker. They moved the entire population of Evorn into a secluded area, away from military operations. Emperor

Jurano ordered that the prisoners be treated well, and the Red Guard complied. Most of the religious order had stayed behind to protect the churches and temples. The humans had no regard for the Utopian belief system, and they tore down the churches or used them for target practice. One elf temple master watched as the humans ripped apart his beloved building and the children that he cared for. The humans moved the children to the concentration camps for safety. The elf was named Aga, a man who protected the main palace church and was also interrogated and tortured by the Red Guard for information.

The next three years, the Utopians had been pushed to the farthest edges of their kingdom and faced imminent defeat. The Utopian Kingdom had never surrendered to anyone before, and they feared what the humans would do. No Utopian weapon could blunt the Consortium's advance, and they had no victories to speak of, and now true terror gripped the kingdom in a great vice. Several noble houses had tried to surrender, but they were taken, beaten, and interrogated. If they were not seen as being connected to something that T'a did not understand then, the humans let them live in concentration camps. T'a did not know what fueled the humans' anger toward them, and none of her advisers would tell her. All the books she had were mute on this subject too. Her allies had abandoned her, her uncle refused to help, and she did not understand why. T'a felt that she was being kept from a revelation that everyone feared. She had lost most of her political power to the generals who could not seem to understand the nature of the foe they fought.

The prime minister told T'a that she still had full access to the all-powerful Roewe Crystals, an ancient gift from the angels to protect them from the next great darkness. To T'a, the humans hardly qualified, but she was tempted and, in insidious ways, was threatened to use them. T'a would commit an act so horrible that she might never be forgiven. She used the incredible power of the Roewe Crystals to curse the Consortium's people with a great dying curse.

Many humans, jewel elves, and dragons fell ill and started to die mysteriously, including Jurano's wife. She died in agony, and this caused Jurano to go into a rage. He and T'eama were close, and they both agreed to use all the Consortium's WMDs in indiscriminate attacks. They also found that the cybers were fully immune to the curse. In an almost religious like declaration the cybers fought a genocidal holy war to avenge their creators.

The order now was to kill any Utopian, no matter the age, status, or condition. The Vanguard was particularly brutal as they used gas and bioweapons on whole defenseless Utopian worlds. If they were going to die, then they would take as many of their enemies down with them. Several worlds ended up cleansed of all life. The curse had made the Consortium go into a berserker-like warpath.

A new leader of the Angel Empire has come to power. Serafus was his name. He had been keeping an eye on the war and saw many things that troubled him. If the two sides killed each other, then their mother, the Great Maker, would damn all angels for all time. Serafus ordered that angels must now interfere to save both sides.

In a massive show of force, angels attacked both sides and forced a temporary ceasefire. Queen T'a and Lady T'eama, in place of the emperor, were sat down to create a peace plan. The process took nearly three years to get right, and during that time, sporadic fighting broke out across the war-torn worlds, though quickly put down by Serafus's forces.

It was at this peace conference that T'a learned many horrible truths. But T'a was given credit for trying to heal old wounds, yet she was never given the chance. T'eama still saw T'a as a monster, as did most of the Consortium. Jurano was dead by then, but he had several children with his first wife, and T'eama had affairs with him too, so she bore several children to him as well. T'a had no children.

The terms of the treaty were that the humans had to dismantle the cybers, as both angels and Utopians saw them as blasphemous, but in return, the humans could keep their WMDs and also keep Evorn and all conquered worlds, and the Utopians had to rent out the planet. The

Human Consortium was forced to merge with the Utopian Kingdom. Serafus's logic suggested that if these two nations could pool their resources together, then they would both survive. Both sides saw the logic, but still, the hatred remained. The humans publicly scrapped the cybers and put all their WMDs in storage. The Roewe Crystals were taken away, and the Utopians could take advantage of the humans' excess food supply.

The Utopians saw this a humiliating defeat and now they had to pay the humans for the right to get Evorn back. The humans built up sections of the palace that they claimed was theirs. Evorn saw advanced industry come, as well as military installations.

Both sides rubbed salt into each other's wounds, and petty fights were common. The Vanguard went into exile to show their opposition to the treaty. Many Utopians formed the Clan and attacked human-occupied worlds in Utopian space as they saw fit. T'eama was now the leader of the Human Consortium and its empress, but she was forced to take the title of countess. She was not allowed the title empress, but she held the power of one. She was, in fact, the most powerful noble in the kingdom and the most heavily armed and was able to dictate some policies. Her stepson, who was Jurano's first son, was an adamant supporter of T'eama, and he secretly rebuilt the Consortium's forces, as his stepmother covered for him.

T'eama took Jurano's family name until she was forced, by royal law, to marry a Utopian noble to seal the final parts of the treaty. She protected the Consortium by giving it all to her stepson.

Known for his brazenness and lack of tact and distrust in the royal court, he often would countermand the royal family's orders, as was his right. T'eama was forced into a quiet and subservient role as wife to one of the wealthier nobles because she abandoned her role as Consortium leader and her stepson controlled it. Now the Utopians were unable to gain control of it. T'eama's stepson hated what was done to her and did what he could to free her, but nothing worked.

The fairies, who had fought the hardest and lost the most in the war, saw virtually nothing and were berated once more as a tiny people. Then the new fairy leadership saw in the royal court decadence and betrayal. So, they started to openly negotiate with the very enemy that once tried to destroy them, the humans. The disgruntled fairies saw in the humans a kindred spirit and sided with them on many subjects.

The Human Consortium refused to share their technology and secrets with the Utopians, but then again, the Utopians wanted no part in human science. The human factories and manufacturing techniques did as many feared; they were changing the economy, and the dwarves and other craftsmen could not keep up. The industrial pollution was horrible, and in some areas, the humans polluted as an act of spite, even though humans had clean technology and pollution was banned. No one cared anymore, and this was evident on Canva Prime. Half the oceans had rising acidic levels, and some of the harbors were heavily polluted with sludge from factories.

The Utopians retaliated too, in small ways. Most humans were denied access to the government programs and from noble activities and limited recruitment into the royal guard.

The more heinous incidents were that some stole human and jewel elf children from their parents. They would even feed them to wild animals or raise them themselves. This sparked the mass production of nuclear power plants everywhere. Nuclear energy generated enough radiation to negate magic temporarily unless breached. These plants were seen as nightly protectors as most humans were not too far away from one. An act of spite, yet again, the humans began construction of a nuclear fusion power plant on Evorn. Officially, it was as a power station for the various things they had already, but secretly it was to make life more difficult for the Utopians.

Queen T'a, as her last act as supreme monarch, ordered that this madness be stopped. She wanted the reactor canceled, but in return, the humans were free to build anything they wanted, as long as it was not nuclear powered. She wanted T'eama's stepson to reinstate the pollution bans, and she would force her court to give humans equal rights. The head of the Consortium agreed to the terms and destroyed the reactor that was under construction. The humans had to clean up their mess; however, the Utopians were ordered, under pain of exile and death, to give them equal rights and treat them as equals.

Queen T'a gave up the throne and her crown in shame. She went into a self-imposed exile on Havaina. There she learned the truth from T'eama's stepson. Her shame and sadness were so great that the noble of the Consortium felt sorry for her. Over the next five hundred years, T'a wandered the Consortium, searching for something, or someone, that could help her. She saw that the whole Consortium hated her and several attempts were made on her life—from ruined humans to angry jewel elves, and even mad dragons. Also, her own who felt that she betrayed them.

She wandered into a temple dedicated to the Hananaka gods. She saw something that changed her life. One of the gods spoke to her and, in front of a once angry mob now in spiritual reverence. T'a saw everything, and this god told her what she needed to do to see redemption, not just for herself, but for her people as well.

Princess Asora listened to T'a's story with mixed feelings. "Were you able to get your people to do what is needed to be done?" Asora asked T'a.

"I do not know. I have lost much influence with my own people because of my support for humans," T'a explained.

T'a looked so sad, and she was truly hurt. She had been carrying this guilt for centuries. Asora could not comprehend that. The princess felt sorry for Lady T'a. She had worked so hard to change things, and she kept hitting a wall. Every time she tried to make it right, people would not allow it, or they made the situation worse. Asora felt closer to T'a then she thought. In a way T'a wants Asora to succeed and do better.

"T'a, I can help you on your quest for forgiveness, if you can help me keep my throne," Asora suggested.

"Yes! Yes, I will! Thank you so very much, my Princess!" T'a sobbed.

T'A'S LESSON

Princess Asora held T'a as her mentor cried for the first time in front of the younger princess. T'a never cried in front of anyone. So, this was unique. Asora wanted to help T'a, Asora did not hold T'a responsible, and she could forgive her. No, she had forgiven her, both Teams and Jurano would have too.

CHAPTER NINETEEN

A SECRET MEETING

Lady Madimoy and Lord Jeia returned from their separate missions. Madimoy and T'ula smelled like ocean water, while Jeia, Frenzen, and Marevin looked horrified and dirty.

Princess Asora had them meet in her private throne room.

"So, Lady Madimoy, Lady T'ula, were you two successful in your mission?" Asora asked.

Madimoy responded by showing her princess the coin of wind. Asora's eyes lit up, but she quickly restored her royal facade. Then Jeia came back with Marevin and Frenzen in tow. The young lord looked exhausted and terrified.

"Jeia, my brother, what happened?" Asora asked, worried for her brother's health.

"It is a very long and ugly story," Jeia responded.

"I would like to hear it, maybe after dinner," the Princess pronounced.

"Our tale will turn your stomach, my princess. Just to warn you," her brother advised.

"What about your new plant?" Asora continued to question.

"It was destroyed in a massive explosion." Jeia almost wept.

"What! What happened? What caused it?" the princess demanded.

Her voice rang with anger. Asora had spent an enormous amount of money to help Jeia build it. She knew of the alien ship, which was the main reason why she helped her brother build it. She knew that the coins of power were not going to be enough to fight Queen Laxur and

A Secret Meeting

her empire. The Princess, like Emperor Jurano before her, wanted to use the aliens' technology to help the kingdom. She was sure that the Hananaka gods would not mind, and Lady T'a had offered to help. T'a was one of the few people that knew of Asora's grand plan to fight Laxur using this combination, though combining the coins of power with the ultra-advanced alien technology would be very difficult.

Later, at dinner, the Princess's private dining room was filled with most of Asora's royal court and privy council. The smell of turkey, potatoes, wine, stuffing, vegetables, and pies filled the room. Princess Asora sat at the end of the table. To her left was Admiral Yane. Also at the table were Lady Madimoy, dressed in a green dinner dress, and Lady T'ula, dressed in the usual aqua-blue gown. Duke Jeia, wearing his brown court suit, sat opposite of Madimoy. He still looked a little spooked, and he was not eating. In fact, he looked slightly ill. Next to Jeia sat Marevin, wearing gray, and he did not look well either. Physically, they were both fine, from what the doctor told them; their troubles were psychological.

"Lady Madimoy, Lady T'ula, would you be so kind to tell us of your adventures on Canva Prime?" Princess Asora asked.

"Of course, Your Highness," the redhead chirped; however, it was T'ula who told the story.

Madimoy remained silent when T'ula was finished, not speaking of the situation between her and Laxur. She decided to tell Asora and Jeia later, in private.

"Very enchanting tale. Thank you. Now, Jeia, Marevin, or Frenzen, would you like to tell us about what happened?" Asora's last word sounded with a hint of anger.

"Should I, Jeia?" Marevin asked Jeia weakly.

"No, I will do it. After all, I was responsible for it. Once you hear what I have to say, you will agree that the plant's destruction was a good thing in the end," Jeia advised, trying to smile.

Jeia's tale was very different from Madimoy's mermaid tale. In fact, what Jeia said was more of a horror story.

"Oh maker! No wonder you look so pale!" Asora exclaimed, no longer upset with Jeia. He might have saved them all from an unspeakable horror.

"I think that I have lost my appetite," Lady T'ula said weakly.

"You are sure that this macro-virus was destroyed?" Admiral Yane demanded.

"If you are not sure, go look at the two-hundred-mile-wide crater where my new plant once stood, and you tell me!" Jeia thundered angrily.

"Enough! Jeia, know your place!" Asora ordered. Dinners were for discussing everything without fear of others mocking you; they were to share opinions amicably.

"Where did this macro-virus come from?" Lady T'a asked with a hint of worry in her voice.

"To be honest, we never found out. As far as we know, the ship had them inside containment units that had Hananaka symbols on it. So, as far as we could determine, the macro-virus was either being studied, or it was imprisoned and contained," Jeia tried to explain.

"The Hananaka?" T'ula asked. "I keep hearing you humans mentioning these Hananaka. What are they?"

"Hananaka translates as the ones from the heavens. The early humans saw them as gods. They brought knowledge, wisdom, power, civilization, and understanding to us. They protected us when they walked our worlds. There were roughly twenty-five known ones," Madimoy explained.

"Twenty-five? Can you name a few?" T'ula asked again.

"Of course," Madimoy started. "There is Praetor, the king of the gods; Imperator, the war god; Esiran, the justice god; and Asora, the sky and storm god."

"Asora? Asora is a name of one of these gods? My Princess, you are named after one of your gods?" T'ula sounded positively baffled.

"Of course, plus the names all have meaning. Like I am named after the god of storms, and the name literally means 'Maiden of the

Sky,'" Asora pointed out.

"Is that common for humans to name their children after these gods?" T'ula asked again.

"Oh yes, it is a form of flattery. The gods thought it was kind of us to do. It became a tradition for the noble humans to name their children after a god of their choosing to show respect," Madimoy interjected.

"Are you named after a god or goddess, Madimoy?" T'ula asked.

"No, unfortunately not. Only the firstborn may have those names, and you must be of noble birth. I was not born originally to nobility, but I was not firstborn. That was given to my brother, who died ten days after his birth. His name was Esiran," Madimoy said in a lower tone.

This was typical of human-naming practices. However, for Asora's family, she got a god's name because her mother insisted. Her father got to name her sister, and he wanted a more charming name for her.

Jeia reached over and folded his hand over her hand, which was clutching her napkin. She smiled gratefully.

"Well, at any rate, Jeia, my dear, were you able to save any of the Hananaka materials?" Madimoy inquired.

"No," Jeia replied flatly.

"Why do we not end this meal and retire for the remainder of the evening?" Princess Asora interjected. Everyone stood up and bowed to Asora.

After she requested her small privy council to retire, she went to her rooms to rest for the night. The Princess had finished a bath, and her fairy ladies-in-waiting dressed her in a lacy white nightgown that hung loosely on her body. Her bed was gigantic and obscenely over decorated in the princess's white, but it was meant for only her. Asora got in and wrapped herself in the many thick, comfortable blankets. Then she was fast asleep.

The next morning, the fairy maids hurried the princess out of bed so that they could do their morning chores. They dressed her in a white dress, and Gourani put a light makeup on her and did her nails. They styled her hair and then put a ribbon in to gently hold it back. The final thing was to put the circlet crown on her head.

After, Princess Asora walked out of her private chambers and toward the dining room for breakfast. She could smell eggs, ham, bacon, and fresh fruit being prepared in the kitchen.

"Ah, princess! There you are!" Frenzen was already enjoying breakfast. They dined together first thing in the morning to discuss the day's itinerary. This was common routine for them.

She sat down and signaled the servant to push her chair in. "Is there something wrong? What is it?"

"It appears that your sister, the Darkcon queen, is coming here to make an attempt to defuse the tense situation between the kingdom and empire," the older elf explained.

"That is rich! Tensions that she started. But then again, this is an excellent opportunity to learn of what else the Darkcons are up to," Asora stated. "Prepare the smaller throne room for her arrival."

"Yes, my princess." Frenzen got up, bowed, and walked away.

"Now for some breakfast," she said to herself, feeling her belly rumble with hunger.

Three hours later, Princess Asora was in the second throne room, standing beside her throne with the entire Utopian royal court behind her and her privy council to her left. They were awaiting the arrival of Queen Laxur and her imperial court. The Darkcon Empire's mightiest ship, the *Sarasen*, had landed in the east garden grounds. The great beast of a ship took up the entire parade field and stretched into the fields beyond. It was hard metal with twelve sharp protrusions. As one soldier had said, it was two black widow spiders back-to-back, with the legs in the air and on the ground.

Joes, Asora's best Knight and Captain of the guard, was to escort the Darkcon Queen to the throne room.

Finally, the doors opened, and the first to walk through was Joes. Behind him was a platoon of royal guardsmen, and behind them were

A Secret Meeting

the Darkcons.

Standing at attention, Joes announced the arrival of the Darkcon Queen. "Presenting the supreme monarch of the Darkcon Empire, Her Majesty, Queen Laxur!"

The dark beauty walked gracefully into the Utopian throne room. Directly behind her was Dari; to her left was Golcon, prime minister and a notorious Darkcon politician; to the Queen's right was General Sysu.

"So nice to see you again, Asora," Laxur greeted. Her words were laced with sarcasm.

"Shall we get started?" Asora responded flatly, yet you could hear the demanding tone in her voice.

"Not a good way to start the negotiations, baby sister. You should know better than that. Or did they forget to teach you proper diplomatic manners?" Laxur taunted Asora.

The Princess could feel the anger rising in her chest. It was taking every ounce of her willpower to repress her feelings.

"Never mind that. Let us get this over with. Now, Queen Laxur, how can we defuse the tensions between our nations?" Asora asked, almost gritting her teeth.

Laxur noticed Asora's frustration and took pleasure from it. She followed her sister to a table.

The table itself was long with chairs on both sides. On one side of the table was the Utopian Kingdom's flag. It was a star with a heart in the middle and the seven insignias of the seven beings of the kingdom inside the points. The other side had the Darkcon Empire's flag. It was a black cross with two swords crossing in the middle. Two chairs stood out among the many at the table. One was Asora's, which was white and taller than the others on the Utopian side. The other was Laxur's, which was the same as Asora's except it was black. She had made it with her magic. After the royalty sat, all the people involved sat, ready to start the debate.

Elsewhere in the Utopian palace, Prince S'tie was sneaking around the castle, looking for Asora's chambers. He had been enchanted by Queen Laxur to do as she willed. He was using an invisibility cloak, which the dark Queen had given him, to move around without being detected. Laxur had spent time breaking the enchantments around the palace while she was on her ship. Only a high witch with incredible powers was able to do this. She was trained over the years in infiltration methods by the military of the Darkcon Empire and the Utopian Kingdom—but here, it was only rudimentary. She had been chosen for this by her natural powerful abilities that came with her unique heritage of being half angel.

Eventually, S'tie located Asora's rooms and saw several fairies buzzing in and out with linens, water, and other things. These were more than likely the Princess's ladies-in-waiting preparing the chambers for when Asora returned.

About ten minutes later, the ladies were finished with their chores and left. Once the fairies were out of sight, S'tie slowly opened the door and squeezed in, closing the door behind him.

"Well now, where would Asora hide a treasure like the coins?" S'tie muttered to himself.

He went to the bedroom and looked around the large room to gauge the possibilities. The prince eyed a vanity mirror, and he started his search there. Gently, S'tie opened the drawers and found only female beautifying products.

He moved away from the vanity mirror to a small jewelry chest on a nightstand next to Asora's bed. He found very expensive jewels, but not coins. S'tie decided to continue the search in her closet. He doubted very much that she would keep them in her sitting room or dining room.

What S'tie did not know was that B'nei was watching him, and she could feel that he had malevolent intent. B'nei had an extra sense that allowed her to see the invisible. The little fairy realized that she could not take on the prince herself. She was going to need her sisters.

A Secret Meeting

Using her wings, B'nei emitted a high-pitch noise that only fairies could hear. To her ears, the wings were making a real racket, but S'tie could not hear a thing.

Across the palace, every fairy could hear B'nei's buzzing for help. The first to arrive were her three sisters, Friea, Gourani, and Rayne.

"Hold it right there, buddy!" Gourani stated authoritatively to S'tie.

The enchanted prince turned to see four angry-looking fairies hovering in front of the door. "And what do you four little girls think that you are doing, hmm?" S'tie asked casually.

"Us? What are you doing here? Are you not supposed to be on Dorien, trying to keep Queen Laxur from making war?" Friea blasted.

"What I am doing does not concern the likes of little fairies," S'tie said insultingly.

"Why you big . . ." Gourani fumed angrily and turned red.

She was getting ready to attack S'tie, until her sisters held her back.

"That is right! You are nothing but cute little bugs." The prince laughed.

"All right! That is, it!" all four fairies said in unison, and they attacked him, using their magic to make him sorry that he was calling them names.

S'tie got a few lucky shots off and swiped them. It was enough to slam the four sisters against the wall. They landed on the floor, and Rayne was unconscious. The prince was about to step on them when a feminine voice boomed from the doorway.

"Leave them alone, now!" Princess Asora thundered. The princess had a sword in her hand. "I thought I heard B'nei's distress call."

"Put that away before you hurt yourself, Asora," S'tie suggested insultingly to the Princess.

"You are the one who is going to get hurt if you do not tell me what it is that you are looking for in *my* room!" Princess Asora demanded.

S'tie suddenly noticed the necklaces that Asora wore. He eyed two coins on two pendants that hung down to her chest. Asora noticed what he was looking at and understood.

"The coins?" Asora questioned. "You and Laxur are after the coins."

"How right you are," Queen Laxur said, appearing right behind Asora in a whiff of purple smoke.

"You are not going to get them!" Asora stated, pointing her sword at Laxur now.

"Get out of my room!" The princess saw her fairy ladies fallen to the floor, unconscious from Laxur's powerful dark magic. She was fighting these two alone.

"Hold her down!" Laxur ordered S'tie.

He grabbed Asora from behind and held her.

"Let me go, you beast!" Asora demanded and screamed.

"Do not embarrass yourself any further, baby sister. It is so unbecoming of a lady like you,"

Laxur taunted as she reached for Asora's two lockets.

"No, please, no!" Asora cried as she struggled.

Then, without warning, S'tie was hit in the back of his head and fell to the floor.

"Miss me, bitch?" Rakon shouted as he showed himself.

He wore his deep-red leather studded outfit.

"You! You are supposed to be dead!" Laxur screeched.

"Guess again!" Rakon snapped.

He lunged at Laxur and crashed right into her, sending them both to the floor. Laxur threw Rakon off her as she tried to get back on her feet. Sarea was now in the Princess's chambers, and she attacked Laxur; however, out of thin air, Dari appeared and used her dark angelic power to stop Sarea.

"I still owe you for Carlon, little girl," Dari thundered down to Sarea. Sarea unsheathed her second sword and was ready to attack Dari.

"Very well then. Let us dance!" Sarea charged at Dari.

Their blades made contact, the sound of metal clanging against metal was heard, and sparks were flying.

In the meantime, Rakon and Asora tackled Laxur. The Princess, at this moment, thought that maybe she could get a hold of Laxur's two coins. Knowing her sister, Asora guessed she would keep them in one of two places: one on her person, the other back on Dorien. If Laxur had the coins with her, they would either be in a pocket or somewhere in her dress. Laxur's strength, however, proved too great for both Asora and Rakon, and she threw them both off her. Asora was not going to be able to get the coins that Laxur had.

"This is an act of aggression, Laxur! You should know this!" Asora thundered.

"A treasure such as the coins of power is too good an opportunity to pass up," Laxur explained coolly.

"It will cost you!" Asora shouted.

Sarea and Rakon came to the Princess's side. All three had swords pointed at Laxur, Dari, and even the Galeron prince.

"You will regret this!" Laxur threatened. With that, the queen and her two companions disappeared in a puff of smoke.

"Well, that was interesting!" Sarea blurted out.

"She was after the coins that the princess has." Rakon pointed to Asora.

"Do not point at her, you foul beast!" Gourani growled as she flew up to Rakon's face. "Get out of my face, you annoying insect!"

"Why, I . . ." Gourani was getting ready to attack Rakon, until Asora stepped in.

"That is enough from both of you!" Asora yelled. "The last thing I need now is to have conflicts within my palace!"

"Yes, my princess," Gourani bowed, hovering in the air.

"Whatever," Rakon said flatly and walked away.

"Hey, get back here, you infidel!" Sarea chased after Rakon. She had her sword drawn, ready for a fight.

"Do not call me an infidel, you lap dog!" Rakon barked at Sarea.

"Should I call you a monster then?" Sarea questioned.

"Leave me alone, you dumb woman!" Rakon blasted and walked into the next room.

"NO!" Asora now roared. She appeared out of a glitter of blue right in front of the demon, who was now in her study.

"Get out of my way, little girl, before you get hurt," Rakon threatened.

"How dare you threaten the princess!" Sarea yelled.

"You can fight, Sarea, but your Princess here is as helpless as a baby," Rakon stated. Asora said nothing, but Sarea was angry. He continued, "Asora, if you think that you are so tough, then strike me, if you can."

"How about you tell me how you heard my lady-in-waiting instead?" Asora kept her sword up. "Also, how were you able to get by my guards?"

"She is an elemental creature. I am an elemental being. That means I can hear her cries. I was near your rooms and knew there was trouble. I figured there would be trouble, since your sister was here. It did not take a genius to figure out that she was up to something. I used what little magic I must transport myself here to find out. Laxur gifted me with the ability to transport myself short distances so that when she called, I could come to her immediately. It is exhausting, so I cannot do it that often. I am sure she is regretting that decision now."

"You were trying to protect the Princess?" Sarea said with interest.

"Anyone who stands against Laxur has my attention." He shifted in his stance and looked Asora in the eyes. "Look, you are no match for Laxur. I know. I trained her. She will eat you alive."

"Then you train me," Asora said.

Rakon burst out laughing. "You?"

"Yes, me. I need someone exactly like you, someone who knows how she thinks, how she moves, and what moves she will make. I know I am not as tall as she and I do not have the muscles that she has, but I can learn to be better than I am now." She lowered her sword.

The demon stared at her for a long moment, when suddenly he struck Asora in the face, and she went down. Sarea moved to gut him when he shouted,

"Lesson 1! Never drop your guard!" The princess motioned Sarea away.

"I will not forget. What is lesson two?" He laughed.

"Lesson two will be tomorrow at dawn. Find a place where we may

A Secret Meeting

practice without the eyes and ears of the court. Sarea may come, but no one else. Do you know of a place?" Asora said.

"Yes, I have the perfect place." She smiled back.

"Tomorrow at dawn then, Your Highness. I will come to your rooms. Be ready. Wear pants and a loose shirt." He bowed and left the women to clean up the mess.

Chapter Twenty
Combat Training

There was a clash of steel followed by the sound of someone falling. "Again! This time swing your blade and use your magic. You will find that it packs a harder punch." Rakon gave Asora a hand back to her feet.

The Princess nodded. "Yes, Rakon. It will be difficult. I have only used one or the other."

The demon growled. "Your sister knows how but is content to use one or the other, so you must use both. You are smaller and more delicately made. You *must* be able to outthink her, and it will be difficult. Since she was twelve years old, she has been in training for the Darkcon military, and she was the best I have ever seen. Come."

He motioned with his hand for her to strike him again on his dull sword. He stood waiting with his heavy tapered blade, which had a dark metallic finish.

She sprang at him. Her sword gleamed white, gold, and blue as it struck his. It reverberated up her arm; she quickly raised her left hand, and Rakon flew into the air, falling several meters backward.

He laughed uproariously as he got back up. "Good. Better, Your Highness. That was a much better spell than the water in the face. If you are going to use water, it should be hard ice. That could cause a concussion. Do you want to try for the ice?"

Asora looked at him in wonder. "But, Shia Rakon, you just said that it could cause a concussion. I cannot hurt you."

"It would not hurt me as much. I am a demon. Therefore, my bony skull would be able to take the blow." He turned toward Sarea. "Tell her."

"Highness, he speaks the truth. When I trained, we used the template of fighting demons because they are the toughest to kill. You will only give him a headache." The bodyguard smiled encouragingly at the Princess.

Asora shook her head. "No, but I will practice on this tree." She flung out her hand, and hard ice shot from her fingertips and took a chunk of tree with it.

"Not bad, but that is not a moving target. And you were not frightened by the movement of a demon coming towards you, yelling with a raised sword."

Rakon stepped back a few paces and came at her again. Asora reached down at her hip and swiftly pulled out her semiautomatic pistol, stopping the demon cold.

"Now that is cheating." He laughed again. "You surprise me, Princess. You do not seem to be a frightened young woman, but one who has known battles. Why is that?"

Asora looked to a smiling Sarea and grinned. "You would not know, but when I went to the royal school, I was known for getting into fights with the female elves and mermaids. They loved to speak down to us barbarian humans. I could not let that go unchallenged, especially when they threw the first punch. I was not going to be like my sister who had taken the beatings until she finally ran away. I was determined that I would not be their punching bag. Jeia taught me how to fight. I did not always win, but I gained enough of a reputation so that the elves left me alone most of the time. I helped Madimoy on several occasions as well. I surprised them by fighting like a man and fighting dirty." Asora thought for a moment. "It was a shame that I could not use the military training. But that was later in my life."

The demon nodded with a slight smile. "I see. You are a strange woman, and Queen Laxur is also strange. She came to me as a hostile child in need of discipline. She was . . . frightened all the time."

Sarea stepped forward. "I was at school with her. All of us humans were taunted and picked on. Laxur, or Asaria as she was called then, was particularly vulnerable to them. At that time, she would not fight back. Violence seemed to make her ill. I and several of the other humans were allowed to go to school there due to our noble births and the angels' insistence that humans be allowed to go. That is why I enlisted in the military—I wanted to defend those that were defenseless."

Rakon nodded. "Admirable. We demons fight for family, honor, and territory. We need a strong leader, one that can keep us in line, or we would fight among ourselves. Laxur can do that. She, however, has taken us into galactic war, and we are dying by the millions for her hatred of the Grand Utopian Kingdom. She has made it into a holy war that will destroy your worlds if she is not stopped. Many of my people will die for her personal grudge, but we will not lose as many as your people will. She only fears the angels and the humans, and both races say that they will not fight for the kingdom."

Sarea tipped her head slightly. "Why do you care about our people, War Master Rakon?"

"*I* care about *my* people. Before the war, Laxur was building new infrastructure: power plants, roads, railroads, schools, hospitals—important things to give the Darkcons a new future. She was building a better future, but now we fight and die by the millions. That is what I oppose." He smiled slightly at Asora. "You have also been kind to me. I believe you are the hope to end this war."

The Princess stared at the demon. "I pray it is so. Your people are very tough, smart opponents. We have yet to prevail over them. You are very loyal to your people. Are you prepared to help us defeat them?"

"In order to save them, I know that it will be necessary for others to die. I am hoping that if the others see me fighting for the Utopians, they will see it is possible to break away from the Queen." He bowed his head and shook it slowly. "The problem is that Laxur has many ways to make you do things that you may not want to do. It is a fact that she holds tremendous control over many in the empire. You need to learn how to break those enchantments. Your friend, Prince S'tie, is one of her latest victims. My friends and family are others. I want to free them, and this is the only way."

Asora sighed heavily. "I saw that. I warned S'tie, but he did not listen."

"It does little good to tell them. The minute she decides that you will be of use to her, your fate is sealed. You must learn to protect yourself and to break her power over others. This may be more important than the sword fighting I am teaching you." Rakon placed his hand on her shoulder and looked into her eyes.

Sarea moved swiftly in front of Asora. "You are not to touch the princess."

Rakon dropped his hand and took a step back, hands outstretched with his sword pointing down. "My apologies, Dame Sarea."

The bodyguard nodded but stayed where she was, until Asora stepped around her.

"I believe that they are equally important. Laxur uses her sword in combat, and though I am her sister, I believe that she would wound or kill me to get what she wants. After all, she was ready to run me through if you had not intervened. I must face that fact." She took a shaky breath, feeling anguish over the fact. She straightened herself and continued. "We will persist with the lessons in combat, but I will speak to T'a and ask her to teach me magic."

"Agreed. The next lesson will be to roll away. Come at me with the sword raised. I want you to swipe at me."

They practiced for another two hours, and then they left the enchanted gardens. This place was only known to the ruling monarch. Asora chose it as the most private place for her lessons. No one could see that she was learning to fight the most dangerous woman in the universe. This way, no spy could report back to Laxur.

She returned them all back to her suite of rooms in the blink of an eye. She invited Rakon to breakfast and summoned T'a to come.

They were partway through their breakfast when the lady elf arrived. She bowed to the sitting Princess, who smiled and indicated that she took a seat.

"Have some breakfast, T'a," Asora encouraged, and T'a smiled, reaching for her food. After she had put some fruit onto her plate, the princess spoke. "Nothing you hear here will leave this room."

T'a swallowed her piece of fruit and nodded. "Of course, Your Highness. Please, go on."

The demon and Princess exchanged a look before Asora spoke. "Shia Rakon and I were speaking about Laxur's tactics, and we believe I need extensive training in protecting myself against dark magic. You have had a great deal of experience in wars with the Darkcons over the centuries." Asora reached over the table to clasp T'a's hand. "I desperately need your help, if we are going to stop the deaths and this war. I must free Prince S'tie and stop Laxur from breaking the spells protecting this palace."

The elf slipped her hand out from under the Princess's. "I agree, but you need to do more than free Prince S'tie and protect the palace. You need to protect yourself and everyone around you."

Rakon growled. "Can she do this? Can she fight Laxur?"

T'a breathed in. "Princess Asora, you have a tremendous amount of raw power within you."

"But can she go against Laxur? Is she powerful enough? I found out that you were a teacher to both. So, tell us. Can she beat her?" The demon thumped his fist hard on the table, upsetting the dishes, while staring at the elf woman.

T'a looked down for a moment before turning her eyes to the other two. "They are the two most powerful beings on this side of the universe. Given time, I would say that Princess Asora has that potential, but Laxur also has the coin of fire."

Asora nodded. "Yes, I know, and I am told by our spies that she has the coin of earth as well. But she is not the only one with coins. I have two as well—the coins of water and wind."

Combat Training

"Excellent! At least we have that. We will need to work with those and learn how to diffuse the coins of fire and earth. I will search out whatever writings we have on the coins and teach you how to use the power of water and wind. They will be your strengths when you go into battle." T'a turned to look at Rakon. "You have been teaching her physical combat. I will need to teach her how to use her powers when she fights."

The demon and princess smiled, and Asora said, "That is what we hoped for."

There was a knock on the door, and the servants on the other side opened it for the prime minister.

"Your Highness." He bowed to her, and the princess motioned for him to sit.

He sat and helped himself to some fruit and a cinnamon bun. "How is the training going?"

She had to let Frenzen know what she was up to so that he can vouch for her absences or her accidents that she had when she appeared hurt.

Asora put her coffee cup down. "We have a strategy. Rakon has spent the early morning working me hard in physical combat, but I need more than that. I need T'a to teach me magical combat. I am years behind Laxur, and I must catch up quickly."

"Yes. Laxur has years of experience in the Darkcon military, learning magical and physical combat. Rakon?" Frenzen poured himself some coffee.

No servants were allowed in while the four of them were together.

"Yes?" The demon swallowed his bite of steak.

"We know that she is not physically equal to Laxur, but are you able to teach her how to use her agile abilities to counter Laxur's bigger powers?" The elf took a bite of the cinnamon roll, waiting for the answer.

"Yes, that was my thought exactly, and we have the two coins of power." Rakon went back to his steak.

T'a lifted a fork. "That is my department. I will teach her how to control her considerable power." She turned to Asora. "Meditation will be your homework. When can we begin?"

Frenzen wiped his mouth with his napkin, swallowing. "The court must not know what we are doing. I do not trust them. I am sure several of them are secretly being paid by the Darkcons for information on you."

T'a laughed harshly. "That is a given. You cannot trust the court. If there is profit, they will sell out their mother, their father, and their children. I speak from experience, and while things change, that remains a constant."

Frenzen waited for Asora to finish her coffee, then said, "You have court all day. I can only suggest you continue to meet in the predawn hours in the gardens. At least there it is not possible to spy on you."

He picked up a banana and ate it, waiting for the others to comment. T'a immediately spoke. "Prime Minister, I will need to train Princess Asora in meditation, so I should see her privately as well. Will that look suspicious if I came every night? It is imperative that she train to control the coins."

Asora thought for a moment. "Perhaps I can say that I am asking you for diplomacy lessons to help me in court, or I need help with dealing with the elves. My schedule is very full, so I can ask for you to come after dinner. It cannot be in the morning because I spend my hours before court with Frenzen going over the day's work. What do you think?"

He nodded. "Yes, I think that should work. It is no secret that you and the elves differ in opinions. Thinking that they are special and that their ideas matter more than others will stroke their egos."

The people at the table snickered at the words. All of them, the elves included, felt that the aristocratic elves of the court were arrogant. The noble elves made it clear on several occasions that they, being the oldest living beings, were more intelligent and should always be listened to. They did not understand that living longer did not always give one wisdom.

It was decided that Asora would practice two hours in the morning and one hour in the evening. It was going to be a long day.

Combat Training

It was about eight in the evening when T'a was admitted into Asora's sitting room with a package in her arms. She curtsied to the Princess, and Asora turned to the fairies, saying, "You may go." They bowed in the air and disappeared.

"We should practice in your bedroom," T'a suggested.

They went to her room, and T'a gave the package to Asora. "Here, these are your training clothes. They will help you meditate and will give you more freedom with your combat lessons."

The princess smiled and looked at the new clothes. They were light, grayish-blue, and made of cotton. The shirt was long, split at the sides, and sleeveless. The bottoms were long and held up with a string.

"How decadent! Pants for a woman! I doubt the court would approve, but it will be better to fight in." She laughed with rosy cheeks. It was scandalous; she loved it! How much easier it would be to practice with the sword. She impulsively hugged the elf woman. "Thank you, T'a. You have made my life easier."

"You're welcome, Princess. They are the meditation clothes of our initiates at the temples on my home world of Galeron. The meditation requires certain movements of the body to bring mind and body together. Would you like me to assist you in changing?" T'a watched as Asora fumbled with her clothing. To be a Princess, one must wear a lot of ceremonial clothing.

Asora smiled with relief. "Yes, please."

They struggled to get her out of her clothes and into the new ones. When they were done, Asora felt much more relaxed and freer to move.

"Thank you. Now where do we begin? In class you taught us meditation before we began learning the spells. What will be different?" The Princess turned away from the mirror she was gazing in and looked at T'a.

"Let us sit upon your bed, in the middle, so that we may face each other," T'a said.

They sat cross-legged in the middle of her bed. T'a began the lesson. "All right, take a deep breath. You have done this before. Now I want you to go to that place in your mind where your power is. Remember, it is your thoughts that direct your magic. I need you to concentrate on the vase by the window. Pick it up and bring it to us. Go ahead and try."

Asora concentrated on the vase, and it exploded in a ball of flame, setting the drapes on fire.

The two stared at the curtains, and T'a said, "Quickly, use your coin of water. Think about putting the fire on the curtains out!"

The Princess grasped the coin around her neck and pictured water putting out the flames.

Water poured from the ceiling, drenching everything, and suddenly, Sarea came bursting into the room with her pistol in her hand.

"Princess! Are you all, right?" She looked at the two women sitting on the soggy bed and realized that she was being rained on. "What has happened? What was the explosion?"

T'a put her hand on Asora's. "Stop the rain, princess. Now, please."

Asora closed her eyes, carefully concentrated, and stopped the rain. She opened her eyes to look at her wreck of a room. "By the Hananaka, I have made a mess."

T'a climbed off the bed and waved her hand. Slowly the water disappeared, and the room turned back to normal.

The Princess sat on her now-dry bed and sighed. "I need to learn how to do that."

T'a stood beside the bodyguard. Turning to the Princess, she said, "It is only one of the thousand things you need to master." She turned to Sarea. "The Princess was practicing her magic. A vase exploded, and she put out the fire. She is fine. Are you not, Princess Asora?"

"Yes, I am fine. Thank you for your concern. You may go now." The disheveled Princess waved her hand dismissively.

Sarea nodded slowly while looking around the room. She holstered her weapon and bowed out of the room.

T'a and Asora looked at each other and started to laugh heartily. T'a sobered up first. "What happened? You had more control when you were my student."

"You never asked me to touch my inner power before. I was able to perform the magic before without thought. Do you think that the coins have magnified my power?" Asora complained.

"You have never used the power of your mind? Have you noticed that your inner power has increased, or is it the same?" T'a was concerned that this woman was more powerful than she thought, more powerful than any witch on record. Asora would need to learn incredible discipline to control her magic. She would, in time, be Laxur's equal or excel her if she could control it.

"There was no change, but I also felt an outward pull of power." Asora's hand went to the two coins around her neck.

T'a nodded. "I think that will be it for tonight. I will see you two hours before dawn. I will meet you and Rakon. Good night."

"All right. I want you to gently make the wind blow with a light rain. Concentrate on the coins." T'a stepped back from the Princess.

At first, nothing happened, and then a wind began to blow, and the skies quickly turned dark. As the wind picked up, lightning cracked around the three.

Rakon looked concerned about the increasing wind and the clouds that now covered the sky. A bolt of electricity speared the ground at his feet, and he yelled over the howling winds. "This would be a perfect weapon against an Army! I can barely stand!"

"Princess! Are you in control? I said a gentle breeze and a light rain!" The elf grabbed ahold of the demon to steady herself.

Asora looked around her with horror. She was hanging on to Rakon as well. She was soaking wet, and her hair was undone from its braid because of the wind. "I-I . . . cannot control it! Help me, T'a!"

"Give me the coins!" the elf woman demanded.

The Princess fumbled with the clasps and handed them over. T'a clasped them, one in each hand. She clutched them tightly and could feel the tremendous urge to open her hands from the pulsating power that was emanating from them. The force of it was almost overwhelming. She calmed and went deep inside her inner self to allow the energy to move and change. The confusion and frustration that Asora felt had been transformed into the storm, and T'a now needed it to calm down. It took an hour to bring the storm under control. They all looked like they had been through a war, as did the garden. There were barren bushes and uprooted trees everywhere.

"What did I do wrong, T'a?" Asora was in tears at the devastation she had wreaked.

Rakon kept his arm around the trembling elf to keep her from falling to the ground. T'a took a shaky breath. "You have an extraordinary amount of pent-up frustration and hostility. The coins responded to it by unleashing this storm. That is why I emphasized meditation—it is to let go of the negative emotions you carry."

Asora sighed deeply, nodding. "Every day I sit on my throne, listening to the court, who belittle me and treat me as if I am burden to them. I am their ruler! I may be young, but they chose me to lead. They think that because I am only seventeen that they can walk all over me, and I have nothing to contribute. I was raised to rule. I have gone to all the schools for leadership. I know what will defeat the Darkcon Empire. Humans have technology in abundance. The court ignores it because the human's border on heresy by believing in the Hananaka, and that they consider the humans barbarians. We are losing the war because they cling to the old ways of fighting. We are losing the war due to their pride! So yes, I am filled with anger and frustration. Can you understand?"

"Yes, *I* understand." Rakon put his arm around Asora.

"I went through something similar before I was banished to Evorn. I tried to tell them not to go to war, to spend the money on our people. Instead, the warmongers, my *own* people, voted against me. They love war to prove that they are best. They are looking for glory. I suspect that your elves, centaurs, and dwarves are looking for the same. They are more like demons than they would like to believe." The Princess laughed harshly and hugged him briefly before pushing away. It was unseemly for royalty to embrace anyone, but she felt a kinship to the demon—something she had needed for a long time.

T'a smiled at the small hug, knowing that Asora desperately needed friends and allies she could trust, even those that were once enemies. She also noticed that Sarea had moved closer to the Princess. It was time to end the lesson for the day. She said as much, and they were transported back to the royal sitting room.

"I must change before Frenzen sees me in these pants. It would scandalize him, and we would not want to do that. I will meet you in the dining room." Asora smiled at the storm-soaked group and disappeared with her fairies into the next room.

"Let me dry you off. It will attract less attention." T'a closed her eyes, and all three of them felt a cleansing mist about them for a few minutes, then they were clean and dry.

"Thank you, Lady T'a." Sarea gave her a brief bow and moved into the dining room, followed by Rakon, who grunted his thanks.

They waited for Asora to return before they took their seats. A few minutes passed when Frenzen came rushing in.

"Your Highness! We must evacuate the coastal cities *immediately*. We have an immense hurricane brewing over the ocean. It struck so suddenly. Some of the others believe that this is an attack by Laxur. You must use the magic eyes to announce the evacuation!"

The other four froze in horror, as they realized what had happened. Asora's use of the coins, even for that brief time, had destabilized the planet.

T'a stood and quietly said, "Prime Minister. I believe I may be able to help. An evacuation may not be necessary. Give us a few minutes, please."

He looked at Asora for confirmation and noticed her white face. Frenzen looked around the table and saw that they were keeping something from him. "What is going on? You know what caused this, do you not, Lady T'a?"

The elf ignored him and said to the princess, "We have time to go to the gardens. I can use the coins again to bring this under control."

"The coins? What coins?" Frenzen demanded.

"Yes, of course. I cannot believe they are so powerful. I only used them for a moment." Asora was ready to cry. She pulled herself together, and in a flash, they were back in the disaster-struck garden.

T'a pulled the coins of water and wind out of her pocket. Frenzen saw them, and he almost fouled his pants. "Those are the coins of power! You were playing with the coins? My maker, no wonder a hurricane is on its way!"

"Quiet! I need to concentrate." The elf held her hands open and let the power wash over her. Through mental discipline, she was able to calm the winds and restore order to the planet's ecosystem. It took hours, and she was exhausted, falling to the ground. Rakon picked her up, and they went back to Asora's rooms to rest.

T'a had not stopped the storm; that would be impossible. She worked to dissipate as much as she could, but the storm still came. While she was fighting the hurricane, they sent elf witches to the coastal towns to evacuate them. Along with them, they sent centaurs to help the towns' elderly and infirmed to move quickly through the portals, which the witches had made.

They took them to the palace, which was on the coast but was protected with spells. T'a had saved the day. Asora knew she had to learn quickly how to control the coins, or she would be as much a danger to her people as the enemy was.

Chapter Twenty-One
Wrath of the Dark Queen

The court of the Grand Utopian Kingdom was packed with anxious and deeply frightened nobles. The hundreds of nobles and representatives of the noble families and great houses were in the Royal Throne Room where the throne of Princess Asora sat and watched. They had heard that a ship with General Jerval had landed in the rose garden. He had been dropped off there, and then they had taken off in a hurry. He was the field marshal, and he had left two days ago for the Xeanix continent to engage Laxur and her forces. The dark queen had invaded Evorn and had beaten back all three attempts to take back the continent of Xeanix. This time, only the field marshal had returned. It did not look good as the general was dirty and his uniform was torn.

The giant doors of the great throne room burst open, and two of the royal house guards carried in the gravely injured dwarf. He was short, even for a dwarf. His wildly curling brown hair had ash, dirt, and blood embedded in it. His blue-and-red uniform was torn, and a bullet hole grazed the epaulette on his right shoulder. The crowd parted for the dirty, bleeding Jerval, as he made his way towards the princess and prime minister. He stopped before the throne and bowed awkwardly, and Asora nodded in recognition.

"Get this man a chair!" Frenzen called to another guardsman.

"And get some water," Asora said to Kika.

Asora raised a finger, and an elegant chair appeared. The men attending to the dwarf helped him sit, and they stood at attention beside the chair. The general did his best to catch his breath. He was in a lot of pain. Kika came back with a pitcher of water and a glass. She poured it and he drank it down fast.

"Welcome, Field Marshal Jerval. Tell us what has happened," Asora demanded.

He began with a tortured breath. "You were right your highness. We should not have tried again. They were even faster, and my men died before my eyes in moments. We cannot win a battle with such an ill-equipped army! They have guns, bullets, and rockets. We have bows, arrows, and spears." He spat the last words and looked beseechingly at his princess.

"You were right!" He strained to look at the aristocrats, glaring at them. "We *need* the humans' technology! They have even better weapons than Queen Laxur's forces, and they have an army. They need to be asked to fight for us, if they will even consider it, considering how badly we treat them. Well, the joke is on us. They either join us, or there will no longer be a Grand Utopian Kingdom!"

There were gasps, but most looked down at their feet to avoid the princess's hard stare. They were the ones that demanded Jerval attack Queen Laxur and her forces, despite the Utopian army being so ill-equipped. Princess Asora had made it clear that the Royal Guard was not ready. No one wanted to listen to her. Now they had no choice.

"I was kept alive by Queen Laxur herself. She wanted to send you a message," the dwarf general stated.

Asora shifted forward. "What was the message?"

"That there is nothing that you can do to make her leave, unless you give her the coins." The dwarf suddenly clutched his right side, which started to bleed through his tattered uniform. He straightened in his chair.

"Thank you, Field Marshal Jerval. I am sending you to the healers now." Asora Said.

She looked at him for a moment, and then he was gone, leaving an empty chair and bloodstains on the marble floor. There was only silence until the clip-clop of a grizzled centaur moved toward the throne.

"Your highness. You warned us. We need to understand that we were arrogant and thought you a child. We should remember that one of the reasons you were chosen was that you scored consistent excellence in military strategy, which surprised the military. You are gifted with the intelligence to take an inferior force and turn it to your advantage. You are what we need. I say that *you* should lead our military, and I say anyone who is against you is a fool." The centaur explained.

Frenzen smiled. "I agree. It is about time."

The centaur, known as Timus the Marquis, turned to look at his fellow nobles, staring them down. "Anyone else?"

There was silence, and then the dwarf with the most followers stepped forward. "I have no problem with this. We agree and will support whatever action you see fit. This invasion must be stopped and stopped now. We are all endangered. What say you, elves, fairies, mer-people, dwarves, sprites?"

Again there was silence, then a voice called out, "First, what are these coins that Queen Laxur wants so badly?"

"I have the coins of power for wind and water," Asora said as she showed two lockets on her necklace.

The court was in shock, and the same elf called out, "You are a coin bearer? You must *never* give her the coins! It would give her tremendous power over the elements of nature itself. We must protect you at any cost! Whatever actions you see fit to protect yourself must be done. As you know, all Xeanix is our holy land. We must have it back. Please, Princess Asora, retake the land before they completely defile it."

There were nods of agreement from everyone and calls to protect the princess and take Xeanix back. This was news to them. Princess Asora was now considered a sacred coin holder and could use the divine elemental powers of more then one.

Bremmer and his colleagues said nothing, nor did the fairies. They knew that this was doomed to fail. Asora also knew this as well.

An hour later the court was dismissed, and Asora called for her inner circle to come to the war room. It contained communication equipment and screens to keep the princess up to date with the war. Normally the war room was filled with magical images and maps. But Asora wanted a technological setup as she trusted machines more. She was also use to this from her days in the Red Guard SDC.

She had chosen fairies, jewel elves, daemons, and humans of the royal military to run all the technology. She also had elements from the Red Guard and SDC present as well. She trusted them to be circumspect, loyal, and better able to understand the technology than the other races. It had been more than a month of training, and she was still not ready. Asora could fight humans with human weapons and tactics, just not magic users too well. She knew how to summon her magical powers and throw it around. However, using them with discipline was harder than it looked.

Her inner circle was comprised of Frenzen, T'a, T'ula, Madimoy, Jeia, Marevin, Yane, Madimoy, Sarea, Joes, and her angelic cousin Dominus. Rakon was now a recent addition to this circle. They took their places at a round table, each one equal and able to see the others. They each had a laptop in front of them. Two chairs were empty.

"Why the empty chairs, princess?" Dominus looked over to his cousin.

"We are waiting for H'dren and Krychel." Asora said.

"Oh! Is the charming mountain elf H'dren coming?" T'a smiled at her.

"He is not a mountain elf," Asora advised.

"What?" She looked dumbfounded around the table. Only Yane nodded, while the others looked just as confused.

"His real name is General Rial Hadren, a human general of our special forces. With him is Sky Marshal Temen Krychel," Yane announced, as there was a knock at the door. Sarea entered with two tall middle-aged human men dressed in the usual garb of mountain elves: brown woolen clothes with a long-hooded cloak.

Sarea stood guard by the door as the men took their seats. She came in right behind them. She was part of the princess's council, but she was also the main guard for them. Joes was also a guard, but he was elsewhere, so guardian duty fell to Sarea this time.

"Good evening, Princess Asora." H'dren smiled and gave a short bow to Asora, and Krychel murmured the same and bowed before they took their seats.

"Princess Asora, what is going on? How are these men here? *Why* are they here?" T'a asked the question everyone, besides Yane, wanted to know.

"When I became princess, I realized that Queen Laxur would start this war. I spoke to Countess Marien, and through much negotiating, I was able to get the human military to come to Evorn."

"They just arrived? I had not heard this, and if I know anything, I know that the court would be in an uproar. You only today got permission to fight." Frenzen was utterly confounded.

"That is true, but they have been here since the beginning of my reign," the brunette girl explained.

"That is barely a year now! Where have you hidden them?" the prime minister continued to question, not with anger, but admiringly.

"They have been in the caves that were carved by the elves during the Great War years with the humans. The palace had been destroyed, towns lost, and the only safe place was the mountains to the east. They used Lake Indigo to dig rooms, passageways, and plumbing. A monumental ocean cave was even created to be used as a subterranean harbor. Now, there is an aircraft carrier inside, as well as several submarines and support ships," Asora stated.

"My maker! How many soldiers do we have, and did you not say that you had a sky marshal as well?" T'a questioned.

"Yes, ma'am. I am here to be sure Queen Laxur's planes never fly again," Krychel announced in a loud voice.

Yane cleared his throat. "The navy will be there too. We have the *Mariah* with us. It is a super-carrier. It is one of the biggest carriers the Consortium has—fifteen hundred meters long. It has one hundred and five jets and one hundred and fifty drones. It has several different types of offensive and defensive gun emplacements. It will easily take on Queen Laxur's navy. And, as Princess Asora said, we have several submarines. With this, we can quickly put an end to this little war."

Asora had a laptop computer in front of her on the desk. She typed on the keyboard, and a picture of Evorn with the continent of Xeanix highlighted popped up on everyone's computer. She wanted to give a visual of what was happening and the plan.

Asora began, "Queen Laxur chose Xeanix because it is the least populated and least guarded continent on this world, but now she has to invade Eradan to get to us. She also wanted to humiliate the elves by taking their holy land. She will be moving soon now that she believes she has effectively wiped out the royal guard. She has, but we have the Red Guard, thank the Hananaka. We can attack her before she begins her campaign against this palace and me. We cannot allow her to get the coins of power or win this war. I appreciate you, General Hadren, Sky Marshal Krychel, and of course you, Admiral Yane. With you gentlemen, we will win this war. How soon can we begin?"

Yane sat forward. "We begin now. I will inform the fairies to get ready to move our ships to the target area. The ones we have on the planet will stay as protection for the palace. It is doubtful that she will get close, but we will have them just in case. We will alert Havaina to fly in ten carriers. They have been awaiting our signal to send them into combat.

"The planes from Havaina should be able to leave in a few hours. By the time they get to Xeanix, it should be an hour before dawn. The fairies are going to be very busy, but they are looking forward to the fight."

General Hadren added, "It is lucky that Queen Laxur has only been here a few days, and the royal guard, though ineffective, were able to keep her busy. I have two divisions ready to go, and I believe that she has the same. My people, however, are better equipped than anyone the Darkcons have ever fought."

"I went over the aerial photos of her campsites where she has been building airfields. It will take her time to make them effective. My people will be taking them out first in the carpet bombing of her forces." The sky marshal looked at Yane. "I believe that you were going to bombard them from the sea, as we bomb by air at dawn. Is that right, sir?"

Asora smiled broadly. "The ambassador for the Darkcons said that the one thing that could stop them would be the Consortium's involvement, but he did not believe that they would ever side with us. I am glad to be a human today. You gentlemen make me proud."

The inner circle stood up and applauded the military men, and they turned red and grinned back. To show their respect to one another.

"Admiral Yane?" The princess turned to her supreme commander.

"Yes, your highness?" Yane asked.

"Get to it. I will be watching from here. I wish you gentlemen good hunting." Asora proclaimed.

Yane cleared his throat. "There is one thing, your highness."

"Yes?" the princess asked demandingly.

"The magical barrier around Evorn that Queen Laxur has put up. Will you have that down by then?" Yane pointed out.

Asora looked to T'a, who nodded. "We will. We go now to tear down her curtain. I will contact you to tell you when to begin."

T'a took out a book and started to read. She was looking for the spells that she believed that Queen Laxur used. She knew of most of them, but the Darkcon queen was very intelligent. The queen also knew of spells, hexes, and curses that T'a may not be familiar with.

Lady T'a thought that the Roewe Crystals might help. However, all but three were taken. One was with the Darkcon Dame Dari, the other two were lost. The angels took the others away after the Great War ended five hundred years ago. T'a learned how to use the crystals during the war. The crystals made T'a so powerful that her own powers dwarfed Queen Laxur's current levels. But all that power turned T'a into an evil monster clouded by rage and sorrow. Because of those damned crystals T'a was hated by Asora's people. Princess Asora herself may have forgiven her, but others like Madimoy had not.

T'a was not sure if Princess Asora would go for looking for the lost Roewe Crystals. Asora was the type of person that did not want more magical power. And there was another danger, Queen Laxur may become tempted to look for them too. Creating a race that Asora cannot afford. And considering Queen Laxur's abilities, that would be a bad idea.

However, T'a could look for them in secret. In Princess Asora's stead. If T'a could find the lost crystals in secret. Give them to Asora and show her how to use them. That would save everyone and keep the Darkcon's at bay for a time.

Though T'a was surprised that Queen Laxur had not utilized Dame Dari as the giant fallen angel warrior woman had a Roewe Crystal in her heart. Dari was a powerhouse. But for some reason Laxur was not using Dari. Could Queen Laxur be unaware? No, she had to be, there was another reason why. What that reason could be, T'a was not sure. She would need to speak to Princess Asora on this in private.

Two hours before dawn, a flash of light came from between two buildings. It was ten humans and one elf, dressed in forest-camouflaged uniforms with bulletproofing. They dodged between tanks driving up and down the streets. The infiltrators' job was to quietly tell villagers to get to the palace using portals before the bombing began.

"You must take it down, your highness. I can tell you how, having used this myself in the war, but Laxur is more powerful than I am," T'a said.

Asora nodded, and T'a explained that it was a bubble with swirls and eddies, which were weak points. She was to focus on those. And she hoped that her plan worked.

Asora reached inside her mind and then looked up, reaching upward in her thoughts, and she could see the barrier in a golden bubble as T'a said. "I can see it! You were right!"

"You must pierce it with your thoughts. With your raw power, you should be able to do it." T'a watched the princess, who had a faraway look, which is what she wanted to see.

"I see a weak spot. It is on the opposite side of the barrier from where Queen Laxur is standing. It is taking a tremendous toll on her, and she is vulnerable. This could be our way in. Our navy can wipe out her ships in the harbor. She will not be able to put a barrier around her ground troops!" Asora exclaimed.

"That is good, but you need to concentrate on making a hole in the barrier and then widening it to get those carriers and the additional troops in. Come on, princess, you can do this." T'a said.

Asora began with a pinprick, felt it give, and soon it was a rift. It grew, but she was tiring from the effort. She took calming breaths so that she could reach deeper inside herself. It worked, and she began again. It was much easier now. Her strength grew as she needed to make this magic trick work. Once done, the Utopian princess stopped and stood back. She watched as her power did its work on the barrier.

"Yane, this is Princess Asora. You have a hole to go through. Queen Laxur should not be able to repair it. She has already used her power on the barrier and has no reserve power. Do it now, before she has a chance to get her forces ready," the princess ordered.

"Understood. Yane out," the admiral acknowledged.

Many Consortium war machines surged through the growing rift that Princess Asora created. She and T'a could hear the attack happening. The Red Guard forces were making themselves known. Princess Asora hoped that this will force Queen Laxur to think twice and hopefully leave.

As the sun began to stretch its light above the horizon, the rain of artillery began with the shriek of aircraft flying toward the Darkcons. The town was obliterated in moments, along with the many tanks that were there.

The carrier, in bright, blossoming lights, appeared outside the harbor and began to attack Laxur's armada. The missiles hit their targets with deadly accuracy, and the wreckage flew into the air as they were obliterated. It took hours to clear the area, and the naval men watched as the aircraft flew overhead to their inland targets.

Queen Laxur watched from her tent in horror at the surprise attack. The Consortium had entered the war on the side of the Utopians! Damn Countess Marien! She would see her pay if it was the last thing she did.

"Golcon! Where is Golcon? The Red Guard are heading for the airfields! Get the guns ready for it and get those airplanes! Damn, where is Sysu?"

Dari appeared, ready to defend her queen. "I saw her racing for your tent. She should be here any minute."

As the bodyguard spoke, the warlord entered the tent. "They came out of nowhere, and my troops are defenseless, but they are manning the guns. The humans will not be unscathed, I promise you that."

"Good. I want as many as you can shot down. Prepare for an assault by their military. It will not be long after the bombing. Have our tanks prepared," Laxur ordered.

"Yes, my queen!" Sysu saluted her and ran out, but not before she looked at S'tie calmly waiting by Laxur. He was an empty husk since the queen ensorcelled him. It was too bad; they could use his knowledge of battle and the humans.

Golcon ran up. "We have to evacuate! The humans are too powerful!" He grasped the queen's arm pleadingly. "You must go back to Dorien. Now!"

Queen Laxur screamed her frustration and overthrew her table, then listened to the explosions outside. She raced outside in the early morning and watched as naval bombardment hit the camp and the jet fighters overhead. At seeing the planes, she reached inside her shirt and grabbed the coin of fire, trying to imbue as much power from it as she could. She shot her hand upward toward the planes to knock them out using fireballs. She knocked one down, but after using most of her power erecting the magical barrier, she had little to give. She collapsed into the dirt, where S'tie found her and carried her back to the tent. He lay her down on the bed.

"My queen, you can do no more. You must go." The grizzled demon stood over her, pleading again.

She climbed off the bed and nodded. "Come, S'tie, we are going. Golcon, have the witches and warlocks get as many of my soldiers home as possible."

She waved a hand, and a portal opened to her fortress. She turned and said, "May the Architect preserve you, Golcon. You and Sysu must follow me quickly if we are not to lose everything."

"Yes, my queen. I shall do as you command."

The campaign was over. The only thing to do was leave the heavy weapons, tanks, and aircraft, and simply to get the soldiers back to Dorien. Laxur would not forget, nor forgive.

Chapter Twenty-Two
The Legend of Rowaton

T'a was in her private palace chambers. Her chambers were like a large apartment with private water closet, tub, and closets. She also had her own private kitchen that she could use to prepare her own meals. T'a also had a large case of books, trinkets, and wooden models. The walls were decorated with pictures, and artworks from throughout her life. This place was made her own. Using the magic in the palace to shape it the way she desired. These chambers were usually for high-ranking nobles who wished to live in the palace. When she was queen long ago, she gave these special chambers to her best friend Queen Atala of the fairy folk kingdoms. But now with Princess Asora, who was allowed to determine the quarter arrangements of the palace. Asora wanted T'a to be nearby and gave these special magical chambers to her. T'a accepted and kept things of Atala in the chambers to give her pleasant memories of her once long-ago best friend. She imagined that Queen Atala's should haunted the palace and lived in these chambers to want to talk to T'a. Atala loved to talk, gossip, and give advice.

It was early evening, and she was making a simple stew for herself. She spoke her prayers of thankfulness over the bubbling brew. She learned these prayers after she abdicated her throne. She had gone into the mountains to seek solace with the monks and nuns, who had monasteries dedicated to the Maker. She had been in desperate need of their kindness and understanding. She spent two hundred years with them, learning their secrets and forgiveness. She learned so much that the former queen was able to gather her courage and travel. She was even able to disguise herself so that she could travel without being recognized and stopped.

She dished out her meal when there was a knock on the door. Thinking it was the princess, she hurried to the door and opened it; however, she found her usual guard standing there with a cloaked figure. It looked like M'quet, her friend from the monastery. He was an elder mountain elf with long graying hair and a strong, lean frame.

"M'quet?" T'a asked.

He flung back his hood and grinned. He had a tremendous sense of humor. He immediately grabbed her and hugged her until the guard stepped in, roughly pushing him away. Normally this would have been unprofessional. But in his monastery, this was a normal way of saying hello. So T'a welcomed this and returned the hug. However, the guard did not seem to think this was appropriate.

"It is all right! I know this man, and he is welcome in my place," T'a ordered. "You can stand at ease." T'a ordered the guard.

The guard visibly relaxed and went back to his post and guarding duties. If T'a was safe and happy, he was calm. Her safety was his primary concern after all.

"I would be delighted, T'a. Show me how you live in such a constrained place," M'quet said.

They walked in, arms entwined. He was taken by her taste in artwork and found her wooden models an odd choice. But he also remembered that these held special meaning to her. T'a loved ships of all kinds. He told her once that she wanted to be a ship's captain rather than a monarch.

"I was about to eat. I should have enough for you." T'a said.

"Excellent!" M'quet said as he put his staff against the wall near the door. "I admit that I have traveled to get here."

"It must be important to take you from your scriptures." She had been smiling but turned serious as she dished him out his portion.

"And make the journey here to see me personally. I must admit I am very flattered."

"What brought you here to the palace?" M'quet took his bowl and sat with her on a couch.

The candlelight illuminated his solemn face. He was in deep thought. T'a had seen this face many times. It was usually a bad omen as T'a learned long ago.

"Two days ago, a monk from the dragon temple came down to bring me this." M'quet said.

He put his hand into his deep pocket and brought out a package. He laid it on the table. He picked up his bowl and began eating after his prayer.

T'a put down her half-eaten food and picked up the package. It was covered by parchment and tied up with string. This was how most Utopians made a wrapped package. It was so plain and uibiqitis that no one would have guessed that it held a special treasure.

"There seems to be writing on it. And what do the men of the temple want with elves? This temple worships the dragons, who have not been seen for over five hundred years." T'a said.

"They asked that I get this to Princess Asora. They must believe that she is the one written of in the prophecies," the elf explained. "I also hope that she is."

"I will present it to her," T'a said.

"Thank you." He sighed as he finished his bowl. "Now tell me, how you have been?"

A few hours later, T'a appeared in the princess's chambers with the package. Asora had said that T'a was welcome to appear in Asora's chambers when she needed to come and see her. Asora had gotten softer on T'a and had begun to see the former queen as a wise mentor. Asora has also started to want T'a closer to her. T'a herself loved that Asora trusted her more now a days. It was certainly different during the academy days where Asora was one of the most rebellious students T'a ever taught. But at the same time Asora was the most intelligent and cunning student. T'a was also instrumental in Asora's rise to becoming the supreme princess and hopefully a successful leader. A leader T'a wished she could have been.

Also in the room was the elemental demon Rakon. The two seemed to have been practicing in private lessons. Rakon was determined to turn Princess Asora into an honorable warrior. He felt that his honor could be restored by Asora. Much like how T'a saw Asora. Many saw Asora as a form of redemption and salvation. T'a hoped she was right on that.

"Lady T'a? What is it?" Asora asked with surprise.

"I received this last night from a monk, a friend from the mountain monastery. It was given to him by a monk from the Temple of the Dragon. The wrapping has writing on it, so do not throw it away." T'a advised.

Asora was not sure what to say, but she opened her hand to receive it. T'a gave it to her, and the she elf and Rakon looked on as she opened it. The box contained a beautiful pendant. It was a glittering sapphire with a curled, pure gold dragon hugging it. The dragon had glowing blue eyes.

"It's gorgeous!" Asora said in an amazed voice.

The princess immediately put it around her neck. It hung above her breasts and glinted in the candlelight. She then turned her attention to the wrapping. It was filled with diagrams. This reminded her of her time in the SDC when she uses to pass messages to Marevin in wrappers. A lesson that the SDC encouraged if you were not caught.

"It is a map starting at the village of Karas," Asora said.

T'a looked at the old paper. "That is the base of Cold Mountain. That is over two hundred and ninety kilometers away."

"It looks as if the people of the dragon want you to go there." Rakon frowned. "That may not be a good idea. You would be away from the palace and its protection. Within these walls you are protected by spells, guards, and walls. This could be a ruse by Queen Laxur to get you to leave this safe environment."

T'a frowned. "I do not think so. I truly believe that my friend would not be a party to that or be taken in by a lie. He is too good a warlock and has lived a long time."

"Hmm." Rakon seemed unconvinced. "You are not prepared if you must defend yourself." He shook his large head. "Archduke Frenzen would not approve. Nor do I."

"I do not have to go now—" Asora started but was cut off by T'a.

"Yes, you do." T'a glared at them both. "M'quet said that the moon will be in the constellation of the dragon in a week. You must be in the temple by then. It is a great omen for this quest."

"Quest? Who said anything about a quest?" The elemental demon glared at the she elf and grabbed her arm. "What are you not telling us?"

"I am not holding anything back!" T'a tried tugging her arm from Rakon's grasp.

"Then tell us, woman. What else do you know?" He growled menacingly.

"Stop it, both of you! Would you have me ask Sarea to break this up?" Asora commanded.

The bodyguard moved away from the wall, with one hand on her dagger and the other her pistol. Sarea was human, but she was a very special human. Rakon had fought Sarea with mixed results. Rakon eyed her and Asora and decided they both meant business, so he let T'a go, reluctantly. The elf walked two paces away.

"Thank you, princess. What my friend said was that the old priest from the Temple of the Dragon told him that it was important that on the day when the moon passed into the constellation of the dragon, you must be in Karas. The old priest said it was urgent that they see you because of the prophecy." T'a explained.

Rakon growled scornfully. "What prophecy?"

Asora, however, was wide-eyed. "*The* prophecy? Do they think that I could be the Dragon Dancer?"

The elemental demon smiled at that knowledge. "What a symbol that would be for this war! Queen Laxur will go mad with jealousy. Only one other Darkcon has been chosen to be one, and that was the first Darkcon ruler, *the* Laxur, the one your sister named herself after. To see her sister riding a dragon into battle will enrage and rattle her. What symbolism it will be to the Darkcon soldiers will be unpredictable, but it will not be in Laxur's favor, I believe."

"The elves would respect—"

"You mean *fear* a dragon dancer," Asora interrupted T'a. "They have not been seen in the last few hundred years, and that was when they were breathing fire on the palace."

"I am aware of that, and it was terrifying as well as magnificent. They seemed like a divine wind come to judge us. If I had not been so frightened, I would have been in wonder. The humans came sweeping down with their weapons made from the scales of dragons. They crashed down with flames, ice, lightning, and vines with steel thorns. They were devastating." T'a's face was white and had a faraway look.

They could see the scene and feel the horror and awe. Was how dragons liked it. Daemons and dragons were one and the same. The Consortium was full of intelligent dragons that were apart of the Consortium's culture and way of life. The dragons that T'a was speaking of were ancient and powerful beings that even the Consortium's dragon population were in awe of.

"I cannot imagine that the ancient dragons will come to our aid this time." Asora shook her head.

"But think if just one were to join us!" Rakon enthusiastically added.

The princess turned to the demon with a smile. "Have you become a believer? Should I go on this quest?"

"Yes, but I want to go along. You will need a fighter by your side." Rakon said.

"Do you think the dragon would choose you?" T'a asked somewhat mockingly.

Rakon looked down then up with a twinkle in his eye. "Why not?" A princess, an elf, and a demon all joined in a laugh.

The following day Prime Minister Frenzen walked into the dining room to find everyone waiting for him. He could tell they were excited, and then he noticed the new pendant that the princess wore. He knew it from old elf lore— the Dragon Dancer King's Pendant. It was an ill omen. Or it could be a great blessing. He took a step back and was almost hit by the door.

"My maker! What are you wearing?" the Prime Minister whispered.

The two were puzzled, but the other elf stood up. "You must not be afraid. There is no danger here. Yes, the Temple of the Dragon has sent for her, but she will not turn against us."

Rakon stood up. "And why not? She has ample reason. Have your people not been contemptuous of her? Have they not spurned her, as they did to T'a?"

Asora now got up. "That is enough, Rakon. Frenzen, please." She gestured to for him to come in and sit.

Frenzen shifted his stiff limbs, pulled out a chair, and sat. The others joined him.

The prime minister cleared his throat. "What has happened, Princess Asora?"

She fiddled with her silverware for a moment before looking up. She did not expect that he would react that way. "We think it has to do with the prophecy."

"The prophecy says there will be great change. We need that, Frenzen, and we have it with the humans joining the war," T'a said breathlessly, pleadingly.

"It also says that there will be great pain and sorrow before this change, and she has not been crowned queen yet. It could mean we do not win this war, or that Queen Laxur has got another weapon or plan—one we cannot fight!" He thumped the table, surprising everyone.

"That is a possibility, but it could mean that we eventually defeat her. Think, Frenzen! There is supposed to be great change, but with it comes great peace." Asora stared at the archduke.

"It also says that the one called must make a quest, a dangerous quest that must be made alone. This you cannot do. You are the princess, and you must be protected at all costs." Frenzen stood up. He was ready to eat, having made his decision, but Asora had to eat first. "Princess, may I get you breakfast?"

"Yes, of course." Asora handed him her plate. "Fruit and yogurt, please, but we have not finished this conversation. I will bring my guard, the fairies, Lady T'ula, and Lord Marevin to guide me. The people of the temple will realize I cannot go alone and will allow me this."

Frenzen handed her the breakfast and got his own. Sitting down, he looked up and sighed. He did not like how this was about to go.

"It is possible, I suppose, if you bring all of them with you. But I do not believe that we should tell the court." He took a bite of food.

Rakon sat down with his food. "I will also go with her."

The prime minister swallowed. "I do not think that would be appropriate with the house guard already going with the princess. It will cause discord."

"I do not agree, because she will need a good swordsman." The demon shook his head.

"That is why Marevin is going," the archduke pointed out. "And T'ula is going as another spell caster, if I understand correctly why Princess Asora chose those two. Did I, Your highness?"

Asora nodded. "Yes, Frenzen, that is correct." She turned to her new friend. "I believe he is correct about the house guard. They are rather upset with your race right now, with the war and all."

"You think that I would allow you to be hurt? I could have done that at any time." Rakon stated.

"But you would have been caught, but if you allow her to fall in a quest, well that is just an accident." The archduke eyed Rakon and then smiled. "I do not believe that, but everyone else will. Also, no one knows that you are training her other than Admiral Yane. He believes that you are doing a good thing. He is very progressive, I have found."

"All right." The demon held up his hands and went back to his breakfast. "As long as no one here believes that."

"How should we proceed, Your Grace?" T'a asked.

"I will inform Admiral Yane to choose the personal guard. I want no one from court to realize you are gone. Between Yane and I, we will figure something out," the archduke stated.

"Better make it quick. I have a feeling that you may be right about Laxur, prime minister." Rakon looked at everyone around the table. "She will not take the humans halting her advance very well. She will be planning something."

"Hmm. I know my sister's temper, and Rakon may be right." Asora sat back with a troubled look on her face. "I believe that we had better hurry."

Frenzen cleared his throat. "You know what this quest really means, who this is really about?"

Asora nodded. "Rowaton, the king of the dragons. He must be ready to be reborn. It is said that he will come alive again at a time of great need."

The prime minister frowned. "That is what is bothering me. Think about it: Laxur has been defeated, the humans are working with us for once, we may still be at war, but we are not doing that badly. What great crisis is coming that we need the god king himself?"

The demon sat forward. "Is it true that he can speak, T'a?"

"Yes. He has a great, deep voice that is cultured. He is quite magical as well. The human king that rode him was able to do magic, when he had not been able to do so before."

"But that is because Rowaton had actually done it." Frenzen shrugged.

"No!" T'a shook her head. "The power was shared through their bond. The king was able to perform great feats of magic, such as breaking the spell of protection of one of my ministers who rode a gryphon. He was then able to use a gun and kill him from a great distance. It took but moments."

"If it happened so fast, how do you know?" Rakon demanded.

T'a answered, "I know because he did it repeatedly around the people that surrounded me, to protect me. They fell over dead all about me, and I would have been as well, but they wanted me alive. I was to pay for starting the war. It was then that the angels came, but Rowaton ended it by eating the prime minister. Rowaton read my heart and knew it to be true. It is the only reason I still live. I have the protection of Rowaton."

"It must be why they contacted you first. Only you can answer the intimate questions regarding Rowaton and the quest," Rakon commented, "such as his ability to read minds."

"He cannot simply read minds. There is more to it than that," Asora explained.

"How else do explain the reading of your heart?" Rakon asked.

"I had to be in physical contact by allowing him to place his hand around me. Rowaton must have physical contact with the person." T'a touched her hand to her chest in remembrance.

"It was quite unnerving," she whispered and then took a deep breath. "He picked me up and brought me up to his face to look me in the eye." She looked around the room. "It was a long way up his muscular body. He is of monstrous size."

"You must have been terrified." The princess put her hand on the elf's.

She looked at the princess's hand on hers and smiled, nodding. "I was, but it was the only way to end the war. I was ready to accept my fate. At that time, I believed I was going to be eaten, but Rowaton refused."

"I had not heard this. I thought the angels were the ones to determine that it was your Prime Minister at fault, and that was why Rowaton burned him. No one has ever mentioned that you were originally on the menu. Was it because the humans wanted your death regardless, or was this before the prime minister was discovered?"

"The humans. They and the dragons wanted me dead without knowing I was tricked. The angels had their say, but they weren't believed. In anger, he picked me up and our minds met. It was horrifying. I felt the overwhelming hatred for me and the deadly want in his thoughts."

Rakon shook his head. "Wait, wait. You said you had to allow him to read your mind. You are saying that you had no choice."

"I did nothing to stop him. I could have defended myself, but I had to stop the war." Asora nodded. "I understand. So, what happened next?"

"I felt his thoughts changing with my own. I felt him begin to understand that I didn't want the war, and he tucked me protectively to his chest and spoke, saying that what the angels said was true, and he would protect me, much to the horror of the humans. I, in turn, created the Temple of the Dragon in the Cold Mountains for Rowaton to have as his home, and I promised to be nearby at all times if needed. I suppose that I am needed now. The quest must mean that a great moment is upon us."

"It must be something we are not expecting. The Darkcons have been quiet—so quiet that they must be building up their strength. They will attack us and attack hard. We simply do not know where," Frenzen said.

Rakon turned to T'a. "What else do you know of Rowaton? What else will Asora gain as his dancer?"

The elf splayed her hands and said, "Only what I have already told you. She will know his thoughts, and he will know hers. They will be able to help each other by sharing power. Both will be stronger for it. Oh, he has the daemons that protect him as he sleeps. They will be with you on the quest. They will test your strength to see whether you can be a Dragon Dancer."

Rakon laughed. "I have heard of this story. I did not know it was true until now. Good to hear it." Frenzen shook his head. "Why daemons as protectors?"

"They were much taken by the dragons and declared themselves to be apostles of them. Do not be mistaken in thinking that these daemons are like the demons that the Darkcon Empire has. These are the ancient daemons, the most powerful ones," T'a calmly explained.

"Hmm. That should make the journey to the temple interesting." Asora sighed.

Chapter Twenty-Three
Into the Mountains

It took two days to figure out how to get Asora to Cold Mountain in secret. Yane and Frenzen argued with the inner circle, but they hammered out an agreement. Princess Asora would get not only her personal guard but also a group of air assault soldiers who specialized in helicopter hit-and-run attacks. They were the best of the best humans for this type of quest.

Princess Asora, the fairies, Lady T'ula, and Lord Marevin, who was excited to be included in his love's quest, went to Asora's room, and transported to the caves where the helicopters were housed. They got in and headed out with the royal guard.

It was soon apparent that the humans and the royal guard had issues. This was however not unexpected. They bickered back and forth, discussing their various training and who was best, much to Yane's amusement. The admiral was only there to make sure that the princess got to Karas.

"That contraption is going to drop out of the sky!" One of the Royal Guard knights complained to his human Red Guard officer counterpart.

"Helicopters have been a reliable form of flight for centuries!" The male human officer complained. "We used them with great effect on your dumbasses during the Great War."

Those other flying machines of yours with wings I can tolerate, but this thing?" The elf knight yelled in frustration.

A jet does not work here without an airfield!" The human officer yelled back.

"Shut it the both of you!" Marevin roared.

The two then jumped to attention once they realized who it was. They also saw the princess herself. They both were sweating. Asora then approached them.

"I take it that you two are having trouble with this machine?" Asora asked as she pointed to the helicopter.

"My counterpart here does not seem to understand the physics behind the helicopter," the Red Guard officer said.

"The helicopter uses lift like a gliding bird. Only that this machine forces lift down and the opposing force causes the craft to go up," Asora pointed out.

"I have tried to explain that" the officer said.

"I am merely concern for your safety, your highness," the knight explained.

"I appreciate your concern. But I have flown these helicopters and certified for combat in them," Asora said almost proudly.

"If you are that comfortable with this thing, then I should be," the knight said.

"Thank you," Asora said with a smile.

"However, I am going to fly this. I would rather fly this then you," the officer then paused. "No offense."

"Of course, this is your chariot. I am merely a passenger," Asora said.

The doors to the helicopter opened up automatically, and a small stair deployed to make getting inside easier. Princess Asora entered first and sat down and buckled up. Behind her was Marevin, Yane, then T'ula. The four fairies then flew in and in Asora's dress. The Red Guard officer then closed the doors and hoped into the cockpit. The Royal Guard knight got into the co-pilot seat. The helicopter powered up and was in the air in moments.

The craft flew into the mountains in the distance. T'ula looked to see that they were hundreds of meters in the air. The noise was deafening, despite the noise dampening and noise cancellation technology used in

Into the Mountains

the hull. Asora and Marvin did not seem bothered by the noise though.

It only took five minutes to come across the village in the mountains. There was an area of flat land just outside the village where the helicopter could land safely. There was no one to tree them as a helicopter was unusual.

Normally when the head of state came to them, they came by carriage and chariot. Flying in by flying machine was scary to them. Asora at this point did not care. It was faster to get to the village by helicopter. She could have used her magic to get here even faster. However, she needed to use her powers sparingly. She needed to use her powers in this quest.

The passengers exited the helicopter once the doors opened. The engine was shut off and the rotor blades stopped. Princess Asora was out first and with T'ula, Yane, and Marevin behind her. Asora was getting use to not being greeted, even though it is an insult. But for the moment she needed to get this quest underway.

They arrived outside the small mountain town, the helicopters creating a whirlwind as they landed. The soldiers immediately sprung out to secure the site before the Princess and her companions could debark. What did surprise her, however, was that a large contingent of specialized Royal Guardsmen were coming up the hill. These knights were specially chosen by Captain Joes as they did respect the princess. Another force came up just below the landing hill, more helicopters full of SDC commandos.

An older knight who was a grizzled elf fairy hybrid and looked to have seen his fair share of fighting in his life came up to Asora. He saluted her sharply, and he showed her respect.

"Your highness, sorry we are late," the knight said.

"Not a problem Lord Cavi, do what you need to do," Asora saluted him back.

Lord Cavi barked out orders to both his special knights and even the SDC commandos. They all went into the town like an invading force. They did not attack but caused enough of a commotion to get the mayor outside.

Lord Cavi was one of those old-time soldiers that did not care who was in charge, you still respected them. Princess Asora was no different. Also, Cavi respected Asora as she sponsored his grandson into the Royal Guard School. Cavi was also one of the very few Royal Guardsmen that knew his trade and tactics, and she could trust to get the job down with minimal losses and waste.

The town was overwhelmed by both the commandos and the royal guard. The mayor was in both a panic and in a rage as he saw the dozens of knights and SDC commandos in his quiet town. Then he became more scared as he saw Princess Asora just outside the town.

The mayor walked up to Yane. "Have we done something to offend the royalty? Are we under arrest?"

"The princess is here to visit your town. You have no cause to be alarmed. We thought you had been told of our coming by the people of the temple," the admiral pronounced.

"We were expecting someone, of course, but not the princess. And we were expecting a visit tomorrow not now! My maker, who would have thought!" The mayor quivered with fear at the thought.

Yane thought the man looked a little too frightened. "Is there something I should know?"

"Know? I-I simply did not expect this! I do not normally deal with the people at the temple. To be honest, they scare me. Dragons do that to us elves, you know."

Yane nodded and dismissed the man and his worried countenance.

"Admiral Yane? Who was that?" Asora walked up in her commando uniform.

It made Yane smile to see the little princess dressed as a soldier in forest camouflage. It was agreed because a long white dress would be in the way. Asora also felt more comfortable in combat fatigues then a white dress. Asora was odd in the sense as she loved her combat boots over her dress shoes.

The Royal Court and other noble ladies often chassis Asora for her choice attire. She was supposed to be the one who representing the kingdom and its beauty. The elegant white dresses, fancy shoes, and expensive jewelry were all meant to make Asora as beautiful as possible. Asora herself however did not think like that. Asora wanted to be seen as intelligent and tough. In the society she came from a military uniform gave that impression.

Asora and her companions began wandering around the town. They were unconcerned about the troops, but the townsfolk were however very concerned. They all hid inside their homes and businesses. The few brave ones looked nervous. This was not what Asora wanted, but she understood why.

"What are we to do? What does the note say, kitty?" Marevin looked around.

Asora sighed and decided to let the nickname go without comment. "No, it does not say anything about this, and it appears that we will receive no help from these villages."

Princess Asora and Lord Marevin walked down the main street. The soldiers lined much of the street to keep Asora and her guests safe. Other soldiers were in civilian clothing moving more easily among the crowds.

The mayor then walked up to them, "Your highness. If you would follow me, we can speak in my office."

Asora, Yane, Marevin, T'ula, and the four fairy sisters followed the mayor to his office. The mayor's office was a small wooden building with a few rooms. It reminded Asora and Marevin of a logged cabin in the forest. It made sense to them considering that this village was deep in the mountainous forest of Evorn. The mayor's office only had a few rooms and the main room was small and had a desk surrounded by book cases full of files.

The mayor sat at his desk, "May I ask the reason for your visit?"

"Tell me about this," Asora gave the paper to the mayor.

The mayor looked at it and hummed to himself. He had seen things like this before. His village was a sort of gateway to the temple.

"The Temple Mount of the Dragon God Rowaton," the mayor said.

"You know of it?" Asora asked.

"This village partly exists as a gateway of sorts. But also, a means for the monks that live in the mountains to view the outside realm. But they rarely come here," the mayor explained. "Where did you get this?"

"Someone came to the palace a few days ago and gave me this," Asora explained as she pointed to the paper.

She was not about to show him the amulet that was in the package. She did not know how he would react.

"What can you tell us about them?" Yane asked.

"The monks? Or the Temple?" The mayor asked.

"Both," Marevin answered.

"Well, the temple is hidden deep in the mountainous forests near the top," the mayor started. "It is said that an egg is at its center and only the legendary Dragon Rider can make it hatch. The one that had been chosen by the god king of the dragons themselves."

"Okay so its a half an hour ride by helicopter to the top," Marevin said.

"No, your human made flying machine cannot go up there. You must traverse the mountain by foot," the mayor said. "Besides, it is not a good idea to fly in the Cold Mountains at this time of year. Or any for that matter."

"Why is that?" Yane asked.

"The Cold Mountains get their name because the whole mountain range extends all the way to the northern polar region of Evorn. They act like a massive funnel that allows the cold air from the distant north to surge down at all times of the year," the mayor explained. "The Palace was built where it is partly because of that. It blocks the bitterly cold air from burying the main village below, as well as protecting the farmland and seas."

"That does make sense actually," Yane said.

"Even during the Great War, the Consortium added to the palace to prevent a glacier surge from coming down," the mayor pointed out. "Good thing they did too."

"What about the monks?" T'ula asked.

"For the most part they stay in the temple, the new ones come down here every so often to gather supplies, and learn about current events," the mayor explained. "Speaking of, did the Royal Guard manage to dislodge the Darkcons off of Evorn?"

"No not yet," Asora answered. "Queen Laxur is far more formidable they we all thought."

"Well, even she would have problems getting past the guardians," the mayor mentioned.

"Guardians?" Yane questioned. "What guardians?"

"The monks?" T'ula asked.

"The monks are more like caretakers and a last line of defense," the mayor pointed out. "The guardians live throughout the mountains, protecting the paths, and all the dark corners. They even defend the temple itself. I have never seen one myself, but I have heard all sorts of strange tales about them."

"What are we dealing with?" Marevin asked.

"Rumor has it that the guardians are a special breed of elemental demons. They draw their power from the mountains, and the surrounding environment themselves," the mayor said as he thought about it.

"How many of these guardians are there?" Asora asked.

"Oh, I do not know," the mayor shrugged. "It can be anywhere between half a dozen to a couple thousands."

"Oh, fucking great," Marevin blurted.

"And they could be elemental too," Yane added.

"The guardians will allow you to pass if you complete their challenges," the mayor said. "Every guardian you encounter will have a challenge unique to them. If you pass, they will not only allow you through. They will also protect you from the others and are honor bound to serve you for all time."

"Oh," Asora said. "That would be helpful." Then she had another thought. "What kind of challenges are we talking about?"

"It could be anything from questions to physical challenges," the mayor said.

"Great," Asora said in a sarcastic tone.

"And we still have Queen Laxur and her forces still on Evorn," T'ula pointed out. "We need to get through this fast."

"This sort of thing cannot be rushed," the mayor said.

"Even with a massive enemy force on the planet?" Bane demanded.

"Even if Evorn is about to be destroyed. Even if Queen Laxur devours our world, the monks and the guardians will move as if it was all normal," the mayor tried to explain.

"Well then," Asora started. "We should get started."

"I recommend that you stay the night. As going into the mountains now would be a deadly prospect. It is best to go in the early morning," the mayor said.

"Very well then," Asora replied. "I and my entourage will need accommodations for the day and night."

"We have a small Inn that can meet all of your needs," the mayor said. "It is the only three-story building in the village."

The entourage of the princess made their way to the Inn which Asora learned was called Dragoona Inn. It was managed by a rare fairy/elf hybrid woman who reminded Asora of an older and crankier Kika. The Inn keeper had never had a noble or a monarch patron her inn.

The inn itself was small and very outdoor in its aesthetic. There was a large dinning hall and pub on the first level. The inn was practically taken over by the Royal Guard. The Inn had not been this full in years.

Princess Asora assured that the Inn keeper would be well compensated for her troubles. The Inn keeper was annoyed by all the soldiers. She also did not know how to take care of the princess. It took the keeper by surprise when Asora was setting a fire in the fireplace. She was stunned by the princess's level of self reliance.

The dinner was also interesting as Asora demanded that her troops be served first. Asora even had her four fairy servants assist the Inn's personnel to make the effort easier. Eventually Princess Asora did get to eat, and the food was not bad, but it was not the best. She did not want to be rude, so she ate it. She really wanted an MRE, but the Inn keeper personally made her meal and she wanted to be a good guest to her.

"You look like you want a cookie," Marevin said when he noticed Asora's look and slow movements on her dinner.

"I am suddenly reminded of boot camp," Asora said. "Remember the three-day march?"

"Oh yeah," Marevin laughed. "You said it was the first time you ever cooked anything yourself."

"Did it show?" Asora asked.

"Do you really want an answer to that?" Marevin asked.

"I suppose not. Now I see what it must have been like for you," Asora said as she ate another bite.

"At least you are being kind to our host," Marevin said. "Here, I will help you."

Marevin took a piece of meat from Asora's plate. She let him as he seemed better able to handle the food then she could. He in turn gave her his bowl of chocolate pudding. Asora loved chocolate pudding and could not resist the temptation for it. To her surprise the pudding was good to her.

Later that night Princess Asora was in her small room reading a book by the candlelight. Gourni had complained that Asora really should try to sleep. Bane said that she had a fairy remedy that could help Asora sleep.

"I will be fine," Asora complained to the four fairies hovering around her.

"We have your camping gear ready, and we also want you to sleep!" Gourni snapped as she landed on the table in front of Asora.

As if to emphasis her point Gourni stomped on the table. She did this every time Asora was doing something she did not like. Things that Asora knew when Gourni was right. The little green fairy was the leader of the quartet and had a commanding personality to match. She was also the one person that Asora respected enough to take orders from.

"I have managed to fit everything into your special backpack," Friea the red dressed fairy said exhausted. "That was a lot of stuff."

"Well other then bathing you have no other reason to be up!" Gourni pointed accusingly at Asora.

"Would you sleep in this situation?" Asora asked Gourni.

"Yes, I would, because I know that I would need all my energy and concentration for the days ahead," Gourni replied matter of factly.

"Okay, I get it," Asora sighed.

The princess was in her lacy night gown and had been ready for bed for a bit already. Both B'nei, and Rayne tucked Asora in. B'nei used her fairy charm to have Asora fall into a deep pleasant sleep.

"She still acts that way. Just like when she was eight," Gourni said exhausted. "I love her, but she has to grow up."

"How motherly of you," Rayne giggled.

"What?" Gourni snapped. "We practically raised her!"

"Except for the SDC part," Friea reminded her sisters. "I am not big on our charge being a member of them. Never was, but it was the law, and she did benefit from it."

Rayne went to the door that led out to the hallway of the Inn. She had heard something odd. The Inn as suppose to be silent at this hour. She thought it could have been one of the knights who were supposed to be on patrol at all times. She looked outside and saw no one in the halls. That was not supposed to be. Rayne's sister then noticed her in the hall and followed her.

"Where are the knights?" Friea asked.

"I do not see any of them," B'nei said.

"They may not like the princess, but they just would not leave their posts," Gourni pointed out. "We need to find them."

"I will get Lord Marevin," Rayne said.

Before they could do anything the last of the candle lights went out. The fairies then felt a warm pressure. The same kind of pressure that their species opposite race gave them, elemental demons. This presence got the fairies into a defensive stance. Rakon gave them this feeling too.

The fairies then lit themselves in the glow of their dominant colors. Green for Gourni, purple of Rayne, blue for B'nei, and red for Friea. Their glow did not go far as the darkness was very pitch black. But they could feel that someone was in the hall with them.

"Show yourself!" Gourni demanded.

The response was a soft breathing, from a female elemental demon. They could tell because female elemental demons tend to be low or quieter. They just could not see this elemental demon. Elemental demons for the most part were members off the Darkcon Empire and thus the enemy.

"Is it possible that this demon has killed the knights?" Bane asked.

"It would not surprise me," Rayne replied.

"But I do not sense or feel death," Friea added.

"We still need to protect the princess," Gourni said.

A letter fell to the floor. Then the feeling of the elemental demon also vanished. The candles then relit themselves. Gourni saw the letter and flew down to it. The letter was bigger than she was. But Gourni opened it to see its contents.

"What is it?" Bane asked.

"It is for Princess Asora," Gourni said. "It says that we are ready for you to come."

The next morning Princess Asora was made aware of what her fairy ladies in waiting encountered. Gourni gave Asora the letter. Asora took it as a good sign and that her quest was granted by either the monks or the guardians.

Lord Marevin was outside on the street with T'ula and Yane. Several of the knights were also around them. When the fairies informed Admiral Yane of what they saw last night. The admiral went on a tear with the knights and demanded to know what the hell they were doing. Yane and the fairies got no real concrete answers.

Princess Asora emerged from the Inn dressed in comfortable fatigues. She was ready to venture into the mountains. She had her backpack on and comfortable boots on. Lady T'ula was with her as well, but she was dressed in a more lady fashion.

"I am ready to go," Asora said as she came up to Marevin and Yane.

"This street leads out into the mountains," Marevin pointed to the path that led up the mountain.

The mountains had a path and there was even a river that was in the distance. The river came down into a waterfall somewhere deep in the valley.

Princess Asora and her entourage walked down the street and out go the village. They continued to wander down a path leading threw of the village. It seemed to go down to a river, and it looked inviting. They were soon out of sight.

Yane looked like the princess walked down the path and was suddenly gone. He followed down the path and felt like he hit a wall. It was some sort of barrier. He could not follow the princess.

"Find me that mayor now!" he bellowed at his troops.

They went on a house-to-house search, wrenching open doors or kicking them down, dragging the elves out. Finally, they found the terrified mayor.

"What just happened?" He grabbed the man by the throat, and the other soldiers pointed guns and swords at him.

"I-I told you! We did not know it would be the princess. These people guard the dragons! What were we to do? They did not tell us that you would not be allowed to go! How were we to know?" the mayor cried out.

"You realize this is treason? That I could put you to death? Tell us all what you know. Now!" Yane ordered.

"Hey! Where did the town go?" T'ula looked up the path and saw nothing but the woods. The town was gone.

Asora turned around, as did Marevin. "I do not know. Let us go back."

"Where are the soldiers? Where is Admiral Yane? He was at the top of the hill." The young lord walked ahead, pulling his sword.

The Princess pulled her pistol, and they walked to the top of the hill and found a wall that separated them from the town.

T'ula tugged on Asora's shirt and whispered, "This must be part of the quest. The soldiers cannot go on with you. It is up to us to guard you now."

The fairies fluttered close to Asora, ready with their magic.

Chapter Twenty-Four
The Princess's Quest

Asora turned around and nodded, swallowing hard. She felt very alone, but she straightened her shoulders. She knew that this was a possibility. She should look at this as liberation. Yes, that was it. It was freeing to be away from the troops. She looked at her protectors and decided that they were very good at what they did. She would be fine. She smiled at them and strode back down the hill to the bridge that forded the river. She could do this, Asora told herself. She had to, to save her kingdom. Her two companions that managed to stay with her, Marevin and T'ula

An hour later Princess Asora, Lord Marevin, and Lady T'ula managed to make their way to the river. It was very cold just like the air around them. But there were a lot of trees, bushes, and grass all over. The watering the river was moving fast, and they could hear the waterfall that was further up stream.

"If it was not so cold this would be a beautiful place," T'ula commented.

"I would feel safer if we had the tin guards," Marevin commented.

Gourni, Rayne, B'nei, and Friea flew out of Asora's dress and looked around. Asora was happy that the four fairy ladies in waiting managed to get through with her. But she noticed that they looked concerned. They orbited Asora in a protective manner.

"What is it?" Asora asked the four concerned fairies.

"We are not alone here," Gourni said.

"There is a bridge further down stream," B'nei pointed to a structure in the distance.

The small troop made their way to the bridge that B'nei saw. The bridge was old looking but it seemed to be sturdy and well kept. Asora thought that perhaps a guardian or a monk took care of it. That could explain the bridge's appearance.

They began to cross when they noticed another figure crossing from the other side. It looked to be a daemon, a stone daemon. *Ah, the first test. It cannot be easy, can it?* the princess thought. *Or I will get my ass kicked. Either way, I will* know *what I am going to deal with.*

The daemon spoke, sounding like rock against rock. "You may not pass until you have defeated me in honorable combat!"

Marevin jumped into action and attempted to attack. He was very quickly knocked sideways by a great stone arm. T'ula ran to Marevin and examined him. Asora thought hard. It was within her to pass the daemon, or she would not have been chosen. It was within her. She had so many depending on her.

"Girls, take over from T'ula," Asora commanded her ladies in waiting.

The four fairies raced to Marevin and T'ula came up next to Asora. "I am here your highness."

"Lady T'ula, hit it with your fire spells and see if you can melt some of it. I will concentrate on using freezing rain and concussion spells with my coins of power. It is something that T'a has been teaching me. It should blast away the stone." Asora commanded.

Asora took a deep breath and calmed herself, as T'ula nodded and began to send torrents of fire at the beast. Marevin got out of the way as the four fairies carried him to safety. They had to paralyze him to prevent him from injuring himself further.

The princess took careful aim at the elemental stone demon and attacked. It hit its mark, and the stone elemental demon was blown backward. Chips blew off, but he came again. He reformed himself using other rocks, sand, and boulders. This allowed the demon to regenerate.

The heat form Tula's fire spells and ever-growing flames had less effect as the demon regenerated. T'ula continued the fire regardless and was barely melting the stone. Then Asora hit it with ice, which settled into the cracks of the rock and exploded.

Again, the demon reformed itself from the surrounding rock, and sand. It managed to throw several boulders at Asora and T'ula. It managed to hit T'ula on her head and knocked her out. The demon then turned to Asora and spat a spew of lava at her. Asora managed to dodge the lava spit. The trees behind her ignited into flames.

T'ula managed to recover as the fairies were carrying her to safety. Friea had used a herb to help T'ula recover. She was placed next to Marevin who looked very annoyed at being paralyzed. T'ula felt as helpless as he did. They could hear the battle still happening. They also saw several trees ignited in flames. They also heard the demon scream in pain. But they could not see the battle.

"Good news, Rayne found a Cerimbria weed," Gourni said. "We will have you two back up and in the fight in a few minutes."

"Good!" Marevin struggled to say.

"How is Princess Asora fairing?" T'ula asked with concern.

"She is holding out, however, Asora needs help," Gourni answered. "Rayne hurry with the potions!"

The princess sent more concussion waves at the demon, sending it back again and again for hours, until it was down on its knees. Asora was breathing heavily.

She had her sword out, "I am still standing."

"So you are," the demon spoke. "You fight with honor."

Just as Asora was nearing exhaustion and was about to collapse, the demon split apart and disintegrated. Asora watched as the demon seemingly vanished. It left behind a tablet, and the fire from the lava burned out. Marevin who had recovered went to get grab the tablet, while T'ula and the fairies held up the tired princess. They guided her to a nearby log to sit down. Meanwhile Marevin read what was on the slab. He came towards the women who looked at him with curious expressions.

Asora whispered to Marevin, "What does it say?"

"It says, The power of stone is yours." The young lord handed her the tablet.

It immediately turned warm in her hands and became a hot liquid. The tablet became lava, and her hands absorbed it. She stood in shock, unable to speak as the hot energy flowed to her brain. It merged with the rest of her power, and she grew lightheaded. Marevin caught her as she fell.

"We must get to the other side and find shelter for the princess. You must carry her, my lord." T'ula walked in front, ready with spells if any other creatures came after them.

The young lord carried his heart's desire tenderly over the bridge. Asora was lighter than he thought she would be. Asora was also so exhausted that she needed to rest. So Marevin would carry her to the next part of their journey.

They followed a path until they came to a clearing and a small icy creek. They were more northward then ever. They also were much higher in elevation of the mountains. Marevin had Asora on his back now. T'ula had put a blanket on Asora to keep her warm. The four fairies were also helping to keep Asora warm as well. Marevin's backpack also gave Asora some comfort and helped Marevin hold Asora up.

"There is a place with grass up here?" T'ula said. "We can rest here for a few minutes."

"Great," Marevin replied.

Marevin gently put Asora down on cool grass. He pulled off his backpack and pulled out a tent. He quickly put it up, and T'ula enchanted it to have the things a princess would need: a bed, bathing room, and so on. The others each got a room, but the fairies insisted on sleeping near the princess. They could keep an eye on her and guard her. This would allow T'ula and Marevin to sleep. Both of them were exhausted. Also the sun was covered and going down.

The tents were made warm by special elf candles that radiated heat like a fireplace could. So as the temperature outside dropped to freezing, the tents were warm.

Asora awakened an hour later to find herself on her bed in a tent. It was very soft and inviting, but she was a little confused. She got up and went outside to see Marevin and T'ula, along with fairies, cooking. They were all bickering about what should go in the soup.

"What is it supposed to be?" Asora clear melodious voice flowed over them, and they leaped up.

"Princess!" T'ula walked up with tears in her eyes and looked her over carefully.

"Kitty!" Marevin stayed by the cooking pot, but a bright smile was on his handsome face.

"I am fine. Let me see what you are cooking." Asora knelt to smell the soup.

"You are a good cook. I had forgotten," Asora said pleased. "Way better then I ever have been."

He looked up. "I have not forgotten our trips together with our parents when we were children."

"They thought we should know one another," Asora smiled stiffly and sighed.

She cared for him, but not like he cared for her. The marriage that they would have would be in a few years, regardless. She did love him and he had been one of her best friends for so long that she was use to him. He also respected her and supported her no matter what. He was always on her side. She stood up, and the fairies surrounded her, fluttering around her head.

"How do you feel?" Marevin asked. "How was holding magical lava?"

"I felt like I was filled with power, and it was too much. I have the power of stone within me now, just as I have the coins of water and wind," Asora tried to explain.

"My princess?" Gourni asked hesitantly.

"Yes?" Asora answered.

"What does that mean? The power of stone?" the fairy chirped.

Asora laughed hard and shrugged her shoulders. That made Marevin, and T'ula nervous. The fairy sisters were more curious.

"I have no idea. I am still learning about wind and water. I wish T'a was here. She would know what I am supposed to do with this new power." Asora went down to the creek bed and lifted her hands above the rocks. Nothing happened. "I guess that it does not work on rocks."

"Maybe it is like that demon, Rakon, you have at the palace. He can create metal out of nothing. I have seen him from time to time, and I understand that he is a metal elemental demon. Those kinds of demons can bend metal into anything they want. Their swords and their metal are magnificent. They control electromagnetism as well. Perhaps, the ability is linked to protection," Marevin pointed out.

"You think that I can make a sword out of stone or lava? Out of my hand?" She stared at her hand, and it began to glow. It itched and felt heavier. "My hand is turning into stone!" Her arm became heavy "What am I going to do?" She shook her hand as if it would drop off, and then it hit her leg. "Ow!"

T'ula screamed next. "My maker! It's growing up your arm!"

"WHAT!" The princess could feel it growing, and she was panicking. Marevin grabbed Asora and held her tight, whispering, "Kitty. You must get yourself under control. You are better than this. Now calm down and *think!*"

She felt his strong arms calming her. He believed that she could handle this, and so she thought about her practices with T'a. She slipped out of Marevin's embrace and stood quietly, breathing deeply. She raised her hand and stared at it. She allowed the power in her mind to soothe. Her arm stopped turning to stone. And then her wrist and her fingers shed the rock. She was free.

"That did it!" She jumped up, and when she hit the ground, the earth trembled. Everyone but the fairies fell. "What was that?" T'ula clung to the grass.

Asora stood shaking, and the harder she shook, the worse the tremors got. She took deep breaths, and slowly the ground began to calm. *This was too hard*, she thought. *I must remain calm. Oh, for the Hananaka's sake.*

Everyone stood up and waited for her to lose control again, but she kept her cool and stayed in one place. "Perhaps, I will stand here for a moment."

"Good idea!" T'ula exclaimed.

"Sounds like a plan," Marevin added in.

"We will bring you what you need," the fairies chirped.

Asora stayed in place for a good hour, before she lightly stepped away from everyone. She really wished that Rakon had come. She could use some advice on dealing with her new changes. The daemon that she fought was a much more powerful being, but it would have helped to have a demon on her side.

The earth did not move, so she felt safe to go to the soup pot where the rest of the group watched her with nervous eyes.

"Princess, are you hungry? I could spoon some out for you." Lady T'ula waited for permission before any of them could eat.

"Yes, that would be delightful. Let us eat." She slowly sat on a blanket that was set with dishes and cutlery.

They ate and talked about the day. Slowly, everyone relaxed as much as they could. They knew that the stone elemental demon was only the first test. They took turns making Asora laugh. Marevin did a fair imitation of Frenzen and Admiral Yane that had everyone cracking up.

When darkness of night fell, the fairies lit tiny candles. The twinkling lights floated above the campers, enchanting them. It also kept everyone warm as the temperature continued to drop. Asora told stories of the Hananaka to amuse Lady T'ula and the fairies, who listened with amazement.

"You mean that the humans pray to these gods? What if the puro were to find out? Your people would be condemned," the elf whispered.

"That you prefer these gods over the Great Maker."

"Oh, the puro knows. It is why he calls us barbarians, but we also pray to the Great Maker as well. There are no temples to the Hananaka, only the stories. Do not worry. You will not be called in to testify." The princess laughed, but T'ula did not. To testify was dangerous for everyone. People disappeared or died. Religion was always a dangerous game to play in politics.

The greatest purge was when all those that believed in the Great Architect went to live on other worlds and became the Darkcons. They had been fighting ever since. Neither the kingdom nor the empire could forgive.

"I think we should rest now," Marevin suggested.

"I do believe you are right," T'ula added.

Asora went into her tent and fell asleep surprisingly quick. Marevin and T'ula went into their tents. The fairies put out the lights outside and lit small candles to warm the tents.

They slept well; there were only minor tremors when Asora was sleeping, but nothing that caused them to wake up. The princess seemed to have some control over it. Just she was not aware.

Eventually it was enough to wake Marevin and T'ula. But by then it was early morning. The sun was mostly covered by the overcast that was common in the mountains.

"Lady T'ula?" Marevin called out to the elf.

"Yes, my lord?" T'ula answered.

"I must strike the tent. You need to get rid of the beddings and such. We must move on," Marevin said.

"Oh, yes, of course." T'ula went inside and closed her eyes.

The tent then returned to normal. They got on the trail and were soon moving deeper into the mountains. It was beautiful, filled with evergreen, deer, and cascading streams. Around noon, however, the sky began to turn ugly. The overcast had turned into a northern storm. This was common in the Cold Mountains. The constant storms were the result of the warm air from the south slamming into the incoming cold air from the north.

The rain was cold, and the wind was powerful. Princess Asora was unable to control it as her talent and experience was not enough. The wind was also strong enough to knock them off the mountains and down deep into the valley below.

As the weather worsened, they found a cave for shelter. T'ula quickly started a fire, and they made themselves comfortable. They felt that they would need to wait out the storm. The storms in the mountains could last from an hour to a week depending on the time of year.

The storm raged outside: wind broke into the cave, flaring the flames of the enchanted fire; lightning struck the mouth of the cave, knocking rock onto the ground, and they could hear women's laughter. Three shadows appeared.

"It is the three sisters!" B'nei suddenly chirped.

"The three sisters? Who are they?" Asora looked from the dangerous wind, driving rain, and lightning to looking at the fairy.

"More demons, Your highness. They are the storm demons. They are deadly. It must be the next part of the quest." B'nei was terrified.

"But you just said they are deadly! Are you insane, sending the princess out there? You will not go, Asora!" Marevin angrily demanded.

"I will forgive your outburst, Lord Marevin, since I know it comes from your need to protect me, but not again," the princess snapped, but the young lord was not backing down.

"You are damn right. I am here to protect you. And you may take me to task, but I will not allow harm to come to you!" Marevin stated dogmatically.

Asora shot him with a paralyzing spell, and he stood stiff with a mutinous look in his eyes. "What about you, Lady T'ula?" The angry princess turned to her other companion.

"I would give my life for yours, but I think that you would turn me to stone as well. Princess, do you have a plan at least?" The elf was nearly in tears as she desperately sought to help her monarch. "Perhaps your coins can help?"

Asora's eyes widened. "Thank you, T'ula. I believe that I can try to control the weather with them, at least the rain and wind. The lightning, however, is going to be dangerous."

"I understand that you want to be a Dragon Dancer, your highness, but please, you are more than that. You are the ruler of the Utopians," T'ula cried out. "You are everything to me."

"Queen Laxur will not take the humans coming to the rescue well. She will hit us hard and soon. I must become a Dragon Dancer to protect the Utopian people, Lady T'ula. I defeated the stone demon, and I was given the power of stone. Now I am being offered the powers of the storms if I am brave enough if I am strong enough. I must do this for our people." Asora said.

She released Marevin, and he walked toward Asora and T'ula. He learned his lesson about defying his sovereign's will. He was tired of being paralyzed.

The four fairies sighed, as did Marevin and T'ula. Asora's words were those of a true monarch. This was not about personal glory or unnecessary risk; it was about a courageous young ruler who knew that she must be as powerful as possible to deal with a very dangerous enemy.

"I must also go out there, because I am the only one that can protect you. The daemons will blow this cave apart. I, at least, have the two coins. The people of the temple would not have chosen me if I did not have the potential to deal with these trials."

She looked at each of them and spoke with a light tremble. "I have never before been so frightened, nor more determined. I know—T'a has said as much—that I have the ability to be a great witch. This is my test." She took a cleansing breath "I will separate the wind and the rain. Without them, there can be no lightning."

Marevin simply nodded. "Good plan. I believe in what you say, but be careful. Lightning kills."

Asora nodded slowly and went to the mouth of the cave. Lightning struck the path in front of her, and she could hear the laughter again.

She went deep inside herself to find calm. She was glad that she wore the camouflage uniform complete with rubber-soled boots, which insulated her from the electricity.

The princess concentrated on the coins and thought about water and wind. She stood silently at the opening of the cave. The storm swirled above her, and she could feel the sister trio demons harassing her. She had to tame them. And she will bring them down.

She felt them fighting her, but she slowly pulled them apart. The wind whipped at her, but after a few hours, it grew calmer. The rain drove into her face, and still she stood silent. Even when lightning scorched the ground in front of her, she stood.

The storm turned violent one more time, and she was blown off her feet as their power entered her. She was unconscious. Marevin ran to catch her. Lady T'ula wrapped the freezing woman in a blanket. The fairies made a mattress to lay her on. They waited for her to awaken to see what power she would have.

Asora slept for hours, and she shook with the storm. The freezing rain was inside of her. The wind blew inside her mind, and the lightning crackled in her spine. The group worried about her and covered her in more blankets.

"We should take her back. This is dangerous." The young lord stared at the princess huddled under the blankets.

"She would never forgive us. She could have us banished, or worse, imprisoned!" the elf shouted. She wrung her hands and stared at the woman.

"She is unconscious, for the Maker's sake!" Marevin shouted back.

"She is sleeping! There is a difference!" T'ula pointed out.

"Then why has she not woken with all of our shouting!" Rayne exclaimed.

They both turned to look at Asora, still shivering under the covers with blue lips.

"What do you think, Gourani?" T'ula asked. "She's as cold as ice, but she's still breathing.

"I think the princess would want to go on. She is stronger than the young lord thinks. She has tremendous power. She simply needs to recuperate. In the meantime, we should make food and wait." Gourni said.

"Agreed." T'ula went to the fire, and Marevin got out the supplies.

Chapter Twenty-Five
Attack on the Palace

Archduke Frenzen looked out the large palace windows. It was raining, and his eyes went to the great mountain in the distance where Princess Asora was. He saw dark, heavy rain clouds smothering the mountain. While he knew that this was a normal occurrence, it did make him worried.

Admiral Yane had returned a day earlier with the contingent of Royal Guardsmen that all accompanied Princess Asora into the Cold Mountains. They were unable to escort her into the mountains as the monks and guardians would not allow it. The admiral was angry about it and Frenzen could not blame him.

Lady T'a walked up to the distracted prime minister. "You are worried for her."

He continued to stare at the mountain. "Yes. It has been two days now. It was a dangerous quest. I should never have agreed to this."

"Do not blame yourself. She had to go. She must have power if she is to be an effective ruler. The court does not respect her yet, but when she comes back, they will see her in a new light," she said.

"You would know. You were chosen to be queen because of the great talent you had," Frenzen reminded T'a. "You were loved, and anyone would do anything for you. I would have preferred that Asora follow your example. Your husband at the time would have done that for you."

"I loved my husband. He was quite powerful as well," she responded. "He also worried about everything too."

Attack on the Palace

Frenzen turned to T'a and saw her ache. He was contrite. He also did not want to bring up old painful memories for his friend. T'a and Frenzen had been friends for so long that they knew each other well. There was no romantic element to their friendship as T'a wanted to stay widowed as a form of penance.

"Of course. I meant you no pain. I was simply stating a fact. You are an extremely powerful woman." Frenzen explained.

"I understand completely," T'a said.

They both turned to the window. The rain pattered on the glass as they continued to watch the lightning strike the mountain. T'a had faith in Asora's abilities. She was T'a's best student during the Royal Academy days. Asora was one of the best campers and the wisest survival expert she had ever seen. Frenzen knew that Asora had military training and so he was not as worried as he normally would be. Asora was the toughest noble or royal woman they knew.

Frenzen was distracted by a commotion down in the village. A great hole had appeared in the sky, and something huge was dropping through it. The thing landed in the middle of the village square.

"By the Maker! What is that?" He pointed to the grotesque shape.

Before T'a could answer, a loud screech blared from the distance. It was ear-splitting. T'a put her hands to her ears, and Darkcon soldiers poured out of what seemed like a thousand portals. They were under attack! Frenzen could barely handle the noise, but he fought through it to get ready for the coming siege.

Admiral Yane came running in. "You have seen it?" Frenzen and T'a nodded. "I am getting the royal guard out there, but I will leave the house guard to protect the palace."

"What about the Red Guard forces who are still here?" the prime minister asked desperately.

"They are here to protect the princess, and they can only be mobilized by her. As per the agreement between Asora and Countess Marien. They cannot help. You were once a soldier, a good one too, so I leave the protection of the palace to you and General D'arris. Now I go to the walls." He paused. "But I can get them to defend sections of the palace." The admiral then ran out to look for Rakon.

He found Rakon sharpening his sword in his quarters. It was intricately carved and had a heavy blade. Rakon did not look up when the admiral walked in. He continued to sit with his back to the door. But he was aware of what was happening.

"You have heard that the Darkcons are attacking?" Yane asked.

"I have heard. I will be waiting for them." The demon continued to hone his blade.

"I want you with me," the Admiral ordered.

That stopped him. He turned and stood up. "Why?"

"You know Queen Laxur and her tactics the best. I would hazard to guess that you were the one to teach her," Yane said. "That is an advantage to me."

"I taught her to be a warrior. That is something I deeply regret," Rakon replied.

"That is why you now train Asora," Yane pointed out.

"The princess is not up to this, unless she has gained years of experience on her short quest," Rakon said. "Becoming a legendary Dragon Dancer will help, but I do not think it will be enough."

"I want your experience with me up on the parapets. It may give us an advantage." Yane looked Rakon in the eye. "We have only seventy thousand soldiers to fight their growing numbers."

The demon sighed and nodded. "I pray your princess returns with a host of dragons, or we are doomed."

The village was a mass of fire and confusion. A gigantic blue gorilla bird was stomping on houses. Yane had instructed the royal guard to hit it with the cannons that were spread out around town. Troops were hurrying to load and fire cannons. The Utopians used heavy artillery cannons, and large crossbow launchers.

The descending Darkcon Army avoided the area around the village and headed for the palace, where Yane was mustering more soldiers. He was wrong in getting the Red Guard forces to help. They were willing to assist the Royal Guard forces if Yane was giving the orders. However, the combined Royal Guard and Red Guard forces were in disarray—the Darkcons took advantage of this and were firing mortars, at the Utopian forces. The screeching from the creature was intimidating.

Rakon noticed their fear and commented to Yane.

"You had better get them to fire those cannons and cast spells, or you can surrender right now!" Rakon shouted.

The human admiral nodded. He was getting frustrated by the lack of coordination between his assembled forces. He turned form Rakon to the dozens of officers behind him.

"Get your heads out of your asses and fire those cannons, or they will overrun us! Get to it now, or by the Maker, my foot in your face will be the last thing you see!" the Admiral shouted at the terrified soldiers until they remembered their professionalism and began doing as they were told.

They loaded the cannons with twenty-four-pound balls and grapeshot. They did damage, but not enough. The Darkcons kept coming. It was like a stampede that shot back.

The admiral then yelled for the spell casters to attack. The arches of lightning and balls of fire came pouring over the parapets and into the enemy ranks. There were a few scattered return volleys, but not many. Queen Laxur's spell casters were too busy keeping the portals open.

Inside the palace, Frenzen sent the court to their rooms and demanded that they send for more troops from their home planets, or they would die in the palace. The courtiers promised to call for reinforcements, but it would take time.

Frenzen had the remaining guards readied for combat in the throne room. It was the largest area in the palace, and he was sure that it was Laxur's primary target. The throne room was the center of power for the kingdom. If Queen Laxur were to step into it she would begin to be fused with the kingdoms great power. Princess Asora experienced this every time she stepped into the throne room. This was meant to make Asora the most powerful magical being in the palace so that she would have power over others. However, if the reigning monarch was away then the next monarch to step into the throne room would gain that power. If Laxur came in she would gain that limitless magical power and if she stayed long enough, she would become the new monarch of the Utopian Kingdom. The horror that Queen Laxur could unleash upon the Utopian people could be devastating.

Archduke Frenzen also sent the elite troops to slow the enemy's way into the throne room. Booby traps were set, and the great stone doors were closed. It would take the Darkcons a while to get there. Well, that was the hope anyway.

It would only slow them down, however. And everyone knew that. The enemy army was like a great ocean. Wave upon wave crashed into the palace gates, and they had brought cannons, explosives, and battering rams. They also brought their determination.

A great explosion erupted, and a crack appeared in the humungous stone gate at the entrance to the palace grounds.

In the village, cannons could be heard along with the shrieking of the thirty-story creature. The gorilla bird swatted the guardsmen and artillery away. Most of the soldiers and villagers were killed.

Those that had run headed for the tunnels in the mountains, where the humans watched helplessly. They were too far away and were under orders to stay put. It was finally decided by the captain of the remaining carrier to stream out and join the fight.

The human general decided to take a back route into the palace. They knew of secret passages; however, it would take many hours to get all his sixty thousand soldiers through.

Yane continued to shout orders on the parapets. He was proud of his soldiers now that they were moving as one. Their faces were grimy from the gunpowder, sweat, and blood. Their usual red wool coats and blue pants were equally dirty. The dead and wounded were quickly pulled away and taken by the healers. New soldiers took their places, but it could not continue indefinitely.

A new wave of Darkcons attacked the walls and gate. The spell casters went to work, raining fire onto the enemy's backs and heads; the fire was sticky and clung to armor and flesh.

"Yane! Rakon! The humans are coming!" the prime minister said breathlessly.

They turned to stare at the archduke. The Admiral asked, "They are? Thank the Maker! When will they get here?"

"That is the bad news. It will take the carrier nine hours to get here, but the planes will be in the air in three. The ground forces will also take some time," Yane informed.

Rakon nodded. "Hmm, yes. It is quite a march from the mountains to here, but it is good news."

Frenzen looked over the parapet and would have had his head blown off if Yane had not pulled him back. "Be careful! They aim for officers."

"Have there been any tanks? Has Queen Laxur appeared?" the elf asked in trepidation.

"No tanks. I doubt she could have transported them. And no, Laxur has not appeared, only her beast in the village. It has crushed the village, and the people have fled for safety in the mountains," Rakon answered.

"Yes. They should have refuge there. I pray my people get here soon. From what I remember of the tunnels, there are several entrances to the palace, so it should be easier to move the troops." Yane looked down briefly.

"They are attacking again. It will not be long before they break through the outer wall. I think we can hold them off for a few more hours. I need to be sure that the royal guard is ready for them below. Please, excuse me." Frenzen said

"If they are breaking through, then I need to get back inside. Good luck. May the Maker bless us." The prime minister ran a hand through his hair.

"May the Architect protect us," Rakon replied.

Frenzen took one more look at the carnage and then hurried down the stairwell.

Hours had passed, and Yane had commanded the guards in the garden to be ready with the cannons and the bowmen to notch their arrows. The spell casters were told to be ready. It would not be long before they faced a slaughter from the Darkcons' guns, but at least they had cannons, grapeshot, and spell casters.

The outer stone gate splintered outward, killing mostly Darkcon soldiers. "Fire!" Yane shouted.

The cannons roared at the enemy trying to climb over the wreckage of the broken stone. It was then that Yane noticed that Laxur's creature had left the village and was at the outer walls, bashing them. It was breaking down another section of wall. Soon there would be another opening for the Darkcons to overwhelm them.

"Rakon? Have you ever seen such a creature? Do you know how to stop it?" The admiral was desperate.

The demon looked over at the grotesque monster pounding on the walls. "It seems familiar, but only because of its resemblance to a creature in a Darkcon story, one that is supposed to scare children. It is called Xercon."

"What destroyed it?" Madimoy asked.

"That is the problem. You do not have the power to defeat it. It simply walks away one day," he answered with a shrug.

"I doubt that will happen. So Queen Laxur's twisted sense of humor created a storybook monster," Madimoy replied.

Rakon shook his head. "It has significance to the Darkcons. It makes them feel more powerful and more courageous. Do not sell it short. We have nothing to stop it. I doubt the humans do either, so perhaps this is why Rowaton is to be reborn."

"By the Maker, I hope you are right," Frenzen said.

They both turned to watch. It was difficult to send soldiers to that section of the wall because the monster was smashing everything; even the Darkcons avoided it. Stones were flying everywhere; it was a death trap. They could only wait to see what the creature and the Darkcons would do. The walls were only forty stories high and four meters wide that encircled the palace, so it would take the beast longer to break through. The walls were also three and half meters thick in some places.

"Soldier!" the admiral called to a centaur. She galloped up and saluted. "I need you to get a message to Duke Frenzen. Tell him that the creature is beating on the walls and will be inside the gardens soon. Got that?"

"Yes, sir!" She galloped off.

The royal guard fought hard, but the thunder of falling stone told them that the wall had been breached. The Darkcons swarmed around the hole. The gorilla bird screeched and began to batter the palace itself.

Yane looked around and saw the hopeless position he and his seventy thousand soldiers were in. He was always a stubborn man. But even he knew when a situation had turned against him.

"Fall back! Fall back into the palace! Now! Get going! Move!" He gestured and heard other officers calling out the orders.

The soldiers fought as they made their way to the stone doors, which the house guard opened for them. The fighting was vicious at the doors. Many Utopians died defending the rest of the retreating royal guard. The great doors slammed shut and were barred. It would take the Darkcons time to set up a battering ram, which gave the admiral time to come up with a new plan. He ordered the royal guard to support the house guard, and he set off with Rakon to find the prime minister. It was over a two- kilometer walk to the throne room. They made notes as they went. They saw checkpoints already set up, and the armory had been utilized. A few human guards had machine guns and grenades piled nearby. These were the few humans that the royal court had allowed Asora to recruit for the house guard. The Admiral was glad for the small force, and Rakon was impressed with their courage.

Frenzen was standing by the throne, speaking to the commander of the house guard. They both turned to see the sweat-soaked, soot-darkened face of the uniformed admiral. They noted a bullet hole in his pants—a near miss. The General, an elf, saluted Yane, his commanding officer. He nodded to Rakon, not sure what to say to a demon.

"The doors have been barred. It will take time for the Darkcons to break them down." the elf informed the Admiral.

Yane turned to the elf. "I saw your preparations, General D'arris. Excellent job. Your people have done a good job. The spell casters were invaluable in keeping the Darkcons out if they have. They were incredibly brave."

"Thank you, Admiral. The humans, with their new weapons, will bottleneck them, and the spell casters will give them hell as well. Do you have any other thoughts?" the elf asked.

"Have you heard from the humans?" Frenzen asked.

"Yes. The airplanes should be here soon. The army and the carrier group will take much longer."

"I will take what I can get. They need to take out that beast of Laxur's. The palace walls may crack from its pounding," Yane suggested.

Frenzen shook his head. "That could kill hundreds, depending on where it is."

"That thumping you hear is the creature. It is banging on this wall." Yane pointed to the wall behind the prime minister. "Somehow it knows where we are, or Laxur has programmed it to find the throne room."

"You sound paranoid," Madimoy pointed out.

"We know that the creature was made by the Queen. Its name is Xercon. It's from a children's story. It is made to terrorize us and bolster the Darkcons," Rakon added.

Yane laughed harshly, as did the General. "I put nothing past Laxur. I underestimated her hatred of the Utopian capital, and now we are paying for our lack of defenses. This was a well-thought-out plot, and I wonder if the quest was part of it. We still have not heard from the Princess. This can only be a takeover. The queen knew when to hit us."

Frenzen growled. "I warned the Princess myself. I told her that this was a possibility. She would not listen. I pray to the Maker that she is still with us."

"Hmm. Perhaps it is best that she is not here. The Princess would have been the target for Laxur," D'arris said.

"You could be right. At least she will not be attacked," Rakon said.

A runner came in, shouting, "The humans have come in their airplanes!"

Outside, thirty planes came, shooting at the beast. Their rockets blew into the creature and the enemy soldiers. They had not expected the creature and were not loaded with many rockets. They expected to strafe the Darkcons and had armed themselves accordingly.

The humans killed hundreds, but the Darkcon portals poured out as many as were killed. They turned around and aimed for the witches and warlocks who were keeping the portals open.

The beast was hit, wounded, and it screamed but kept pounding on the wall. The pilots were out of ammunition and had to return to the carrier.

Without the spell casters to stop the demons from using the battering ram, it took less time to break the stone doors. They were soon clearing the broken doors, and the Darkcons were in the palace. It had been eight hours since the beginning of the attack.

"They have broken through, General D'arris!" a frightened officer told the elf.

"That is it then." D'arris turned to speak to the waiting soldiers. "We fight to the last person. Remember, we are Utopians. We are strong and will give them hell! Send them to their Architect!"

"YES, SIR!" The Utopians raised their fists into the air.

"Get into position! The humans have set up areas that will bottleneck the Darkcons, but they only have so much ammunition, so keep sharp!" the General shouted, and they waited.

The humans aimed and fired their machine guns. The bodies of the Darkcons piled up, and those that went to fetch the dead were mowed down as well. The Darkcon soldiers could only climb over the corpses to be killed themselves.

The first group of humans and their spell casters were out of ammunition, and they retreated to the next nest. It was another killing zone, until they ran out of bullets and grenades and pulled back to another nest. This kept up for the next few hours, until they came up against the last of the stone doors into the throne room.

After several hours of agonizingly waiting, the door was blown out. The flying rubble killed and wounded hundreds of Utopians. The remaining nineteen thousand of the house and royal guard stood ready against the fifty thousand Darkcons.

The Utopians killed a thousand in hand-to-hand combat but could do little against the gun- toting enemy. The Darkcons had proved to be experts with these more advanced.

When the guards were on their knees with rifles pointed at their heads, a great cheer went up from the Darkcons. There was a stir at the broken door, and with another cheer, in came Queen Laxur.

She wore her black armor with a black cape and a golden phoenix across her chest. She looked around the room and smiled at the defeated Utopians. It amused her to see her foes in this state. How she waited for this moment.

The queen walked up to a disheveled and battle shocked Frenzen and raised her hand for him to move. She languidly waved her hand over the throne, and it was transformed. It was now a duplicate of her throne on Dorien. She turned and sat down. She felt the power in the throne room start to fill her with more power. It was a wonderful and even pleasurable feeling to her. The tiny hundred stars that floated above the royal seat fizzed out. The queen looked around and had one question.

"And where is Asora?" Laxur asked with a smirk.

Chapter Twenty-Six
The Temple Mount

Princess Asora woke in the early afternoon. The sun was barely visible from behind the clouds. She had a splitting headache and she held her head and moaned in pain. It took her eyes a few moments to adjust to the light. She got out of her sleeping bag and saw that she was alone in the tent. Asora could hear the fairies talking to Marevin and T'ula. The princess came out of her tent and got the attention of her companions.

"Your highness! You are awake! How are you?" T'ula asked coming up to her.

The first thing Asora did was sneeze snow. She kept sneezing and more snow came out of the princess. Asora created a tiny blizzard around them. However, she able to stop. When Asora stopped and took a few breaths, she created small violent hurricanes that blew T'ula and Marevin back. Asora stopped and covered her mouth in fear of causing more damage.

"Oh my," Asora blurted.

"Wow, all that power gave you a hell of a chest," Marevin commented without thinking.

Lady T'ula gave him a slap to the side of his head. "How vulgar!"

"I was talking about her lungs! Asora can make storms so easily!" Marevin said in an apologetic tone.

"I am so sorry," Asora said. "I am trying to control all this power. They are coming out of me in so many ways."

"If this journey is to continue," Gourani started. "You must learn to control your new powers."

"We do not have that kind of time!" Asora pointed out. "I will just have to learn on the way."

"That is very dangerous to do," T'ula said as she climbed down from the boulder that she was blown on top of.

"The Darkcons are still of Evorn. If we wait, then Queen Laxur will have taken over!" Asora said.

"Very well then, "T'ula said. "I know of some meditation techniques that can help and they can be done within minutes or as you humans say, on the fly."

"Good, I can do that," Asora said.

The two ladies sat down on a flat rock. T'ula closed her eyes. "Do as I say."

Princess Asora sat just has T'ula had. The princess inhaled and exhaled. She closed her eyes as T'ula had done.

"Now what?" Asora asked.

"Envision the two coins you have in your thrall," T'ula said.

Asora envisioned the coins of water and wind. The two coins in Asora's mind were much more then large golden coins.

"Now see them as they are," T'ula said.

"What?" Asora questioned.

"The Coin of Water is power of water, so see it as it is," T'ula spoke.

This cryptic line made Asora aggravated as she did not see why this was always the case with magic. She mused that mystics must enjoy riddles. Only to make things more difficult to show off. But none the less Asora thought hard on her two coins.

The Coin of Water then turned into a blue liquid energy. The blue liquid enveloped Asora but it did not harm her. It felt cool, not cold. Then it turned warm like a shower or a bath. Again, it did not hurt, but it felt good. The blue liquid then turned into a blue princess gown. Asora found it attractive as the patterns on the fabric were that of water. Rivers, lakes, and oceans. The dress also felt like a warm and pleasant shower.

"Now channel your power of water to do what you want it to do," Tulsa's voice rang out in Asora's mind.

Princess Asora focused, and water formed from nothing in her mind. However, instead of a wild surge of power. The power was greater but controlled and refined. She then saw a tidal wave coming towards her. She put her hand up and the massive wave stopped. Asora lowered her hand, and the wave flattened no longer a threat. Then Asora raised her hand again and a new tidal wave formed. But it refused to threaten her, and Asora could sense that. The destructive force obeyed her. The rain from the clouds that just formed above her merely fell around her. It was a tropical rainstorm but Asora was dry and safe. Then the rain stopped in mid fall and became stopped.

"Am I doing this?" Asora asked.

"Yes," T'ula replied. "Water is your loyal servant. And all the power that comes with it."

Asora then made the water turn into a small cat. The watery cat meowed at Asora and acted like on too. Asora pet it and giggled. The power of water embraced her in the form of this watery cat.

"Okay, time for the Coin of Wind," Asora called out.

"Indeed," Tulsa's voice said.

The watery cat disappeared as did all the water around her. The air then became heavy, and Asora felt a sort of arrogant challenge to Asora's authority. Powerful gale force winds attempted to force Asora around. The princess stood her ground equally as defiant.

"What is this?" Asora demanded.

"The power of wind is new to you, and it is defiant of you," T'ula said. "You have to tame it, or it will blow you away."

The wind then took the form of Asora herself. A dark cloudy shape of Asora. It laughed at Asora as it mocked her. It did not speak but Asora got the meaning of its jests. The wind Asora inhaled, and her chest expanded to many times her size. It reminded Asora of an exaggerated cartoon move when those things wanted to blow wind.

The wind Asora blew the actual Asora across the skies.

Princess Asora then crashed into something solid. The princess looked and saw the rock demon. She was in his hand and the giant merely looked at her. Asora knew that this demon meant no harm to her.

"Focus!" The demon spoke.

"I cannot," Asora said. "The wind the air it is too much."

"Steel yourself, become its power," the demon's powerful rocky voice spoke.

The cloudy wind Asora came towards them both, laughing like an evil banshee. She crashed into Asora again and blasted her off the giant rock demon's hand.

As she flew, Asora was reminded of an ancient saying about wind. "No matter how the wind howls, the mountain shall never bow to it."

Asora looked at the rock demon and it nodded to her. It was telling her that she was right. Asora unfurled her white angelic wings. She managed to stop herself, and she flew back to the giant rock demon.

"What is this?" T'ula's voice asked.

"A new power is being born within me," Asora said.

Princess Asora flew up to the giant rock demon. He then turned into an avalanche to stones, rocks, sand, and minerals. It all flew to Asora and enveloped her. In place of the giant rock demon was a giant Princess Asora made of stone. She towered over everything. The dark cloudy Asora also grew to gigantic sizes. The cloudy Asora then punched at the stone Asora. This time however the punches did nothing to Asora.

"Just like in the ancient saying," Asora said.

Asora's movements were very sluggish, but extremely powerful. The cloudy Asora used her speed and tried to blow the giant rock Asora away. This failed miserably as rock Asora barely noticed. Rock Asora attempted to swipe at the cloudy attacker. After a few attempts she managed to smack the cloud. The cloud crashed into an invisible wall.

Rock Asora then vanished, and the princess walked up to her cloudy doppelgänger. The cloudy Asora looked up at Asora. She was still and even submissive. She held out her hand and Asora took it. The cloud

Asora then vanished as the wind enveloped the princess. Asora now wore a dress that was grey and blue. It had patterns of wind, tornadoes, and swaying grass.

"The power of the wind itself," Asora said to herself.

The princess then held her hands out in front of her and in between them a magical ball of wind formed. She had contained wind. Then she blew and it transformed into a hurricane. Asora then raised her arms and the hurricane turned into a tornado. It moved as she told it to move. Once she put her hands down the tornado vanished and the realm was still.

"I have it," Asora said.

Princess Asora opened her eyes and she saw Lady T'ula looking at her curiously. She seemed to be studying her.

"You have a basic mastery of water and wind now," T'ula said.

"And I have a guardian too," Asora said.

"Guardian?" Marevin asked.

"That rock demon. He is now my guardian. He is apart of me now," Asora said. "He protects me."

"Elemental Demons are some of the most loyal beings. To have one as a guardian is a great honor," T'ula said.

"You mean we have to share Asora with more demons?" Friea complained.

"Relax Friea," Asora said. "He does not mind fairies."

"What is his name?" Marevin asked.

Asora closed her eyes, "Roll."

"Roll?" B'nei questioned.

"Like Rock and Roll," Marevin laughed.

"What is that?" T'ula asked.

"It is a type of music," Marevin said. "I will let you listen to some of my favorites when we get back to the palace."

"Oh, I love Rock and Roll," Gourni said.

"Really?" Asora asked with an odd tone in her voice.

"What?" Gourni asked. "I like modern human music."

"Well," T'ula started. "Princess Asora should rest for a few moments and practice her newly mastered powers."

This time Asora's body and mind were able to incorporate her new powers more easily. She felt strong and ready to continue the quest. She used her hands to make water and wind magic. It was entertaining to the fairies. The princess was able to make a full-sized watery version of herself. The watery Asora went up to Marevin and kissed him. It then evaporated into steam. The steam enveloped Marevin and blew around him. Then another duplicate Asora made from micro tornados formed. It smiled and stood triumphant in front of him. It then vanished back into Asora's hands.

"Neat," Marevin said.

Asora giggled and winked at him. "I thought you might enjoy that."

They ate a snack quickly and continued their way. The path was steep but climbable. It was a clear, beautiful day, but their eyes were constantly searching for demons. They could not relax.

Up the mountain trail they walked. The trees were becoming larger the thicker. the air was still fresh but cold. The fairies pulled out coats and fuzzy boats for everyone. They were quick to get everyone covered up. They also made warm clothes appear on themselves as well. The four fairy sisters then went inside Asora's thick dress coat.

"How much further?" Marevin asked.

"A few more kilometers?" T'ula answered in a questioning tone.

"Horizontally? Or vertically?" Marevin quipped.

"Seriously?" Asora asked annoyed. "They are going to be like this all the way up." Asora said to herself.

As the day wore on the air became cold. As they got closer to the summit, they stopped, looked around, but found no more demons. It was nerve-racking and exhausting. They rarely spoke because they were intent on watching for danger.

They turned a sharp bend and found a cabin near the top of the mountain. They walked around it to be sure it was not a hiding place for anything. Marevin slowly opened the door, with his pistol drawn.

The Temple Mount

T'ula went in next with a glow ball to light up the room. To their relief it was empty.

It was a one-room cabin with a great stone fireplace. There was also a small corner that looked to be a kitchen. There were beds that reminded Asora and Marevin of army cots. There was no electrical lighting or anything modern in the small cabin. Asora lifted a finger, and a fire started behind the grate of the fireplace.

"We can stay here for the night," Asora said.

"Has anyone heard from the palace?" Marevin asked.

"No, it is all quiet," T'ula said. "But I have a very bad feeling about this."

The princess sat at the fireplace and stared into the flickering flames. A temple suddenly flashed in her mind. It was a wooden structure with a high ceiling and four columns on each side of a great room. It had highly polished dark-wood flooring. The walls and pillars were red with black and gold accents. Dragons were depicted everywhere; there were statues of them in jade, stone, crystal, wood, steel, silver, and gold. Bowls and goblets of fire lit the room. In the center of the room was an altar with a dragon relief, which was painted in gold. A golden egg was nestled in the center of the altar, and two massive pillars of fire on both sides of the altar lit it. Two statues of demons loyal to Rowaton, the dragon king, stood next to the pillars of fire. Behind the egg was a golden armor.

Just as quickly, the vision vanished, but she knew what she had to do. "There is a temple farther up the path. I must go alone. You must stay here. It is the final test." Asora informed.

The elf, lord, and fairies opened their mouths to protest, but they quickly shut them and nodded. They knew they must let her go. This must be done if Asora is to convince the mightiest of dragons to aid them. Rowaton was a god king and respected honor and strength.

The princess took her backpack, turned, and walked out the door, and Marevin quietly closed it.

"She will be fine," T'ula said comfortingly. "She is strong, and you know it."

"I know, but I cannot stop worrying," Marevin said. "What kind of man would i be if i allow her to get hurt?"

"A man that knows when your lady needs to do what is needed," T'ula said. "You two are in love and it is natural for you to have these thought."

"That may be," Marevin said as he walked past T'ula to the fireplace. "That does not mean i have to like it."

The path led upward. Princess Asora felt the night come quickly. it was very dangerous to be this deep into the mountains at this time. However, she did not have a choice. Her breath could be seen as the air temperature continued to drop. It did bother her, but the warm clothes kept her safe from freezing to death.

She then heard something moving in the bushes and up in the tall trees. She also felt that she was not alone. Asora had her angelic sword ready but not drawn. Asora continued to walk up the path.

Then there was a distant rumbling. A lightning strike hit the path directly in front of the princess. It made her stop in shock. Then she heard wolf howls. A lot of them. Asora turned to see behind her was a large pack of mountain grey wolves. Then on Asora's other side she saw a being made of lightning land on the path.

"Only the worthy may pass me," the lighting demon said.

"I am worthy!" Asora roared.

"The wolves smell fear on you little girl," the demon said.

"That is not fear, that is determination," Asora said.

"You are right, not fear. You are desperate," the lightning demon said.

The pack leader then attempted to attack Asora. The princess moved fast enough to dodge the attack. Another wolf came at Asora. The princess was able to punch the wolf on its nose. She knocked the lead female wolf out, but the male wolf managed to ram Asora to the ground.

"Submit to defeat little one," the demon commanded.

"Never!" Asora snarled.

Princess Asora slowly and painfully got back onto her feet. She then channeled the power of water and wind. She created a small tornado and sent it against the wolf pack. The wolves ran around in a panic as the tornado chased them. Once it caught them it spun them and then tossed the wolves in random directions.

"You do not kill them?" The demon asked.

"They are just hungry, I am not going to kill them for that," Asora snapped.

Once the demon heard that it stopped. The tall demon then kneeled before the princess. The tornado stopped and vanished. The remaining wolves then approached Asora and the lightning demon. But this time the wolves approached like puppies would. They were now non-threatening and wanted Asora to pet them. Asora petted the lead male wolf.

"Tell me, what test it this?" Asora asked.

"This was to show what power you are and desire. You desire power to use to benefit others. You also showed that you will use your power to merely defend and not take vengeance," the demon explained.

"And these wolves?" Asora asked.

"They are a group of guardians, and they test anyone who desires the power of the god of dragons," the demon explained. "They also had to test you to make sure. You did not take their lives. That showed that you are a noble being."

The female wolf looked at Asora like she was still mad about being punched in the nose. Asora used a spell to remove the pain from the she wolf. The she wolf was still unimpressed and begrudgingly allows Asora to pet her.

"You may proceed to the Temple Mount of Rowaton," the lightning demon said.

The lightning demon then vanished, and the wolves ran back into the forest. Princess Asora was left alone, and the path was clear. The rain started to pour, and the air was as cold as ever.

An hour later Princess Asora came to a nondescript building. It had the steep roof she saw in her dream and two wooden doors. Asora walked up to the doors. She pushed them open, and she saw the temple exactly as she remembered.

Once she walked inside, the doors blew closed, and she walked alone to the egg, which she knew would be Rowaton reborn.

The pillars of fire began to flare up, and suddenly a column of flames lit up in front of her. It was a fire daemon, and it shot flames at her. She backed up hurriedly. She called forth the stone daemon, and it appeared before her, blocking the attack. The daemon attacked again and again. Asora had to think of a way to defuse the fire daemon, so she called to the storm.

The ceiling was instantly covered in black clouds, punctuated with lightning and a howling wind, attacking the fire daemon. The storm wildly went out of control. Asora added ice to the rain, and the fire daemon screeched. This went on for hours, but neither side was winning. Finally, it occurred to her that like the other demons, she must use the power inside her to conquer it.

The princess pushed forward to the fire daemon, who smiled and sent out flames to engulf her. The other daemons pounced on him, but it was too late. She was on fire. The heat seared her, but she stood her ground and opened her mind. Her mind accepted this new power, and the flames began to form a halo around her. The scalding temperature turned to warmth. She opened a fist, and a ball of fire rested inside of it.

The fire demon sent a conflagration at her. She held up her other hand to grab it, watching it move over her arm like water, yet she was unharmed.

Seeing this, the fire daemon bowed to her, saying, "Now the power of fire is within you, and so am I. You may proceed."

The daemon moved and allowed the princess to go to the altar. She approached it with reverence. She caressed the egg and watched as it splintered and erupted into fire, a golden flame, billowing ever outward.

Chapter Twenty-Seven

The Rule of the Dark Queen

"Where is my sister, Frenzen?" Laxur sighed at the muted archduke and turned to the admiral. "Yane? Where is my sister? Not talking either." She sighed. "All right, where is Duke Jeia?" She looked around the room. "Nobody?"

S'tie walked up to the two silent men. "Let me get the information from them."

Sysu walked up to Laxur, who was lounging on her throne of leather and steel. "Let me get the information from them, my queen. They will tell you anything you want to know when I am done."

The dark beauty shook her head. "They will tell you nothing, whether you use torture or magic. They would die first, and I still have plans for them. What you can do for me is find the courtiers, especially the ruling hundred. Send the troops to find them." Sysu turned to go, when Laxur suddenly smiled. "Oh, and find me the Puro. Bring him to me in chains. I promised a friend that I would see him on his knees."

"Yes, Majesty, as you command." The tall, coldly fascinating vampire snapped her fingers, bringing the officers to attention. "You heard your queen. Move out and find these Utopian pigs."

"General Sysu, one more thing." Laxur waved her over. "I want you to find Jeia. He is our greatest threat right now. He will be mounting a counterattack. He has a way of speaking that encourages others to do as he says. I do not want him hurt. I simply want him brought to me."

"Of course." The general nodded. "He is your brother and will be treated as such. I will send my best soldiers for him. With your permission, I will arrange for the other prisoners to be brought to you."

"You have my leave." Laxur nodded. "And check the remaining royal guard to see if they know where Princess Asora is. Do not feed on them until you have the information."

"Yes, my queen." Sysu bowed low then left to confer with her officers.

"What do you plan to do, Laxur?" Frenzen demanded, and the dark elf holding him punched him between the shoulder blades.

"You will speak with respect to your new ruler. You will address her as Queen Laxur or Your Majesty." The dark elf snarled, pulling the prime minister's arms up his back sharply, causing the elf to wince.

The dark beauty smiled nastily at Frenzen. "Careful, duke. This is my throne now, not my naive sister's. What I plan is to redecorate this drab room. First, we get rid of these white drapes." She smiled as the billowy drapes changed from white to black.

Obsidian pushed his way in, wearing a blood-stained Utopian uniform, as did the rest of his pack.

The Queen smiled widely at her general. "Found some clothes, I see."

He shrugged, returning her smile. "They had no further use for them, and we did not want to come to you naked." He bowed low, and she raised him up with a casual wave of her hand.

"Yes, I think you would shock these Utopians if you appeared in all of your glory. Has the rest of the royal guard been found?" Laxur laughed.

"We have them corralled in the garden, and we have taken away their arms. It was easy. They only had lances, bows, and arrows," Obsidian informed his queen.

"The humans? I thought I saw some of them when I came through," Laxur asked demandingly.

"They have dispersed. We are searching for them. In the meantime, we have their new machine guns to study. I have sent them with a few dozen of my wolves to Dorien. I also saw that they wear a vest that can stop a bullet. I took them off the dead spell casters that the humans were protecting. They did a great deal of damage until we overwhelmed them."

"You mean when they finally ran out of ammunition." She sneered.

Obsidian lowered his head. "Yes, my queen. That is why I have sent these new weapons back to Dorien. We will learn why they are so advanced."

"You have the soldiers that operated them in custody? Or are these the humans that have eluded you?" the Queen asked snidely.

"We have not found them. I do not understand how they got away," Obsidian explained with his head bowed.

"The spell casters helped them, of course. And you have killed the spell casters, thereby destroying any hope of finding them alive." The dark beauty fumed.

"True, but my soldiers and General Sysu's had no choice. They made it impossible to capture them."

"They goaded your people into killing them! They cannot take their own lives, but they can force you to." Laxur sat back down in a huff, drumming her fingers on the armrest. "It is unfortunate that it occurred, but remember, I want the humans alive. Your soldiers know that they are not to harm them?"

"They have strict instructions. They know that they will have to face my wrath as well as yours, and that is something that they do not want," the werewolf commander said, growling.

"I must have their secrets of warfare, and Countess Marien may pay to get them back, not that I would return them. She will pay for getting involved with the other Utopians." Laxur looked around the cavernous room with the new drapes. "S'tie, what do you think of this throne room?"

"It is too pristine, too sterile. It lacks your touch." The enchanted Prince smiled at his enchanter.

She smiled. "I agree." The queen took a deep breath and closed her eyes.

The room began to shimmer. The marble columns turned black with a metallic sheen. The floor became a shadow where she sat, and it spread outward until all the white marble turned black.

S'tie smiled at her. "Much better, my love. It goes better with your throne."

She opened her eyes and smiled. "And one more thing, to be sure they know who their Queen is."

She stood up and walked down the steps from the throne. She turned to face the wall behind it, and a huge portrait of Laxur suddenly appeared. She was sitting on the Darkcon throne in a long black dress with the golden eagle across her impressive chest, contrasting her tight black leather pants and jacket.

General Sysu walked in with twenty soldiers who were pulling thirty Utopian courtiers in chains behind them. They were elves, centaurs, and dwarves; the women had tears in their eyes, and the men had fury in theirs.

The queen smiled nastily and sat back down. "Nobles! I am so glad you have accepted my invitation to join us."

"Archduke Frenzen, help us!" the elf Baron Casar begged, and he was pushed to his knees.

"He cannot help you. No one can help you. I have looked forward to this day for a long time. Last I was here, you people shamed me, humiliated me, and physically abused me. I have come to do the same to you. I would tell you that you are the newest members of the Darkcon Empire, but that would give you rights within the empire, and you have none." She looked at each one of them.

"I may go easier on you if you tell me where my sister is. Anyone?" Her smile slipped away. "Do you think that I will not torture you for the information?"

"Your Majesty!" Frenzen called out. "You do not need to torture them. You can use your magic or your vampires'. Please, Queen Laxur."

The queen looked at the archduke in amazement.

"You would protect these evil creatures? I know from my spies that you have been fighting with them over their disrespect of my sister. They have done everything in their power to stop Asora from upgrading her army. They are the cause of their own downfall for refusing new weaponry and training. By the Architect, they are corrupt and disgusting in both mind and soul. I have spies in the noble houses—they were happy to take our money and sell you out. They are traitors! Why do you think so many were against you rearming your kingdom? They think that I will reward them for their efforts."

"Instead, you will kill them for their betrayal. You must, because that means that they might do the same to you. Am I right, Queen Laxur?" Frenzen calmly said.

She smiled again. "You think I should reward them?"

"I think that they did a tremendous job and were loyal to you," Frenzen said.

"You defend them?" the Queen asked demandingly.

"Perhaps they agree with the Darkcons. Perhaps they believe in your empire and did not do it for money," the Prime Minister suggested.

Laxur thought about that. "It is a thought. Thank you, Archduke Frenzen. I shall investigate that thought. It will be interesting to find out what drove them, but then again, I doubt I will find it to be true. They did it for the money, and they expect more money and titles." She looked intently at the Prime Minister.

"Again, why do you care? They betrayed you, and they have made your life and Asora's miserable. Do you care so little about that?" Laxur asked.

"I care about the nobles. They are not all traitors, and perhaps they were trying to make changes in their own way." Frenzen said.

"By subjugating you under my rule?" Laxur declared.

"Are you suggesting that Darkcons do not have good lives? That your rule does not have advantages? You have built temples, schools, hospitals, and roads for your new automobiles," Frenzen said ingratiatingly. "Of course, you have also brought war and death to billions in your personal quest to wreak vengeance on the Utopians."

"You think I am the only one who hates the kingdom? We get more people from the kingdom every year, refugees. Others, such as dark elves and fallen angels, have paid the price for their crimes, but they are not welcomed back into society. They have nowhere to go. They are shunned and become lost souls until they come to us." Laxur explained.

Frenzen sighed. "And you take them in."

"Yes, and they are put into the military to give them structure, discipline, and a sense of belonging. We teach them to use their powers to the best of their abilities." Laxur said. "It also helps that they have grudge against the kingdom."

Laxur relaxed back in her throne. "Naturally. Let us face it, my dear archduke. The Utopians make it easy. Your Puro is a disgusting, self-important tyrant. He is no holy man, and you know that. And your government is weak-willed and vain. You have not been able to pull them into the modern world because of their arrogance, and they took bribes to keep it that way."

"Not everyone loves the empire," Madimoy said from her knees.

"Do you mean Rakon?" Laxur demanded.

"He does seem less than joyous about it. I believe he felt that you should pay more attention to the people," the redheaded girl said.

"I thought you praised my treatment. You even mentioned my building new schools, temples, and hospitals." She smiled and arched a brow.

"All for the military's benefit. The schools are for more intelligent soldiers, the temples to emphasize the Architect over the Maker, and you need hospitals to save your troops," Frenzen pointed out.

"Rakon has made his feelings clear. Where is he, by the way?" Laxur asked.

"I do not know." The duke suddenly found his chin grabbed and Sysu staring intently into his eyes.

"He does not know," the vampire said to her queen.

Laxur sat forward. "What about T'a and Jeia?"

Frenzen tried twisting away, but the vampire held him firm. "Tell us what you know. Now!" Sysu's hypnotic gaze worked, and Frenzen blurted out, "T'a is in the temple. Jeia, is probably hiding in the tower of Canva Prime. It has the most guards."

The dark queen nodded to her general, who immediately gave orders to take the tower and find T'a.

Obsidian dragged in a middle-aged man wearing the robe of the high Priest. "At least she is in the temple. We found this one with a suitcase full of money, throwing nuns at the troops, hoping we would find them more to our liking. He even told us where to find the abbey, hoping that we would let him go."

"How much money did he have?" Sysu asked.

"A couple million crowns," the werewolf answered. Laxur waved her hand, and Obsidian brought Puro Aga forward. "That is a lot of money, but I would say it is just a small portion of what you have hidden off-world. We will find it."

"You will burn in hell for this! I am a holy man, and the Maker will punish you!" Aga shouted. The Queen stood up and walked up to the Puro. She looked down from her two meter-plus height to the meter and a half tall Priest. "You think that I will burn? You think that the Maker will punish me and that you are a holy man?" She leaned forward to whisper in his ear. "I know your secrets. I know what you do to young women, girls, and even little boys. I will be doing God's work in enslaving you. Do not ever say that you are a holy man again."

Golcon strode into the room with T'a in tow. He pushed the elf down to her knees. "Queen Laxur? We found T'a in the tower. She had many guards, but it did not take too long before we were able to capture her."

"Headmistress T'a, I am so glad that you are here. I want to show you the justice I was denied by the school. Remember all the times I went to you and told you about the abuse I suffered by the elite children of the elves, centaurs, and dwarves?" Laxur asked snidely.

"I punished them! You said yourself that they left you alone!" T'a was confused and frightened.

"I said that because they threatened me and my sister for telling you! You should have realized that!" Laxur roared in T'a's face.

"I saw no more bruises on your face and arms. I thought that they had stopped." T'a cried.

"The reason you saw no more was because they beat my torso. You failed as a headmistress. Now you will watch my justice." She turned to Golcon. "The list of names I gave you—find the families and bring them here."

"If they put up a struggle?" Golcon asked.

"Kill them. It will not matter to the universe if some loathsome families are no longer with us. I want Jeia found!" Laxur demanded.

S'tie had wandered over to the small privy room. Something inside him remembered being in there and that it had been important to him. He opened the door. He was suddenly dragged through the doorway. It was Rakon, and he had a sword ready to thrust at the prince.

He spun away from the demon and pulled his own sword. They clashed with a great ring of steel. They dodged and parried around the small room, and S'tie was pushed back out the door.

They were suddenly in the throne room, and Laxur stopped to watch the battle. She smiled malignantly at the pair, as they fought viciously back and forth.

The prince and demon were dodging between soldiers and captured prisoners. Rakon banged into Yane and his captor, and the Admiral took the opportunity to punch the dark elf who was holding him. He escaped, using Rakon and his sword for cover.

"It is a trick! Get them!" Laxur realized that they bolted for the privy room, and the soldiers ran after them, only to have the door slam, locking them out.

The Queen got up and used her magic to splinter the door in every direction. She looked in, and instead of two cowering prisoners, she found an empty room. They had escaped!

The Rule of the Dark Queen

Duke Jeia and Sarea were checking on the secret passageways that led the human army into the palace. They were in an old, unused room with an enormous fireplace. The bodyguard pushed the correct stone, and the back of the fireplace yawned open.

A high-ranking soldier poked his head out and smiled. "I did not want to come out until I knew that you were friendly."

The duke shook hands with him. "Colonel Fuston. Good to see you. Have you been able to get the army through the passages?"

"Only half went through the passages. The other half is on the other side of the wall, waiting for orders," the human commander informed Jeia.

"How many altogether?" Sarea asked.

"About sixty thousand in the tunnels and sixty thousand at the walls. I believe that makes us even with Laxur. The problem is that psychotic bird. I hear the carrier group will be here soon, and they will need to take care of it. We do not have the heavy armaments that are needed. Let me check with the other leaders," Jeia stated.

"Are you going to wait until the carrier group is here to leave the tunnels, or are you going to mount a counterstrike now, before more innocent lives are lost?" Sarea asked impatiently.

"Innocent? Those freaks! I agree with Laxur on this part. The court will be a better place without them. They prey on the weak and any human, looking down on us. You must agree on this too, Sarea. I know that you had a hard time," Jeia complained.

"Yes, I took classes at the Royal Academy for the female military. It was hard, but I learned a great deal. It was an honor to learn magic."

"Oh please, Sarea. You should have been allowed to learn because you have the ability, but you were only chosen to protect a woman candidate. Otherwise, you would have been jailed for your gifts," Jeia said.

"I am doing what the princess would want, and that is protecting all of the court," the female soldier stated.

"She may have to because of politics, but I do not. I say let them be punished." Jeia turned to Fuston. "How long before everyone is in position?"

"It will take two hours to get ready to take the palace back. That should give the carrier group time to get here. We need to stall. I checked with the other officers."

"Duke Jeia and I will lead them away from the passages. It should not be that difficult. The other four are in little-used rooms, except for the one in the wine cellar, and Laxur is known for her drinking," Sarea warned.

"Get down there and warn them," Jeia ordered.

"We already have. We were ten steps away from the servants that were followed by soldiers into the cellar. The radios may work," Sarea suggested.

The Colonel raised the radio to his ear. "Hadren? Are you there? What is your situation?"

"We are not quite in position. There is a lot of activity in the cellar. I have talked to Prunin and Winsem, and they must clear a lot of debris from their passages. It will take three and a half hours," a voice said over the radio.

"You have to be ready," Fuston said.

There was a heavy sigh. "We will do our best."

"No. You will do it in two hours. That is when the carrier group arrives. We must be ready."

"Yes, sir." There was a pause. "May I ask where Admiral Yane is? I got a radio message to take orders from you as if he were giving them, but I have received no intel that he has been killed or taken prisoner."

"He is going around to the nobles to make sure that they are contacting their home worlds for more troops, per their treaties. It has not been easy. Most of them have crawled under their beds. From what he has said, it will take a few hours for most of the planets to send additional troops. We must try to stay out of the Darkcons' hands. Everything hinges on this. I will see you in a few hours, Hadren."

They both swung the heavy door closed, and Jeia with Sarea ran off to spy on Laxur.

The Queen smiled as two noble dwarves were brought to her. The young couple looked in horror at Laxur. They knew that they had turned away while elves beat her. They had not helped her or gone to a teacher. They simply walked away.

"We did nothing to you!" the female cried out, and the Darkcon who held her squeezed her neck viciously.

"Yes, you did nothing, all right. Absolutely nothing as those monsters beat me, tore my clothing, and pushed me down. You did nothing, like animals that see others fighting. You are nothing but pigs, and so shall you be," Laxur thundered in rage.

The dwarves disappeared, and pigs appeared and began to root around while Laxur giggled. The werewolves that were still in wolf form began to chase them around the cavernous room, making the rest of the Darkcons laugh.

An elf family was pushed forward with a whip, hurrying their movements. They were a typical family of three: a mother, a father, and a child—in this case, a twenty-five-year-old daughter who had gone to school with Laxur.

The Queen could feel rage sweep over her. G'lisel was a haughty and cruel young elf. She went out of her way to torment Laxur. The elf made sure that the other elves played nasty tricks on her. She pushed her down the stairs of the academy and fought her in the hallways, calling her a disgusting human. There had been other humans at the Royal School, and they were all treated like shit on her shoes.

G'lisel raised her chin. "I suppose you will turn us into pigs for your amusement as well." "No. I have something else in mind for you. General Sysu!"

"Yes, my Queen?" The vampire approached the throne.

"I have new candidates for your family." Laxur pointed to the elf family.

"Hardly regal, are they? Pathetic fighters, but I will take them in." Sysu looked them over ravenously.

The elves clung to each other, now realizing what Laxur had planned. Forever would they be Darkcons, and forever they would serve Laxur through Sysu.

"Hold them," the general ordered the angel fallen angels that had the elves. They pulled their heads back so that Sysu could more easily turn them into vampires.

As the elves were screaming and struggling, Laxur noticed that Dari was bringing Madimoy, wearing a torn moss-green dress, in through the crowd. She watched the elves agonizingly become vampires with joy, and the redhead was coming closer.

She called out to Dari, "Where did you find her?"

"She was in her office, crashing her computers." The giant fallen angel bowed to Laxur with Madimoy in hand.

"Were you able to see what she had been up to?" Laxur demanded.

"No, Your Majesty," Dari said weakly.

The Queen got up from her throne and walked to Madimoy, striking her hard across her face and knocking her to the ground. "What were you doing? Were you in contact with the humans? Did you call them for help?" Madimoy wiped the blood from her mouth but said nothing.

Dari yanked her up. "Answer your Queen!"

"She is not my Queen. Princess Asora is the monarch here," Madimoy said defiantly.

Laxur grabbed her face, staring intently into her desperate eyes. "And where exactly is your monarch?" She looked around the room. "I do not see her here, so where is she? And where are the humans? Have you been in contact with them? That you have computers must mean that your system is important. The nobles either do not know, or you are in possession of highly classified secrets. You must be the contact for the humans. Is that why you crashed the computers?"

The queen turned to General Obsidian. "Find me a corrupt human who has computer training. We must have some."

"I will check with the magic users." The general growled and loped off.

Laxur turned back to Madimoy. "You still have not answered my question—where is Asora? And I also want to know where your fiancé is. It will be less painful if you simply answer the question."

The lady looked at the prime minister, who was being held by a troll. "She does not know."

Laxur punched him in the stomach. "I did not ask you. I asked Lady Madimoy. Now, answer the questions."

"I do not know, you hag! Last I heard, Princess Asora was hiking in the mountains. I have not seen Jeia since the battle began, I swear it!" Madimoy cried in pain.

The Queen smiled. "The mountains are what my spies told me. She left me with the perfect opportunity." Her smile slid off as she walked over to Frenzen. "I still want to know where Jeia is."

"I do not know," Frenzen spat out.

"And the humans? Either of you? No?" She punched Madimoy in the head. "What do you know of them?"

"I know you are scared of them!" Madimoy spat her blood in Laxur's face.

Laxur crashed a fist into her stomach, and Madimoy doubled over from the impact.

Frenzen struggled with the troll, but the foul-smelling brute held fast. "The humans cannot act without explicit instructions from Princess Asora. All we have are the few soldiers allowed in the house guard."

"Is that where the airplanes came from?" Laxur asked in anger.

Suddenly, a huge ball of fire erupted in the center of the throne room. As the flames dispersed, a giant golden dragon appeared with Asora, wearing full golden armor, riding on his shoulders. T'ula, Marevin, the fairies, the airborne assault team, and a set of strange and ancient-looking elemental daemons stood behind her.

The Princess, wielding her new slim sword, pointed at Laxur. "Get off my throne, usurper!"

Chapter Twenty-Eight

Asora, the Dragon Dancer

Laxur stared in amazement at the scene in front of her. Asora was adorn in powerful golden armor. Then an overwhelming rage of jealously took over the dark queen. "Never! Evorn is mine! The kingdom is mine!"

"No, my kingdom will not fear you and your rage," Asora said.

The dragon flexed his tail where T'ula was and the airborne assault team, and Marevin were riding. They slipped down and headed for the exits, out of the way of the gigantic Rowaton. He then snapped at Laxur, who punched him in the snout while using her wings to fly out of the way of his jaws. The queen's attack did nothing to the massive dragon.

The Darkcon soldiers could not believe the size of this dragon. The glow from the divine beast was enough to make the Darkcons turn away in pain from the light and heat. Queen Laxur however was able to handle it.

"You are not the only one who can call upon legends! Behold Xercon!" Laxur laughed.

A flash of blue flame erupted beside Rowaton, and the monstrous gorilla ape appeared. It stood at roughly the same height as the divine dragon. The two giant beasts stared each other down.

Asora was stunned. "You have mutated your beautiful phoenix spirit into a corrupt creature."

Laxur shot a ball of fire at her sister and unleashed her sword with her other hand. She floated by one of the chandeliers. She fired lightning at Asora. The princess jumped off Rowaton's head and floated a few meters from Laxur. Laxur shot lightning again and it struck Asora. However, the powerful lightning was absorbed by Asora's armor. The princess then pointed her sword at Laxur and fired the lightning back at her older sister. Laxur was struck and was blown back.

"Your power is as great as mine?" Laxur asked.

"We are equals now," Asora said in a commanding voice.

"Oh yes, we are," Laxur chuckled. "And I love it."

Laxur pointed her sword to the sky and lightning struck it as to charge it up for a new attack. She then swung her sword and a wave of electrical energy surged towards Asora. A golden shield that covered her wings magically formed in front of the princess and protected her. The electrical energy washed over Asora, and she felt no pain from it.

The queen then opened her free hand and a fire ball formed in her fist. Once it was the size of a large ball, she threw it at the golden armored princess.

The princess dodged the flames and unfurled her wings, pulling her new sword out. "I will send you back to Dorien. You and your creature!"

Asora sent out a wave of blue lightning at Xercon. The lightning was powerful enough to knock the giant monster back. It crashed into a large structure that was a palace tower.

Laxur tackled Asora in mid air. The two powerful sisters went flying across the skies above the palace and the two giant monsters. The two monarchs were more then a kilometer above the palace using their inherited angelic magic to fly and fight.

Asora slammed her fists into Laxur's back causing the queen to lose her grip and fall a few meters. Laxur caught the wind and flew back up to Asora. Laxur's massive demonic sword glowed with purple light. Asora's golden sword was smaller but easier to handle.

Laxur slammed her sword at Asora. The princess intercepts Laxur's strike and deflects it. Both sisters unleash lightning blasts on each other.

Laxur's purple lightning burned and caused lingering pain. Asora's lightning was blue and was quick and blunt. Asora's golden armor absorbed the purple lightning without getting Asora harmed. Laxur was able to absorb the blue lightning and use it as a temporary boost to her magic and physical strength. It was painful but she took it.

"Why are you fighting me?" Laxur asked.

"Really?" Asora demanded incredulously. "You are asking me why?"

"You and I are sisters. I do not hate you. I see you as a powerful lady like me. You and I are the two most powerful beings in the realm. We rule it! And we should rule it. We are power itself incarnate; we are goddesses." Laxur then pointed down to the palace. "And everyone knows it. You and I are growing, young goddesses. We are more then they are."

"And that is why I oppose you," Asora said. "You and I are powerful, we may be the two most powerful beings in the realm. But we are responsible to govern with wisdom. Not tyranny."

Queen Laxur bursted out laughing, "Have you forgotten how these inbred monsters have treated us? Both of us. I know that they despise you, they hurt you and defy you constantly. They only understand power and force. You are the most powerful Utopian alive. You can force them to do as you please. But you allow them to walk all over you, spit in your face, and defy you."

"I am not a tyrant. I am change and change is always hard. Am I angry about how they treat me, yes. Do I hate them? No. And I do not hate you either. We are sisters, I still love you, I still see you as Asaria."

"You do not hate them? I hate how they treat you. I hate that they hurt you. They hate us, they are jealous of us. We are the future, you, and me. Join me and we will unite the realm in our image." Laxur offered.

"I want to unite the realm and hope that you will help me in that. But not like this," Asora said.

A tear of sadness went down Laxur's cheek. She truly wanted Asora at her side. She believed in her words. Then she thought that her little sister must have been manipulated in some fashion.

"No, you and I should be together and rule together. I will beat the evil manipulation out of you!" Laxur then flew at Asora and tackled her hard.

In the battle scared palace Frenzen ran for the stairs leading up to the balcony, with Sysu, Golcon, and Obsidian following closely behind. They watched the monarch sisters battling with with immense power in the skies above.

Obsidian and Sysu stood before Frenzen. Sysu has a black onyx saber at the ready. Obsidian morphed into his wolf form. Frenzen made a sword appear in his right hand. It was silver and with intricate designs of mountains.

"You are not usually this stupid to come at us by yourself," Sysu hissed.

Obsidian sniffed the air. "He is not. He has company."

"Damned straight," Frenzen said.

Three Utopian knights along with Admiral Yane and Captain Joes came up behind Frenzen.

"You were saying?" Frenzen asked Sysu.

"I am glad that you have not so foolish," Sysu said. "I have looked forward to defeating you!"

Sysu charged at Frenzen and slashed as hard as she could at Frenzen. The taller male elf was able to block the female vampire's charge and slash. Obsidian charged at Yane, however Joes intercepted the running wolf and attempted to trample the Darkcon under his hooves.

The palace rocked with the battle of the two giant beasts fighting each other. Xercon rammed itself into Rowaton. It was enough to force the dragon backwards and into a tower. Rowaton got up and shook off the debris on his armored scales.

The animals attacked each other, and the thirty-story-tall bird pushed the dragon over while biting his upper right limb, causing both Rowaton and Asora to cry out, bleeding.

Rowaton, on his back, used his claws to open up Xercon's lower abdomen. Now the bird and Laxur cried out; the spirit animals and their masters felt and bled the same.

Now the dragon pushed the bird back, and he rose onto his back legs, giving his hands the chance to attack. Laxur fell against the chains of the chandelier. Asora stopped the downward stroke of her sword because she saw blood on her sister's black leather sleeve. Laxur, however, threw a vicious stab that Asora barely avoided.

Xercon grabbed Rowaton by the neck and leg, throwing him through the wall. The dragon crashed into the garden outside, sending Darkcon soldiers running for their lives and killing the ones that were not fast enough.

A combination of Utopian Royal Guard conscripts and Red Guard attacked fleeing Darkcon soldiers. Magical arrows and depleted uranium rounds went flying. The Utopian knights also tackled several large Darkcon warrior officers.

From above Queen Laxur shot lightning at the Utopian forces to allow her troops a clear escape path. Then the queen landed in front of a Utopian knight. The knight charged at Laxur only to have his sword cut in two. Despite being half his size, Queen Laxur was able to high kick the large dwarf knight into the air. Once the knight crashed to the floor, Laxur rammed her sword into his head and killed him in an instant. Then arrows and bullets struck Laxur's wings. Fortunately to Laxur her wings were covered in a strong metal that made her impervious to armor piercing bullets and deadly magical arrows. Laxur unleashed another wave of lightning to stop the constant barrage on her.

Princess Asora suddenly dived and slammed into her sister. This caught Laxur off guard as Asora broke the sound barrier. Asora slammed Laxur into a wall. Once the sonic boom caught up it was enough to blow Laxur back down after she got back up.

Queen Laxur was hurting, and blood was slowly trickling form her mouth. The queen rubbed her mouth and saw the blood, her blood. Laxur chuckled evilly as her needs for violence grew.

"Stop this," Asora commanded.

"Why? I am enjoying this," Laxur laughed. She got back up to her feet. "You are only making me stronger!"

Laxur flew out and into the skies, and Asora gave chase. The two powerful sisters flew above the two giant monsters that were still fighting. The princess and the queen hovered above their spirit animals as they attacked each other, both animals snapping ferociously.

The queen moved toward the princess and crashed into her. Laxur started to ferociously pound Asora savagely with her larger, heavier sword. Asora, using a new whip-like weapon made from the sharp scales of her dragon, countered and slashed Laxur's right hand. She was able to tangle Laxur's massive sword ands forced Laxur to stop. Then Asora punched Laxur in her diaphragm. Laxur vomited a little bit of blood, and she cried in pain.

Xercon cried out as blood seeped from its right hand. The animal punched Rowaton in the face, causing both him and the princess to reel backward. Xercon then grabbed the neck of the dragon, choking him. Asora gagged, and Rowaton moved his body under the bird, using all four of his claws to rip at Xercon's exposed belly.

Laxur screamed and held her stomach as she felt the pain in her body. She quickly recovered and pummeled Asora with her free fist, driving the princess backward. The young woman whipped her sword back, but Laxur shrugged it off by slapping the princess's sword aside. Asora electrified her sword, and the dark queen was paralyzed for a moment. Asora flew close and punched her sister hard, sending her falling from the sky. At the last minute, she regained her wits and was able to zoom upward with her sharp sword, aiming straight for the princess's heart.

The mad queen summoned a super hot fire and blasted the princess, and she was shocked to see Asora absorbing the flames. Suddenly, the princess convulsed, and out came a fiery creature—the fire demon. It doubled in size as Laxur's coin fed its flame. It floated between the two monarchs, blocking the attack.

"As the old saying goes, time to fight fire with fire," Asora said.

The fire demon then smaller into Laxur, using the queen's fire powers to fuel itself. Laxur felt the demon's flames but was largely unharmed by it. However, the demon was holding her down. It roared in defiance in her face. The heat made Laxur sweat, and she could barely breath. But Laxur was able to shove the demon off her. The cold air was refreshing but she was still sweating. Laxur's armor had also been melted away, leaving her in her black and purple uniform and boots.

Asora called upon the water coin as well as her wind coin. This allowed her to sent ice shards flying toward her sister. They sizzled and cooled the flames that still surrounded Laxur. A bank of steam kept the queen hot and dizzy. She did better in fog, but Asora knew to make steam. Asora then fused with the steam.

As steam Asora was able to attack Laxur without sustaining any serious injuries. But her own attacks were weaker. However, Asora could attack far more frequently and could even fuse or go inside Laxur and attack from within. Queen Laxur was getting angry and just unleashed an explosion of dark energy to disperse the steam. Princess Asora then reformed and was flying backwards as if shows punched hard.

The queen then summoned her own coin of fire. Her fists turned into balls of blue flame. She threw these balls of blue fire at Asora. The fire demon intercepted the fireballs and absorbed them.

Seeing that the coin was now useless against Asora, Laxur searched wildly around to find some way to destroy this wretched place. She took hold of her coin of earth and flew to the ground, stomping her feet. The palace quaked, sending both armies crashing to their knees.

The animal spirits were entangled, snapping and snarling. The dragon kept raking Xercon with his claws, causing Xercon to bleed and let go of Rowaton. Xercon was exhausted. But the monstrous beast was not defeated yet. Xercon got back up and forced itself into Rowaton. The giant golden dragon crashed back first onto the ground. Xercon was on top of Rowaton trying to crash the dragon's armored scales. In retaliation Rowaton bit down hard on Xercon's thick neck.

Queen Laxur felt her spirit animal in tremendous pain as it came crashing to the ground, no longer able to fight. It rolled off Rowaton and the dragon released the bird beast. She felt its pain—an unbearable pain in her belly and neck. Laxur knew she must do something. She must sever her connection with her creation. Her connection to Xercon was very deep. This monster was a piece of the queen in a way. She had to free herself of this pain, and there was one way to do that. The only way was the one way she did not want to do. It broke her heart, but it needed to be done.

Queen Laxur reached into her pocket that was in her corset and took out a green potion. The vial was large enough to require Laxur to hold it in her full fist. This was her favorite potion; she opened the top and drank it. Its sweet, sweet taste was something of an addictive treat. The sweet potion felt good as it sank deeper into her. The potion interacted with Laxur's powers and body causing powerful, and pleasurable explosions inside the queen.

Laxur felt her belly churn, and a feeling of raw power began to overcome her whole body. A faint glow could be seen on Laxur's skin. Then she began to grow larger.

Queen Laxur bursted from her armor like a click hatching from an egg. Electrical arcs erupted from her. When her clothes tore away, her coin of fire created a sort of one-piece swimsuit like covering made of red and orange fire to cover and protect Laxur as she grew into her giantess form. The Coin of Fire also fashioned weapons that could be wielded by the growing Laxur.

The growing queen erupted from the palace violently and was on fire. Her massive black wings also burned with dark flames that made her nearly invulnerable to any attacker that was smaller than her. The heat from her flames burned anything close to her, and even ignited people both Utopians and Darkcons alike. Anything that burned fed Laxur's growing body.

The massive half a kilometer tall queen stomped her way out. Every step caused a localized quake. The world of Evorn trembled beneath her. Lightning constantly struck Laxur, but it caused her no form of discomfort. In fact, it was a power source that Laxur was using to sustain herself as she moved about.

Queen Laxur felt that she was being struck by powerful cannons. At this size the powerful and devastating cannons did nothing to Laxur except annoy her. She raised her giant hand and out came a wave of powerful purple lightning. Laxur destroyed everything around her. She did not care who or what she struck. Even her own troops ran for cover as the lightning wave came at them too.

The flames that covered Laxur's torso grew to cover her wings, giving her demonic look. The fire on Laxur's body shaped itself into streams of flame to burn flying attackers. Then Laxur created a maelstrom of fire around her to be used as a shield of sorts.

Princess Asora was the only one powerful enough to get through the storm of flames that surrounded Queen Laxur. However, the heat and pressure of the flames was enough to knock Asora around the firestorm protecting Laxur.

Laxur managed to grab ahold of Asora and held her. Asora could not break Laxur's grip, and it did not help that Laxur's hand was many times larger then Asora was.

Laxur's laugher sounded like powerful booms like cannons, "Struggle to break my grip all you like. In the end even you will bow to me."

"Maybe, but not today!" Asora roared.

The princess was able to summon a blast of energy. It was so strong it nearly broke the bones in Laxur's hand. The giant queen released Asora. The princess used her angelic wings to fly to the edge of the fire maelstrom surrounding them. Then Queen Laxur using her vast size and strength punched Asora hard. Asora crashed through the fire and slammed into a gardener's shed.

The flames then closed in and around Laxur. The flames collapsed back into Laxur's fiery covering. She could see that so much was on fire now. That meant that ere was more to feed her power and growth. She looked to see both Rowaton and Xercon still fighting. Laxur made her way towards them.

Rowaton had finally exhausted Xercon, and head butted him to the ground. Now that she was as big as Xercon. Laxur saw the suffering creature and thrust her sword into the heart of her spirit animal. It roared in agony. This agony could be felt by the queen and her animal spirit seemed to beg her to not do what she was about to do.

Asora was more horrified then stunned. Her sister had killed her spirit animal—a part of herself. The monster was still apart of the queen. Now Laxur would truly be alone and without protection. Everyone else stared in dismay. No one in their right mind would kill their spirit animal. It was such a sacrilege that even the Darkcon's themselves questioned their queen's sanity.

The princess could not believe how far Laxur had fallen. Was there anything human in her anymore? Xercon then drew its last breath and vanished. Its energy and life force then recombined with Laxur, which made her grow larger and more powerful. The flames that covered Laxur also grew in intensity. Her muscles also inflated to become larger. The queen's now even more massive size made her slower physically, but she made up for that with so much defensive magic.

Queen Laxur created a sword made of black flames out of the sword she had already and slashed out at Asora with the bloody and in flamed sword. She dodged it in time, and Rowaton turned to the queen. He stood on his back feet and reached out with his claws to rip at her. She swiped at him with her sword, keeping him at bay. Laxur may have stood taller than Rowaton now, but he was quicker then the giant queen.

Rowaton unleashed a blast of fire. This flame was only absorbed by Laxur. The divine flame actually fed her, and this caused Laxur to grow even more. This was however temporary as the evil queen could barely handle Rowaton's power. The fires on Laxur burned hotter as she grew larger and stronger.

Now, Laxur was far taller than Rowaton, and both he and Asora were in great danger. The princess used her new powers to call upon the demon of fire to attack her sister. It appeared, but he was not powerful enough to give her more than a blister. The demon could feel Laxur's pull on him. Laxur devoured flames and this made the demon of fire scared of being food for some insane fallen angel monarch.

Rowaton roared in rage as it charged at Laxur. The mighty dragon slammed his full weight into the much larger Laxur. This was enough to send the queen stumbling backwards.

The queen turned on the dragon. She grabbed him by one of his claws and threw him back, then drove her sword into his chest. Asora felt the pain and fell to the ground. She must heal Rowaton! She crawled over and put her hand on him, calling her ability to heal. It flowed down her hand and into her dragon.

Laxur was stunned by what she saw. Why would Asora use her energy to save her dying dragon? It was doing nothing but taking her life force from her. There had to be something she was missing here.

Exasperated, she asked, "What are you doing? Kill it, and you will be well! The paint will stop."

"He is part of me now! He is my spirit animal and must be saved, or I will never be whole." Asora said.

Suddenly, human forces from the mountains surrounded them. Flying machines like jet fighters and attack helicopters from the carrier group had arrived in the harbor. The carrier sent its planes, drones, and missiles at Laxur; soldiers fired rocket launchers at her. With her great size, they did little but irritate her. But she was a very easy target. Impossible to miss something that big.

Laxur swatted at the fighter jets but missed them, so she stomped over the town to get to the harbor. She jumped into the harbor and caused a tidal wave that crashed over the carrier which destroyed the support vessels. But the combat vessel continued their attacks on the queen and only her.

This gave Asora time to heal Rowaton. The wounds on Rowaton's chest healed and he got back up onto his feet. The mighty golden dragon flew up into the sky and slammed into Laxur again. Only this time he latched onto the queen's wrist with his jaws. His grip made her bleed heavily. He was draining the queen's power, and this caused her to shrink. Once small enough Rowaton used his jaws and swung the still shrinking Laxur into the air and she flew and crashed into the palace courtyard.

Queen Laxur, now back to her normal two-meter-tall size, found herself surrounded by Utopian and human soldiers. She knew she could not keep Evorn. She had lost as her own soldiers were in retreat. Princess Asora floated down nearby still in her battle armor. The queen bowed her head to Asora and disappeared, taking Golcon, Sysu, and Obsidian with her. Portals began to open, and the Darkcon soldiers that were able to run escaped.

Chapter Twenty-Nine

Rebuild

Princess Asora turned to her spirit animal. "Thank you, Rowaton. I could not have done it without you. What was it that you did to Laxur? How were you able to shrink her?"

He sat back, and in a deep booming voice, he answered, "I know great magic. We dragons were one of the first made, like the angels. I have seen magic like the type she used. It is a compound potion, but I know its antidote. Our bodies make much magic, and I used a spell as well. It is that simple. Luckily, she did not know that I would be joining you."

"It is lucky indeed. Will you wait here in the garden while we round up the rest of the Darkcons?" Asora asked.

"I will be here to protect you," Rowaton promised. "And your realm."

The golden armor that adorned Asora vanished. A white dress then formed on her body. She was disappointed that her combat fatigues did not appear. The palace still had power as did the crown on her head. And both made sure that Asora was always in virgin white.

Asora looked around at the destroyed garden, palace, and ruined village beyond. She saw the dead and dying everywhere. There was so much work to do. It brought tears to her eyes to see the beautiful world of Evorn destroyed so thoroughly. The first thing she needed to do was find her friends.

The Consortium and Utopian guards bowed to the princess as she passed. They flanked her as she made her way inside the remains of the palace. She flew over the broken masonry, while the soldiers climbed over it. The wounded also were everywhere. So many injured. Not just soldiers, but maids, servants, nobles, commoners, and even a few priests. All moaning in agony on the floor. Asora also saw the ones who were not injured from every walk of life lending aid wherever they could.

That made Princess Asora hopeful. To see her people coming together and helping one another. Some of the nobles gave first aid to commoners, and soldiers tended to wounded priests. Soldiers ran around getting supplies and materials needed. Doctors and healers were starting to drop from were exhaustion.

"I said I can handle it!" Someone cursed.

Princess Asora looked to see Admiral Yane yelling at Puro Aga. The puro was helping to tend to the injured. Asora smirked and approached. Both men spotted Asora approaching them.

"Ah, princess," Yane started. "Can you tell this robbed maniac to get the hell away from me!"

"I am tending to his wounds. He has several broken bones," Aga explained.

"Good work Puro Aga. You may continue to tend to the fussy admiral," Asora said with a grin.

"What?" Yane blurted flabbergasted.

"You heard her highness, now sit down," Aga laughed as he forced the old human admiral on the floor.

Asora chuckled to herself and shook her head. It was funny, but Aga was doing some good now at the very least. She continued to look around at the casualties. Everyone looked up at her with pride and respect.

She was now a legendary dragon dancer. Warrior men and women of epic power and courage. The Utopian Kingdom's best legends even by Asora's standards revolved around the dragon dancers. The last one was several hundred thousand years ago. Legend said that this last rider was the one who landed the killing blow to the evil Dark Lord Abaddon. But Abaddon was able to kill this dancer. The dancer's sacrificed himself to save the kingdom.

Princess Asora now inherited this legacy. A legacy of hero's and legends. Even Asora most hardened critics could not muster the opposition strong enough to go against her. At least for the moment. Puro Aga was possibly the best example of this.

High Priestess Nona who was covered in dirt and blood came up to Princess Asora. The priestess did not seem to care that she was filthy, but Asora allowed it to slide.

"Your highness," Nona started. "I am honored to be in your presence."

"Did you want something from me?" Asora asked.

"We need to get the palace repaired so that there is shelter. Otherwise, the wounded will become sick," Nona said.

Princess Asora knew that Nona was right. The palace was more than large enough to house everyone and keep the people safe during the recovery process.

"I will get to it at once," Asora said.

"Thank you, your highness," Nona bowed.

Asora then walked away and towards another bed at the far end of the room. There she found Madimoy being treated by a human medic for her broken jaw. Asora gently placed her hand on her friend's face, and it warmed under her hand as she healed the bones. Asora's magic was quite gentle when used to heal. Asora's healing magic did not use her life-force energy like most magical healers do. A sharing of life-force energy was seen as a noble act. But it was also a very dangerous act too as the healer could kill themselves to save another. To be able to use their magic instead showed just how powerful or experienced the magical being was.

The redhead young woman smiled in her gratitude and then shrieked in joy as Jeia came into view. He was surrounded by the human troops that he had let into the palace. Jeia and Madimoy embraced, kissing passionately.

Yane who was finally allowed to walk and had his arm in a sling walked over. He was cradling his dislocated arm despite being in a sling. He was just happy to be able to walk around.

"Your highness, I am grateful that you are well. It was a good thing that you went on your quest. Rowaton was needed. It is as if the people at the temple knew what Queen Laxur was planning," Yane said happily.

Asora smiled tiredly. "Perhaps they did. Let me heal your shoulder."

"I had forgotten that you excelled at healing as a student. I appreciate whatever you can do." Yane said.

She moved to his side and lifted her arm high to reach his shoulder. With gentle pressure, he felt the arm slide back into position and the pain dim. The golden glow of Asora's healing magic was as soothing in its feel as it was a sight.

"Thank you, Your highness," Yane said.

"Now that that is done, where is Archduke Frenzen?" Asora asked.

The admiral pointed to the old elf, who was being looked over by a human military doctor. But unlike Yane, Frenzen was not resisting the human's attaempts to heal him. There was an elf healer with him as well.

"He broke his leg in the fighting." An elf healer said as he went over to Frenzen, and the doctor walked away to help someone else.

"Thank you," Asora replied.

"Your grace? If I may?" The archduke nodded painfully.

Another elf healer came up to Frenzen and knelt. Closing her eyes, she touched the aching, shattered limb. It glowed, and the archduke sighed in relief. The healer walked away to the next patient.

The last hour had been both depressing but hopeful. Her people truly came together to save each other. There were a few Darkcons that could not escape with their comrades. They were rounded up by the Royal Guard and taken away.

Some of the remaining Darkcons's remained defiant and attempt to fight the Royal Guard. But are quickly subdued. One Darkcon, a small troll managed to escape the Royal Guard and slammed into a butler. He almost escaped when he ran in front of Princess Asora herself.

"Out of my way pretty girl!" The troll barked.

To the troll's surprise Asora does not move. In fact, she does not seem to be afraid of him. The troll may not have any weapons, but he believed that he could overpower the princess and maybe take her prisoner.

"Your highness! Get clear!" One of the knights pleaded to Asora.

The troll then lunged at Asora. The princess simply side stepped, and the troll crashed into a pillar that was behind Asora. The troll lost consciousness as he hit the pillar a bit too hard. The knights then ran up to the princess.

"Are you well for highness?" The knight asked.

"Yes. I am well. Just take your prisoner and carry on," Asora commanded serenely.

The knights took the troll away. Asora waited for them to leave. Once out of sight, Asora continued her tour.

Four balls or light then floated towards them. One was green, one blue, one purple, and one red. These balls of light then transformed into the four fairy ladies in waiting, Gourni, Rayne, Friea, and B'nei.

"There you four are," Asora said happily.

Princess Asora held her right hand out. This was an invitation to fairies to land on Asora's hand. All four sixteen-centimeter-tall fairy women landed not just on Asora's palm, but also her right arm.

"We are so happy that you won!" B'nei said.

"And that you are well," Friea added.

"Just do not take on the queen again without us," Gourni demanded.

Asora chuckled, "Yes ma'am."

Asora and the other fairies giggled. Gourni folded her arms over her chest. She was being serious. She loved Asora and hated when she was in peril. It was Gourni's job to serve and protect the princess. She helped to raise Asora when she was born. Gourni sometimes thought of Asora as her child. Asora was aware of this and loved Gourni and her sisters as if they were her sisters too.

"I am being serious," Gourni said. "I care about you too much to see you get hurt!"

"I know Gourni," Asora said kindly. "You are the perfect big sister."

Princess Asora kissed Gourni on her tiny cheek. That caused Gourni to calm down. And the leader of the fairies relaxed and breathed.

Rayne then floated to Asora's head and corrected the crown on Asora's head. She also cleaned up Asora's hair that had become wilder then she would have liked. Rayne's touch always made Asora feel good. The purple dressed fairy was so good at making Asora look beautiful that the princess only allowed Rayne to tend to her beautification needs. Rayne always knew what Asora wanted. She also knew what Asora saw as beautiful.

"We should go and see the Privy Council," B'nei said.

"Oh yes," Asora said.

The four fairies then hoped into the air and orbited Princess Asora as she walked down the halls to the council chambers.

Asora went into the privy council room through the splintered door. She found a body tied up with rope. The man looked familiar. She moved closer. It was S'tie. The princess saw the dark spell swimming in his eyes. She passed a hand over his face slowly, and a black film was peeled off him.

Rakon and T'ula were in the room as well. They were the ones who tied him up. They seemed to have been interrogating him. Princess Asora approached Prince S'tie.

"Stop! He is enchanted!" Rakon ordered.

"I know, Rakon. I am taking away the spell. He will be fine in a moment. Help me untie him." Asora commanded.

The metal elemental demon pulled out a long dagger and slit the coils of rope. S'tie sat up with a confused look on his face.

"Why am I tied up? And where am I? The last thing I remember was greeting Laxur." The prince was staring desperately.

Asora helped him to stand. "That was months ago. You were enchanted. I should never have let you go."

"My maker, what have I done that you needed to tie me up?" He stood up, yanking down his Darkcon uniform. "By the Maker, what am I wearing? A Darkcon uniform? What have I been doing?"

"That will take some time—" Asora started.

"I will tell you." Rakon cut off the princess. "The princess is needed elsewhere. Go ahead, your highness. I will be as gentle as I can. One can only pity him now."

She nodded as the princess knew that Rakon was right. Asora and T'ula walked back to the throne room.

"I am very glad you came back to help us," T'ula said. "I was so worried about you."

"Thank you for believing in me too," Asora said.

"I have always believed in you," T'ula replied.

The princess, T'ula, and the four fairies came into another large chamber. There they see General D'arris was organizing the capture of the remaining enemy soldiers. He was shouting orders when a part of the room's ceiling began to crumble. T'ula looked up to see where the debris was coming from. A large stone block fell, knocking the elf to the ground. Fortunately, he dove between two fractured tiles that tilted upward, and he was unhurt.

Asora realized that the structural integrity of the room was dangerously unstable, but she believed that she had the answer. She called forth the stone demon.

It appeared and bowed to her. "Master demon of stone and craft, the palace is in danger of falling apart. You must rebuild it."

The large stone demon looked around and saw what he needed to do. It stood and raised its arms high, and the ceiling began to rise again. The wall was back to holding the weight of ceiling, and the danger passed, but the demon was not finished. It went around the palace, repairing the broken masonry. It would have to work for days, and the demon was going to exhaust itself when it would have to return to the sacred mountain.

An hour later, Princess Asora and those escorting her made it to the Privy Council where the others were meeting. Admiral Yane, Lady T'a, Lord Marevin, Prime Minister Frenzen, Lord Jeia, Lady Madimoy,

High Priestess Nona, Captain Joes, Puro Aga, Dame Sarea, and Shia Rakon had gathered.

"Well, how badly damaged are we?" Asora asked to the crowd.

"Not as bad overall," Frenzen said. "The palace itself took the brunt of the damage."

"What about the village?" T'ula asked.

"It will be easier to rebuild the village then the palace," Marevin spoke.

"It will take months to fully rebuild both," T'a said.

"There is also another concern," Yane said.

"What is it?" Asora asked.

"The Darkcons have taken some things from the palace. They ignored the village and its treasures," Yane said.

Asora looked at the centaur Joes, "Captain have an inventory taken."

"Yes, our highness," Joes replied.

"Begin the reconstruction efforts and I want Evorn to be reinforced," Asora commanded.

The council bowed to Asora as they acknowledge her commands. Then everyone filed out to carry out Asora orders.

A day later the Utopian military took control of the Darkcons' dropped armaments. Admiral Yane wanted to reverse engineer them, and he campaigned in court to update the military's weapons. Pointing out that again they had to rely on the humans to battle the advanced Darkcons. This time he had more votes, but they came only from the royal guardsmen that were willing to use the advanced weapons. He, Frenzen, and Asora had to be satisfied with that small victory.

Plus, after being raided and humiliated the Royal Court approved the admiral's plan. What also wanted to show that they were doing something to prevent this from happening again. Also, there was an air of Yane and Mister Arton for being right. Human ego tended to be insufferable to many, especially when they are right.

When the court met again nearly three months after they took their world back, the princess took to task the representatives of the hundred planets that had sworn to protect the palace but sent no soldiers to fight. Frenzen told her about the families, which were unnamed, that had taken money from Queen Laxur to hold off upgrading weapons and troops. Frenzen had been doing some investigations into these rumors.

"Why did they send no guardsmen? Why did the humans have to disregard the court's order and help us? They showed more love of the Utopian Kingdom than all of you. Why is this? Answer me!" Asora yelled in rage.

There were none that came forward; they all looked at their shoes. They all could not give an answer that would not give Asora the option to have them hanged.

"By the Maker, you were left here to die with the rest of us. Does this mean nothing to you?" Asora shouted again, demanding answers.

Still, they muttered awkwardly. They had no answer for her. Asora now knew what it was like for her mother when she did something wrong when she was a small child. It was so annoying and Asora was not sure what to do. She could have them tried and exiled, but that would not do much of anything.

"It is clear that they believed that Queen Laxur would have won and they did not want to provoke her anger. They were cowards, and so are all of you for not standing up for yourselves. She would have killed you all! Again, I ask, does this mean nothing to you? What do these rulers say to me?" Asora's angry voice echoed.

A centaur walked forward slowly. "They say they are happy that the battle went well and was won in the end. You had no need for their soldiers, who were needed at home, in case Queen Laxur attacked them next."

"Really? With Evorn, the home world for all the worlds of the kingdom, in Darkcon hands, she would then attack the outer worlds?" Asora struggled to keep control.

"With Evorn gone, the rest would follow! We are the center of commerce and the home of the royal guard. The realm's center for the monarchy. The outer worlds would be easy picking. You all know this. They would surrender." Asora got up off her throne. "Cowards."

Frenzen, Yane, T'ula, and T'a walked out with her. They showed their solidarity to the princess. As Asora and her supporters walked out she could hear Bremer Arton start yelling and cursing. He loved starting political fights, and he took Asora's words personally. Even though Asora saw Arton as one of her most powerful allies in the court. She left it to him to straighten the Royal Court out.

Later that night, Asora was in her bed chambers alone. She sat in her nightgown before her vanity mirror, combing out her long dark hair. Asora noticed that her hair was longer and fuller. She loved having her hair combed as it gave her comfort. She loved the art of hair making. The ladies of the Utopian Kingdom had their hair done up in unique styles. Asora did like that and asked her fairy maids to come up with new but lovely designs for her hair and crown. The fairies were well renowned for such things. But at this moment she wanted her hair to be free and flowing.

The mirror in front of Asora then turned pitch black. Asora's image also vanished. The candlelight that lit her room also dimmed. The mirror then started to change to allow another image to form of Asora. At first her image began to blur. A new image appeared. It was a smiling Queen Laxur in all her beautiful and deadly glory.

"Sister, what brings you to my vanity? You know this is so fairy tale. Makes you look like one of those evil queen's," Asora droned unimpressed.

"Well, baby sister, you won this round, but next time, you will not be so lucky," Laxur threatened.

"Unless you have something that can beat a god. I do not see how you can fight me too effectively," Asora boasted.

Laxur chuckled, "You cannot rely on your pet dragon forever." The queen paused for a moment. "I did mean what I said to you."

"You said quite a bit," Asora pointed out. "You will need to be more specific."

The image of the queen then came out of the mirror like a holographic image. Asora could feel Laxur's touch on her face.

"I still love you and believe that we should be one," Laxur said in a lower tone.

"I love you too," Asora started. "But I cannot be at your side like this."

"One day you will be at my side, and we will rule the realm at the most powerful beings to live. As the goddesses that we are," Laxur said. "This will happen. Like it or not my little sister. We will reign."

The image of Queen Laxur faded away. The room then was filled with light once more. The mirror also returned to normal. Asora was left with a queasy feeling. It was not over.

Asora retired to her bed and fell to sleep. Rayne extinguished the only remaining light in the room. All was black and still.

Chapter Thirty

The True Plot

On her capitol world of Dorien, the queen dwelled. In a dark room deep inside the great Onyx Palace, the queen of the empire had just turned away from one of her many powerful and useful magic mirrors.

Magic mirrors had always been a staple of stories and for reigning monarchs. Princess Asora used them, but Laxur loved them. Even the bad ones had their uses. They also had their secrets, secrets only known to the queens of the realm. There was always a history in the realm between queens and mirrors, in a similar vain for kings and swords. Or prince's and crowns, or princesses and palaces. Mirrors were instruments of wisdom and craft as well as showing what was needed or unknown.

Mirrors were most responsive to queens with great power or will. And since Laxur was the most powerful queen she knew more about the mirrors and could harness their powers. Laxur was an empress, but she preferred the title of queen as it made her sound powerful and wise. An empress made her sound too old and uncaring. She wanted to be seen as the woman of everyone's dreams and powerful. Someone that was lusted for and desired more than any other. But at the same time wise, passionate, and powerful. All these magic mirrors did that for her.

The mirrors also kept the queen updated like a computerized security system about events or anything that could endanger her or her rule. While she would have preferred technology, it came off as rather scary and even a source of horror to her people. And she could understand why. Machines, and advanced technology had a very menacing factor to them. Magic, sorcery, witchcraft, alchemy, and supernatural powers were more familiar to the realm. Whereas science, technology, bioengineering, and physics were relatively new and only really embraced by the Consortium state of the Utopian Kingdom.

Queen Laxur was a master in the arts of witchcraft, magic, sorcery, and alchemy. But she also knew a great deal of science and technology. She wanted to use all of this in her rule over the realm. After all it was her destiny to conquer and rule over not just the Darkcon Empire, but also over the smaller kingdoms, princedoms, bishoprics, city-states, minor powers, and even that vast Utopian Kingdom. All of this was meant to be hers. To rule over as not as a queen, or an empress, but at an all-powerful goddess.

And to that end she was on a quest to make this a reality. Gathering all the most powerful relics, learning the most powerful spells, learning ancient secrets. While adding into the mix the newest technologies, and the newly discovered sciences. All to add to her and to give Laxur what she truly desires.

So, war was also a necessary step. Princess Asora was surprisingly successful at first at thwarting Laxur's actions that would bring war to the realm for the first time in five hundred years. But in the end Asora's efforts were a waste. As was defying Laxur's will and destiny.

It was thought that Queen Laxur had lost the battle of Evorn and was defeated by Princess Asora, but this was not true. In fact, she had completed her objectives. She never wanted to take and conquer Evorn. Not yet at least. She needed something to cover her true motives and actions.

The temporary takeover of the Utopian palace was just a little bit of fun, but completely unnecessary. What Laxur was truly after was a document hidden in the palace's library. She had her soldiers rip it apart, and they eventually found several scrolls. This was her true objective. She made this all known to her Inner Imperial Council. They were the ones who helped Queen Laxur devise a way to obtain the scrolls.

The True Plot

It would also allow the Darkcons to vent some much-needed rage on the Utopians. And Laxur could not blame them as she enjoyed her people tormenting the Utopians.

The powerful dark beauty was in her private laboratory, reclining in a comfortable chair, reading one of the stolen scrolls. It was old and held together with ancient magic. This one was more of a historical document. Written in a language that had eventually evolved into the modern Utopian common language. Laxur was able to read it through a spell that was called Rosimer. This steel could translate any magical language into a form that the reader could understand. Surprisingly it also worked on ehan, the human's main language. It should not because the human language was not magical, but natural. Queen Laxur suspected that perhaps in the very distant and forgotten past that humans were once a powerful magical race that simply forgot it.

The scroll itself spoke of an ancient battle between two powerful beings. Both gods, and one managed to imprison the other. It did not say where of course. But it mentioned that the victorious goddess whose man Laxur could not read as that part of the scroll had been damaged over time. She fused her own power with the one of the defeated gods and took it back to where they came from. Only the one who was chosen by destiny could have it and its limitless growing power.

Laxur knew that was herself. This power would be hers and she would make sure that she was worthy. But how true was this?

"I see you found them, my queen," a beautiful feminine voice in the darkness said.

"Yes, I did. They were where you said it would be. Asora was completely unaware of their existence," Laxur responded. "And the Utopians have not noticed them missing."

"Phase one is complete. What does phase two entails, if you do not mind me asking?" the young female voice asked.

"Phase two is to have Asora retrieve the remaining coins and then find a way to make her give them to me." Laxur said.

The woman in the shadows walked into the laboratory so that Queen Laxur could see her. She was a blond haired, green eyed, average height, slim, and athletic in build. She wore a long black dress and a corset over her torso. She also had green trim on her dress. She was younger than the queen but no less as lovely and as dangerous. She also looked human with a divine feel to her. This young woman was what Laxur would consider attractive to her.

The queen women as attractive as men. She desired both and felt that only being attractive to one gender over the other was too limiting. While Laxur herself was seen by so many as the ultimate woman, the queen herself preferred to have other females that were more average as a comfort companion. But this woman was very different and Laxur treated her differently too.

"Make yourself comfortable. You are, after all, an expert on magical items, Polea," Laxur said to her companion. "And my best expert on these."

"True, my queen." Polea extended her hand, and Laxur handed over one of the other scrolls.

The blonde took out a pair of reading glasses, put them on, and began to read the parchment. These glasses were not enchanted, but normal seeing glasses. Polea had weak eyes and she needed her glasses, but she hated to wear them. Laxur tried to help her once before, but Polea had a very rare eye condition that not even magic could cure. Only divine powers could help her. Laxur then cast a spell on the glasses that Pole was wearing so she could read the scroll's words more easily.

Laxur was very fond of Polea for many reasons. One reason was that she was, as Laxur was, a human-angel hybrid. Laxur found Polea to be a kindred spirit, and she trusted her. Laxur, Polea, and Asora were the only one of their kind known. Like Laxur herself and Asora, Polea was extremely powerful and unlike other magical beings who could get exhausted after using their magical abilities too much. Polea's magic regenerated almost instantly, giving her a greater endurance that even Queen Laxur could not match. It was believed that Laxur, Asora, and

The True Plot

Polea each had a unique feature that made them better then the rest. Something that Laxur believed in fully as did Polea.

"What can you tell me about what is written on that scroll?" Laxur asked her farsighted friend.

"Interesting. It says that the last remaining coins are hidden in a book," Polea whispered.

"A book? How is that interesting?" Laxur said. "Does it say which one?"

"No, it does not. But it does say that the master of the Utopian kingdom will hold it," Polea said.

"So, Princess Asora may have it?" Laxur asked.

"In order to get the last few coins, one must enter into the story of the book. One must play along with separate stories for each of the coins," Polea read out loud.

"Let me get this straight. In order to get the remaining three coins, we have to go through three different stories in a book. Who the hell thought that up?" Laxur complained.

"The former Queen T'a of the Utopian Kingdom, that's who," Polea responded dully.

"Figures. So where is this book of stories?" Laxur asked.

"The book is kept nearby the current monarch." Laxur said.

"I did not see this book in Asora's possession, nor in the library," Laxur said. "But if I can make her get the coins for us. All I need is an idea," Laxur whispered.

"We will need to think of something, since Asora is the only one allowed to retrieve the final three coins," the blonde pointed out.

"Which ones are left?" the dark queen asked. "The final three are the coins of light, life, and darkness."

"I heard a rumor of an eighth coin once, long ago. What was it? What happened to it?" Laxur asked.

"The eighth coin was rumored to be the most powerful of all the coins. The power it held was the power of time. It was said that a mysterious deity stole the coin eons ago. The deity took it because it was afraid of someone abusing its awesome power," Polea explained.

"A coin that could control time. That *is* the greatest of all powers. I thought that the coins gave a person control over just nature?" the Darkcon monarch questioned.

"Time is a part of nature, and it is also the most dangerous if fooled with." Polea said. "I can understand why this entity would take it, if it was the responsible type."

"Eight coins once existed," Laxur thought out loud.

"There was a myth once that there were in fact thirteen in all. Only the Empyrean themselves could wield them. But over time mortals could as the Empyrean needed help," Polea said.

"Thirteen in all? One for each other thirteen Empyrean," Laxur said. "It was only a myth, too bad."

"It is possible that all thirteen still exist. There was once a being who quested to collect all thirteen," Poles said.

"What happened?" Laxur asked curiously.

"No one knows, the quester never returned," Polea said. "It was only a myth."

"We can discuss that one later. Right now, I need to concentrate on getting the three coins from the book, and the two that my little sister has," Laxur said.

The queen got up off her chair and walked to her workbench. She grabbed a tool and mixed liquid in a beaker. She took ingredients from shelves and racks and mixed them. This was very calming to the queen as she worked her magic on these potions. In reality she did not need them, but she loved alchemy and using potions helped preserve her power.

"Are you making more of those green elixirs that you are so fond of?" Polea asked, catching a glimpse of her queen's actions.

"Yes, I am. Would you like to try it sometime? It feels good," Laxur said suggestively.

She was holding a vial and offering it to Polea. Normally, Queen Laxur would not do this, but Polea was a special case. She loved Polea in

The True Plot

a similar manner that she did to Asora. Others like herself were beyond rare and in the queen's mind her kind are the only ones destined and by divine right to lord over all. Asora and Polea should rule with Laxur and being big would help too. If she could make it permanent, she would, but growing into a giantess as fun and pleasurable as it might be, it was very draining. After the fight with Rowaton, Queen Laxur was exhausted and slept for days. If she could find a way around that drawback, then Laxur would be having more of her ideal fun.

"Of course, Your Majesty, but I will not use it now. Maybe later. I do not want to damage this new home of mine," Polea said.

Polea then took the vial and putt it in her pocket. She watched the seductive queen place several vials into her pockets that were all over her dress. Polea could not help but be envious of Laxur and her curves, and her other sensuous attributes. How she wished that she could have a form like hers. Pole saw Laxur as the feminine form perfected. Laxur was flawless and powerful. Her strength was hidden behind her tall sexy body. The queen was dangerous and alluring to the point that made her divine.

The young blond woman was cursed with her limited and weak body. Perhaps she should use the potion, but it would only last an hour and was meant to make a person bigger. While she loved to watch the queen grow. Polea felt that she needed to improve her appearance before she would make herself grow. Maybe she could ask the queen if she could make a potion that would make her as sexy, strong, and deadly as the dark beauty was permanently.

A knock at the door. Laxur gave her command to enter. In stepped the powerful Dame Dari. The greatest warrior of the Darkcon Empire and Queen Laxur's personal bodyguard. Polea found Dari to be as equally as attractive as Laxur.

"Lady Polea," Dari nodded to Polea.

"Yes Dari?" Laxur asked.

"Your Inner Council is ready. And the House of Lords wants an update," Dari informed.

"Finally," Laxur replied. "Polea, gather the scrolls and follow us."

"Yes, your majesty," Polea bowed.

The blonde woman then ran around collecting and rolling up the scrolls as fast as she could. Dari watched the small blonde woman work. She smiled as Polea worked. Dari enjoyed women like Polea. Dari waited for Polea to finish before she escorted both to the Inner Council Chambers.

Minutes later the three women arrived at an average sized door that was made of stone and metal. Dari opened it up to allow Laxur and Polea through. In the dimly lit room there was Prime Minister Golcon, General's Sysu, and Obsidian, Master Herenian, and Priest Illumin were all present. They all sat at a large circular table with a small throne at its center. Queen Laxur sat upon the throne, and it moved around to all her to see the others. Polea and Dari sat down in two available seats at the table.

"We have all gathered as your requested," Golcon said.

"Excellent," Laxur replied. "Polea, show us the scrolls."

Polea laid out several of the scrolls on the large table. They were passed around.

"We wasted our time for scrolls?" Golcon snapped angrily.

"We did not waste anything," Obsidian barked. "This was our main objective."

"Though it would have been nice to have taken Evorn and hold," Sysu commented calmly.

"It would have been nice but unnecessary," Laxur said. "Our true goals were achieved."

"And they were?" Golcon demanded.

Laxur had not told her council everything. Only Dari and Polea were aware of Laxur's true aims. As the queen needed their expertise for her quest. The others only needed to do what they do best.

"I too would like to know," Illumin spoke.

"Knowing our mighty queen," Herenian started. "It will be something quite epic."

The True Plot

"And what do I tell the House of Lords?" Golcon demanded. "That some random and unseen factor has been achieved? You know as well as I do that will not fly!" Goclon pounded the table in frustration.

"Calm down," Sysu said annoyed. "We all knew that attacking Evorn was the easy part. Holding it was going to be impossible with our current state."

"Again, what am I suppose to tell them? And also, that our people are a bit confused at the moment," Golcon said.

"Confused on what?" Dari asked.

"How the hell did we get to Evorn and not just kick the Utopian rats out?" Golcon replied.

"Their princess has a dragon," Herenian pointed out.

"More than that," Illumin started. "Rowaton no less."

"I could have defeated all the Utopians on Evorn by myself," Laxur boasted. "But fighting the dragon's god king is beyond even me. For now."

"What the hell does that mean?" Golcon snapped.

"Trying to read the scrolls before you burn them," Polea said.

"And who the hell is this blonde pipsqueak?" Golcon roared pointing at Polea.

"She is one of us now," Laxur said in a very threatening tone. "If you have an issue with her, I suggest you keep it to yourself."

"How many more lost pets are you planning to bring in?" Golcon said without fear of the queen.

"As many as I please," Laxur replied. "Now pay attention and I am sure you will think of something to say to the House of Lords."

Obsidian was reading the scrolls. Unlike everyone else Obsidian was very good at reading ancient languages. It was one of his non-martial skills that he enjoyed. He read over them and then looked for another.

"Fascinating," Obsidian said. "All thirteen of these scrolls are meant to be read together."

"Explain?" Laxur commanded.

"The scrolls were written in a way as to put them together like child's puzzle," Obsidian explained. "Give me your copies."

The werewolf general then placed all thirteen scrolls in front of him and rearranged them on the table. Everyone gathered around them. The scrolls did form a larger message. But the spells normally used for translation did not work. One had to know what was being said.

"Amazing," Polea said.

"Can you read it?" Laxur asked.

"I think only the two of us can," Obsidian said.

"He is right," Polea replied. "Only ones who can read this language can truly understand its meaning."

"Well then," Herenian started. "Do not keep us in suspense you two."

Both Polea and Obsidian read and reread the now united scrolls. They talked in between themselves as they spoke the ancient foreign language out loud. Polea and Obsidian also debated on how to pronounce some of the words. Because the pronunciation of the words has meaning on what they are trying to say.

"Well?" Laxur asked. "What can you two tell me?"

"It speaks of a vast power. But to learn of it and where it is to be found," Obsidian started.

"Seven of the thirteen are needed," Polea finished.

"Seven of thirteen what?" Golcon demanded.

"Shut up for a moment and we will tell you," Obsidian barked.

"Coins," Polea answered.

"Coins? Like from the treasury or like the ones that her majesty has?" Golcon asked.

"Like the ones I have," Laxur showed the two coins she possessed. "Asora has two as well.

"That makes four," Illumin. What about the other three?"

"They are hidden in a divine object that is disguised as a book. A book that is in the hands of the most powerful Utopian," Polea answered.

"So, Princess Asora has this divine book," Golcon asked. "Are we going to have to attack Evorn again to get it?"

"I hope not," Laxur said.

That made Golcon blink in surprise. He was not disappointed more

THE TRUE PLOT

like relieved. While he wanted to attack the Utopian Kingdom like any Darkcon. A costly attack like on Evorn was too much. Even for him.

"Can we lure her somewhere then?" Sysu asked.

"The princess herself?" Illumin started. "Not likely. After the Evorn campaign I would assume that the Utopians will be far more cautious now."

"Also, there is Rowaton to contend with now," Obsidian said.

"And that Asora is now a Dragon Dancer. Mighty warriors that fought for the Utopian Kingdom," Dari spoke.

"You fought them and won," Polea said.

"It took more power than I originally was born with to take on a whole team of them," Dari pointed out. "Asora is the most powerful Dragon Dancer that has ever existed. To have Rowaton himself as her dragon means that Asora herself is beyond even me."

"Really?" Golcon questioned. "I remember you able to take down hundreds of Dragons Dancers in the past. What makes Asora different?"

"Princess Asora," Laxur started with an emphasis on Asora's title. "Is bounded to a god king. The first of her king, and the makes her a divine warrior. A Paladin of the gods. It would take a god to fight a god."

"So, we need a god on our side," Illumin said.

"Why do you think I went to so much trouble to get these scrolls?" Laxur asked.

"They show where you can find one?" Herenian asked.

"No," Golcon said in awe now. "They show you how to become one."

Queen Laxur merely smiled evilly. That was the answer that Golcon had. He now knew what to tell the House of Lords. And he believed that he could spin this into a greater story. He was going to tell the House of Lords that Evorn was a necessary move so that Queen Laxur could gain the true prize. And to cover her tracks to prevent the Utopians from figuring out her grand plan, the invasion needed to be done. The Utopians would assume that the actual objectives were destroyed, and that the Utopians victory was in fact quite hollow.

It had been six months since the invasion of Evorn when Laxur felt ready to complete her quest for the coins. But she still had not created a good enough plan to get them. It had to be done a certain way otherwise Asora would simply deny Laxur her prize. The queen was in her darkened bed chambers still up and plotting. She looked at one of her many magic mirrors.

"Where is Princess Asora now?" Laxur asked the magic mirror.

"The maiden you seeks on Evorn," the mirror said.

"I never thought that you, of all people, would use a magic mirror. It seems so old-fashioned," Polea said.

"All queens have a magic mirror, my friend. I find it useful," Laxur responded. "Besides they are a symbol of queens and queendoms. Plus, I like them."

"If you say so," Polea said.

"Hallows Eve is coming," Laxur said. "Will you come to my costume party?"

"I would love too," Polea replied.

Part Two

The Swaye Family

Chapter Thirty-One
Laxur's Costume Party

On Dorien the capitol world of the Darkcon Empire and the seat of power for their all-powerful Queen Laxur. The fall season had come. On Dorien a world of perpetual night with bioluminescent plants and some glowing creatures. The temperature mostly became colder mostly. This also caused powerful storms near the Onyx Palace.

These storms had been helpful once long ago as a defense of the palace from attackers. But now a days they were a big problem. The Onyx Palace was the only structure on Dorien able to withstand the most powerful of storms on the planet. The giant black colored palace also doubled as an emergency shelter for much of the planet's population. The Onyx Place rivaled its Utopian Kingdom's counterpart on Evorn in sheer size and majesty. But many considered the Onyx Palace to be a work of art.

Normally the Onyx Palace was the most dominating structure on all of Dorien. But under Queen Laxur the economy had exploded, and the tiny villages and small settlements now resembled human scale cities and even a mega city formed around the Onyx Palace. The Darkcon's first mega city put the Onyx Palace at its center. Several million people lived outside the palace in comfort. But still the storms were punishing, and the Onyx Palace was still the safest place to go.

As was custom around this time the Onyx Palace was open to the public. For the week was Hallows Eve. One if not the biggest Darkcon holiday. Queen Laxur also put a pause on the war with the Utopian Kingdom to allow her people to celebrate it. Laxur absolutely loved Hallows Eve. Everything about it was what she loved about celebrating.

Costumes, treats, surprise scares, fun, and storytelling. Laxur loved to celebrate the day and followed in past ruler's footsteps and opened the palace to the festivities. The gremlin workers were putting the finishing touches on the decorations. The queen gave freedom to how her home would be decorated to those that served her.

It was also customary for the ruling king or queen to dress up as a very obscure person or being from history. And to get the people to guess who they were. The one who got it right was given a great prize.

Laxur looked out of her window and saw the vast numbers of her people coming into the palace to celebrate with her. She saw a huge number of girls and women dressed like her. It made Laxur smile to know that she was so loved and admired by her people. While Laxur herself could not join in the contests. She was however the judge of all the costumes, games, and stories. She was the one for whom you must impress and try to scare. Laxur is not easy to fright, but she could be allowed to put on a show of scare.

A knock at her door. "Come," Laxur commanded.

Dame Dari stepped through the door. She was already dressed up like Princess Asora of all things. Laxur held a hand over her mouth to stop from laughing. But she could not. Dari also laughed as she knew this would make her queen laugh.

"Lovely," Laxur laughed.

"I thought so," Dari said. "She is a darling."

"That she is," Laxur said.

"Why are you not dressed?" Dari asked.

"I do not know who to dress as," Laxur admitted.

"You do this every year," Dari sighed.

"I know," Laxur said. "I do come up with something last minute. It just must be something special."

"Perhaps you should dress as Golcon?" Dari said.

The two tall women burst out laughing.

"I need something historical or scary. Not a rabid screamer," Laxur laughed.

"Good point," Dari said. "Besides Golcon is going as General Thrasus," Dari paused. "Believe it or not he did a good job this time."

"General Threasus? Really? Laxur thought. "Damn. That is a good idea."

"Just do not go as Aethina," Dari asked.

"Oh, I would not do that to you," Laxur said. "That witch was a monster, and I would not be caught dead in her dresses."

"Thank you," Dari said.

Queen Aethina was the first queen of the Utopian Kingdom and was Dari's main rival. The two clashed during the Great Sundering thousands of years ago. Aethina was a monster of a woman. More beautiful then Laxur was, but such an evil beast. Aethina was so evil that she took Dari's only child from her. But in the end Aethina was destroyed, and Dari was free of her nightmare, but she could never see her child again. Laxur promised her once that she would help her find her lost child and reunite them. Dari served Laxur for this hope.

"Maybe I should do an animal theme this year?" Laxur pondered out loud.

"That would be different," Dari said.

"But of what?" Laxur asked herself. She looked around at the books on her large bookshelf. A book of animals that lived on Dorien caught her eye. She opened it and saw one that caught her eye. "Ah this will do."

"What?" Dari asked.

"A Syrican," Laxur said.

"A Syrican is just like a Scylla-Mermaid," Dari pointed out.

"My mermaid form is a Scylla type," Laxur said. "Besides, tentacles are fun."

Laxur sashayed to her dressing corner. Dari watched as the queen transformed herself into her mermaid form. Which indeed had dozens of long and strong tentacles like that of an octopus or a squid. The biggest difference between a Syrican and a Scylla-Mermaid were that the Syrican's had armored skin that more resembled a human war submarine. The skin was metallic, and they had crab pinchers along with human like arms. They were also bald. Laxur transformed her long black hair into armor like skin and extra pinchers under her arms. Also, the Syricans had something in common with coconut crabs. In that Syricans were not water-based life forms but lived on the coastal areas and near bodies of water but could not go into water.

Queen Laxur emerged from her dressing corner looking like a hideous beach dweller. Her skin looked to have been made of steel and her pincher arms were massive. Her tentacles also wiggled and seemed to struggle to hold her up. To help Laxur made her normal legs reform under her mass of tentacles.

"How do I look?" Laxur asked confidently.

"Like a monstrous Syrican," Dari smiled.

"Excellent," Laxur replied. "Now let us go and party!"

As the two left, the book was still opened, and it showed that the Syrican's had one known natural predator. The Dorien Black Basilisk. A water snake like creature that was twenty meters long with a mouth full of sharp bladed teeth. Skin as hard as steel, and it had electrode organs. Basically, it could zap its prey with electricity. It also had six eyes that glowed in three different colors. One pair saw in normal light, another pair in infrared, and the third pair in ultraviolet. It was classified but the Dorien Institute of Biology as a super predator. While endangered due to habitat loss, it has been classified as extremely dangerous. Only certain experts were trained on how to deal with them.

Queen Laxur and Dame Dari came out into the vast and heavily decorated courtyard. It was made to resemble an old, haunted mansion. Though pulling that off with millions of people in the palace was impossible.

Tours were going on as were a lot of games and vendors selling treats all in the theme of a spooky holiday. When Queen Laxur came out of the palace tower everyone roared in approval and cheers. Today no one was to bow to her, but to treat her as more of an honored guest. This was a custom of the holiday and one that Laxur respected.

There were thousands of children running around. Queen Laxur loved children, and to see so many running around, playing, and dancing made the dark queen smile. There were games, and rides as well as tents of portable kitchens. The massive and imposing Onyx Palace tonight more resembled a carnival or theme park.

Laxur was reminded of a theme park back on her home world. A theme park that her father took her to many times when's he was a little girl. She enjoyed those days. She secretly wanted to recapture that wonderful feeling and give that feeling to her people. She saw them as her children now. She was more then a queen, and she wanted to be more.

Prime Minister Golcon was in a surprisingly good mood. He managed to sell Queen Laxur's plan to the House of Lords and was interested in celebrating. This surprised Laxur as he normally opposed her holiday plans. So, the queen approached the now drunk hell spawn demon.

"I am glad that you are enjoying yourself for once," Laxur said.

"Well, I have a reason to celebrate this time," Golcon said. "I managed to pull off the best sell of a plan in our history!"

"Just like I planned," Laxur said.

Prime Minister Golcon merely walked off to continue his drinking. Laxur should feel slighted, but she allowed it to slide. Today is a good day or night as the darkness of night was hard to determine at this time of year. Unless you were aware of the time. One of the towers in the palace was a clock tower. It showed that it was indeed mid evening.

As the Onyx Palace was alive and everyone was heading to it. At the nearby shores of the land, the black sea roiled and bubbled. A large creature from the depths poked its head out in the darkness. Unlike the Darkcon people, this thing could see in the dark. It could sense the heat of so many creatures. This would be a feast. The creature then moved closer.

On the beach five Darkcon's in armor were in a newly purchased beach comber vehicle. It was new to them so only one of them know how to drive the motor vehicle. A dark she elf with one missing ear. Her companions were holding on for dear life as the driver was piloting their beachcomber like a maniac.

"Slow down you damned maniac!" One of the Darkcon soldiers yelled in fright.

"I'm getting sand in my mouth!" Another yelled.

The beachcomber suddenly stopped and all, but the driver went flying off the vehicle. The four soldiers crashed and slowly picked themselves up off the black sand.

"Shasu, are you drunk?" A big troll complained as he wiped off the sand from his face.

"Hey, you said you wanted to see what this thing could do," Shasu the dark elf woman complained. "It's not my fault that you can't handle it!"

As the two argued, the smallest of the five noticed the waves moving in a way they were not supposed to. Cautiously he took out his machete of a sword. He hoped it was just one of the sea critters that came onto the beach to lay eggs.

"Hey Bors!" One of the other soldiers came up to the small soldier. "What is it?"

"Something's wrong with the waves," Bors said.

"Something wrong with the waves?" The fellow soldier asked. "Man, you're paranoid. Let's get back before the sergeant eats Shasu again."

As the two soldiers walked away from the ocean. Something slowly made its way to the beach. Bors then heard something and looked back to the water. He could not see in the pitch-black night. The only light visible was coming from the carnival that was open at the Onyx Palace a few kilometers away. That did nothing to light up the beach. Bors looked for his flashlight in one of his pockets.

Then he heard a large monstrous creature was very close to him.

He could the light that was to attach to his gun, but that was back in the beachcomber. He still had his machete.

Back at the beachcomber the sergeant and Shasu were still arguing. But their argument was cut short when the machete of Bors landed on the ground in front of them with a clang. It was snapped in two. Then came the grumbling and moaning of a large beast.

The driver grabbed her gun and was about to open fire. A deadly poisonous acid was spat at the four. The acid spit melted the beachcomber and killed one of the soldiers. The sergeant took out his sword and swung at the thing in the dark. Only to have his head bitten off.

Shasu heard her companions scream and then go silent. The dark she elf attempted to run to a cropping of rocks. She fell to the ground as something thick and slimy wrapped itself around her left leg. Shasu was then lifted up and as she was tossed up and started to free fall. The last thing she saw was a massive maw of teeth and eyes of red and black in a ring around a hideous head.

Back at the Onyx Palace General Sysu refused to dress up in costume as she felt it was embarrassing. So, she wore her military dress uniform with all her medals, ribbons, awards, and ropes. She was not a festive person nor was she in the mood. Her family or coven of vampires were in their bat or cat forms. All joining the celebrations. Some of the men in her coven had families and they brought them to the palace to have fun.

"Really? Just your dress uniform?" Laxur asked Sysu.

"Why not? It is the only thing I feel is worthy of me this day," Sysu said.

"Obsidian was right, you are a bore at parties," Laxur said.

The queen had a large tankard full of ale or beer. Sysu could not tell. She knew that her queen was a very big lover of alcohol and drank a lot. More then most men could. It honestly shocked the old vampire warrior woman. But she at least picked a decent costume.

The music was being played by an actual music band famous for their holiday music. It was a very large band and they spread out across the vast courtyard so that their music could carry and be heard.

The large wheel ride was full of people. Other rides now had large lines. All in the theme of a spooky fun holiday. This was new and almost all of it was possible because of the queen herself.

A small troll boy was chasing a toy he dropped. He ran into the queen and did not realize it. He crashed into her leg, and she merely lunged forward. She looked to see the small boy looking up at her in fear. She did not like that. So Laxur kneeled grabbed the toy and cleaned it. She smiled like a loving mother to him and gave it to him.

"Here you go, be careful next time," Laxur said sweetly.

"Thank you, your majesty," the boy said.

Queen Laxur kissed him on his forehead. She gave him a pat on the head and sent him on his way. The boy ran to his family and Laxur watched them walk to the nearby food court. Laxur sighed in sadness. She envied all the families that surrounded her. This was why she wanted these celebrations. This brought them all together. They brought them all to her.

Barking from little werewolf puppies came up to Laxur. She smiled and giggled as they came up to her and wanted to play. Then their father, General Obsidian in her wolf form came up looking exhausted.

"Sorry, the kids are a handful," Obsidian said.

"Oh, it is quite alright," Laxur said. "Your children are just adorable."

Obsidian barked to get his children's attention. They stopped trying to climb up Laxur's legs and sat at attention in front of their father. Then another werewolf came up. A she wolf who was all black. She looked menacing and ready to fight. She rubbed her head on Obsidian's neck.

"Our apologizes your majesty," the female werewolf said.

"Oh, it is no trouble, your children are just the cutest," Laxur said.

"Coal," Obsidian said to the female werewolf. "Let's go get a cafob."

"We need to get the kids that cotton candy first," Coal said.

"I can do that for you," Laxur offered.

"Oh, we cannot impose on you your majesty," Coal said.

"It is no trouble. I need some cotton candy too," Laxur said.

"Really?" Obsidian asked.

"Please!" The dozen werewolf puppies begged. "We'll be good for the queen!"

"I will take care of them for a few minutes," Laxur said.

Obsidian snorted to Coal and the werewolf couple walked off. The dozen small playful puppies jumped and ran around Laxur very excitedly. Laxur chuckled with delight as the playful puppies moved about.

"You all will be some fearsome attack troops one day," Laxur said as she made her way to the stand that sold cotton candy.

"Yeah. I'm going to be you captain!" The oldest of the young puppies said.

"Oh really?" Laxur asked impressed. "You have the energy of a battle-hardened knight."

"I want to be her assassin!" A girl puppy said as she bounced on top of the oldest.

"I have many assassins. You are going to need to be extra sneaky," Laxur said with a smile.

Werewolves were born as dogs or wolves would be. They started out as four legged puppies and learned to transform from wolf to human shape. They could talk like a person and learned just as easily. Most of a werewolf's magic was devoted to hunting, fighting, and searching. The Utopians believed that werewolf bites made you into one of them. That was not true, that was how infections spread, but not how werewolves reproduced. Werewolves were normal magical mammals.

The gremlin in a pick uniform and white apron managed the machines that made the cotton candy at the stand. The hyperactive creature looked like a nightmarish critter normally. But Queen Laxur found them to be fun and very effective at any job they are put in.

"Order?" The gremlin asked.

"Thirteen sticks," Laxur said. "One of each flavor."

"Coming up!" The gremlin vendor chuckled out.

It disappeared behind the stand. A comedic wave of noises came from the stand as the hyperactive gremlin worked. A few funny screams and the crashing of pots. Laxur was tempted to see if the vendor was alright. Then a moment later thirteen sticks full of different colored cotton candy appeared with a scaly fist holding them. The queen took them and gave twelve to the puppies. They instantly started eating. Laxur gave the fidgeting gremlin a small sack full of gold coins. The gremlin opened the sack and inspected the coins. It was happy with the payment and disappeared back behind its counter.

Laxur enjoyed her traditional pick stick of cotton candy. It brought back pleasant memories of her father when she was small like the puppies. Her father took her to carnivals all the time and bought her cotton candy. Pink was always her favorite and he mad it a point to make sure she got one.

"Thank you," one of the younger puppies said.

"You are so very welcome," Laxur petted the puppy on his head.

Laxur sat at a park bench and the twelve puppies were on the ground in front of her playing and enjoying their royal treat. Obsidian and Coal came back to see their queen enjoying a large stick of cotton candy as their children played at her feet. She even was allowing two of the puppies to play fight one of her feet.

"Thank you for watching them your majesty," Coal said.

"It was my pleasure," Laxur said. "You are welcome to come to the Onyx Palace any time. Bring the family."

"I may take you up on that offer," Obsidian said.

Int he palace storeroom several workers were getting another barrel of mead out to the vendors. The large trolls and orcs also were picking other supplies to bring up.

"What the hell is that smell?" One of the orcs complained.

"It ain't me!" A troll said as he sniffed himself.

"Did the toilets back up again?" Another troll asked.

"No, it do not smell like a toilet! This smell is like dead fish or a corpse!" Another orc said.

"Just find the dead animal and get rid of it. The queen likes to have the palace clean!" The biggest troll ordered while holding his nose.

"What's that noise?" A smaller troll asked.

It was a hissing sound and the sound of leather moving on stone. The lone electrical light then went out after some foul-smelling liquid hit it.

"Blimey get a torch!" Someone complained.

Then someone screamed. That was enough to get the others attention. But before they could do anything, they too screamed as they were devoured.

Outside of the storeroom the palace staff heard a panicked commotion from below. Something then started to rumble. Then the floor below them exploded. The lights were knocked out inside the palace.

In the courtyard the whole palace and the ground shook. The artificial lighting flickered as the shaking continued. Then a section of the palace wall exploded. Several dozen people screamed in horror as a beastly roar came. They could not see it against the backdrop of the black sky. But the carnival lights were able to show some of the beast.

"A Black Basilisk!" Sysu said.

The master was easily twenty meters tall. It had a snake like head with hundreds of horns coming out of its flesh. It also has a three jawed mouth that was lined with rows upon rows of long teeth. It also has a ring of many red eyes around its head. It also had a dozen hissing tongues that tasted the air around it.

It then spat at the wheel ride causing it to fall over. Then like a snake it lashed out and got a mouth full of victims. Arrows, and bullets were fired at it the monster only for them to pounce off the armored scales. A rocket struck it from the side, fired by a random soldier from a tower. The blast merely knocked the giant basilisk to the side.

The monster saw the young child play area full of tiny Darkcon children. An easy prey for it. But before it could come at its prey, hot flames crawled up its body. Its red glowing eyes were blind by the fire.

But it managed to see Queen Laxur shooting fire from her hands at it.

"Get the heavier weapons out!" Laxur commanded. "I will keep it busy!"

The basilisk let out an ear-piercing scream that made Laxur stop and cover her ears in shock. The flames vanished from the monster but now it wanted the queen as its next meal. Queen Laxur then transformed herself back into her normal form. This allowed her to unfurl her large black wings. She jumped into the air and flew up into the skies. The basilisk was trying to reach her. Laxur then launched fireballs at the beast every time it opened its gapping maw of a mouth at her. It almost had her, but Laxur was able to fly away at the last minute. But she did get badly cut and she bleed on one of the monster's teeth.

Laxur landed on the ground. The giant Black Basilisk then looked down at the queen with sword in hand. The creature then convulsed and shrank down and transformed into an all-black copy of Queen Laxur herself. But this copy was only a copy in shape only. It had Laxur's feminine curves and wings, but its mouth was still in three parts and full of fangs. Its ring of red glowing eyes became three rows of red eyes from her face up to the top of its forehead. It also had the snake tongues hissing.

"Delicious blood," the creature spoke in a poorly mimicked version of Laxur's voice. "You are delicious. I need to feed."

It then lunged at Laxur. The queen jumped int the air and watched the copy of her crash into a wall. It went through it as if it was not there. It turned and then also flew into the air. The black copy of Laxur grabbed hold of her and held on to her like a snake would its prey. It was attempting to constrict and crush Laxur. The queen then ignited her body turning herself into a plasma fire. The heat and pain burned the monster and it fell away agony.

The Basilisk Laxur crashed to the ground. It slowly and painfully got back up. It was convulsing again. It grew larger and huge horns and spikes grew from its body. The mimicked hair turned into huge quills and stingers. The Basilisk Laxur still in the queen's image grew to twenty meters in size. And it let out an ear-piercing scream. It swung its massive arm and it slammed into Laxur herself. This sent her flying out to sea and far away from the palace. The beast then looked back at all its prey. It enjoyed this form and made more enhancements. Its neck extended to allow its head to move about.

Dozens of rockets and missiles as well as large grenades hit the beast from every direction. Hundreds of Imperial Guardsmen armed with rocket launchers opened fire. The beast then unleashed a mist of deadly acid. Its breath was so corrosive that it reduced metal of any kind to rust. It burned flesh, and poisoned water. Stone could even be made soft and the air itself rotten. The mist also had a paralyzing affect on living things.

Just as the Black Laxur Basilisk was about to gorge itself on the meal it now had. Several powerful quakes struck the land from the sea. They sounded like footsteps of something massive approaching. The basilisk turned to see a tidal wave was coming. A wave that crested at least a hundred meters high. There was also a bluish-purple light at the center.

The wave struck the palace and washed away much of the poison mist. Then the whole land shook as a massive object arose from, he sea. It was a creature with hundreds of massive tentacles, that could generate tidal waves all on their own. From the center of this mass arose a huge being. It was Queen Laxur herself. Her angelic wings were so vast that she covered the skies itself. She had transformed herself into her mermaid form.

Queen Laxur could change herself into other beings. Her mermaid form was that of a scylla type mermaid. The kind that had tentacles instead of fins. But Laxur also used one of her potions to grow large. In this form she was the largest that she had ever become. She had hundreds of tidal waves making tentacles coming out of her waist, and her wings created hurricane force winds. She also towered over the palace itself by many orders of magnitude. She was so large that she could shake the ground for hundreds of kilometers. This was Leviathan Laxur.

The basilisk was in awe and horror at this coming super beast.

Leviathan Laxur lashed out like a vicious predator. She roared and bellowed like a beast as well. Her roar could be heard across all of Dorien. Her chest glowed orange and red. Then from her mouth Laxur belched a wave of plasma flame. Her fire was so destructive that it caused the ocean around her to ignite and become a sea of fire.

Leviathan Laxur flexed and expanded to double in mass. She then unleashed another wave of plasma fire. The Basilisk Laxur took to the air and flew straight for the face of the giant sea monster. At this size Leviathan Laxur was very slow and the basilisk was able to dodge the arms and tentacles coming at it. The Basilisk was able to cut off some of the massive tentacles causing them to gush out hot red blood. Leviathan Laxur roared in agony. But it was only for a moment as the damage the massive Laxur endured healed in an instant. From the stump of one tentacle came ten more. Eventually the basilisk stopped cutting tentacles as more just kept growing and Leviathan Laxur became a forest of of the things.

And this was what the massive sea monster wanted. There was no way to dodge them all. Leviathan Laxur then grasped the Basilisk Laxur. In one move she crushed the life out of it. She then tossed it out to sea.

What everyone did not know was at this size Laxur had no higher brain function. She was in a sense a mindless beast. She roared in triumph and her roar was heard across the world. She then turned to the land and made her way ashore. She still had her two legs, but they were like mountains. Each step was a quake, and her movements created many tidal waves. She was heading for the power station, not the palace.

"Great Architect," Golcon said partly somber. "It is just like out of those old cheesy human giant monster movies!"

"Why is she attacking us now?" Sysu asked.

"At that size she may not realize it. The larger one grows the more animal like you become," Dari explained. "Right now, our queen is a giant rampaging monster."

"That came make planet breaking quakes and continent sinking tidal waves," Golcon added. "How do we stop her?"

"We have to wait for the spell to wear off," Dari answered.

"That could be any hour or days!" Sysu snapped.

"Why is she heading for the power station?" Obsidian asked.

"Electricity would add to her. Making the spell stronger and her even bigger and stronger," Dari said.

"Uh oh," Obsidian said in a low and panicked tone.

At the power station a corrupt human worker was off shift and walking to his car. Then the ground beneath him split open. He fell to the ground in horror as he looked to see a wall of armored flesh that seemed to tower kilometers into the sky. He looked up and saw this tall beast roar in a low but still loud tone. It surveyed the power station. It then started walking. The worker was crushed in an instant.

The quaking from Leviathan Laxur caused the station to go into an emergency alert. The loudspeakers and klaxons were blaring to shut down the generators. The power plant was a hydro-electric dam for a nearby river that flowed into the sea.

Leviathan Laxur stomped her way through the complex seeming. Unaware that she was crushing it and killing. The explosions from the electric generators did not bother her. Her hundreds of tentacles snaked through the building and pathways as she moved. Several of her tentacles destroyed the gate controls that would have shut down the generators. Now the generators could not be stopped, and the titanic beast made her way to the dam.

The dam itself was one of the largest projects the Darkcons ever did. It was Queen Laxur who designed it and gave the resources and funding needed to make it a reality. The dam was so large that the river the largest on Dorien could for the first time be controlled. She easily towered over the massive dam. Laxur was blinded by pure animalistic instinct and needed to feed. Electricity was what she craved now.

There was then an irritating noise that causer the giant beast's attention. She turned to see Dari holding a megaphone.

"Oh crap," was all Dari could say to herself.

Leviathan Laxur roared in rage but followed Dari as she moved out to sea. Dari floated in the air many kilometers up to make sure that the giant beast did not loose sight of her.

Dame Dari was shocked by the sheer mass that made up this beast. The hundreds of tentacles, the hurricane generating wings, and the many kilometers tall central body of the queen. She turned herself into a giant monster to defeat another. Dari just had to tire Laxur out and she would hopefully revert to normal.

It did not take long before Leviathan Laxur started to tire out and slowed down. She was still trying to grab Dari, but the fallen angel was too fast. The giant beast was now breathing heavily as she stopped in the middle of the ocean.

The beast then sighed and in an explosion of light vanished. Dari looked to see Queen Laxur back in her normal form and size floating face up in the ocean. Dari flew down as fast as she could and scooped the queen up.

As Dari landed, Laxur regained consciousness. She had the worst headache and complained about it the whole way down. Sysu had a towel ready for Laxur as she was now naked. The queen also wrapped herself in her wings to further cover herself. Everyone was clapping and cheering as Laxur got back to her feet.

"What are you all so happy about?" Laxur asked.

"Now that was an event," Obsidian said.

"Giant monster fights are new," Coal laughed.

Queen Laxur then thought about it. Then she realized that Coal was right. This was a unique addition to the holiday. Haunted houses and slashers were one thing. But monsters from the dark, and of course giant monsters were equally as fun.

However, Laxur looked around and saw only damage. She could only imagine the carnage that had resulted. But everyone did not seem to pay any mind to it. At least they did not show it to her.

"Do it again!" One of the girl puppies barked happily at Laxur. "You were awesome!"

"I was, was I?" Laxur asked with a smirk. "I did like being the biggest thing in the world. But I did not like that fact that I was a mindless beast."

"Well, we now have a new story to add to the day," Dari said.

"Let's clean this up and take note," Laxur said. "I do however wish to continue the celebration." Laxur paused for a moment. "Hallows Eve has only just begun."

Chapter Thirty-Two
Asora's Holiday Mystery

It was the princess's favorite time of year. The snow was gently coming down. Trees were being decorated, and the evergreens smelled wonderfully everywhere. The candles and the electric lights made both the palace and the village come alive and feel warm. Feasts were being made and specialty treats were baking in nearly every home.

This time of year, long ago, every race had a major holiday; however, the Utopians, for the last five hundred years, have called this time of year the Great Holiday Winter's Born. This allowed for more unity in the kingdom, and everyone celebrated together.

In the village the snow covered the roofs of most buildings. The main downtown district was alive with shoppers, workers, guests, and soldiers. The newly built park was full of children skating on the frozen lake that was there. The trees were decorated or in the process of being decorated with lights, both candles, and electric, as well as designed glass bobbles of different colors.

The symbol of the holiday was a green wreath with red bobbles, yellow lights, and blue wrappings. Each door across the village had its own unique take on the wreath symbols. This wreath also showed others that you welcome them or can help them.

At the docks the pubs and restaurants also used wreaths made of seaweed and chains. While this gave it a demonic appearance. This was an old Utopian sailor's belief that these evil looking wreaths scared off evil spirits and anyone who wanted to cause harm during winters born.

The Royal Guardsmen that marched through the village also wore small wreaths of their own on their right shoulders. The Royal Guard's wreaths were mostly bare. This symbolized the bare necessities that the Royal Guard believed they needed to make this holiday theirs.

As for the humans, Winters Born was relativity new, but the consortium also had a unique wreath made up of mostly multicolored electrical lights. This symbolized their scientific and industrial power. But at the same time a very playful nature with so many colors.

Angel wreaths were white as snow with black wings that covered the wreath in a protective manner. This was the angel's symbol to show that they see this day as sacred.

The noble families of the Utopian kingdom all have their own unique spin on wreath designs and colors. And it came as a surprise that Princess Asora did not have one ready. It was not that she did not want it. Quite the contrary, she loved this Utopian holiday. She was mad because she could not come up with one unique wreath design all her own. One that could symbolize her as the Princess of the Utopian Kingdom. In fact, it was the duty of a royal princess to design these things. One duty that Asora had been looking forward to all season.

On the table in front of Asora was a large bare wreath that High Priestess Nona had brought to her earlier. The blonde elf priestess was still with her. As it was her responsibility to make sure Asora fulfilled hers.

High Priestess Nona on the surface did not seem to care for the holiday. But you would be very wrong. Nona loved the holiday deeply and she even born just before the holiday week itself was to start. That start was a week away.

"Would you like to use my wreath as a bases?" Nona asked.

"No, I do not want to copy your unique designs," Asora said.

Nona's wreath was green with hints of white and gold light. She also had red bobbles, and blue snowflakes on it. She had added to hers over the years but its themes of the cold hiding a secret remained.

"Perhaps you are going about this all wrong?" Nona thought out loud.

"What do you mean?" Asora asked.

"What represents you?" Nona asked. "And what is it that people see in you and what is underneath?"

Princess Asora thought for a moment, "Well I have authority is what most would say."

"That is not what I mean," Nona said. "When I look at you, I see a beautiful girl with glowing potential. And underneath a divine hidden power."

Asora looked at Nona with amazement. "Incredible, you are better at this then me."

"I have been at this for five hundred years," Nona pointed out. "Plus, my birthday is just before the week of Winters Born. So, I take it seriously."

"Your Birthday?" Asora gasped. "Why did you not tell me?"

"It should not concern you," Nona said. "The special days of the minions who serve you."

"I take pride in getting to know my minions as you say," Asora said. "Do you have plans?"

"Normally I have to work in the chapel on my day," Nona said.

"Well, I am giving you the option of having your special day off," Asora said.

"Thank you, your highness," Nona said.

"Is there anyone special you celebrate with?" Asora asked.

"Unfortunately, no," Nona answered.

"Can I celebrate it with you?" Asora asked. "It could be a great way to get to know each other better?"

"Why would you bother?" Nona asked.

"Honestly Nona. All I know about you is that you are the highest-ranking priestess and second only to the Puro himself. You are an excellent alchemist, and you are in my honest opinion creepy. But I suspect that is because you are lonely," Asora said.

"Me, creepy?" Nona asked bewildered.

"I have heard a lot of rumors about you too. I tend to believe that they are either exaggerated or outright lies. Given the tendencies of the Royal Court," Asora said. "I think they see you as big a threat to them as I am."

"It would not surprise me," Nona said.

"So, you and I are the two most dangerous women in the eyes of the Royal Court," Asora said.

Both Princess Asora and High Priestess Nona laughed together. This was a rare moment for both. Asora imagined that was the spirit of this holiday. Then a thought came to her mind. The princess then had a great idea. She looked around for small flat disks. She did not find any, but she came across thirteen pieces of metal ingots.

"Can you give me those molds over on the shelf marked, smelting?" Asora asked.

Nona arched her eyebrow in confusion but did as she was told. Nona found thirteen small molds meant for minting coins. But these were blank. Nona gave them to Asora, and the princess used a magical etch to make some very intricate designs. Designs that reminded Nona of the Coins of Power.

"Should I go and get a foundry?" Nona asked.

"I can make one," Asora said with confidence.

The princess then used her magic to make a small metal furnace appear. Over the next hour Asora used her limited smelting skills to forge thirteen duplicates of the Coins of Power. Each in a different metal or alloy. Once done she cooled them down and cleaned them until they shined.

Then Asora took electric light strings and put them in. She also gave the fake coins the ability to glow in a unique color. She then used pinecones and mistletoe with berries to finish her decoration.

Once finished she showed it to Nona. The high priestess pretended to be a through inspector and hummed to herself as she examined it closely. After a moment she came up to Asora's eye level and gave her a thumbs up. That was the first time Asora saw Nona do that. Marevin, Jeia, and Sarea did that.

"It is you," Nona said.

"Thank you," Asora said with a smile. "Now to find a proper place to put it."

Princess Asora and High Priestess Nona walked out into the palace's main hallways. The halls were full of people running around doing their duties. There were also others decorating the halls and the various columns and artworks. The smell of pine and cinnamon made the palace feel more like a home then a place Asora was forced to work.

"If I had known that you were a fan of this holiday. I would not have to supervise you so much," Nona said. "If only you gave this much excitement to the rest of your duties."

"Nona, there is only so much I can tolerate form the day-to-day activities. But this is a holiday and that means change," Asora said. "If you do not wish to be with me that is your choice. I am not keeping you here."

"It is my duty to be with you currently and advice you. As well as guide and teach," Nona said.

"Well, I do appreciate it," Asora said. "And Will you allow me to be with you on your birthday?"

"If you can bake a cake, I will demand that you celebrate with me," Nona said jokingly.

"You are on," Asora said.

Nona stopped walking and turned to Asora. "I beg your pardon?"

"I will make you a cake," Asora said. "Though do not ask Marevin about it. It is best that you do not know."

"That has me worried," Nona said.

"Oh relax," Asora said humorously. "I learned from the last time. Marevin was only in the hospital for a week. After they reset his arm and got the shrapnel out."

That made Nona very worried. "I hope that is human humor."

"It is as long as you do not talk to Marevin or Sarea," Asora winked.

As the two passed through the halls and into the larger rooms of the palace. There were large gangs of professional decorators that the palace employed to get the palace ready for the days. Special candles were being lit, and the new electrical strings of lights were being put up too. Asora and Nona looked up to see angels lighting up the palace halls with their luminosities. Fairies also flew high above spreading fairy dust, which gave everything it touched a warm glow.

Asora looked behind her to see Lady T'ula with her trademark clipboard, making notes and looking busy. Both Asora and Nona walked up to her. Nona following Asora. T'ula saw both coming.

"You know you do not have to do all the planning yourself," Asora smiled at her close adviser.

"I prefer to do this myself to ensure that everything is as it should be," T'ula stated.

Asora took T'ula's clipboard from her and held it away. Then Nona took it from the princess. She did not bother to read it as T'ula's handwriting gave Nona a headache. And she could not understand half of what the taller dark-haired elf wrote down anyway.

"I am ordering you to relax and have some fun." The four fairies that served Asora flew over with a massive box full of decorations. Asora reached in and tossed a beautifully decorated ornament to T'ula. "Now, let's get our hands dirty and help decorate. I love this part of the holiday."

"As you wish your highness," Nona said.

T'ula sighed as she could not get around this. "Can I at least have my clipboard back?"

Nona gave T'ula back her clipboard without a word. The three women then found a box full of decorations.

It took the whole day, but the palace was finished decorating and it was time for the traditional first lighting. This was reserved only for the crowned princess. And since Asora was that only she got to light the palace up. This year there were two ways to do this. One was the traditional way by lighting a starter candle. This candle would then send its small flame to all the other enchanted candles all hung up across the vast palace. The second was to flip an electrical switch for the electric lighting. With her right hand Asora shot a magical flame at the starter candle, and with her left she flipped a switch.

In mere moments the palace exploded with holiday lighting. Fireplaces even lit themselves up. The temperature inside the palace went up to what Asora felt was comfortable. All around her the lights danced across the ceiling as light art moved showing so many images. Asora found it enchanting as the light art shined with history.

Several courtiers were fathers and mother to families of all sizes. They brought their children here and they were as amazed as Asora was. The fathers told their children what the light art was trying to say.

"Beautiful," was all Asora could say.

"Do you know what the lights are saying?" Nona asked.

"No, please tell me," Asora asked.

Nona then told both Asora and T'ula that the lights were telling the history of Winters Born. When the first king of the Utopian Kingdom had the palace built, the cold of winter threatened the people. So, he invited everyone in to stay warm, and shared his feasts with them. The people made him wreaths to thank him as it was all they had. Where normally statues of great leaders would normally go, he put the wreaths in their place for the winter. The people lived through the cold and continued building the Utopian Kingdom once spring returned.

"Nice," T'ula said.

"There is more to it but that is the basic tale," Nona explained.

"I like it," Asora said. The princess felt her belly rumble. "I am hungry. Let us go eat."

The trio then made their way to the dining hall where a feast was waiting for them.

The next day the giant trees were being put up and decorated across the palace. Where wreaths were a personal symbol, trees were symbols for whole groups. In the palace main courtyard, Princess Asora, Lady T'ula, High Priestess Nona, and Lord Marevin were helping the decoration teams set up the tree. Marevin who loved to decorate things was practically directing and commanding the efforts of everyone. Princess Asora loved seeing him so into this. She had always asked him to help in these matters. T'ula on the other hand looked to be ready to smack him with her clipboard. She was in charge here and she will not have Marevin disrupting her work. Nona could care less what those two wanted. So, Nona and Asora worked as Marevin and T'ula argued.

"Should we stop them?" Nona asked Asora.

"You are welcome to try to," Asora offered.

Nona looked at Marevin and T'ula as their yelling and cursing had elevated for everyone to hear them. T'ula took a swipe at Marevin who merely bounced out of the way.

"I see why you wish to leave them be," Nona said.

"Let us just get this tree up before those two murders each other," Asora said.

Nona arched an eyebrow at that. But she did as the princess commanded. The tree was as tall as a five-story building and required several people who could fly. Princess Asora was one of these people. She easily flew up and decorated the top portions of the tree.

Several hours later as the sun was setting. Princess Asora took the tree topper which was a golden star. She flew up to the top and placed it on the treetop. The tree exploded with light, and it lit up the courtyard. The hundreds of people who were present clapped and cheered as Asora landed on the ground.

"Now the weeklong holiday can begin!" Asora proclaimed.

On the following day the tree was hosted to gifts that the nobles wished to gift to others. Mostly their heirs or lovers. However, the servants noticed that many gifts and parts of the feast were going missing. This was known to happen in the village every few years but not in the palace.

This was enough to get much of the Royal Court upset. They at first went to the Royal Guardsmen Captain Joes to solve this. He could not find anything clues as to who may be doing this. But he did detect powerful magic that was beyond him or his knights. He did say that Princess Asora would be able to solve it at this point. That was because Asora was the most powerful being in the kingdom.

So, the Royal Court called a special session of court and summoned Princess Asora only. This confused the princess as this was not normal. So, she grabbed High Priestess Nona and wanted someone there to witness whatever the court wanted.

"Your grace, I believe that there is a Thief Ring operating in the palace," a dwarf said to the princess as she turned to look at him.

"A Thief Ring? Do you have proof?" Asora asked.

"Well, over fifty thousand Krowns' worth of gifts, food, and other materials have vanished. The servants and maids have been searched, and they are all clear, so there is another presence here," the servant said.

"That is a lot of stolen things," Nona said. "Where is the Prime Minister? And Lady T'ula?"

"This does not need to concern them, yet" another courtier said.

"Funny, I have not sensed any form of malevolence anywhere in the palace. Perhaps you have misplaced them?" Asora suggested.

"It would not be the first time," Nona added.

"I will investigate your suggestion, Your Highness," the dwarf turned around and walked out.

"Interesting," Asora said to herself. "Anyone else?"

Later, Asora and Nona came across Lady T'ula and Prime Minister Frenzen, who were arguing with a number of courtiers. Instead of interfering, Asora decided to hide behind a pillar to listen in. Nona followed Asora's lead and hid with her. Lady T'a had just walked up to the crowd around Frenzen and T'ula.

Frenzen and T'ula were talking about the missing things that the dwarf servant was talking to her about earlier. Apparently, many items were gifts to the courtiers' loved ones and children. Both T'ula and Frenzen, and now T'a, said that they could afford to buy replacements for them; the shops were not exactly out of gifts. And that they should just keep this quiet and tell Asora and Nona to not bother.

That appeared to not faze the nobles as it was the principle of the matter. There was a thief or thieves running around the palace, and they wanted the thief or thieves caught. If the gifts were not returned or the thieves caught, then the court would use their influence to cancel the whole holiday month. Frenzen pointed out that only Princess Asora had that authority and ability to do so. And she was unlikely to such a thing.

Asora and Nona looked at each other. The two made sure no one could see them.

"Would you?" Nona asked.

"Would I what?" Asora asked.

"Cancel the holiday?" Nona asked.

"No way," Asora reassured. "If anything, I agree with Frenzen."

The courtiers promised to force the princess to do this. As they were confident in their power over the princess. But the law said that princesses had full authority over all holiday matters no matter what. So, forcing Asora to cancel the holiday would be difficult.

T'ula said, "Good luck with that."

Asora and Nona then snuck back into the servant's corridor and made their way to the throne room.

"What should we do?" Nona asked.

Asora pondered for a moment. "We could stake out the scene?"

"What does that mean?" Nona asked.

"Have you ever read any crime novels?" Asora asked.

"Oh yes," Nona said happily. "But not the kind the humans write. Too technical and too heavy on action."

"Well, the idea is that we make covert observations and lay out bait," Asora said.

"This should be fun," Nona replied.

Even though the royal court was dismissed for the holiday, they all came to Princess Asora unofficially as she was decorating the throne room with her privy council. Asora had taken to her duties as host and mistress of all Utopian holidays. She stopped once the nobles all started to come to her again.

"I understand that you are all upset about the random misplacement of your gifts, but I will not, under any circumstances, cancel the holidays!" Asora stated firmly. "And if you threaten me, I promise to make your holidays as miserable as you have made it for everyone around you."

"I am sure you can," a courtier said.

"Do you know what a Cold War is?" Bremer Arton asked the courtier.

"No," was all she said.

"It goes like this," Arton paused. "You force her to cancel Winters Born, then she retaliates in some way like slapping you with fines or a nasty tax bill so she can pay the workers to remove everything early."

"He is right," Asora added. "And he is only telling you the nicest things I will do to you."

"What more can you do?" Nona asked as she came up to Asora.

"A Cold Slide," Asora said.

"You would not dare," someone snapped.

"Try me," Asora said. "We will hold court outside every day until spring. I hate the cold, but I bet I can out last you." Asora paused. "So, I will not cancel Winters Born. I will solve this mystery. And you will make no more attempts to 'convince me' otherwise. Do I make myself clear?"

"Yes, Your Highness," the court seemed to bow, and they talked among themselves. It was obvious that they were not going to be able to get Asora to cancel the holidays, but they came up with another idea. "Princess Asora! We request that you investigate why things are randomly disappearing personally. This is our right, as you know. We will hold you responsible."

"Yes, it is, unfortunately. I will conduct this investigation. Whatever I find will be the official findings. Do you accept the results of whatever

I find in this investigation?" Asora said.

"Of course," a mermaid spoke.

"Good, I shall get to work," the princess left the throne room with Nona right behind her. "Damned crashes."

The four fairy ladies in waiting that served Asora flew up to her. Gourani, Rayne, B'nei, and Friea. They were all wearing coats and fuzzy boots. All in their traditional colors.

"So where do we start?" asked B'nei.

"We shall start in the Courtyard where the Great Holiday tree is," Asora pointed out.

Nona, and Asora along with the fairy quartet made their way outside. The snow was starting to fall gently. Asora was not a fan of the cold, but she was dressed for it. Nona likewise was not thrilled about it, but she could tolerate it better than the princess could. The four fairy sisters on the other hand loved the snow.

Once at the tree Asora spread a spell throughout the entire area to reveal prints and/or other magic or spirits. "No evidence of spirits, but I sense dark magic at work here."

"Dark magic? The Darkcons!" Rayne cried out.

"But why?" Nona asked. "They have nothing to gain."

"Maybe, but it is not their style, and why would they?" Asora thought out loud. "Nona could be right."

"Perhaps you should ask," Gourani suggested.

"Is that wise?" Nona asked. "We could end up offending Queen Laxur?"

"We are at war with her and the Darkcon now. Offending her is not high on our list of priorities," Friea explained.

Asora, Nona, and the four fairies went to the princess's room. Nona had the fairies lock it down and wait outside to prevent anyone from disturbing her. Nona felt that Asora could use help if Laxur wished to be difficult.

The princess removed the covers from a large vanity mirror on her dresser. She waved her hand across it without touching it. She conjured an image of her older sister, the dark queen herself, the ruler of the Darkcon Empire, Queen Laxur. Her image came into form in the mirror.

"Well, baby sister, come to wish me a happy holiday?" Laxur smiled. "And you brought a pet too." Laxur was referring to Nona.

"I have an interesting dilemma, and I think that either you or someone in your circle is behind it," Asora accused.

"You mean, if I or anyone in my empire is responsible for all the disappearing items from your little white palace?" Laxur asked with mock innocence.

"Did you?" Asora pointed out.

"First off, how dare you accuse me of something so juvenile? I have plenty of gifts and food and decorations, and not to mention, we Darkcons are in a joyful holiday mood. We are not in the business of ruining this sacred time of year," Laxur stated, now faking an upset voice.

"I have found traces of dark magic that has Darkcon written all over it." Asora showed her spell to Laxur.

Queen Laxur who looked rather surprised. From here, Asora seriously doubted that Laxur or the Darkcons had any involvement. Plus, Laxur would have nothing to gain from this mischief as Nona pointed out earlier.

"Well, this is odd, but there is one thing wrong here," Laxur said. "This is mine, but I have not left Dorien in weeks. You can even check on that yourself, you know how," Laxur said.

Nona looked at a magical log that she made appear in her hands. She looked over the notes. Then the priestess nodded to Asora that Laxur was telling the truth.

"For once I believe you, but I will check," Asora said. As Laxur's image was about to disappear. "Oh, sister, one more thing." Laxur stopped.

"Happy holidays." Both sisters smiled, and the image vanished.

"We can rule out the Darkcons?" Nona asked.

"Yes," Asora answered. "They are not a factor in this."

Asora and Nona came out of the princess's chambers, puzzled. The fairy sisters looked as if they were confused too.

"That did not take long," B'nei said.

"So what happened?" Friea asked.

"I know it was not Laxur or any Darkcon, so it may, in fact, be someone using stolen spells from her," Asora explained.

"Or someone with magic similar to hers," Nona pointed out.

"Who in their right mind would steal some of Laxur's magic?" Rayne thought out loud.

"That is the only thing that I could think of," Asora said.

"I only know of one person whose magic is very similar to the queen's," Nona said. "Lady T'ula."

"Why would T'ula steal gifts and food?" Asora asked.

"As much as I dislike her. She does not strike me as someone who would do this. At least without reason," Nona said.

Hours later, as the sun set and the feast was about to be served, Asora noticed something amiss. High Priestess Nona was the only high-ranking member of the Privy Council who was present. The fairies were also confused. Gourani then spotted people moving about the halls. Nona made a hand signal to have Gourani and B'nei to go and see what they were up to. Rayne and Friea stayed with Asora and Nona. B'nei signaled that it was safe for Asora and Nona to come and see.

Asora, Nona and the fairies saw Archduke Frenzen and Ladies T'ula and T'a in the ballroom by themselves, and they were moving the presents, or better yet, they were taking them.

"So, it was them, but why?" Friea asked in a whisper to Asora.

"I do not know," Asora said. "Let us go find out."

Asora, Nona and the fairies followed them with an invisibility spell. The three elves gathered and picked up huge sacks full of things that could not be seen. They looked around nervously as they made their way through the palace.

Once outside under the cover of darkness, Asora, Nona and the four fairies saw the three elves leave the palace grounds and move toward the village. They took one of the carriages, where Marevin was waiting for them. He and Madimoy were loading it with presents and half the feast from the kitchen. Asora, Nona and her fairies saw the the five get in once everything was loaded up. Madimoy and Frenzen were driving the horses pulling the carriage. The Royal Guard let them through as they assumed that they were going out for official business.

Asora, Nona, and the fairies kept their invisibility spell on, but their shadows were not cloaked. So, they had to stay to the darkness. That was going to be difficult since the candles and electrical lights threw out lighter than was normal.

The guards did notice the shadows and had their new recruit to go and inspect. Nona had the idea of using the light wind and wreaths. The recruit saw that several wreaths handing on a pole that was casting the moving shadows. The recruit shrugged and went back to inform his comrades.

Once gone, Asora, Nona, and the fairies managed to get past the guards. This made Asora a bit miffed as it was so easy to slip by the guards. She made a mental note about that. And she would have to get Captain Joes to run more in-depth security drills.

The carriage entered the village on the main street or broadway. Then the carriage made a turn that led them into the lower end areas. This was the part of the village were the lowest income earners lived.

The carriage stopped in front of the only orphanage in the village. Asora's curiosity perked up. Nona was familiar with the orphanage.

"I come here every month," Nona said.

"As part of your services?" Gourni asked.

"Of course," Nona replied. "Many of the children are also very sick."

"I think I know what is happening," Asora added.

They looked through the window and saw Frenzen dressed up as the Jolly Gift Giver of the holidays. T'a and T'ula were also dressed up as joyful givers. Madimoy and Marevin were serving specially made meals and treats. The smiles on the faces of so many children warmed Asora's heart. Nona held Asora like a loving sister as even with her darkness, this made even her warm. The fairies did their best to keep the snow from burying them.

It might be snowing, but the orphanage was warm. T'ula helped to dish out a great feast for the children, as T'a used her magic to make the room more festive. Frenzen passed out gifts to the youngest first. Madimoy started to sing, while Marevin was putting together the opened gifts that the children got.

"So that is what happened, how precious!" Gourani and the other fairies fawned.

"Indeed," Asora responded.

"How will we explain this?" Nona questioned.

"I have a scientific idea, ludicrous enough that the court will accept," Asora said.

"I would love to see how you will pull this off," Nona said.

The next day, Asora had the nobles and courtiers, along with her privy council gather to discuss her findings. She had been working on what to say.

"Well, princess? What do you have to report?" a courtier asked.

"You may be surprised why things have been disappearing. Ever hear of an artificial quantum singularity?" Asora asked.

"A what?" they asked.

High Priestess Nona looked at Princess Asora with a curious expression. Asora had not told her of what she had planned. But she was told to back her up on the story that she was going to conjure.

"During the Great War, when the Consortium had full control of Evorn, they began experiments. One of them was to generate a tiny black hole to use to power the new scientific instruments to conduct research. One result was that it generated a black hole outside the containment. It escaped and it has wandered Evorn ever since. It is harmless to organic matter as far as it looks, and only appears once the powerful magical energies leave an area," Asora explained, as above their heads to confuse them.

At this point Admiral Yane, the princess's main military minister, came next to her and whispered into her ear. "Uh, your highness, we did not conduct such a test. I do not even think it is possible to make a black hole even today."

"I know, I will explain later, just back me up," Asora whispered back.

"A black hole?" A courtier asked.

"An astronomical phenomenon that is normally found in the center of galaxies," Nona answered.

"I know what a black is, but how can one be here?" The courtier barked at Nona. "Would it not have destroyed Evorn when it was created?"

"If the black hole was the size of you, yes, but it was smaller than that diamond on your ring," Nona pointed out.

"So, we should have someone around at all times who is powerful, magically, to prevent this black hole from taking anything more?" another courtier asked.

Asora nodded, confirming the answer. As did Nona. But even this priestess knew that black holes did not work like that. Nona found it amusing that Asora could create such an outrageous lie. She admired the princess for that. And it was a lie that is worth spinning.

"Very well then, princess, will you provide guards during the holidays?" another courtier asked.

"I will, you need not worry, unless they are interfered with," Asora warned.

"Is it possible to get the things back?" Another courtier asked.

"A black hole destroys anything that enters its event horizon. Even if I could get it all back. They would all be compressed to the size of an atom," Asora explained.

"It would be best if you replace everything," Nona added. "The shops and makers still have everything available."

The courtier all left, satisfied with their sovereign's answer. They did not like that they would need to buy these items again. But they would give her no more trouble.

"Frenzen, T'a, Marevin, Madimoy, and T'ula, please remain," Asora ordered.

Admiral Yane stayed as well. Once everyone left, Asora had her fairies lock the room down. Nona, Gourni, Rayne, B'nei, and Friea also remained and were at Yane's side. He was a bit curious as to what the hell was going on. But he suspected that he was about to find out.

"So, how are the children?" Asora asked.

"You know?" Frenzen asked, shocked.

T'a and T'ula were also shocked. Marevin and Madimoy looked worried and embarrassed.

"Yes, after much investigation, I, and Nona found you five committing the theft. However, your motives were worthy of the holiday's spirits, and I will not discipline you. I wish that you had come to me first," Asora said.

"It would have made our days easier," Nona pointed out.

"Wait, these five were responsible?" Yane asked. "Personally, you should have gone for the bigger ticket items."

"Yes, admiral, but for good reasons, and thanks to the courtiers ignorance of history. I was able to craft this deception. Now, Yane, I will need you to keep taking the guards that I station away every so often so that they can finish their holiday mission," Asora ordered.

"You will allow this to continue?" Nona asked.

"This holiday needs a new tradition to be added. Those people out there should be giving to those less fortunate. They lied to me, and some in my circle are keeping them honest," Asora said.

"Yes, your highness," Yane said.

"As for you five," Asora started. "Give each child one of these." Asora made special magical toys for the little boys and girls.

"Yes, your highness. Thank you." T'ula smiled.

"Happy Winters Born," Nona said.

The following day only parts of the feast now disappeared, but the gifts stayed put and the food was not so expensive. And much of it was leftovers anyway. Princess Asora ordered the gates open so all could come in and warm up by the various fireplaces and fill their bellies with good, royal food. She even asked that the orphanage allow their children to come and see the palace and meet the princess. These holidays were especially joyous, and this was what Princess Asora wanted for these days.

Chapter Thirty-Three

The House of Countess Marien

Far away from both Dorien and Evorn was the human world Havaina. Orbiting it were many vast complexes, space stations, satellites, spaceships, three moons, and a ring. Havaina was a blue- and-green world with vast oceans and mighty continents. The planet was larger than an average inhabited world.

Winter had come to Havaina's Northern Hemisphere. This world was familiar to the supreme monarch, who had come to visit her true home. The snow was falling, and a white wonderland had overtaken the city of Aunsborg, home of the largest spaceport on the planet. Aunsborg was a large harbor city with an enormous sound for boats, ships, and giant landing towers for spacecraft. It was an ancient city of timber and brick, contrasted by its modern areas of steel, concrete, and glass.

The name Aunsborg meant "mountain city" for the vast Auns mountain range that enveloped the city limits next to the oceans. The city was the largest of Havaina's cities, as well as the capital for all humanity.

Princess Asora and her privy council drifted toward a privately owned harbor. They were landing on the human home world onboard the royal Utopian flying vessel HMS *Alandrya*.

T'ula peeked out a window, looking to the world below in curiosity. "I have never seen a city so big. Is it the capital? Where does Countess

Marien live?"

Asora was in an elegant white dress with beautifully styled hair, looked at T'ula. "The population is roughly thirteen million people. As for where Countess Marien lives, we will be landing, and we shall arrive soon."

The *Alandrya* set down in a small bay just outside the city limits, and snow covered all the land and structures. The water had not frozen over. The wind gusted up, and the temperatures dropped as they disembarked.

"Careful, everyone, the temperatures can go below freezing this time of year," Jeia warned.

"We know, Jeia. This must be the millionth time that you have reminded us," his red-haired fiancée said, exasperated.

"Only making sure, Madimoy," Jeia responded.

Princess Asora was the first of the royal council to leave after her guards had disembarked to stand guard on the ground below. Nine members of her privy council followed the Princess outside into the cold, windy air. Behind them were four little fairies, using their magic to keep snow from falling on Asora and her guests. Servants emerged from the ship, carrying massive amounts of baggage.

"Be very careful with that trunk. It has the gifts in it," Gourani ordered.

Asora saw Countess Marien's honor guard waiting for her. A man in a black Army uniform greeted the Utopian Princess and escorted her to a limousine, which was ready to take her and the privy council to the mansion where the countess awaited them. The servants loaded the cars with the luggage as the privy members entered the limousine. The soldiers and honor guards packed themselves into utility trucks and vans. The Utopian soldiers were in front of the convoy, while the human honor guards were in the back.

Because of a landslide, it was taking longer than usual to get up the mountain where the mansion stood.

"Why? Has it done that before?" another elf woman with brunette hair and almond-shaped blue eyes asked.

"The landslides are common in the winter, but not around here," Rayne, the fairy, answered.

"Hope they clear it up soon," Jeia said casually.

"Why? You looking to go somewhere?" the old demon spoke up.

"No. I just do not like to be cooped up in a car with snow and wind."

"I hope they clear it up soon too. The thought of spending the trip in this mobile tomb with you is aggravating enough," Rakon complained. "Then again, watching you soil yourself at the thought of freezing to death in this thing is rather entertaining."

The demon laughed at his own humor, and Jeia charged and started to pummel him. It made Rakon laugh even harder.

"Stop it, you two. What the hell is wrong with you boys?" Asora screamed, but she could not help but laugh too.

Lady T'ula, annoyed after she had a drink spilled on her new purple dress, decided to stop them the hard way. With an electrical spell, the elf pointed her fingers at Jeia and Rakon. She released a charge of energy that shocked the two fighting men and turned them charred and smoking. They stopped fighting from the shock of electrocution, and they both fell over, twitching and squealing.

"Grow up, you two oversized babies," T'ula said harshly.

"Nice job, T'ula. But next time, not so much energy." Madimoy laughed.

"It is either high voltage or nothing with me. I like it powerful. In fact, I like anything powerful," T'ula stated triumphantly.

The angel man, Dominus, leaned over to her. "You know, Lady T'ula, there is real danger in power. It can and will corrupt you."

"You are a captain fun kill, Dominus," a dark-skinned human wearing a black naval uniform spoke.

"Even you, Admiral Yane, have to agree with that," Dominus spoke calmly.

"Oh, I do, sir. But Lady T'ula likes powerful things and only Maker knows what else. That is just who she is. Everyone learns the follies of their ways eventually," Yane responded.

"I will accept your answer," Dominus shrugged.

"Damn straight." Yane turned to T'ula. "So, you like powerful things. Does that include anything?"

"Yes, it does. Why?" the elf asked, curious about what the admiral was getting at.

"Well, how would you like to get a load of my powerful long arm guns?" Yane said almost suggestively to the young woman.

The sexual pun was lost on T'ula and most of the council, except for Asora, Jeia, and Marevin. The Princess sighed disgustedly.

"I do not understand what you mean, Admiral," T'ula wryly said.

"Good! Admiral, you, and I are going to have a little chat later," Asora said in a very threatening tone.

"You're right, Your Highness. I was just in the spirit of the occasion." Yane smiled ingratiatingly.

"I will put my fist in your spirit if you pull something like that again." Asora balled her hand into a fist and posed it in front of Yane. She turned to T'ula. "He meant the guns on his ships, of course."

"My Princess, there is no need for threats like that," T'ula said soothingly. "You do realize what that meant, right?" Marevin asked T'ula.

"No, why?" she questioned.

"I will tell you later," the Princess told the elf girl.

The four fairy girls were looking out a window onto the scenery of white. "It is so pretty. I love this time of year," the little fairy B'nei remarked.

An hour later, the convoy of vehicles parked in front of a massive mansion. The mansion was called La Deonig Manor, named for the family of La Deonig, who helped found the Human Consortium's social democratic system. The manor was the main dwelling for Countess Marien, the leader of all humanity, as well as daemons and jewel elves.

The mansion was four stories tall and made of red brick and stone. A large portico of white greeted the Princess and her retinue, as they

The House of Countess Marien

walked past the countess's rangers, who were standing at attention.

The double doors were opened ceremoniously as the Princess approached. The countess stood inside. For the occasion, she had foregone the Utopian long dress for a fine wool business suit of cerulean blue and her diamond tiara with her diamond pin. Her fine blond hair was set in an elegant bun. Her emerald eyes were hard.

"Welcome, Princess Asora. It has been a long time since I have seen you—not since your coronation," Marien commented coolly.

"Criticism taken, Mother. However, you must know I have been busy, but I am here for your birthday. Are you going to let me in?" Asora smiled as she walked up to the door.

Marien broke into a smile and held out her arms. "Of course. And of course, I know you have been busy, but you could call more often."

"Can the rest of us come in, Marien?" the angel asked, looking at the embracing pair. She waved her in-law in, along with everyone else.

The doors closed to the cheers of "Happy birthday, Countess!"

"Thank you all for coming. Now, all of you come into the living room. You look cold. Jeia, come give me a hug." Marien grinned at the young man.

"I was wondering if that business suit of yours was your way of telling me I need to change out of the court clothes. I cannot wait to get into my jeans." He smiled as he hugged her and walked her into the living room.

The room was large but warm, with the great fireplace ablaze. The walls were mellow wood tones with dark-red velvet curtains. The floor was covered in a deep white carpet. The sofas were heavily padded and comfortable, and they all sank down into them, except for Yane, Rakon, T'ula, and T'a. They each took armchairs, also comfortable but away from the family scene.

Marien, still standing and smiling, turned to her children and Madimoy. "You can go and change now that the ceremony is over. I believe I will change as well. As for the rest of you, I will have refreshments, and the servants should have brought your luggage to your rooms."

They all stood, and Yane grinned. "As always, Marien, you are the supreme hostess. I would love to change out of this uniform and into more comfortable clothes."

They walked out to see a contingency of servants ready to show them to their rooms.

Jeia was the first down, and he picked at the plates of sandwiches, cookies, small cakes, and vegetables. He was dressed in his comfortable jeans and beige sweater, and then Madimoy came down in her jeans.

He grinned leeringly at her. "I love you in a tight blue sweater." He grabbed her, making her squeal.

"Can you not wait until you are alone, you two?" Asora sauntered in, wearing denim as well.

She wore a soft yellow sweater. It felt good to wear colors again. Jeia, taking his head out of Madimoy's shoulder, groaned. "We were alone until you came down." They stepped slightly away from each other, still entangled in each other's arms.

"The rest should be down soon. Try to be more social," his sister remarked as she went over to the refreshments.

"We were being social, just not your kind of social," he responded with a wink.

"You have to give us a break. It is hard to be alone at the palace," Madimoy complained.

"You two are rarely there! You are here with your companions. It is I who should be complaining. And do you hear me complaining?" Asora bit into a cookie.

"Yes, just now, and whenever we are alone." Jeia took the cookie from her and ate it.

"Hey! I was eating that!" The Princess put her hands on her hips just as Marien, wearing a casually elegant sweater and jeans, entered the room.

"Already at it, you two? How long have you been alone, five minutes?" Their mother shook her head.

"He took my cookie," Asora complained.

"And she was interrupting . . . something. And complaining," he said, pointing at his sister.

"I was not complaining." She turned to her mother. "I do not complain. I am a Princess, and we do not complain."

"That would be the royal we, and they complain as well." Jeia laughed at Asora.

"Stop laughing!" she yelled back and tossed a pillow at his face.

"Here is another cookie, Asora." Madimoy handed her the goodie, and the Princess smiled at her, taking it. Chewing happily, she walked away toward the fireplace.

"How are you, Madimoy?" Marien hugged her.

"Fine, but we have something to ask of you, before everyone else comes down," the redhead said.

"I hope that does not include me?" Marevin walked in. He was comfortable in gray slacks and a shirt with a suit coat.

Madimoy and Jeia smiled at him. "Of course not. You need to hear it too." Jeia motioned him in closer.

"What is it?" Marien asked.

"We want you to marry us," Jeia announced jubilantly. That got Asora's attention, and she raced over to embrace her brother and Madimoy.

"You have waited long enough! This is wonderful. Of course, Mother will marry you!" Marien swallowed hard. It was very emotional for her.

Her son wanted her to marry him to the love of his life. She was overcome but choked out, "Asora is right. Of course, I will marry the two of you." Wiping tears from her eyes, she called out for champagne.

"Quickly, please." The servants ran to obey, as the rest of the group came down the stairs into the room.

Yane was dressed like Marevin, in a casual suit of navy blue. T'a and T'ula wore the typical Utopian long dresses of elves, but they were comfortable, casual gowns. Rakon was the only one dressed in leather and steel.

Yane looked at the champagne and asked, "What are we celebrating? Is this for your birthday?"

"We are getting married!" Madimoy joyfully announced.

"Congratulations!" T'a called out.

"You do not have to attend," the redhead said cuttingly.

"Madimoy, she is a guest," Marien said softly.

"You, of all people, should understand why she should not be attending, Marien," the bride-to-be wailed.

"She is a part of your Princess's life—your friend. I do not excuse her for her part in the war, but I do appreciate what she has done for my daughter," the countess calmly and firmly told Madimoy, who bowed her head to Marien in acquiescence.

T'a said nothing but smiled softly at the countess. Marien nodded at her. The elf sat down in the farthest chair.

"I say congratulations as well." Yane clapped Jeia on the back, who grinned inanely.

"I add mine as well." Rakon slammed his hand on Jeia's back, sending him to the floor. Madimoy quickly helped him up.

"Madimoy, how joyful for you! You have wanted this for so long. It is wonderful." T'ula embraced Madimoy as she stood up.

"Champagne!" Marien called out as the servants poured glasses. They were toasting the new couple when there was a slam on the door. Marien called out to her butler, "Jeeves, see who is at the door."

The old servant bowed and exited the room, but soon they were hearing raised voices.

"I must see her at once! This cannot wait! It has significance to her guests!" There were more murmurings when the same irate male voice called out, "Countess, it is General Tobrin! I must see you!"

Marien sighed. "Excuse me. It must be important."

She walked into the hall, and they could see her walking to her study with a highly decorated military man with brown hair, which was graying at the temples.

"He mentioned us. Yane, were there any threats coming from

Havaina to the Princess?" Rakon demanded, thumping over to the admiral.

"The usual for a monarch, but she is also the countess's daughter. A human threat is less to her and more towards the authority that she is." Yane backed away from the irate demon.

"She is priceless! Her welfare should be your prime consideration. You are even out of uniform!" Rakon sneered. He slammed his fist into his chest. "I, at least, still wear my armor."

"We should wait until my mother returns before we panic, Rakon. Please." Asora placed her hand on his bulging upper arm.

He looked down into her pleading face and relented. He walked away from Yane and took a chair close to T'a.

They all waited in silence until the countess came back out. They could hear her and the general talking, but not the words. When she came back in, she was grim.

"The Vanguard attacked one of our army posts and stole weapons about three hours ago. The general is worried about who the target is. We are not on the best terms with the Utopian Kingdom, as you all know, and it is certain that the Vanguard will attack an elf, dwarf, or centaur outpost," she informed them.

"Who is this Vanguard, and what threat are they to Princess Asora?" Rakon demanded.

"You are new to the Utopian Kingdom, so you do not know who or what they are," Asora began.

"Long ago, during the Great War between the human and Utopian forces, many elite forces existed. The Vanguard was an elite military unit that protected the emperor. Then one day, when the then Queen T'a used the Roewe Crystals on us, a general by the name of Messerstal began rounding up the Utopian prisoners. He kept them in camps and began torturing them and doing horrible experiments on them. He was trying to create biological weapons to wipe out the elves, dwarves, mer-people, fairies, and centaurs. He wanted them exterminated. When it was discovered what they were doing, it was the end of the war.

However, the general and all his followers went underground and have been fighting us and whomever they consider inferior ever since. The current leader of the Vanguard is a man by the name of Irantanco. I met him once, and I must say he scared me to death." Marien shuddered.

"You met him? How? When? Where?" Asora asked in horror.

"I met him years ago, when you were only five years old. It was at a social function. He was there as a guest. He is from one of the older families and had only started on his path to hate. He wanted to know why I had married something that was beneath me. I can still remember the pathological look in his eyes." She looked around the room.

"He was asked to leave when the host overheard. I have not seen him since, but I have been attacked verbally by them in the past—that is why General Tobrin was concerned with all of you here. They are increasing the military presence here, however, so do not worry."

"Has my security been notified?" Asora questioned urgently.

She knew these people as well. They had been hitting outer worlds for centuries. They were terrorists, and the only good thing about them was that they harassed the Hydra Clan. They despised each other and fought constantly. Out of the two, it was difficult to say who was worse, but most leaned toward the Vanguard. Both groups murdered and tortured people, one for money and the other for the sheer joy of it. The Hydra did not kill without a reason, but the Vanguard did.

The princess spoke her concern. "The soldiers with us will need to be advised."

"Yes, darling, the general is seeing to it. Joes and Sarea will be advised," Marien answered.

Yane stood up. "The question is who is going to be hit?"

"I need to talk to Frenzen. I may have to leave." Asora ran to the hall.

"I already told him! He said that he is on top of it. The alerts are going out, and he said to have a great time here!" Marien called out. Asora hesitated for a moment in the hall.

"No, I should speak to him myself." She took off to her room.

"And we have spoken to the head families of the others. They know what to do. Princess, this is not the first time this has happened. They have never stolen arms before, but they have attacked us." Frenzen smiled wryly at Asora through the magic eye. "I was the Prime Minister with the last monarchy. Enjoy your time with your mother. You have not seen her for over eight months, and it is her birthday."

Asora smiled back dryly. "It does not hurt that you want to keep good relations with the countess and the humans, does it?"

"They are an important part of the kingdom." Frenzen sighed heavily. "Princess Asora, if we need you, we know where to find you. You have planned this for some time. We have planned for every contingency, including terrorist attacks. You are needed, but we can function without your immediate presence for a few days."

"All right. I will stay here. But Frenzen, you contact me as soon as something happens, the Maker forbid." Asora drew her hand over the eye, and the duke faded from view.

She sat for a moment at the desk in her room, thinking. She felt torn. She wanted to be here with her mother and friends, especially with Jeia and Madimoy getting married, but her responsibilities as head of state also weighed on her. She sighed; the duke was right. She had earned the time off. She was only eighteen, and she had the right to have some fun. She slid off the chair and headed down.

Asora made it to the living room and found everyone talking softly and worriedly about the Vanguard. Rakon was listening with a wicked look in his eyes.

The demon spoke. "Let us change the subject, or we allow the Vanguard to win. I have seen they're like many times, and they are all the same. The right people must put them down, but we at this time are not the right people—your generals, Joes, Sarea, and the countess's security are the right people."

"Sword Master Rakon is right. Enough of the speculation. It will do no good." The blond countess smiled at the demon.

The group agreed and began talking about the wedding. The younger people did not notice that the countess and the demon spoke mostly together. Rakon even smiled at Marien.

Chapter Thirty-Four
Shadows of the Vanguard

On the other side of Havaina, in the hot, searing desert known as Fire Valley, was a small fort, but this was only a facade. This was also an ancient place long believed were the ancient Hananaka gods had first landed. So, this region n of Havaina was sacred to many. So much to this desert was empty of cities and towns. There were temples and very small travel huts, and a few historical places.

The fort was one of the larger still standing facilities still in the valley. It was a walled series of buildings made of stone and some wood. This was from a time when the advanced technology that the Consortium as known for did not exist.

In the fort several men and women lived and worked here. But their true workplace was not in the fort itself. It was below. A huge underground base was built without anyone noticing. It was the perfect place for a vicious terrorist group to plot. This was one of the many bases for the Vanguard.

The Vanguard was an old renegade organization that was founded just after the Great War five hundred years ago. The modern Consortium labeled the Vanguard a terrorist organization for its acts of sabotage. It attacked mainly the Utopian Kingdom, but on occasion attacked Consortium targets as well. They saw themselves as the continuation of the war and that the Eleventh-Hour Treaty was a mistake.

The Vanguard was not the only terrorist force in the realm. Their main rival the Clan, a Utopian Kingdom version of the Vanguard also waged war against the Consortium and the Vanguard. The two would clash in the shadows mostly as nether one could truly match the full might of the Consortium or the kingdom.

Almost a kilometer underground was a vast complex that was once used by the Hananaka gods of old. Now was one of the main headquarters of the Vanguard. Thousands of humans, jewel elf, and daemon men and women worked, and lived. Unlike at the surface were the temperature reached fifty degrees Celsius regularly. Underground the temperature was much cooler.

The large command and control center were hundreds of operators directed operations across the realm. If you were to look at the displays screens you would see that the Vanguards network spanned every world that bore life. They even had operations going on inside the Darkcon Empire itself.

The Vanguard was not stupid. They would on occasion work with Consortium, Utopian, and even Darkcon leaders to complete their objectives. If they aligned just right. Which was not often.

Queen Laxur was known of hiring them for specific missions. Normally they would not but the queen was a very high paying client that did not care how they did their jobs only that it got done and it could not be traced back to her. Because of that the Vanguard ended up with a large number of corrupt humans in their ranks. Most of Laxur's jobs were assassination missions against her own government. Some were high profile lords that opposed her. The ones they could not assassinate, Laxur would have them dig up or out right fabricate scandals that would allow her to act how she saw fit. So yeah, the queen of the Darkcon Empire used them as a means of maintaining her power and even growing it more.

As for the Utopian Kingdom, the Vanguard's most hated foe. They slowed or out right stopped attacking the central Utopian government since Princess Asora took the throne. Asora was very well known to the Vanguard and seen as an opportunity by the Vanguard leadership. The same displays in the command-and-control center showed that they had operatives in the Royal Palace on Evorn.

The leader of the Vanguard had scaled back their actions against the Utopians since Asora took power. Many felt that he was going to attempt to recruit Princess Asora herself. This made sense to the Vanguard personal. Princess Asora for the most part shared many of their views and she was what they consider a good candidate. The problem was that Asora was stubborn and set in her ways, and that also included seeing the Vanguard as a terrorist force. But Asora has also not done much if anything against them. So, it was much more difficult to gauge her intentions. Nevertheless, they had agents looking after her.

Now when it came to attacking Consortium targets, this created a lot of anger. The Vanguard was founded from the surviving elements of the old Black, White, and Grey Guards of the old Consortium. So, they still saw themselves as loyal to the Consortium, and that the Red Guard were still their comrades. Even the Red Guard has a hard time fighting them because of the long history they shared.

In recent years a fanatical extremist right wing group called the Freedom First Movement or FFM had no issue with murdering Consortium civilians and attempting to assassinate political leaders. The Red Guard was unable to effectively fight them. However, the Vanguard could. In exchange for certain privileges, the Vanguard fought the FMM into near annihilation. Elements of the radical organization still wrecked havoc across the Consortium, and the Vanguard had to be ready for them.

This arrangement had worked out for the Vanguard for the last few years. And they do not see it changing anytime soon. That suited them just fine.

In a small room near the command and control center a blond man of middle years, wearing a black suit, sat at a desk. He was watching numbers and letters going by on a flat-panel computer screen. He was reviewing the intelligence reports coming from Aunsborg. He was researching codes that had come his way from various associates.

His name was Irantanco. The current leader of the Vanguard. In the outer office, he had hundreds of people working on various things. He ran the organization more like a bureaucracy then a terrorist cell.

While he was the main leader of the Vanguard, he was not the only leader. Dozens of others across the realm lead their cells into combat or other clandestine operations. It was Irantanco's job to keep them informed, and in line.

Being the leader or as this title was Supreme Commander or SC was always a position that was vulnerable. Assassination of the SC was not an unheard-of fate for his many predecessors. But Irantanco was able to get to his position mostly by sheer dumb luck and good timing.

Under his leadership, the Financial woes that had plagued the Vanguard for many decades had vanished. He did this by expanding the Vanguards scope of operations to include various black-market operations, jobs for hire and so on. He was so good at it that the Vanguard could theoretically rival Fusion Corp itself in financial gains.

At first the other cell leaders hated his approach to modernization as he called it. But after seeing the results most quickly had their tunes changed. He had to kill out right a few to get his way. While Irantanco was an advocate for democracy, only while it suited his agenda. He was not above using some good old fashion iron fisted approaches to get his way.

"Well?" Someone in shadow asked from the computer display on Irantanco's screen. "Does this work?"

"It does," Irantanco said. "But did you really need to blow up a whole power plant? It would have been cheaper to just shot him."

"The parasite didn't give me the option and the opportunity presented itself. So, I took it," the man on the small side screen replied.

"And how many people did you end up killing this time?" A woman's voice demanded.

"Does it matter?" The other man asked. "They're filthy merks.

Utopian scum should burn. They are funny to watch screaming and running around like headless chickens!"

"You are sick," another man said. "Killing is an art that only should be used as a scalpel. Not a sledgehammer!"

"Like I said, does it matter? The job is done," the first man snapped.

"We are not the FFM!" Another man said as he injected himself into the conversation. "We do not go around mass murdering people who do not deserve it!"

"That's surprising coming from a jewel elf. You guys rightfully hate the other elf species. I would have thought that you'd appreciate it," the first man said.

"I apparently have a high value on life!" The last man said.

"Enough!" Irantanco barked into the computer. "The job is done. However, the collateral damage is unacceptable! I'll give you what you are owed. But no bonus."

"Whatever," the first man said bored.

"Anyway," Irantanco said. "Back to the matter at hand."

"Why are we bothering to spy on Queen Laxur?" A second female voice asked. "She is one of our highest paying customers. And I do understand why we want to keep an eye on her. But for an extremely specific reason doesn't seem worth it."

"That power hungry wench is up to something. You don't just attack Evorn and leave without any resistance," another voice said.

"And I agree," Irantanco added. "We cannot leave Laxur unattended."

"Agreed," seven out of the fifteen meeting attendance said.

"Supreme Commander," a third female voice called up. "We are eating our time on this. We should move on."

"No," Irantanco said. "This is something that will concern us one way or another."

"What about Princess Asora?" The woman asked. "She would be the most valuable asset if we can get her on our side."

"She requires a great amount of convincing. Plus, she is basically her mother's daughter," Irantanco said. "I haven't given up on her though."

"Never do," the first man said. "She is a good person."

"That's surprising coming from you. I thought you hated us magic users?" The first woman asked.

"Jewel elves, and daemons are the only acceptations," the first man said. "Asora is more human than angel. Hell, she holds a lot of our views. I like her policies too."

"She is an ongoing project," Irantanco reminded them. "Once she is betrayed by her own Royal Court, and it will happen it's only a matter of when." He passed for effect. "And we will be there to take her in."

"Hopefully it's soon," another voice added.

"Anyway, that is all for today. We will go over the updates and plans for the next campaign in a month," Irantanco then closed the communications line.

Irantanco then sighed and relaxed back into his chair. The computer mojito on his desk then changed to its normal desktop with the symbol of the Vanguard. It was of three swords. One black, one white, and one grey. Each a representation of the guard forces that formed the Vanguard centuries ago. They were pointed up and arrayed form a center at the bottom. They were also inside a shield of gold and silver. It was a bit much for him, but Irantanco did not design the seal himself.

On his desk he had a picture of the beautiful Countess Marien in a golden frame. She looked younger in the image with near flawless skin and beautiful eyes, and her long and full golden blonde hair. Her smile made anyone fall for her.

He had once been in love with her. They were once best friends, then lovers as they got older together. They were once apart of a quintet of kids that stuck together and looked out for one another. Marien was always the smartest of them. Irantnaco once made a crown of flowers for her, and she refused to take it off her head. It made her very adorable. That was Marien in a nutshell back when they were children. She was the most adorable little girl. Then she became the most beautiful human woman.

They did have adventures together. He also was the only one to believe her when her mother was an evil witch that wanted to kill Marien for whatever reason. This partly explained why Marien was so beautiful. She was part magical, but she did everything in her power to hide it. She was afraid of what others would think of her. But Irantanco did not care. He loved her and showed her that he did.

He could not understand why she had allowed herself to be polluted by an angel and had given birth to two freaks. At least that is how the others in the Vanguard saw it. And for a time, he did too. Unfortunately, these two freaks practically ruled the known universe. But where they freak? Or were they an extension of Marien herself?

He wondered if the gods could best cruel in their humor towards the love of mortals. Despite what happened between Marien and Irantanco in the past. He still loved her and kept her in his heart. He would never allow any attacks or jobs that went against her. It also helped that Countess Marien was popular with the Vanguard as she was seen as the toughest leader of the Consortium since Emperor Jurano himself five centuries earlier. It made sense since Marien was an in family descendent of the old emperor. So, she had all his fighting spirit and stubborn resolve. That also showed up in all her children.

At this moment, an older blond woman in rough jeans and a shirt, with a scar across her throat, came in. She was Desal. Seen as a secretary to the SC. But she was more then that. Desal was widely believed to be the next SC as Irantanco was grooming her for the position one day. She was very aggressive and Irantanco has had to teach her patience many times.

"Sir. Are you aware of the Utopian trash in Aunsborg?" she asked.

"Yes, I am. The question is what to do about it," the leader said.

"We could kidnap them and hold them for ransom. Force the Utopians into terms," Desal plotted.

"There is a problem with that method," Irantanco pointed out. Desal looked at him with confusion. "Those fat inbreeds in the Utopian court will not lift a finger to save their princess. Maybe the two elves on her privy council, but not her."

Irantanco pulled up a profile and a picture of Asora on his computer screen. It showed the Vanguard's whole wealth of knowledge they had on Asora. It was a surprisingly large file as Asora was a recent fixation for the whole organization.

"Too bad, really. Out of all the daughters of Marien, she is more human. According to the genetic profiles, Asora is over seventy percent human. Her sister is not even forty percent. Asora is less of a freak and more tolerable, unlike her nutcase bitch of a sister, Asaria. Maybe she has too much contaminated blood in her," Irantanco said.

"But how would that work? I would think that they would both be fifty-fifty," Desal said as she sat down in a chair in front of Irantanco's desk.

"According to the medical records, when that angel mated with Marien, he became energy and became a part of her. While inside her, he was able to manipulate the DNA of the egg, and this is how the first human-angel hybrid was made. But then, they found that Asaria was extremely receptive of emotions, even more than the average angel. They tried again with a similar method. Asora was born more human, and she was far less receptive to emotions. She is able resist their influence, unlike her sister, to whom emotions are like a drug." Irantanco said s he read the file on the genetics notes.

"It sounds like genetic manipulation of our race to me. Those two are an abomination!" Desal spat. "But I will give Asora this. She has as much love for the other Utopians as we do."

"You ought to pity the two girls and blame the father. He should have made them fully human, or he should have known that this would happen. It is not Asora's, nor Asaria's, fault at all," he pointed out.

"Are you aware of the ancient explorer theory?" Irantanco asked, and Desal shook her head to show that she did not know.

"To be honest I don't take much stock into myth," Desal said.

"Well, it is said that we are all descended from the angels or another race just like them. They were the only race in the universe, or so it was believed. They went out into space and explored the worlds. As they did, they settled them and began to change. Some figured out that they could change to match their environment, and this is how the centaurs and mer-people came to be. On other worlds, the food affected and shrank them. This is how the dwarves and fairies were born. The elves came about from the nature of the worlds that the angel explorers went to. Powerful magical forces that gave them great powers heavily influenced these worlds. As for the dark forces, well, the darkness does some rather strange things to the angels." Irantanco explained from memory.

"Interesting," Desal said.

"Well, we humans came from one of these explorer groups too. However, the worlds that we humans inhabit have much higher radiation levels. Instead of killing the angels, the radiation mutated them and made them solid and intelligent. Magic is still possible in radioactive environments, but it is different and harder to do. The groups lost contact with each other and their home and were forced to survive on the worlds that they all went to. The radiation affected some of the newly formed humans to the point that they became mind walkers, but after a great cataclysm, they went away millions of years ago. All of this happened tens of millions of years ago. That is the reason why the two girls have angel DNA in them. Their father could not manufacture them like a human can, but he could activate those ancient genes," Irantanco explained.

"I would not spread that around if I were you. To think that we would have something in common with those winged, freakish parasites is disgusting," Desal pointed out.

"Perhaps," Irantanco said. "But it is worth bearing in mind as we indulge in our base thoughts."

"What do you have planned for the Utopians? Do you believe that they could open the vault? They are here, so we might as well make the best of this opportunity," Desal asked.

The vault was a place where the Consortium was forced to store its super weapons and other powerful technologies from the Great War era. A sort of great treasure that only a handful of people could access. Countess Marien was one such person. It was also believed that Lord Jeia and Princess Asora could have access too.

"I hope that the rumors are true about the cybers," Desal said.

"What about them?" Irantanco asked.

"That the Consortium only dismantled them and not destroyed them," Desal said. "Imagine the Vanguard with millions of legions of robot soldiers. We would never have to worry about being outnumbered anymore."

"The cybers would be a magnificent prize. And I know for a fact that the cybers were only dismantled. Lord T'eama herself back then falsely said that she had them all destroyed. Only to have their plans, parts, and the cybers themselves put into storage," Irantanco said.

"I've always loved T'eama. She was one of the greatest leaders. And the most badass," Desal said. "My whole task force knows her speeches by heart."

"But it was not she who founded us," Irantanco reminded her.

"I know, but she also made sure that we could exist," Desal added.

"While our Financial situation is fine. We cannot keep incurring losses," Irantanco said. "Mass damage casualties are not profitable."

"Agreed," Desal said. "What happened in the empire was unfortunate. And I think Queen Laxur will not be happy once she finds out."

"She knows already," Irantanco said. "She voiced her disappointment last night. But she was willing to overlook this."

"In exchange for what?" Desal asked.

"She didn't say," Irantanco said. "And to be honest she's more of a bitch then ever."

"I'm surprise you've tolerated her this long," Desal said. "She must be really attractive if yo are willing to do business with her for this long."

"She's a power-hungry tyrant. And she is not my idea of attractive. She's too sultry for my taste and a bit too devious."

"I don't know. She is easy on the eyes," Desal said. "But I do get what you are saying about working with her."

"If I get the chance, I will make my displeasure to her known," Irantanco said.

Desal laughed at that, "Good luck with that."

"Evil tyrants like her are all the same in the end," Irantanco reminded Desal.

"But, you are right about one thing. We should take advantage of this opportunity." Irantanco opened a drawer and took out a box that had a magical talisman incased in a bracelet inside.

"What is that?" Desal asked.

"A nullifier stone. It was made by the Havaina police force with fairy magic to stop magic- using criminals like witches and warlocks. We will use this on Asora and bring her here," he said. "I want to make our offer to her."

"What about the others?" the woman asked.

"Knockout gas, then we take Asora, along with Marien, to the vault on Doraboss," Irantanco explained. "Then we can take the nuclear weapons, and the cybers from the vault and use them as we see fit."

"Now that is more like it," Desal said.

"Now you see, Desal," Irantnaco said as he got to his feet. "Assemble the number four squadron for this mission," Irantanco ordered.

"Yes, sir!" Desal stood up and walked out of his office, smiling.

Chapter Thirty-Five

Father Dear

The powerful master of the Darkcon Empire, Queen Laxur was also on Havaina. She came incognito and alone. The reasons were hers and hers alone. She also wished to be alone here and did not wish to draw unwanted attention.

Unlike her little sister Princess Asora, the wickedly beautiful Laxur mystically transported herself to her home planet. Normally this was not recommended to do because it was very draining of one's magical powers. And would require a day or so of rest.

Laxur, however, was not going to the mansion where her mother lived. Instead, she had appeared and had gone to walk through a graveyard. She meandered through without fear, unlike other beings; the other life forms of the kingdom would quiver in terror and run from the graveyards. It was in graves and monuments where the ghosts could be found. These spirits were rarely happy.

Many would not be if they were doomed to be dead. Who would not be? The souls of the people who dwelled here in limbo were always unhappy. Laxur could care less, as they could do nothing to her. These ghosts could not harm anyone who carried angelic blood within them. Laxur was one such individual. She was more angel then human and that has been both a gift and a curse all in one package. That package being herself and who she was now.

Obsidian had snarled over her going by herself. He felt he or one of his pack members should have gone with her. He salivated at the chance to taste Utopian meat, which was why she told him that she would go alone. But bringing them with her would have drawn too much attention to her.

Now was not the time to alert her mother to her presence. More importantly, Obsidian had been changing humans into werewolves to bulk up his pack since the disaster at Evorn a few months ago. So, the Red Guard would be on the alert for werewolves and could stop Laxur's purpose.

But a graveyard was a strange place for a powerful magical queen. However, this place was special to Laxur. She did not want others interfering or causing problems. Obsidian might amuse her, but she refused to have anyone observe her at this time, for in this graveyard was something special to her. This place held someone here that she made a point to come and see on special days.

She passed by several hundred tombstones. They came in many sizes and designs. These were she spotted a tall hill, and at the top was what she wanted. There was a very special mausoleum. It took Laxur a few minutes to get to the top of the hill. The people who were buried here were mostly the upper or wealthier people of Havaina. She had to weave around dead plants, fences, and tombstones. The ghosts of the people cringed as she passed. They could do nothing to her, and she was not frightened of them.

She finally made it to the crest of the hill where the royal Swaye family vault was. But not just the Swaye family, but others who married or became apart of the royal family of the Consortium. It was made of smooth white marble with a large, imposing edifice. The inside honeycombed throughout the surrounding hillside. It contained all her dead ancestors, going millenniums back.

One of its best named residences of the mausoleum was the last emperor of the Consortium, Emperor Jurano. There was also the famous Lady T'eama the warrior politician and the governess of the Swaye Family. Others whose names were only remembered by history books. A few were so ancient that their names were only known by the stones that bore their names. Their deeds lost to time.

She opened the extremely heavy stone doors with gold and silver trim and wording. Only family could enter and see what was within. A magical spell had been placed upon it by Lady T'eama ages ago to protect those within. Laxur was mourning, and her face was somber. She had a bouquet of flowers in her hands. She was also family and allowed in.

Inside the massive mausoleum it was dark and cool with a slight breeze and a heavy scent of dust and decay. There were torches in holders that were out and only needed a light to make them burn. She had to go deeper into the catacombs, passing many ancestors.

Laxur took one of the unlit torches and used her power over fire to light it. It came to life and gave Laxur light and warmth. It then walked deeper into the tomb. She came to an intricately engraved white marble sarcophagus that seemed to glow within from the eternal flame that burned inside. It glowed when Laxur came close. Her power over fire allowed it to recharge her magic and light the normally dark room. Laxur then placed the torch on a holder mounted on the wall.

Queen Laxur kneeled before this glowing marble in honor of its occupant. She lit incense she brought with her to soothe the ancestral spirits. She removed the dead bouquets that lay in front of the grave, tossing them disdainfully on the door. He did not need her mother's or Asora's flowers. He did not love them as he loved her. This she told herself in her heart.

"Hello, Father. I brought you our favorite flowers, like I always do," she said to the stone.

The bouquet was a mix of roses of all colors with mixed greenery. It was large and magnificent. Laxur spent days assembling the bouquet of flowers. She also used the finest silks to tie the flowers and greens together.

His daughter's voice was very soft, almost childlike. Laxur touched the marble that had been etched with the late Taral Serafus. He had been a tall man, with black hair and powerful white wings. The angel who gave Laxur her angelic blood. His hypnotic eyes had been a deep blue, like Asora's. Laxur looked a great deal like her father, but she had her mother's eyes. She also had his empathic nature and warrior skills. She could feel others, and she could feel what they planned to do next. It was the reason that she could overcome her foes so easily, except for her sister.

Her immense power was also a gift to her as was the coin of fire itself. He gifted the coin to her as a reminder of him to her. It granted her the power over all fire. He wanted to protect Laxur when she was younger and more vulnerable. He taught her how to use the power of this coin and the tales of the others that were out there.

Somehow, Asora could block her thoughts from others. It made life interesting, if not irritating. The empathy also made the queen unstable. The emotions of everyone around her could also be used to empower her further. But if she lost control, she could become dangerous to everyone around her and even to herself.

She brushed her hand over the marble that covered her father, softly whispering her vow to break her sister and bend her to her will. Tears slid down her cheeks for her lost father. He was the one person in the whole universe whom she truly trusted, admired, and loved. She had so many fond memories of him. There were days where Laxur wondered if he would be proud of her. Would he have prevented her from falling into darkness. Or would he have wanted to her to grow into the woman that she was now?

"It has been a long time since I have been here to visit you. I really missed coming here and talking to you," Laxur said in her sweet and tender voice, a voice that no one had ever heard before.

Laxur was on both of her knees, resting on the balls of her feet. She looked like an innocent child. She loved coming to this place to talk to the crypt that held her father. Nobody would disturb them; nobody would see her here. Tears flowed from her eyes as she talked to the cold stone. She caressed the letters as she spoke. At times, she wished that she could stay forever in his presence, even if it was only to touch the stone where he lay. She draped her whole body over the tomb, caressing it.

Her thoughts were of happy memories. But her heart was full of sadness. She believed that her father lived within her. He was protecting her in some way. She then moved around and rested her back up against the crypt and held herself. She wanted to feel her father's warmth and strong embrace. She was always safe, warm, and loved whenever he did that for her.

She still had wonderful memories of her father, despite her painful childhood. Laxur's mind went back into those days. It had been an appalling childhood for her. She was constantly bullied and humiliated, and it cut deeply at the young angel human hybrid child. She was intelligent when it was not popular to be so. She was the most beautiful in face and form. Her family was noble and respected. They were loved for their generous nature and political savvy. She had the best genetics of both human and angel. Again, the other children resented it, except for her brother Jeia, who had tried to fight her battles, but he was too small or too busy to do much good.

Angels were very sensitive to others' pain, as well as their own. They could sometimes hear the thoughts of others when they became excited. She knew when people were lying. It was why angels rarely left home. It took years to learn how to block others' emotions. For these reasons, she was often beaten and the target of nasty pranks. Few wanted to be friends with someone who could read their emotions so well. Her empathic powers were strong even for an angel. In fact, Laxur's powers even at a young age were vastly greater then most adult angels. As a result, even angels avoided her, both the older and younger ones.

She hated her early years and the beings that she had to endure. Her father's gentle and warm hand and heart were the only exceptions. She always believed that her father was the only one in the universe that really cared and loved her, other than her brother and sister. When her father died, she fell into extreme depression, and she never recovered. Her small fragile world fell apart. The light of her life had left her. She sank into darkness. It had been unfortunate that at the same time of Taral Serafus's death, when she had been called away from their school on Evorn to go home, the boy, S'tie, was not there to stop the beginning of her transformation to Laxur. Jeia and Asora had been too young or not around to stop it as well. Who else could she turn to?

The dark beauty came out of her memories and found herself in tears. No one in the universe had ever seen her like this before except for the one in the ground below her feet. Laxur's own heart was in pain as she showed her true emotions to the stone. She had become Asaria again.

She hated this universe. He hated how cold and unsympathetic it was to her. It did not care, the people who dwelled within it did not care. The Great Maker of the Realm and the one whom the Utopians worshipped was nothing more then a jealous goddess to Laxur. Even the Darkcon's God the Great Architect was equally as cold and, in her opinion, useless. Why worship gods who were unconcerned with mortals unless they pray and worship them? The realm was still a cold and cruel place.

If Laxur was a god, she would force the universe to be what she believed it was supposed to be. This warmed her blood back up as anger boiled within her. She wanted to punish the deity that was the creator of death and cruelty. If she could have all that power, Laxur would force the universe to bend to her will. She would undo all the injustices. She would also destroy those who deserved to be punished. She wished for a power that could allow her to bring her father back from the beyond.

Over the next few hours, the young night turned darker and the wind colder. It began to snow when Laxur, still on her hands and knees on the icy stone, began to feel the cold. The dampness got Laxur's attention, and she snapped out of her crying fit. She then realized how much time had passed.

Laxur was used to the cold and snow, but this felt different. It was more bitter than she was used to. She tested her magic and found that her powers were still exhausted. Her fire magic was also having trouble in this cold.

She was tired physically, and she began to feel chills in her body. Laxur got to her feet, forcing her frozen muscles to move, and started to walk off. She tried to create a magical portal, but the storm, which was growing in strength, caused her powers to fail her. The fight with her sister had diminished her, and the death of her spirit animal would continue to weaken her until she got the coins. Add to that her journey to Havaina using only her powers added to her weakened state.

Laxur stamped her feet and walked into the night to make a portal. She raised her left arm, and powerful energy swirled outward, but a sudden lightning strike destabilized it. She tried again, but the same thing happened. The storm had too much energy, and she was too weak to counter it. Until the storm passed, she was stuck on her home world. She could not stay in the mausoleum either as there was no protection from the bitter wind.

She had no place to go to wait out the storm. She folded her arms around her chest, trying to keep warm. She was not wearing her imperial dress, which would have kept her warm. She was wearing jeans and a tight black sweater with an overcoat to avoid being identified too easily.

Laxur wandered into the nearest town, which was near the mansion that she used to call home. The small town was mostly a mountain town that was more of a supply dump for the chateau where she was born.

Laxur saw no one out in the storm on the streets. Everyone was inside their warm homes. The dark queen looked in a window of a small home. There was a mother playing with her children and a man tending to dinner on the stove. It was a loving scene. She could feel the love and happiness from this family.

The scene upset Laxur. She was distressed as she walked through the town. She saw the same thing in many homes, and she knew she was not welcome. She knew if they had the chance, they would kill her for the things she had done to them. She barked a laugh at their pathetic lives.

Then she came across a shop that was more of a gas and charging station. She saw a man cleaning up inside and a woman at the cashier's station inside. The lights were still on inside. She thought about going in, but she had no money and her magic was not strong enough to cast spells. She did not want to risk it as those two could be armed. It would not surprise her if they were. So Laxur continued through the cold wet streets.

A kind of rage began to grow inside Laxur's heart as she moved on, soaked by the snow. No one would be willing to help or shelter her. Her hate for not just this world, but all the worlds in the realm. How she desired to be more powerful and force the realm to bend to her will.

A thought came to her. She knew of an old shed on the grounds of her ancient home. She could probably spend the night there. Her anger ran deep and grew uncontrollably at the sight of the warmth of these people. It now disgusted her. Oh, what she would give to see them all suffer like her. She wanted to punish them for it. A flood and a plague sounded just right.

No, her empathic powers were growing in intensity. And she felt a sort of feedback from her own sadness and rage. She could also feel everyone else's as she passed by. Laxur could inflict her emotions upon others, but it was deadly. Magical beings could become dark and eviller. As for humans they could become suicidally depressed or out right savagely violent. Both were preferable to her at this point.

She did after all use her incredible empathic powers to great effect on the Darkcon people. It was how she was able to endure herself to them and made them love her and willing to follow her. Their love for her was partly the result of her growing empathic powers. Her power had grown to the point that she could envelop a whole empire and a massive swath of the realm. She suspected that soon her empathic powers would grow to the point were the whole realm could feel her and she could feel it. By that point Laxur suspected that she would rule all or all would desire her. Both thoughts were satisfying to her.

The queen finally reached the mansion's gates and garden walls. Moving stealthily and using a small spell, Laxur maneuvered around the guards and looked for the shed. What she found was that recent construction had been done on the mansion. She found several new rooms had been added. One had glass doors that opened out to the garden patio.

"Better than an old shack." Laxur smiled to herself.

She did not need to use her magic to open the doors. These were the new smart doors. Marien always loved the new big thing in home automation. Laxur could not blame her on that. Even the queen found the new technology very fascinating. The smart doors opened to her which made her nervous. But when nothing else happened, Laxur figured that not all the bugs had been worked out yet.

She entered the new bedchamber and locked the doors behind her. The last thing she needed was to be discovered. She also kept the lights out and used the small and dimmed LED lighting to see what her was around.

In the room, she found had a bed already made, as if her mother was expecting guests to use it. That could be awkward if she were discovered here. So, she looked around to see what else was in the room. She needed to know if luggage had been delivered. The maids could have put the clothing away. She briefly scanned the room for fairies as well. Her quick check revealed that no one and no luggage were there. It was just made to be ready on notice. That was normal for noble homes.

The bedroom was like the rest of the house. It was paneled with polished, warm wood. It had the tall, whitewashed ceiling, but this one had purple plush velvet curtains instead of the red like in the rest of the house. They were closed over the floor-to-ceiling windows.

The cold chill returned to Laxur, and she shivered. She also felt dirty. She needed a bath as Laxur could smell herself. She smelled like a flowerpot in her opinion. As luck would have it, there was a bathroom complete with a large tub.

"Oh yes, just what a queen like me needs," Laxur said to herself.

She made sure that light could not leave the guest house. So, she found small candles and used matches to light them. It created a romantic mood of her. This made her more depressed as she wished for a lover to be with her. One person in this romantic setting. Prince S'tie was another person she wanted back with her. Even though she placed a powerful spell on him, she still wanted him. The spell was to make sure that he stayed with her no matter what.

The water filled the tub with warm clean water. She stripped off her clothes and put them on a warm rack to dry them out. She then sank herself into the hot water. She found soaps, and shampoos to wash herself with and used them. As she continued her bath, she began to reflect on her past. She had been doing this a lot recently, and her bitterness had only grown.

After an hour, she got out and dried off. She decided to wait for her clothes to dry, and she wrapped herself in a fluffy large white robe left in the bathroom. It was not her favorite color, but it will do. It was white, why could it not be purple? She found that some of her magic had returned. She then caused the tiny candles to float and follow her around.

Laxur went into the bedroom and sat at the vanity mirror to work on her hair. Her thick long blue-black hair reached her lower back, and it took an hour to brush it out and dry it. She found a hair drier, and it was silent which was a surprise to her.

She looked in the drawers of the vanity desk and found brand-new cosmetics. She put only a light touch of makeup on. She could have done it with her magic, but she liked to do these things by herself. She might be homicidal, but she was still a woman. And it made her feel better.

She turned back to her clothes. They felt they were dry. She used her magic to make them clean and warm and slipped back into them. She walked over to the bed and lay down, thinking that it felt as comfortable as the old bed that she slept on as a child.

She remembered that her father would often read her a story before bedtime. When she was little, she enjoyed those moments, but now those times were gone forever. Before she knew it, tears welled up and fell from her eyes down her soft pale-pink cheeks. She felt alone in the universe, unlike Asora, who had a lot of friends and a better life.

The dark queen had to scheme to get the respect she felt she was due. She ruled with terror and an iron fist. But she also had her empathic powers that made her rule over others easier. So, it was very interesting to see those she condemned enjoy it just to see her and make her feel better.

She did not need friends, because she had great power. The Darkcon Empire was vast, and it was all hers. However, the thought of her little sister made her blood boil. She would add her birthplace, along with all the Grand Utopian Kingdom, to the Darkcon Empire. It would all one day be hers to do with as she pleased.

Laxur heard a loud crash and great deal of laughter from inside the mansion. She sat up and looked out the window. From the room, she could see the reception room, where everyone was. It was not far from her room, and she could hear some of what was going on.

What she saw disgusted her: Asora, her friends, and the one person in the whole universe that she hated even more than Asora—her mother, Marien. Was that Rakon there too? Damn that traitor! They were all laughing and having a good time, while she suffered, as usual. The scene tore into what was left of her heart. She was a fallen angel, and darkness filled her. Rage and anger were emotions that gave her strength and power. Ever since her father was taken from her.

"Before I rip them all apart, I have to know if my powers work again." Laxur said to herself.

She took a breath, and after twenty minutes of experimenting, some of her powers had returned. She allowed her anger and sadness to grow and empower her. It worked as the magic that she was used to returned with so much force.

"My father is dead, cold in his grave. I want all of you to know the agony that I feel, the terror I went through at the Royal Academy. It is time for all of you to suffer as I suffer." Laxur swore to herself.

The queen, now satisfied with what powers she still possessed, went out into the storm. She moved silently, weaving spells to incapacitate the soldiers and guards. She was concocting a grand entrance to her family's home.

About three hundred meters below Laxur, there was a six-person team, all wearing black, moving toward the mansion in an underground tunnel known only to the Vanguard. These people had, at one time, been the personal royal guards of the ruling family. They took their knowledge of these underground networks with them when they rebelled against the humans becoming part of the Grand Utopian Kingdom.

"Irantanco knows that we only have five people, does he not?" the fourth person down the line, the powerful magic user Deron, questioned with humor.

The leader heard and cracked back, "That is why we have you, explosives, guns, and rope."

"Me? I am not sure if I can match Asora's power." Deron was rather alarmed. "That girl has been practicing magic since she was three. I practiced with Illumin before he had to run off, but still, I do not know if I can match her."

The single-file line stopped. They were making sure that they were still alone.

"Well, you had better be tough enough to handle her, because our plan will fall apart fast if you aren't," Irantanco stated with steel in his voice. He looked down the line at Desal, who was last. "Are you thinking this is ill-advised too?"

"No, I do not, Irey." She laughed. "It is not like we have not done insane things before. Remember the attack on the Hydra at Eltas?"

He laughed, and the others joined in. Tolan, who was second in line, punched his leader, saying, "They should never have attacked a human colony, eh?"

"Hey!" a wiry blonde, third in line, said. "Do we know where we are?" She was Neeyako.

The fourth in line, a teenager named Maluse, spoke up with a surprisingly deep voice. "We are below the gardens. The entrance is a few more meters. We should find the way climbing upward." He lit up a map with his flashlight.

They began their careful trek and found the stairwell quickly. It wound steeply around for three hundred meters, and they ended up in a large empty concrete chamber. Irantanco moved forward to the four-foot-thick round door with a hand wheel crank on the side.

"This should take us to the bomb shelter of the mansion."

Neeyako moved up to him. "They do not know this exists? Even now?"

Irantanco grunted. "No. This was known only to the Vanguard because of what it inherited from the old Grey Guard to protect the family if any of them were subject to kidnapping, assassination, or bombing. This is the secondary site. They only know of the primary site."

Maluse now asked, "Why do they not know?"

"To prevent any information being leaked." Desal laughed abruptly. "They did not trust the family to keep their mouths shut. That is priceless!" The group laughed, and Irantanco cranked the door open with a rumble.

Chapter Thirty-Six
The Wrath of Laxur

In the La Deiong Mansion, everyone was celebrating the lovely countess's birthday. They were singing a birthday song and feasting on treats like cake and ice cream. The fairies that served Asora were also able to celebrate. Just as they took care of Asora, they once helped raise Marien when she was younger. Marien had asked the four fairy sisters to care for Asora as a gift.

Countess Marien was also known for her love of hats. She loved any hat that was unique in design or even use. She had everything from large feather and furs with moving flowers, to the Red Guard battle helmets. Marien collected military helmets from every battalion, squad, company, service, and fleets. It was one of her many playful quarks. If you were to investigate her biggest closets you would walk into a museum collection of hats from all across the realm.

Princess Asora, Dame Sarea, and Lord Jeia had worked on making a very large hat. It was their gift to Marien. They had put together a large hat with real clouds that moved about it. Asora used her magic to make the clouds, while Jeia made the actual hat. Sarea made the various fabrics and tied it all together.

Rakon then came up toe Jeia with a lot of things in his hands. Never missing a chance to make Jeia's day a living hell. He came up to him.

"Boy, take these to the women." Rakon said.

The metal elemental demon had placed the dirty dishes into the hands of servants, shoved a tray full of fruit and cheese in front of Jeia.

He took them with a grunt and grumbled to himself as he walked off. Jeia walked through the room where everyone was having a good time.

"Oh, Jeia, thank you. You have turned into such a nice young man," Marien commented.

The countess's remark was making him blush slightly. The other three women giggled at her comment.

"What?" Jeia demanded.

"Oh, you are such a nice young man, Jeia," Asora mocked her mother's words.

This was making Jeia shake his head at his adoptive family. He had been a baby when he had been brought to Marien and Taral. Asora had yet to be born, but Asaria had doted on him, even though Jeia was older.

"I would rather deal with Rakon than this," Jeia said to himself, and he walked back to the demon.

"Back so soon?" Rakon asked.

"Those women are vicious," Jeia replied.

"Oh, please. These girls are gentle compared to the ones in the empire," Rakon replied.

"The only one that comes to mind is that 'fabulous queen' of theirs." Jeia said.

Rakon looked Jeia straight in the eye. "Not everyone in the empire wants her on the throne. The Darkcons have lost their way."

"I could have told you that," Jeia said. "But still I wish she would be Asaria and come back home. Like she use to."

"I remember when I first saw her," Rakon said. "I thought that she was yet another Utopian woman wanting to escape the kingdom's various faults."

"If I had known I would have helped her," Jeia said.

"Oh, I imagine you would have, but given how savage Utopian noble women are," Rakon said. "I am surprised that she survived it at all."

"What did the Darkcons do to her?" Jeia asked.

"We did not do what you think," Rakon explained. "She had great potential, and we gave her the power to show us and make grow as a better person."

"She grew alright, into a deadly monster," Jeia said.

"I did not have a say in it. I only did as I was told," Rakon pointed out.

"I know. I do not blame you," Jeia said.

"You seem to," Rakon said.

As if on cue, the lights went out. And the temperature suddenly dropped. The two men quickly moved to find their way back to the living room. The mansion was in total darkness. They came across confused servants and soldiers.

Jeia came across a team of technicians examining the mansion's server rack and power panel. They seemed to be as lost as everyone else.

"What happened?" Jeia asked.

"We do not know yet sir," the small daemon in a technician's vest said as he did not look away from the server rack.

Rakon looked at a small jewel elf woman also in a technician's vest. She was testing the power panel for electricity. She as shaking her head in confusion.

"What is it?" Rakon asked.

"I am detecting electrical power in the panel. So, there is electricity incoming. It is just not moving past the main breaker," the technician explained. "The storm outside has not cut the power."

"What can do that?" Rakon asked.

"Technically nothing mechanical or electrical," the female tech said. "Very powerful magic can, but only a hand full of known magic users have this kind of power."

Both Jeia and Rakon looked at one another. They knew of one person that was that powerful.

"Keep at it," Jeia said.

Both Rakon and Jeia then ran down the hallway to the main living room where the countess and her guests were.

"It is the storm, everyone. It is only a power outage due to the wind and ice. Asora, would you be dear and give us some light with your magic?" Marien asked.

"Yes, Mother." Asora snapped her fingers.

Princess Asora herself now glowed brightly. She used her warm magic to not just light the room but give off warmth so that the cold did not get to them. Sarea then found a large stick and wrapped it in paper soaked in gas.

"Your highness," Sarea held the stick to Asora.

The princess touched it and the stick turned into a torch. At the same time the fairies made their glows brighter and looked for candles.

"Thank you, Asora. Now, the servants will find the power box or the emergency generator," Marien assured them.

"You forgot the fireplace, Asora," Lady Madimoy commented.

With a flick of her wrist and a snap and crackle, the fire flamed back on. Warmth seeped back into the room. Abruptly, they heard the front doors blow open and someone walk in.

Everyone ran into the main hall, and they were shocked to see the queen of the Darkcon Empire standing in the doorway. The servants were frozen in place. The security guards pointed their weapons at Laxur. Only for the queen to simply snap her fingers and turn their weapons into puddles of goo.

A large daemon charged at Laxur only to be tackled in return. Laxur had enough strength in her charge to knock the big guard down. Then three female Human and jewel elves in security vests attempted to use martial arts to force Laxur back. One of the female human guards had a shock baton and swung at Laxur.

To the amazement of the three women, Queen Laxur was blindingly fast. She grabbed the extended arm of one guard and tossed her over the shoulder. The guard with the baton swung as hard as she could. While the other guard attempted to high kick Laxur in the back.

The large black wings that Laxur was famous for came out of her back and blocked the guard from hitting her in the back. Then Laxur allowed the shock baton to hit her in her right arm. It was painful and paralyzing. Laxur fought the pain and used her left hand and slammed her fist into the guard's head as hard as she could. The guard with the baton went down and was unconscious.

Laxur took the shock baton and used it to fight off the last guard. As she battled the last standing female guard, the first one, the large male daemon recovered. He roared in a primal way that showed that he was going to charge at the queen. He did charge but did not complete it. He instead slides on the floor slammed his full weight into Laxur sending her into a wall.

Her wings absorbed the impact, but it was still disorienting for Laxur. She quickly got back up to her feet and swung the shock baton at the larger guard. He was not fazed by it as most daemons can handle electric shocks. So Laxur used more martial means. She struck the guard's leg tendons. That sent him crashing to the floor.

Before Laxur could knock him out, the last female guard came up from behind. She grabbed Laxur and placed her in a hold that was supposed to immobilize her. To Laxur's surprise this small woman was amazingly strong.

"I've got you," the female guard said.

"Do you?" Laxur asked with a hint of humor. "I think you need to look again."

Queen Laxur then used her left leg and tripped the guard. As the guard fell, she pulled Laxur with her. This was what the queen wanted. The guard took not only the full force of her fall but also Laxur's. And to add to it Laxur made sure to hit down extra hard. Laxur heard some snapping and a bone or two break in the guard. It was also enough to knock the wind out of her and render the female guard unconscious. This released her grip on the queen.

Laxur then got back onto her feet, "I enjoyed that dance."

She did not encounter anymore guards as Laxur moved through the mansion. It was dark and cold. Just how she liked it. And this was how it should be.

Queen Laxur happened upon several maids and butlers. Both Utopian and Consortium personnel. The pathetic fools tried to stand up to her. Laxur just had to laugh at them.

"We all know that none of you are match for me in any way. So, move aside," Laxur commanded.

"Never," one of the butters said.

"Have it your way," Laxur replied.

She held out her hand and unleashed a wave of purple lightning energy at the servants. Laxur was not trying to kill them but drain them of their energy. She pulled out all their energy and took it int herself. The dozens of servants then dropped to the floor from sheer exhaustion. Their energy was enough to satisfy her need for more. For the moment anyway. For what she had planned would require a lot of power.

All that stood in her way now was a very large and most likely barricaded set of intricately decorated double door. She could hear people on the other side. Then with one mighty kick Laxur kicked down the doors and she merely walked in.

Dame Sarea was the last person who stood in Queen Laxur's way. Laxur towered over Sarea, but that did not intimidate the dame at all.

"Ready for round two?" Sarea snarled.

"As much as I enjoy knocking you around," Laxur said. "But I am not here for you."

With a wave of her hand, Laxur generated a wave of purple energy. The wave slammed into Sarea, and it knocked her aside. Madimoy then ran to Sarea to check her and try to protect her. Fortunately for Sarea and Madimoy, Laxur was not interested in finishing them off.

"No!" everyone yelled in unison, except the mother. Marien stayed silent and looked at her eldest daughter with sadness in her eyes as she beheld her for the first time in many years.

"What do you want? Come to wish your mother a happy birthday too?" Madimoy questioned the queen. "If you did you have the worst way of showing up!"

"You stay out of this, you little bitch. This is between me, my sister, and my mother," Laxur hissed.

Jeia and Rakon come into the room through the back door and

saw Laxur in the main entry way. Admiral Yane was also near the door ready to organize an escape for the countess and her family.

"Now we know the cause," Rakon said.

"My older sister is not here for a good time. This is going to get ugly," Jeia whispered to Yane, nodded.

Laxur's sword magically appeared in her left hand, and she pointed it at Asora's friends. She also charged it up with her iconic purple magical lightning energy.

"All of you, into the main master living room and do not come out," Laxur commanded.

"Since when do we take orders from you?" Madimoy retorted.

Laxur smiled evilly. With her free hand she seemingly reached out to Jeia. He vanished from his position and reappeared in front of Laxur. Jeia found that he could not move. She took hold of Jeia, pulled him in front of her, and put her sword to his neck. She held him in a headlock in front of her, like a shield. She said, "If you do not, Jeia is going to have a few permanent health problems."

T'a, Madimoy, T'ula, Yane, Rakon, Dominus, and Marevin backed off into the living room, with their eyes locked on Jeia's reddening, grimacing face.

Sarea did manage to recover and was ready to strike. But she saw that Jeia was being held in a headlock and any sudden moved could end his life.

"Get over there with them," Laxur barked at Sarea.

The dame raised her hands to show that she dropped her weapons and slowly followed the others.

Once they were in, Laxur picked up Jeia by the back of his shirt and threw him into the living room, where he crashed onto the table. Laxur cast a spell from her sword and magically locked the room with a magical barrier. She kept the doors open so that they could see what she intended to do.

"Now then, it is just us three." Laxur proudly stood alone.

Marien could not find words to express her sadness for her oldest daughter. Such a beautiful woman she was, so full of hate and evil. Marien still remembered a time when she was Asaria, the perfect daughter. But now a deadly monster and mad with power.

"How dare you break in on our mother's special day and continue this feud here?" Asora hissed.

"How dare I? Well, let me think. Because I can, that is why," Laxur answered. Asora stepped in front of Marien.

"Oh please, Asora. You think you can protect her? You just barely beat me last time. What are you going to try, hmm?" Laxur asked.

Asora did not answer, but she stood her ground, "But I still won that time. I can do it again."

"Fortunately for you, my anger is at our dear mother and not you, baby sister." Laxur moved to stand adjacent to Marien.

"Funny, I always thought you were angry with everyone," Asora said quietly.

She did not want her sister to become more unhinged than she already was. She suddenly flicked her eyes behind Laxur. There was movement in the darkness, and it was not someone that even Laxur seem dot be expecting. Her elder sister turned just in time to see a fist connect with her jaw, but Laxur was tough and did not fall. She stumbled and looked up to see Irantanco's massive two-and-a-half-meter muscular form standing beside her.

"I agree. You do have a problem with positive emotions. You are not the warm and fuzzy type of person," he rumbled.

Laxur took a step back to get her footing. She then sneered. "Irantanco, I could say the same thing about a terrorist." In a flash, she punched him in the head, crashing him against the wall, and then she kicked high into his stomach, knocking the wind from him. She brought her sword up under his chin. "Twitch, and I will push this through your skull."

"Look down and you will see that you will die with me, little girl," Irantanco whispered.

His dagger's blade was perched at her chest, ready to kill. This was no ordinary blade. Laxur could feel the deadly radioactive energy from it.

"A dagger made of plutonium?" Laxur asked.

"Yep, just in case," Irantanco said. "Like this."

Queen Laxur moved away from him and backed away. Like nearly all magical beings any sufficiently high radioactive sources can nullify magic. That plutonium dagger would have killed Laxur in a matter of weeks and there was no way to stop it. Best to release him and deal with him another way.

"What are you doing here, Irantanco? I know my mother did not invite you any more than she invited me," Laxur demanded.

The Vanguard leader had no intention of telling the homicidal witch anything about his true plan, so he smiled and said, "I was on my way to Aunsborg and thought I would stop off to do some shopping for the holidays and get something for the countess here. I just wanted to know what she would like."

"Bullshit," Laxur snapped. "You are here for either my mother or my sister, but I will be the one to take them. However, that does not mean that you must be excluded from the festivities." She reached out with her hand, and Irantanco flew into the wall. He crashed and crumpled to the floor. "So much for the terrorist. Now for you two!"

"Believe what you want. It still doesn't change the fact that I'm here now," Irantanco pointed out.

Queen Laxur waved her demonic sword. "Move!"

"No! You tell me why you are doing this. Now!" Asora shouted at Laxur.

Laxur smiled wickedly. She walked toward Marien, and both Asora and Marien took two steps back. Irantanco however looked to be trying to circle around for another attack.

"A series of trials to determine the fate of our dear mother," Laxur answered.

A gunshot rang in the room, and the dark queen fell to the floor, holding her left shoulder. The bullet Las passed through her wing. Causing sever pain and damaging her ability to fly.

Irantanco had pulled out a handgun that was concealed in his coat. "Word of advice, cow, never turn your back on a Vanguard operative. It could be fatal," the Vanguard leader said.

"I will remember that," Laxur said with pain in her voice.

"Now stay down, witch, and you will live to see tomorrow." The terrorist continued to point his gun at the queen as he moved toward Marien and Asora.

When Irantanco was not looking, Laxur reached into a pocket near her injured arm. She pulled out a purple magical stone that was known for its healing abilities. She muttered a spell in an ancient language. In a matter of seconds, the bullet in her flesh was gone, and the wound vanished. The pain was no more.

The queen stood up with a whip in hand. She planned to hit Irantanco in his head, but she was struck on her head by a blunt object. She went down with a nasty headache. Laxur was still conscious and was growling in anger.

"That's what you get for not taking the man's advice, you whore," Rakon thundered.

He had hit her with the stock of his sword. The human terrorist now pointed his gun at Rakon. In response, the elemental demon used his powers to take the gun away. He then took hold of it.

"Really? Do you think that your toy here will hurt me?" Then Rakon smashed the handgun with his brute strength. "If you want to kill me with something made of metal, I recommend something that can move faster than I can."

Queen Laxur moaned and staggered back to her feet angrily. Summoning her most evil of magical powers, Laxur unleashed a primal scream. She projected a beam of purple energy at Marien, and then the countess vanished.

"Now for you three!" Laxur proclaimed.

The dark queen unleashed another wave of purple energy. This time, Princess Asora countered with a blast of wind and water. It broke Laxur's onslaught. The wave of energy did damage the rest of the room.

But Asora, Rakon, and Irantanco were unharmed.

"You will need to do better than that, sister," Asora said triumphantly.

"You are right about that, little princess. So, I think that this will do." Laxur snapped her fingers, and Marien appeared, restrained in what looked like a spiderweb.

"Mother!" Asora screamed. "Let her go, or I will—"

"Or you will do what? The way I see it, you three idiots have two choices: either you ignore me, and the web will drain her life away, or you find me the last three coins of power," Laxur stated.

"Even if wanted to, none of us know where the last three coins are," Asora said.

"I do." Laxur now held a book in her hand.

It was Asora's little storybook that their father gave her when she was very young. She had carried it with her as a talisman. She loved this book. It was magical to her but not in the way that Laxur might have been thinking. Or so Asora thought.

"Unfortunately, I cannot get to them, but you can, Asora. So, the deal is you retrieve the final three, which are hidden in here, and I will release Mother from the web." Then the mad Queen added, "Oh, and do not take too long. I am not too sure how much energy our dear mother has left."

She zapped Asora, Irantanco, and Rakon with a wave of black energy, and they disappeared into Asora's storybook. Queen Laxur laughed evilly.

Chapter Thirty-Seven
Inside Asora's Storybook: Ela

Asora, now wearing a long pale silver gown, opened her eyes and was greeted by a scene from her book. It was a field of tall grass and rolling hills. There was a forest that bordered the field not too far away. She could even smell the forest, grass, flowers, and wind. Beside her was Irantanco, now dressed in the Utopian garb of a long black frock coat and black pants. Rakon was still wearing his red studded leather uniform and was unconscious. The human terrorist was the first to wake up.

"Where the hell are we?" he demanded.

"This scene does look very familiar to me, but in order to be sure, we need to go into that forest." Asora pointed to the trees.

"That damned witch actually did it. We are in a stupid storybook," Irantanco babbled.

"Did anyone catch the number of that tank that ran me over?" Rakon muttered, holding his head as he got up.

"Glad to see that you are awake finally, demon," Irantanco said dully.

"Yeah, nice to see you too, bastard," Rakon barked back.

"Knock it off. You two can fight later. Right now, we need to get into the forest." Asora walked to the forest, and Rakon followed behind her. Irantanco did not.

"I do not think so. Why should I care what happens to Countess

Marien?" The terrorist stood with a nasty smile.

Rakon turned. "You will never get what you came for."

The smile left Irantanco's face. "Oh, I think I will. My people will come for me and for the Countess and Princess."

"You are trapped in here as much as we are. I doubt your *friends* will be able to find you. I doubt that they will even get by Laxur. You are dangerous, but she is more so, and she has us in a storybook. Think your buddies will think to look in here? I prefer you stay here, lost in this book, so good-bye." Asora sneered.

Irantanco growled and trudged after Rakon and Asora. An hour passed, and they came across nothing but more trees.

"Where exactly are we going, fangut?" the terrorist complained.

"It was not funny the first nine times you whined about it. We get there when we get there. Now shut up!" Asora yelled.

Rakon stopped and heard something—someone singing.

"What is that?" the demon asked.

"Look over there." The terrorist pointed to a large building in the woods.

"That, gentlemen, I believe, is what we are looking for," the Princess said.

The trio ducked behind a series of bushes to observe the property. It turned out to be a large house—a mansion. They saw a lone elf maiden hanging laundry on a clothesline. She was singing a lovely but sad song that the three could barely make out. She looked about sixteen, was small and thin, and had long blond hair and pale-green eyes. She wore a faded long blue dress.

"I think I recognize this from one of the stories," Asora spoke softly.

"Well, do not keep us in suspense. What story is it?" Rakon demanded.

"I think that this could be from the Winter Maiden," Asora whispered back.

"The what?" Irantanco asked, dumbfounded.

"The Winter Maiden, you dummy. Honestly, did your mother ever read to you when you were little?" Asora fired.

"My mother died when I was three, and my dad was a wasted drunk," Irantanco said flatly.

"My stepmother, my old governess, was very pro-human, almost religiously. She would have never read these fairy tales filled with witches, fairies, and elves. The military academy does not read your fairy tales either." Ela said.

"Oh, well, that does explain a lot, actually," Asora said in a calmer tone.

"Oh, boohoo. Cry me a river. You two can have your little therapy session later, after we get this over with," Rakon said, annoyed.

A couple of animals were roaming around the girl as she hung laundry up.

"Poor girl. Perhaps we can help her," Asora said.

"Help do laundry? I think not," Irantanco sneered.

"No, not that. That." Asora pointed to an older woman, with four other girls in tow, coming out of the mansion, complaining about the chores not being done.

"What a bitch!" Rakon said after about three minutes of watching this woman complain to the tired young girl.

"Why must we do anything? We are supposed to be looking for three stupid coins, not playing fairy godmother to some little mouse girl. She is an elf, after all. Let her suffer." Irantanco growled with a gleam in his eye.

"For all we know, that is what we need to do in order make the coins appear," Rakon barked back.

The five wicked females reentered the house, leaving the tired maiden to tend the rest of the laundry. The maiden then heard voices coming from the bushes on the other side of the yard. She slowly made her way toward the voices. They did not notice her as they were bickering among each other. She found a very well-dressed girl that looked like a Princess, an elemental demon, and a human in an odd-looking military uniform.

"Who are you people?" the maiden asked.

Inside Asora's Storybook: Ela

Suddenly, the trio stopped arguing and turned.

"Oh crap!" Irantanco exclaimed. "Get away, fangut."

"Be nice!" Asora barked.

"You kind of caught us at an awkward moment. Just give us a second," Rakon said to the maiden.

"Of course, I guess," the maiden said hesitantly.

"Our apologies, Ms. Ela. We are looking for something, and our search brought us here," Asora attempted to explain.

"I am Asora Serafus of Havaina, the elemental demon is called Shia Rakon, and that is Irantanco." Asora introduced all of them.

"Why do you have a demon with you?" Ela asked.

"He is my ally," Asora replied.

"Is this Irantanco a prince or something?" Ela asked.

"More like a dangerous, racist terrorist," Asora responded.

"So what do a Princess, a demon, and a terrorist want here?" Ela demanded.

"How did you know that I was a Princess?" Asora asked. "The way you talk, and the magical powers that you seem to have."

"I guess I do stick out," Asora said with a light laugh.

"Yes, you do. Now, can you please explain to her why we are here?" Irantanco complained.

"You allow this man to speak to you this way?" Ela asked Asora.

"He is a lowlife terrorist. There are no explaining manners to him," Asora said.

"We are looking for three special coins that have magical properties," Rakon added in.

"Three magical coins? I have never seen anything like that before," Ela answered.

"Well, she is a big help. Can we go now, Princess?" Irantanco asked.

"No! We are staying," Asora ordered.

"I hate to agree with the virus here, but he is right. There is nothing to be gained here," Rakon said to Asora.

"We are going to help her. I think that is what we need to do,"

Asora proclaimed.

"How long do you think this will go on?" Rakon asked Irantanco.

"How long before we lose our minds is more like it," the terrorist replied.

Asora, Irantanco, and Rakon were in the attic, hiding from Ela's mother and sisters. Asora began explaining the story of the Winter Maiden.

"Okay, so the girl lives with a rotten mother and greedy sisters, so what?" Irantanco butted in.

"You are missing the point. See that palace out there in the distance? There is going to be a ball tonight, and we must see to it that Ela gets there," Asora explained.

"You believe that one of the coins is in the palace, and the easiest way to get to it is by going to this ball, am I right?" Rakon pondered.

"You are very right about that, Rakon. What better place? Now help me put this dress together for Ela." Asora threw needles and thread to Rakon and Irantanco.

"You're kidding, right?" the terrorist asked.

"The vermin are making me nervous." Rakon pointed to the small singing birds, mice, kittens, and puppies.

"They are not vermin. They are cute." Asora smiled. Then she picked up a kitten, held it in her arms, and began to pet it.

"Great. Just frickin' great," Rakon complained as he started sewing a sleeve on the pink-and- white dress.

"If I was not *stuck* in this book, I would burn this house down with those elves in it. Give me that damn dress!" Irantanco viciously ripped the cloth from Asora's hands.

Later that night, Ela was surprised by the dress that the trio of visitors helped put together.

"Oh, it is so beautiful. Thank you, Asora!"

"Well, you should thank these two boys here. They did most of the work, and the terrorist is quite the fashion designer," Asora teased Irantanco.

"No, I am not. And do not say that ever again," Irantanco warned, turning red.

"Whatever, Mr. Sew." Rakon chuckled, sitting back in a chair.

"Well, Ela, put it on," Asora suggested. "Out, boys," Asora ordered Rakon and Irantanco.

They left and closed the door. To hide, they went into a dark cellar and played with a deck of old cards. Rakon never took his eyes off the terrorist, and Irantanco watched the demon. It was an uneasy alliance.

Moments later, Ela emerged from her little room with Asora behind her. "Pretty," Irantanco said flatly.

"You really think so?" Ela asked hopefully.

"Probably," the terrorist responded flatly again.

Asora slapped Irantanco upside his head for his rudeness.

"What the hell was that for?" Irantanco growled, rubbing his head. "If you touch me again, I will break you!"

"You think you can get by me?" Rakon rumbled.

A carriage pulled up, driven by several horses and a coachman.

"The carriage is here! I must get going. Thank you, all of you." Ela ran outside. Asora had a worried look on her face; she knew what happened next.

"What's wrong, Princess?" Rakon asked.

"She will not be going to the ball. Not with them anyway," Asora said.

"Now what?" Irantanco complained as he heard raised voices from outside.

The trio watched as the sisters of Ela ripped her dress. Rakon looked rather upset.

"You knew that this would happen, Princess?" Irantanco said. She nodded in acknowledgment. "Then why the hell did we waste our time making the damn dress?"

Asora did not answer the terrorist as she watched the girls devastated Ela. They left in the carriage, and poor Ela was on her knees, crying.

"Well, that was a complete fiasco. What do we do now?" the

terrorist demanded.

"I do not know. Play fairy godmother?" Rakon said, annoyed.

"Come with me, you two," Asora ordered. The two men sighed and followed Asora as she ran outside.

Two hours later, many families were arriving to the ball in carriages. Princess Asora showed up as her title entailed, a Princess, and Ela posed as a fellow Princess. Asora used her magic to repair Ela's dress, and Asora wore a pale-blue ball gown. Rakon and Irantanco were disguised as a lord and a soldier.

"You two search the palace. I will search the people in the main hall," Asora ordered quietly to Rakon and Irantanco. They nodded and left the carriage.

Asora planned to use a special magical power that she rarely used—a power that would allow her to see the coin through any material in a room. She had no intention of dancing, but she wanted to make sure that Ela had a good time.

Rakon went into the lower chambers where the cellar and dungeons were. After knocking out several guards, he searched the rooms and cells.

Irantanco went into the towers, moving past the guards. He found the king's room and searched it.

Asora was in the main hall, secretly using her magical sight to see if the coin was on any person or hidden in the room, but she found nothing. She was getting frustrated. What made it worse was that many noblemen wanted to dance with her. Asora was not part of the fairy tale, and they should be going to Ela, not Asora. Asora needed time alone to search for the coins, so she placed a spell upon the men trying to win her affection. It worked, and they left the Princess alone and moved on to Ela. Hours passed, but none of the three had any luck. They met in the lobby, outside the sight of the palace guards.

"Any luck?" Asora asked, but she knew the answer.

"No, this place is simply too vast for the three of us to search," Irantanco said.

"The coins of power are too small to be noticed," Rakon pointed out.

"I think that we are going about this the wrong way," Asora thought out loud.

"How so?" Rakon asked.

"Perhaps this coin cannot be found by looking for it. Maybe it will come to us?" the Princess postulated.

"Come to us, really? Uh, half breed, I think you need to spend a little more time in reality," Irantanco commented.

"Very funny, terrorist. Remember that each of these coins is to be found in a unique way. Perhaps that is the way this one will be found," the Princess said, a little irritated.

"What is going on over there?" Rakon said as he looked toward the great hall.

"That would be Ela running from the prince before the magic that made her beautiful wears out," Asora explained. "We should follow her. I still think that Ela will lead us to the coins."

The Princess hustled after Ela. Irantanco and Rakon followed the Princess out of the palace.

Then something went wrong. Ela was stopped from leaving by her own mother. She ripped the remainder of Ela's beautiful dress and revealed Ela as a common servant to the prince and all the nobles.

"Stop!" Asora roared and stomped toward Ela.

"Who are you?" the wicked mother demanded.

"I do not need to answer to the likes of you, cow!" Asora said.

"How dare you, you stupid child!" The wicked mother stated.

"You stupid old woman, you have no idea whom you are dealing with. Now, get out of the way," Asora ordered.

The older woman attempted to slap Asora but failed, and the Princess caught her hand and threw it back. Asora accidentally unfurled her wings, revealing her angelic nature.

"Oh, great," Irantanco mumbled.

The terrorist pulled out his point forty-five caliber revolver. He pointed it at the wicked woman, trying to threaten her even though these people had never seen a gun before.

"Do you really believe that that toy of yours is going to do any good?" The prince laughed.

In response, Irantanco shot a guard that was coming toward him. The terrorist shot him in the head, and the guard's head exploded. The thunderous roar rang through the halls for a few moments.

"Great Maker, Irantanco, are you trying to deafen us all?" Rakon yelled, holding his ears in pain.

The rest of the people ran from the gory display.

"You just had to do that?" Asora exclaimed.

He went past Asora and pointed his gun at the wicked mother's forehead. "Now you bitch, we are looking for three special coins. If you give them to us, I will leave. If you do not tell me what I want to hear, then you have a very serious problem. Understand?"

"What coins, sir?" the woman cried as Rakon restrained her.

"These coins." Asora showed her a magical picture of the last three coins of power. She did not like Irantanco's approach, but it was now or never. "Like he said, the sooner we get these coins, the sooner we will leave."

"I know where that one is." The woman pointed to the coin of darkness. "It is part of Ela's inheritance."

Ela and Asora looked surprised, and Asora spoke. "Ela has an inheritance? And she never knew. Let me guess—it's from her father, and you wanted it for yourself." This was not in the original story; they were making it up as they went along.

They went to Ela's home, and the mother went into a closet. Irantanco was right behind her with his gun at the back of her head.

"That is right, no funny business," the terrorist warned. She got a medium-size black box with red seams.

"Here it is. Now take it and leave!" the woman pleaded.

"Oh no, you said that you knew where the others were. Where are they?" Asora demanded.

The Princess took the box from the woman and opened it. It was the coin of darkness. The two coins that Asora had begun to react to the newly discovered coin.

"Go north to the kingdom of Galalu. The next coin is there. Now just leave, you madmen!" the woman cried.

"Galalu, huh? That sounds familiar. Come on, Rakon and Irantanco. Let us get going," Asora ordered.

"Wait. Please, wait!" Ela cried.

"What is it, elf?" the terrorist demanded.

"Please, take me with you," Ela pleaded.

"Your place is here," Rakon reminded the fairy-tale character.

"No, let us bring her. She may be able to locate the other two coins," Asora pronounced.

Chapter Thirty-Eight

Inside Asora's Storybook: A Pirates Life

The prince loaned them a carriage after Irantanco "persuaded" him to do so. It turned out that Princess Asora was uncomfortable on horseback, and it was more comfortable to travel to Galalu this way. The trip took roughly three days.

"I wonder if time moves faster in this book than it does in our realm," Rakon asked.

"Maybe it does. It would make sense. Otherwise, my sister would be in here telling us to hurry up," Asora pointed out.

"Good point. I guess we will know once the last two coins are found," Irantanco said.

"We have entered the realm of Galalu, your royal highness," Ela said to Asora.

They told Ela about who they really were—that Asora was a princess from another realm. This amazed Ela that there were other worlds beyond her own. And that these three strangers were from it. She never thought that she would meet a powerful and beautiful princess like Asora. Though the elemental demon was quite the contrast. However, Asora was comfortable around Rakon and that told Ela all she needed to know. The human man on the other hand was something of a mystery. Both Asora and Rakon kept referring to him as a terrorist. Ela had no idea what that meant. Irantanco did explain that he fought for rights and to avenge injustices. Princess Asora's rather snarky comments however made his claims a bit suspicious.

Galalu greeted them with mountains, trees, and a sea. An island in the distance was where they wanted to go. If this story was what Asora thought it was, then they had to look for a playful boy about twelve or thirteen years old. He would have a fairy friend who was also his guardian. The mere mention of a fairy made Rakon groan with annoyance. Irantanco was having trouble putting his finger on what story this could be.

They arrived at a port city on the sea. It was like any other in the Utopian Kingdom that Asora had seen. It had docks, shops, bars, workmen's area, and so forth. The day was sunny, so the ocean seemed to sparkle. What got Asora was how colorful it was. Unlike in the village back on Evorn where the dominant color of the harbor was grey, white, and black. Here it had yellows, browns, blues, reds, whites, pinks, and so many more. It made it look like a child had colored in the buildings with colored marker. The people also seemed to be more colorful than what Asora was used to. Most did not seem to be paying attention to them. That suited Asora just fine. Rakon and Ela got a few funny looks. Rakon merely growled and most got the hint to leave him alone. Ela however was not too lucky. She and Asora were the two most attractive ladies in the harbor.

A few cat calls for the princess came. She merely zapped them with a low energy lightning and set their pants on fire. That prompted them to scream and jump into the oceans to put out the fire.

"Really?" Irantanco asked annoyed.

"Why not? If they learn that it was worth it," Asora shrugged.

"And it is a good way to attract the pirated here," Rakon pointed out.

"I am just not in the mood to deal with pirates," Asora said.

"Pirates?" Irantanco asked.

"This story involves pirates and a magical boy with a fairy," Asora warned.

"Sounds far more fun than the last one," Rakon remarked wryly.

"Damn fairies."

"The last story was messed up, and I have a bad feeling that this one will be too. And besides, Irantanco here is enough of an outlaw for me," Asora said.

"Just remember that I am deadly," Irantanco growled, fingering his weapon.

"Whatever," Asora said dismissively.

Asora directed the carriage to take them to a nearby duty free exchange store. The four got out and the princess was the first inside. Ela looked around at the fancy store and marveled at everything on sale. Rakon and Irantanco looked very annoyed. They even eyed each other showing that they really did not want to be here.

"Come," Ela said as she pulled Rakon's arm.

Irantanco felt someone yank on his arm. It was Asora and she used more force then was necessary to hauled him towards fine clothing.

"What the hell?" Irantanco demanded.

"We need to blend in more," Asora said.

"You have magic, use it," Irantanco complained.

"I could, but this is way more fun," Asora said.

"Your mother is in danger," Irantanco pointed out.

"I am well aware of that," Asora said.

The princess held a newly acquired gun in her hands. Then Irantanco understood why Asora wanted to come here. She did not want clothes, she wanted weapons and supplies. That made him feel better. Once Asora saw in Irantanco's face that he finally understood. For fun and for laughed Asora planted a large rural cowboy hat on his head. He took it off with an annoyed expression.

"Cute," Irantanco said in the most sarcastic voice he could muster.

"I am not going to waste any opportunity," Asora said as she put some more items in the shop basket.

The four then gathered at the cashier till. The cashier said that the price was forty pieces. That got everyone's attention as they had no idea what that was. Asora took out forty Utopian Krowns. Small coins of gold, copper, silver, nickel, platinum, and cobalt. The cashier looked at the coins and thought it was funny looking foreign currency. After Asora explained that the three gold coins were solid gold, the cashier tested it. To his amazement it was gold. He bagged their items and bid them a good day.

The four then got back onboard the carriage and it took them towards the ships that were berthed nearby.

"Does Utopian currency work here?" Rakon asked.

"It seems so," Asora answered.

"Where those real gold and silver?" Ela asked.

"Of course," Asora said. "Our coins are called Krowns."

"The most basic currency in the realm if you ask me," Irantanco said.

"Unfortunately, I agree with you," Asora said.

The carriage then stopped near the ships at their docks. They departed the carriage at the busy docks. Asora and Ela were dressed like rich ladies, while Rakon and Irantanco looked like gentlemen. They did stand out, even for the wealthier patrons that walked about the berths.

"Come, boys, we have a ship to hire," Asora ordered playfully.

The four followed Asora as she walked in the direction of a ship at the farthest pier. She had a commanding presence that was not appreciated by a few of the dock workers or sailors. Rakon was on alert for any trouble. Irantanco thought this was hilarious, but he kept that to himself. But being the pragmatic man he was, Irantanco looked around at the other people. He knew these types well. He dealt with these sorts all the time.

"These people that you are planning on hiring do not look like the reputable type," Irantanco pointed out to the princess.

"You would know, terrorist. So, if they try to swindle me, I imagine that you will come to my aid," Asora said, knowing that he would, if he wanted to get out of this storybook.

"You take a lot of risks, half breed." The terrorist followed her down the pier.

Asora smiled to herself, but she knew that he was right about that.

Besides she knew what was happening and what needed to be done. So, in her mind she was the leader.

A grizzled old man was sleeping on the floor between boxes and barrels. This was whom she was looking for. The man that had the ship she needed, and who also just happened to be a key character in this tale.

"Are you sure he is the one?" Ela asked, a little worried.

"Yes, the old Captain Tuke of the RMS *Keysky*. We will need him to take us to that island just beyond the horizon." Asora pointed to a spot out at sea.

Rakon walked up to the passed-out man and stomped his foot to wake the captain. The old man in response broke wind and it stunk. Irantanco and Asora were holding back fits of laughter. Rakon was now annoyed and had lost patience. He did it again when the old man failed to wake up. Rakon was about to punch him until Irantanco grabbed his hand. Then Irantanco took out his handgun and shot a barrel right next to the old man. He woke with a start.

"What are you trying to do, you maniac, give me a heart attack?" the old man roared in confusion and terror.

"Got your attention, didn't?" the terrorist said with a hint of humor.

"What do you people want?" Tuke demanded.

"We wish to hire you, captain, to take up to the island of Som," Asora said.

"And who are you, woman?" Tuke asked, curious about Asora.

A lady had never hired him. He just was not use to it. But he had to admit both ladies were the most attractive he had ever seen. One he could swear had to be a princess, or an angel. The other looked like a beautiful young scullery maid.

"My name is Asora, and these are my associates, Rakon, Irantanco, and Ela." She pointed and introduced them.

"And why do you want to go to the island?" the old man asked. "Why?"

"I am looking for a boy named Smika," Asora said.

"Why would you want to look for that little brat? Did he steal something from you too?" The old man said.

"I believe that he may know about something that I need," the princess replied.

The old man perked up. "Is there a reward for it?"

Irantanco came within centimeters of the old man and stared at him with a glare so terrifying that it would have scared ghosts. He knew what kind of man this was. And he knew how to deal with them.

"Are you going to rent us a damn boat, or are we going to have to kill you and take it ourselves?" Irantanco threatened.

The captain swallowed painfully. "I will take you. No need to get lethal."

"Good, now get to it!" the terrorist bolstered.

"But first my fee," the captain said.

Irantanco rolled his eyes. Asora reached into her pocket and took out nine pieces of gold and silver Utopian krowns. She tossed them at Tuke, and he caught them.

"I don't foreign money," Take said.

"Just look at them," Asora said.

He did and to his utter amazement these were pure gold and silver. More then enough to get them where they wanted to go. He also suspected he could get more, but the have mean human and the equally scary elemental demon with the girls were a problem.

"Come and climb aboard my humble little ship," the captain bowed and ushered them to the gainway.

It did not take long to set sail and head to the small island out beyond the bay. They arrived on the island at dusk. They thought it may be dangerous on shore, so they stayed on board for the night. The sailors stood guard, for they knew as well as Asora did that there were pirates around the island. But she knew that they were safe tonight.

At dawn's first light, Irantanco was awake and looking at the island. He was looking at the geological features and mapping it in his mind. He wanted to be ready for anything.

Rakon was already on the sandy beach, looking for anything that he could use as either a tool or a weapon. He was mapping out what he saw around him as well.

Asora persuaded a sailor to give her a set of loose sailor clothes, and she would use this outfit on the warm island. She put her hair up and wore a brown wide-brimmed leather hat that shaded the feminine features of her face. She convinced Ela to do the same. She told her that a dress was not ideal for this environment. She wore khaki pants and a loose white shirt with a wide hat to cover her face. The sailors suggested bikkni's or swimsuits for the ladies. Ela had no idea what those where, but Asora did. She told her to not do it here.

The women joined Rakon on the beach, with Irantanco disembarking the ship behind them. The tropical jungle was very warm, at least thirty-seven degrees Celsius. Asora felt warm but in a good way. She loved the beach, and wished she could swim. But now was not the time.

"So where is this damned Smika?" Irantanco cursed as he wiped the sweat off his face.

"It will depend on what day it is," Asora responded.

"What is that noise?" Rakon spoke up, hearing chanting in the distance.

"What noise?" the human terrorist asked, pulling out his handgun.

A weight fell onto Irantanco's shoulders, knocking him to the ground. "What the hell?"

"There he is," Asora said, smiling.

"Yep, and he is it. Now time to play tag!" the boy said.

He was a twelve-year-old boy, slim, with golden eyes, russet hair, and a grubby smile. He looked like a young teenager or was about to become one. But being almost alone on an island would warp someone like him.

"Get off of me, you fangut!" Irantanco yelled as he tried to get up.

Ela picked the young boy off Irantanco and put him on the ground. She also wiped the sand off the young man.

"There you are, Smika," Asora said politely

"You know my name? Who are you, lady?" Smika asked.

"Of course I know who you are. My name is Asora, Princess Asora. And my friends are Ela, Rakon, and Irantanco," Asora said.

"You're a princess? What are you doing here?" Smika asked with confusion and suspicion. "I didn't take anything from you."

"I know," Asora said. "But I needed to come and see you."

A fairy brushed by Rakon and stopped in front of Smika. She was a bit taller than the fairies that Asora was normally use to dealing with. This one had short brown hair and rainbow glittery wings as big her whole body.

"What have I told you about talking to strangers, Smika!" the fairy scolded the boy.

"Never talk to them, for they could be pirates," the boy said dully.

The fairy gave a serious look as she floated around him and then around Asora. The fairy was surprised by Asora specifically.

"No way you can be a pirate," the fairy was to Asora.

"We are not pirates," Ela said.

"Maybe he is, sort of," Rakon pointed to Irantanco.

"I am a political activist," the human terrorist insisted.

"No, you are a terrorist, but that is the same thing," Asora interjected.

Asora turned to the fairy, "We are looking for a special coin. We are wondering if you might have seen it."

Smika looked at a picture that Asora gave him. The fairy also looked and seemed to know what it was. Smika looked to the fairy for guidance.

"Why do you want this?" the fairy demanded.

"Lives are at stake, and that coin can help us save them," the princess said, trying her best to not give all the information away.

The princess stared at them for a long while. The fairy was obviously thinking about it and trying to figure out what to do.

"The pirates have it. It is in Captain Rows's room," the fairy said.

"That figures. I knew that this would not be easy," Asora said.

"I take it that this Captain Rows is the main antagonist in this story," Irantanco said.

"Smika, have you ever been able to get onto the ship without the captain finding you?" Ela asked.

"Of course I have. That old fart would never find me unless I want to be found!" Smika boasted proudly.

"I think we should get in, take the coin, and get out," Rakon said.

"Is he a demon?" the boy asked the princess, pointing to Rakon.

"Yes, he is. He is a metal elemental demon." Asora said. "He is on my side."

"That is beside the point. Why are we asking this kid to infiltrate a pirate's vessel? I can get in and retrieve the coin," Irantanco stated. "And work off some undue stress."

"And if they see you?" Rakon asked with a smirk.

"I kill them," the terrorist explained.

He walked to the front of the group, looking for the coast where the pirate's ship was. He made sure that his weapons were at the ready when he would need them.

An hour later, they found a massive wooden ship flying the flag of a pirate captain. Irantanco told everyone to stay put while he went in. He did not want Princess Asora to come because he was not sure if her magic would work at a critical time. Plus, she would make things more difficult for him if he turned out to be right about her magic. Asora admitted that she could not guarantee it would work. The others agreed that Irantanco should go alone. He was the most experienced, and it was not right to have a kid do a mission like this.

He managed to climb the hull to the weather decks. The terrorist moved across the deck without being seen. He calculated that there were roughly eighty pirates on board. As the last pirate of a group walked past, Irantanco climbed up and moved to the top of the weather deck where the helm was. Behind the helm wheel was a large door that was innately decorated. He figured that this was the entrance to the captain's quarters. Before going in, he investigated the small porthole that was next to the door. He saw no one inside, and he opened the door and quietly closed it as he went in.

He figured that the captain would keep the coin either in a chest or on his person. There were three chests of various sizes next to the bed: one was at the foot of the bed, another was used at a bedside table, and the last one was against the wall below a porthole. He went to the one used as a table first. He kept one ear open and an eye toward the door.

After ten minutes of searching through all three chests, he had no luck. He even rifled through the captain's desk. "Damn! He must have it on him. I will wait for him to come in then."

Three minutes later, a large, bearded man came in, cursing.

"Where is that damned lamp?" the old man roared.

He found it and lit it. The captain was surprised to see another man sitting at his desk, pointing a strange-looking gun at him. The captain only stood there in bewilderment.

"Hey, fat man, have I got a question for you," Irantanco said with a grin.

"Who the hell are you?" the captain demanded.

"Answer my question first, then I will answer yours, if I feel like it," Irantanco said. The captain nodded. "I am looking for this." He put a picture of the two remaining coins on the desk.

"I do not know what you are talking about. What would I know of a specific gold coin like this?" Captain Rows said cagily.

"I am willing to bet that you do know and that you have one, and," Irantanco said, still pointing his gun at the captain, "I am also willing to bet that that necklace you have holds one of these."

"Even if I did, what value is it to you?" Captain Rows demanded.

"That doesn't concern you. What should concern you is what I am going to do to you if you fail to give me what I want," Irantanco threatened.

Irantanco noticed Captain Rows slowly reaching for his sword and decided to act. The terrorist kicked the desk at Rows, forcing the captain back. Irantanco jumped off his chair, swung around behind Rows, and put him in a chokehold.

"All right, fat ass, give me that damn coin, or I will break your worthless neck!" Irantanco threatened.

The terrorist ripped the coin from the man's neck, and with the butt of his pistol, Irantanco put the captain down. He crashed hard onto the deck causing a very loud and heavy thump.

The pirates heard the loud thump from the captain's quarters. They figured that the captain was too drunk and collapsed on the floor. They merely went back to their duties.

Irantanco opened a window and dove into the water. He swam ashore, where Asora, Smika, Rakon, and Ela were waiting.

"Did you get it?" Asora asked.

"Yes, I did, now help me up," the terrorist demanded as he tripped in the water.

The coin in Irantanco's pocket glowed brightly. In a blinding light, they all vanished.

Chapter Thirty-Nine

Inside Asora's Storybook: The Games Afoot

A police whistle woke Asora up. She found herself in the streets of old Aunsborg when it was beginning its industrialization period. That meant cobblestone streets, with cement grey sidewalks, and buildings made of wood. Streetlamps that burned oil, and the newest invention the telephone was being installed for mass public use. A combination of horse and buggy and very old-fashioned automobiles cruised the streets.

She looked around and saw no one else. Her dress had changed yet again. Her dress matched the time that she was in. She wore a fancy light brown dress with a high collar and knee-high boots.

She found the others, and they were still unconscious on the cobblestone street buried in fog. Smika and the fairy Hyea were also with them as well as Ela. This was strange as if Asora and her allies were making time jumps and pulling others with them.

An explosion crashed through the area. It came from a large twelve-story building. Several people ran from the giant whole in the wall. They were dressed in black suits and wore masks. They were yelling at each other in a dialect of Ehan that had not been heard in centuries.

The rest woke up from the explosion, and they were all dressed differently. Ela and Hyea were all dressed like Asora. Rakon, Smika, and Irantanco wore suits of black and grey, and black dress shoes.

"What the hell was that?" Irantanco asked.

"An explosion, you moron," Smika said.

A man ran over Irantanco and tripped over Rakon. The terrorist looked at the man and recognized him from a story that he read when he was young. The man then ran off, as more people poured out of the large hole in the wall.

"Is this what I think it is?" Irantanco muttered to himself.

"It is. This is the 'Adventures of Detective Heralin,'" Asora answered.

"Then that guy over there should be either Heralin or his partner, Joen," Irantanco said.

A gunshot was heard, and the man fell. He fell somewhere in the thick fog. Asora ran over to him and used her magic to heal him. She kept her magic as concealed as she could.

It was Joen, the main character's partner. He was still injured and was out of the fight. This was not supposed to happen. He was supposed to dodge the bullet. So that meant that something or someone else was here interfering.

"You there, woman, what has happened to Corporal Joen?" a tall man in a black suit demanded of Asora.

"He was shot, but the bullet did not hit anything critical," Asora reassured the detective.

Asora did not notice that Rakon and Irantanco were dressed as police detectives like Joen and Heralin. Heralin thought that these two men were new in the police department. Ela and Asora were dressed as ladies of high society, in long gowns of browns, pinks and grays, respectively. Smika looked like a child of privilege in a dark blue almost black suit.

"Damn. Corgan got away with whatever it was he took." Heralin cursed.

"We can help you, and we know what he took too," Irantanco said.

"How do you know that?" the detective demanded.

Asora quickly and violently pulled Irantanco to her. She was very worried and frustrated.

"Excuse us for one moment," Asora said with a polite smile.

"Uh? Irantanco! Why did you say that? Now we must tell him things that I really do not want to tell him," Asora scolded the terrorist.

"What? I'm moving this along. And you know as well as me that Joen was not supposed to be shot," Irantanco pointed out.

"If you two know something, then you are required to tell me," Heralin demanded.

Asora slapped her hand on her head in embarrassment and frustration. She had to agree with Irantanco on this one.

"Very well, Mr. Heralin, I will tell you. Corgan ran off with the plans for the military's new flying machine, the gas-powered airplane," Asora said.

"They stole top-secret war plans again. Great." Heralin sighed.

"We know where they are and whom to find." Irantanco again.

He knew that he went over Asora's head to Detective Heralin. In response, the princess punched Irantanco in the back of his head. Detective Heralin was a hero to both Princess Asora and Irantanco, but the way Irantanco was acting was shameful to her.

The terrorist grabbed Asora hand, snarling. "Touch me like that again and I will cut off those disgusting wings."

"You will not touch her again." Rakon dug his dagger into Irantanco's coat.

"Are you six together?" the detective asked as the others surround him.

"Yes, we are, sir," Ela said.

"An elf girl? Why the hell is she here?" Heralin asked.

"I am a lost child," Ela said.

"No offense, girl, but this is not for you." The detective turned to Asora, Irantanco, and Rakon. "You three, on the other hand, are coming with me."

"What about Ela and Smika?" Asora demanded.

"This is too dangerous for an elf girl, a fairy, and a child," the detective reminded Asora.

Asora decided to flex her status to Heralin. She had to keep them all together. And there was no telling what could happen if Smika, Hyea, and Ela were let loose in the streets of old Aunsborg.

"I am ordering you to allow them with us. I, Princess Asora Serafus, demand it," Asora commanded.

Detective Heralin was surprised and had no choice but to obey the Utopian princess. But he was now suspicious of her and the others. He reluctantly allowed Ela and Smika with them on the adventure.

Days later, they were in one of the slums of old Aunsborg, a suburb known for its dark-hour activities. Asora and Ela were not in a good place, for women in that neighborhood were usually prostitutes. Or were prime targets for murders or psychos.

As for Smika he had not been exposed to this sort of situation and was very nervous. His own magic was not useful in these dark streets with so many insane humans. Hyea also did not know what to do in these sorts of situations. She spent most of her time in Smika's pocket. Only coming out if he was in danger.

Rakon had to protect them from a host of lustful men and even some crazed women. But it was here where they could get the information that they needed to find Corgan and his gang. Rakon was throwing men all over the place for trying to harass Ela, but Asora knew how to protect herself.

The princess liked to scare the drunks with her magic, angel wings, and golden armor. She even made herself look like a demon witch at one point, just to have some fun. At one point she took a page from Queen Laxur's books and grew taller.

Irantanco took to just knocking others out. For the most part however, he used his knowledge of the societal underbelly to get information. He even gambled and went into a fighting ring to get information.

Later, the seven of them left for the largest industrial center in

Aunsborg, the infamous Shrow District. In Asora's time, it was the most highly developed center known for green technology; however, in this time, it was a slum. The factories with large smokestacks and power plants were unspeakably ugly, and it was even dangerous to breathe at certain points of the day. Fortunately, it was night, and night was the safest time to come into the district, with regards to the air. Also, the number of people around was far fewer.

A bright light shone on them from a nearby tower. It was a watch tower used by security forces of the day. The area had a lot of military style private security details that roamed the alleyways and dark corners. Looking for troublemakers, and spies. Like them.

"I must admit, Heralin, you have assembled quite a collection of misfits: a terrorist, a demon, a princess, an elf girl, a fairy, and a boy? Wow, I am impressed!" a man yelled from another tower above them.

"And how do you know that, Corgan?" Heralin demanded.

From behind Corgan, a tall, dark woman appeared. It was Queen Laxur. She had decided to inject herself into the story for a bit of fun. She was also a fan of these stories. But tried not to show it. She also was impatient if Asora did not know better.

"We know now," Rakon spoke.

"Who is that? She is beautiful," Ela commented.

"Do not let that fool you. She is very evil. In fact, she is the queen of darkness," Irantanco explained. The elf girl was shocked, but not as shocked as Asora.

"What are you doing here, Laxur?" Asora demanded.

"I want to have some fun. I got bored reading this book," the queen said with a smirk. "Also, I wanted to meet all these characters like you have been."

"I'm surprise you can read," Irantanco commented.

"I am more highly educated then you are," Laxur laughed.

Smika and Hyea were very taken by Laxur's beauty and power. Smika asked his fairy friend if that was what an angel looked like. Hyea's response was a firm yes. But she feels dark and cold. Her power was overwhelming to Hyea, but the queen was not using her power. Smika kept commenting on Laxur's beauty and how young she looked for a queen. He always thought that queens were older women in stuffy dresses. Laxur looked more like a dark, tall, and young princess or better yet, an angel.

"Remember your promise, your majesty," Corgan said in a lower tone.

"Yes, yes, Corgan," Laxur said with an annoyed tone in her voice.

Asora used her magic to enhance her hearing, and she heard the criminal speaking to her sister. So Laxur had to make deals with the characters. That could be useful.

"And what promise would that be?" Asora asked with force.

"Corgan here wants to leave this storybook and come to our world. In exchange for his help, I will grant him life in our universe," Laxur explained.

"You do not have that kind of power." Asora turned to Corgan. "You should be smart enough to know that."

"How do you explain them," Laxur pointed to Ela, Smika, and Hyea.

"If you believe that she can do that, then you are extremely deluded. I bet that you think that you can win her affections, and you are very wrong. You are nothing more than a toy to her." She looked back to Laxur.

"What makes you say that princess?" Corgan asked.

"You obviously did not mention to him that your power is very limited in here," Asora said.

"Actually, he knows that. However, I have something else that is valuable to his cause," Laxur said.

"And that would be?" Irantanco demanded with a growl.

"More advanced avionics knowledge than what the Consortium has been developing," Laxur stated. "Our modern aircraft, and even spacecraft from Fusion Corp.

"Fusion Corp? It still exists and it is outside this world?" Herlian asked.

"Yeah," Rakon said cautiously.

"What do you plan to do, give him the knowledge to create a fighter jet?" Asora inquired. "Starships?"

"Nothing as complex as that, dear baby sister," the queen said.

"What are you trying to accomplish?" the younger sister demanded.

"I will make some of my intentions known to you, but not all, baby sister. I obviously want the coins that you have retrieved for me so far. And I got tired of waiting for you, so I decided to have some fun," Laxur explained.

"You do realize that your interference will delay us further, right?" Asora pointed out.

"Unfortunately, yes, I am aware of that minor inconvenience. Still, I want some entertainment, and what better way than at your expense? Besides, I do not care if mother dies or not," Laxur stated. "In the end I win no matter what."

"We should go," Heralin said.

"Listen to the detective. Now, run along, like the good little mice, before the cats get you." She laughed.

Corgan's men then began to shoot at them. They fired single shot pistols, and some had machine guns. Asora, Heralin, Smika, Ela, Rakon, Hyea, and Irantanco ran for their lives into an alleyway in between two very large buildings. They fled the scene entirely and ended up under a bridge that crossed the massive river running through Aunsborg. They got underneath the bridge and hide in its shadow to be kept from being seen by the gunmen.

"Why is that witch here? I thought that she could not get in here. Is this not your book?" Rakon asked Asora.

"I thought that she could not either. She is either more powerful than we ever thought, or she found a way to break into the book," Asora postulated.

"What are we going to do about this witch then, madam?" Heralin asked Asora. "And why did she not attack us?"

"I think I know why," Rakon said.

"Since this is your book, Laxur has no real power in here, but you do, Asora. Her mere presence was enough to disturb us, but, she is helpless. This could help us." Rakon said.

"Do you really think so?" Irantanco asked.

"Why not?" the demon replied.

"She may be able to use her potions and other magical items that do not require her magic," Asora said.

"What can she do?" Smika asked.

"She has too many abilities to list, and too much of herself to get into," Rakon answered.

"If she had power, she could have waved her hand, devastated us, and taken the coins, but she did not. I do not think that she can get the coins while in this book. That is why she sent us in here to get them. So, her being here is merely motivation for us to find the final coin." Asora postulated.

"Asora, some of your magic works now? Why not use it?" Irantanco suggested.

"And do what?" Asora demanded. "This book seems to be unable to make up its mind if I can use magic or not. I would not trust it."

"Take their weapons, kill them, or destroy the whole area," the terrorist brainstormed.

"I will only kill as a last resort. As for taking their weapons, that is a very difficult trick to do with machine guns. It is easy with swords, but not with guns or anything as complicated. And I really do not want to destroy the entire industrial complex of Aunsborg," Asora explained.

"Well, you have limited our options then my princess. But if you are to retrieve these coins, and if I am to get the plans for the aircraft back, you must be willing to commit some collateral damage," Heralin pointed out, hoping to convince Asora to act.

"Besides," Rakon added. "We are in a book. Time to do a little power fantasy."

"Fine then. Prepare for a spectacle of magic and flying bricks," Asora pronounced.

Meanwhile, Queen Laxur and Corgan were in an office. It was of normal size. It had large windows and was well decorated in red and white. Not really Laxur's colors, but Corgan did as he pleased. He also seemed to have a thing for plants, and in particular roses.

Laxur knew that in the stories Corgan used the red rose as his calling card. He would gift the rose to an intended victim, and later in some creative way they would be killed. Laxur admired his commitment to the craft of assassination and research. But it was usually for a higher purpose, or so he believed.

"Here you are, your majesty. The coin you so graciously requested." Corgan held up the final coin of power. As Laxur reached for it, Corgan pulled it back from her. "No, no, no. Not yet, my queen."

"What? You dare!" Laxur said, raising her voice.

"You gave me the knowledge to build a better aircraft, but I want the other thing that you promised me: freedom from this book," Corgan demanded.

"Yes, yes, yes, I know you want meaning to your worthless existence. Give me that coin, and I will grant you your wish," Laxur demanded, getting rather irritated.

Then a low rumble was heard and felt by Laxur and Corgan. Outside through the window, they saw a massive wall of water coming toward the industrial complex. It was like a slow-motion cresting wave of seawater.

"It is a tidal wave!" Laxur cried out. She knew that it was Asora. She was using her coin of water to manipulate the sea nearby. "Damn."

On the streets that led to the facility's docks Princess Asora was walking at the base of the tidal wave. Her hair became liquid energy, her skin was blue, and her eyes were glowing a bright aqua. She had summoned the powers of her coin of water. She now had full control over all liquids on the planet.

Everyone inside the industrial center ran for their lives when they saw the one-hundred-story tidal wave coming at them. Water from within the pipes also burst out and flowed to Asora like a loyal pet.

All the water, even the dirty and contaminated water came to her and danced around the princess.

Laxur and Corgan, along with several dozen armed thugs, came out to confront the angry teenage princess. Though there was not much they could do as Asora controlled all the liquid around them.

Asora surrounded them with the wave. She readied her other coins. She wanted to make it known that she was ready to fight and use some very destructive moves on them.

"I am only going to ask you once. Give me the coin of life!" Asora demanded as she powered up the coin of wind.

The wind and water started to interact and create ice. The dirty contaminated water formed toxic rubble. Asora shot these toxic ice balls at the gunmen, and they ran in terror. The ice also started to cover everything around Asora. The ice then formed an icy armor upon Asora's body. This ice did not require cold, but pressure. A pressure that forced water into a solid. It was this ice that Asora wore, as this ice was as hard as steel.

Queen Laxur was powerless inside the storybook. But if she could get the coin before Asora did and get out, then Asora, Rakon, and Irantanco would be trapped in here forever. Doomed to wander its pages and tales. However, Asora was known for being very quick to react.

Corgan decided to run, leaving Laxur to face her sister alone. He knew when to get away, and Asora was a foe that he could not beat.

"You bastard!" Laxur shrieked. "Get back here!"

Asora created a tornado of water and wind and sent it after him. The storm ripped apart the workers and buildings that guarded Corgan. Corgan was swiped up by the winds and brought to his knees in front of the princess.

"Give me the coin, or I will send you on a very unpleasant ride," Asora warned.

She squeezed her hand, and thunder and lightning erupted from her fist. Her threatening appearance did not do much to persuade Corgan to hand over the coin.

Inside Asora's Storybook: The Games Afoot

The villain of the story was too stunned to speak. When her display of power failed to make him surrender, Detective Heralin came up behind Corgan and punched him from the side of the head. The coin went flying, and Asora caught it with her left hand.

All seven coins in such proximity caused Laxur's spell to break, and a vortex opened up. The dark queen was blown out of the book and back into the real world. Corgan was buried in the tidal wave. Asora, Irantanco, Rakon, Heralin, Ela, and Smika were sucked into the vortex.

Chapter Forty

A Glimpse of the Future

The darkness passed, and lightning erupted. Princess Asora was face down in the dirt of some world. There was also a hint of sea water in the air. She also could hear distant thunder. No not thunder, gun and cannon fire. She knew that sound well from her short time in the Red Guard before she was crowned princess. The smell of sea water so potent suggested that Asora was in a cave next to some sea.

Asora tried to move only to be hit with powerful pain in her back, chest, and head. She thought that she had a concussion. She had in her hand the coin of life. Asora could not control her voluntary muscle movement and she started to panic. Then a moment later she managed to gain some control and closed her fist around the coin. The coin's power then in moments filled Asora with a healing energy. The pain vanished and Asora could move again.

Princess Asora then slowly sat up and looked around. She saw a dark room in a ramshackle shack with all her companions inside. The shack was on a beach and had no floor but used the beach sand as its floor. That explained the dirt she was face down in earlier.

The others were still with her. Irantanco, Rakon, Ela, Hyea, and Heralin were still unconscious. Smika was up and was at the only window in the shack. Smika was struggling to look out a window at a scene that he could not understand. He noticed that Asora was now awake. She came up to him and helped him to the window.

"The lightning sounds close, princess," Smika said.

An explosion rocked the shack. Asora knew that was not lightning. It was from artillery fire and missiles exploding.

"That is not lightning. It is cannon fire, human cannon fire," Asora replied. "Missiles, and artillery fire."

The next explosion was so close that it awakened the others. Rakon looked around and saw a newspaper. It was the *Canva Times*, the human colony's newspaper on the mer-people's world. He took it and started to read it.

"Uh, Princess? You may want to read this." Rakon handed Asora the newspaper.

She noticed that the date was odd it was a year and a half in the future. It described a war with an enemy that she had never heard of, but the paper was mostly ruined, and the name of the enemy was erased. She did know for sure that it was not the Darkcon Empire. From what she was able to glide from the paper. This new war had been going on for nearly a year now. And whoever it was had been advancing deeper into the Utopian Kingdom at a rate faster than the Consortium did five hundred years ago during the Great War.

"What the hell is going on?" Asora asked.

"What is it?" Irantanco asked.

"Take a look," Asora handed the newspaper to him.

Irantanco looked shocked. He saw the date and it made no sense. This should not be possible.

"We're a year and half in the future?" Irantanco asked. "Wait? We're outside of the book now?"

"Does time travel factor into your magic?" Heralin asked.

"No," Asora said. "Time travel is in the realm of science fiction."

"Great Architect! What is that thing?" Rakon stated.

As Rakon opened the door and looked out onto the scene in the distance. Everyone rushed over to look out the window. They all went outside, and they saw something that none of them had ever seen before. And it horrified all who saw it.

A massive city-like structure hovered in the sky above the ocean, moving toward the land. It seemed to be shaped like a nine-pointed star from underneath. On top it had many towers of various shapes and heights. Surrounding it was a massive swarm of flying machines. The whole thing was in hues of grey's blues, and blacks. It had several glowing lines. It even had whole sections that floated around it like icebergs an ocean.

"I have no idea what that thing is or who would built it," Irantanco commented in awe. "But it's incredible."

"I am more worried about what it is for," Rakon added.

"Why are we here? I thought that we got all the coins?" Ela said.

"So did I. I know that we are on Canva Prime, but why here and at this time?" Asora pondered.

"Perhaps there is some even here in this time that managed to intersect your mission and that even pulled us forward," Heralin postulated.

"That makes no sense," Hyea said.

"Who are those who built that floating city?" Heralin asked.

"It does not fit any known design I know of," Asora said.

"It sure as hell is not Darkcon," Rakon pointed out.

"Nor human," Irantanco said.

"Also, not Utopian either," Asora interjected.

"So, there is a new faction that arises?" Ela asked. "And they are completely new. Where could they have possibly come from?"

"There is no place in the realm from where those who built that thing could have come from," Rakon said.

"Then they came from beyond the realm," Asora said. She turned to Irantanco. "Ever hear of the Greater Theory?"

"Yes," Irantanco replied. "It was the theory that there is a greater universe beyond the Great Void that surrounds the whole realm."

"I bet that these new people came from beyond the realm, beyond the Great Void," Asora theorized.

"That is scary," Irantanco said.

A Glimpse of the Future

A huge squadron of human and new types of jet fighters flew overhead at Mach speed, heading toward the massive floating structure. It was a massive number of them. More then both Asora and Irantanco had ever seen before. They fired missiles at the massive floating object. The strange thing was that these fighters did not have Human Consortium markings; rather, they had Utopian Kingdom markings. The seal on them was not that of the Royal Guard, but of a modified version of Princess Asora's Royal Seal.

Behind the jets was an enormous wave of thousands of flying battle drones. They too were armed with missiles. They opened fire on the smaller objects that orbited the massive floating city ship.

Out at sea a fleet of ships bearing the same seal as the jets came into view in the distance. They opened with their massive guns and missiles. Large flattop carriers launched more aircraft into the skies.

The floating city seemed to have energy shields and energy weapons. The shields glowed with each impact. However, some of the fire from the Utopians was getting through impacting its hull. The energy weapons were a red glow and beams. The beam weapons made short work of their targets on the ocean and land. The aerial targets however seem to be too quick to be hit.

"Since when has the Utopian Kingdom used fighter jets?" Rakon commented. "And battle drones?"

"Well, maybe in two years they start to, or this is the first battle that they use them in," Heralin suggested.

He did not know this world, but it seemed obvious to him. He could only speculate on the events he was seeing. This world was so fascinating. He was in another world now. Granted it was a violent one and as he learned, in a future that is not too far off.

Princess Asora managed to cast a spell to make them invisible so that they could not be seen. Once that was done, they made there way to a large formation of Utopian troops. It looked to be a large battalion of infantry, mechanized, and other forces. They had the feel of a Red Guard not the Royal Guard.

Overhead, they watched as the missiles impacted an invisible wall of energy that was surrounding the floating city. Over a hill, a battle was getting ready to rage. Utopian soldiers dressed like human troops were fortifying a position on the beach. There were humans among them. As well as daemons, and jewel elves.

It was so odd seeing Utopian Conscripts in Red Guard style battlefield uniforms. Asora was able to see that they did not have the seal of the Royal Guard nor the Red Guard. They also bore the modified seal of Princess Asora.

The seal of Princess Asora was of a golden dragon in a pentagon of silver. The modified seal on the aircraft had this same seal but with the addition of an upward delta arrow in black. The naval ships had a blue anchor. The troops had two swords crossed inane X shape.

"They are all wearing your seal?" Rakon said. "You were right, it works."

"Indeed," Asora said.

A familiar voice came from the front of the formation. It was Admiral Yane himself. He was dressed in a similar uniform to the troops. He looked to have been in fight earlier. Asora assumed that it was it this new enemy.

"Here they come, everyone. Remember, the Feds will not show any mercy, so give no mercy yourselves," the human commander bellowed.

As he spoke to the Utopian troops, who look as if they just got out of training and sent into the field. They looked nervous but determined. This enemy struck real fear into them that many would rather run. But not these men and women. They came to blunt the enemy advanced. Even at the possibility of their own deaths. This gave Asora hope. She had plans, and it looked as if some of her plans panned out.

"The Feds? Ever hear of them?" Irantanco asked Asora. She shook her head a firm no.

"We may want to leave before these Feds show up," Asora said promptly and started to walk away.

"Considering what is being thrown around us," Ela commented.

A Glimpse of the Future

"How far can we get?"

"We should be able to get to a nearby mermaid safe place. Ah grottos I believe they are called," Asora said.

"Great," Irantanco said. "Do you happen to know where one is?"

"The thought of fish stench," Rakon gagged.

"It cannot be that bad?" Ela asked.

Princess Asora said no more and led everyone away from the formation. They followed an old trail that led to a more secluded area of the beach. They did not see anyone on or near it. But Asora knew better then to let her guard down. She had been in war before and knew what dangers awaited the foolish. Fortunately, she also had Rakon and Irantanco with ehr whom cold help as they had greater experience on the battlefield.

"I am curious," Heralin started. "Who are these Feds?"

"I have no idea," Irantanco answered. "They're new."

"And they have managed to create giant floating cities," Heralin added. "I must say that is impressive."

"You also said that this is a future time," Smika said.

"One possible future," Asora said.

"What do you mean?" Hyea asked for Smika.

"Temporal mechanics is a new and very difficult subject," Asora explained. "We are most likely seeing one of an infinite possible future. We can never know for sure."

"Spoken like a true theoretical physicist," Irantanco commented.

"At least i read about it," Asora snapped.

"I read too, just things that matter," Irantanco defended. "Like new techniques on metal forging, the latest new rifles, economics. Things like that."

"How boring," Smika commented.

"To you maybe young man," Irantanco said. "But as you get older you start to see this for what it is."

"I hope to never get that old," Smika said.

"No choice on that one kid," Irantanco replied.

"So where are we?" Heralin asked Asora.

"We are on a world called Canva Prime," Asora said. "It is a mostly water world with a lot of small islands a two small continents. It is home to mostly mer-people and a few million humans."

"An ocean-going world?" Heralin asked. "I imagine it is a complicated place to live."

"Humans and Mermaids do not get along well for the most part," Asora pointed out. "One over builds, the other deprives of resources, and one gets accused of mass pollution, and so on." Asora groaned at all the times in court that the mer-king complained about the humans on the islands. "Canva Prime was conquered by the Consortium during the Great War five centuries ago. The Consortium still claims Canva Prime, but the mer-people living here also claim it."

"I see," Heralin said. "So, it is a constant source of irritation for you then? Your highness."

"You have no idea," Asora sighed. "But now. It is just sad."

Hours later, they were kilometers away from the defenses on the beach. They could still hear the firepower roaring in the distance. Though the frequency of explosions had intensified, they were getting less and less loud. Rakon said that the battles seem to be waged in certain locations and it does not seem planet wide. But then again, they could only be in an area that has either been attacked already, is is about to be.

"I wonder what these Feds look like or who or where they are," Ela said.

"I personally do not want to know. After hearing that human commander speak to his troops that way, I sure as hell do not," Heralin interjected. "They seem like the violent and out right hostile folk."

"I imagine that we will find out in a year or so. We need to find a way back to our time," Asora said. "And prepare for this."

"Agreed," Rakon replied.

Asora wanted to be ready for the coming of this new foe. Rakon was not too worried about Asora succeeding. It was obvious that some of her plans had evolved and came to fruition.

They came to a hill that separated the beach from the inland regions. Asora hoped for a road or a small home, or even better a working vehicle. They climbed over to see another segregated area of the beach.

They then saw this secluded beach filled with dead mermaids and mermen. It looked as if they died from a sudden trauma. Their eyes and ears were gushing red blood. Their bones had also been smashed to dust. So many of them were skin and water.

The princess remembered her old uncle telling her stories about the Great War. In which the Consortium used their ships' sonar rays on them. The resulting sonic shock wave in the water crushed their organs. That was exactly what this looked like.

"It looks like someone used a very powerful sonar blast on them." Irantanco looked around. "That is a painful way to die."

"That is what I believe as well," Asora said.

"Hyea?" Smika asked his fairy friend. "What happened to all the mer-folk?"

"The princess and her companion there said someone about a sound weapon used in water," Hyea tried to sum up what Asora and Irantanco were talking about.

"This is horrible," Smika said.

"I agree," Hyea said. She turned to Rakon. "Could these Feds have done this?"

"Most likely," was all Rakon said.

"Sonar? What is that?" Ela asked.

"A device that sends out waves of powerful noise into the water. The sound waves bounce off all the surfaces in the area, and the returning waves are analyzed by either a human ear or a computer," Asora explained. "Some marine mammals use it to hunt. More advanced naval forces use to as a tool and as a weapon."

"So how does it kill mer-people?" Ela asked again.

"The sound waves are so strong that they are capable of disrupting nervous systems, crushing bones, and even imploding organs," Irantanco explained.

"Great Maker, what a horrible thing," Ela commented.

Asora and Irantanco did not bother to answer back. They continued to move through the field of mer-death as it would be called. But as they moved further across the beach, they started to see humans. Humans with massive holes in their bodies that seemed to have been caused by a plasma or electrical explosion.

"Even the humans were killed," Hyea said.

"Yes," Irantanco started. "But by different means." He turned a corpse of a human male over to see that his body had been chard. "Take a look at this."

"It looks as if he was electrified," Asora pointed out. "By a plasma beam?"

"I don't know anything that could do that," Irantanco said. "Only you and your sister could do something like this. But I seriously doubt either she or you did this to him."

Princess Asora looked around and saw a large build in the distance. It was made of coral and volcanic stone. But it lacked the glow and color that was normally associated with mermaid and merman castles. This did not bow well for them. Plus, it was on the beach and not under the waves like any other undersea palace.

The group then walked closer to see what awaited them. As they came closer, they saw more evidence of a massive battle that took place. More dead bodies of mer-people from all levels of their society. Humans and fairies as well as elves, dwarves, and centaurs in the same strange military uniforms littered the sands and waves.

"Strange that we do not see any Fed bodies," Heralin said.

"We do not even know who or what these Feds look like," Asora pointed out. "We do not have all the contexts about what is happening here."

As the palace came into better view, they also saw the mer-people's palace uprooted onto the shoreline. It was done by either the mer-people themselves or the mysterious foe, but they did not know. The palace

A Glimpse of the Future

was full of holes and burn damage.

"I feel an incredible power coming from the inside. It could be the coins," Asora pointed out.

"Why do I have a very bad feeling about this?" Rakon commented.

They all walked inside and found more dead mer-people on the floor, killed by what looked like heat or energy-based weapons. Asora followed the great power that was drawing her. It was like following a light only she could see.

Eventually, they entered the darkened throne room. The missing seven coins were sitting on a table; however, the group was not alone. They hid behind a broken wall and saw something horrible moving in the shadows. A mermaid that was just barely alive was trying to crawl away from a creature that none of them had ever seen before.

The beast was three and half meters tall, black skinned, and had powerful-looking claws that could probably shred armor. Its blood glowed bright blue in the darkness. The shriek it made was shrill enough to make blood freeze.

It grabbed the mermaid, ready to kill her. Irantanco jumped into the air and kicked the monster in the head. The mermaid was dropped, and she rolled away. Asora and Ela grabbed the mermaid and pulled her to safety. Smika and his fairy were too frightened to move. Rakon jumped into action to help Irantanco.

The creature shoved them both aside. Asora stood in its way with her angelic sword. The creature spat at Asora. The acid it spat melted her sword and parts of her dress. The four black eyes of this monster made Asora fall to her knees in terror; she could not move.

The creature froze in place, and its eyes went white. This sudden stop made everyone even more nervous. Asora could not feel any magical power that could do this.

"That's enough!" an unfamiliar male voice thundered.

Asora noticed a man in the shadows. He had all the coins in his hand, and they started to float in front of him. They still could not see his face as he was mostly in shadow. Then all seven coins floated down to Asora.

"Consider it a gift, princess. I have no use for them," the man said.

"Who are you?" Asora asked.

"You'll find out, but for now, I'll send you all back to your own time." Then the man revealed another coin—the lost eighth coin, the coin of time. It glowed a bright gray, and they all disappeared.

Chapter Forty-One

The Coins of Power

Asora, Irantanco, and Rakon woke up in Countess Marien's mansion. They were shocked to find that Smika, his fairy Hyea, Heralin, and Ela were with them, outside of Asora's storybook.

"How are you outside the book?" Irantanco demanded.

"You tell me, terrorist. So, this is your world. Not much to look at," Heralin commented as he looked around.

"That is because the lights are out, you idiot," Rakon retorted.

Then they heard feminine laughter coming from one of the dark hallways. It was not Queen Laxur's, but it was just as creepy.

"Oh my, Asora, you and your companions are so infantile." A woman laughed as she watched them.

"Who the hell are you?" Irantanco demanded angrily.

"Well, since you asked." The woman stepped out of the shadows and into the light.

She was blond haired and green eyed, roughly the same height and age as Asora.

"Why are you here, Polea?" Asora demanded.

"I am free to go where I please. Besides, I was invited," Polea boasted arrogantly.

"I do not remember your name on the guest list," Rakon said.

"The countess was not the one who let me in," Polea pointed out.

Then another taller figure came in behind Polea. It was Queen Laxur.

"Fangut," Irantanco spat out, not thrilled to see the witch queen.

"Glad to see you too, terrorist. I see that you all came out of the book with a few companions." Laxur looked at the characters from the book, and then she chuckled darkly.

"Worthless little bugs, are they not?" Asora, using her magic, made her dragon sword and golden armor appear. In her free hand, she gathered the energy from the wind, readying for an attack.

"Sister, release everyone now. And you, Polea, get lost!" Asora ordered forcefully.

"You have some nerve to order us around, little princess." Polea raised her chin. She then turned to her ally, the Darkcon queen. "What should we do with the extras?"

"What threat does a whinny little elf girl, a bratty boy with a stupid fairy, and a has-been detective pose to me?" Laxur asked as she chuckled.

"Did you forget that you have a metal demon and a terrorist, not to mention a tough, magical princess to deal with, witch?" Irantanco spoke.

Laxur and Polea laughed at Irantanco's comment.

"If you are done entertaining me, human, surrender the five coins that you have to me, now!" Laxur demanded and stopped laughing.

Asora held up a gray pouch with the five large coins inside. The dark queen could feel the raw power of the coins that Asora possessed.

"No" was all Asora said.

"What was that? Did I hear you correctly, baby sister? You do not want to save mother and the others?" Laxur giggled.

"I want to save everyone from your madness, but I will not allow you to have the powers of all seven coins," Asora fired back.

"You will not allow?" Laxur laughed again. "You must not have noticed, but you are puny compared to me."

"But not compared to us, witch!" Rakon roared.

Rakon, Irantanco, and Heralin charged at the mad queen, tackling her to the floor. Asora powered her enchanted golden armor and struck at Polea with her angelic sword. Polea was ready; she had a magical sword of her own. She slashed back, but Polea could not see. She put on a pair of glasses with a strap to hold them on her head during the fight.

"Wow, those are some thick glasses that you have, Polea," Asora commented rather rudely.

"Shove it, you cow!" Polea swung again, and her katana slammed into Asora's torso armor. It blew the Princess off her feet. On her back, Asora looked up to see Polea readying for another strike. Smika stood in front of Polea, blocking her path to the Princess.

"No!" the boy cried out.

"Move, you brat, or I will hurt you!" Polea threatened.

"I had not figured you for someone that would hurt children, you witch," Asora said, getting up in a hurry. Smika pulled out a slingshot and rocks. He fired a large one at Polea's stomach, and she reeled in pain.

"You little brat!" Polea shrieked, and then she got hit again in the head. The rock cut her forehead and drew blood. She growled in anger and pain. Asora landed a punch in Polea's chest and grabbed Smika.

Meanwhile, Irantanco had Laxur in a chokehold, while Rakon and Heralin had a hold for her arms; however, even with three men on her, Laxur was able to overpower them with her mystically enchanted strength. She swung the men, still on her arms, into one another, knocking them out. She grabbed the terrorist and flipped him over her head, and Irantanco was slammed hard into the ground.

The evil queen laughed at the three men trying, pathetically, to restrain her. "Are you three done? I still want to play," she said with a laugh. She was then struck in the back of her head with a blunt wood object. She fell to the floor.

"Down, bitch!" a woman's voice echoed. She was familiar to Irantanco; she was one of his fighters.

"Yeoa, where are the others?" Irantanco asked a black-skinned woman in a Vanguard military uniform.

"They're dealing with Laxur's friend with the thick glasses," Yeoa said.

"Good, but I need them to free the hostages. Please, Yeoa, rescue the countess," Irantanco ordered.

"She will be touched to know that you care so much, terrorist," Laxur said as she rose to her feet. The witch queen punched Yeoa. "You will go down, cow," the Queen roared at Yeoa.

"Uh-oh, the bitch is mad," the human woman taunted.

Then she pulled out a gun to hold off the queen.

"You really think that your little pistol will stop me, you pathetic little human?" Laxur boasted.

"Yeah, something like that," Yeoa threatened, still in a standoff with the Queen.

Then Yeoa shot Laxur in her left shoulder. However, the bullet bounced off Laxur's clothes. "That was not supposed to happen."

"Yes, I imagine so," Laxur stated and zapped Yeoa with a blast of dark energy. Yeoa was blown to the floor, and Irantanco grabbed her and helped her up again.

"Now may be a good time to retreat," Irantanco said as he pulled his injured comrade to safety. Rakon and Heralin did as Irantanco suggested and fell back.

Marien saw someone quietly move a floorboard inside her living room. It was a human man in a Vanguard uniform.

"My queen, you and the others get in here before that mad Darkcon queen and her lackey discover us," he begged the countess.

"Of course. Do as he say and get in," Marien ordered to all that were being held by Laxur.

"You all would not be trying to escape, would you?" Polea said with a wicked smile, waving a katana.

"Polea, please do not do this," Marien pleaded.

"Oh yes, I will, countess," Polea said, and she revealed a pair of angelic wings that sprouted from her back.

"You are like my daughters? But how?" Marien said, shocked.

"I am full of surprises. Now, little countess, I cannot let you or your guests leave," Polea said.

"I am not going to give you that option, witch!" the man threatened

Polea, unsheathing a katana of his own.

"It looks like I have a wannabe hero to contend with. And what might your name be?" Polea questioned.

"I am known as Reaper," he said.

"I meant your real name, you fangut," Polea insulted.

"I have no name. The Vanguard gave me the name Reaper. And last I checked, a fangut cannot do this!" Reaper jumped into the air and rammed his foot into Polea's chest, sending her flying.

"You will pay for that, Reaper," Polea spat.

She got up, but not fast enough. Reaper rammed his whole body into Polea, knocking her back to the floor. Polea slashed at Reaper while she was down. She used her wings to blow Reaper back, giving her time to get back up. Reaper was now on the floor with a headache. Polea stepped on the arm that held his katana. "I told you that I would make you pay, little man."

Before she could stab Reaper, she was struck with a metal fireplace poker. Admiral Yane was responsible for the strike. "You have some nerve, Admiral, to strike at me."

"You are too full of yourself, and you are a loud mouth," Yane said, trying to distract her. Polea growled with anger and attacked Yane.

"Smika! Smika, where are you?" Asora yelled for the boy that she had lost track of.

Smika had lost Asora while she was trying to get away from the nasty blond lady.

"Ms. Asora, where are you?" Smika asked, scared. He was alone; even his fairy was nowhere to be found. The boy huddled into a corner, shivering.

"Why so frightened, little boy?" a dark feminine voice asked Smika in a friendly way.

"I'm lost, and a bad lady is out to get me," Smika whimpered. "Oh, I am here, and I will not allow anyone to hurt you." Then she picked up Smika and held him close, like a mother would.

"Who are you?" Smika asked as he embraced her.

"I am called Laxur, and I am a Queen," Laxur said gently to the boy.

"That's an odd name for a pretty lady like you. I like your hair."

"Oh, well, thank you, young man." She waved her hair around to show it off to the boy. "Come, you need not be afraid of me."

Ela woke up in handcuffs with a gag in her mouth. She had been captured by the Vanguard. She managed to get the gag out of her mouth. Her captors were humans. Ela had never seen humans before today; she had only heard about them. But these people were fanatics. They kept calling her an animal, a primitive. Compared to their technology, that might be true, but their actions suggested the opposite. She had nothing against humanity, but these people were giving her a bad image of their species.

"Why is she tied up?" a human woman demanded.

"This savage was found wandering the mansion halls. We stopped her, and she is being detained for questioning," another human woman explained.

"Release her now. She is not the problem, you psychos!" Marien thundered in rage. Irantanco was behind Marien, and he made his team release Ela.

Yane went flying through a thin wall. Polea came in after him.

"You want to call me a fat, four eyes again, you stupid little worm of a man?" Polea roared.

"I called you no such thing. I will, however, call you fangut," Yane retorted.

"Fangut, fangut, fangut! I will kill you, you worthless bug!" Polea fumed.

"Good luck with that. I have faced down better foes than you," Yane said back.

A gunshot rang through the air of the room. It was Jeia. He had gotten a hold of a handgun and was pointing it at Polea.

"You may be tough, girl, but I am betting that you are not capable of dodging a bullet," Jeia pronounced. The nobleman was shocked by dark energy.

"Well, we cannot have that, now can we, brother?" Laxur said as she entered the room with Smika in her arms.

"Since when do you have a child?" Jeia asked with a shocked look.

"He is not my child, but I have decided to care for him," Laxur said sweetly. Polea looked at the boy with dismay, but to make her mistress happy, she would obey. Laxur looked around and saw that several people were missing. "Polea, where are the others?"

"That rat Irantanco managed to get a few out, including that elf from the storybook," Polea informed her mistress.

"I think of you even lower, you parasite!" Irantanco blasted as he threw a boomerang at the blonde.

It hit Polea in her chest and slammed into Laxur as she raised her arm to protect her and Smika from it. "Release Smika before I put you down like the mad dog that you are."

Smika used his slingshot and fired a magical bolt at Irantanco. Laxur gave them to him. She was aware of Smika's tale and how good of an archer he was.

"I will put you down so you can deal with the riffraff," Laxur cooed.

She placed the boy on the ground so he could do his duty. Laxur had put a very powerful spell upon the boy; it was almost unbreakable. She knew that Irantanco would not harm a child, even if the child was fighting him.

A wash of water and wind blew through the mansion. Princess Asora was using her magic to fight Queen Laxur.

"Back away, now!" Asora ordered forcefully. Her power, however, faltered, because Smika snuck by and stole the pouch that held the coins. "No! Smika, give them back, please!"

Laxur chuckled as the boy gave the pouch to her. "Thank you, my boy. You have served me well." She opened it and the five coins were there.

The dark monarch put her two coins inside the pouch. Queen Laxur had all seven known coins of power, and she wanted to test them out on her little sister. She allowed the power to pulse through her, and she turned to face Asora. "Now, baby sister, let's see what these coins can do."

"Not today, bitch!" Yeoa yelled out as she threw a contact grenade at the mad queen.

The explosion blew out the whole first level and parts of the second level of the mansion. Everyone inside was thrown out into the cold and snow.

Asora slowly got up from the snow. She saw Polea getting back up.

"This is just some friendly advice, Polea. I recommend that you stay down," Asora suggested as the guards and others in her company gathered around the Princess.

Polea growled with anger, as she, Smika, and his fairy guardian backed up. Polea had placed a spell upon the fairy. Just then, the ground began to shake.

"It seems that your problems have just gotten bigger," Polea said with a chuckle.

A mass of snow and dirt rushed out in a tidal wave. A powerful feminine roar erupted, and a massive being grew out of the ground. It was Queen Laxur in all her terrible glory. She grew several dozen meters tall, and with her increasing size came greater power and strength. The massive woman stopped growing, and she looked down at all the tiny people below her.

"You pathetic bugs are so annoying to me," Laxur bellowed, and she raised her foot, readying to crush everyone. Laxur towered over the mansion, the mountains, everything. Her foot was large enough to smash most of the mansion.

Before she could crush anyone, a wave of fire and wind washed over the massive Laxur.

"Look at what I have," Asora's voice thundered out.

She now had the pouch full of the coins. Laxur scowled at Asora in her moment of triumph. Asora remade her golden armor and revealed both her angelic and dragon swords. Her wings gave her the power of flight.

The giant queen blasted the airborne Asora with powerful dark energy. The princess's armor was not powerful enough to withstand her sister's attack. The dark energy also destroyed the coins of power, and their powers were released. Asora crashed into ground, still wearing her broken golden armor.

"How pathetic, baby sister," Laxur commented in her massive voice.

Just then, the powers of the coins surged into Asora. She was empowered with the energies of the elements. The power rebuilt her golden armor.

"Arise, guardians of the dragon king! Come to my aid!" Asora commanded. Five beings appeared.

"Guardians, stop Laxur!" The five monsters attacked the oversized woman.

The golden armor that enveloped the Princess grew, and it changed colors, depending on which power she used. She took to the skies once again and came right up to Laxur, who was busy battling the Princess's guardians.

"What are you planning to do, Asora?" Laxur asked in rage.

"This!" Asora's golden armor changed color, and a storm formed right above Laxur.

The storm made it hard for Laxur to breathe, but the massive queen raised her hand and smashed into Asora from below. The princess flipped into the air, out of control. Confused and dizzy, Asora fell and crashed right in between Laxur's large breasts; she was stuck. "Sister, must you really expose so much of your skin?"

"What is the matter, baby sister? Jealous?" Laxur snickered.

The wind daemon guardian pulled Asora free, but they were caught on something. Several pieces of string were acting with wills of their own and were tying themselves to Asora and the wind daemon. The strings were from Laxur's clothes, which were enchanted. The Princess cut them with her katana, but more came up and enveloped her. The wind daemon escaped and went to get another to help him free Asora.

"You look very stuck, Asora. You will not be going anywhere,"

Laxur said with a laugh.

A beastly roar erupted from the cold night, and a wave of fire descended from the skies. The dragon lord Rowaton emerged from the flames, and he was angry. The mighty beast snarled and roared at the giant Queen Laxur. Even though he was only half her size, he was still a great danger to her.

"Do not attack me, beast, for I have your charge within my grasp," Laxur warned Rowaton.

"I am well aware of that, witch," a powerful male voice thundered from the dragon. "Release Asora now, or face my wrath."

While Rowaton and Laxur bantered back and forth, Asora became further buried in Laxur's enchanted strings. Her strength was almost gone; she felt weak. A gust of cold wind woke Asora, and she spotted a set of green vials. The Princess remembered that Laxur always had potions with her. The green vials made a person grow into a giant and increased their powers and strength. If Asora could get to one of them and drink it, she would become as big and as powerful as her sister.

The problem was that the vials were far from her, and for her to get to them, she had to cut herself loose and run across a terrain of soft and sensitive skin. The running part would only be for a few seconds; it was the strings and Laxur's heightened sense of touch that Asora had to watch out for.

Rowaton's daemon guardians came to the aid of the dragon lord and helped him battle the giant witch, Queen. Laxur was pounded from all sides with fire, ice, wind, water, rock, lightning, plants, and energy. The attacks seemed to have little effect on the Queen, and she brushed it all off.

Her attacks, on the other hand, were devastating to Rowaton's daemons. Rowaton himself suffered little from Laxur's dark magic; however, the giant woman's strength was a problem for the dragon lord. She was ten times his strength. She grabbed a hold of the dragon's thick neck and began to squeeze.

"Time for you to pass into the next world, Rowaton," Laxur stated.

Rowaton wrapped his tail around her arm, and he tried to scratch and bite her, but to no avail. The daemons again charged at Laxur, but this time at her face. They were trying to distract her long enough for Asora to escape.

They, however, were not aware that the princess had another plan. Asora wiggled out of her armor and made it shrink and reappear upon her body. With all her strength, Asora ran full tilt to the green vials stored in Laxur's corset. The magical strings were chasing her, but Laxur had not noticed, for she was busy trying to fight off the daemons.

Laxur slammed Rowaton's back into the ground, and he let go, just as she did. The daemons continued their attacks. Asora ran right into the fabric of the giant corset and looked for the green vials of growth potions. Laxur's clothes, jewels, and weapons grew with her, except for her vials of potions because the magic in them cannot have their sizes altered so radically. This prevents the user from making too much of the potion. These must be made and not twisted; otherwise, it could cause harm. Asora, in a mad hurry, grabbed ten vials and drank one of them. It tasted sweet, like nectarines. Suddenly, Asora felt something churning in her belly, and she felt like it was growing. Then, Asora was overcome by a feeling of ecstasy; she had never felt so good. She thought that this was why Laxur liked to do this; it was almost addicting. Before she knew it, Asora began to grow.

Queen Laxur's chest felt heavier than usual. She looked down at her large breasts and saw Asora growing. She expanded so fast that she broke through Laxur's corset, and the newly enlarged Princess Asora was still getting bigger. Laxur magically mended the front of her corset back together as she watched Asora grow. The princess finally stopped growing, and she was the exact size as Laxur.

Asora had never been so big; it felt so odd, and it felt good. Her wings exploded out, bigger and stronger than ever. The golden armor, however, seemed to be having trouble covering parts of her body, but it covered her enough to be decent. The Princess could also feel her powers grow exponentially. Her strength was beyond anything that she ever felt. She understood why her sister enjoyed this—the power, the intensity. It all felt so good; her body felt good, and it was very addicting. Asora wanted more, but she had to concentrate on the matter at hand.

"You dare use my potions to aid you! I will crush you for this." Laxur used her magic to make her sword appear out of thin air, and she slashed at her little sister.

"You are damn right I would dare! To stop you! I can see why you enjoy this so much, though." Asora's voice boomed. She sounded so powerful; both sisters' voices echoed through the area for hundreds of miles.

The fighting was even. Both sisters were equally matched in strength, power, and speed, and neither one would give up.

Rowaton recovered enough to fly again. The dragon rammed right into Laxur's side, knocking her over, and this gave the Princess the opening she needed to land a powerful blow to the queen. Asora slammed her fist into Laxur's head, knocking her to the ground.

Laxur crashed face-first into the snow-covered ground, causing a massive quake felt for miles. With one pound from her fist, the queen caused another quake, and she shrank back down to normal size. Polea, Smika, and his fairy surrounded their fallen queen, and in a flash of light, they disappeared.

It took an hour for Princess Asora to shrink back to her normal size. She spent the hour freezing in the snow; the growth potion was the only thing keeping her warm. She felt weak and empty now; the rush of power and strength was gone. She felt tired, and her hands trembled lightly, but she hid this from everyone. She still had nine of the green vials.

In the meantime, during her enlarged state, Asora put her magic to use by repairing the damaged mansion. The Vanguard agents, along with Irantanco, had fled. Heralin and Ela could not be returned to the storybook from where they came, so Countess Marien took it upon herself to let them stay with her and work for her. She could always us a personal detective/spy and a mistress. The rest of Marien's birthday party went on without incident.

Chapter Forty-Two

For Laxur's Heart

The winter storm began to intensify with greater winds, thunder, lightning, rain, and snow mixed with hail. The mega city Aunsborg had seen such weather before. Its towers, buildings, and other structures were well suited in withstanding it. The smaller towns, however, are much more vulnerable.

Far outside Aunsborg, deep in the mountains, and away from the chateau and town. A small cave was occupied. There was a small campfire going to keep the occupants warm and give them light. Polea had taken her queen, Smika, and his fairy, Hyea, there to hide. She wished to keep Laxur safe.

They were unable to leave Havaina because of the storm. Until it was over, they were trapped there. Smika started a fire with wood that Hyea found. Polea was impressed by the young man's ability to use the magical gifts. He obviously had something to show or prove.

At first Polea thought that Smika was trying to impress her. As it turned out it was not her, but Laxur. He was trying to prove himself to Laxur. Polea was not sure how to feel about that. The blonde lady was not particularly impressed by men, but Smika has managed that feat and quite well.

The queen was laid out on the ground on a special pad. She was also covered in a sleeping bag near the fire to keep her warm. Polea was able to handle the cold, but the others around her could not. Also, the danger of the cold on a sleeping person was very great. Even for the queen a cold sleep would be a death sentence. Polea would not allow Laxur to die. And she was not alone in this. Smika and Hyea seemed devoted to Laxur. That was good to Polea.

Queen Laxur had been asleep ever since they arrived at the cave. Polea and Smika tried to wake her up, but they had no luck. Polea made blankets and had a sleeping bag for Laxur and moved her near Smika's fire to prevent her from freezing. Polea wanted Laxur to be comfortable.

"Smika, I will be back in an hour. I am going to see if I can find some food for us," Polea said to the young boy.

"Can you use your magic to make food?" Hyea asked.

"For some reason, my magic is even weaker now. It could be the storm, but the point is, I do not have much magic left. I need to save it," Polea responded.

She put on a heavy black hooded coat and left. Hyea went with Polea in case she needed help. Smika could hold his own, and the cave was well concealed. Polea wore a black cloak and had Hyea inside to keep each other warm.

"Polea," Hyea called out.

"Yes?" Polea asked.

"We need to get some food," Hyea said.

"I saw a store nearby," Polea said.

Polea made her way through the cold, wind, and snow. She got pelted by hail and her skin felt raw and dry. But she did come across the store that she saw earlier. It was what humans called a truck and supply stop. It was a place for those large semi-trucks that roamed all Havaina's roads. They carried everything from cargo, supplies, livestock, and who knew what else. This store was also a rest stop for those trucks, and anyone who needed a place to stop for a night or two.

This store was large, but its parking lot was surprisingly empty. This made Polea curious as she had an image in her mind that these places were always full and had dirty and fat humans roaming these places. But this place looked deserted. That suited Polea fine. It meant that no one would disturb her and Hyea.

Polea came up to the door. There was a window built into it and it was dark. The door was obviously locked. So Polea made a point on her finger that glowed a jade green. She inserted the point into the key lock and the lock opened. Polea then let herself in. She took off her hood and used her powerful angelic senses to feel for any other life around her other then Hyea.

Like Queen Laxur, and Princess Asora, Polea also had powerful angelic powers. She was as close to being an angel then a human, but she appeared more human. Polea had the power to feel for whatever she wanted. She felt five others in the building. She knew that they were not yet aware of her. Three of them were men and two were women. All five were humans, and they seemed to be drunk. That would make things easier as they would be more interested in whatever they were doing.

Hyea flew out of Polea's cloak and looked for the food section. The small fairy was confused by the packaging of the processed foods and the odd-looking meals. None of it looked appetizing to her. Some looked out right disgusting. She could not understand how humans and the others of the Consortium could stand it let alone eat it.

"What is this garbage?" Hyea asked as she pulled out a package from a shelf.

"That is beef jerky," Polea said as she read the package details. "It may not look good, but it is good for camping. Get a few of the packages."

"If you say so," Hyea said.

The fairy took the packages that were twice the size she was. She made them smaller and put them into her magical backpack. Hyea really wanted to find something that looked more appetizing. So far, she only found more odd and disgusting foods. That was until she came across a candy called gummies. The colors alone drew her to them. She opened on pack and the sweetness of the gummies made her want more.

Polea made her way around the store. It was surprisingly large for a truck stop. It held more then just food. There were clothes, trinkets, maps, books, magazines, and toys. Polea was drawn to the toys. She loved them and collected them. Boy's toys, girls toys, baby's toys, games, and puzzles. It did not matter she loved them all.

"Who the hell are you?" A mans voice rang out at Polea.

A powerfully lit flashlight is shined in Polea's face. It momentarily blinded her. Polea covered her face to get the light out of her face. Polea could now feel three of the five now near her. One woman and two men, and one of them was drunk.

"I am so sorry, I am lost," Polea tried to lie.

"Yeah right," the woman said. "A teenage chick broke into the store."

"Get her," the third person said.

The two men charged at Polea. Before they could get to her, the blonde girl jumped into the next isle. She needed some distance to get ready.

"Get the lights!" The first man yelled at one of his fellows.

As the third man went to the lighting controls. He was hit by a ball of rainbow light. It was a fairy who was attacking him by punching him in the face.

Hyea was surprised by how well she was doing against this fat human. She needed to protect Polea. So Hyea used a spell to destroy the lighting controls to prevent them from turning on the lights in the store.

Polea meanwhile had to put her glasses on so she could see what she was up against. She could easily take them out with her magic. However, she wanted to play with them. She then looked at all the children's toys and got an idea.

"Damn it there's a damn crazy fairy in here!" The third man yelled back.

"She is not your only problem," Polea called out.

The blonde girl took off her cloak and unfurled her grey wings. This made her look a lot bigger than she really was. In her hand was a jade and gold glowing whip sword. She cracked her razor whip making it glow a menacing green.

"She's a merk!" The woman cried.

"Shot her!" The third man yelled.

The first man had a handgun and he opened fire on Polea. What they did not know was that Polea had a barrier made of compressed sound. She knew how to deflect small bullets using a combination of magic and science. She also swung her razor whip to deflect to the other bullets. This had a very intimidating effect on the three humans that Polea rather enjoyed.

"Oh, I am more then that," Polea hissed. "I am you doom."

Polea used her free hand to cast a spell on the store. The toys in the store then suddenly came to life. They made sounds that you would expect from children's toys. But Polea added a creepy factor to them. As the toys grabbed knives, tools, and guns from the other isles. They jumped on the shelves and crawled along the walls like insects. All while speaking in innocent voices.

"Now who is outnumbered?" Polea laughed. "Seize them!"

The hundreds of armed small toys suddenly jumped and attacked. The third man was stabbed, slashed, and ran threw hundreds of times. He was left a bloodied mass of pulverized meat in mere moments.

Polea laughed evilly as she unleashed a bolt of lightning at the two humans. She cracked her whip again and destroyed a display stand. She also sent out a pulse of green electricity.

"What is the matter?" Polea laughed evilly. "Do you two not want to play with me?"

"You're fucking insane!" The woman yelled in a panic.

"Well, I do play rough I will admit," Polea laughed. "But it is very satisfying."

The woman took out a large shot gun and aimed it at Polea. However, before she could fire Polea used her razor whip and chopped the gun into small pieces. The gun fell apart in the woman's hands.

"You will need to do better then that," Polea said.

Then a bat struck Polea on the back of her head. The blonde angel girl went to the floor. The bat was in the hands of one of the drunk men who was asleep when Polea used her lightning. He then started to pound on Polea's back and wings to try and keep her down.

Polea then was grabbed by the other man and held forcefully. The man with the bat struck her again. The toys were not here because they had dragged her into another room. She could hear the toy army trying to get in to help Polea. The woman then punched Polea in the face.

"You fucking sick bitch," the woman snarled. "You're going to pay for murdering him."

"Pigs like him deserve to be put to death," Polea spat.

The woman punched Polea again. Blood came from her nose and lip. Mixed in her blood were her tears. She was angry and scared all in one.

"Let's see how you like it when you are cut to pieces," the woman said.

Polea had daggers hidden in her sleeves. She made them pop out and she stabbed her capture in between his legs. He roared in agony and was forced to release Polea. She then rammed her blades into the man's face. Once he dropped dead, she blasted the door opened.

"Kill them all!" Polea commanded the toy swarm.

The hundreds on fanatically insane toys armed with every assortment of weaponry in the store charged in like an attacking army. Polea watched with glee as the humans were torn limb from limb. She laughed and walked back out into the store. Hyea had been watching and was in shock at what Polea had done.

"Why did you do that?" Hyea asked.

"Do you know what rape is?" Polea asked.

"No," Hyea replied.

"Then you are fortunate," Polea said.

"But you did not need to kill them," Hyea pleaded.

"They were going to kill me, and you. And that would leave our queen vulnerable," Polea explained.

Hyea said nothing. It was obvious to her that Polea had some trauma in her past. And this could be why she felt that this was necessary. Polea also said that she was also protecting her as well. It made Hyea feel a bit odd that Polea went this way to protect herself and Hyea as well.

"I think we have everything we need," Hyea said.

"Good," Polea said. Then she looked at the small fairy. "Are you afraid of me?"

"Honestly," Hyea said. "Yes."

Polea's eyes looked hurt. But she should have seen that coming. Hyea was from a story where the horrors of the real universe did not happen.

"I am sorry that you fear me. You have nothing to fear from me," Polea said.

"Then make those toys stop moving," Hyea asked.

Polea raised her hand and drew the enchantment from all the toys. They all fell to the floors. They were inanimate objects again and they dropped whatever they were carrying.

"Better?" Polea asked kindly.

"I suppose," Hyea said. "It is just that acting like a pirate does not suit you."

Polea laughed kindly. "Me, a pirate?"

Polea made several mock pirate grunts and sounds. It made Hyea laugh. But she could not forget how scary her tall blonde companion was now. Polea made her wings vanish into her back. She also put her cloak back on and put the hood over her head. Hyea went inside Polea's cloak, and they exited the store.

No doubt in Polea's mind that once the storm passed that the local authorities would investigate the store. But they would find nothing of value. She hoped that they would be long gone by then. The wind and snow covered her tracks as Polea walked off into the darkness.

Back at the hidden cave, Smika was tending to the campfire. He had just placed another log on it. He earlier had to fend off a wolf that tried to eat him and the sleeping Laxur. Fortunately, Smika was good with fending off hungry predators.

Smika thought that he heard Laxur move. She was still. He piled another blanket at the entrance to keep out the cold wind and snow. He sat near the queen and investigated the fire. He poked at the fire to keep it burning brightly.

He turned around to look at Laxur. Even to a boy his age, she was extremely beautiful. Smika could not help but be attracted by such beauty. Smika had covered her with a thick blanket to keep her warm. He was very impressed by her fighting power, her size, her beauty, her strength, and her kindness toward him. He made his blanket into a pillow for Queen Laxur to rest her head on. Her skin looked smooth and lightly pale; her hair was long, thick, and pure black; her lips were as red as blood. Smika was lost in Laxur's beauty, and he could not help but kiss her on the lips. He always wondered what it would be like to kiss a girl. Laxur would not mind if he got one little kiss from her; what harm could that bring?

Before he did, he stopped. He kept hearing noises, but it was always the wind and the movement of the black out blankets. Smika turned back to Laxur and wondered if she was dreaming. If she was, then of what? He knew that he would be dreaming of her for a long time. Her steady breathing was very rhythmic and soft.

He wondered if all queens were as beautiful as Laxur was. He knew that she was not exactly good, but in a twisted way. That made her more exciting to him. He had never felt this way about a girl or a lady before. Smika wondered if this was that love that Hyea kept talking to him about.

Smika then started to fantasy about what would life be like if he stayed with her. Was it possible to earn this queen's heart and love. But what could he offer this perfect woman that some other man could? All he could do was keep watch over her and protect her. And yet he wanted to be closer to her.

So, Smika leaned down to Laxur's resting face. He could hear her breathing lightly. Then, very slowly, he placed his lips upon hers, and he tried to replicate the same actions that he saw when adult men and women kissed back in his world.

After what seemed like an eternity, Smika pulled away from the queen's face. Laxur began to stir and moan, her eyes slowly fluttered open, and she saw him leaning over her. She smiled at him. That made him feel good. She was not upset, but glad to see him.

"You managed to awaken me. Thank you, Smika," Laxur said sweetly to the boy.

She then sat up with the blanket on her. She was still a bit cold. She looked around to see where she and Smika were.

"Was that your first time kissing a lady?" Laxur asked.

Smika nodded in acknowledgment, "I'm sorry if it offended you."

Laxur smiled kindly at him. "You are pretty good at it for your first time."

"Thank you," Smika said blushing.

That made Laxur chuckle as she could make this young man's heart flutter. Then she noticed that he had no blanket and no other means of keeping himself warm.

"Are you not cold?" She asked, concerned when she saw Smika shivering. He again nodded. "Here then. Come and cuddle next to me. I will help keep you warm. It is very cold outside."

Smika accepted Laxur's offer and slowly crawled under the blanket with the beautiful woman. She was right; he was very cold, if not freezing to death. This boy saved her life, and she wanted to repay his kindness by saving his. She liked him. She used her body heat to warm him back up. She covered him except his face. Laxur sat him in her lap and enveloped him in her arms.

To Smika, Laxur felt so comfortable. His mind drifted to a time so long ago when he was a baby. He remembered his own mother holding him just like this when he was sad. Laxur felt so comforting. An evil person did not feel like this. Laxur was not evil like everyone says she is.

"Feel better?" Laxur asked.

"I do, your majesty," Smika said.

Laxur chuckled. "If it is just, you me or Polea and Hyea, you can call me Laxur. You can skip the formality."

"I like you too much to do that," Smika said.

"Oh really?" Laxur asked playfully. "You like me huh?" Laxur held him closer. "Did you enjoy my battles?"

"How big can you grow?" Smika asked.

"I have grown bigger than that," Laxur said. "Once I grew well over a kilometer tall. And I was able to dominate."

"Wow," Smika said impressed. "You're no queen. You're a goddess."

Laxur chuckled. "I hope to be one."

"You should," Smika said. "And I will help you."

Queen Laxur smiled at Smika. She gently kissed him on her forehead. She did not cast any spell on him. She had no need to. Laxur could feel this young man's love and absolute loyalty to her. She did not need to worry about him. Laxur needed more allies like him. He was good at magical trickery. Laxur was aware of his story and was not a fan of it. But she was learning that Smika was someone she could count on.

"Where are Polea and Hyea?" Laxur asked as Smika continued to adjust his body to hers.

"She said that they were going to get some food. She cannot make her magic work right, so they went out to get some," Smika answered. "I think she said something about a store a few kilometers away."

"Well, I guess it is only you and me then," Laxur said with a smile and a kind voice.

Smika could not believe that this lovely woman was supposed to be an evil witch. If anything, she was simply powerful and protective. If she were the queen of darkness, then that was fine with him.

Laxur laid back against the cave wall, she still held Smika gently. Smika felt so much warmth from her; he also felt safe. Laxur's body was soft, like an extravagant pillow. He stopped shaking and sank deeper into her. She allowed him to fall deeper into her embrace.

"Relax, Smika. I will keep you safe. I will keep you warm. You saved me, after all, so I am in your debt. I will not let any harm come to you," Laxur repeated.

"Thank you, my queen," Smika said very lightly.

He said it so low he thought that no one could have heard, but it was enough for Laxur to hear. She smiled and laughed lightly. Smika was the little brother she always wanted. She knew that he felt differently.

Hours later, Polea and Hyea returned with baskets of food covered in snow. They saw that Laxur was now awake and keeping Smika warm. "Welcome back ladies," Laxur said.

Chapter Forty-Three

The Wraith

The mansion was restored, but the snowstorm had prevented anyone from leaving. Countess Marien had the guest rooms readied for long storm days. She frequently had guests over longer than planned, which was perfectly fine with the human monarch.

Jeia, Marevin, and Yane were playing a card game with Asora. The four were trying to teach T'ula how to play an old human game called twenty-one. So far, T'ula looked like she had a handle on the basics. The numbers on the cards tell you the value. The person that got closest to twenty- one was the victor.

Marien and Madimoy were in the kitchen with the cooks, baking a cake for everyone. Sarea and Rakon were sparring in the gym. Heralin and Ela were in Marien's private library. Lady T'a was in her room, sleeping peacefully. Dominus was out doing Maker knew what. He was an angel after all, and they liked being mysterious.

An hour later, a knock came at the door, and one of the countess's servants opened it. In walked a tan-skinned woman in a blue military uniform with a black cloth covering her hair.

"Supreme Sky Marshal Alianzu? What brings you to my home this day?" Marien asked the sky marshal.

"My Queen, I have just come from the Hiyadrome. They sent me to convey wishes for your birthday." Alianzu bowed to Marien.

"Well, thank you for coming all this way, my dear Sky Marshal.

When you return to the Hiyadrome, tell the other Generals, Admirals, and Sky Marshals that I appreciate this," Marien said, welcoming in the highly decorated military woman. Alianzu had a small box topped with a ribbon.

"I would have been here yesterday, but I was busy. Here you are, my queen. From all of us at the Hiyadrome." Alianzu gave Marien the box.

Marien opened it, and she found several beautifully handcrafted coins, one from each of the military forces that served her: a jade coin from the Army, a blue gold coin from the Navy, a yellow gold coin from the Air Force, a platinum coin from the Special Forces, a diamond coin from the Cyber Defense Force, a palladium coin from the Coast Guard, a copper coin from the Defense Forces, and a germanium coin from the Space Command.

Marien was a well-known coin collector, and her military knew it.

"They are each one of a kind. They are our souls in your hands, my Queen," Alianzu said with a smile.

"Oh, thank you, Alianzu. I will treasure them," Marien responded. She took them to a case with many other coins that the countess had collected over the course of her life.

"Alianzu? What brings you here?" Asora saw the sky marshal.

"Wanted to wish your mother a happy birthday, and so does the Hiyadrome," the highly decorated woman said sharply. "Before I forget, my Queen, Fleet Admiral Yane and Vice Admiral Corgol have managed a joint fleet exercise next week. It will be a good show. This will be our chance to show you our newest warships."

"I would love to see them." Marien turned to her daughter, who loved the shows of military strength. "Would you and your privy council like to stay an extra week and see the OCIA Fleet exercises?"

"I would love to, but I have to check with the others before I say yes," Asora said and walked out.

Asora, along with Alianzu and Marien, walked into the living room from the other room, where everyone from the Princess's council, except Dominus, was gathered. T'a had just woken up, still looked tired, and was very cranky.

"Who would like to see the OCIA war games next week?" Asora asked.

"We are back on Evorn next week, my Princess. Unless you want to extend our stay here until then," Madimoy said.

"I do. So, who wants to see the naval war games?" Asora asked, almost demanding an affirmative response.

"I believe we should. It would be a good distraction from the events of the last few days. Besides, after Laxur's rampage, I would not mind seeing some machines that are stronger and are more helpful to us," Lady T'ula said, helping Asora.

"When is OCIA?" Jeia asked. He knew what it was. To him, these war games were boring. He could not go home because this was a part of Countess Marien's birthday celebration.

"It is in five days, my lord," Alianzu replied sharply.

The rest agreed to Asora's demand to go and see the war games.

"Wonderful. Sky Marshal Alianzu informed me that the supercarrier, *Tycon*, will host us when the war games begin," Marien said.

"What is a supercarrier?" Ela asked.

"Do you know what an aircraft carrier is?" Jeia asked. Ela shook her head no.

"A supercarrier is an aircraft carrier that is far larger than normal. It looks flat on top with a tower-like structure on the starboard side. It launches and lands jet aircraft. It is basically a floating city of steel," Admiral Yane explained in the simplest way he could.

"A floating city made entirely of steel? Great Maker!" was all Ela could say.

"Wait until you see one close up. They are huge machines," Asora said to Ela and then held out a picture to show her what the *Tycon* looked like.

"That is an odd-looking ship. Where are the sails, and why does it have a tower on one side?" the shocked elf asked.

"It is powered by a massive steam turbine plant. The propellers can push the ship up to thirty knots or faster. The steam plants are far better than sails. The tower is both a bridge and a jet control tower," Asora explained.

"It should be interesting to see this beast of a ship in person," Ela said with amazement in her voice.

A family night was underway between Marien, Asora, and Jeia, along with Madimoy. Madimoy and Jeia were due to be wed in the next few months, and Marien was giving Madimoy the customary speech from mother to future daughter-in-law. The four fairies that served Asora who also served Marien as servants, maids, and spies. and they were grilling Madimoy's fairy servant, Rentha, in a similar way.

Marevin, T'ula, and T'a were in the room, observing the family ritual.

"Are you going to have to go through this as well, Marevin?" T'a asked.

"Eventually, I will. Thankfully, not right now," Marevin replied sheepishly.

"It looks painful to have the mother interrogate you," T'ula added.

"Do you elves have something like this, where your parents interrogate your fiancées?" Marevin asked.

"No. Most elves are arranged for marriage. So that eliminates the need for such a ritual," T'ula said.

"Wow, that kind of takes the fun out things," the human man stated.

"Marriage is not supposed to be fun. It is for convenience and to help the families create alliances," T'a replied with a bored sound in her voice.

"Not all of us elves are arranged for marriage. Some of us are either not worthy or forgotten," T'ula said with a hint of regret.

"That is sad. And I take it from your tone that you are one of those that were forgotten?" Marevin asked.

"Not forgotten. I have been told that I am not worthy of any man of nobility," T'ula said sadly.

"That is rather hard to believe, Lady T'ula," T'a added in. "Why is that?"

"Because I am an embarrassment to my stepparents. Also, I have an inheritance from my real mother."

"An embarrassment? How? You are young, powerful, beautiful, and talented. You are more a lady than your stepmother," Marevin said.

"Well, for starters, I am half human," T'ula admitted. She showed them her shorter–than–normal elf ears under her thick hair.

"My real parents were wonderful people. My mother was once one of the wealthiest and most loved nobles in the kingdom. My father was a human businessman that had a garage, I believe it was called. He fixed things for a living. He saved my mother from a snowstorm, and she fell madly in love with him. A few months later, I was conceived, but there was a problem." T'ula paused for a moment.

"What was the problem?" T'a asked.

"The problem was that my mother was already married to another man—my stepfather," T'ula answered.

"That would pose a problem. So, what happened?" Marevin asked.

"When I was born, my mother gave me everything. My stepfather had no choice but to accept me. My real father was a wonderful man. He taught me everything he knew. I have very fond memories of him." T'ula stopped.

"What happened to your real parents?" T'a asked.

"My father died in an accident, and my mother" —T'ula started to weep—"my mother burned in the palace fire a few decades ago."

"Oh my maker, you poor dear," Marevin said sorrowfully.

"My stepfather remarried the woman that you know. I am tolerated by them because my birth mother gave me her entire fortune, and they practically live off that," T'ula said begrudgingly.

"Okay, I get it. They do not allow you to marry because it would take their fortune away, and they would be poor. And the fact that they know that you are half human makes it embarrassing to them and easier to justify your chastity," Marevin speculated.

"You are very right, Marevin. I can watch others with love between them, but I am not allowed to have love myself. It is very painful deep inside my heart," T'ula said.

Countess Marien was finally finished "interrogating" Madimoy, as was the duty of the mother. Asora noticed Marevin talking to T'ula and T'a.

"And what are you three discussing?" Asora asked kindly.

"We were curious about why your mother was questioning Lady Madimoy so intensely," T'ula answered.

"Well, Mother wants Madimoy to be the right woman for her son. It only makes sense to have them sit down and talk about things." Asora shrugged.

"I believe that would make sense, since you humans normally do not have arranged marriages, except within high nobility," T'a added, "such as yourself. You are of the nobility and therefore are subject to this rule."

"Dinner will be served in an hour. What do you three want to do?" Asora asked. "What were you planning on doing, my Princess?" T'ula asked.

Countess Marien heard a knock at her door, and one of her servants opened it. Marien was in the foyer when she heard a voice that made her cringe with hate; it was him, the damned Puro, in her house. Behind him was a priest and three priestesses, all dressed in white.

"What are you doing here?" Marien demanded.

"The Utopian Princess is days overdue, and I am here to escort her and her court back to Evorn," Puro Aga explained snidely.

"Really? Because I think that you are here to annoy me," the countess responded.

"You are the one who is annoying, Countess," Aga retaliated.

Marien and Aga stared each other down, both gleaming with hatred. It was no secret that these two were rivals, in every sense of the word.

Princess Asora entered the room, and her spirit plummeted when she saw the Puro.

"Why have you not returned, Princess?" Aga demanded.

"It is winter here, and the storms have a tendency to disrupt magical portals. So, I take it that you are stuck here too?" Asora pointed out.

"Unfortunately, the ship that I came in was hit by an Astrostorm, and Havaina was the closest world to land on for a safe harbor," Puro Aga explained.

"Wonderful. That means you are here for the next week to give me a giant headache, and just after my birthday no less," Marien complained.

"A pleasure as always," Aga said with a smirk.

"Well, you and your Priests and Priestesses are not staying here. There is a hotel in Aunsborg that you can stay in," Marien commanded.

Just then, the electrical power went out in the mansion.

"What happened?" Jeia asked as he entered the room.

"The power went out. Have Jyals go out and reset the breakers," Marien told a maid. The young girl bowed and ran out.

An hour had passed with no power.

"I wonder what is taking the human so long to fix this problem?" a priestess asked. She was an elf of middling years with coffee hair and eyes.

"It does not take this long to reset a few breakers. Jeia, could you see what happened?" Asora asked her brother.

"Of course. I would rather do that than spend another hour with that dirtbag." Jeia pointed to Aga and left.

Jeia, Asora, Sarea, T'ula, Yane and the elf Priestess ventured outside to the utility shed. They found the door to the shed open and the snow-stained red.

"Oh no!" Asora cried out. Yane pulled out his point forty-five revolver, looking around. He was not going to be caught off guard again.

Jeia looked inside and saw nobody, and the breakers looked to have been tripped by an electrical surge from an outside source.

"It looks like a lightning bolt or a laser hit the breakers and fused them completely." Jeia turned to Asora. "Is there another utility shed?"

"I believe so, but it is for the emergency generator," Asora pointed out.

"How long will the generators last?" T'ula asked.

"About nine days," Jeia responded.

"Why do you care?" the priestess asked snidely.

"I do not need to explain myself to you, T'fala," T'ula stated harshly.

They all heard a noise in the snow-covered forest behind the mansion. It sounded like someone moving through brush and snow. Sarea readied her sword and her gun.

"Whatever it is, it is getting closer," Sarea said.

"Do you think that it is Queen Laxur again?" T'ula asked.

"I think not. I do not feel the dark magic from whatever it is," Asora said with a hint of worry in her voice.

Jeia and Sarea slowly walked into the snow-drenched forest. Admiral Yane stayed to protect the Princess and the others.

A few meters into the forest, Sarea could smell death. Jeia saw blood dripping and looked up to find a body hanging from a branch.

Sarea looked up. "By the Hananaka. Who or what did this?"

"I seriously doubt that Laxur or Polea could or would do this," Jeia added in.

A bolt of energy surged toward Jeia and Sarea. The two humans jumped out of the way, and the energy ball hit a tree and set it ablaze.

"What the hell was that?" Jeia screamed.

Another ball of energy streaked toward them. For a moment, Sarea could have sworn that she saw a shimmer in the darkness. Asora, T'ula, Yane, and T'fala came running in.

Being one of the few humans allowed to learn magic, Sarea chanted a spell that lit up the area, and the pulse revealed what was attacking them. Electricity sparked and arced around the body of a ten-foot machine.

"What is that thing?" T'fala demanded.

"You have me there," Jeia retorted.

The machine launched another energy bolt, this time aimed at the Princess. Asora was quick enough to duck out of the way, and the bolt missed her. Yane fired his weapon at the machine. The bullets bounced off what sounded like metal armor. It roared inside its mask, and the thing made a run for the mansion.

"If it gets inside, it will kill everyone in there!" Jeia yelled.

"Move your asses!" Yane yelled back, running in the same direction as the monster. He had a gun in each hand, ready for battle.

Once back at the mansion, the group saw Rakon fighting with the creature. The metal demon tried to use his mastery of metal on the beast; however, the metal it wore did not respond to Rakon's magic. The monster bashed Rakon on the head, knocking him down, and plowed into the mansion.

Asora and T'ula helped Rakon back to his feet. At the same time, Jeia and Yane ran past them and after the creature.

"What is happening?" Marien said when she saw them. Admiral Yane grabbed Marien and pulled her to the wall with his hand over her mouth.

"A monster just broke down the back wall and is running around your home. Please be calm and whisper if you need to speak," Yane whispered into the countess's ear.

She nodded in acknowledgment, and the admiral released her.

A few minutes later, the three heard the machine rummaging around the upstairs computer lab.

Quietly, they moved upstairs and down the hall. By a broken door, they saw a dead elf priest and a badly hurt Puro Aga holding a magical blade covered in blood.

"What happened?" Marien whispered.

"I and Talbor heard a strange noise and came out to investigate. The next thing we knew, a monstrous metal beast came out of the shadows, ambushed us, killed my priest, and went into your accursed machine shop here. I did manage a few swipes at it with this." Aga held up his knife. "But it did not scream or even flinch when I tried to stab it."

"Well then, you and the countess stay here. The admiral and I will go in," Jeia whispered his plan.

"Go in? And do what exactly?" Yane asked, dumbfounded.

"I do not know. I am making this up as I go along," Jeia answered back.

"That is very reassuring," the admiral retorted.

"Do you have a better idea, sea ape?" Jeia shot out.

Yane slapped Jeia in his face. "You call me that again and I will kick your ass so bad that we will need surgery to have my foot removed from your butt."

"How about you two argue later and go in and kill the creature?" Aga spat.

Yane and Jeia looked at each other and shrugged. Jeia peered through a hole in the wall to observe the creature. It looked like it was accessing the computers; it had already gotten past all the security programs and firewalls that protected the machines.

"It looks like it's trying to send a signal," Jeia said.

"We cannot let it do that," Yane said, loading his revolvers. Jeia loaded a clip into his pistol. The two men nodded to each other.

In a flash, Yane and Jeia jumped up from their cover and opened fire. They unloaded several rounds at point-blank range. The attack destroyed the computer and prevented the monster from accessing it. A roar of rage was heard, and it charged at the two men. They jumped to either side, out of the path of their angry opponent. It crashed through the wall.

"Does this thing not believe in doors or something?" Jeia cracked.

"If you were that pissed, would you?" Yane responded.

"Good point."

A loud thud was heard while Yane and Jeia chased after it. It had jumped down two and a half stories and punched its way past the guards.

A young soldier with a large shotgun did manage to briefly stop the intruder with a solid shot. When he got too close, the monster ripped the gun away and snapped it in two. The young man was shoved so hard that he was knocked out cold.

Then the creature broke down the main doors to the outside to find Princess Asora in her golden dragon armor with her angel wings unfurled. Lady T'ula was there with a dueling sword and blue-black armor, and Priestess T'fala stood chanting a spell.

"You are going nowhere, creature," T'ula pronounced.

Asora powered all seven of the coins of power. She could feel raw power coursing through her; it felt warm and cool at the same time. She felt energized and more powerful than ever before. Lifting her sword into the sky, she summoned a thunderstorm.

"Cold and fear! Attack thy foe with all the fury of the elements!" Asora's voice boomed in the wind.

The hail made had no effect on the creature, and it ran toward T'ula and Asora. Dame Sarea did a flying kick and landed powerfully against the monster, sending it flying backward. The machine made what sounded like gagging noises. A shotgun blast knocked the machine to the ground. Marevin loaded another shell into his shotgun.

Yane and Jeia came running out with Rakon and Aga in tow.

"Nice shot," Yane complimented Marevin. T'a and Madimoy came running around a corner to see the gathering of people.

Jeia examined the armored machine more closely and discovered something interesting. "This does not look like any metal that I have ever seen." He picked up an arm to look more closely. "It looks a lot like plastic or carbon nano-tubing."

"Carbon nano-tubing? Plastic? What are those?" Aga demanded.

"Nonmetals, you dolt," Marien retorted.

"Carbon nanotubes are nanoscopic filaments of carbon fibers that, when weaved together, produce a fabric stronger than any form of steel," Yane added.

"Plastic is an oil-like, solidified form. It can be as hard as metal if there is enough of it, and it is much lighter," T'ula said, demonstrating her scientific knowledge.

"That explains why my powers did not work on it," Rakon commented.

Aga turned to T'ula. "How do you know all this?"

"Because she does something that you do not, and that is study," Marien said to Aga.

Yane noticed that the faceplate was a mask, and it was removable. Slowly, he pried off the wires and tubes holding the mask on. Once he removed the final wire, he wrenched the mask free and pulled it away to reveal what was underneath.

What was revealed was something that none of them had ever seen before. A lizard-like freak with a mouth full of razor-harp teeth and what looked like head-up displays covering its eyes.

"This is one ugly freak," Yane said in a low tone.

In one move, the monster's arm shot up and grabbed Yane by his shirt; it opened its eyes and roared into his face. Yane was screaming along with everyone else. It tossed the Admiral ten meters away and grabbed Marevin's shotgun, and everyone quickly backed away. It shattered the shotgun on a rock, and it threw the rock at Marevin.

It turned to Asora and pulled a circular flying blade from its back. The blade glowed red and self-guided toward the Princess. Asora took to the skies and tried to outfly it. The beast then took a cannon-like device from its shoulder and snapped another piece to it to make what looked like a large gun. A single blast of hot plasma streaked by, sending people and shrapnel flying in all directions.

Princess Asora was doing her best to outfly the missile-like disk that was trying to cut her down. She pulled her sword, but the disk cut her sword in half and sliced through her armor and a little bit of her flesh in her left arm.

"Enough of this!" Asora said with anger.

"I call forth the daemon of lightning." In a flash of lightning, a creature that was destined to forever serve Asora appeared next to her.

"Destroy that disk!" Asora ordered the daemon. The daemon fired many bolts of superheated electrical arcs at the disk. Attracted to the disk's metal, the lightning had no problem finding its target. The disk was destroyed, and the daemon disappeared.

Asora looked down and saw everyone behind trees and rocks for cover. She had to end this fast, and there was one definite way to do this. The Princess had one of the stolen vials of potion with her. With this, she would be almost invulnerable to the monster's weapons, and she could destroy it in an instant. But then she would have to explain why she had the potion, and for a reason she did not understand, she did not want to explain or share the potion. At this point, however, her friends and family needed help, and she had to do something. She pulled out the potion from her pocket and drank it.

The monster snarled as it continued to fire on its adversaries.

"We need to get behind it!" Jeia shouted.

"Great plan, smartass. How you plan to do that?" Yane yelled back.

Suddenly, a massive object landed behind the monster, causing a quake in the ground. The monster turned to see a giant Asora. The giant Princess grabbed the monster's back and lifted it.

"Try picking on me now, you little bug," Asora's voice boomed in the face of the beast.

It pointed its plasma weapon at Asora, but she grabbed the weapon and ripped it out of the monster's hands, crushing it with a snap of her fingers. She formed a magical cage around the monster, but it failed to hold it. It broke free of Asora's grasp and jumped onto her arm, running toward her head. She tried to swat it off her, but the thing was too fast. It jumped into the air, going for her head, but the five daemons that served her intercepted it. The daemons tossed the monster dozens of meters in front of the giant Asora. With one blast of white light, she destroyed it.

An hour later, Asora shrank back down to her normal size, and her mother was demanding an explanation.

"I thought you only had one of those growth potions. Why do you have another? Or should I ask, how many more do you have?" Countess Marien demanded of her daughter.

"That was my only one. I only managed to grab two of them from Laxur," Asora lied.

Asora did not want anyone to take away something that gave her such pleasure. She was going to need more of it, and soon.

Lady T'a looked at Asora and knew something was going on.

The night was turning late, and what remained of the mansion was put back together, temporarily, to allow every weary fighter a chance to rest—except one.

In her old room, Princess Asora pulled out the seven remaining vials from her dresser drawer. She desired more. It felt so good to use potions. She understood the raw power, incredible strength, invincible feeling, and even the sexual appeal that Laxur enjoyed. It was doubtful that Laxur would give her more. Maybe she could steal them from her sister again.

"What is that thing that our Princess has?" Rayne asked her sisters, who were trying to sleep.

"I do not care right now, Rayne. Just go to sleep," B'nei complained.

She turned away and fell asleep.

Rayne looked back to her Princess, and she worried for her.

Chapter Forty-Four

Other Voices

Two days later, the snowstorm stopped long enough to allow Countess Marien and the others to travel to the famous Jalio Islands on the other side of Havaina, where the OCIA war games were being held. First, there was to be a military parade in honor of the human Queen.

A beautiful island city called Toniwe was where the fleet was assembling, and the countess, Asora, and her privy council were staying in a fancy hotel. Outside, the main street was lined with police officers in black uniforms and Marien's personal guard, known as the high guard, in heavily armored dark-blue uniforms.

From the outdoor balcony of the city's main building, the Utopian and human nobles sat and looked down at the massive street below. Marien and Asora were flanked by dozens of human generals, admirals, and sky marshals.

The anthem of the Human Consortium played over a series of loudspeakers. Every human either stood up or saluted, as an honor guard of seven troops holding flags came marching down the street in the ceremonial dress uniforms of the Army, Navy, Air Force, Cyber Defense, Special Operations, Coast Guard, and Space Command. Once they passed, another tune was played over the loudspeakers. Lady T'a recognized it and cringed, for she had heard it before during the Great War. It was known as the "March of the Consortium" to the humans; to the elves, it was the "March of Carnage."

A rhythmic rumble and thumping could be felt and heard by all. A long row of human military officers in army green was the first to come forth. Men and women goose stepped by Queen Marien and saluted her as they passed. This went on for the rest of the service, as troops marched by the people and their Queen. Four hundred thousand troops passed by the humans' queen.

Next was a procession of military machinery. Hundreds of tanks, each with one troop standing out of turret hatch, passed by, and the troops saluted Marien. After the tanks, a series of machines came forth. They were missile trucks carrying a massive ICBM. Another set of trucks with strange devices upon them fired off powerful laser light beams. The many Navy jets and combat drones darkened the skies. Hundreds of ships were in the cove—aircraft carriers, advanced destroyers, attack submarines, super battleships, and their support vessels.

Hours later, Marien, Asora, and the rest of the menagerie were taken to a Navy helicopter that transported them to the super-carrier *Tycon*. The ship was three hundred and a half meters long and a hundred and twenty meters wide. Asora had always wanted to see it, and Jeia was proud of it; his company built the thing, after all. It was a massive city of steel, with five thousand souls on board and over a hundred aircraft.

"I have always wondered what it would be like to be inside one of these beasts," Lady T'a muttered.

"Considering that ships like this one destroyed how many of your former fleets?" Madimoy taunted the former elf, queen.

"That was low, Lady Madimoy. Stop reminding her of past mistakes," Marien scolded.

They eventually entered the Command-and-Control Center, or CIC, of the mammoth warship. An Admiral with four large stars on his blue-and-gray digital camouflage uniform was inside.

"Admiral Herantano, good to see you again." Marien shook the man's hand.

"You as well, my Queen," the Admiral said.

Other Voices

He was looking straight into Marien's eyes, and then he turned back to stare out at the sea. All ships full steamed out to the open sea to begin OCIA.

Hundreds of ships fanned out and moved into formation away in the staging area. An hour later, the fleet of three hundred warships was sixty miles from the coast.

"It is going to take about a day to get everything ready for the exercise," the Admiral said. "So I invite you and your company to the wardroom and any entertainment we have to offer."

"Thank you," Asora said. She looked around for a door and went too it.

Later, the sun had gone down, and the ships intercom blared. "Darken ship. A fix all Circe Zebra fittings, close all hatches, doors, and portals to the weather-decks. Engage all darken ship lights and observe quiet hours. Now Darken Ship."

Asora was on the weather-deck and could barely see anything. She could hear the sailors hard at work readying the ship for the night cruise. Asora chanted a spell to herself, and her eyes glowed for only an instant. Her pupils had widened so much that she could see better. But not only that, but special nerves in her eyes also gave her the power to see in the dark. She could now see as clearly in day light.

"Your highness. You should be below. There is a movie and ice cream night on the mess decks," an officer said.

"Thank you. I was just enjoying the sights," Asora said.

"What sights? All I see is black," the officer said.

"I can see more," Asora said.

Inside the ship on its mess deck dozens of sailors were in line for their treats. There were games going on and a small dance off in the corner. Jeia was rattling off numbers to a game of bingo.

Rakon was in line for ice cream. He was surprised to see Countess Marien behind the counter with several of the ships highest ranking officers and chiefs serving the snack.

"What are you doing back there?" Rakon asked Marien.

"They asked for volunteers and ice cream is one of my favorite treats," Marien smiled. "So what will you have?"

Rakon pointed to three different flavors and watched Marien scoop and top the ice cream for him. "Enjoy."

At another part of the mess decks T'ula and a female sailor were dancing like a duet tango. They looked like an exotic couple. T'ula was showing this young female sailor how to be a romantic dancer and how to show romance.

"I don't suppose you could be my ball escort?" the sailor asked T'ula.

"I would love to come to the Navy Ball. And you are a very lovely lady. But I am not the right woman for you," T'ula said.

The sailor gently kissed T'ula on the lips to show her affections. "Are you sure?"

T'ula returned the kiss. "You are meant to enchant someone else. I can feel that. But I am more than happy to teach you how."

"Elegant lady," a sailor said to Marevin, who was at a table playing bingo.

"She is. Men and women lust for her as much as they do for Queen Laxur. I suppose it is a curse and a blessing all in one," Marevin said.

"Does she like only women?" the sailor asked.

"No. I like both. Lady T'ula is a very diverse woman," Marevin said.

"Do you like her?" the sailor asked.

"As a friend only. She is not my type," Marevin replied. Jeia called out a number and Marevin cursed.

"Ah damnit!" Marevin tossed the card away. He lost this round.

Princess Asora wondered into the ship's store and found a very bored sailor at the register. He was on his smartphone probably playing a game. Once he saw Asora, he straightened up and practically tossed his phone aside.

"Welcome to the ship's store, how can I help you?" the sailor asked.

"I was wondering if you had any of those shipboard uniforms

available?" Asora asked.

"We do. I'll just need to take your measurements and gather all the patches," the sailor said.

"Very well," Asora raised her arms up for the sailor who just grabbed his tailor's kit.

He took out his measuring tape and wrote down Asora's measurement. He looked up the measurements in the computer at the register and found a blue fire-retardant coverall set that would fit her. He went into the back to grab the coveralls, boots, patches, belt, socks, ball cap, and a few other items. He came out a few minutes later with a hand full of items. He asked Asora to up on the uniform to see how it fit. He said that she could use the back room to change but Asora used her magic to swap out her dress for the coveralls. The boots fit themselves onto her feet and tied themselves. Asora gave him permission to touch her as needed. The sailor put the belt on Asora's waist. It was khaki in color and had a gold belt buckle with the ship's seal on it. The sailor then had a three-dimensional printer make a patch with her name on it in gold. He took the patch and attached it to the coveralls. Asora's name was in gold on the right breast, and the letters H.C. NAVY on the left breast. On the top part of the patch was a gold stenciled medal that Asora had from her days as a Colonel. And below was a medal that was given to her by her brother that was an official navy medal. On the collar where the rank insignia was supposed to be the sailor made a pair of special seals that were of Asora. One of her family and the other of the Utopian crowned Princess. On the middle of her ball cap her insignia of colonel was patched.

Once the sailor storekeeper was done, he showed Asora a mirror so she could see. Asora looked like the admiral. The storekeeper did a wonderful job.

"Excellent work my good man. I will take it," Asora smiled.

"Great," the store keeper said. "Do you want anything else?"

"What else would I need to complete the sailor look?" Asora asked.

"Well the chiefs are always carrying around coffee mugs?" the sailor store keeper said.

"Very well then," Asora looked to the mugs and picked one with the ship's seal on it in blue. "This one."

Hours later the sun started to rise.

"Admiral Herantano, radar has detected a large unknown object twenty miles northeast of the fleet. It seems that it is admitting high energy waves!" a female sailor yelled out across the CIC to the Admiral.

"Very well. Dispatch the *Haerl, Lant, Coran, Yeowl,* and *Zaltan* to investigate the object," Herantano ordered the fleet captain next to him, an older man. "We will also go with them. The *Maria* will be the flagship until we return."

"Yes, sir," the man said, and he went to a computer to send the order.

Four destroyers, one advanced destroyer, and the *Tycon* super-carrier broke away from the fleet and headed northeast of the fleet's position.

Princess Asoa and Countess Marien walked into the CIC with two marines behind them. Princess Asora was wearing her brand-new coveralls and had a large coffee mug full of coffee from the ship's wardroom. She looked like a ship's captain.

Asora looked at the tactical display as figured out what was happening as did Marien.

"How long before we reach the target?" Marien asked.

"Twelve minutes, but we are in visual range. On screen," Herantano ordered.

An image appeared on the large screen. It showed a tall, flat island-like platform with a tower jutting out.

"What the hell is that?" Admiral Yane asked.

"You have me at a loss sir," Herantano said to Yane, his superior.

"Commander Solk, dispatch a boarding team to the object," Admiral Herantano ordered a younger man.

"Yes, sir," Solk responded and picked up a headset to communicate with the boarding team.

Thirty minutes later, the advance destroyer *Zaltan* launched a small boat with four humans to investigate the strange object. They came up next to it, and it was a metal structure of unknown design.

"What the hell is this thing?" the only woman in the group asked, bewildered. She was of medium build and height with black hair and skin.

"Steady, Jiala," the leader of the group ordered. He was a fierce blond man with a crew cut. "Salic, go and see what is up there."

The young man grabbed a medium-size rifle and climbed up to the metal object. His black hair was cut short.

"There is nothing up here except a big tower!" Salic yelled over the wind.

"We are coming up, ensign!" the commander yelled. The other three climbed up to the platform. The four human sailors and officers walked toward the tower.

"Interesting building, is it not?" one sailor commented.

"Yes, it is!" a powerful feminine voice echoed from above.

The humans looked above to see Queen Laxur and Princess Polea floating in the air with their wings unfurled. Polea had a child in her arms, and a fairy was buzzing around them.

"What do you want, witch?" the commander demanded forcefully.

"Is that any way to speak to your superior sovereign?" Laxur said mockingly.

"Superior my ass, you freak!" the woman soldier blasted, and then she opened fire on the Darkcons.

Both Polea and Laxur flew around, avoiding the bullets flying at them. Laxur pointed a finger at the woman and blasted her gun out of her hands. The other men opened fire, aiming at Polea. The blond Darkcon created a magical whip, and she used it to destroy the humans' weapons.

"You boys would not be trying to hurt little me and my helper here, would you?" Polea said teasingly.

"Let the kid go, witch, and I will let you live!" the commander yelled at Polea.

"I am not holding him hostage. He is my little helper," Polea said, and then Smika threw a magical bomb at the commander.

"We cannot shoot the kid," Salic pointed out.

"We cannot just let these bitches take the monolith!" the woman, Jiala, shrieked.

"We will not! But we cannot kill them to save it," the commander stated.

A door rumbled open from the tower. The four humans and Darkcons stopped fighting to watch the door open.

Laxur and Polea flew in, with Smika in Polea's arms. The humans followed them inside. Inside was a giant dark room with towering structures that seemed to go on forever.

"Who built this place, princess?" Smika asked Polea.

"I do not know. Whoever did was a bit excessive, though," Polea responded, as she and Laxur landed gracefully on the metal floor.

"Well, we are not going to let you Darkcon whores take this thing," the commander said, and the other three humans held their backup guns to the Darkcons.

"That is a bad move, little man," Laxur snarled.

Her sword appeared in her hand. Polea had her magical whip, and Smika had more magical grenades ready. Hyea, the fairy, grew to human size. The massive metal doors slammed shut, and a low humming noise could be heard rumbling below their feet. Eight tall pillars rose from the floor. One white light beamed out from each of the pillars. The next thing that they knew, they were all pulled up by a powerful invisible force and restrained at the tops of the pillars, roughly four meters above the deck.

"What is this? What kind of magic is this?" Hyea asked.

"You got me there," Jiala retorted.

Red light swirled above and came together to form a ghostly face that looked down upon them all.

"Calderan?" the humans said in unison. Calderan was a mythical figure from human mythology—a titan that came to defend humanity during its first dark times.

"There is no form to explain our existence," the ghostly image said. Calderan was also known for punishing humans for their wicked ways.

"Why are you here?" Queen Laxur demanded.

"You and your adversaries have damaged this colony, and now the planetary defense grid is in active," the image stated coldly.

"We can fix whatever was damaged," the commander begged the ghost.

"We are not interested. The planetary defense grid is now coming online to purge the colony," the image stated.

"Purge the colony of what?" Laxur demanded.

"The creatures of Z'yon have contaminated the colony." It looked at Queen Laxur and turned back to the humans. "This will result in a sterilization effect."

"You cannot do that! You have no right!" the commander shouted at the image.

"We have no choice. The danger is far greater than you could imagine. We are sorry, but this must be done to prevent the horror that is to come. Begin the termination sequence."

The image disappeared, and the whole room lit up brightly. The pillars shattered, and the eight prisoners were free to escape.

From the decks of the *Tycon*, everyone saw the massive structure begin to glow, and it sprouted a wall of energy. It cut off the six ships from the rest of Havaina. The massive structure began to transform. Admirals Yane and Herantano ordered all six ships to open fire.

The four humans hurried back to the *Tycon*, for it was the closest ship to them. Queen Laxur and Princess Polea, along with Smika and Hyea, crashed onto the flight deck of the massive supercarrier.

"Send up as many Marines as possible to the flight deck! We have hostiles on board!" Herantano yelled into a gray communication box.

Suddenly, hundreds of human troops poured onto the flight deck, surrounding the Darkcons.

"We are not the ones that you humans should be worried about,"

Laxur said, pointing to the changing structure.

Three things came off the object that looked like flying ships. They hovered above the waves, looking at the human warships.

"Get the jets up here now!" Herantano ordered.

Everyone hurried off the flight deck. Several Marines forced the Darkcons into the tower with the admiral. In an instant, the elevators roared to life, loaded with jet aircraft and ammunition. The *Tycon* was carrying roughly a hundred jet fighter craft and two dozen support planes. As soon as the jets were topside and armed, they were launched.

The largest of the three alien ships opened fire and destroyed the *Lant* with a barrage of red energy. The other destroyers opened fire with their six-inch cannons and antiaircraft guns. One of the smaller enemy ships thrust forward toward the *Coran*. The old destroyer was blown to pieces by multiple missiles strikes. What was left of the *Coran* was still moving, and the inflamed wreck rammed right into the enemy that destroyed it. Both ships were destroyed and sank beneath the waves.

Zaltan, the advanced destroyer, powered up its newly installed particle cannon. The captain of the *Zaltan*, a young woman named Abiea, ordered her ship to full power, and it charged at the second small enemy ship. The alien ship did the same maneuver, charging at the *Zaltan* at an unheard of sixty knots. At point-blank range, the *Zaltan* fired a massive beam of blue and gray energy. The aggressor vessel was stopped dead and exploded. The *Zaltan* plowed right through the wreckage of its sinking foe, only to come face-to-face with the largest alien warship. This time, the particle cannon's beam bounced off an energy barrier protecting the enemy ship.

"What the hell? A force field?" an officer blurted out.

"No shit. How do we break it?" Abiea screamed.

Back on the *Tycon*, everyone was worried. "Can you not get a hold of anyone outside the energy barrier?" Asora screamed at Herantano.

"No, we cannot. Can you not?" the hysterical admiral fired back.

"This barrier is not magical. It is technological, and my powers have no effect on it!" the Utopian Princess blasted.

"Well, do something. Anything!" Herantano roared. "And what would you have me do?"

"Hit the deck!" Jeia shouted, and he and a few others dropped to the floor as a big fireball surged by and struck the bridge.

It sent glass and metal shrapnel in all directions. After a minute, the bridge crew and other personnel dug themselves out of the debris to find that the bridge was destroyed. Asora popped up from under a plastic board, and she was covered in filth. She coughed and spat out more filth from her mouth. Her arm ached. She looked at it and found that it was broken in two places.

T'ula and Jeia were stuck behind a steel beam that pinned them to what remained of a bulkhead. T'ula was bleeding badly, and Jeia was out cold. The elf woman turned around to see the massive flight deck below on fire. There were still people on deck fighting the unrelenting alien fire.

Below deck, Laxur, Polea, Smika, and Hyea were thrown across the passageway, and the overheads collapsed on them. Three of the four Marines that were escorting them were killed from the mass of steel that fell on them. The fourth Marine was badly injured and could not move.

"Let us get out of here!" Smika cried out.

"I agree. Before we end up like these poor bastards." Laxur pointed to the bodies of the fallen Marines.

The queen walked down the passageway with the other three right behind her. They saw most of the crew fighting fires and trying to control flooding. They were too busy fighting the ship to bother with the Darkcons. The four made it to the hangar deck after climbing several flights of ladders.

Fires were everywhere, and the smell of jet fuel was in the air. An explosion erupted, killing several crewmembers near a drone fighter at the aft end of the hangar deck. The explosion blasted six people into the air, and one of them landed back-first in front of the Queen. He was a young man, burned badly, covered in jet fuel and blood, and crying from the pain.

Laxur hesitated. She could leave him there to die and escape with Polea, Smika, and Hyea, or she could help him and risk getting herself killed. Smika was shaking, and Polea held and tried to soothe him.

Another explosion erupted, but this time, it came from the outside. Something had blown its way in. It was an alien machine, and it opened fire on the people, jets, and drones on the hangar deck.

Laxur grabbed the crippled human, and they ducked behind a fallen piece of steel. Polea, Smika, and Hyea followed, and three other humans followed them.

"What the hell is that thing?" a woman screamed.

"Another one of those creepy machines," a male retorted.

The third human noticed the Darkcons, and his reaction was surprising. "What are you sitting here for? Do your thing, you crazy woman!"

"Do not speak to me in that fashion, you human!" Laxur stated harshly.

A projectile went flying by.

"Are you seriously lecturing me on royal etiquette right now?" the man said, dumbfounded by Laxur's arrogance.

"Why do you not heal Usac here? You can bash me later." He pointed to the seriously injured man.

Laxur looked to blow the crippled young man a kiss, but it was in fact part of a healing spell that she cast. In moments, Usac's injuries vanished, and the pain was gone.

"Happy, human?" Laxur asked snidely.

Another explosion blasted the group out from their hiding spot. They came face-to-face with a twelve-foot machine. It threw steel and piping aside and started after them.

Hyea was trapped under a plate of thick steel. Smika was using all his strength to try to free the enlarged fairy. The machine came up from behind Smika, ready to kill the kid.

Laxur blasted the metal monster with a powerful force of dark energy. She then cast a spell upon her body to make herself grow as big as the machine. She was now five meters tall, and the Queen slammed her fist into the metal. Her skin and bone were much stronger at this size, and she was able to shred metal like paper. Using all her knowledge, Laxur cast as many enhancement spells as she knew of. Laxur made herself stronger and faster than ever before. She wanted to protect Smika and her two other companions. The crewmen grabbed guns from the fallen Marines, and they helped Laxur by shooting at the machine. Eventually, the Queen tore down the monster with her bare hands.

The metal monster was destroyed and in pieces all over the deck. "Glad to see that you decided to stay and help, sister!" Asora yelled up to Laxur.

"I did not have much of a choice, little sister," Laxur said. "Are you going to stick around and help us with the rest of them?"

Chapter Forty-Five

Clash of the War Machines

The massive alien device unleashed four smaller vessels. Other human ships managed to break down the force field by using their energy weapons and came charging in. Nine aircraft carriers sent hundreds of fighter jets and drones into the skies. The *Tycon* could not launch aircraft because of its damaged decks.

The fires were being put out by the flight deck crews. The Tycon's flight deck also had a few explosions going off from bombs and small munitions that caught fire. Fortunately, the Tycon had an armored deck that could handle it. However, that did not mean that the fire could not spread. The Tycon was still moving on the sea as fast as it could to keep from getting hit by more enemy weapons fire.

The half a dozen destroyers blasted the alien vessels with a fury of lead and fire. The enemy ships returned fire with advanced energy weapons that ripped through the metal hulls of the destroyers. One destroyer was clever in two and exploded apart. Another destroyer simply capsized. A third destroyer just sank. However, the fourth destroyer though heavily damaged was still steaming and firing its main forward gun like a defiant and indignant soldier. The fifth and sixth destroyers were undamaged due to their zig zag courses at high speeds.

Princess Asora watched as the destroyers battled their adversaries. The alien device finally landed mortal blow to the fifth destroyer. But just like the fourth destroyer the fifth was still steaming. However, its super structure was gone. It had been reduced to a high-speed hull. The sixth destroyer then rammed itself into the alien machine. To Asora's surprise the ramming severely damaged the alien machine, at the cost of the sixth destroyer. The resulting explosion was so powerful that the shockwave shoved the Tycon back.

A sudden thunderous explosion rocked in the distance and ripped through another alien device's shields, crippling the main ship. It appeared to Asora that the Red Guard Navy had been doing some serious damage to these alien machines. Then a very large and powerful salvo of impacts and multi kiloton explosions tore through much of the enemy defenses.

Asora smiled wickedly, for she knew where those shells came from. "Finally, the mighty battleships are here," she whispered to herself.

From a distance, nine large vessels of human design approached menacingly. These vessels were over three hundred meters long and had massive four barrel per turret cannons. And each one had four turrets. Two in the front and two in the back. They also sported dozens of smaller secondary dual gun turrets, and a vast battery of missile launchers and laser cannons. They were steaming into battle at speeds far above any normal vessel of the sea could move. These nuclear-powered monster ships started to draw the alien weapons away from the battered fleet.

Lady T'a saw the mighty battleships coming from the wrecked bridge. Only once before had she seen these monsters, the dreaded human battleships. But now she was happy to see them charging into battle. She hoped that they could turn the tide of battle. Like they once did five centuries ago.

They formed a line in front of the alien machines and opened up with their thirty-centimeter guns. The firepower blew the ships back several meters. It was like a wall of guns, rounds, and fire erupted to life and ripped apart anything they hit.

The concentrated fire overwhelmed the shields of one of the machines. It could not survive the relentless barrage of naval gun fire. In five furious minutes the singled out alien machine exploded violently. The shockwave tore through the ocean and the fleet. It also generated a powerful tidal wave that washed over the larger ships and the other alien machines. The smaller vessels on the other hand were not so fortunate. The tidal wave swept many ships away.

The surging tidal wave slammed into the shoreline. The fifteen-meter-high wave hit the coastline with such force that ripped up stone, concrete fortifications and smashed smaller buildings. Thousands of people were torn apart by the sudden slam of water.

Moments later after getting hundreds of meters inland, the torrent of water retreated to the ocean. As the water moved back it took with it builds, cars, vehicles, and bodies. Trees, and boulders were also torn away and taken into the depths.

Onboard the lead battleship *Rowtan*, an admiral watched as they approached the next target. Next to him was Irantanco, kept under guard by the ship's security detail. He had been found on a small ship a few hours ago, and the admiral wanted to keep an eye on him.

Allied or not, Irantanco was a terrorist. Not just any but one of the Vanguard's leaders. The admiral hoped that bringing him in would be helpful. But that was not a priority for him right now.

The admiral was an older human man with a grey beard and worn skin. He wore his blue, grey, and green naval combat fatigues. His rank was symbolized with three golden six-pointed starts on his shoulders.

"Admiral, the *Tycon* is carrying Empress Marien, her court, and the Utopian head council. We must be careful with our shooting," the captain informed.

The captain was a male jewel elf in a similar uniform to the admiral. Only his rank was symbolized by a single silver star with three unbroken lines below it. The man had short black hair and only one very pointed ear. The other had been cut off years ago in a fight and was only a stump of healed flesh.

"Very well," the admiral replied. "Captain, make you course to bring us along side the Tycon."

"Aye sir," the captain said.

"We cannot allow those ships to leave the area!" Irantanco shouted.

"With our empress in there? I think not!" the admiral roared back.

"Well, you have to do something, you idiot!" Irantanco shouted back. "We need to capture it and study it."

The admiral punched the terrorist in the face to silence him. Irantanco fell to the deck holding his jaw. The old man could punch hard.

"Challenge me again terrorist," the admiral snarled. "And I'll personally fire you out of one of those main guns!"

"Aye, sir," Irantanco said bitterly and still on the deck.

"Gun master! Target the largest alien vessel," the admiral stated. "We need to break it's shields!"

"Sir, yes, sir!" The female daemon who was the ship's gun master relied loudly.

"We have have bearing on target," the ship's XO called out to the captain.

"Prepare a spread of torpedos!" The captain yelled. "We don't wan them pulling any surprises on us!"

The massive guns of the lead battleship swung and took aim at the largest alien warship. The giant guns opened on their foe, but unlike the other smaller ships, the largest one got its shields back up. The massive shells slammed into the shields. But it was enough to knock the alien machine back a few meters. It turned to face the battleships. Ready to the next round.

"Launch aerial attack drones!" The captain yelled.

Dozens of small tube canisters erupted into jets of flame as they launched their drones. The dozens of tiny robots charged at the alien devices spraying the shielded machines with small caliber rounds. Some drones fired missiles and deep penetrator explosives.

The largest of the alien machines became distracted by the dozens of smaller drones. It then popped out from the tallest part of it a rod. This rod emitted a blast of electrical arcs that destroyed the drones in a few seconds. But that was all the time that was needed.

The nine large battleships had begun steaming up in a chaotic formation. They were throwing up a massive storm of radar, EM energy waves, and a healthy dose of rapid secondary gun fire. Three battleships took aim at wanting one would consider point blank range. In unison the three closest battleships opened fire with their four mean guns. It was not enough to break the shield of the alien machine, but it was enough to knock it back a few dozen meters.

"Damn!" The admiral complained. "What is it going to take to break that fucking shield?"

Suddenly, a powerful gust of wind kicked up, and the skies darkened. The wind turned into a hurricane and blew up massive waves. Several waterspouts appeared in the water. The spouts danced at first across the ocean. They then rushed toward the alien flagship at a terrifying speed. The spouts grew as they fused with one another. The now super waterspout slammed violently into the smaller of the alien machines. The smaller alien machine was then torn to pieces by the violent storm. However, the largest of the machines remained.

Back at the *Tycon*, Princess Asora was using her water and wind coins to conjure the chaos. She was out on the ship's bridge wing that was several decks above the main weather deck. Asora glowed and appeared to be made of both clouds and water. She directed the storms around the battlefield like a conductor of an orchestra. Lightning occasionally struck her. It was not painful; it was a means of her controlling so much power.

"Let us see you bastards withstand nature's fury," Asora pronounced.

The two coins were glowing brightly in her hands. They infused their power into the princess. The power obeyed her will. So, the ocean and sky turned its rage on the alien machines. Asora then reached out into the water, and this created a new wave.

A massive tidal wave formed from Asora's will. It surged past the human battle lines in a very controlled way and slammed into the alien ships. All but one was destroyed; the one that survived was the flagship. The largest of the alien machines was stubbornly still functioning.

"Damn it! Why are you not dead?" Asora cursed.

"Maybe I should handle this thing, baby sister?" The voice of Laxur said mockingly.

The Darkcon queen had appeared next to Asora on the ship's bridge wing. Her sudden appearance scared the sailor that was at the doorway to the bridge. Asora however was not impressed by Laxur.

"That 'thing' will tear you apart, even if you are a kilometer high!" Asora stated.

"And what makes you say that?" Laxur demanded.

"Because that ship has guns that do not care that you are magical," Asora said in a rather irritated tone. "It can rip apart warship hulls!"

"We will see about that," Laxur said.

Laxur's large black wings appeared and covered her. She then disappeared disappeared into thin air and into the chaos.

"Yes, we will," Asora whispered to herself.

The princess turned her attention back to the battle scene. The menacing foe towered over the human ships and defended itself from the superstorm that Asora created. She put one of the coins in her left hand, and with her right hand, she reached into her pocket and pulled out another green vial.

"Maybe she has a point. Perhaps size will make all the difference." Asora said to herself.

She bit off the cork, spat it out, and drank the whole vial of potion. The princess then jumped off the flight deck into the water. She splashed into the sea with the bridge officers in a panic at her actions. It was Asora's hope that a larger size with increased power and energy would be enough.

The sea began to churn and rumble beneath the waves. Two massive and towering white objects came shooting up from below. They were wings, giant angel wings. They moved ever so slightly. As they did, they generated powerful waves and powerful winds.

A moment later, a giant person emerged Princess Asora Asora, standing over one kilometer tall. She was bathed in a white and gold glowing light. She let out a primal roar that caused the skies to thunder. She put the two coins on her necklace, and she activated her golden dragon armor. In her hands were her dragon katana and her angelic sword. Her hair moved about as if she was under water. Her blue eyes glowed a powerful deeper blue. Her size and power made her feel like a goddess.

Missile, and energy beam weapons fire hit Asora. They were coming from the alien machine that still defied her. It was not enough to critically harm Asora, but the attacks did sting and knocked her back. Despite being many times larger than it was, Asora was still getting pushed around by the machine. With one mighty flap of her wings, Asora created a powerful hurricane that moved with super sonic speed.

This was powerful enough to blow the machine back several hundred meters. Asora also unintentionally damaged the fleet of Consortium warships. They were all now trying to get out of Asora's way. Now the giantess princess did not care. She moved closer.

Her footsteps sounded like thunder in the distance as she marched toward the alien war machine. The machine recovered enough to see it massive opponent coming right at it. Asora slammed her angelic sword right into the shield, and it did nothing. She then swiped as hard as she could again and still the shields of the machine deflected the attack.

The princess put her angelic sword away; next was the golden katana. With both hands and all her might, Asora swung the massive blade and swiped the ship up into the air. The shields were still intact, but she was able to knock it back. She hit the shields so hard that they exploded with a shower of sparks. It also went flying further out to sea. It crashed nearly four kilometers away. Asora then made her way towards it.

The alien machine then righted itself just as Asora violently slammed her fist into it. Her fist was armored so she could inflicted greater damage. Each strike she made created explosions of fire and lightning. For her, it was like punching a very thick balloon that would not pop. This was making her angry and increasing her adrenaline levels as well as her hostility. The potion tended to make its users easily irritable. Asora thought of drinking another vial to help amplify her strength; however, she could not see the vial due to her enormous size.

The princess allowed her anger to override her judgment. She wanted this defiant thing to explode. In blind anger, Asora pounded on the alien ship like a crazy person. Her attacks did not give the alien machine any time to respond.

"Why, will you not die!" Asora bellowed in pure rage.

A large shadow was then cast over Asora and the alien machine. It was so vast that it covered much of the ocean around them. Asora turned to see her sister, Laxur. She had the look of amusement on her face.

"Having fun, sister?" Laxur boomed from behind Asora's back.

"What do you want?" Asora demanded fiercely.

"Thought I would help. But it looks like you are having too much fun," Queen Laxur said mockingly.

"I do not need your help!" Asora thundered, getting even madder.

"Of course not, baby sister. But with that attitude, you are likely to explode. I personally would not mind seeing the Utopian princess lose her cool, but you are an exception." Laxur had an enlarged vial of potion in her hand. "Perhaps you would like this?"

Asora turned around and eyed the vial greedily. Lady T'ula from the deck of a ship that had not gotten away, was paying attention to the whole ordeal.

"Oh no, you do not, you witch," T'ula said to herself.

She conjured up an attack spell with a bolt of lightning. She shot the giant vial, and it exploded all over Laxur. Asora looked disappointed. Neither sister knew where the lightning bolt came from. And this made Asora frustrated. Laxur was also very annoyed by this. Both looked around to see who or what destroyed the vial.

Meanwhile, the alien machine reoriented itself and opened fire on the oversized sisters with a powerful particle weapon. Asora was protected by her golden armor, but Laxur was not. The queen's skin was burning, and her garment caught fire. Her black wings appeared to cool her skin off. She kept the flames on her burning and turned it into a sort of armor of fire to protect herself.

The alien machine then mimicked Asora's tactics. It rammed itself into Asora's belly and crashed her into Laxur. Both sisters then fell backwards into the ocean. The machine then reoriented itself back up right again. Asora then kicked it as hard as she could. The machine was knocked back and ended up crashing into the wreck of a sinking ship. The explosion bounced it back to the sisters.

Laxur had managed to force Asora off her and stand back up. She opened her arms up and caught the shielded machine and held it like a giant beach ball. Interestingly the shield made it feel like an inflated ball. The machine inside it was held in place by the shield projectors. To Laxur this machine was surprisingly heavy, and she fell backwards into the ocean. But she still had a hold of it.

On the battleship *Rowtan* blasted the alien ship with a new weapon a zero-energy penetrator projectile. This was a special type of munitions that had to be fired from a rail gun that the Rowton was equipped with. It looked like a conical needle with strips of glowing lines that generate a special field around the munitions. Launched at a speed of mach ten it was active the very nano second it left the launcher. In mere seconds it impacted the shield of the alien machine and cut through the barrier into the machine's hull. It was enough to penetrate the ship's inner defenses. The resulting explosion caused the machine to stop moving and it fell on top of Laxur.

The admiral onboard the battleship gave Asora a quick salute, and she nodded with a slight smile. With her katana, Asora swiped at the alien ship and made a clean cut through the hull. The ship exploded violently from the force. The explosion did not harm Asora or Laxur, but the heat was brutal.

The pieces of the alien machine then fell into the sea. A moment later Laxur arose from the sea like a mighty leviathan. She shook herself and forced the pieces off her. The queen looked around and seemed pleased.

Asora was exhausted now. She sat down in the ocean and allowed the fleet to gather near her. A thunderous clapping could be heard from Laxur. She was pleased with her little sister's actions.

"Nice work," Laxur commented.

As night fell, Asora began to shrink back to her normal height. Queen Laxur was not far behind. Asora and Laxur walked onto a nearby beach as they shrank back down.

"Well, this was fun," Laxur started. "But now I and my allies will take our leave of you."

Queen Laxur then vanished in a cloud of black and purple fog. Asora and T'ula could feel that Laxur had left Havaina. Her powerful magical presence could no longer be felt. T'ula let out a sigh of relief.

Asora then sat down on a large rock. She had Lady T'ula by her side, and they were alone on the beach.

"You do realize that your mother will be furious with you for lying to her," T'ula pointed out.

"I know," Asora said.

"How many of those vials do you have?" T'ula demanded.

"Six," Asora answered.

"Give them to me," T'ula ordered.

"Since when do you give me orders?" Asora demanded.

"Since I am your friend and adviser. It is my job to look after you and do things that are in your best interest," T'ula pointed out.

"I think these will be useful," Asora said.

"I do not want you to follow your sister on the path of darkness. I want you here. I believe that you can change the kingdom for the better," T'ula said. "And you cannot do that if you use your sister's tactics."

Asora did not quite know what to say. So, she kept quiet. T'ula as usual was right and Asora both loved and hated her for that. But Asora knew that T'ula was right.

"Asora, I do care for you. You are like the little sister that I have always wanted. I love you like an elder sister would. That is why I will not allow you to be ruined," the jewel elf woman stated forcefully.

Asora thought long and hard about what T'ula said. This elf was more than an adviser and a friend; she was the sister that Asora wanted. She felt comfortable telling T'ula her most intimate secrets. T'ula had been there for her, and she was now protecting her. Asora wanted to give T'ula the vials, but something in her mind was preventing the princess from doing the right thing.

She refused, and T'ula was disappointed. But T'ula was true to her word, and she would break Asora of her addiction, one way or another. T'ula cast a spell upon Asora that put her to sleep, just as Countess Marien and a few others came up to them.

"Are you sure that you can do this, T'ula?" Marien asked.

"I will do all in my power to free her from this curse," T'ula promised.

Chapter Forty-Six

In Her Torment

Princess Asora awoke in her childhood room in her home on Havaina. Her bed felt so soft and smelled clean. Asora sat up to look around. She was surrounded by all her old toys and personal effects from her early years. Stuffed animals, posters, games, and a child's computer that was dressed as a space station all surrounded her. Even her old cat was also there, meowing at Asora to play with him. He hoped up on the bed to get closer to Asora.

"Bulau! You naughty kitty, where have you been?" Asora said.

She happily as she opened her arms, and the cat jumped to her. The cat jumped into Asora's lap, purring loudly as the Princess pet him behind his ears. Bulau was a black cat with white paws, a white belly, and a white-tipped tail. He purred loudly as he rubbed himself on Asora. The cat was very happy to see her again. Asora loved animals like cats, and dogs.

"Aww, I missed you too," Asora cooed as she held her pet cat.

She found a cat toy on a nearby nightstand. Asora took it and dangled it over Bulau's head. The cat wanted to play now. He tried to take playful swipes. Asora giggled as the cat rolled on her lap playing with her.

What Asora did not realize was that she was being watched by two elf women and her mother. They were observing her through a security camera system. The cameras were hidden in various places throughout the room. Here was also an observation window that was disguised as a mirror. These were all very recent additions and where not originally apart of Asora's bedroom.

"Hope this works, T'a," T'ula started. "Because if it does not, she will react violently."

"Were you able to get all of those damned vials and the coins away from her, T'ula?" Marien demanded.

"I did retrieve all seven coins as she slept. I found all but two of the vials on her person. I have no clue where the last two vials are. If she still has them, then curing her of this addiction will be very dangerous," T'ula said.

"I know the dangers. I am her mother, after all." Marien paused for a moment all allow her commanding noble image to melt away. Now she had the look of a very worried mother. "I cannot believe that two of my baby girls are going through this," Marien said, almost was crying. "Why is this happening to them?"

"We can save Asora. We will worry about Asaria later," T'a said, sounding almost cold.

"Asaria I am afraid could be too far gone," T'a said.

"No," Marien said. "I will not give up on them."

"Good," T'a replied. "Asora has to be cured and returned to Evorn more powerful."

"How is Asora's standing?" Marien asked T'a.

"At the moment, stable," T'a then paused. "However, if this were to get out, her position and standing will be very badly damaged."

"I have Admiral Yane, Lord Marevin, and and Lady Madimoy working to keep this covered up form the public," T'ula said.

"What about the battle?" Marien asked.

"That is already public knowledge," T'ula said. "That is not an issue. In fact, it might help Princess Asora's standing in the future."

"Having a princess that can grow into a giant monster version of herself and able to defeat both a giantess Queen Laxur, and a machine horror does add to the princess," T'a pointed out.

"Evorn is aware of the incident," T'ula said. "And As I thought.

Asora being seen defeating Laxur at her own game has helped."

"It is all for nothing if she is addicted to potions that are needed for it," Marien pointed out. "King Adium told me more about these potions." Marien paused for a second. "Only fairies cannot get addicted, to anyone else it is like a drug addiction. One can be helped weaned off. If caught in time."

"So, Princess Asora can be helped according to King Adium?" T'ula asked.

"What about Asaria?" T'a asked.

"That," Marien paused to breath deeply. "Is going to be an even greater battle."

"Our focus right now is to be Asora," T'a stated.

"Did King Adium tell you how to get Princess Asora back to normal?" T'ula asked Marien.

"He did, and that is why we are doing what we are doing here," Marien said. "This is the first step in saving Asora from Asaria's fate."

Asora was petting her cat happily as he purred. Asora was enjoying the purr as it felt good to her. A knock at the door was heard.

"Come in," Asora said gently.

It was Lady T'ula. She came in and sat on the edge of the bed with a smile on her face. She petted the cat too. The cat liked T'ula too as it could sense that the jewel elf had good intentions. At some level the cat knew what was happening and was as determined as Countess Marien was to save Asora.

"I like cats. I always wanted one myself," T'ula commented happily. "But I was never allowed to have one."

"Why is that?" Asora asked.

"My adopted parents especially my stepmother had allergies to cat and dog fur," T'ula explained. "But I was able to help strays with getting food and fresh water."

"How kind," Asora said.

Asora then felt her neck and noticed that her necklace was gone.

She started to look around the bed. She then looked at the nightstand, and in the drawers. T'ula knew what Asora was looking for. So, she prepared herself for the coming violence from the princess.

"T'ula," Asora began. The elf looked at the princess. "Where are my coins?"

"I and your mother have them. We needed to keep them safe," T'ula reassured Asora.

"Keep them safe? From what or whom?" the princess demanded.

T'ula looked at her sovereign sternly and full of concern. She formulated her response as carefully as she could. But for this situation she knew that no matter what she said, Asora was going to get angry.

"Keep them safe from you," was all T'ula said.

"From me?" Asora began to think about what her friend said.

"You have a problem, and we cannot afford you using that great power to feed the addiction that is now plaguing you. It is also for your protection," T'ula pointed out.

"I do not have an addiction, T'ula!" Asora roared in anger.

The cat jumped away from the angry princess. The cat jumped away with an angry meow. He did not like being in the middle of a violent interaction.

"Yes, you do!" T'ula fired back. "And I can prove it." She went into a pocket in her dress and pulled out one of the green vials. "If you are not addicted, then you will have no problem with disposing of this."

Asora looked at the vial and tuned out T'ula's voice. She wanted it so badly now. She wanted to be strong, powerful, and big. She needed to get it out of T'ula's hands. T'ula noticed Asora's attention, and she moved the vial around, watching Asora follow it.

"I thought so. So, I will do it," T'ula said.

"No!" Asora cried.

The princess tackled T'ula off the bed. She was trying to wrestle the vial away from T'ula before she could destroy it. T'ula was much stronger than Asora, but the princess was quicker. T'ula knew that if someone was desperate enough, the adrenaline rush could magnify her strength.

And that was true here. Princess Asora summoned hidden strength and managed to force her hands to T'ula's arm. The jewel elf was getting tired quickly as Asora forced her to heel. Then Asora elbowed T'ula's arm to make her bend closer.

"Give me that!" Asora demanded.

"No," T'ula replied. "You cannot do this."

"Watch me!" Asora snapped.

Asora then head butted T'ula and forced the taller woman down. This weakened T'ula's arm. The vial went flying and bounced gently on the carpeted floor. It rolled and stopped in front of the dresser. Asora then attempted to break into a run. T'ula grabbed Asora's leg and tripped her. Asora went face first into the floor. Just a few meters from the desired vial of green potion goodness. Asora snarled in anger as she tried to free herself from T'ula.

T'ula then pulled hard and Asora came back into T'ula's grasp. She managed to put Asora into a bear hug and that made Asora struggle. T'ula stood back up on her feet and still with Asora in the bear hug. T'ula then slammed Asora into a nearby wall. The princess seemed to collapse to the floor. T'ula then went over to grab the vial. She was tackled again by Asora who recovered in a very crazed state.

"I will have that!" Asora snarled.

"Not as long as I am here," T'ula replied.

"Let us fix that!" Asora snapped.

Asora kneed T'ula in her back. The jewel elf screamed in pain. But despite the pain T'ula held the vial out of Asora's reach.

"I will have this!" Asora shouted.

T'ula managed to get one arm free, and she tossed the vial into the air. With the same hand, she fired a magical ball of fire at the vial, and it burned away. The green smoke then vanished into the air.

Asora, in blind anger, started to pound on T'ula, but with one powerful punch. T'ula hit Asora in her face, and the princess went down to the floor. She was crying in rage and humiliation. She wanted to move but found that she could not.

Little did Asora know what that she was shot with an electric stun gun. A weapon designed to paralyze a violent criminal or an insane person. The person who shot her was Countess Marien herself.

"Was that part of your plan?" Marien asked.

"That did not work. Let's try something else," T'ula said to herself.

"I would prefer something that will not result in painful fights," Marien said.

Asora woke back up in a chair and groggily saw T'ula talking to the princess's four ladies in waiting fairies. The fairies looked worried as T'ula spoke to them. Asora also found that she was strapped to the chair. She also found that it was hard to move about. Asora then decided to listen into whatever T'ula was talking about to the fairies.

"And how is this powder made?" T'ula asked one of the fairies.

"All the ingredients are on the world of Fae Tern. This potion is very powerful on non-fairies and, as you have seen, extremely addictive. Curing our princess will be more difficult than curing a normal person. The more powerful a person is, the harder it is to cure the addiction, and the more potent the cure needs to be," Gourani explained.

"But the poor princess is going to be dealing with this addiction for the rest of her life. She is the most powerful being in the whole kingdom, after all. The powder will only be partially effective on her," Friea pointed out.

"Then this will become a new addiction," Rayne pointed out. "And if we run out of the powder, we will have to tie the princess up again."

"And that will cause some really bad problems if the Royal Court finds out," B'nei said. "And it could also be very awkward if they see us tying her up to her throne."

"Even in the Consortium that would be a very inappropriate thing to do to her," Friea added.

"And one can only imagine the stories and conspiracy theories. And not to mention what Laxur could do once Asora looses credibility,"

Rayne said.

"Let me worry about that," Asora said as she staggered back to her feet.

Asora had cut threw her binds using her nails and magical cutting spells. She also looked more sober. But T'ula suspected that Asora was doing her best to appear better. She rubbed the bruise on her cheek that she got from T'ula. She was not mad at the elf, for she knew why she attacked her.

"I will give you whatever you need to get this magical powder. I do not want this addiction to plague me anymore," Asora said.

T'ula and the fairies smiled at their ruler. They truly hoped that Asora was doing better. If not, then they have allowed a danger loose once more. There is one way to make sure.

"My lady, we will do all in our power to help you in this uneasy time," T'ula said. "We will preserve your dignity."

"I appreciate that," Asora said.

"Just know we are doing this not because you are more then our leader," T'ula started. "You are our friend. We also love you."

Tears welled up in Asora's eyes, and she began to cry. T'ula opened her arms to the princess, and the tall elf embraced the smaller hybrid. Asora cried into T'ula's chest and held her close. The fairies also came in and hugged Asora in her head and snuggled into her hair. Asora had never known anyone outside her family that was this close to her. T'ula was the one person that had been there for the princess, and she was the one person outside her family who was intimately close to her.

The fairies were as close to Asora as sister's could be. They did also raise Asora too. They were very loving and Asora cannot dream of being without them. They had done their best to keep her out of trouble.

As for T'ula, she was just like Asaria when the sisters were younger. Looks were not the only thing that T'ula and Asaria shared; they were both also loving. T'ula had become what Asaria should have been. Asora could feel T'ula's sister-like love for her. Asora felt comfortable with T'ula.

"Thank you, T'ula. Please help me. I will do whatever you need." Asora cried. "I am so sorry for what I did to you."

"I understand," T'ula replied. "But next time, try not to bruise my organs and bones."

"I really was not in my right state of mind," Asora explained. "What can I do to make it up to you?"

"All I want from you is to be strong. I know you are strong, but I need you to be stronger. I will free you of this. We all need you. I need you," T'ula whispered.

"I will do all that I can to live up to our expectations," Asora said. "All of you."

An hour later, the four fairy sisters returned with sacks of the special powder made from a rare diamond only found on Fae Tern, one of the fairies' home worlds. T'ula was still holding Asora in her arms, comforting her like a big sister. She did not want to tie up the princess again. She was calmer now then she was earlier.

"We have it. Are you ready, my princess?" Rayne asked.

Asora nodded. She wanted to be rid of this addiction. She could only imagine what Asaria's condition could be with years of this.

"You will need to eat this powder, and I must warn you. It tastes nasty," B'nei warned.

"I do not care. I want to be free of this problem," Asora said weakly.

"Hopefully you only need one of two doses," Rayne explained. "If this works you should be fine."

"Very well then," Gourani said.

The leader of the fairies gave Asora the sack of powder. The princess devoured the four sacks that were given to her. As B'nei warned, it was foul tasting. She felt like gagging, and it made her mouth burn. When she swallowed it, her whole body felt weird. Her belly felt like it was about to explode. Asora broke free of T'ula's gentle embrace, holding her mouth. She ran to the bathroom. A moment later, vomiting could be heard.

"Is that supposed to happen?" T'ula asked Rayne.

The four fairies nodded in confirmation. They knew that this would happen. It was part of the treatment process. The powder was repulsive to the potions used by the fairies and others. It forced out the ingredients from a body. For a complex living being, that would result in violent evacuation of one's insides of foreign materials as the fairies explained for one another.

"It is cleansing her body, and that will make it harder for the addiction to dictate her thinking," B'nei explained.

"Yeah, but it is a painful process," Gourni added.

"And smelly," Friea said as she held her nose.

"I forgot about that," Rayne said.

The smell from the bathroom was staring to float out like a fog bank. The fairies did warn that the powder would be painful, and that the smell would be offensive for a day or two. But that is a small price to pay for being cured of this madness.

After a half an hour of vomiting, Asora emerged from her bathing chamber pale and completely exhausted. She was like a zombie as she moved across the room. She was so tired and felt sick.

"The reports of my death have been greatly exaggerated," Asora whimpered as she slumped into a chair.

"You may feel bad now, but in the end, it will all be worth it," Gourani pointed out.

"I hope so. I do not know how much of that I can take," Asora responded.

Countess Marien was watching the whole thing from another room. She left the room suddenly at the beckoning of a top general.

"Well, Tansl? What were you able to find out about the alien technology?" the human queen asked with a hint of excitement.

"This technology is older than the Hananaka. It is millions of years older than they are. We were able to translate only a few phrases on some of the devices and interfaces," Tansl answered.

"What did they say?" Marien asked.

"From what sense we could make of it, they pointed to a region of the universe, and then they said something like beginning of all," the general said.

"Beginning of all?" the countess inquired.

"Tera, my queen. It mentions Tera itself," Tansl said with caution.

"Tera? For eons that world has been but a myth. But if these devices arose from Tera, then Z'yon could be true as well," Marien thought out loud.

"If it is, my queen, then we must move soon," Tansl warned.

"Yes, we must. Before either the Darkcons or the Utopians figure it out." Marien thought for a moment.

"General, find out where Tera and Z'yon are located. Then put together a strike team to secure them. Especially Tera," Marien ordered.

"It will be done, my queen." Tansl saluted Marien and walked away.

Part Three

The Dark Goddess

Chapter Forty-Seven

The Legend of Z'yon and Tera

It was said that many millions of years ago, all intelligent life arose from two worlds: Z'yon and Tera. These two worlds were mythical in the minds of all who knew their story. A story that had become myth over the countless eons. So much of what is known cannot be believed. What might surprise many is that the Human Consortium knew only as much about these ancient worlds as the Utopians and Darkcons did.

The libraries of many worlds throughout the realm had very little information about the twin worlds. They do not exist on any star map. The name of the star that they orbited has been lost to most except for a select few. Countess Marien did learn this ancient star's name, Sol. Tried as she might, no star map or text mention this name Sol. Tera and Z'yon are likewise a mystery.

How Marien came across this knowledge was classified to all but a select few. A few years ago, she came across ancient vessels from a time long forgotten. And some of these vessels had living ancient humans onboard. They spoke of another world called Earth, and its star Sol. Tera was an alternate name for Earth billions of years ago. These ancient humans were granted freedom and allowed to live on Havaina in peace. As for what was known about Z'yon.

Z'yon was the world where all the magical beings were born. Magic itself was born on this world. How this came about was a mystery that no one could know. Those that tried were driven mad. The High Priestess Nona claimed not too long ago to have figured it out. However, she never mentioned how she came across this knowledge or what it was. Nona and Marien often traded information for some benefit or simple knowledge exchange. But this was one secret that the elf priestess never told her.

Upon this ancient magical world was where elves learned, fairies played, dwarves built, centaurs hunted, demons conjured, and merpeople swam. Many others also came into being here, like elemental demons, daemons, werewolves, ents, trolls, goblins, and sages. A balance of light and dark forces coexisted. Good and evil lived in harmony with one another. A perfect balance that existed for countless millennia. That was until something happened. What that something was is a constant debate.

The most accepted theory was that in those ancient times the gods called the Empyrean and others walked among the mortal races. Several of the gods were said to have gone mad. They destroyed the balance of good and evil. What transpired in those times could only be imagined.

Then there was Tera. The world where all nonmagical beings evolved. Intelligence and advanced ingenuity sprung from this world. It was from this world that the humans and many other nonmagical races emerged. Here, technology was so advanced that humans and the other races could play with the stars and galaxies. Grand cities towered into the skies, and populations outnumbered most races on Z'yon. In legend humans and other species of Tera had vast empires that ruled over so many whole galaxies, it boggled the imagination. Wars were thought to have been common but fought across space and other realms of reality.

Light and darkness kept the balance of Z'yon; on Tera, peace and war maintained the balance of power between the empires. Magic was used on Z'yon, technology was used on Tera as well.

For millennia, the peoples of Z'yon and Tera never interacted. But the worlds shared the same planetary system and even orbited the same sun, which gave life to both. Again no one knew why this was. It was believed that the empires of Tera knew of Z'yon and its people. But for some unknown reason none of Tera's people ventured to Z'yon until the final years of the myth.

However, in the fourth age of Z'yon's existence, a ship carrying the children of Tera landed upon Z'yon's soil. The humans were greeted with open arms by the reigning elves. The humans were so advanced that they ruled millions of other worlds and could control whole galaxies. They showed off their great technological marvels to what they believed were primitive beings of Z'yon. The elves, by contrast, could manipulate the energy around them and create their own energy.

Technologically and scientifically, the elves were primitive compared to humans. However, the humans were unable to feel the joys from magic and the other forms of fantastical energy of the world. It was said that the humans defeated the fallen gods who dwelled on Z'yon. This was said to have led to a new age.

The many peoples of Tera wanted to build cities on Z'yon—one for each race from Tera. At first, the council of Z'yon decided to allow this, but they soon regretted their decision. Billions flooded into Z'yon to build these great cities, which were the size of small kingdoms—cities that towered into the skies and expanded into the oceans. Many of the people of Z'yon also left their world for the first time as well to explore the universe that was under Tera rule.

These amazing feats made many in the councils of Z'yon nervous. The most conservative people wanted the immigrants from Tera gone, especially the humans. Humans, however, were too powerful. To oppose them would mean extinction. So, these vocal minorities felt that they traded one oppressive ruler for another.

As the myths and legends did mention that there were riots, protests, and savage attacks erupted all across Z'yon. They targeted any people of Tera that were on their world. Several of the aliens fought back with brutal and devastating efficiency, killing hundreds of thousands. The riots and fighting were quickly and constantly put down.

Many humans were killed, and the human leaders on Tera, furious about the attacks, ordered the near extermination of all magical races. They planned to genetically bottleneck all the magical races to permanently subdue the uprising. Or so the legend went. But there were other stories that countered these tales as well. So, what truly happened will be a mystery for the rest of time.

In one year, Z'yon went from a population of ten billion magical beings to a mere one hundred thousand. The empires of Tera took control of Z'yon and the magical races. Some were more merciful than others. At the same time a myth said that the Realm itself was being created. By whom or what was a mystery. The myth did say that the people of Z'yon were migrating to the early Realm to escape the oppression of Tera.

In this atmosphere, a great evil was reborn. The evil recruited the children of Z'yon to rebuild their numbers and start a holy war against the empires of Tera. At first, the humans and others won the battles, but they soon lost ground and were eventually driven from Z'yon.

In the wake of their departure, Z'yon fell into the shadow of evil. Light and darkness became unhinged, and the balance was forever destroyed. Good and evil became enemy's eternal to destroy one another.

Another ten thousand years passed, and the torment of Z'yon only grew. Many found ways to escape the planet, but they also found only angry humans and aliens who would not allow Z'yon to escape its misery. The exodus to the Realm had stopped as no one was able to escape Z'yon anymore.

Legend spoke of an elf queen and a fairy found their way to Tera to speak to the new masters of Tera. Some of the gods lived on Tera at the time as well. One was chosen to be the leader of a then fully united Tera.

Not much is known of what happened after that, only that the evil was defeated and locked away. A great and terrible war eventually destroyed both Z'yon and Tera, and all the people were forced to leave and settle on other worlds. The evil's legacy remained strong, and the hate still lingered between the races.

Most of the people of Z'yon did find their way to the Realm and eventually would found the Utopian Kingdom. And the rest was history. Well known history from then on out. As for Tera only a small fraction of humanity found its way to the Realm. The rest vanished with the rest of the races of Tera.

Countess Marien read these stories countless times, both Utopian/Darkcon and human versions. If these two worlds still existed, she wanted them and to keep them from the Utopians and Darkcons. The legends stated that the humans from Tera were so powerful and advanced that they were able to manipulate entire galaxies, and they colonized trillions of worlds. Their race was said to number in the hundreds of quintillions.

All that power, knowledge, and who knew what else had been lost so long ago. To Marien this was heresy. Such a lose should never have been allowed.

The countess had spent a large portion of her life looking for any evidence of Tera. Anything even if it was mere myth and legend. She wanted to learn of its location. And know what happened, and possibly rebuild it.

Marien thought that sovereignty over such an ancient and vast super empire would have been glorious. She aimed to resurrect this ancient state of humanity and restore her people to greatness. She would no longer need to be shackled to the Utopian crown.

Her daughter may be the supreme monarch now, but there was no telling how long that will last. Asora was too radical for the Utopian Royal Court. Asora would be seen as an average politician in the Consortium Senate. For Marien it was only a matter of time before the Utopians lose their nerve. They will find some way of getting rid of Asora and putting someone else that they can control upon the throne. That is just the nature of their craft.

However, that threat can be mitigated nearly completely if Marien could locate not just Tera, but Z'yon as well. Z'yon could be used as a powerful bargaining tool. Utopian scholars had been obsessed with finding Z'yon for as long as the kingdom itself has existed.

Countess Marien was in her study. She allowed both Lady's T'a and T'ula to cure her daughter Asora of her addiction. She trusted them as did Asora herself. Marien still worried about her family.

Someone came up to Marien and put a plate of cookies next to her. She looked up to see Asora's bodyguard looking back at her lovingly.

"You look hungry," Dame Sarea said.

"Oh, thank you my dear," Marien said kindly.

Marien started nibbling at one of the cookies. She went back to the book on the desk in front of her. Sarea was curious about the topic matter.

"What are you reading about?" Sarea asked.

"I am making another attempt at figuring out the location of Sol," Marien said.

"Oh mother," Sarea sighed. "You cannot keep doing this to yourself."

"You may be my true eldest daughter, but you should be more understanding," Marien pointed out.

Dame Sarea was in fact Marien's oldest daughter and her second born child. Sarea was also the biggest child Marien ever had. Like her brother, Marien had Sarea outside of her last marriage. Sarea would have inherited everything that Asora and Asaria did if it was not for one thing. Sarea was a human that could practice and wield magic.

Humans did not care that other species practiced magic, but humans in general were believed to be unsuited for magic. The ones that could were seen as witches, warlocks, or something else. A half human that practiced magic was considered okay, but not pure-blooded humans. The Consortium had very strict laws about pure humans practicing magic. And Ironically Marien was partly responsible for those laws. Like most humans, Marien grew up with the understanding that humans and magic did not go well together. Any pure-blooded human that could wield magic at any level was to be quarantined and studied. This people had no privacy and were under constant monitoring.

Witches and warlocks not too long ago always fought against the Consortium and used whatever they could to fight back. They even sided with the Utopian Kingdom during the Great War. Ever since then magical humans were regarded as traitors and constantly persecuted. The last time a rebellion happened was a few years ago when Marien first took control of the Consortium. These witches and warlocks were defeated. Marien ordered that they be expelled or terminated. No one in the Senate or in the Consortium in general had a problem with this.

That was until Marien gave birth to Sarea. Both of Sarea's parents were humans with no magic. So Sarea was unique in the fact that she was born with magical powers. Marien suddenly realized that her own daughter could be destroyed if it was found out that Sarea was magical. Marien was forced to disown Sarea and was taken into an adoptive jewel elf family who were very close to Marien's family.

Despite that Sarea knew who she was. And what surprised Marien was that Sarea understood why. Marien tried to be involved in Sarea's early years. Sarea was told that she was adopted because her true parents did not want her to suffer. Sarea grew up powerful, strong, and very independent. She wanted to come to Marien as a powerful and loving daughter who could now take care of herself.

Marien at the time thought that Sarea wanted revenge for getting rid of her. What Marien got instead was a powerful hug and a woman that wanted to prove to all that magical humans were no threat. Sarea was proof if raised right that they could be useful to the Consortium. Sarea also hid the fact that she was Marien's daughter. For the same reason why, she was given away. Sarea did not want Marien to suffer.

This brought them closer as Sarea wished to be the most powerful magical woman and the mightiest warrior. Sarea also got along with Asora in her younger years and was the one to teach Asora how to use magic. Asora never knew that Sarea was her oldest sister, and neither did Asaria.

Sarea's desire to protect Asora led her to this point. Sarea was respected in the Consortium, and many believed her to be the only good magical human. Everyone believed that she was abandoned by witches because she was not evil like that were. And that Marien took her in to help. Sarea had also been getting closer to Marien and wished to help her.

The obsession with Sol and finding Z'yon also was a hobby to Sarea. But that was it a hobby. She did not like seeing Marien wasting all her time looking for some mythical star.

"I understand well, mother," Sarea said. "But if what we do know of Sol is right. It is most likely a white dwarf by now."

"I know," Marien said. "But there is a chance that both Z'yon and Tera survived. Plus, the ancient empires of Tera could have extended the star's life."

"If they did, according to legend, then it would have to be regularly maintained," Sarea pointed out. "Tera and Z'yon were abandoned billions of years ago."

"There would still be remains," Marien said. "Type four and five civilizations arose and ruled on Tera. Humans were once one of those. Perhaps we were the most powerful then?"

"Perhaps," Sarea added. "But what good does it do us now?"

"That is why I want to find it," Marien said. "We can reverse engineer what we find."

"Just like the message that our people found five hundred years ago?" Sarea asked.

Dame Sarea was referring to a very classified incident from the middle of the Great War. At the time a brand-new discovery of a hidden alien message. Some of the message did eventually lead to new technologies and sciences. But the idea of aliens from beyond the void was something so frightening that it could not be comprehended. As a result, Marien's great, great, great grandfather, the last great Emperor Jurano classified it.

"Yes, just like that," Marien said. "But there is a political advantage in controlling it all and having it before the others can find it."

"What about Z'yon?" Sarea asked. "The ancient home of all magical things."

"I want Z'yon too," Marien said. "It has a purpose too."

"Are you speaking of the great ancient power that can turn one into a god?" Sarea asked.

"That is part of it," Marien added. "But only a magical being can have that power."

"Like me or Asora," Sarea asked.

"Yes, very much so," Marien looked at Sarea.

"I do not want to be a god," Sarea said. "I want to be a great hero."

"I know, I will not force you to be," Marien said.

"Asora could use it," Sarea pointed out. "She would be a powerful goddess and a great needed bringer of change."

"And it would not hurt to have the technology of a type five civilization to back her up too," Marien added.

There was an old scale on how a civilization was measured. When Marien was referring to Tera having nothing but type four and five civilization she was referring to what humans saw them as. A type one was a civilization that fully ruled and controlled a whole world. A type two was a civilization that controlled whole planetary or multiple planetary and star systems. A type three controlled a whole galaxy and have some ability to colonize other galaxies. A type four ruled and could control a super cluster or millions of galaxies. A type five reigned over a double-digit percentage of the visible universe. The scale went up to six and seven, but it was not clear if such levels were even possible.

By using this the Utopian Kingdom may own and claim dominion over many galaxies worth of worlds. The Utopians were classified as a type one at best. The Darkcons also fell into this category. The Consortium by contrast was a type two at most.

Countess Marien then got an update from her astronomy department. It came as a computer message on her electronic tablet. Marien read the message and her yes lit up.

"What is it?" Sarea asked.

"An entire galaxy just emerged from the void. It has finished drifting in and is fully visible," Marien said.

Marien showed the data on the tablet to Sarea. She was as amazed as her mother was about this.

"It is massive," Sarea said. "Almost a trillion stars."

"And it is ancient," Marien added.

"The astronomers believe that it was once several galaxies that merged. Three large spiral types, and several smaller ones," Sarea read. "That fits with how it looks, and its core make up."

Marien thought for a moment. She remembered having a conversation once a few years ago when discussing about Tera and Z'yon. It was said that the galaxy that Sol was in was on the verge of merging with other galaxies in its local group. She got up and walked to a nearby bookshelf looking for a book that had maps.

She found it and took it back to her desk. She also took the tablet from Sarea. The maps on this book were very different from the rest. Sarea brought a small laptop computer to Marien.

"Plug these numbers in," Marien showed Sarea the information.

Sarea typed away as Marien looked more closely at the images of the new galaxy. It was a massive elliptical galaxy that looked to have once been a spiral galaxy. But it had three massive centers at its core. That told Marien that this was once three large galaxies. And the orbiting globular clusters were the remains of smaller orbiting irregular and elliptical galaxies.

The computer came back with a message. The kind of message and prediction she Sarea was not expecting.

"Mother," Sarea said. "It says that there is a match."

"What?" Marien asked. "Are you certain?"

"I am running the calculations again," Sarea said.

The dame re-entered the information and waited for the response. It came back as a secondary confirmation. Marien as watching from over Sarea's shoulder. The countess was in awe.

"Confirmed," Sarea said. "That could be it."

"Sol is somewhere in that ancient galaxy," Marien marveled. "Can we figure out which star could be Sol?"

"We do not have enough information on this galaxy. But the estimates of the different star types are only that. An estimation," Sarea clarified. "We do not even know what Sol was or in what condition it was in when all left it."

"I learned some time ago that Sol was a yellow main sequence star," Marien said. "It was middle aged then. According to them."

"And nine billion years have past since they came," Sarea said. "That means that Sol could be a white dwarf now with several burnt planets and is shrouded in a small colorful nebula."

"We can start with that," Marien said.

"How many other planets orbited Sol other then Tera and Z'yon?" Sarea asked.

"I think they said seven others," Marien thought out loud. "Three other rocky worlds, two gas giants, two ice giants. Then there were two asteroid regions and many dwarf worlds."

"It may take centuries to fully look at this new galaxy to figure that one out," Sarea said. "And multiple galaxy mergers can reshape even planetary systems if they are hit the right way."

"I know," Marien said. "But this is the first true evidence of Sol. And with it Z'yon and Tera." Marien thought long and hard. "Classify this. I want that galaxy."

Countess Marine's dream of restoring her people to its true place in the universe has come at long last. She will have both worlds. The divine powers of Z'yon, and the hyper advanced technology and Tera. All hers, but this had to be done quietly. And quickly otherwise someone else could try at her prize.

Chapter Forty-Eight

The Chase

In her royal chambers deep inside the Darkcon Onyx Palace, Queen Laxur was relaxing to soothing music and drinking a very intoxicating wine. She was trying to relax after a rough week. Polea had promised her that she could handle the day-to-day operations, and she told the queen that she should take a week off. So far, Polea had done wonderfully. To Laxur, Polea was one of the best stateswomen she had ever seen. The queen felt comfortable letting Polea take the reins, for she did not fear a hostile takeover. Polea was a loyal friend and was under Laxur's seduction. Not that it took much. Polea had been loyal to Laxur for far longer than many would expect.

A knock at the door disrupted the queen's thoughts. At first, she was mad, until she realized it sounded like a child knocking. Her anger faded at the thought that it could be Smika. She hoped it was as she could use someone friendly to talk to.

"Enter!" Laxur commanded.

As she expected, it was Smika. A smile rose on Laxur's face. She liked Smika a lot—he was smart, brave, and gullible. She asked the young boy to do some research in the great library. Another reason she liked him was that he could keep a secret; he was also in love with her, and he was willing to do whatever she wanted. Queen Laxur thought the young love was cute and useful.

"What were you able to find, dear?" Laxur asked kindly to the tween boy.

The Chase

She had asked him to find something that could enhance her powers. She felt weak, and Asora was now too powerful to handle. But she needed to keep up the image of being all powerful. This was not as hard as Laxur thought. If she did this sparingly.

"You may find this interesting, my queen," Smika said as he gave Laxur a very old scroll.

The queen took the scroll and read it. It was the legend of Z'yon and Tera. She remembered her mother and father telling her these legends when she was a little girl. Like Countess Marien, Queen Laxur loved these legends, and she wanted very much for Z'yon to exist. Then she noticed a section that told of an ancient royal family that knew the location of Z'yon. The family's name was Haiso.

"Haiso? That is familiar," Laxur pondered.

"That is because deep in the former King Tarmin lineage, he was related to the Haiso line," another female voice spoke.

It was Polea. The young blonde came into the dark, fire-lit room.

"I guess that you would know that, since they had no child of their own and you were adopted by them. Did they tell you, their secrets?" Laxur asked with a hint of excitement.

"They did," Polea answered shortly.

"Why have you not told me this?" Laxur demanded.

"Because I was sworn to secrecy, and a powerful spell was put upon me to punish me if I told anyone. I was hoping that if you were able to obtain the great power, you could remove it from me," Polea said.

"Why did you not go and get it yourself?" Smika asked.

Polea looked at the boy. "I could never handle such power."

"What power?" Laxur asked.

"On Z'yon, there is a power that can give a person the powers of a god. It was left there after the first Great War. It defeated the dark evil and left its divine energy in a grand temple," Polea explained.

"Why would a god give up their power like that?" Laxur asked, interested.

"The story that is not in the legend says that when the great evil reemerges, a special being will be chosen to inherit the divine powers of the Maker," Polea said.

Laxur's eyes widened. "It is the power of the Maker?"

"So if someone takes this power, they become like the Maker?" Smika asked.

"In a way, yes. But not anyone, only someone chosen by destiny may have this great power," Polea explained.

"What would happen if someone not chosen tried to take the power?" Smika questioned.

"I do not know. I would imagine that the power would destroy the false one," the blonde said. "It might be possible to trick it, however, to think that you, my queen, are the chosen one."

Laxur was now in her own thoughts. She was imagining herself as powerful as the Maker, an equal to the Maker. The possibilities were endless. She would be invincible; she would rule all.

She was snapped out of her thoughts when Polea called her attention to another scroll. The Princess made another scroll appear in her hands in a puff of brown smoke.

"My queen, this should be useful for you in any quest that you wish to pursue," Polea said, holding the scroll.

The queen took the scroll, opened it, and began to read. "Is this the only copy?" Laxur asked.

"Yes, it is. That is why none of the past quests have been successful. But with this, it is possible," Polea replied.

"Yes! Oh, Polea, you are beautiful. Gather up our best and most powerful vessels. We are going to Z'yon."

On Evorn, Princess Asora was practicing her new powers from the coins. She now had mastery of fire, water, wind, earth, light, dark, and life. She had so much power coursing through her that it made her feel invincible. She was the most magically powerful being in the known universe.

Walls of fire formed from nothing. Tidal waves surged out of thin air. Hurricane winds blew through the magical gardens. Powerful quakes shook the floor; light and heat blasted. Dark and cool energies flooded the area. New trees, bushes, flowers, and grass reformed.

Feeling strong about her abilities, Asora stopped training for the day. Rakon and Marevin had been teaching their Princess.

"As of today, my Princess, you can beat the Darkcon witches all by yourself," Marevin said with a smile.

Asora wiped the sweat from her forehead with a white towel, and she smiled at Marevin's words. His confidence made Asora feel strong.

"Clean yourself up, princess, and you are free for the rest of the day," Rakon said, and then he left.

Later, Asora and Marevin were walking down the grand hallway toward the princess's chambers. They were jubilant and talkative. They arrived at the massive doors that led to Asora's private rooms. Countess Marien stood in front of her doors and startled the pair. She smiled when she saw Asora and Marevin together like young lovers.

"Mother? What are you doing here?" Asora asked.

"I need to talk to you. Marevin may want to hear this too." Marien had the four fairy sisters open the doors.

The three went inside, and the fairies joined them in the princess's white sitting room. Marien's face was no longer smiling; instead, she looked dead serious.

"My queen, what is the matter?" Marevin asked respectfully.

"It would appear that your sister has found Z'yon and is on her way to it," Marien said.

A shiver ran down Asora's spine, and Marevin's face became pale.

Marevin started, "That is not good. If she finds the great power, there . . ."

"We cannot let that happen," Asora barked. "She would turn all of nature insane. We must beat her to it. Rayne, B'nei, Gourani, Friea!"

"Yes, my princess?" The fairies bowed in midair.

"Have the privy council assemble my best and most trusted

guardsmen," Asora ordered.

The fairies bowed their heads, and they flew out.

Marevin held Asora's hand to calm her down. She was shaking just thinking about what could happen if Laxur obtained that kind of power.

An hour later, in a small room near the throne room, Asora's and Marien's privy councils gathered. On Asora's side were Frenzen, T'ula, T'a, Jeia, Madimoy, Yane, Marevin, Rakon, Ela, and Heralin. On Marien's side were five humans, three military and two in civilian clothes: General Tansl of the Consortium Armies; Admiral Kiala of the Consortium Navy; Sky Marshal Jasina of the Consortium Air Force; Semanal, the prime minister of the Consortium; and Secretary of State Athea.

"I am sure that my mother has told you what has happened. I have arranged for a fleet of ships and a couple of battalions of guardsmen to intercept the Darkcon force heading for Z'yon," Asora informed.

"We better make sure that we can overpower the Darkcons and secure the world," Frenzen suggested.

"I am going to make sure of it, Frenzen. I think two hundred million troops and four thousand ships should do the job," Asora pointed out.

"That is the largest military force that the Utopian Kingdom has mustered since the Great War," T'a pointed out.

"Mother, could the Consortium send some forces too?" Asora asked Marien.

General Tansl answered for her. "We would be willing to add about another two hundred million troops, five hundred ships, seven thousand jets, and nine hundred thousand drones."

"So we have a grand total of four hundred million troops, four thousand five hundred ships, and other military equipment. What do the Darkcons have?" Rakon thought out loud.

"We do not know, but I imagine Queen Laxur is taking every precaution to make sure she gets what she wants," T'ula pointed out.

The Chase

One week later, a fleet of Darkcon ships were nearing the edge of an unknown galaxy near the Great Void. Onboard the *Sarasen*, the Darkcon Empire's flagship, Queen Laxur sat in a room, looking out into darkness, watching her fleet move through space. She had been lost in her thoughts since they left Dorien one week ago. She had been so consumed with what she could do with this divine power that she had been forgetting to eat and sleep. Her powers had been weakening, and her strength was lowering. Polea and Smika were very worried about Laxur. They feared that her health might be in decline.

Hyea and Dari were in the dark room, serving their queen. Hyea was now Laxur's personal servant, and she admired the queen. But she was worried about Laxur's mental health.

"My queen? Do you require any sustenance?" the fairy asked Laxur, hovering in front of her face.

"No, now leave. Both you and Dari leave me. I will summon you when I need you," Laxur said in a dreamlike state.

They both fell into the shadows, leaving the queen to her loneliness. Laxur fell into a deep slumber and began to dream.

She was walking down a dark road in the middle of the night. She saw nothing in front or behind her.

"Is anyone out there?" Laxur yelled out into the dark void.

At first, no one answered, and she heard nothing. Then she heard a noise—footsteps walking toward her. The queen made her right-hand glow to shine a light on the approaching person. It was Asora.

"Sister?" Laxur said. Asora said nothing, and she looked dirty, beaten, tired, and angry. "What happened to you?"

"You have doomed us. You have killed me. You are a monster," Asora muttered.

"What are you talking about? I have not done anything," Laxur pointed out.

"You will kill us all!" Asora yelled and charged at Laxur. She disappeared in a wisp of smoke, leaving the queen alone.

Another noise could be heard. It sounded like a child crying and a woman moaning in her death throes. She turned around to see Smika dead on the ground and Hyea crying as she was dying.

"What happened?" Laxur asked, worried for them.

"Please, my queen. Do not hurt us anymore. Please!" Hyea begged.

"What are you talking about? I did not do this," Laxur stated.

Hyea shielded herself and the corpse of the young boy.

They vanished, and Laxur was alone again. She looked around, trying to find another person, and she found a man in the shadows. Laxur had never seen him before, and the Queen could not make out what he looked like, but some of his features were visible. As far as Laxur could tell, this man was judging her, and he hated her.

"Who are you?" Laxur demanded.

He did not answer; he just continued to stare her down.

"Answer me!" The man punched her in the stomach and then grabbed her arm and threw her to the ground.

"You will burn" was all the man said, and then he vanished.

Queen Laxur woke up in a cold sweat.

"Hyea! Dari! Polea! Smika!" Laxur cried out. No one came. "Please! I need you!"

Hyea finally flew in to see the queen on the floor in a fit of pain.

"My queen!" Hyea cried out.

She landed, drank a small green vial, and grew to a size bigger than Laxur. Hyea was nearly four meters tall, and she picked up Laxur and put her back onto the moving throne.

"Hyea, please do not leave me," Laxur begged the fairy.

She grabbed the fairy's shirt, keeping hold of her.

"I will not leave you, my queen." Hyea held Laxur close to her.

"I do not want to hurt you. I never will. Please remember that" Laxur babbled.

Only Laxur's privy council—Hyea, Polea, Dari, and Smika—had ever seen her like this. They all appeared and held her together.

A buzzing noise came from a gray box mounted on a pole next to Queen Laxur's mobile throne. Dari pushed a button and picked up headphones to answer the call.

"What is it?" Dari demanded. Only she could hear what was being said. "What? How many? Great Architect!"

"What is happening?" Laxur demanded.

"The Human Consortium and Utopian Kingdom have sent a massive force, about forty-five hundred ships, to intercept us," Dari said.

"They outnumber us five to one. How far ahead of them are we?" Hyea asked.

"We have only a few hours head start. Their ships have always been faster," Polea pointed out.

"So in one hour, they will overtake us?" Smika asked.

"Pretty much," Dari answered.

"How far is Z'yon from our current position?" Laxur asked.

"About two days," Polea said after she looked at a magical map.

"Two days versus one hour. Great choices." Laxur looked at Polea's map. "We can go into that nebula on the other end of this galaxy's border. I will have several of my ships intercept and fight the Utopians long enough for us to escape into the nebula."

Three dozen Darkcon ships broke formation and charged straight at the Utopian and human ships.

On board a human warship called the *Tricore*, Princess Asora and her privy council, along with Countess Marien, were watching the Darkcons coming right at them.

"Are those idiots insane?" Frenzen questioned.

"They have to know that they will be destroyed, so why?" Madimoy asked.

"They are either desperate or . . ." T'ula had an idea. She turned to a computer monitor at the rear of the bridge. "What is in that galactic nebula?"

"It is mostly hydrogen gas and dust, as far as we know," Jeia answered. "It is also at the edge of the galaxy where Z'yon is rumored to be."

"Could Laxur use this nebula to sneak past and get inside more easily?" T'a asked.

"Yes, she can. Have the destroyer escorts engage those ships coming at us. The rest will continue to follow and intercept the main Darkcon force," Asora ordered. Ninety small human ships broke formation to attack the oncoming Darkcon ships.

Outnumbered, the Darkcons opened fire on the human ships. They blasted the humans with powerful dark energies and froze them. The humans returned fire with laser and particle weapons, as well as a solid rod missile. The rods slammed into the Darkcon ships at high speeds, shattering the hulls of the enemy ships.

Meanwhile, the Darkcon fleet managed to get inside the nebula after Laxur sent another flock of ships to slow the Utopian-human fleet down. They dove into the red and orange gas clouds that stretched for thousands of light-years. The Utopians followed them in and fanned out to find the Darkcons. Princess Asora would rather have them all killed than allow them to find Z'yon. The *Tricore* had managed to lock on to the *Sarasen* and follow it. The *Tricore* was faster; it was a powerful super dreadnought designed for speed and hard-hitting power. The *Sarasen* was a warship too, but not as powerful as the *Tricore*. The only advantage the *Sarasen* had was the magical energies it used, which were strong enough to damage the *Tricore*. But the *Tricore* had powerful, energy-based weapons and a new breed of nuclear missiles; however, firing energies or nuclear weapons would set much of the nebula ablaze and cause a powerful, supernova-like explosion.

Nine days later, the *Sarasen* had evaded the *Tricore* and emerged from the nebula into an ancient planetary system.

"There it is. Z'yon," Laxur said with excitement. "It is the third planet from the star, the one with green skies."

"It has a breathable atmosphere but little water, and it appears to be a covered in desert," Polea stated.

"Desert or not, Polea, the divine power that I am looking for is down there, and I want it," Laxur said. "Land!"

The Chase

The *Sarasen* descended into the atmosphere. At the same time, the *Tricore* emerged, and it saw the *Sarasen* entering the atmosphere of the third planet.

"Get down there and get the troops loose on the planet surface!" Asora barked out her orders.

The Utopians and humans rushed around, getting ready to fight. They ordered the other ships to get out of the nebula and follow the *Tricore* to Z'yon.

The *Tricore* entered the atmosphere near where the *Sarasen* landed.

Chapter Forty-Nine
The Challenges

From the darkness inside the *Sarasen*, Queen Laxur and her court emerged with an array of soldiers. The black clad queen, wearing a large-brimmed hat, looked out upon the landscape and saw only endless desert and hot sand.

"Are you sure that you should be wearing black, my queen?" Smika asked to her. He was wearing the Darkcon black pants, tunic, and boots, all lightweight.

"I will be fine, my dear. Polea, where do we go from here?" Laxur asked.

The blond girl, in beige cotton, put on her much-hated glasses to read a magical map.

"Out there to those mountain ranges in the distance." She pointed to a long line of mountains that were barely visible.

The queen had a motorized chariot deployed to transport her and her court to what Polea said was a massive castle beyond the mountains. They could not land next to it because the mountains were too high.

The motorized chariot was a long jeep-like car. It was black and brown emboldened with the imperial symbol.

Queen Laxur, Princess Polea, Minister Golcon, Heranian, Smika, Hyea, Dari, Sysu, and Obsidian were escorted into the chariot; it was started, and they were gone.

The *Tricore* landed roughly two hundred miles away from the *Sarasen* in a field clear of sand dunes. Doors to the hangar bay opened,

The Challenges

and human pilots manned their jets and other aircraft.

Princess Asora looked out from the hangar bay to the planet of Z'yon. Asora could feel a great power here, and it was beginning to affect her. It made her feel wild, almost primal.

"The Comancor has just reported in!" Admiral Yane yelled out as he approached Asora. "These are orbital photos of the *Sarasen* taken twelve minutes ago."

"Looks like they took a chariot and went by ground. We will go by air and intercept them," Asora said.

Yane noticed something a tad different and, being the blunt naval officer that he was, said, "Are you okay, Princess? You look like you are about to lose your head."

"I am fine, Admiral. Thank you for your concern," Asora said dully. "Now get the P-Ninety Seven into the air. And ready the long-range bomber. I am taking that."

"Are you sure?" Yane asked.

"I have always wanted to ride in a hypersonic nuclear bomber, Admiral, you know that," Asora said with a smile. She was right; Asora had been dying to fly inside a powerful military aircraft.

The P-Ninety-Seven was what the humans called a sixth-generation stealth jet fighter. It was a two-seater with advanced electronics and avionics. The missiles and guns were all stored inside the aircraft. It was capable of hypersonic flight and suborbital combat.

The bomber was called the Thunderer B-fifty-five. This massive aircraft had eight turbo high-speed engines pushing this beast to a speed of Mach ten. It carried so many bombs and missiles that it could lay waste to a nation or a whole continent by itself.

"You are planning to strike Laxur from the air?" Lady T'ula asked as she walked up to her Princess.

"And knock out the *Sarasen* once and for all, while I am at it," Asora pointed out.

"One mission at a time, my Princess," T'ula reminded her.

Then an announcement could be heard over the intercom.

"Attention. All craft, prepare for electronic launch. All personnel, to your fighters and bombers."

"Let us go, T'ula. Today will be our first day in a hypersonic bomber," Asora pronounced.

Nine jet fighters were launched from an electromagnetic rail system inside the hangar bay. Next was the massive Thunderer carrying Asora, T'ula, and the rest of her privy council. They were strapped into benches lined against the hull.

In seven minutes, the fighters spotted the Darkcon ground convoy.

"Strike Eagle Four to Thunder Giant. Have located ground bogies headed northeast towards a large mountain range," the flight leader reported.

"This is Thunder Giant. You have authorization for weapons release. Fire at will," the sky marshal ordered.

The jets fired off a barrage of missiles at the Darkcons below.

On the ground, Queen Laxur heard several whistling noises, and then several explosions erupted around her and the convoy.

"Where are those bombs coming from!" Laxur roared.

She looked up and saw nine P-ninety sevens' flying at subsonic speeds. She knew all about these warplanes, and she knew that at subsonic speeds, they were on high alert. Surprising them will be difficult.

"Shoot them down!" Polea ordered. As she said that, another series of explosions rattled the escort chariot that held the Darkcon privy council. "Is Asora actually trying to kill us?"

From the bomber orbiting seventeen thousand meters above the scene, Princess Asora watched the P-ninety seven's strafe the Darkcons.

"Do not kill the privy council. I want them alive. You can destroy the rest of the Darkcons," Asora ordered.

The Darkcons continued to be rattled by human and Utopian firepower from the air. The last missile overturned the escort chariot. Laxur and Polea were thrown into the sand. Queen Laxur watched as her troops tried to fight against the jets, but they could not land a single hit. The dark queen ran for the mountain range a few miles away.

The Challenges

"My queen! Wait for me!" Polea begged as she staggered back up and followed Laxur.

Hyea, wearing Darkcon black, flew at the Queen's side. Dari grabbed Smika, and they ran after Laxur.

The pilots in the P-ninety sevens could not see the five escaping Darkcons, and they continued to pound away at the convoy.

Scanners on the bomber, however, detected the five fleeing Darkcons.

"Follow them! Have the fighters finish off the others. We will deal with those five," Asora stated.

The Thunderer slowly turned and followed Queen Laxur. They were too high up for the escaping Darkcons to see or hear, and that was what Asora was counting on. She ordered the bomb doors open. Asora made her white wings appear, and her gold dragon armor formed around her body. The Princess jumped off the platform and into the Z'yon sky. At Mach speed, Asora descended kilometers toward the surface. She powered all seven coins and readied herself for battle.

A fire ball surged past Queen Laxur and made the ground shake, causing her to fall flat on her hide.

"This is going to end, Asaria!" Asora stated forcefully.

"You are right. This will end!" Laxur fired back. She fired a bolt of dark energy at Asora. It vaporized on Asora's armor, and the Princess did not even feel it.

"Is that all, sister?" Asora asked mockingly.

"Damn it," Laxur said.

A glowing, golden whip wrapped around Asora, restraining her arms against her torso. "What?" Asora spat. She turned, and it was Polea.

"Nothing is ever that easy, little Princess," Polea said mockingly.

Then Smika and Hyea attacked Asora with rocks and magical bolts.

The sound of a motorcycle roared toward the scene. It was Jeia with an old-fashioned side sword. He sliced the whip, freeing Asora and distracting Hyea and Smika.

"Let us make this a double date, shall we?" Jeia mocked.

He then tossed Asora a shotgun with a pack of electric bullets designed to stun people.

"Thank you, brother," Asora said, and she loaded it as fast as she could.

Jeia punched Polea in her face, sending her flying into the sand.

"Stay down, whore!" Jeia said forcefully.

"Funny that you say that. Maybe I should tell Madimoy about a few of your, or should I say our, adventures together," Polea said with a wicked smile.

Jeia kicked sand into Polea's face, blinding her long enough for Jeia to punch her again. Then he grabbed her by the front of her corset and lifted her up. A rock hit Jeia in the head, and he released Polea. Smika, with a fist full of rocks, readied another.

Then Jeia was hit with a beam of dark energy from his sister, Queen Laxur.

"That was not nice, brother," Laxur said.

"Neither is this." Asora shot a fireball and a lightning bolt at Laxur. The queen was blown back into the sand, and her dress was partly on fire. Asora pointed her sword at Laxur. "Surrender and I promise to be lenient."

Princess Asora was knocked down and rendered unconscious by a powerful blow to her head.

"My queen, come!" Dari said, holding out her hand.

"Thank you, Dari. Polea, Hyea, Smika, let us leave for the mountains." Laxur zapped Jeia with another beam of dark energy. He was out cold too. The five then disappeared in a purple fog that formed around Laxur.

Princess Asora woke up in an emergency medical bed with scanning equipment hooked up to her skin.

"What happened?" the Princess demanded, with her head throbbing.

"You acted when you should not have, again!" T'a said, disappointed.

T'a crossed her arms. Asora growled in anger, and then she looked to the other side of her, where her brother was still sleeping and recovering from his injuries.

The Challenges

"Where is Laxur?" Asora demanded.

"We lost track of her somewhere in the foothills of the mountains," T'a said.

"WHAT!" Asora shouted and then held her head in pain.

"Relax. We are looking for them now. In fact, T'ula and Marevin say that they may have picked up where they went," T'a informed.

"What about the rest of the Darkcons?" Asora asked.

"We managed to round up roughly forty percent of them. As for the rest, they have either gone back to repair the *Sarasen* or fanned out across the planet. We are trying to track them now," T'a reported.

"Very well then. Leave me," Asora ordered.

Dusk had begun its debut to the new visitors of Z'yon. Lady T'ula and Lord Marevin, with a contingent of human and Utopian soldiers, entered the mountain's foothills. T'ula could not help but admire the sun going down on the horizon.

"Hey, lady elf! We must track down the Darkcons before they find whatever it is that they are looking for!" Marevin yelled to T'ula.

"I happen to enjoy dusk. And the Darkcons are looking for a fortress that spans from horizon to horizon," T'ula said melodically.

"Whatever. Let's just get moving," Marevin said dully.

"Tell me again, Marevin, why are we out here?" T'ula said with a smirk, antagonizing Marevin.

"Are you kidding me?" Marevin spat.

"Watch and learn, young man," T'ula said, and she revealed tracks in the sand near a rock. "You sneaky—"

"You're welcome, dear," T'ula said, smiling.

"Let us go!" Marevin ordered to the several dozen troops.

At the *Sarasen*, the Darkcon religious leader, Illumin, was leading a ragtag band of Darkcon soldiers, civilians, and technicians in the defense of their ship. For a religious human, Illumin was quite the skilled warrior. He had knowledge of most human technology and most Utopian magic.

The Utopians set up a defense perimeter around a human ship that landed. The Puro was ordered by Princess Asora to greet the countess because he was the only one available to do so. Countess Marien, dressed in jeans and hiking boots, was present, as was Puro Aga, along with dozens of human and Utopian troops.

Illumin jumped up high and slammed his staff into the ground, causing a quake and a wave of dirt to decimate the invaders. Marien had a military-grade mask that looked like a gas mask without the canister. Aga made a magical barrier around his face to shield his eyes and mouth.

Aga blasted Illumin with a ball of green energy; however, the Darkcon clergyman deflected the blast with his staff.

"Care to try again, animal?" Illumin said snidely.

"You blasphemous imp! You will fall. I will see to that." Aga spat.

"Oh, I am so scared," Illumin mocked.

"I fear Queen Marien more than you, animal." Illumin fired a bolt of purple lightning at the Puro.

Marien pulled out a handgun and joined her guards in shooting at the Darkcons.

"I am flattered that you think of me as a greater threat than this dirtbag. But I would suggest that you surrender," Marien ordered.

"I think not." Illumin spat, and then a Darkcon solider jumped over him and took to the sky.

The fallen angel blasted the human guards and Marien with lightning bolts. Illumin, yelling at the top of his lungs, charged at Marien and Aga. The clergyman slammed his fists into the Puro's stomach and the countess's face.

"Come on. I can take you both on," Illumin pronounced triumphantly. He then punched Aga in the face, as Aga's guards were getting trampled by Darkcon troops.

Marien was now mad. She landed a powerful kick into Illumin's stomach. Illumin doubled over in pain.

"You are going to pay for touching me, Darkcon," Marien growled.

The Challenges

"You are going to make me pay, because I think I am now," Illumin held his stomach in pain.

"What are you waiting for, you damn woman? Kill him," Aga ordered Marien.

"You do not give me orders, you beast," Marien spat to her rival.

"You two fight like an old married couple. Maybe you should consider it," Illumin suggested insultingly.

He got back up and was picked up by one of his followers, a female fallen angel. She took him inside the *Sarasen* as the rest of the Darkcons fought on.

"We must evacuate the *Sarasen* and locate our queen," Illumin ordered to the fallen angel.

"Yes, sir," she said and bowed to him. The fallen angel walked away.

The ship shook from the raging battle outside.

"My lord, we have located our queen. She and four others are in the mountains, about one day's march from here. She may need our help," a follower said.

"Yes, she does need help," Illumin said ominously.

The sun had now set over the horizon. Queen Laxur was worried about the cooler temperatures, and she was tired. Princess Polea sent Dari looking for shelter. Hyea was tending to the Queen, while Smika was helping Polea look for anything to burn for a fire. The temperature had dropped from comfortably warm in the sunlight to dangerously cold in the darkness. The queen's garments were not enough to hold her body heat.

"My queen!" Dari called out. "I have found a large old building that is structurally sound."

"Where?" Polea demanded.

"Roughly three kilometers from here," Dari reported.

"Very well. Take us to it," Polea ordered.

Dari grabbed Laxur, while Polea took Smika, and Hyea flew. For roughly twenty minutes, they flew deep into the mountains. As Dari said, a single large building sat in a tiny valley. It appeared to be a church or some kind of religious building. Dari, Polea, and Hyea landed, and Dari released Laxur.

"What is this place?" Polea asked.

"It looks like a place where people worshiped," Smika said.

"How fitting," Laxur said quietly.

She was thinking about the powers that she would gain, and this place gave her ideas about how people would serve and worship her.

Polea opened the ancient stone doors with a spell.

"We can burn the cloth here for a fire," Polea pointed out. "The night can last eighteen hours, according to what the techs said."

"Make it happen, Polea," Laxur ordered.

Polea and Dari began to collect old cloth from around the cathedral. Hyea started to make a place for them all to sleep. Queen Laxur and Smika were in another room, looking around for anything of value. Smika enjoyed being this close to the lovely dark queen. He found the queen incredible, and he had fallen for her. He wanted to please her in any way he could.

"My queen, look at this," Smika said as he pulled out a small stone slab.

"What did you find, my dear?" Laxur asked. She took the slab; it had strange writing and pictures on it. "What is this?"

"Could it have something to do with the powers you want, my queen?" Smika asked.

"I believe it does," Laxur responded. She could read a few words, and they were very enticing.

She looked to Smika with a dark smile. She gently ran her cold hand across the young man's face. "My dear, you have just granted me the divine. Keep this to yourself. It will be our little secret."

Smika did not want to argue. He liked sharing a secret with her, and he would do as she asked. He was pleased to see her smile and was glad to make her happy.

Later, Laxur and Smika emerged from the other room to see that

The Challenges

Polea had managed to get a fire going. Dari was sitting on a stone slab, beginning to nod off. Polea sat on a bench facing the fire. Hyea was nowhere to be seen. Laxur assumed that she shrank down and was buzzing around somewhere.

"My Queen, come sit here and sleep. Hyea is outside, watching the perimeter," Polea said.

Laxur sat down next to Polea, and Smika sat next to Laxur. The three began to fall asleep.

Princess Asora had dispatched the Huusaud—Special Forces troops from the Utopian royal guard. They were loyal to the Princess, not the court, and were made up mostly of jewel elves, fairies, rare daemons, smelting dwarves, and sage humans. They were assassins, saboteurs, soldiers, spies, and police.

"I want Queen Laxur and her privy council captured alive. You can dispose of the rest," was the Princess's order to the Huusaud.

S'tie stood behind Asora with a report on the *Sarasen*. Despite her mother's and Aga's antics, they captured the ship.

Chapter Fifty
Rise of the Malicious Goddess

At first light, Queen Laxur, Princess Polea, Dame Dari, Hyea, and Smika traveled on foot through the foothills toward the edge of the range. An hour later, they were on a cliff overlooking the other side of the mountains. Laxur's excitement aroused when she saw a massive fortress that seemed to stretch from horizon to horizon.

"That's it! Come, everyone. We must get to it before the Utopians do," Queen Laxur ordered.

"Yes, my queen," the four said in unison.

Dari and Polea, with Smika in her arms, took to the winds, and Queen Laxur jumped into the air and unfurled her black wings. They were flying toward and around the massive fortress. It took them two hours to fly to it, and they saw only a small part of the fortress.

"This thing is enormous. And I do not see any place to enter," Dari complained.

"If I had to guess, I would say that this fortress is one hundred miles long and wide," Polea said.

"Who would build such a place?" Smika asked.

"It was made for a god or goddess, and all things are big for them," Laxur said.

The Queen got tired of flying, so she landed near the giant wall.

"I would say that this wall is ten kilometers high too, at least at this end and the outer edge," Polea added.

"That is big!" Hyea commented and whistled.

Laxur took out the small stone slab that Smika gave her, and she began to decipher it. As she did, the same writing from the slab began to appear on the wall in front of her.

"It is a door?" Laxur said curiously.

She had figured that if she touched the symbols in a certain way, a door would form. A gunshot echoed past and cratered in the wall. The five Darkcons turned around to see the dreaded Huusaud, Princess Asora, and her entourage.

"The next one will not miss. I guarantee you that!" Marevin yelled out.

"You would not dare harm me, insect," Laxur hissed.

"In order to keep you from getting in there, it is an option," Asora pronounced.

"So it is like that, is it?" Laxur said with a frown. She was not surprised by Asora's comment.

She kind of expected something along that line. "Well, I am sorry to disappoint you then, baby sister, but I will have this power. There is nothing that you can do to stop me."

The Darkcon queen walked through the wall and vanished. Hyea, Smika, Polea, and Dari also vanished into the wall.

The Utopians were shocked. Lady T'ula went up to the wall and found it to be solid.

"What are we going to do?" the elf lady asked, worried.

"Break down the wall!" Aga yelled out.

"I imagine the walls are several centimeters thick in order to support such a large construction," Jeia pointed out.

"What do you suggest?" the Puro asked.

"These symbols? Did anyone see which ones Laxur tapped?" Asora asked as she moved toward the wall and observed the symbols.

"I managed to capture a few pictures on my camera," Countess

Marien said as she pulled out her camera. "We can look at these later."

It was a small black brick-like object. She opened it up and a screen came to life, showing an image of Queen Laxur pointing to seven specific symbols. Princess Asora took the camera in one hand, and with the other, she tapped the same symbols. All of a sudden, the wall felt empty, and her arm fell in. Asora walked through and vanished. T'ula, Jeia, Madimoy, and the Huusaud troops ran in. Countess Marien, Puro Aga, and the rest of the Utopians and humans remained outside.

Queen Laxur and her privy council were walking down a long, dark corridor. Hyea shrank and was glowing brightly so they could see. The halls were not exactly tight; in fact, there was almost a hundred meters between the walls, and the ceiling seemed to be a kilometer high.

"Truly a worthy home for a goddess," Laxur said with confidence.

She looked at the slab to find the symbol that would point her to the powers of Z'yon. The stone slab began to glow. Laxur turned one direction and the glow dimmed. When she turned another way, its glow brightened. She assumed that if the glow stayed bright, they were on the right path.

"Come, everyone. We are to go this way." more than anything. Polea was trying to conjure a spell to see if she could get them to the center of the fortress.

"Any luck, princess?" Dari asked.

"Not yet," Polea replied.

Smika was looking deep into the dark like a sentinel.

"What is it?" Hyea asked him.

"We are being followed," Smika responded.

"I know. They have been on our trail for the last three days. We just happen to be faster," Laxur added in. "But fortunately, I think that we are very close to the center, according to this symbol."

"So how much farther is it, my queen?" Polea asked.

"On the other side of this wall," Laxur said, pointing to a massive black-coated wall with no entry point. "I just need to figure out how to get in."

"Can we tunnel through the wall?" Smika asked.

"It may be possible," Hyea thought out loud.

"My powers have become limited. Polea, do you think that you can do it?" Laxur asked.

"I can do it. It will take me a few hours, though," Polea said. The blond lady whispered a spell that allowed her to remove rock as if it were whipped cream, and light from her hands cleared the bricks and rocks from her path.

"Maybe you should go into construction and demolition," Laxur commented as she watched Princess Asora's golden armor was glowing so she and the thirteen others could see.

"Any ideas where they went?" Jeia asked.

"That way," Marevin said.

He pointed to a particular direction after he noticed a set of tracks in the Princess Asora made two balls of light appear in her hands. She sent them to find the walls, and she sent a third to find the ceiling. All three balls disappeared.

"Well, that was interesting," Asora said in a wonder.

"This place has to be miles in all directions," T'ula thought out loud.

"I think you are right," Asora responded. "Let us go and follow Marevin."

Days passed and Laxur was getting frustrated. Her powers were weak, and she wanted this Polea work. She was very thankful that she had Polea. The queen intended to reward the blonde greatly with whatever her heart desired. She owed Polea that much.

Two hours later, Polea reached the other end of the wall, and what she saw was incredible. This room was very brightly lit. It was huge—Polea could not even see the other side of the room or its center. Laxur, Hyea, Dari, and Smika followed directly behind Polea.

"Where is the light coming from?" Hyea asked.

"From the center," Dari added.

"And that is where we are going," Laxur said, and she started walking toward the source of the light.

The other four walked forward to follow their aueen. Laxur could feel the great power of the Maker herself. It was intense, and she wanted more and more. The feeling was indescribable, and it felt better and better the closer she got to it.

After another three hours, the five Darkcons saw the center of the room. At the center, they saw a great table of gold, jade, and diamond. A big blue glowing crystal-like object floated above the table. That was the source of the light and power that Laxur was feeling.

The queen's eyes widened, and her breathing increased. She licked her lips in satisfaction. She had finally made it.

A bolt of lightning hit Dari square in her back, and she went down, screaming in pain. The Darkcons turned around to see Princess Asora with five daemons, one golden, as well as T'ula, Jeia, Marevin, and a dozen Huusaud troops.

"The next one is for you, sister. Now stop this, or so help me I will shoot you," Asora warned.

"No!" Laxur roared.

She zapped Asora with the last of her dark energy, and it temporarily blinded the Utopians. Then she took off, running as fast as her long legs could carry her.

Asora cleared the dark mist to see her sister running faster than she had ever seen anyone move.

The golden daemon grew wings and flew after her, and Asora followed.

"Rowaton, do what you must to stop her!" Asora ordered to Rowaton in his daemon form.

"Yes, Princess," Rowaton acknowledged.

Asora and Rowaton were having a hard time catching up to Laxur. The queen was known for many things, and being one of the fastest known runners was one of them.

"Great Maker, she is fast," Asora commented to herself. Asora gave herself a burst of speed in the air, and she tackled her sister just before she could get to the table.

The two sisters were fighting each other tooth and nail.

"Get off of me, you bitch!" Laxur roared in anger and exhaustion.

Asora responded by punching Laxur in her face. The fact that the princess had armor on made it more difficult for Laxur to withstand Asora's forceful blows. The queen stopped moving to recover from the painful blow. Asora got off Laxur, confident in her victory. She looked around and saw Rowaton coming toward her. Then a powerful blow to the back of Asora's head sent her to the floor.

Queen Laxur was standing back up, and she used all her strength to hit her sister. Asora was on the ground and pulled Laxur to the ground with her. Laxur was lying on top of Asora, and she used her weight to exhaust Asora.

"You are fortunate that you are my sister, and I love you very dearly. I will remember this, and I will remember that you are my sister as I transcend into godhood," Laxur pronounced.

She got off the Utopian Princess and walked to the base of the giant table toward the crystal. Her hunger for power was growing as she moved closer to it.

On top of the high steps, Queen Laxur found a vast table of gold, silver, jade, and obsidian stone. The crystal spun slowly around on an axis. It was small enough to fit into both of Laxur's palms. She did, however, notice that the crystal seemed to only be half there, as if half of it were missing.

Laxur hopped onto the table and walked to the crystal. Princess Asora got back up and saw Laxur heading toward the object.

"No" was all Asora could muster herself to say.

Queen Laxur touched the crystal, and something happened. A massive pulse of energy surged into the Queen's body. Laxur screamed in agony as an unfathomable amount of power entered her and began to change her. Queen Laxur's body began to grow—every part of her. Her hair became longer and thicker, her muscles expanded and became more pronounced, her black wings unfurled themselves, her breasts grew bigger, and her legs became longer. As she grew, her dress was torn, leaving only a tight medium-size black corset to keep her somewhat decent. After twenty agonizing seconds, Queen Laxur let go of the crystal, and she found that her form and powers had changed greatly.

Princess Asora and Rowaton were in shock from what they saw. The queen now stood four meters tall and had a heavier muscle build and more curves than ever before.

"Oh yes! This is power! This is greatness. It is everything that I have imagined." Laxur moaned in pleasure as her new powers coursed through her reformed body. Her voice was now deeper and godlike. She looked down at Asora and Rowaton. "Oh yes, you two."

"What happened to you, sister?" Asora asked, worried.

"I have become the most powerful being in the universe," Laxur boomed. "And in a few minutes, I will become as powerful as the Maker and Architect."

Those words haunted Asora and Rowaton.

"So now you have become a bigger headache than before!" T'ula yelled out as she caught up to Asora.

"You will be on your knees praying to me soon, elf," Laxur boomed again.

"I think not, witch," the elf lady fired back.

Then she shot a bolt of purple energy at Laxur. It impacted her stomach and did nothing. Laxur laughed menacingly at T'ula, as the elf fired again and again. She stopped when she realized it was not doing anything.

"I should thank you, elf. I absorbed every pulse of energy you shot at me, and I learned all your spells. I must say, you are quite advanced. But now, all your skills are mine," Laxur said.

Then the massive queen blasted T'ula, Asora, and Rowaton with the same spell that T'ula tried to attack Laxur with. She returned it to them tenfold, blowing them down the steps. Laxur's evil laugh echoed throughout the giant room.

Gunshots fired and peppered Laxur's body. She could feel every bullet strike her, but they caused her no pain, for none of the bullets were able to pierce her elegant skin. The Huusaud were firing a multitude of arms and magical attack spells. They were stunned by the negligible effect they were having on the oversized half-naked Darkcon beauty.

"Nice try, boys and girls. But all your might amounts to nothing." Laxur proclaimed.

She zapped them all with powerful lightning bolts. She killed the thirteen Huusaud troops in one blow. The queen laughed at the sight.

Rowaton roared, and a wall of flames enveloped Laxur. The enchanted flame was enough to hurt the mighty Darkcon woman, but it also angered her. She fought her way through the wall of fire and slammed her fist into the smaller daemon's head, knocking him out.

Asora powered all seven of her coins and readied herself to block her deranged sister.

"My princess, the queen's lackeys are coming," T'ula said as she saw Polea, Smika, Hyea, and Dari coming toward them.

"Can you handle them, T'ula?" Asora asked.

"They are pathetic to me. It is Laxur I am worried about. So yes, I can take them," T'ula responded, and she charged at the four approaching Darkcons, saber in hand.

T'ula ran right for Dari and kicked her in the stomach. The force knocked the oversized fallen angel onto her backside, and then the elf launched herself at Hyea. The fairy was human-sized but not strong enough to withstand T'ula's saber strike. The elf cut into Hyea's skin, drawing blood. In anger, Smika threw rocks at T'ula, but the elf lady, ever graceful, caught the rocks and tossed them right back at Smika. The boy backed off, badly hurt and unable to fight back. Hyea dropped to her knees and surrendered to T'ula. Only Polea was left.

"You were never a match for me in anything, Polea. What makes you think that this time will be different?" T'ula boasted.

"I have a few new tricks up my sleeves," Polea said. She made a sword of enchanted jade appear in her hand; it had depictions of bears and a forest. The nearsighted blonde charged at the lady elf with great energy; however, T'ula, being much stronger than Polea, had the upper hand in this contest.

Princess Asora faced down Queen Laxur. She was ready to defend herself against the massive woman.

"So what do you think of me now, baby sister?" Laxur asked confidently.

"I think you are a mess. You need to stop this," Asora replied.

Laxur laughed, and it echoed deeply. "Oh, baby sister. You could never understand what it is like to have this power. It is the most incredible thing, the most incredible feeling." Laxur waved her hands over every curve of her enhanced form.

"You are right. I never will," Asora said sadly.

"I am, however, willing to share with you this ultimate power. Together we can rule the universe as loving sisters. We can make all the wrongs right and make things the way we see fit," Laxur promised evilly.

"This is not how to do it," Asora retorted.

"Fine, have it your way," Laxur replied.

The big queen then surprised Asora by grabbing hold of her, raising the Princess to her chest, and hugging the smaller girl hard. Laxur was squeezing Asora deep into her torso and starting to drown her in her flesh. Asora could not breathe as her sister increased her grip. Asora's face was trapped in between Laxur's enormous breasts. The Princess did the only thing that she could think of. She powered up her seven coins, and in an incredible burst of energy, the mad queen released her grip on the Princess. Asora was dropped to the floor, gasping for air. Her sister was laughing evilly.

"What are you so happy about?" Asora coughed.

"You did exactly what I wanted you to do," Laxur chuckled.

Asora realized what Laxur meant.

"By using all seven coins to break my grip, you gave me the power that they and you possessed.

I have your mastery of these powers now. Except with me, it is many times stronger." Laxur laughed confidently.

Asora, realizing that all her advantages were gone, knew that she was beaten. Laxur sent a pulsing wave of fire and wind directly at Asora. The heat from the flame was so intense that it began to melt her golden armor. Then wind blew Asora across the floor as if she were in a hurricane.

"That ought to hold you for a little while" —the massive queen turned to the crystal—"while I obtain the rest of this great power."

Laxur walked back up the steps toward the crystal of Z'yon. Asora was in too much pain to get back up. Then Marevin came in and jumped right in front of Laxur with a katana in one hand and a pistol in the other.

"Oh? And what do you think that you are doing, little man?" Laxur chuckled.

She always thought that Marevin was cute, especially when he tried to impress her baby sister.

"What does it look like?" Marevin retorted.

"It looks like you are making a fool of yourself, trying to impress my little sister," Laxur said with a grin.

"Wrong. This!" Marevin shot Laxur in the head with a bullet made of uranium.

It blew Laxur off her feet and down the steps. The super queen was cursing in pain and about to get back up, so Marevin kicked Laxur back down and jumped on her back.

"Now stay down, you bitch. I have got a lot more uranium bullets with your name on them. That last one may not have gone into your brain, but the next one will go into your chest. I do not care how big your breasts are. They cannot stop a U-two thirty-four projectile."

"Is that so, you miserable pest?" Laxur fumed.

Marevin put his foot on the back of Laxur's head and pointed his gun at her neck.

"If I have to kill you to save the universe, then so be it," Marevin declared.

"Asora would never forgive you," Laxur said forcefully.

"I will understand," Asora said as she slowly walked up to them.

In a wave of wind and water, Marevin was forced off Laxur's back and into Asora's arms. They were both knocked down by the impact. As Laxur got back up, another blow hit her, this time into her stomach, with a force strong enough to knock her onto her butt. Lady T'ula was the one that attacked the queen this time.

"Do what Lord Marevin said and stay down!" T'ula said forcefully.

"You have been nothing but a pain in my backside for years, T'ula," Laxur growled.

"Funny, because your backside is the largest that I have ever seen. I figured that it would be used to it," T'ula said with a grin.

Laxur was offended by T'ula's offhanded comment; she must have learned that from Jeia. Then with one massive kick, Laxur sent T'ula flying backward and into the steps, breaking her back. T'ula cried out in pain. Asora and Marevin crawled up to her to help. Asora used a healing spell to mend T'ula's spine, and she stopped screaming.

Laxur, however, had made it back up to the table and was just about to grab the crystal, when the room began to shake violently.

"What the. . ." Laxur demanded. She turned around to see Asora using her rock coin to cause a powerful quake. She destroyed the table, and Laxur's legs and waist were trapped in solid rock. "You cannot stop me. I am a force of the universe now. There is nothing that can stop me!"

With all her strength, Laxur broke free of her rocky restraints and saw the table and the crystal hovering in the air.

Asora's neck was restrained by Polea's golden whip. The blonde was bloodied and dirty, and her dress was torn from her fight with T'ula.

"You are going to pay for that," Polea hissed. "Go, my queen!"

T'ula fired off multiple bolts of magical lights that bounced off the floating objects. She and Marevin were trying to destroy the crystal. Asora was choking and trying to fight Polea.

Laxur jumped up into the floating debris field, hopping on and off large fragments, fighting her way to the crystal. She was hit many times by T'ula and Marevin. Laxur flashed a bright light long enough for her to grab hold of the crystal, and she had an idea. She broke it into three small pieces and then ate them.

Laxur landed in a corner away from the others, and she relaxed. As she swallowed the three pieces, and they slid down her throat and settled in her belly, she could feel the raw divine power pulse through her. She had never felt this kind of power before. It felt so good, not painful like last time. It was better than sex. The queen breathed heavily as the power inside her grew. It was out of control, but she did not care. She wanted it; she wanted limitless power, and she was willing to endure anything to get it.

"Where is the crystal?" Asora yelled out.

Laxur stood up, laughing evilly. She felt the power growing and changing her. "It is where it belongs," Laxur said as she moved her hands over her belly. "It is inside of me now."

"No! What have you done?" T'ula roared.

"I am now as the Great Maker is. You will all bow down and worship me as you do her," Laxur boomed.

The queen's belly began to glow white as the power surged inside her. Suddenly, Laxur's belly glowed so bright it was blinding, and Laxur fell to the floor in such ecstasy that she lost control of herself for a moment.

"Oh yes! Yes! Yes! Yes!" Laxur moaned in a completely pleasured state. "The power inside me. It is growing!" Her breathing increased, and she began to change again; she was growing even more. "And I am growing!"

The dark queen expanded rapidly in all directions. She was moaning, and her power could be felt by all in the room. Her stomach was glowing brightly.

"We better get out of here!" T'ula warned Asora.

"Yeah, I think that you are right," Asora responded, stepping back as she watched her sister get bigger.

In an hour, Queen Laxur's body filled the giant room. Her head hit the ceiling that was so far up. Laxur was now tens of times larger than she had ever been. Her wings were cramped in the cavernous room. Her moaning increased and grew more intense. The room had been abandoned.

"More, more, give me all. I want it all," Laxur moaned to herself. In response, her glowing belly brightened even more. The queen felt the sudden surge of even greater power. "Oh yes!"

Outside, the ground shook violently, and the fortress looked as if it were going to explode. Two massive black wings seemed to sprout out from the middle of the giant building. The wings towered kilometers into the sky, blocking out the sun. Then the gigantic Laxur sat up and rose from the fortress, covered by a purple glow. She laughed evilly, and her deep and powerful voice echoed across the whole of Z'yon.

The gigantic goddess queen looked down with arrogance and darkness.

"Let us balance the sides in my favor now!" Laxur boomed, and she raised her hand. From her fingertips, dark lightning erupted and surged into her troops.

The Darkcons grew big. They all became massively muscled, magically supercharged, and three meters tall.

The poor humans and Utopians were no match for the supersized Darkcon warriors. Utopian magic was absorbed by the Darkcons, and human bullets bounced off their skin and muscles.

Queen Laxur, still growing, was enjoying the show that her forces were giving. She noticed all the dead Darkcons, and this did not sit well with her. Laxur knew that she now had the power to restore life. A surge of black energy erupted from her other hand, and the dead Darkcons returned to life.

"Now, my children, destroy all who oppose me!" Laxur's order boomed all over.

The giant resurrected Darkcons slew the humans and Utopians that were at arm's length. The humans used grenades and bombs to slow the insane Darkcon warriors, and the Utopian troops used all their magical powers to stop them.

Queen Laxur laughed as she watched the "entertainment" below. She continued to grow even larger, and her power grew more intense as new skills and magic were added to her arsenal. The glowing continued around her, lifting her off the ground and protecting the beings below from her growing body.

A tiny fireball hit her in her cheek. She barely noticed it, but it was enough to draw her attention. She turned to see Princess Asora, Rowaton, T'ula, and Sarea. All four were giants themselves, but they were as big as they could get, which was puny compared to the queen. They were about as big as her nose.

"So you have decided to enjoy the show too?" Laxur chuckled.

"Stop this!" Asora yelled.

"I cannot. I am a goddess, and there is no such thing as limits to me. I am invincible!" Laxur thundered.

"Stop growing and fight fair!" Sarea roared.

Laxur laughed at the woman's words. "You simple, tiny fools. Even if I wanted to stop growing, I cannot. The power inside me is changing me into the new Maker. And the best part is, I do not want it to stop. I want more." Laxur bellowed.

"You are insane," Asora cried out.

"Maybe, but you are in no position to stop me," Laxur boomed.

"We will see about that," T'ula threatened. She jumped off Rowaton's back to Laxur's expanding face. She rammed a tall spear into her eye. Unfortunately for T'ula, it did not have the desired effect. Laxur laughed and swatted the tiny T'ula away. Sarea, on Rowaton's back, swooped down and the magical human woman grabbed T'ula. She pulled the elf up behind her on Rowaton's back.

Laxur got a rather twisted idea for these four. She spat out a fireball from her mouth like spit. They were only hundreds of meters away from Laxur's face, but from her perspective, they seemed mere centimeters. The ball hit them hard, and the four fell and crashed onto Laxur's large chest.

The four Utopians recovered and noticed that something was not quite right. "What happened?" Sarea asked.

"Where are we?" T'ula looked around and felt the ground below them.

"Oh, you have got to be kidding me," Asora blurted out.

"What is it?" Sarea asked, almost afraid to hear the answer.

"We are on Laxur's skin," T'ula answered for Asora as she looked up. They looked up to see the still growing Laxur looking out onto the world.

Polea, Dari, Hyea, and Smika appeared, ready to fight.

"Our great queen has asked us to subdue you, intruders," Polea decreed.

"You people have lost your minds. It is true what they say," T'ula stated.

"And that is?" Smika asked mockingly.

"Absolute power corrupts absolutely," T'ula said to the young man.

"That is a stupid saying, elf witch," Smika retorted.

"But it is a true saying." T'ula pointed up to Laxur. "That is proof."

"You are full of it, elf," Dari roared, and she blasted T'ula with a powerful energy bolt. It was far stronger than Dari's normal attack.

"That felt different," T'ula said, getting back up.

"They must be enchanted with Laxur's new power," Asora postulated.

"And you would be right about that, Princess," Polea said. Then the giant blonde shot electricity from her jade sword at Asora, but Asora's sword absorbed Polea's attack.

However, the amount of energy from Polea was unlike anything that she had ever withstood. Hyea then attacked Asora with powerful magic. Fortunately for Asora, her golden armor was able to withstand her attacks, though barely.

A low rumble was felt.

"What was that?" Sarea asked, worried.

The floor below them shook as the power inside Laxur's still-growing body suddenly accelerated, causing Laxur to grow faster, and her moans rumbled in the chests of all that were on her flesh.

Sarea slammed her whole body into Dari. T'ula slashed Smika with powerful slaps. Rowaton opened fire on Hyea. Asora and Polea were in a vicious fistfight and sword battle.

"You will join us, Asora," Polea whispered in a crazed-like state.

"I do not want this power," Asora reminded.

"Do not lie. I can see it in your eyes. You too lust for this great power. You also want to be a goddess. If you stop this and accept Laxur, you will be a goddess too," Polea said.

"My personal life is of no concern of yours. Why do you even care? I would have thought that you would want this. Why would you want to share with me?" Asora asked, struggling.

"We are only three of a kind. Our kind should rule the universe. Who better? Besides, I happen to love you very dearly, with all my heart. But I hate that damned thing on your head," Polea admitted.

She moved uncomfortably close to Asora. Polea was only centimeters from Asora's face, staring directly into her eyes. Polea kissed Asora on the lips to show her fellow Princess her affection for her. This shocked and disturbed Asora. Polea could be trying to influence her, or she could be sincere; Asora did not know.

Asora, in embarrassment, forced herself away from Polea.

"Oh no, you do not. I am not like that. I prefer the opposite sex to the same," Asora stated.

"Oh, what is wrong, little princess? Cannot stand a little affection? Even from your own twin sister? Am I too uncomfortable for you? I cannot help but show my affection to people I really like or love," Polea said rather sultry.

"I do not care about your romances. I am just not comfortable. And besides, you and I are foes!" Asora yelled, and she tried to jump into the air. Unfortunately, Laxur moved ever so slightly, causing the flesh on her chest to ripple. Asora was knocked back down at Polea's feet. The blonde was laughing at the embarrassed Utopian princess.

"Come back for more, my dear?" Polea chuckled. Asora growled at Polea.

"She needs some more dark love, Polea," Laxur said as she appeared in a puff of purple smoke.

"Okay, this is odd," Sarea commented when she saw the queen.

"How is this odd? You are fighting on my body. If anything, this is odd for me." Laxur thought for a moment. "But then again, having all of you moving around on my breast is rather enjoyable."

"You are very sick," T'ula commented.

"You should try it, elf. You and my sister will enjoy it too," Laxur said sleazily.

Wanting to make her uncomfortable, she moved up to T'ula in the same manner that Polea had done with Asora. She looked T'ula up and down.

Meanwhile, Rowaton and Sarea were fighting Dari, Hyea, and Smika. The dragon had the upper hand against Dari, the massive fallen angel. Rowaton had harder skin and scales, and Dari's weapons could not punch through. Sarea had a tag team problem, so she had to be quick. Hyea kept shrinking and growing, which made battling the fairy difficult. Sarea did not want to hurt Smika; he was young and naive and probably under a spell, but this young man was making things difficult with his spells and magical attacks. He was formidable in a magical battle. Sarea, for once, had underestimated someone. Sarea had been more concerned about Hyea, but it turned out it was Smika that she needed to focus on. Smika made a glowing purple sword and charged at Sarea. His skill was surprising; it was the level of a master. That takes years, and this kid was outperforming her in swordsmanship. Polea had given him the ability to learn anything quickly.

Princess Asora and the now Princess Polea were clashing with their swords: Asora and her golden dragon against Polea and her jade bear.

Laxur and T'ula watched their friends fight each other. T'ula was worried greatly, but Laxur was enjoying the show. The queen walked around her elven counterpart very closely, almost sexually.

"Polea was right. You look just like me in every way: your curves, dimensions, shape, body, beauty, powers. You and I are virtually identical in every manner except your face. I like that," Laxur whispered into T'ula's ear. Then Laxur kissed T'ula's neck to seduce her.

"But your body is no longer equal to mine now, is it? Is it, cousin?" Laxur rounded T'ula and was face-to-face with her. T'ula was breathing heavily; she was nervous about what this mad woman planned to do to her. Laxur's evil smile made T'ula panic. Laxur was now skin-to-skin with her. "But I do need you for a test. I do not want to hurt Polea or Asora, but you, as much as I find you attractive, are expendable. Sorry, cousin, or should I say, twin sister. Nothing personal."

Queen Laxur grabbed T'ula by her face and kissed her hard. Laxur was doing an experiment and having fun at the same time. The queen was in fact injecting tiny pieces of herself into T'ula.

The elf woman shook violently from the struggle. Asora managed to get away from Polea to see the horror that Laxur was doing to T'ula. The Utopian princess did not understand what Laxur was doing, but T'ula looked as if she was in pain.

Asora flew straight at Laxur. T'ula felt an unimaginable surge of power course through her. She did not know why Laxur was doing this. She could feel something growing in her belly. It was the Z'yon powers that Laxur had. But why was she giving them to T'ula?

Laxur was torn away from T'ula, and the queen disappeared, laughing in a puff of purple smoke. Asora ran over to T'ula to see what happened. The elf was in serious pain and crying.

"What is happening to me?" T'ula cried.

Asora held T'ula, and she could feel the same power that Laxur had.

"Did she put her power inside you?" Asora asked, dumbfounded. "Is she mad?"

"She said something about an experiment," T'ula sobbed.

A sudden jolt of pain surged through T'ula's body, and it was causing her to change. Her body was beginning to expand, like Laxur's did. She ripped up her dress. Her hair was longer and thicker, her body was taller, her breasts were larger, and her muscles were more pronounced. T'ula, however, managed to stop growing because she had a disciplined mind. "What is this?"

"She made you into a near perfect copy of herself," Asora commented.

"So it worked. That is good," Polea said, excited.

Asora gave T'ula her cape to cover her exposed body.

"We have to get off of this giant now!" Sarea yelled.

"I agree. Rowaton, grab and hold T'ula. Sarea, hop on my back," Asora ordered.

Rowaton grasped T'ula and held her in his hands. Sarea climbed onto Asora's back and was holding on tightly. They launched, and Laxur's growing body was catching up to them quickly. Sarea looked back at Laxur, and she was stunned by the immense size of the queen. She had to be several dozen kilometers high by now, and she was sitting down in the ruins of the once great fortress. Laxur's belly was glowing as brightly as the sun. The skies were darkening because of Laxur's power and form. She was emitting a dark cloud, and it grew as she grew.

The Utopian and human warships were leaving.

"Rowaton, give me T'ula and take Sarea to my mother," Asora ordered. Asora had given Sarea a message to give to Marien only.

Asora and Rowaton traded passengers, and they again flew as fast as they could.

Laxur noticed them trying to escape. She did not want Asora and T'ula to get away. The others were immaterial. With the point of her finger, Laxur made a hole in the sky. Asora and Rowaton tried to avoid it by flying back toward Laxur, but Rowaton was hit by debris and fell toward the ground.

The last Utopian ship caught the falling dragon and his passenger. However, Asora and T'ula were not as lucky. Asora was trying to avoid the black hole in the sky. She figured that she and T'ula could take their chances with Laxur again.

The massive queen began to reach out to grab her sister when another piece of debris hit the Princess. It sent Asora and T'ula into the hole and launched them into the unknown.

Queen Laxur was disappointed, but she would worry about it later. Another pulsing surge, from deep within her, erupted. This one was the most powerful yet. It caused her to expand at a faster pace. She was now able to see blackness on the horizon. Laxur thought that she had grown to over two hundred kilometers tall. She could not be more excited. Laxur had never been so immense, and it felt so good. She wanted more, and this power seemed to be granting her wish. She did not want it to end.

The queen's head was now in space, and she could see the moons from her vantage point. The moons seemed to be getting closer to her. In minutes, the queen's body began to cover half the world of Z'yon. The raw power was sheer pleasure to Laxur as she now lay upon the planet. Her moans of pleasure echoed throughout the regional planetary system.

Laxur's body then began to completely glow white. The blinding light could be seen for light-years. Then suddenly, her body seemed to explode, sending out a wave of energy into space, telling the universe that a new divine being had been born.

Queen Laxur was light and energy now. But she wanted to be seen and worshipped. That was one of the reasons why she did this. So, she willed herself to be corporeal once more, and then back down to her near-normal size, but she was changed because she wanted to be changed. Size had so many benefits; she felt tight but good. In a blinding light, Laxur had reformed back in the wreckage of the fortress. It was starting to rebuild itself around her.

"My queen! Are you well?" Polea came up to the moaning queen.

Princess Polea noticed that Laxur had been changed. As Polea helped Laxur back up to her feet, Dari came in to cover the now-naked queen.

"Yes, Polea. I have never been so well." Laxur moaned and groaned in pleasure.

Queen Laxur was no longer two meters tall; she was now three meters. Every curve she had was larger, her muscles were more pronounced, and her hair was longer and thicker. Her wings were grander with a greater span.

The fortress finished rebuilding the grand room, where Laxur gained the great power. A massive throne formed where the giant table once stood.

"This place is reacting to my thoughts and will. I am in complete control in here." Laxur grinned at this realization.

She had Dari and Hyea cover her goddess-like body to make her more decent. The truth was she did not mind being naked; the queen found it not scandalous but flattering. She now had in her mind the perfect form; she was the perfect woman. To her minions, that seemed to be true; but to the ones that she wanted to impress, that was yet to be answered.

Queen Laxur sat upon her new supreme throne, and the comfort was so extreme that she did not want to get up.

"It is now time for my word to be the law of the universe. Have my forces march forth in every direction and conquer the whole of creation for me," Laxur ordered. The three women before her bowed and left.

The power within her was still growing and changing her. She loved it, yet Laxur did not want to be alone. She wanted to share it with someone. These four close companions would do nicely.

Chapter Fifty-One

The Other Laxur's

The divine Queen Laxur sat upon her now vast and dark throne. Z'yon was slowly transforming into her ideal world. She was its newest master. The power coming from her belly and surging throughout her body gave her more abilities than she knew what to do with. Even the act of just sitting upon her throne gave her pleasure that equaled sexual satisfaction. It just would not stop, but then again, she did not want it to stop. She wanted to learn what new powers she now possessed.

One ability was obvious. She could things to obey her. The inanimate objects around her whereas devoted to her as her four closest companions. The great ancient fortress was back to being a grand palace for just herself. Another power was that Z'yon itself was hers. It desired her as much as she desired it.

To Polea, Dari, Smika, and Hyea. Their queen looked to be enjoying herself. She was glowing still and breathing heavily but pleased. Energy then built up around the throne room and surged to the queen. Laxur felt more pleasure as she was being filled with more.

"Never stop this!" Laxur command din a deep booming voice. "I wish for this to never stop."

The four companions of the queen could feel her pleasure and lust. To Polea it was satisfaction incarnate. For Dari it was a mission completed. For Hyea she was proud to be in the presence of a goddess. Smika's love for Laxur was now absolute and he would do anything to just make her smile for him.

"You must really enjoy this," Polea said. "Anyone who gained that much power do not normally survive it."

Laxur chuckled, "True, but I am no ordinary woman." Laxur slowly stood up. "I was destined for this. I can feel my new powers speaking to me."

"It is conscious?" Hyea asked.

"Oh yes," Laxur said. "And Z'yon as waited for me. I am its chosen one. The one it has loved and wishes to unite the universe to it. Through me."

"Incredible," Smika said.

"But first I need time to master all of these new powers and abilities that I am growing now," Laxur said. "I require loneliness to make this work."

"We will keep you safe," Dari said.

"For when I re-emerge. Your goddess queen will be ready to fulfill her divine mission," Laxur proclaimed.

Dari, Smika, Polea, and Hyea all bowed to Laxur and left the throne room. They locked the doors to ensure that she would not be disturbed.

Laxur looked around and could hardly believe that one hour earlier she filled these cities sized room up with her own form. That growth was so good that she honestly wanted to remain large. Oh, it was so good, it was honestly better then sex or any mortal pleasure that she was used to. Laxur liked thinking of herself as a goddess now.

She commanded a full body mirror into existence. She wanted to see with her own eyes what she looked like now. What looked back at her made her feel perfect. She was taller, bustier, fuller, just all around bigger and better. A full meter taller and with hair as black as space itself and so full that she could darken everything around her. Her wings came out and were several times larger than she was.

An angel's wings showed and talked so much about them. The color told you what type they were. In Laxur's case she was a fallen angel because they all had black feathery wings. The size of an angel's wings showed one how powerful they were. The larger the more powerful. Laxur's wings were now the largest that had ever graced an angel of any kind. Her wings were larger than her father's. Angel wings were also a sign of beauty for angels of both genders. Male angels had strong and rigid and colorful wings. Female angels had flexible and intricate designs in their wings.

Laxur continued to look at herself in the mirror. She loved what she saw. Every single bit of her.

"Feminine perfection," Laxur said to herself.

She took off the dress she had on so she could view her name body in all its glory. It only got better for her as she saw only a perfect woman. She was the curviest of beautiful women. The most powerful being in the Realm. She was only going to grow stronger and become the Realm's one and only master.

She wondered if she could shape herself into an even more attractive form. Or if she could create new forms for herself. Laxur transformed herself into her mermaid form. Her mermaid form was a scylla type, which meant that she had tentacles instead of a fin. Laxur preferred tentacles and had as many as twelve. But she wanted to look more dangerous, but at the same time attractive.

That was how the Dorien Purple Octopus hunted. They made themselves look inviting and attractive. Only to insnare its prey in its dozens of tentacles. These little octopuses tended to grow a lot if they were in a food rich area. Laxur kept one as a pet and it grew as big, she was. This was how she gained her mermaid form. The octopus was used in a spell that Laxur needed. It gave itself to her as this allowed Laxur to transform into a tiny leviathan of attractiveness and danger.

Laxur's aquatic form then grew many more times as many tentacles as she was normally used to. She ended up with a hundred. Her normal legs were underneath all the wiggling appendages. The huge number of tentacles did make her heavier, but she could handle it as her muscles became more inflated to support her new mass.

She then noticed that the glow in her belly was gone. But the power remained. This meant that Laxur had fully digested the crystal shards. That meant that the power was not permanently hers and could never be taken. Laxur could only chuckle in delight and amusement as she was now invincible. Dozens of her tentacles moved all over her body to make her feel good. Her bellows covers by several of them. Then she commanded her tentacles to become as hard as titanium but in the shape of an elegant purple dress. This was not a new ability; she was able to do this before. But not with this many tentacles.

"I have the perfect human form, the perfect angel form, and the perfect mermaid form," Laxur said to herself. "What form should I make next?" She thought for a moment. "Fairy, demoness, beast, vampire, werewolf, elf, or something more?" She flexed to show herself off. "Maybe a giantess form. I have two kinds I can become. Myself just bigger, or a monster form. Oh yes."

As Queen Laxur continued to admire herself in the full body mirror, she noticed something moving. She did not sense it and looked to see what it was. Whatever it was, it could only be seen in the mirror, and in the shadows.

"Who is there?" Laxur demanded.

There was no answer. Again, she could not feel or sense anyone else in the room with her. Laxur then turned back to the mirror to continue to examine herself. But this time she could not shake the feeling that she was being observed. How would that even be possible? Her powers are beyond the peak of what was possible. She felt no one around her, she was alone. Her empathic abilities sensed no one. But still the feeling remained.

There it was again, movement in the shadows. Laxur quickly turned around and created light from her body. She shined like a bright young star. Still nothing in the shadows that burned away. There was no one around.

"Am I seeing things?" Laxur asked herself.

She turned the light of her body off, and the room returned to normal. She turned back to the mirror to examine herself. She was going to ignore the feeling. If she was being watched, then she will give them a show. After all it was now dangerous to observe the queen in her glory now. Her body was so seductive that it could cast a spell upon any who gazed upon her. So, she would figure out who was spying on her eventually.

Laxur turned around and her image in the mirror did not move. The divine queen noticed that her reflection was not following her. She knew that this was not an enchanted mirror.

"What is this?" Laxur demanded.

The image of Laxur in the mirror cracked a cruel grin, "What do you believe I am?"

"You can speak?" Laxur asked in amazement.

"So can you," the mirror Laxur laughed. "But to be honest I am the true one."

"You are a fool," Laxur said. "I am the god queen here!"

Mirror Laxur laughed, "Are you sure about that?"

The mirror Laxur sounded exactly like the queen. But her laughter was starting to get on the queen's nerves. She recognized that kind of laughter. The same kind of mockery laughter she was forced to endure when she was little. The kind that others poked fun at her. Making her feel like a worthless mess. Rage boiled over within her and Laxur punched the mirror to make the reflection stop.

The mirror shattered into many pieces onto the floor. All the mirror shards had a piece of Laxur within them. The queen for a moment looked down to see the many shards looking back at her. Laxur breathed heavily as she tried to regain her wits.

Suddenly she felt others in her presence suddenly. A great many others. These were familiar to her. The mirror shards then started to move and grow. Laxur watched as the dozens of fragments transformed themselves into different versions of herself. She counted at least thirteen different beings whom all bore a perfect resemblance to the queen.

The mermaid form of Laxur was the first to develop fully. She stretched and flexed. She looked around and saw the queen. She merely smirked at the amazed queen.

"So, do I fit your ideal form of sexual incising configuration?" The mermaid Laxur asked in a sultry voice.

"Who are you?" Laxur demanded.

"Who do I look like?" Mermaid Laxur asked in the same sexy voice.

Another shard finished morphing into a form that Laxur had never used of seen before. This one looked like a woman with obsidian skin and purple glowing veins. Purple glowing eyes and fangs for teeth.

No Laxur recognized this form from her childhood. This was an alien form she thought up for a costume once. She was inspired by an old movie that Jeia and Asora watched with her. An old science fiction horror tale of a deadly alien virus that mutated people into radioactive monsters like this. This was what Laxur thought she would look like as an alien mutant.

Alien Laxur looked at the queen but had no malice in her face. If that was what she was seeing? It merely looked at Laxur inquisitively.

"What are you supposed to be?" Laxur demanded.

"The part of you that you do not understand," Alien Laxur answered.

Mermaid Laxur laughed, "She does not know herself well enough as it is!"

A third shard then formed into a full human version of Laxur. Equal in height and shape but no powers or wings as far as the queen could tell.

"I know you all too well," Laxur said. "Asaria."

The human woman looked up at Laxur with a look of sadness. "And I know you all too well too."

"Go back into the shadows where you belong," Laxur commanded.

"No," Asaria said. "You do not command me."

Laxur created a fireball in her hand. "You want to bet on that?"

Mermaid Laxur put the fireball out with a splash of water. "Now, now. Play nice with your other selves."

Alien Laxur then growled like an angry dog at Laxur herself. She took a defensive stance next to Asaria.

"Leave her be," Alien Laxur snarled.

A fourth shard of the mirror had then formed into a pure angel form of Laxur. This one with one white wing, and one black wing. She was taller than the others and Laxur could feel power from this one. She was very beautiful, and radiated power.

"I take it that you are Angel Laxur?" Laxur asked.

"I am Angel Asaria," she said looking sadly at the human. "I am her. The one that loves her and you."

Mermaid Laxur laughed again. "Oh, I missed you. But where is your more fun half?"

A fifth shard had just finished forming. This one was a sexy demonic horror version of the queen. She sported large fleshy wings and a scaly snake like tail. Her fingers were human like, but her feet were more like claws of a bird. Her skin was orangish red, and her eyes burned red.

"I live once more," Demon Laxur said with a satisfied groan.

"Oh, I missed you," Mermaid Laxur laughed.

Demon Laxur looked at that queen. She smiled evilly and sashayed towards Laxur. She seemed to examine the queen.

"So, you actually did it?" Demon Laxur asked with a sleazy tone.

Laxur did nothing as she allowed the demonic version of herself to look at her. Five out of the thirteen shards had finished.

The sixth shard however was different. A version of Laxur that appeared more like flower or a tree. A very plant like version of her with red and pink hair. Her eyes were as green as Laxur's herself. From her legs came a carpet of grass and flowers.

"Oh please, the flower girl?" Demon Laxur complained.

"I am nature and the nature of us," Nature Laxur stated.

"Oh please," Mermaid Laxur said annoyed. "You are the most annoying of us."

"I like her," Asaria said.

The seventh shard had finished transforming into centaur version of Laxur. All black and heavily muscular. She looked like a warrior ready for battle.

Alien Laxur hissed at Centaur Laxur. The larger centaur version jumped onto her back legs and let down a powerful charge.

"Out of my way you foul monster!" Centaur Laxur spoke.

"You die first," Alien Laxur snarled.

"Oh, what fun. A fight," Demon Laxur laughed.

Laxur then noticed that the eighth shard had finished in silence. The queen approached it to see what this one became. It was dropped in a black cloak and had a ghostly feel to it. It turned to look at the queen and what Laxur saw was a pale ghost. No not a ghost a phantom, an undead being who bore all Laxur's ills.

"A phantom," Laxur said.

The others looked at the Phantom Laxur and all froze in fear. Even Demon Laxur was afraid of it. Alien Laxur backed away in caution. Angel Asaria covered and held Asaria herself.

"What ill possessed you this time?" Demon Laxur demanded.

Phantom Laxur said nothing. She merely looked around at the others. Then she looked at the queen. No emotion on her face.

Queen Laxur heard a noise from one of the remaining shards. This one was something that she did not expect. What arose from the ninth shard was a mass of disgusting flesh and horror. This Laxur reminded her of victims of a nuclear reactor meltdown. A walking cancer that suffered greatly and spread radioactive horror wherever it went.

"Twisted and cruel. This is what you made me," Mutant Laxur spoke.

"What the hell is that?" Mermaid Laxur asked.

"I am the pain," Mutant Laxur snarled. "We are fragments of that." She pointed to the queen. "And more to come."

"You seem to know this? How?" Laxur asked.

Mutant Laxur then pointed to the tenth shard that had just finished forming. This Laxur was made completely of metal. It reminded Laxur or a cyber. A race of machines that the Consortium used during the Great War centuries ago. It was cobalt blue and silver. Its eyes glowed red, and the armored wiring also glowed red.

"One piece of you that only knows logic," Machine Laxur explained.

The Other Laxur's

"I figured that one out," Laxur said.

Machine Laxur looked around uncaring about the others. Mermaid Laxur's tentacles felt the machine to see what she could understand of it.

"To think we are all a part of your broken psyche," Mermaid Laxur said.

"And what do you represent?" Asaria asked. "My cruelty?"

"Actually, I am the seductive one," Mermaid Laxur said as she showed off her body.

"Correct," Machine Laxur said.

The eleventh shard then transformed into someone that Laxur had never seen before but felt like she knew all too well. This woman had the look and feel of a goddess. The very same thing that Laxur herself was trying to emulate. This one looked around with a look of concern.

"What the hell is this?" She demanded.

"Who are you?" Angel Asaria asked.

"A goddess from long ago," the goddess said. "I was the original owner of this power that now flows through you." She looked at Laxur.

"I know enough about you," Laxur said. "This is only half of you. But all your power and powers of others."

"She put the power on Z'yon," Asaria said.

"I did," the goddess said. "And you have one hell of a fragmented mind." The goddess then looked at the twelfth mirror shard. "Here comes another one."

This shard had transformed into a seemingly perfect copy of the queen. However, upon closer inspection revealed this one had light and heavy scars. She also was the only one other then Asaria and Angel Asaria that was dressed. But she reminded Laxur or a pirate captain. The rogue or rebellious part of the queen. The one who wished to defy all.

"Well, this is quite something," Pirate Laxur said. "Which one of you is the fool who made us all up?"

Machine Laxur pointed to the queen. Pirate Laxur then made her way to the queen. She looked ready to fight.

"Back away your filthy pirate," Laxur commanded.

Pirate Laxur burst into laughter. "You the hell do you think you are to give me orders?"

"I am queen, and I am a goddess. I am the lord and master of all of you!" Laxur proclaimed forcefully.

Pirate Laxur laughed again. "We are you."

"I am the goddess. Who's powers you have consumed and are using," the goddess corrected.

"I am the goddess now. You re all fragments that make up me!" The queen snarled.

"Okay," Mermaid Laxur started. "What about that one?"

Mermaid Laxur pointed to the thirteenth and final shard. The largest of all of them. It was still forming and growing. They all watched as this mirror fragment transformed into an amalgamation of all of them. A giant monster version of Laxur herself. It towered over all of the others and the queen felt that this thing was more powerful than she was.

"Oh great," the goddess said. "The most dominant part of you."

"That thing is me?" The queen asked in horror.

The central torso was Laxur's, but this thing had legs of a human, horse, and crab. It also had hundreds of tentacles, and many arms. Its mouth split into three parts as it roared. It also had metal skin, both angel and demon wings. Its hair was long and flowing as if it was under water. Its eyes glowed a deadly green.

"That thing is a monster," Laxur said.

"Actually," Angel Asaria began. "That thing is actually you."

"You lie!" Laxur snapped.

"She is right," the goddess said.

"Damn, you are ugly," Pirate Laxur quipped.

"That is not the true me!" Laxur roared.

The giant monster Laxur then lashed out at everyone around it. But its primary focus was on the queen. It slammed its mighty arm onto the ground to cause it to quake. The whole room shook. The twelve Laxur's ran as far to the other side of the city sized room as they could. Laxur herself jumped into the air to get away from the mass of flesh, tentacles, and deadly hair. As the giant monster Laxur moved it giggled and caused the room to shake.

Laxur was surprised that no one from the outside noticed. Normally Dari would have come in to check. But nothing happened. The doors were still sealed. If no one will come to help, then she would need to defeat this beast herself.

A spear struck the Monster Laxur in the head. Then another and another. Laxur saw that the centaur version of herself was throwing spears and all were hitting their mark. Laxur assumed that Centaur Laxur was her martial self. Which made sense.

Angel Asaria picked up Asaria and flew up next to Laxur. Seeing Asaria out and about made Laxur feel both angry and regretful. How can she feel both at once?

"You have to stop that thing," Angel Asaria said.

"How?" Laxur demanded.

Demon Laxur then flew up to them. "Think of something fast!"

Monster Laxur then opened its vast mouth. A long flexible tongue launched out at Demon Laxur. It wrapped itself around the demon and pull her in. Monster Laxur then swallowed Demon Laxur whole. A moment later Monster Laxur quivered and convulsed. It grew larger and from its back exploded a new pair of demonic wings.

"If it eats any of us then it gains ours everything?" Asaria said. "That is, you."

"That is not me!" Laxur roared.

A series of explosions shook the giant monster. Laxur looked down to see Machine Laxur using hidden weaponry in her arms to attack. She fought alongside Centaur Laxur, and Pirate Laxur who was armed with old fashioned pistols.

Meanwhile both Alien Laxur and Mermaid Laxur were looking for weapons to use. They were also trying to avoid getting wrapped in the monster's many appendages. Laxur herself flew down to them.

"What are you two looking for?" Laxur asked.

"Anything that can help," Mermaid Laxur complained.

A scream came from the three fighting Laxur's. The queen turned to see that Centaur Laxur, Machine Laxur, and Pirate Laxur are all wrapped in tentacles being drawn to Monster Laxur's vast maw of a mouth. The three were then forced in.

Like before Monster Laxur then convulsed painfully and changed further. As it changed it sent out more tentacles at the last of the Laxur's. It grabbed hold of Angel Asaria and Asaria herself. Then it grabbed Alien and Mermaid Laxur's. They were all drawn into Monster Laxur's mouth. It grew larger and the noises were piercing.

The goddess then grabbed Laxur and flew her to safety. They went up to the ceiling that was far above the mass below.

"What is happening?" Laxur asked.

"It is putting you back together. But under its influence," the goddess said. "That is, you that is what you have become."

"No, that is not true!" Laxur said.

Before the goddess could continue her foot was grabbed by hair form the monster below. It pulled the goddess down into the mass of flesh and energy. The beast below quaked and sent shockwaves across the room.

Moments later the mass then reformed into an identical version of Queen Laxur. The very same thing that looked back at her in the mirror. The queen looked at her monster self in shock.

"Am I still the greatest thing you have ever seen?" Monster Laxur asked with a laugh in a voice completely identical to the queens.

"What are you?" Laxur demanded.

"You have been told this so many times," Monster Laxur said. "How many more times must it be repeated?"

"I refuse to believe that you are me!" Laxur snapped.

"You damned fool. I am the real you. And you are the mirror image," Monster Laxur said. "The part of us that is the weak one. The one that wishes for love, pleasure, and safety." Monster Laxur paused for a moment. "I am the one that is power, strength, and cunning."

"I am the one who holds the power," Laxur said. "I am the one in control!"

Monster Laxur laughed deeply, "You are so amazing. That very power is the reason why I can be here today. And once I consume you, I will be complete once more."

"Fat chance," the queen said.

"I happen to enjoy growth and will be you once more," Monster Laxur said.

Monster Laxur's body started to grow larger. As she got bigger all her other appendages exploded from her body. Tentacles, wings, legs, arms, and now armored skin. She grew to fill the vast room. This gave Laxur no room to move as she was not trapped. The queen's powers were having no effect on this monster.

Queen Laxur was pinned between Monster Laxur's flesh and the main back wall of the throne room. Monster Laxur's face formed in front of the queen. It was as big as Laxur was currently.

"All that power and no control," Monster Laxur quipped. "But I can make it all work."

"Never!" Queen Laxur yelled.

"So, say the queen," Monster Laxur laughed.

Monster Laxur's mouth then opened wide and her tongue split into dozens of snakes like whip tongues. They wrapped themselves around the queen and Laxur was pulled in. And everything went dark.

Queen Laxur opened her eyes and found herself sitting upon her throne. There was no damage to the room at all. No evidence of any battle, and no evidence of the mirror.

"Did I dream all that?" Laxur asked herself.

She thought about what she had dreamed. She looked and saw the full body mirror at the far end of the room. Laxur got up off her throne and went to it. Laxur also noticed that she was dressed in her black skintight dress. She came up to the mirror and saw her reflection. It flowed and moved with her. She felt relieved and made it go into the corner of the room where it would not interfere with her.

As the mirror went to the corner, the image of Laxur did not vanish. It looked out at the limited view it had of the throne room and of Laxur walking back to her throne. All it could do was watch.

Chapter Fifty-Two
Revenge of the Empire

A few days had passed since the now-divine Queen Laxur became a mighty goddess. She had been alone, trying to master her ever-increasing powers. It took her a day, but she finally mastered most of her new abilities.

"My great queen! You summoned us?" Smika asked. He, Dari, Hyea, and Polea stood before their goddess queen.

"Yes, I did. You four have been with me the whole time. You have proven to be my most valuable, noble, and loyal allies, friends, and in some cases, more." Laxur paused.

"I wish to reward each of you. I have the power to grant you a divine wish. What do your heart's desire the most?"

Queen Laxur looked at Dari, who knew what she desired, and Laxur had an idea what it was.

"My great queen, I desire to be the most powerful of all angels as well as the strongest and biggest." Dari bowed in reverence to her goddess.

"I thought that you would ask for that. And I love that idea." Laxur got up and walked to her great protector.

Laxur raised her palm, and in it a red ball of energy formed. The queen gently blew the energy ball at Dari.

The already-massive angel started to grow. Her wings doubled in size and became not only black but also red, gray, and silver. Her muscles expanded to a greater size than normal, and her height was increasing. Dari normally stood more than three meters; now she stood five meters tall.

When it was all over, Dari stood towering over the others around her. Dari's wish had been granted, and she loved it.

"Oh, thank you, my goddess queen," Dari said happily. She stood behind Laxur's throne.

Hyea flew up to her queen to ask if she could get a wish. "And what do you desire, my favorite lady-in-waiting?"

"Only to serve you, my queen," Hyea said nervously.

Laxur cocked an eyebrow, looking at the fairy. "Really? Well, thank you, and I do desire you too. But still, is there anything that you yourself desire most of all?"

Hyea blushed and turned away shyly. She did want something but was too shy to ask, especially in front of Smika, whom she liked dearly. Laxur looked at Smika and back to Hyea as she sat back down on her throne.

"I would like to be a more powerful and prettier fairy," Hyea finally answered.

Queen Laxur grinned. "Well, I do need my lady-in-waiting to be a very strong, powerful woman, as well as a great beauty. So, I will grant you this." Laxur raised her hand again, and a purple energy ball formed.

Hyea flew into it and stood in her palm. She absorbed the energy and began to change. Her clothes changed. Her wings became clear, and instead of one pair, she developed three pairs. An additional four wings sprout from her back. Her face became more mature, as did her body. She still had an ice-blue complexion, but it glowed more. Hyea felt a massive surge of energy pulse through her tiny body. With her six wings, Hyea zipped away and flew around the room at a speed that she had never achieved. Hyea felt incredible, and she loved her new powers that were gifted to her from her queen.

"Smika, what do you desire the most?" Laxur asked while Hyea flew around them, enjoying her gifts.

"I do not know yet. Could I come to you later?" Smika asked bashfully.

"Of course you can, my dear," Laxur said ever so sweetly to the young man.

She then turned to Polea, her best friend and closest female companion. "And you, Polea, my love. What do you desire the most?"

"I want your body," Polea said in a low voice.

Laxur was taken aback by Polea's response. "You want my body?"

"I mean, I want to look like you. I want to be as strong, as powerful, and as seductive as you are, my divine queen, and I do not want to wear glasses," Polea explained.

Laxur grinned and chuckled, for she now understood what Polea wanted.

"You are right. Our kind should be the definition of feminine perfection. I will give you this, and I will enjoy this as much as you will." Laxur seemed to moan as she came up to Polea.

Queen Laxur towered over Polea. Laxur held Polea in a gentle embrace. Polea could feel Laxur's warm body. The queen lowered her head down to Polea, and they kissed. Laxur was feeding Polea small pieces of herself. It was known that Laxur and Polea were very close, but no one knew how close. It was rumored that they were both bisexual and that they might be lovers. Both were enjoying this, but Polea was enjoying it more. The blonde could feel an unimaginable power surge into her, more than she had ever felt before. After a few seconds, Polea broke the embrace in a fit of pleasure. Laxur had put so much power into Polea; she might have overdone it. Polea was moaning and yelling loudly as she began to change. Polea's blond hair became golden and grew so long that it covered her. Polea was on her knees, holding herself. She could not tell if she was in pain or pleasured. Her body had expanded to a larger size. In a minute, the feeling stopped, and Polea had been permanently changed. Like Queen Laxur, Princess Polea had morphed into a goddess-like woman. Her body mirrored the queens, except that Polea was not as tall as Laxur. Queen Laxur stood three meters, and Princess Polea went from being more than one and half meters tall to more than two and half meters high. Polea's size tore through her dress, and she used her long, thick golden hair to cover herself.

"I overdid it, but it looks so good for you," Laxur commented, looking Polea over.

"Oh, my queen, I feel so mighty and perfect." Polea moaned as she felt her new curves.

"Indeed, you do. I have given you more than you think." Laxur smiled. She sat back down and made a tight black corset form over Polea's new body. "You are the only one who is a match for me. As of now, you are the most powerful mortal."

Polea could not believe that her queen would give her such great gifts. She loved them all—she loved her new body, her new powers, and she loved Laxur for this gift.

"Now to business. The Utopian Kingdom must be conquered and brought into my control. I want the universe to bow to me and accept me as their new god," Laxur commanded.

"How may we serve you?" Smika asked.

"My forces are to be empowered with my new magic," Laxur stated.

A knife formed in her hand, and she cut her fingers, causing little drops of blood to seep out.

She flicked the blood on the floor. Hundreds of drops on the floor began to grow and form into the shapes of bodies. Female demonic-like creatures were born—soulless, seductive, and deadly.

"What are these?" Smika asked.

"These are succubi. They are my newest soldiers and servants," Laxur explained to Smika.

"Rather sleazy-looking creatures, my queen," Hyea commented.

"That is the idea, Hyea. They are made to seduce and then kill their victims," Laxur said.

"That works on men, but what about women?" Smika questioned.

"They can seduce women too. But you do have a point, so . . ." Laxur trailed off, and then she bled her other hand.

She again flung her blood into hundreds of droplets on the floor. The divine red blood grew and changed into dark male-like beings. They were muscular and tall. Polea, Hyea, and Dari were taken aback by these male creatures; even the succubi were excited.

"Behold my incubi. They will do the same to their women victims that the succubi will do to their male victims," Laxur explained.

Then Queen Laxur stood back up. "Go, my children, to Evorn and ravage that world!"

Her succubi and incubi vanished into nothingness. Laxur chuckled at the thoughts of the mayhem that her "children" would cause. Then images of Utopians crawling around in the sands of Z'yon came to her. She smiled evilly.

"It would appear that there are many Utopians and humans left here. Have the imperial guard round them up," Laxur ordered Dari.

"Yes, my queen." The giantess Dari bowed and vanished in the dark.

"S'tie is here too. He got left behind when the Utopians pulled out," Laxur said. "I want S'tie. Bring him to my chambers, unharmed and well treated."

Hyea left to carry out her divine queen's order. When she did, others entered the room: Sysu, Obsidian, Golcon, Illumin, Heranian, and many other Darkcon nobles.

"You summoned us . . ." Illumin trailed off when he looked at his queen in her new form.

The other Darkcons were shocked but taken by their queen's new appearance.

"Do you all like what you see?" Laxur asked them sleazily. "I will take your silence as a yes." She sat back down.

"I did summon you. You are all aware of my goal of conquering the Utopian Kingdom. Well, today that will be so. There is going to be a change in the monarchy." Obsidian said.

"What do you mean?" Golcon asked.

"Princess Polea will be your new monarch and leader. You are all her subjects now," Laxur This bombshell shocked everyone, except for Polea.

The golden-blond beauty grinned.

"Her? This little girl is an unproven, spoiled little brat,"

Golcon complained.

"You are brave and stupid," Heranian commented, chuckling nervously.

"I look forward to being her new monarch. And for those that do not believe in me, you will." Polea grinned as she walked in front of the group.

"What about you, my queen?" Obsidian asked in his wolf form.

"Polea will rule all, but I am a god, and I will be a god to all. I will be worshiped, loved, admired, desired, and everyone will be willing to die for me," Laxur said in a low and seductive tone.

"You wish to take the place of the Maker and Architect?" Illumin asked carefully.

"I do. And you, Illumin, will be my highest priest and will spread my faith," Laxur said.

She then reappeared behind Illumin and gently coercing him. She was so close to him that her skin rubbed on his clothes, and he could feel her power and mighty curves through his black robes. She was arousing him, making him love her the way she wanted. Laxur disappeared and reappeared on her throne.

"I will accept you as my princess." Illumin turned to face Polea.

She smiled at Illumin's loyal creed to her. Polea distrusted men, except for Illumin. He was completely different to her from other men; he was the only man she trusted. He healed her broken heart in a different way than Laxur did. He was the only one that she wanted loyalty from.

"What are we going to do with the remaining Utopian roaches crawling around your world, my queen?" Sysu asked.

"I have sent the imperial guard out to round them up. Princess Polea will decide their fate if they do not accept me as their god," Laxur answered.

"I really want to punish them myself, my queen. Why does the lovely princess get to have all the fun?" Sysu asked, smiling evilly.

"I can let you have a little fun with a few of them. I imagine that you would like to grow your 'family.' Obsidian can join in the fun too. Your pack needs a few more pups." Polea chuckled, looking at her new Generals.

She then turned to Golcon, her sharpest critic.

"As for you. I will be your monarch. You will either love me, or I will make life a true hell for you," the golden-blond woman threatened.

Queen Laxur watched Princess Polea take charge. She no longer needed to worry about ruling. Polea had power and was using it, but Laxur still had to protect her most loyal friend from their foes.

On Evorn, many human and Utopian ships landed and crashed around the planet. People were running everywhere, and chaos ruled the world.

Archduke Frenzen looked out at the turmoil below from the giant glass windows in the throne room. Countess Marien and Rakon walked up to him.

"I take it that the mission failed," Frenzen said without turning to face them.

"And you would be correct. Queen Laxur has become like the Maker," Marien said with regret.

Frenzen shook his head in disappointment.

"Where is Princess Asora?" he asked, now turning to look at them.

"She was lost in the conflict," Rakon broke the news.

"Lost! What do you mean *lost*?" Frenzen roared in anger.

"I mean, she did not fall to Laxur, but we lost sight of her when she and T'ula charged back to fight the insane witch," Rakon barked back.

"That is not good. We need to find them," Lady T'a said, now coming into view.

"Can you track them?" Frenzen demanded of T'a.

"I cannot feel them. They are either in a place where I cannot go, or they are dead," T'a explained.

"I know that my daughter is not dead," Marien stated sternly.

"How do you know that?" T'a asked.

"Motherly intuition. I know also that Asaria would never kill Asora," Marien said.

"With all due respect, Countess, your first daughter is now insane. She is not the same little girl that you once knew," T'a reminded Marien.

The countess growled at T'a.

"Enough, both of you. The problem now is what do we do?" Frenzen ordered sternly.

"Who is in charge?" Sarea asked.

"Until we figure out what happened to Princess Asora, I am in charge. I am Prime Minister," Frenzen reminded everyone.

"My lord, my lord, there is news!" A guardsman ran up to the prime minister.

"What is it?" Marien answered for Frenzen.

"Creatures from Z'yon have appeared on several of our worlds across the kingdom," the guardsman explained.

"What kind of creatures?" Frenzen demanded.

"I have never seen them before, but they say that the creatures have seduced many to Queen Laxur's side," the man said.

"Great," Frenzen said dully. "So she has made the first move."

"We have to stop this," Marien said.

"Yes, I know," Frenzen commented. "Muster your troops, and I will gather mine as well. We will meet this threat head-on."

"Of course," Marien said.

Then the countess pulled out a device from her pocket and talked into it. This device, Frenzen learned, was what the humans called a smart cell phone. It allowed the humans to communicate with each other from any place on a world if there were satellites in orbit and towers on the ground. Frenzen found the devices silly, but they worked.

"We will make our first stand at Goban Tipu," Frenzen said.

"Agreed. The mountainous terrain makes it easily defensible against any foe," Marien said.

An army of ninety-three million Utopian troops—comprised of elves, fairies, dwarves, mer- people in landform, centaurs, daemons, and local spirits known as sprites—gathered in the mountains. The humans built a massive base, which could launch aircraft and drones, and deployed their mechanized forces designed for mountain warfare. Sixty-two million human troops added to the defense of Goban Tipu, the Utopian Kingdom's most formidable defensive world and first line of defense against the Darkcon Empire.

Two days after the defenses were completed, a horde of two hundred million Darkcons descended upon them. These were not the typical Darkcon; these two species were new: female demon-like creatures with wings and larger male beasts that looked like more attractive trolls. To the defenders, these creatures were attractive and disarming.

Not a single shot was fired. The seductive creatures took Goban Tipu without a fight. They seduced the defenders with their appearance. The millions of succubi either drained men's souls or corrupted them so that they were mindless slaves to their Queen. The incubi made the women weak with love and impassioned them into mindless slavery. The incubi did not take the women's souls because they found them more entertaining intact.

From Evorn, Frenzen and Marien watched in horror as Goban Tipu fell to Queen Laxur's forces.

"That is not good," Frenzen commented.

"No shit, Detective" was all Marien could say.

"Something must be done. Can we counter the seductive spells of those creatures?" Frenzen questioned.

"The only thing that I can think of is to either use our new drones or bomb them," Marien suggested.

"I prefer the drone option. The bombs you have may be too much, and we should save them as a last resort," Frenzen said sternly.

"Very well then. I will need to have Jeia's company produce as many drones as they can as fast as possible," Marien stated.

Over the next few weeks, the humans' drones wreaked havoc on the succubi and incubi, but they could not produce them fast enough to keep up with the new Darkcon races. Queen Laxur had been able to produce millions of her new children a day, while the humans could only build a thousand drones a week. Even though the drones were causing incredible damage to the Darkcons, they were unable to stop them; they could only slow them down. The Utopians liked the humans' drone weapons, but they were disappointed by the humans' production rate.

On Z'yon, the remaining Utopians had been captured and imprisoned, including Prince S'tie.

Princess Polea's hatred for the Utopians came to light when she decided to have a little fun with a couple of humans and elves that were trying to escape.

Four prisoners in a dark room saw the black-dressed Darkcon Princess enter. She was so beautiful, seductive, and powerful that all four wanted her. Only one of the prisoners was a man an elf. The other three were two human females and a mermaid in landform. The golden Princess sat in a chair that she conjured with her great magic.

"So you four do not like the hospitality of my goddess and I? I have to say I am hurt," Polea mocked.

"We are prisoners. How do you expect us to act, you bimbo?" the mermaid cursed.

Polea smiled evilly at them. "So you think I am a bimbo? Well, I should thank you for such a compliment."

Polea gently removed her dress and revealed a tight corset. Her large breasts were pushed up to give her more cleavage. She forced the mermaid into another chair and sat on her lap.

"Get off of her, you oversized bimbo!" one of the humans yelled and punched Polea in the face.

It knocked Polea off the mermaid's lap onto the floor.

Polea chuckled and got back up. "You are strong. I like that." Polea jerked her head around.

The elf man came up from behind Polea and restrained her tightly. "Oh my, you are a strong man. Trying to impress the ladies?"

"Not really. I thought that I would hold you down long enough for them to escape," the male elf hissed.

"You think that you are a hero, do you? Too bad it will not work," Polea said sleazily.

She used her nails to dig into his skin, and she sent a pulse of energy into him. It paralyzed him, and he fell to the floor in a spasm. "You are brave. I will give you that. But I am your Princess now, and you will obey me."

Polea put her hand over his face, and he screamed in pain.

"Stop it!" the other human woman demanded.

"Why? He is only a man, an elf, which is even worse," Polea said wickedly.

Then Polea noticed something, and her smile faded.

"You are in love with him?" Polea got off the elf and looked back at them.

"Then you four will spend all of eternity together." Polea unleashed a wave of energy, and the four Utopians screamed in agony.

Princess Polea walked into the throne room, where Queen Laxur was reading a book.

"Did you have fun with the prisoners?" Laxur asked her female companion.

Polea showed four little dolls to her goddess queen.

"You and your dolls, Polea." Laxur put the book down. "Did you get what you wanted before you added them to your toy collection?"

"I had fun with them. Though they did make me angry." Polea pouted.

"How did they make you angry?" Laxur asked.

"Two of them loved each other, and that, for some reason, infuriated me," Polea explained.

"Why? I thought that you enjoyed love?" Laxur asked, now skin-to-skin with Polea.

"Because this elf was able to resist my seduction spells," Polea said, holding up one of the dolls.

"You are the most beautiful mortal woman to ever live. There are bound to be some men that can resist, but most will submit to you like they do to me." The Queen embraced the blonde Princess in a powerful and loving hug.

"I will see to it that you are the most powerful and beautiful woman to ever exist. I want you to be beautiful. I want you to be loved like I love you." Laxur said.

"I am yours, my divine goddess," Polea said, and then she buried her face into Laxur's chest.

"If you do not mind, Polea, I would like to have some time alone with S'tie," Laxur told her female companion.

"Of course, if I can have more fun," Polea responded.

Laxur nodded in acknowledgment. Polea was released from Laxur's loving hug and walked away.

Princess Polea walked through the crowded halls of the giant fortress. She moved toward a large room that was crowded with millions of people. They were all listening to one man—Illumin, the Darkcon Empire's highest priest and religious edict. Princess Polea was a regular to his sermons and an admirer of his theology. Polea was a known man hater, but Illumin was very different. He was very moving, and he had tried to heal her in a time of need.

"We give thanks to our new goddess Laxur. She has been given powers beyond mortals or immortals. The Maker left this power to the one that was to bring in the new era. We Darkcons should celebrate, for has she not already given us new strength and mightier magic? Do you not feel more energized? The Utopians will fall before us and our new goddess. It is our time! Now, on your knees and thank her for all that you have been given." Illumin said.

Polea watched as thousands sank down with their heads touching the floor. *Laxur will love this*, she thought, but Illumin was obviously struggling. *Well, he is new to this. It will come.*

An hour later, the sermon was done, and the people slowly left. Princess Polea remained, hoping to catch Illumin in private. When the time was right, the golden princess walked all nine stories down to the stage where Illumin was writing on a white marker board.

"Your sermons are as wonderful as ever, my love," Polea commented lovingly to the religious man.

"Thank you, my princess. How can I help you today, my love?" Illumin smiled back to Polea.

Polea was smiling shyly at him. Polea and Illumin were lovers themselves. They were so alike that they felt akin to each other.

Like Polea, Illumin was once a hater of women. When he was in the Utopian Kingdom, he fell so in love with a beautiful woman that he risked everything for. She betrayed him and exposed his secrets, and he fled the kingdom in humiliation and terror. Every woman that he encountered did this to him, except Polea.

Both Polea and Illumin had many similarities and mutual interests. Polea collected toys and dolls. Illumin did not make fun of her for it; instead, he added to it by making things for her. He liked to write stories but was too shy to let anyone read them. He had been ridiculed before, but Polea loved his poetry.

"I would like to hear your latest poem," Polea said kindly.

"If I could hear you sing," Illumin responded.

Polea's smile turned into a giggle. She loved to sing for him. He said that her voice was so beautiful that the Architect would be enchanted by her. Polea sang in a language that only angels knew, and it ensorcelled Illumin. After a few minutes, she finished, and Illumin read her a short poem that moved Polea's soul.

"Where did you get those new dolls on your lap?" Illumin asked.

"These were Utopian prisoners that tried to escape. They were rather aggravating to me," Polea explained.

"You can turn people into dolls now?" Illumin asked, rather shocked. Polea nodded.

"Give them to me, and I will keep them safe." Polea did as Illumin asked. She knew that he might try to free them, but she did not care. He put them in a cabinet and turned back to Polea. He sat down very close to her. She pulled her body so close to him that they were touching skin. "What else can you do now?"

Polea leaned close and kissed him passionately. "I will take great joy in showing you all of my powers, abilities, and skills." Polea chuckled and kissed him again.

Illumin broke the kiss for a moment. "Perhaps we should go somewhere more private."

"You are right. We will go to my chambers." Polea pulled Illumin's head to her face and kissed him more, and they both disappeared in a golden light.

Prince S'tie was thrown into a dark room lit by a large fireplace. It was cold until he came close to the fire. S'tie was badly injured, his energy was low, and he ached a great deal. He saw a large couch in front of the fireplace. He could hear someone breathing and moving in the dark.

"Are you enjoying my bedchambers?" a familiar feminine voice asked.

"Asaria? Where are you?" S'tie asked.

"Over here, my one true love," Laxur said as her voice became concentrated enough for S'tie to find the source.

A light from Laxur's body revealed her to the injured prince.

Queen Laxur had become far more infatuating to the prince. She glowed, and she looked ready for sex. She was dressed in a very tight black corset and nothing else. Her body was very muscular. Her breasts were larger than he remembered, and her hair was so long that it reached the floor. She was now equal in height to him. She wore a smile of pure seduction and love. She took his hand and guided him to her bed.

"Oh, this must hurt so much, my love. Allow me." Laxur gently placed her hand on his broken leg and the gashes on his torso.

They healed right before his eyes, and then Laxur passionately kissed him. As she did, all his pain melted away, and all his injuries healed. She loosened the top of her corset, and her chest expanded as she breathed. Minutes later, she broke the kiss and left the prince so aroused that it was painful to not be touched by her.

"There, all better. How do you feel, my love?" Laxur smiled as she continued to slowly loosen her corset.

"My injuries and wounds are gone," was all S'tie could say. He had found himself lost in Laxur's form and incredible passion.

"That is all?" Laxur mocked a hurt tone.

"Then I need to" —Laxur forced herself on top of him—"intensify my passion for you."

"You never needed to do that," S'tie said. Laxur was taken aback by his comment. "What do you mean?" Laxur asked.

"Asaria, I have always loved you. You never needed to use spells on me or use your body like a whore. You have always had my love," S'tie explained.

Laxur was at a loss. She wanted to be the ultimate woman and the ultimate mate for S'tie. She loved him so much that she would do anything to make him want her. He was the only one allowed to call her Asaria; he was the only man that could truly be hers and hers alone.

"My love, I gained godlike powers and endured so much. I want you to love me like you did when we were young," Laxur said.

"You do not need this great power to have me. I have always wanted to be by your side, and I want to be by your side now." S'tie gently took her hand and held it to his face.

"You would willingly join my empire and be my king?" Laxur's face lit up.

"If I can be with you, I will do anything you want." S'tie kissed Laxur with all the love and passion he had.

Queen Laxur could feel his lust, his love, and his need for her. Laxur held him, and they fell onto the giant, cold bed. Laxur made S'tie's clothes vanish, leaving him completely naked. Laxur removed her corset, and she was naked too. They made such passionate love that Laxur's powers again began to grow beyond what she could control.

Her powers were affecting her empire. They made her forces so strong that they were overwhelming the Utopians.

After a few days, S'tie decided to find Illumin. He needed someone to talk to about Laxur being a goddess. The prince was told to look for him in one of the great rooms. It was nine stories tall with a vast stage surrounded by stadium seating.

He walked down the stairs to the dais, where he could see Illumin walking back and forth and muttering.

"Illumin," S'tie called out as he walked up to the black-frocked priest.

"S'tie." Illumin clapped him on the shoulder.

"I see Laxur brought you back from death's door. I heard you had been pretty badly wounded. I am glad to see that you are well. What do you think of the temple?" Illumin said.

"It is, um, well . . ." S'tie looked around at the great empty room and grinned back at the priest. "It is large."

Illumin sighed heavily. "Yes, it is that. I fill it every day with those that want things from Laxur." He shook his head. "I am keeping a list, but I have not the nerve to bring it to Laxur." He looked down and then up at the prince. "You know what the difference is between being a priest for the Architect and for Laxur?"

S'tie loathed hearing the answer, but that was why he was there.

"The difference is that when you pray to the Architect, you have to take some personal responsibility for your wishes or dreams, but Laxur can grant them in a whim—or take them away on a whim." He looked at the prince with a wry smile. "You understand?"

"I understand." S'tie put his hand on Illumin's shoulder. "Believe me, I understand. Do you want to hear something worse?"

"I think I had better. You have the look of a man who seeks confession or a good friend. Why do we not talk back in my rooms. They are not far." Illumin motioned for the prince to follow him.

Illumin picked up his staff, which had a ball of light at the tip, and went to the back of the stone wall. He tapped the wall, a door opened, and the two men slipped through to a wide hallway illuminated by torches. They passed by his offices and storage rooms. At the end of the hall was Illumin's suite of rooms.

They sat in his living room. It was large and dark, so Illumin lit the fireplace and several candles.

"The temple needs statues of Laxur, do you not think? Large ones that can be seen from the farthest seats. I am not sure if I should have craftsmen make them or just suggest it to the goddess." Illumin poured whiskey for S'tie, who took it gratefully.

The priest sighed heavily as he sat in his soft chair across the prince, who sat staring at the fire. "You are uneasy."

"Yes. My maker, she made herself a goddess and is having you call for her worship! Does that not bother you?" S'tie asked.

"Hey, you sleep with her." Illumin smiled and took a drink.

"And you sleep with her blond twin." S'tie got up and tossed back the drink with a cough.

He put his glass out for his host to refill, and Illumin poured a small portion.

"So what does that make us, other than two scared little boys?" Illumin laughed hysterically.

S'tie joined in and then moaned. "I am scared, all right. She says she did this for me. For me, Illumin. What does *that* say? I did not want her this way. I wanted her as Asaria."

"And who is Asaria? I mean to you?" Illumin asked.

"Asaria was light and sweet. She was gentle, loving. Flowers bloomed for her." The prince sighed.

"They bloom for her now, too." The priest held up his hand as his guest gave him a look. "All right, I know what you mean, but if I remember this story right, you were her protector until you were called back home."

"And then something terrible happened, and she disappeared then reappeared in the empire, and Rakon became her protector." S'tie slammed his glass down.

"And she did not need you anymore. Well, I will tell you this, my Prince. *We*, the Darkcon people, *need you*. *I* need you. You are all that stands between madness and some semblance of sanity. Laxur is a flipping nutcase with enormous power. Polea so loves Laxur that she cannot see the danger." Illumin leaned over S'tie, grasping his hand.

"Polea will do anything for Laxur. She was the one who found me dying out in the sand and brought me to Laxur. She did not heal me because Laxur wanted to. So, I had to wait and watch the others die around me. Polea and Sysu shot everyone around me, smiling, then picked me up gently as if I were—"

Illumin cut S'tie off, "A doll?"

"I was a doll. I am still just a doll to Asaria. I do not even think she sees me as a man. I am more of a possession." S'tie motioned for more whiskey.

Illumin complied and had a gulp himself. "You have got to be more than a possession, S'tie. We need you to be her conscience. You will have to be careful though. I do not know how far you can push her. It could be dangerous."

S'tie shook his head. "I doubt that. She does not listen to what I say. She says she is only happy that I am here."

"Nothing like being a kept man. I am sure she loves you for your mind." Illumin poured another glass, a little sloppily. "So what do you think? Get craftsmen to make the statues? It will take a while, and I do not believe the goddess can wait to be worshipped properly."

The fire began to smoke outward in heavy billows, drowning the room. Behind them, a form reaching the top of the twelve-meter ceiling appeared. It was covered by a black cowl, but two glowing red eyes could be seen.

"Gentlemen, I am the Architect," the deep, bone-jarring voice announced to the quivering men, who each stumbled a bit and bowed low. The god sighed at the drunken men. "Listen to what I have to say."

Illumin tried to sober up and dropped to his knees. "I have disappointed you. I—"

"No, Illumin. You are where you are supposed to be." The Architect turned to the distraught S'tie.

"You are where you are needed. You both will be needed to guide Asaria into behaving as a goddess should. She is acting like a child—killing and creating life haphazardly, destroying the balance. You need to guide her through this."

S'tie, more inebriated than Illumin, got up and asked somewhat belligerently, "Why can you not say these things to her?"

"It was not my essence that was left. It was my mate's, and she believes the child Asaria will be fine. I do not. I believe she is already having difficulties with her new abilities. She needs *sober* guidance. Do not let her powers guide her. She needs command over them, or they will get out of control. I do not want to have to fix the multiverse. Gentlemen, I will be watching, and I suggest you do not speak of this to the child. She cannot rely on me to help her. What she wants to do is in direct conflict with me. I do not believe she would want my total and undivided attention. There are things that can be done, but she is young. It would be a great pity, and Illumin, it will not be only Asaria, but Polea as well. Gentlemen, I rely on you, and so do your women. You need to shepherd them well."

The smoke suddenly flew up the chimney, and Illumin and S'tie were alone.

"This is serious." Illumin sat down.

S'tie glared at his friend and sat. "You think so, Illumin? I mean, really? If we do not tone down Asaria, she will be attacked by the Architect. He expects that she will become out of control—"

"More than she already has? Making soldiers, reanimating the dead, making Polea look like her?" Illumin got up to brew some coffee.

"Polea was the one who wanted that." Watching his friend, he called out, "Illumin, do you have any food?"

The priest picked up some fruit, cheese, ham, and bread with butter.

"Yes, we should eat something to sober up." Illumin placed the platter on a table and motioned for S'tie to join him as the water boiled for coffee.

"I got pretty sober when I saw the Architect. I would have thought I would be more terrified. I must be used to the terror of being with beings that can turn me into paste with a thought. I wonder if that is a good thing or a bad thing," S'tie ruminated as he sat down at the table.

"Pretty standard when you work with Laxur. I wonder from time to time if it is really an advantage to catch her eye." Illumin cut the bread.

"What do you mean 'catch her eye'?" S'tie asked suspiciously.

Illumin burst out laughing. It took him a minute to calm down, and he put his hand on his friend's shoulder. "Not that way. I have been useful to her with the humans, and Polea likes my sermons, so Laxur has listened on occasions. Nothing sexual. I am not her type, and I will be honest and say that the Queen is a little too high maintenance for me. No offense."

S'tie nodded with relief. "Thank you, Illumin, for being honest. Yes, she is high maintenance, but I love her as much as I am afraid of her. I please her now, but what if those changes? And now I must be her conscience."

"You would be her conscience anyway, S'tie. We must be smart about this," the priest said. "We cannot seem to be criticizing. She will not take that very well."

"I cannot simply agree with her on everything. She has created monsters to destroy my worlds. How can I say nothing?" S'tie made himself a sandwich and took some coffee.

"You think I want humans subjugated? Beaten and humiliated?" Illumin asked.

"She will do worse to my elf relatives, and I doubt anything I say will change that." S'tie slammed his fist down on the table.

"Maybe we can convince her that they will worship her instead," the Priest suggested. "It could be more satisfying for her."

"Worshipping her—I am having trouble with that. She's, my lover." The prince sighed.

"She is your goddess. Remember that and live, my friend." Illumin took a bite of his sandwich.

Polea's rooms were like a dark, twisted dollhouse. The walls were black, as Laxur had changed the stone of the castle from beige to onyx. The curtains on the windows were candy red, as were her throw rugs and bedspread. Along the walls were shelves of dolls, stuffed animals, and board games. There were blocks that interconnected and picture books. The Princess, dressed in a long blue gown, was lying on a rug while she threw jacks on the floor. She was seventeen, but she still loved toys, girls, or boys. She was now turning left-behind humans and Utopians into her new toys to be played with.

A glittering white light materialized in the center of the room, blinding her. She sat up as a figure in dazzling white appeared. She had pale skin and light-blue eyes, and she wore a veil over her white hair. Polea knew instantly that it was the Maker, and she froze.

"Polea, I have come to talk with you, child." The voice was soft and musical.

The Princess stood up. "Why would you talk to me and not Laxur?"

"Do you have less value than Asaria?" The Maker smiled gently.

"Yes. I am not a goddess as you and Laxur are. Why talk to me?" she asked again.

"You are just as important. You are Asaria's friend," the Maker said.

"Oh, now I understand. You want me to tell her something for you?" Polea asked with a smirk.

"I am concerned with you and only you. You have changed your appearance to look like Asaria because you hoped to become powerful and seductive. Has this made you happy?" The Maker spoke gently.

"What does this have to do with anything?" Polea asked as she picked up her jacks. She straightened and looked at the Maker. "Why do you care?"

"Are you happy? Are you content now that you have changed? Illumin loved you before you became as you are," the Maker insisted.

Polea frowned. She had not thought of her lover and what his reaction would be. Now she had doubts. "Are you saying he does not love me or want me anymore? We have made love since, and he did not seem bothered."

"Illumin loves you and understands that you felt you needed to change, and he is accepting of that. He is a good man," the white vision assured. "You still have not answered my question: are you happy?"

"Of course I am. I have everything I desire." Polea nodded.

"Do you love yourself?" the Maker unexpectedly asked.

"What are you talking about! What has this to do with anything?" the Princess yelled in frustration. She walked away from the vision to look out the window into emptiness.

"It is a simple question, but" — the Maker paused—"not so simple to answer. It is a painful one, I think."

"Laxur and Illumin love me. That is enough," Polea said softly.

The Maker sighed and moved closer to the Princess. "That is not true. You have come so far, and it is little wonder that they adore you. You give all of yourself to those that you love. Illumin has done much to help you heal, but you still have anger—"

"Damn straight! Where were you when I needed love and protection? You were not there when I begged for mercy from my parents and your high priest, that disgusting Puro! No, it was the Architect who took my hand. Where is *he*?" Polea demanded.

"He is concerned and works in other ways. That is what concerns me. I see great danger and anguish if you cannot find contentment and love for yourself. Only in that way can you help Asaria find her own and be the goddess she was meant to be," the Maker advised.

"So this is about Laxur. Will the Architect attack her?" Polea asked hesitantly.

"You need to heed my words, Polea, and be that friend to her. Help her to see that her powers come with a price. She must control herself, or the power will control her. The way is to be content and to love oneself. The rest will follow, and greater things will come," the Maker said. The white light flashed again, and the vision was gone.

Polea stared at the place where the Maker had been standing. She did not take it lightly. The goddess did not appear to simply have a chat. There was deep meaning there. It must have galactic import. She needed to see Illumin.

She transported herself to the temple and found no one, so she walked to his rooms, where she found S'tie and Illumin.

"Polea!" The priest rose from the table and went to her.

He gently took her face in his hands and kissed her tenderly.

The Princess smiled against his lips. "Illumin." She sighed. "I needed to see you. Do you love me the way I am, even though I have changed my looks?"

"Polea, I love you however you look. It is your heart that I love." The priest kissed her on each cheek and then her lips.

"I suppose I had better go." S'tie stood up.

The Princess laughed at S'tie's awkwardness. Polea waved him to sit down. "No, I will join you two gentlemen. What are you having?"

"Coffee and sandwiches, as well as a little philosophy." Illumin pulled a chair out for his lover.

Polea sat and smiled at the two men.

"Philosophy? How so?"

S'tie frowned at Illumin, then shrugged. "Just figuring out life."

"Yes, you know, how we got to this point in life and what comes next," Illumin added. He believed that now was the time to begin to map out what to do. He was not going to lose Polea to the Architect.

The Princess frowned at the prince and priest. "You are here because Laxur is a goddess and she will rule the universe. Well, she will not rule. I will rule, but she will be worshipped by all."

"We were talking about that. It will be better to take over the universe and have everyone worship Laxur instead of killing everyone." Illumin smiled at Polea, who smiled back.

"Yes, that is why Laxur has created the succubi and incubi—to seduce the beings of the universe into slavery." She looked happily at the two men, who tried not to frown. S'tie rubbed his hand down his face and sighed.

"Yeah, into slavery," Illumin said.

Polea frowned at the prince and said sharply, "You do not sound happy with her plans. You should be grateful to her for saving your life. She loves you."

"And I love her. That is exactly the thing, Polea. Asaria is *better* than slavery and needing worship. She should be exploring what good things she can do with her powers. Instead, she is intent on destruction." S'tie agonized.

Polea slammed her fist on the table. "They deserve it! And she deserves to be worshipped!"

S'tie stood up. "Why? What has she done, Polea? Has she created the universe, the ground beneath our feet?" S'tie put his hand up to stop her from speaking.

"Yes, she has created life, but did she create their souls? No. She wanted them compliant and not to think for themselves. She created slaves. She could have so much more. She could have real beings believe in her. They might come to worship her if they could see her as we do, and not this dark, twisted image. I worry for her, do you see?" Illumin said.

Polea was silent, thinking about what the Maker said. "Do you think that it is blasphemy and that the Architect will punish her?"

Illumin and S'tie looked at each other sharply before Illumin answered.

"It is possible. I am, or was, the high priest for the Architect, and he was for law and order." The priest paused to gauge Polea's reaction, which was a slight narrowing of her green eyes.

"Laxur was good for the empire by giving us law and order. She was harsh, but that was what it took to keep our people in line. The Architect had no issues with her. Now Laxur has taken powers that were meant for a great cataclysm. I would say that he will be watching her."

Polea stood up and walked behind her chair, placing her hands on its back. "She should be a match for him, being a goddess, as well."

"Are you sure? If I were a god, I would make sure that I was still the top god, even if I needed someone with extreme power. I would make sure I had something the other did not," the priest suggested.

Polea frowned. "She deserves what she has. This is not fair. They cannot take it back or punish her for taking what was lying around."

"Nothing has happened yet." Illumin tried calming the distraught woman.

"We will all try to help Asaria to do the right thing," S'tie began, "to control her power before—"

"Before the power controls her," Polea interrupted with a smile and tears in her eyes.

"Yes. We could do that. The three of us must help her. We will make a pact to help guide Laxur to control her powers. That should please the Architect."

"It pleases me as well. I love Asaria, and I believe that she is worthy of her powers if she will follow her true heart." S'tie smiled and reached over to clasp Polea's hand.

"So we are agreed?" Illumin asked. "Agreed, for Laxur," Polea responded. "For Asaria."

Chapter Fifty-Three

The Shadows of Tera

A hole in a dark, rainy sky opened. It was more than a kilometer in the skies of another world. A world that was not Z'yon. Two beings dropped out of it and fell uncontrollably to the ground below. Princess Asora and Lady T'ula were tumbling down. Asora unfurled her wings and raced down to grab hold of T'ula. The jewel elf held onto Asora for dear life. Asora attempted to slow their descent to the ground. Her white wings were having trouble stopping their fall. Asora then maxed her wings length and used them to glide. Both women then crashed into a nearby hillside and into the soggy mud below.

Asora popped up from the mud and spat out the dirt. T'ula was not in sight but Asora could feel her. Asora looked around to make sure that they were safe. Then she looked at herself to see what damage she took.

"Uh, Maker me," Princess Asora complained.

She was wiping away the wet dirt from her golden armor and dress. She picked herself up from the mud and muck to look around again. She spotted T'ula a few meters away. She was hunched over, holding herself as if she were in pain.

"T'ula, are you well?" Asora asked.

"I feel as if I am going to explode!" T'ula cried.

She felt all the power that Laxur had put in her. It was growing inside her, and she was losing her concentration. T'ula now looked nearly identical to Laxur in body, and size. The only real way to tell them apart now were their eyes and ears. T'ula had long and pointy elf ears, and now blue eyes.

"You have to regain control, or you will do what Laxur did and grow to the size of a planet," Asora reminded T'ula.

"Yes, I know. I do not want to grow that big. I hate being big," T'ula said.

"You can do it T'ula, I know you can," Asora encouraged her companion.

Asora held T'ula's trembling hand. After a minute, T'ula stopped trembling, and the exploding feeling inside her was gone for now. It was enough of a relief that T'ula could now concentrate on her surroundings.

"Thank you, my sovereign." T'ula looked around. "Where are we?"

"I do not know. We need to get out of the rain and wind before we freeze," Asora said with a shiver.

She helped up the larger T'ula. The elf woman was almost naked, and she looked cold. She was shivering like Asora was. Asora tore her dress up and took off her cape. She wrapped T'ula as much as she could. The noble lady looked like she was wearing rags, but it was much better than being naked and freezing. Asora still had on her golden armor, so she was fine.

"This place is not Z'yon," T'ula said.

"No, it is not," Asora answered. "I do not feel any magic here."

We should figure out where we are," T'ula said.

The two started to walk down the hill. There was nothing but dark mud and puddles of rainwater everywhere. Like on Z'yon, no trees, grass, or plants. But unlike Z'yon which was a blasted hot desert. This place was cold, rainy, and too wet. The opposite to Z'yon. Asora wanted to start a conversation, so she did not have to think about their predicament.

"Why do you think Laxur did this to you? Is she insane to give you this power?" Asora asked.

"She called me cousin, no, twin sister," T'ula said.

"Twin sister? Polea said that about me and her. I think the both have lost their minds," Asora commented. "Though it may explain why you look so much like Laxur, but you are a jewel elf, and Laxur is an angel human. It does not make sense."

"Would not your mother have known and said something?" T'ula asked.

"She would have said that you and Polea were related to me and Asaria," Asora pointed out.

The princess looked ahead and saw a cliff edge. She and T'ula made their way to it. Asora climbed up to get a better look at what laid beyond. From the cliff, Asora and T'ula saw a city in the distance. It had lights, just like a human city on Havaina. And it looked vast, even bigger then Aunsborg did. The lights were powerful enough to reflect off the cloud and aimed below.

"I wonder who could live on a world like this," T'ula said.

"I do not know, and quite frankly, I do not care. We need their help," Asora stated as she walked toward the city.

"Wait! We should seek shelter and wait for the rain to stop," T'ula recommended.

"You are right. Do you have a place in mind?" Asora asked, looking around.

"Right here, my princess." T'ula pointed to a tiny cave.

Asora jumped down and saw that it was large enough for them if they squeezed in together. It would be very tight, but they could share body heat and keep warm until the storm passed. If it did pass?

"It will be warm with the two of us, that is for sure," Asora commented.

"You first, my sovereign," T'ula offered.

Asora went in first, and then T'ula tried to squeeze her larger body inside. She had a tough time, and Asora tried to make room for her. Asora was up against a solid piece of rock that was cold, but Asora's armor was creating a barrier to shielder back. T'ula was now fully in front of her and holding onto Asora like a child would its stuffed animal. T'ula barely fit inside the cave. Asora tried to make her squeeze in more.

The princess had not seen any insects or animals of any kind. But still, she just could not leave T'ula so vulnerable. So Asora detached the front parts of her armor and used them to cover T'ula's exposed body and protect her from the elements.

"I am sorry." T'ula said apologetically.

"Do not be. Here." Asora dug into the dirt to make more room for T'ula.

"I really hate being bigger than normal. I hate that I am stuck like this forever." T'ula began to cry.

"You should not look at this as a curse. If you can get a hold of these new powers, you could be my best bet against Laxur. You could be her equal in some way. And the queen may not have realized it. You should embrace this," Asora suggested warmly.

Asora noticed something about T'ula. "T'ula, you feel incredibly warm, like you are a steam kettle. And you are not shivering even though the exit is almost completely covered by your form."

Asora looked to make sure that her armor was still on T'ula's body. It was and was giving T'ula cover from the winds and rain. Asora wanted T'ula to feel good about herself. She hoped that Laxur was so foolish that she might have accidentally shared her powers with T'ula.

"I do not feel cold at all anymore. The powers inside of me are keeping me warm. I have begun to explore what I can do. This appears to be one of the few things that I can use on this world. I can only use the powers that work on the inside on this world," T'ula said.

She had earlier experimented with her new magic to see if it would work or what she could now do. It was odd that only the magic that could be used inside her body worked. Any real powers for use outside her body failed. T'ula wondered if it had something to do with this strange world in some way.

Asora was crammed in, but she felt warm against T'ula's body. T'ula felt just like her mother. T'ula's skin was soft and warm, and it made Asora feel comfortable and safe, like a baby in her mother's arms. This feeling was beautiful to Asora.

"I am doing my best to make you comfortable, my princess. I want to help," T'ula said sorrowfully.

"You are hardly uncomfortable. In fact, being this close to you makes me feel like I am being held by a loving mother," Asora said.

That made T'ula smile. T'ula was thankful that the princess was warm and safe. Also, that Asora cared for her so much.

"I do wish for one thing that Laxur said was true," Asora said.

"What is that?" T'ula asked.

"That you are in fact apart of my family in some way," Asora said.

"I wish for that too," T'ula admitted.

"I would love it if you and I were truly related," Asora added.

T'ula held Asora closer to her. Both women enjoyed each other's company and protected one another. They were sisters now in a way. This they wished to make real.

Hours later, the rain stopped, and the dim light of the sun was shining in the distance. T'ula and Asora woke up and flexed their aching muscles. They stretched and felt the air warm up only a bit. The sky as still covered in dense clouds. As Asora examined the clouds, she noticed how artificial they seemed. These clouds were ancient and seemed to cover the whole planet. That could be the reason why no plant life existed. Dorien the capitol world of the Darkcon Empire had a similar feature, but Dorien had plant life. This place did not as far as Asora could tell.

"Let us go to the city and see if anyone is home," Asora said.

"Of course, my princess. I will follow you," T'ula offered.

The two noble ladies walked for hours in the cool air of the strange, darkened world. The environment was as unchanging as they walked. No plants, animals, or anything. Only that strange city in the distance. T'ula saw that they were walking down a mountain range into this city. As they got closer, they could make out more details.

Nine hours passed, and they reached the outermost border of the giant city. Asora was amazed by its size and magnificence. The cities on

The Shadows of Tera

Havaina were nowhere near this enormous. This one had a dense forest of massive skyscrapers near its dozen centers. More unique buildings were near edges of what Asora assumed use to be great lakes or an edge to an ocean. This world once had a vast ocean. It made T'ula and Asora wonder what it was like once.

"My princess! How are we to move around this massive place?" T'ula asked as she looked around.

"I wonder if there is a vehicle nearby," Asora said.

The two ladies gazed around and saw what looked like a ground vehicle. It had wheels and an enclosed cabin big enough to hold both. Asora found that the doors were unlocked. She opened the door and started looking around.

"This will do," Asora said.

"Can you make it work?" T'ula asked.

"I think I can," Asora reassured. "It looks fairly similar to a vehicle from Havaina."

Asora eventually figured out how to make the cabin and the internals work. There were two more doors that led in from the rear. It had only four seats for four people. Unfortunately for T'ula, it was built for people who were Asora's size. The oversized jewel elf had to squeezed in and had her knees near her face. Her weight was also noticeable when she sat inside; T'ula was nearly twice her normal weight. The vehicle, however, came to life and reoriented itself to compensate for T'ula's heavier form.

"I really hate this," T'ula mumbled.

"Do not let it get to you. Are you able to, see?" Asora asked.

"Yes, I can," T'ula replied. "What are you doing?"

"I am studying how this thing works. It looks like a car to me. It should be just as easy," Asora said.

"I hope so. This car is very uncomfortable," T'ula complained.

Asora placed her hand on T'ula's shoulder. The two smiled as Asora shared her strength with the jewel elf. T'ula very much appreciated Asora and her compassion. Asora was the perfect little sister in T'ula's eyes.

Eventually, Asora figured out that the car was electric and was kept charged by the road itself. That fascinated Asora greatly. She wondered what other technological wonders existed here. This technology was fairly like Consortium technology, but it was far older. So that ruled out this being some lost Consortium colony world.

Asora activated the car. The rain started up again and was pounding outside, but the climate controls adjusted automatically to make the air warmer. The water was cleared by a set of wipers. The manual controls were easy for Asora to learn, and the car was off. She was surprised by the technology on how it responded to her commands and controls. She directed the vehicle to take them into the city itself.

The city was well lit, but no one could be seen. Asora saw what looked like a massive multi story shopping district. She piloted the car into a slot for parking. The two exited and went inside the giant building. T'ula spotted what looked like a shop for clothes. The clothes varied widely, from fancy to commoner to dodgy to scandalous. T'ula liked to wear dresses, but there were none, yet there was something that looked like human garb commonly seen on Havaina—a pair of black jeans, a thick blue sweater, and a pair of comfortable walking shoes that were black and white.

So T'ula went inside and found no one. She also saw nothing to stop her from trying out the clothes. So, she took what she liked and found that they adjusted themselves to her. It felt comfortable on her skin.

Asora decided to keep her armor on. It kept her warm and safe. T'ula needed new clothes badly. T'ula also found a jacket that was made to be worn in the rain. Asora watched as T'ula seemed to be giggling as the clothes were automatically adjusting to her body. Some of the clothes looked too small for her in fact made themselves fit her.

T'ula came out in what looked to be jeans, a sweater, boots, all black and purple. It made T'ula look like an actress from Havaina. Asora honestly thought she looked very attractive in that outfit.

"I like it," Asora said.

T'ula blushed and spun around, "As do I. These clothes are kind to me. This science is as magical and magic."

"I saw that it form fitted to you," Asora said. "At least you are warm and protected now."

Asora then looked out into the shopping building. She could have sworn she saw something moving in the distance. At first Asora thought that it was one of those dancing and singing robots that were on display in one of the stores. Then she felt that feeling. The feeling that someone was watching them.

"What is it?" T'ula asked.

"I do not think we are alone," Asora said.

"We have not seen anyone here," T'ula pointed out.

"That has me worried," Asora replied.

The two exited the shopping building. As Asora feared they were not alone after all. Outside the street was covered in things that were moving like worker insects all over the place. It reminded both Asora and T'ula of honeybees in a way. They saw an army of little mechanized machines in the streets. They were fixing, repairing, upgrading, cleaning, etc. The machines worked in the cold rain, keeping up the cleaning, working appearance of the empty city.

Music and songs in an alien language echoed in the air. Asora thought it was catchy and memorable. The car they used had disappeared by dematerializing in a blue light in front of them. So, they were forced to walk to the downtown district. Asora figured it was because cars were not allowed to go any farther into the city, or there was a malfunction somewhere.

Toward the center of the city, there was a series of towers they hoped they would find answers there. T'ula noticed a bunch of giant screens with dancing pictures. To Asora, they looked like advanced high-definition television screens. The written language looked like an odd form of human characters and symbols. The screens echoed in a language that sounded like the human language of Ehan.

"I wonder what it is saying," T'ula commented.

"I have no idea, but it looks like a commercial for a service," Asora said, looking at the display.

"What kind of service?" T'ula asked.

"Best I can figure, building repair," Asora said.

The image changed to what Asora thought was a news message. The language was frustrating for Asora and T'ula. They wanted to know what the oddly dressed human was saying. It was obviously a recording, and he was somber. Asora listened to the image of the man on the screen and his words. From what Asora could gather was that there was an incident on a nearby planet that had gotten out of control. The princess was unable to understand the rest. She sighed in frustration and studied the images. One looked to have been a picture from Z'yon of all places. Or it could have been a desert on this planet long ago. Asora could not tell.

The two walked away toward the center of the skyscraper forest. The towers were all connected through a series of bridges near their mid sections.

"So, they are all connected to one another," T'ula said.

"It would make transiting a lot easier," Asora said. "We do not even do that."

Suddenly, a powerful roar erupted from behind the two women. Then they saw it—a massive beast of unique and terrifying form. It stood four meters tall on six legs. It had four pairs of arms and a pair of claws. Its skin looked black and leathery.

"What in the Maker's universe is that?" T'ula said, shocked at the beast.

It opened its massive mouth to reveal rows of teeth like those of a shark. It hissed and snarled like a very angry animal.

"Angry, that is what it is!" Asora yelled and ran toward the towers.

T'ula quickly followed her princess. They ran as fast as they could hoping that they were faster. Asora tried to make her wings come out and fly, but she was unable to. Her powers were there but it was as if they were turned off.

The giant beast gave chase and was just about to overtake them, then it was attacked by smaller and more terrifying monsters. These creatures were also black, and they looked machine-like, but they were organic. They had two sets of eyes and a small mouth within a larger one. They had many teeth that looked like snake fangs. In minutes, they killed the larger beast and began to eat the body.

"Are these the dominant creatures of this world?" T'ula asked.

"I think we should leave," Asora pointed out.

"Agreed," T'ula said.

As they turned, another one of those monsters came up behind them and trapped Asora and T'ula. The creature grabbed Asora and lifted her up. The smell was horrid, and its mouth was drooling. Another lower-toned roar erupted from the towers. Instead of killing the princess, the monster closed its mouth and dragged Asora to the tower. Another creature grabbed T'ula and took her along.

A few minutes later, Asora and T'ula were taken deep within the tower complex. They were thrown into a large room that had many structures and statues. What these were once, Asora and T'ula did not know.

"Where are we?" T'ula asked, shaking from fear.

"What is that noise?" Asora heard breathing.

Another monstrous beast with black and brown skin that looked mechanical came forward. It was four meters tall, and it had a humanoid face but was closer to a human skull wrapped in skin. The body looked to have been wrapped in melted flesh. It had two legs and two arms.

Asora and T'ula were restrained by wires in midair. The beast came up to Asora and seemed to sniff her. It looked oddly at the princess and released her. Asora rubbed her arms to relax herself. But T'ula was still restrained. The other creatures backed away from Asora and the creature in front of her.

"Ox Hos aj kup nax of loerh!" the creature said to Asora.

"I do not understand you," Asora said.

Again, it looked oddly at Asora. It turned to a computer-like console and typed. The computer beeped a few times. The creature sighed in what Asora thought was irritation.

"Do you understand me now?" it asked.

"Yes, I do. Who are you? What do you want?" Asora asked, worried.

"I am known as the Historian. To answer your second question, I want to know why you are here. Why do you have this Z'yonist parasite with you?" the Historian said.

"Z'yonist?" Asora asked, looking at T'ula. "What do you mean?"

The Historian pointed to T'ula. "That thing is from Z'yon, correct?"

"She is from Taliano. We did, however, escape from Z'yon. Where are we?" Asora asked.

"This world is called Tera. Are you not part of a returning human race?" the Historian asked.

"This is Tera?" Asora asked in amazement.

"You humans built me and this city eons ago," the Historian stated. "I have been its leading caretaker."

"What is the name of this city?" Asora had so many questions now.

"This was once the capital of the most powerful human nation that ever existed, the United Republics. This is its capital mega city, Washilang. You should know this." The Historian was now curious about Asora.

"We came here by accident. No one knows about Tera, except in myth. But to see this and know that it is real! It is incredible. You must come with me to Evorn," Asora said.

"Evorn?" The Historian asked. "Who are you?"

Then she remembered. "Oh, where are my manners? I am Princess Asora Serafus Swaye of Havaina. I am the Great Monarch of the Utopian Kingdom."

"Utopian Kingdom? What is that?" the Historian asked.

"Could you release my friend? She is harmless to you," Asora asked.

The Historian released T'ula from her bonds. T'ula was very afraid of her surroundings. But seeing her princess so brave gave T'ula strength.

"It is a collection of magical creatures and nations under one major governance. It includes the humans as well," T'ula answered for Asora.

"Humans obeying others? That is unheard of," Historian whispered.

"I am curious, Historian. Could you tell us about this place, the humans, and what happened?" Asora asked.

"I could, but it is not to leave these rooms. Understood?" the Historian demanded.

Asora, T'ula, and the Historian exchanged information, history, and ideas. The Historian was built by ancient humans to be a memory of their civilization and knowledge. He had existed for untold eons, alone. He built the Uridan to help him. The various bio-mechanical creatures that now roamed Tera. Unlike Z'yon, where nothing lived, Tera had beings that survived and evolved to be extremely hostile. Washilang was rebuilt and became a sanctuary for the Historian, his knowledge, and collections, and it became home to the Uridan. The monstrous Uridan had been helping supply a technological, organic-like ship with parts and equipment. They worked to the day they hoped that their creators would return.

"Sir Historian! Are you aware of anything that could stop Queen Laxur?" T'ula asked, curious.

"I told your princess, but I guess you could know too. There is a piece of technology that can render magical powers inert, either temporarily or permanently," Historian began.

"He does require hydrogen bomb's with a powerful-enough explosive yield," Asora added in as she eavesdropped. "That we have too."

"Hydrogen bomb? Those are deadly. What kind of weapon is this?" T'ula asked.

She knew what nuclear weapons were. The Consortium was notorious for using those magic-killing devices frequently during the Great War. The one thing that the Utopians had never figured out was how to defend against them.

"We humans have two types of nuclear weapons, but apparently, there is a third. This one is powerful enough to affect the dark matter and energy around an object in space," Asora pointed out.

Asora and the Historian explained to T'ula what they had in mind. To say that T'ula was now more afraid then ever would be an understatement.

The Historian and hundreds of now friendly Uridans escorted the two women out of the room and into a hallway. They went into another room, and it was a large assembly bay. It had a large and very advanced ship in it. The Historian promised to assist Asora in her mission. He also wanted to learn more about what was going on.

They boarded the ship with thousands of Uridans. Both Asora and T'ula found the ship to be very creepy. The walls, ceiling, and decks felt warm and somewhat squishy. It was of organic material.

"I do not like this place, my princess. It is like something out of a nightmare," T'ula complained, looking around, paranoid of the Uridan.

"I know, but the Historian is being nice and letting us use his ship," Asora replied.

The ship jolted and began to move. The giant, strange organic mass floated into the dark skies of Tera. The ride was smooth after that, and they could not tell if they were lifting off or just stationary. The Historian had a window form to allow the Utopian women to look outside.

Once in orbit, they found a structure of ancient alien design orbiting Tera. The ship was heading toward it. The structure was a giant circle flanked by smaller satellites. The ship entered the circle as it powered up, and a hole in space formed inside it. And from here the universe seemed to disappear.

Chapter Fifty-Four

The Vault

In the palace on Evorn, the Royal Court had gathered. They were in a heated discussion about what to do. The Darkcons have blasted through all the defenses. Even the Consortium could not hold them back. Magical images showed Royal Guardsmen and Red Guard personnel forced to retreat on many worlds. Survivors and refugees being loaded onto ships of Utopian and Consortium design. They barely had time to enter the Heavenly Gateways.

"How could this have happened?" A courtier demanded.

"Queen Laxur is truly invincible!" Another said.

"She even murdered Princess Asora. Her own sister!" A third yelled.

"Prime Minister!" Someone called to Frenzen. "What shall we do?"

Archduke Frenzen was looking out the large window at someone horrible outside. A dark shadow had been cast. This shadow was in the shape of a person. It then transformed into a flock of horrors that Frenzen had only seen in stories.

Hundreds of succubi and incubi had descended upon the citizens of Evorn. Both the palace and the village had come under attack. The royal guards were either slain or seduced. The people of the village and palace staff were subjected to the same thing. Three in ten people managed to escape, two in ten were killed, and the rest were under the most powerful seduction spell ever conjured. Those under spells were turned into slaves or food.

The palace had become a refugee camp. Both Royal Guard and Red

Guard forces were able to fight off the flock of sedition horrors. Millions of people were already inside. They were in the many basements, and the under-rooms were full. They had everything they could carry with them. They could hear the battle being waged outside and around them. Families huddled together trying to give each other comfort as the soldiers fought on.

Both the Royal Guard and Red Guard forces were preparing the palace's defenses. Elves armed themselves with swords and magical armor; humans readied their guns, advanced armor, and technology for the coming battle. Everyone else used whatever they could find that could be used as a weapon.

The typical elf warrior's armor was thin, almost paper-like, and silver, gold for the officers. The armor was, however, deceptively tough. Elf women were allowed to fight, but only as archers or on cannon crews. The males were foot soldiers and cavalry. The weapons were magical swords, arrows, spears, axes, and maces, all forged of magical elf metal called Urganto.

A typical Red Guard fighter, either man or woman, had very advanced armor made of a blend of metal mesh, fabric, and hardened ceramic. Their helmets had what were known as head-up displays. This armor was far heavier than the elf armor, but it protected better and assisted the wearer in battle. The humans, jewel elves, and daemons had advanced rifles, bombs, lasers, grenades, battle knives, and personal battle drones.

This was the first time that the Royal Guard and Red Guard had worked together. It had raised hopes, but prejudice was not forgotten. But in this moment, they were brothers and sisters in arms. Ready to fight and die.

A wave of darkness covered the moons above and the Darkcon queen's minions as they headed for the palace. They practically covered the skies with their numbers. They kept multiplying front he clouds and out of thin air. Yet another power from the Darkcon goddess queen.

From the throne room, Frenzen watched the invaders coming

toward the palace. He wore his old suit of battle armor and was ready with his sword. He had not been in a real battle like this in years. But some skills you do not easily forget.

"T'a, have the spell casters power the barrier." The archduke turned to Marien. "Marien, have your technicians prepare those new shield generators that you brought."

Both women bowed to the prime minister and had their aides carry out the orders. They had their aids break off and ran as fast as they could to carry out Frenzen's orders.

"Frenzen, you do realize that my spell casters' magic is useless against Queen Laxur's powers now," T'a reminded the old man.

"That is why he is hoping that my new shield technology can hold them off. This tech is unaffected by magic. The nuclear generators should be enough to protect us," Marien explained to T'a.

"You brought nuclear technology here? You know how that crap affects us!" T'a yelled.

"I was the one who told her to bring it," Frenzen interjected.

"The prime minister was smart enough to know that this 'crap' may be the only thing that can hold them off," Marien said to T'a.

"We need to work as one to defeat Queen Laxur and her forces," Frenzen reminded Marien and T'a.

"As you wish." T'a replied.

An explosion rocked the palace. Cannons of both elf and human design fired on a dark cloud approaching the palace. The cloud was thousands more succubi and incubi. Arrows and bullets hold were fired into the mass of these new Darkcons. The shields and magical barriers were up, and the invaders bounced off the walls. The incubi tried to break the wall with brute strength; the succubi tried to dig in the dirt below. They both broke down the magical barrier, but another stronger and toxic barrier greeted them. The incubi and succubi began to feel sick.

"It looks like the human shield generators are working," Frenzen noticed. It held for a few minutes, and then the shield began to malfunction, and then it dropped. "What is happening?" Frenzen demanded.

"Someone broke into the generator and damaged it," Marien said.

The countess was next to an officer from the Red Guard who was holding the emergence phone to her ear and repeating what she was being told.

"How?" T'a demanded.

"It seems that a succubus got through and seduced the entire crew. Then she commanded them to destroy the shield unit. The commandos then killed her, but the crews went mad, and a fight is now in progress," Marien informed.

"Damn them!" Frenzen cursed.

The door and walls were broken open, and thousands of incubi and succubi flooded in. The demonic flock flew in and scooped up their victims. They liked to carry them off up into the rafters high above.

Countess Marien was grabbed by a flying succubus and raised in the air. She then tried to reach for her knife that she kept in her belt.

"Put me down, you filthy whore!" Marien demanded.

"I do not think so. But I kind of like what I see. My goddess wants to see you," the succubus teased and then licked Marien's cheek.

The flock of demonic horrors had overwhelmed the throne room, with the guards and servants and other defenders unable to stop the onslaught. Frenzen was exhausted after getting hit several times. He had cut down four incubus and two succubus before they resorted to hit and run strikes. T'a was tackled to the ground and getting her dress ripped apart, and her skin torn. The screaming of the people was hard to listen to. But the noises that the flock of monsters made was too hard to hear.

A rumble was heard, and a large black object appeared in the skies. It hovered in an orbital pattern. Just above the palace. This thing was not from the Darkcons. The Incubus and succubus were confused by this thing.

A beam of gold and silver light illuminated the throne room.

Princess Asora and Lady T'ula formed from the light. The princess's armor was glowing golden, and her great power illuminated the room. She looked up to see her mother being held. Lady T'ula zapped the succubus with a very potent electric spell. Frenzen had just ran an incubus through its chest.

"You freaks will leave my kingdom NOW!" Princess Asora ordered forcefully.

The succubi and incubi laughed at the little princess. While Asora's golden armor was attractive to them and made her look tough. They doubted that Asora would fair about as well as the rest of her people.

"And what are you going to do if we do not? Last we checked, you were no match for us," a succubus gloated.

Asora smiled wickedly, for she had a secret weapon that they were unaware of. She wanted to see what was about to come.

"I did not come back from the dead alone," Asora said ominously.

Another light beam, this one gray, glowed brightly, and behind Asora, a four-meter freakish behemoth formed. It snarled in rage as it looked around. Baring teeth and looking like a predator that just found its favorite prey. Then more hideous creatures formed behind T'ula and the Historian. These animalistic monsters stared down the incubus and succubus.

"I want you all to meet a new friend of mine. He calls himself the Historian." Asora looked around and then ordered, "Uridan! Destroy the succubi and incubi!"

The monstrous black and brown fleshy beasts launched themselves into the air and began to slay the demons. The Uridan were impossible to kill and were unaffected by any magic. They easily tore into the enemy lines. One Uridan was able to cut to pieces several dozen succubus without trouble.

Asora pointed her sword into the air and formed a lightning storm in the throne room. The lightning fatally electrocuted hundreds of the incubus and succubus monsters. Marien fell from several stories up. The Historian casually caught her. Marien was so sacred by the creature that she passed out. The Historian handed Marien to T'ula to deal with. The Historian also casually snagged a retreating succubus out of the air. He then crushed its skull like a human could a breakfast egg.

Within twenty minutes, the Uridan finished the butchery of the demonic invaders. The black and brown freaks seemed to be obedient to Princess Asora and the larger monster called the Historian. The only survivors of the incubus and succubus attackers escaped into the skies and vanished.

The Historian walked awkwardly toward Frenzen. It lowered its head to eye level and looked as if it were sniffing him. He did not like the smell of elves. Or any magical being for that matter.

"Z'yonic freak," the Historian said in the language that Asora taught him.

"Who are you calling a freak, monster?" Frenzen retaliated.

"Disgusting pointed-ear bugs. Your kind was an infection in the classical times, and you apparently still are," the Historian commented.

"You know nothing about us," T'a cried as she listened in.

"I can tell you stories about your kind from the classical period that will make anyone's skin crawl," the Historian said.

"You make my skin crawl," T'a retorted.

"Primitive savage," the Historian said back to T'a.

"Enough! All of you! Historian, you said that you could fashion weapons that can neutralize the divine powers of Z'yon?" Asora said authoritatively.

"Yes, of course, Asora. I need access to the human nuclear fusion weapons arsenal," Historian informed.

"What exactly are you going to use them for?" Marien demanded.

"Who are you?" Historian returned.

"I am Marien Serafus Swaye, ruler of the Human Consortium. But I am referred to by as countess," Marien introduced herself.

"You rule the human race now? You are certainly different than the last one I knew," Historian said curiously.

The Vault

"Historian! We need to get these weapons built and deployed," Asora said.

"Asora, be kind to him," Marien scolded her daughter.

Asora growled in frustration. She was the one in charge and it was her kingdom that was in danger. She was also the one who found the Historian. How dare her mother do this to her now.

"So you will need to gain access to my arsenal vault. I want to know what you are going to do before I give you access," Marien stated.

"Ah, you *are* like your predecessors, you know that, Countess?" Historian commented.

"Thank you . . . I think." Marien replied.

The Historian rose back up and spoke in the language that Asora taught him. He had learned it surprisingly fast. He spoke as if he always had.

"A high yield thermonuclear weapon of at least one hundred megatons minimum can be modified to affect the space around an interstellar object." The Historian had a device that projected a hologram to show what he intended to do. "You are familiar with two types of particle manipulation, fission and fusion. But in fact, there is a third contraction. In this process, you can literally crush the atoms of light elements. When the subatomic particles collide with one another, a powerful energy is released. It is like colliding matter and antimatter. The explosion can affect the dark energy and matter in space. The major side effects are high levels of gamma radiation and low levels of epsilon. It is that radiation that will cancel out magical energies. But to stop this Laxur, you will need at least a one-hundred-thousand-megaton explosive."

"Interesting. So, you plan to convert my most powerful nuclear weapons into atomic crushing devices," Marien thought out loud.

"I want you to open the vaults for him, Mother," Asora demanded.

"Wait just a moment. I am not about to let the Utopians get a hold of our ultimate planetary weapons," Marien scolded Asora.

"The Utopians do not want to have anything to do with those

things. I want the Historian to have a few of them to make the Darkcons and Laxur stop this madness," Asora stated. "At the very least this can give us an equalizer."

"Or they will put an end to this Darkcon Empire," Historian pointed out. "Either outcome is suitable to me."

"At this point, it does not matter. Do it," Asora ordered.

Even though Marien was Asora's mother, Asora outranked her and could order her. Asora did have some authority over Marien. In moments of external crisis Asora can command any noble to do what was demanded of them.

"As you wish, my daughter. But I will remind you of this later," Marien warned.

Asora ignored her mother's warning, and Marien gave Asora a black and red keycard. It had "N. Vault" written on it.

"There are two," Asora said. "Where is the other one?"

"It will be waiting for us at the vault," Marien said with a sigh.

A week later, on a human-owned world named Geocom, the Utopian court, Royal Guard, human government officials, Red Guard, and vault technicians all gathered by a large mountain with a military base built into it. Asora found out that it required two people to open the nuclear vault. It was revealed then that the other codes and keycard were stolen over a month ago. The princess was furious. But she had to figure out how to break in.

Princess Asora stood at the entrance to the vault. She paced around like an angry guard dog. Her anger was getting to her. The Historian was fascinated by Asora, but he also was as annoyed as she was.

"I believe this is what you want, my princess," a familiar male voice said from the shadows.

It was Irantanco, and he held out a keycard like Asora's. He was the thief. To Asora that figured, but right now she could not let him go.

"You! How did you get that?" Asora demanded.

"Now, that is not nice. I am here to help you," the terrorist said.

Then several heavily armed Vanguard warriors appeared. They looked to be ready for a fight if Irantanco and Asora came to blows.

"Who are these people?" Historian asked Asora.

"Terrorists and nothing more," Marien stated bluntly.

"Really? I guess some things never change," Historian said dully.

"What are your terms?" Asora asked coolly.

"Asora!" Marien scolded.

"Not now," Asora ordered.

"I wish to help you. And I place the aid of the Vanguard at your disposal. I just want to see a victory against the Darkcon Empire," Irantanco said kindly to the princess.

"Really? Is that all?" Asora sounded suspicious.

"That is all, princess," the terrorist reassured the young lady.

"He lies," the Historian said.

"I know he is," Asora replied.

"What it that?" Irantanco asked.

"He is called the Historian, and he can rip your head off and i can get the key that way," Asora pointed out.

"I like this," Irantanco said. "You've changed. That is what you need to run an empire."

"Whatever," Asora said.

The terrorist leader smiled ingratiatingly. Asora looked him over with caution and agreed. Both Asora and Irantanco went up to a control panel on either side of the giant metal door. They both slid their keycards in the slots, the computer beeped, and the door unlocked. The giant door creaked open, and the inside of the room was dark. A technician found a switch and flipped it. White lights flickered on section by section. Eventually, the giant room was fully lit up, and it revealed its contents.

Thousands of warehouse shelves, kilometers in every direction, were fully loaded with different types of containers and canisters with sizes ranging from people-sized to the size of giant missiles. They were all marked with radiation and lethal symbols.

"And so they laid out the instruments of annihilation across the land from east to west, top to bottom. From darkness they brought light of the end," T'a recited an old elf poem.

"What was the meaning of that verse?" the Historian asked.

"It is from the Epulam, our holy scripture. The verse is from the final chapter and talks about the end days and the horror that our greatest enemies will use on us," T'a replied ominously.

"End days? Irrelevant. There is no such thing. Time marches forward into the never-ending abyss. That is a proven fact of the multiverse," Historian pointed out.

"That may be, but it fits with this. I fear that Princess Asora will go too far with these weapons," T'a said sadly.

"What do you mean?" the Historian asked.

"I have seen these weapons in action before, and they gave me such nightmares. I saw billions of my loyal soldiers and subjects burn in an instant in the giant mushroom clouds." T'a remembered the horror.

"Hmm," the Historian mused. "Such power can never be ignored for long."

"Historian, will this one do?" Asora asked as she had a human servant cart over a large crate with human military markings. "This is a one hundred and twenty-two megaton thermonuclear bomb."

"It is more than enough. I will require three of your days to make the appropriate modifications to it. Then you can test it," the Historian said.

"Do what you must," Asora said.

The Historian, several Uridans, and the human technician took the crate to a workroom. Princess Asora turned back to the massive nuclear arsenal. She went from being lost, fearful, and powerless against her sister to having the deadliest weapons arsenal ever created. She felt powerful, and she wanted to show Queen Laxur that she could hold her own against her siege. Billions of nuclear weapons were now at her command, and she wanted to use them. She wanted to bring the Darkcon Empire to the brink of extinction as punishment for what Laxur had done. And she will see to it that this would come to pass.

Chapter Fifty-Five

The Historian

On the Utopian/Consortium world of Geocom, deep inside the Consortium military control zone the Historian and his Uridan worked. The Utopian officials could only watch as the biomechanics creatures moved about to and through. They took parts and supplies from their ship to create workstations out of organic materials.

Countess Marien and Archduke Frenzen were next to the Historian. They were very curious about him and his origins. The Historian was very uncomfortable around what he called Z'yonics. Frenzen learned that this was a term that the ancient human's and other races of Tera used to refer to any being from Z'yon or a being of magic. It was a racist term to be sure. But it did reveal some piece of lost history.

Marien was more fascinated by Tera itself and its history. Her daughter Asora described a dark, cold, and wet world. But it had a fully functioning city, the Historian said that hundreds of cities of various sizes throughout the planet. Asora and T'ula only saw one. And it happened to have been the ancient capitol of the UR.

"This UR," Marien asked. "Was this the greatest of human nations?"

"In your limited understanding yes," the Historian said.

The Historian continued to work as he talked to his two companions asking him questions. The Historian did not mind, he did find having intelligent company as comfortable. While he did not like the Utopians themselves, he did respect them. So, he was willing to answer any questions they had. Of course, answering what he knew.

"What does UR stand for?" Frenzen asked.

"United Republics," the Historian answered. "A mid tier type five civilization that started on the northwest continent in the western hemisphere. It was an evolution of an even earlier nation from before the final ice age."

"What was this ancient nation?" Frenzen asked.

"That information was unknown even to the UR at the time. There was a great exploration of history to figure out what Tera was like before the final ice age," the Historian said honestly.

"So even the mighty UR did not know what came before?" Frenzen asked.

"There were theories," the Historian corrected. "A great many in fact. To the point of insanity inducing."

"Did anyone from Z'yon have anything like the UR?" Frenzen asked.

"No, they didn't," the Historian said. "The closest they had was something called the Barundur Imperium."

"Barundur existed?" Frenzen asked amazed.

"Why?" The Historian asked.

"Barundur was a myth to the Utopians and Darkcons for as long as their history is," Marien added. "It was believed to be a place of myth."

"Some myth," the Historian snorted. "Baurndur was some worthless type zero civilization that was planet bound and easily wiped out."

"By the UR?" Frenzen asked.

"The first Barundur Imperium or half of it, yes," the Historian said. "That was after First Contact."

"The UR destroyed our greatest civilization," Frenzen repeated.

"Barundur was geocoding your kind and all the other species in your current kingdom," the Historian pointed out. "When First Contact between the Lesser Races as your kind were referred to as, and the UR exploratory expedition the exchange was peaceful."

"Wait? Elves, mer-people, dwarves, fairies, and everyone else was being exterminated by the Barundur Imperium?" Frenzen asked horrified.

"Oh yes," the Historian said. "I was online and about when First Contact was made." The Historian continued his work on the device on the desk in front of him. "Humanity of the UR became righteous and believed it was their duty to save your kind. But there were laws, and the other civilizations of Tera were not happy about the UR going to Z'yon."

"What happened next?" Marien asked.

"I think it was an elf woman a queen, I think. She was the first to set foot on Tera and speak to the UR government. In exchange for citizenship the UR would descend upon the Baurndur Imperium and burn it away," the Historian explained. "It only took one year."

"So, we humans saved them?" Marien asked with a smug smile.

"For more than five thousand years the UR ruled Z'yon surprisingly peacefully and well," the Historian said.

"Then how did it all fall apart?" Frenzen asked.

"That is an extremely complex story," the Historian warned. "But the short answer is that one of the leaders of the old Barundur Imperium managed to evade UR authorities and quietly reassembled the old imperium. A very long series of wars broke out. The last of the UR forces knocked Z'yon out of its normal orbit and reduced it to a burnt desert. Then the fighting on Tera became so deadly that they were forced to darken the skies to render it uninhabitable."

"So that is what happened," Marien said. "What about all the races of Tera? The UR and the other civilizations? Where did they go?"

"The shattered remains of all two hundred Tera civilizations gathered in giant fleets and fled to the unknown reach of the universe," the Historian said.

Archduke Frenzen formed another question that he hoped that the Historian could answer. "Did the UR or some other nation of Tera ever list the Realm?"

"The Realm?" The Historian asked now looking at the old elf with a curious expression.

"He is referring to what we view as the universe," Marien clarified.

The Historian looked dumbfounded for a moment. He turned to a computer and merely placed his hand upon it. It came back with a series of noises and tones that reminded Marien of a data network modem.

"Oh, this region that is surrounded by a dark matter void," the Historian asked in understanding. "Yes, the UR built this whole region."

"Wait a moment!" Frenzen said in shock. "The UR built the Realm?"

"Yes," the Historian said. "It was their final ultra stellar engineering project. It was an experiment in creating sanctuary zones. In the end they gave it to the Z'yonics that were considered harmless and helped the UR in its final years."

"Humans built the Realm," Marien could not get over that fact. "Out of dark matter and moved whole galaxies around."

"They used a nearby galaxy cluster and isolated it from everything around and moved the rest away. They then generated a massive dark matter void to fully isolate and insulate it. A form of protection from the larger universe," the Historian said.

"And it was all an experiment?" Frenzen asked.

"A working concept prototype if you will," the Historian said. "As far as I know, this was the only one of its kind. It was prohibitively expensive and resource intensive."

"I can imagine," Marien said.

"The humans who lived in the region were more of less low-level citizens that worked the worlds and did scientific research. As well as live more primitive lives to escape the chaos of the central UR authority," the Historian said.

"My people were colonists, farmers, scientists, and spiritualists?" Marien asked.

"More or less," the Historian answered. "The kind that wanted a simpler life. And had no say in the matter when the UR built this zone."

"So, we were here first truly," Marien said still grinning from ear to ear.

"Correct," the Historian said. "This was UR territory originally. But the UR at the time was also friendly to the lesser races of Z'yon and wanted them to evolve. So, they segregated this portion of their territory as a sort of reservation at first. In the long term it was to be handed over to the lesser races of Z'yon as a gift."

"The UR owned the Realm, but it was destined to be a gift for us," Frenzen said.

"Also correct," the Historian said as he went back to work.

"May I ask you two questions?" the Historian asked.

"Of course, you may," Marien said.

"This Utopian Kingdom," the Historian started. "How old is it?"

"This is currently the sixth iteration. And it is roughly one hundred million years old," Frenzen said.

"Sixth iteration?" the Historian asked. "What happened to the others?"

"In the very early history of the Realm a great dark lord destroyed the first five," Frenzen explained. "Abaddon the Dark Lord and right-hand man to Sargon himself."

"I know of the Empyrean Sargon," the Historian said. "But this Abaddon, I do not know."

"Abaddon was a creation of Sargon that outlived him," Frenzen said. "Abaddon was searching for his master and believed him to be somewhere in the Realm."

"I assume he was unsuccessful?" The Historian asked.

"You assume correctly," Marien added. "Then there was his daughter Aethinea."

"It bred?" The Historian asked. "How?"

"Aethinea and her purpose were never truly known. But she finally died during the Great War," Frenzen said.

"I keep hearing about this Great War, Asora explained some of it during our travel to Evorn. But I'm curious about your interpretation of it," the Historian asked.

"Princess Asora's telling was most likely from a bias point of view," Frenzen said.

"She told me that," the Historian pointed to Lady T'a. "She

was the ruler at the time and was tricked and confused by grief and misunderstanding."

"I am surprised that she said that" Frenzen said.

"Asora has a lot of confidence and faith in her," the Historian noted. "She reminds me of the first elf to set foot on UR ground."

"The one who came to the UR senate?" Marien asked.

"Yes," the Historian replied. "That T'a woman looks very similar. Maybe they're related?"

"Perhaps," Marien replied.

While the Historian worked and answered Marien and Frenzen's questions. Princess Asora was examining several components of an older nuclear weapon. She was looking for a few pieces. The work bench she was at was cluttered with parts and tools. All of which were familiar to her.

"Here, you could use this," Irantanco said offering Asora a cup of coffee. She eyed it suspiciously. "Relax it's not poisoned. You do me no good dead."

"Uh huh," Asora said unenthusiastically. She took the cup and drank it. "Not bad."

"What are you doing?" Irantanco asked.

"What does it look like?" Asora replied.

"You look to be dismantling several nuclear warheads and attempting to put them back together," Irantanco answered.

"That is part of it," Asora said. She then thought for a moment. "Have you ever read my thesis on potential forced nuclear power generation and release?"

"You wrote that?" Irantanco looked surprised. "Holy crap! You're more dangerous then i gave you credit for."

"And that is why?" A new voice asked.

High Priestess Nona walked up to the two. She looked at Irantanco with contempt. The human terrorist returned the stare. He was not going anywhere.

"What is it?" Asora demanded of Nona.

"I wish to know what you are doing and to make sure that this," Nona pointed at Irantanco. "Man does not harm you."

"According to him I am more beneficial alive," Asora said. "And as for what I am doing. I am building a prototype based on a research paper I wrote during my time in the Red Guard SDC Super-weapons Forces."

"I am still trying to get over the fact that you were a warrior in the SDC," Nona said.

"And I'm trying to get over the fact that you wrote and researched a potential new form of nuclear and anti-matter firepower," Irantanco added.

"What?" Nona asked.

"My thesis was based on a combination of nuclear fusion using anti-matter versions of normal matter hydrogen," Asora said.

"I do not understand," Nona said.

"Do you know how a nuclear weapon works?" Irantanco asked.

"Her highness did explain in detail during the Royal Academy. Much to the dismay of the teachers and faculty," Nona remembered.

"Ah yes," Asora said with a grin. "I remember those days."

"You said something about fusing hydrogen into helium and with no stabilization causes a supernova like event. The result was a nuclear explosion," Nona said trying to remember.

"A thermonuclear explosion is the result of the fusion process that is not contained," Asora said in an annoyed tone.

Asora was not annoyed with Nona. More like she was not able to find a certain component. She was looking all over the desk.

"Is it safe to be working on nuclear devices?" Nona asked.

"As long as the cores are contained and you use the proper PPE, it's safe," Irantanco said.

"Is it safe on what Asora is working on?" Nona asked in a very worried tone. "I remember these weapons and the power plants from the Great War. This is a science that is not to be taken lightly."

"You are very correct," Irantanco said. "But from what I can see, there is no core here."

"It is over there," Asora pointed to a large grey box that was marked with many biohazards, radiation source, and deadly contents stickers. "What I need now is a particle accelerator."

"A what?" Nona asked.

"A very large device that is used to smash atoms and particles at near light speed," Irantanco answered.

"Why?" Nona asked.

"It is the best way we humans know how to manufacture anti-matter," Irantanco said. "But how are you going to contain and control it? Anti-Matter is the most volatile substance in the universe."

"A magnetic bottle," Asora replied.

"The only magnets I know of that can hold anti-matter samples the size of a grain of sugar. These are giant electro-magnets that was as big as this vault," Irantanco pointed out.

"The Historian gave me some pointers on how to scale it down," Asora said.

Irantanco was at a loss for words. He was not sure how to approach this. One thought came to him as they were about to trade one tyrant for another. Queen Laxur was a terrifying tyrant now and showed it. Asora is whole different kind. So, this made Irantanco believe that both Asora and Laxur were not as different as they appeared. Laxur used magic, Asora was about to unleash nuclear and anti-matter death.

"There must be another way to stop Queen Laxur," Nona said.

"Can a tyrant be negotiated with?" Asora asked.

"One must try," Nona said.

Both Asora and Irantanco laughed at that. This was where the differences in Utopian and Consortium thinking diverged. Utopians did believe in trying diplomacy first. Even if they believed it it would fail. The Consortium by contrast have the mindset of what to expect and react accordingly. Meaning that the Consortium judges you based on what they see and make assumptions.

"Someone like Queen Laxur only understands force," Irantnaco said.

"And these old super weapons are the definition of force," Asora said. "They worked well during the Great War."

"What makes you think that these weapons will have any effect on Laxur?" Nona asked. "The deadly energy from these things do not always work on gods."

"That is why I am modifying these weapons," the Historian said walking up to the three.

Nona looked at the towering bio-mechanical monster and backed away to Asora. The Historian then placed a device on Asora's work desk.

"The Z'yonic pointy ear has a point," the Historian said.

"What?" Irantanco asked.

"Empyrean and the others like them were not always beaten by standard ionizing radiation-based weaponry," the Historian explained.

"I assume that the UR found a way?" Asora asked.

"They did, but rarely needed to use them," the Historian said. "They tried in their final years. But never had the chance."

"Well then," Asora started. "Time to see if they would have worked."

Hours later as the day turned to evening, the work still moved forward. Princess Asora was asleep at her desk. She was exhausted and could not keep up anymore. She did stir and found that she was alone. Not physically alone, there were thousands of workers and engineers still in the vault doing their jobs. The ones who were always around her were gone. Asora looked up at a clock and found that it was one hour from midnight.

The princess got up and walked out of the vault and into the main office complex. She saw dozens of Uridan moving about doing what ever it was that they did. She then saw the Historian carrying a large device from his organic ship. He then handed the device to some of the Uridan for them to take it to the vault. He saw Asora and approached her.

"You look to be tired?" The Historian asked.

"I am. Have been trying to get my new device ready," Asora said.

"Your anti-matter fusion weapon," the Historian asked. "You are attempting to create something that event he UR's best scientists could not even achieve."

"But it is possible," Asora said.

"It is. The math says it is possible," the Historian pointed out.

Princess Asora sighed in exasperation. She was tired and could barely think straight. The Historian picked up on this and had a thought.

"Do you have a backup plan?" The Historian asked.

"What?" Asora asked.

"Do you have an alternate plan in case this fails?" The Historian asked.

"No, I do not," Asora said. "And I am disturbed by that."

"I may have something that could function as a backup plan," the Historian said. "Follow me."

The Historian went back to his ship and Princess Asora was right behind him. The organic like vessel was lit up and was cooler to the touch. The humidity was also less brutal. The Historian led Asora into another chamber that opened into what could only be described as a cross between a computer lab and a brain in the centers linked up by neurons.

"I found that a sector of the old UR military network was recently activated," the Historian said. "It had been damaged and is nearly fully repaired now."

"Are you referring to the incident on Havaina?" Asora asked.

"Yes," the Historian said.

The Historian projected a holographic image of Asora back on Haviana a few months ago as a giantess. She was pounding on and trying to destroy the various alien machines.

"Those things are repaired. By whom?" Asora asked.

"By the automated maintenance system," the Historian answered. "That sector was activated by accident. And without an operator it will happen again."

"Can it be stopped?" Asora asked.

"Yes, and this fits into my idea for your lack of a backup plan," the Historian said. "I am able to turn control of the entire UR defense grid in this region over to you."

Princess Asora marveled at such an idea. But then other ideas and thoughts came to her. But the mere idea of controlling such vast and ancient technology was appealing to her.

"Can it handle Laxur?" Asora asked.

"She was stupid in how to deal with just malfunctioning devices," the Historian said. "With an actual mind behind them that can understand her. Even the Empyrean feared this entire system."

"Laxur has the power of an Empyrean," Asora said.

"And you know her," the Historian pointed out. "I recommend that you keep this control as a secret. A final solution or last ditch back up."

"Agreed," Asora said. "So, how do I gain control over this defense system? And what is its reach?"

"To answer your second question first," the Historian started. "The entire region that you refer to as the Realm. It has these UR defense platforms installed across it. Once you have control you will know." The Historian then took out a canister from a containment unit on the bulkhead. "To answer your first question. You gain control just like the other UR flag officers did."

"With that?" Asora pointed to the canister.

"With the nanites inside," the Historian corrected. "These nanites will make you completely compatible with UR technology and allow you full access and control of it."

"Nanites? You want to put machines into my body?" Asora asked.

"The Nanites will be fused to your nervous system and take residence in your brain. It will not rewire you more like they settle in her brain and intemperate your commands. Your entire nervous system becomes a kind of wireless command and control system of all UR technology. You would be recognized as a UR flag officer and have full access," the Historian explained. "The nanites would be completely symbiotic to you. They will do their best to keep your health, while you give them a place to live. They are alive after all. So, they may make you a bit hungry then what you are normally use to. But other then that the rest of you will be unaffected."

"Will I be able to see all the knowledge and information that the UR has?" Asora asked.

"Only what the defense grid has in its various databases. But you would be in full control of it all," the Historian pointed out.

"Speak of this to no one," Asora commanded. "And you may put these nanites into me."

The Historian then had Asora go to a table that formed form the ceiling. The princess laid down on it and did what she could to relax. She then heard a hiss and she fell into a very deep sleep.

When she awoke two days later. Princess Asora did not feel any different. She was in a cot in the Red Guard barracks on Geocom. That surprised her since she knew that the fairies would be throwing a hissy fit over Asora's sleeping accommodations.

She did have an odd feeling in her head. It was not a headache but more like a pressure. It was not completely unpleasant. She also had a surge of ideals, thoughts, and images all coursing through her mind.

"You recovered faster then I would have thought," the Historian said as he entered the room.

"How long was I out?" Asora asked.

"Two days," the Historian said casually. "Normally recovery takes a week. You are far more resilient than any human I've ever known."

"Is this feeling in my head normal?" Asora asked.

"The light pressure?" The Historian asked. "Yes, and the flood of information and ideas is also normal. Your brain is adjusting to its new abilities now. The neural network is also adapting itself to your requirements."

"The UR technology is making itself better able to be used by me?" Asora asked. "Incredible."

"Indeed," the Historian said. "Remember this is to be a final solution."

Princess Asora thought about those words for a moment. A final solution, for if or when her true and original plans fail. She thought about what the Historian's plans could be? There had to be more to this. Why was she only now thinking about this?

"I am hopeful that the modified weapons you are building for me will be enough," Asora said.

"They will work, they did before," the Historian reassured. "This Laxur is ignorant of the past. The Empyrean were partly immune to ionizing radiation, but that required them to know what to do. Laxur should be unaware of this ancient Empyrean procedure."

"Queen Laxur is far more cunning than you think she is," Asora said.

"It's been my experience that when any being, not just humans that gain so much power they tend to become arrogant, blind to other dangers, and devolve into tyrannical idiots," the Historian said.

"I bet you have a lot of stories about that sort of thing," Asora said.

"I have nearly four point four billion years' worth," the Historian corrected.

"Wow," Asora exclaimed quietly. "That is a very long time."

"And I've been alone of Tera for just as long," the Historian added.

"You are welcome to stay in my kingdom," Asora offered.

"I better not," the Historian said. "I wish to stay on Tera and await the return of those who truly built me."

"As you wish," Asora replied.

Four days later, the Historian finished his modifications to the nuclear warheads. He had put all his mods inside, so nothing looked like it was modified. He explained the internal dynamics, how it worked, and its expected power to the princess. Others were with Asora and the Historian, like Marien, Frenzen, Nona, and T'a.

"So where would you suggest I deploy this weapon, Historian?" Asora asked.

She was looking over the weapon, which was as big as she was. The princess was impressed and, on some level, could feel its raw power. She saw this as her greatest weapon now.

"For a weapon this massive, unless you plan on cracking the planet, I recommend detonating it in orbit, in between the planet and its orbiting satellite," the Historian suggested.

"What good would that do?" Irantanco asked.

"It might knock the planet out of its orbit, which is a very possible side effect. The high gamma radiation levels will contaminate the planet's atmosphere, and that will result in inhabitability and permanent magical neutralization," the Historian informed.

"Either is a good thing for us, princess," Irantanco commented.

"I want the Darkcon Empire on its knees and Queen Laxur and Princess Polea in an asylum," Asora pointed out. "Killing them will be a last resort."

Marien looked at Asora with a horrified expression. Has Asora lost her mind now? All this power has now corrupting her two most powerful children. But what could she do?

"I agree with you. They need to be stopped and locked away," the terrorist said.

Asora looked at him with suspicion, and she was not willing to turn her back on him. He did, after all, call her a freak of nature, and he said that she should not exist. He made Asora nervous, but right now, she needed his help. His organization could move the device that she needed into the correct position.

Another month passed, and the Uridan modified over two thousand thermonuclear bombs. Many Utopians were nervous about the forbidden human super weapons. They tried to get them banned many times before, but the humans, ever defiant, refused. These weapons killed billions during the Great War; however, this time the Utopians were not on the receiving end.

Chapter Fifty-Six

Asora's Nuclear Firestorm

On the now-occupied Darkcon world called Ebanaoia, a fleet of Utopian ships and a few human warships entered orbit for a field test that Princess Asora had ordered. The Utopian royal Admiral Farkon, an older elf, was put in charge of the operation. He was ordered to detonate the weapon on the surface and record the results after the blast. He did not care much for the Darkcons, but he was alive during the Great War. He remembered the humans firing their nuclear weapons. His wife's world was burned and left radioactive for the next ten millennia by these weapons. He hated these things, but he studied what little information there was about them. And what he learned scared him to death.

Now the Utopian Kingdom was calling upon these horrifying weapons to fight the newly divinely enchanted Darkcon forces. The admiral did not know how to feel about that. These weapons may indeed be the only thing that can stop the Darkcons now, but there had to be a better alternative.

The ship carrying the admiral and the prototype weapon was a very elegantly designed Ship of the Line. A multi-mast sailing vessel that used the solar winds to move through the stars. A crew of two hundred and an additional one hundred more guests were out on the main deck watching the events unfold.

Above his ship there was a Consortium destroyer. Unlike the majestic Utopian Ship of the Line, the Consortium destroyer was a metal grey box with a lot of antennas sticking out of it. As well as large rockets strapped to its aft section. It also did not have the rotating sections of the larger Consortium battleships. Instead from what Admiral Farkon understood of Consortium space naval engineering, they generated gravity by using thrust. The destroyer was laid out like a tower and not like his ship was. The Utopian ship had more guns on paper, but the destroyer's weapons were more destructive.

The admiral also knew this type of ship well. They were very common during the Great War and were a pain to fight. This one was from that time too. It was one of the oldest ships still in service. The commanding officer of the destroyer was someone that Farkon knew and liked. A jewel elf woman that was more interested in studying stars then combat.

The admiral had a Consortium communications device and an officer from the destroyer on his ship to be able to communicate between the two ships. The human communications officer was new as he was still shocked by the Utopian vessel's appearance and abilities. And he was still trying to get over the fact that there was an atmosphere and gravity on the ship. He was accustomed to having to work and live inside a large metal box with pressure and gravity machinery.

"First time on a ship like this?" Farkon asked the human.

"Yes, sir," the male human replied still looking around.

"You really need to get out of those metal boxes," Farkon said.

Another officer then approached. This was a small male fairy dressed as a Royal Guard naval officer. He was in a blue and grey dress uniform. He was also in his normal diary size of sixteen centimeters.

"The weapon is ready to be deployed, sir," an officer said.

"Very well. Shoot the missile at the surface and take us to a safe distance. I do not want to be anywhere near the explosion," the admiral stated. "Communications, tell the destroyer of our actions."

The human communications officer relayed the message. The

console beeped with a reply. And showed him the message.

"Message acknowledged," the communications officer said. "They are also moving to a safe distance."

The reason for the Utopian vessel to have the weapon and not the destroyer was simply that the destroyer did not have the needed space nor the required equipment. That struck Farkon as strange, and he suspected an alterer motive behind Princess Asora's thinking here. But he was here to do his duty.

The ship launched a large cylindrical missile at the planet's surface. The device was atop a modified missile that rockets the device to many times the speed of sound. Even if the weapon failed to work, the physical impact would be enough to level the continent that it was racing to on the planet below.

Within minutes, the missile entered the atmosphere, and a blinding light could be seen from space. The crews of the ships were stunned by the brightness. A few moments later the blinding light vanished, and a towering mushroom cloud appeared.

The sight gave Admiral Farkon flashbacks to the Great War when Consortium forces rained down nuclear destruction upon many Utopian worlds in a similar way. Though none of them were as powerful as the one his ship just launched.

This mushroom cloud covered nearly the whole continent and sent several worldwide quakes and shockwaves. They could even see towering tidal waves of radioactive water surging from the epicenter. The lands below seemed to shake and crack with fire.

All of this made it look as if the planet below was struck by a very big and fast-moving meteor. The cloud was now able to reach into space and spread its deadly cloud into the high atmosphere.

Princess Asora was watching the events unfold from the far end of the deck of the Utopian ship. Unlike everyone else who looked on with horror. Princess Asora was grinning with a smug satisfaction. She now had a weapon that could allow her to fight back. A weapon that can deny her foes magic and even challenge gods. All she had to do now was make sure that only she controlled this vast and deadly arsenal of super weapons. For she had more to come.

Three days later, the destroyer personnel were on the surface, covered from head to toe in radioactive resistant suits. They took bodies and samples back to their ship in orbit. Inside the research ship, the Consortium scientists examined the corpses and soil samples behind safe walls. The planet was still experiencing the aftereffects of a nuclear attack.

"As expected, the victims' internals were heavily radiated, and the organic matter had melted," a female scientist proclaimed.

"Confirmed. The soil samples show higher than normal radiation levels from a conventional hydrogen bomb. The levels are nine times higher than normal. Levels are almost above the gamma radiation spectrum," a male scientist said as he typed on a computer.

"The princess wants to know the results from your tests," a military officer said as he entered.

"Well, you can tell her royal highness that these things take time and to keep her corset on. She will get it in due time," a technician complained.

"I will tell her that. I want that data. The next test is going to begin in three days," the officer stated, and then he left.

"Damn, I know we are in a corner, but this is too fast," the scientist said.

"I'm not the one giving the orders," the officer said. "This is coming from her royal highness."

"What is she planning on? A full-scale nuclear war?" The scientist asked.

"I think that is what she has in mind," the officer answered. "And we are all going to see this on a regular basis now."

"Maybe she will only use them a few times? You know to get the Darkcons to think twice?" The scientist suggested.

"Someone under that much stress?" The officer asked. "Is going to make these sorts of weapons their go to choose instrument."

"I hope you're wrong on that," the scientist replied.

Three days later, another Utopian warship, captained by a dwarf named Sauwan, was orbiting another Darkcon world. He was ordered by the princess herself to detonate a nuclear bomb in orbit of this world, which was once owned by a dwarf noble who was killed in the Darkcon invasion. Sauwan did not care what this weapon was, or who built it; if it killed Darkcons and avenged the fallen dwarf noble, then he supported it.

He heard about this weapon from the humans and jewel elves who loaded onto his ship a few days ago. They were trying to scare him and his crew. He could tell that. But in reality, the information actually made him more fascinated by it.

A weapon that could for an instant make a tiny star. Then that power can be thrown at the enemy in a wave of light and fire. How poetic Sauwan thought. He was warned though to keep at a safe standoff distance when deploying this human super weapon.

"Captain," a small, enchanted weasel in a dress uniform skittered up to the captain. "We are in position."

"Fire!" Sauwan ordered.

The missile was launched from the deck of his ship. The target was the space on the opposite side of the planet's biggest moon. An explosion larger than the dwarf had ever seen erupted. The moon was shattered like glass in blue and fiery light. The massive debris field slammed into the planet. The radioactive debris ignited the atmosphere of the planet. It was burned away in a matter of minutes. Some of the larger debris chunks from the moon crashed into the planet. This took out huge swaths of the continents and oceans. The rest was ejected into space. The event was so powerful that it altered the orbit of the planet. The remains of the planet were thrown onto a collision course with the star that the planet orbited. In one year, it would burn up. The crew of the ship cheered as the Darkcon interlopers were gone. They did not care about the planet anymore.

A human onboard the Utopian ship captured the test on camera. He was stunned by the spectacle. To him this was a planet killing weapon. More powerful than anything the Consortium ever fielded. He was scared.

From a hidden room Princess Asora watched the video and saw the pictures of the second test, and she had also recently received the results from the first test. She was impressed, but deep inside, she was scared. But at the same time, she was excited. She finally had a weapon, not an answer to Laxur and her power and madness. But if she was not careful, she would be just like Laxur. A mad tyrant that would not hesitate to use extreme force.

The Historian and his Uridans were touring Evorn with Countess Marien. She had learned that Evorn was once a human colony when humans lived on Tera. Evorn was once known as Tamotan, an ancient human word meaning "a world of sea and land."

An elf asked what worlds were once theirs. The Historian told her only one—Z'yon. The elves, dwarves, fairies, and all the rest of the magical creatures only had one world. Humans and many other unknown races once spanned the universe with vast interstellar empires. The humans were once more advanced than they were during Asora's time, and they were like gods to the primitive magical peoples.

Princess Asora came out of the secret room with a fist full of papers. They were data readouts and intelligence reports. She also was looking for another site. She saw Archduke Frenzen nearby. She approached and as he bowed to her.

"I want another test," Asora commanded.

"Of course, Your Highness. Where?" Frenzen asked.

"This one will be at Hailospont," Asora said.

"Uh? Are you sure?" Frenzen asked concerned.

"Yes, I am sure, damn it!" Asora yelled in anger.

She had lost sleep and was running on coffee, magic, and adrenaline. That was not good for health or temperament. For any species really. It was showing on Asora now.

"As you wish, my princess," Frenzen said coldly and left.

Asora went into another room. The war room. Here Princess Asora was alone in this large room filled with maps, papers, and two computers. She was frustrated with the resistance that she was getting from the court. They were concerned and that angered Asora.

"You should not push so hard, my child," an unknown voice said gently.

"Who is there?" Asora demanded. "Show yourself!"

A bright light appeared on a chair, and a beautiful woman formed. The woman had white hair, pale skin, and icy blue eyes. She wore a white dress with a transparent veil. Princess Asora felt incredible power from her, just like Laxur with Z'yon, but she was different.

"Who are you?" Asora demanded.

"You should know, my dear. You pray to me almost every day," she said with a gentle motherly smile.

"You. The . . . the Maker?" Asora stuttered, and then she dropped to her knees and bowed. "Please forgive me."

"Please, Asora. Rise to your feet. I wish to speak to you," the Maker said.

"Of course, my maker. What do you wish to speak to me about?" Asora asked politely.

"I am afraid for you and your sister, Asaria," the Maker began.

"My sister has stolen divine powers. I will do what I can to stop—" Asora was then cut off.

"That power was, in fact, meant for Asaria," the Maker interrupted. "Unfortunately, she has become too irresponsible and unstable for it. She is at risk of being controlled by her new powers."

"Why? Why give her that power? You knew that she would turn into a vile witch," Asora seemed to complain.

"It was her destiny. I also said I fear for you as well," the Maker said.

"For me? If it was not for you giving that power to Laxur, you would not have to fear for me," Asora stated rudely.

"I fear for you for a different reason, my dear. You are now on a similar path with a force that you do not understand. The super weapons you plan on using will kill more than your enemies. Your own people will die, and you will be to blame," the Maker explained.

"And what do you want me to do? Just let Queen Laxur steamroll over me?" Asora stated rudely.

"Of course not. You must find a better way. A nuclear holocaust is not the answer," the Maker said.

"And how can I challenge her? I am not a goddess. You sound a little crazy," Asora complained.

"That is your belief. There are other ways. You are just not seeing them," the Maker scolded Asora.

"You're insane!" Asora yelled.

"DO NOT TALK THAT WAY TO ME!" The Maker's voices roared. "I am the one that gave all your ancestors life. I am the reason you exist! I have the wisdom of a trillion lifetimes! You are a mere child. If you do not heed my warning, you will suffer the consequences," the Maker then disappeared.

"Crazy old bat," Asora said. "How the hell am i suppose to fight someone who is so full of power and drunk on it?"

Days later, another test was scheduled at Hailospont, a world near the angels' territory. Dominus had officially delivered a protest from the monarchy of the angels to his cousin, Asora. The Utopian princess ignored the protest and continued the test. She had no time for their antics.

She was on location to witness the test for herself. She was going to see the power of these weapons firsthand. She was tired of only seeing them through computer monitors and data readouts.

The angels were angry, and they had threatened numerous times to fight their fellow Utopians if Asora continued her nuclear firestorm tests as they called them. Asora was doing things that she would not normally do. She used her coins on the angels and overwhelmed them. The angels were defeated, and Dominus was told by the monarchy to submit to the princess before she decided to use her new weapon on them. They would never be able to defend against such devastation.

When the Utopians and the rest of the universe saw Princess Asora alone defeat a billion angels, no one dared question her or her developing madness for these nuclear weapons. She would be allowed to have her way, but there would be a terrible price to pay.

The next model of the modified weapon was deployed from a ship in orbit. This one was the smaller of the test devices and incased in a missile housing. Princess Asora watched as the missile then took off and towards the planet Hailospont.

The test began with a bang, literally. The planet Hailospont was destroyed by a shockwave of energy and flying debris. The explosion was so powerful it affected the star nearby. The surface of the planet was stripped away and uprooted like a peel of an orange. The tectonic plates lifted into space and the edged burned with fire. Most of the pieces of the planet crashed into the small star causing a powerful corona mass ejection.

In her room on board the human flagship, the HCS *Thundercon*, Princess Asora read more reports. She was impressed by this new weapon, but she looked bored. Everyone else looked horrified. The angels were now both angry and scared for the first time in ages.

Tired, Asora went into the bathroom to wash up. Unable to fight her sleepiness anymore, Asora decided to go to bed, and she put her own nightgown on. Her fairies were unable to come on board because of the nuclear fusion reactor that powered the ship. Fairies were very susceptible to nuclear radiation, even in the smallest amount. So Asora had to do a lot on her own.

Asora took off her dress and corset, rendering her naked. She looked at herself in the mirror and for a moment imagined herself like her sister. What would it be like to be a goddess? To have all that power, the perfect body, perfect beauty, strength, and only the Maker knows what else. Asora imagined herself looking just like Laxur: two and a half meters tall, the most beautiful face in the universe, the strength of ten knights, beauty so intense that no man could resist her whims, magical powers that were on par with the gods themselves.

She snapped out of her imagination and put on a thin white robe after she covered herself with a bra and underwear. She felt the cold chill from being undressed for so long.

She then felt another cold chill down her spine. A dark cloud flowed into an empty chair, and a being formed, scaring Asora. She thought that it was Laxur; instead, it was a man in a black robe. Asora could not see the man's face.

"Who are you?" Asora demanded, screaming, and covering herself.

"Relax, princess. I am not here to harm you. I am here to offer advice," the man said in a deep voice.

Asora relaxed somewhat, as she could feel that this man had the same aura and power as the Maker. She had an idea of who this could be. "Very well. What do you want?"

"I am known as the Architect, and you are now a part of my plan. My mate gave you a hard time, but in my opinion, her logic is flawed. You have the right idea," the Architect said.

"I have the right idea? You mean my super weapons? What Plan?" Asora questioned.

"Asaria runs the risk of damaging the universe. If she cannot be changed, then I will force those changes my way. I am tired of cleaning up messes," the man complained.

"How could Asaria be made to change?" Asora asked.

"Three terrors will descend upon her and the whole realm. You are the first terror. The second terror is on the way. The third, hopefully, will not be needed," the Architect informed her.

"I am one of your infamous terrors? And why would you want to help me?" Asora demanded.

"You hold my powers and gifts. Those coins that dangle from your neck are my gifts and powers. Those coins have accepted you, and so do I," he said.

"Unfortunately, Laxur has these powers now," Asora said sorrowfully. "Plus, whatever else she has."

"She may have all those powers, but they are not as powerful as what you have," he reassured the princess.

"So, my weapons are able to deal with her then," Asora said.

He got up and stood in front of the smaller girl. He seemed less like a god and more like a father. He placed his hands upon her shoulders. "Do what you need to, and no more. I will help you when I can."

The Architect vanished in a cloud of black mist, which enveloped Asora. She felt a very great power course through her. The god that the Darkcons worshipped was now helping her. How ironic Asora thought.

Chapter Fifty-Seven

The Second Battle of Z'yon

"The test at Hailospont has confirmed what you thought, Your highness. The powerful magical forces protecting that world failed. They could not stand up to the modified nuclear blast," Marevin explained.

The Historian was on board and was fascinated with the events. He had been studying the tests and adjusting without a care for what the weapons were going to be used for. He felt that the modifications were complete and successful.

"Good. That means that your modifications are sufficient to attack Z'yon successfully," Asora responded.

"Are you sure that you want to do that?" Dominus asked.

He had been ordered to be always around Asora, except in her chambers. The angels were now worried and could no longer take any chances if Asora wished to turn her weapons on others for any reason. It was hoped that Dominus could stop her.

"I do not want to destroy Z'yon itself, but if Laxur does not leave it for the Tervi system, I will have no choice but to destroy it," Asora stated.

Heralin and Jeia looked at the plans that they had for a magical and scientific prison that they were building on a world in the Tervi planetary system for Laxur and Polea. It was lightly populated and near the Great Void.

T'ula, Ela, and T'a were preparing their magic for the coming battle, while Rakon and Marien were with Asora in the battle room of the *Thundercon*'s command and control center. The Historian and a few Uridan where with him too.

"Asora, is the prison completed? Are you sure of the calculations for the weapon you are planning to use?" Marien demanded from her youngest daughter.

"Yes, Mother," Asora answered dully.

"The prison is the fourth planet in the Tervi system. Laxur and Polea will have a whole planet to themselves, after it is lightly radiated," Asora explained. "Or at the least isolated."

"You had better hope that works, or your sister is going to go on a warpath for you," Rakon warned, "or die of radiation poisoning."

"That is a bad thing why?" The Historian asked.

"Are you two finished?" Asora demanded coldly.

"I think that we are," Marien said, and she left.

After a minute, only the Historian remained. The rest had followed Countess Marien out of the room. The Uridan also went out at the Historian's command.

"That could have gone better," the Historian commented.

"I do not care right now. Do you have the final bomb?" Asora asked.

"Here. It has been miniaturized so you can carry it. Only you can activate and deactivate it, even Laxur cannot turn it off." The Historian explained.

He held out a medium-size black ball with four red buttons. He placed it in Asora's hands. The princess took the weapon, and she admired the power that she held in her hands: the power to destroy, the power to cause fear, the power to control.

"Let Asaria have Z'yon. I have this," Asora said to herself.

She was holding the ultimate super weapon. The Historian looked curiously at Asora. She reminded him of so many famous leaders of the UR. One came to mind to him. He kept that to himself.

"It is a strange thing, to hold such power over the destiny and fate of so many. From the smallest single cell organism to the fate of whole worlds," Asora said. "And now the fate of the Realm is either slavery or burn in fire."

"Very poetic," the Historian said.

Deep inside the fortress on Z'yon, Smika was wandering around the halls, looking for his goddess queen. He was bored, and the queen usually enjoyed his company. She was not in her bed chambers. Prince S'tie was out with Illumin, and Heranian was in the desert. That suited Smika well. That meant he can spend some time with Laxur.

He was ready to share his wish with Laxur. He was embarrassed the first time to ask this. But now he had his chance, and he was going to take it.

An hour later, Smika figured out where she was. She was in a room a kilometer from her royal chambers. The young man opened the door. Inside, he saw Laxur lying facedown on a special table and being massaged by six succubi.

She looked up and saw Smika looking from the door. She smiled in delight. She stretched up but only enough to keep herself decent in front of Smika.

"Come in, my dear. Would you like a massage too?" Laxur asked him gently.

"I guess?" Smika seemed nervous.

It was not Laxur that made him nervous, but the succubi. They were big, seductive, and ravenous. And he found them very hideous. Especially when compared to Laxur. Who was in Smika's mind as perfect.

"Do not be afraid of them. You are under my word, and they will not harm you in any way, my dear," Laxur reassured the young man. "They will also reframe from making you uncomfortable."

Two succubi escorted Smika to another table that had just appeared. It was directly in front of the queen's so she could face him. They took his clothes except for his underwear. They laid him facedown and placed a thin blanket over his legs. The two succubi began to massage the boy's back.

"Feels good, does it not?" Laxur asked.

"Yes, it does, my queen," Smika replied politely.

Laxur liked the fact that this boy was so well-behaved. He was one of her most loyal servants, but he was not a servant; he was her only male acolyte. He was the only one that did not request a special divine gift. She wanted him to have one, but he was too shy to ask her. That gave him a very cute feel to her. She also could feel his attraction to her.

"Smika, have you thought about what gift you want?" Laxur asked sweetly.

"Yes, I have, my queen," the boy said. Laxur looked at him as if she were demanding to know. "I want you."

That took the dark beauty by surprise, but she should not have been. He was at that age where he was beginning to find women attractive. And Laxur was in reality a very attractive woman. Possibility the most beautiful. She enticed everyone around her with her mere form.

"Oh my. As flattered as I am, and I really am, I am too old for you. I could have a lady of your age found for you, or I could create a woman just for you," Laxur suggested.

"You asked what I wanted. I find you to be the greatest and most lovely woman that ever lived. I do not care that you are older or bigger than me," Smika said quickly. "I love you."

Again, Queen Laxur was taken aback. This young man was madly in love with her. Her love and seduction spell were meant for older men, so the spell upon her body was working too well.

"I am sorry, my dear Smika. I cannot do that, but I can do something that will satisfy your wish," Laxur suggested. Smika looked both sad and confused. "I have an idea what you may like."

"I am sorry if I make you uncomfortable," Smika said.

"It is not that, my dear," Laxur reassured. "I feel you deserve better."

A few hours later, Queen Laxur was in her new lab using her divine magic. On a platform, the body of a young girl began to form. She was making a girl for Smika, but this girl, this creation, would be different from her others—this one had a soul. She made this girl to resemble herself. She had blue-black hair and was tall, roughly more then a meter and a half. Slightly taller than Smika. The queen gave this girl blue eyes and great mortal powers. She could do everything LAxur herself could but on a lower level of power and skill. She was voluptuous for a female teenager human/angel hybrid, and her muscles were light, unlike Laxur's, which were powerful.

"My queen. What is that?" Princess Polea formed nearby in the lab.

"This young lady is for Smika," Laxur said.

"Why are you going to all this trouble for him?" Polea asked.

"Because, Polea, I want Smika to have a companion his age," Laxur replied, looking back to her creation.

"Again, my queen, why?" Polea asked insistently.

The dark queen decided to tell the blond princess. "Because, Polea, Smika just admitted to me that he is in love with me."

Polea had a face of understanding, and she realized Laxur's intentions. "Oh my. He is really shooting high. I must give him points for trying, but then again, you are the ultimate catch for any male."

"Smika is far too young for me," Laxur began. "Besides he deserves a very dedicated lady."

"I can understand that. Plus, you are far too big for him too—like four times his size," Polea mumbled. "And a goddess."

"Thanks," Laxur said dully. "So this girl will be a perfect alternative for Smika. I will see to it that she loves him and is loyal to him."

"But what if she does not turn out to be what you or Smika want? What if she turns traitor on us, or worse, hurts Smika?" Polea asked all her questions at once.

"If I have to, I will use my most powerful spells on her. She will be the woman of his dreams, one way or the other," Laxur stated.

"What if Smika does not love her even if she loves him?" Polea added in.

"That is a risk that I am willing to take. Now what do you think of her? Any ideas for a name?" Laxur asked.

"I think she is very pretty. I like her hair. She reminds me of a fragile china doll. As for a name, now that is a tough one," Polea said thoughtfully. The blond princess was in deep thought. "Oh, I have an idea for a name. How about Aladynia?"

"Aladynia? You really want me to give her an ancient elf word for a name?" Laxur questioned.

"Aladynia, it means 'new.' Or you can use the human meaning behind it. Humans and elves have many similar words," Polea suggested. "New."

"But the human translation is more of an insult. The word means 'prototype,'" Laxur pointed out. "So New Prototype?"

"If you think about it, my queen, it fits her well," Polea said.

"You are right. All right then, Aladynia it is," Laxur proclaimed.

Two days later, Smika was looking for Princess Polea. Usually, he and she played games with Hyea, but Hyea was out now, so only Polea was around. He remembered at first, he and Polea met. They had a rocky start, but they became friends, and he enjoyed playing the games that she had. Polea was a very pretty woman just like Laxur, but Polea was more of a child, and that made her easy to get along with. And was more of a best friend to him. Laxur was far more mature.

The princess was usually around the queen, so he went to the throne room but did not find them there. He went to the dining room because Queen Laxur liked to eat and drink a lot. How she could maintain her sexy figure was beyond Smika's understanding. She was not there, and neither was Polea. He could go to the queen's sleeping chambers, but she usually had 'suitors' there.

A purple glowing ball hovered in front of Smika's face. It seemed to beckon him to follow. He followed it for an hour, and it vanished behind a set of giant doors. These were the doors to the queen's bedchambers. Perhaps Queen Laxur wished to see him about his gift. The doors opened, and he slowly walked in. He hoped to see Laxur, but he wondered what she wanted. He had begun to have fantasies about the queen recently. He could hear several heartbeats—all but one was familiar. Smika had the unique ability of ultra-sensitive hearing. He also had an excellent memory, and he memorized everyone's noises, especially the queen's heartbeat.

Queen Laxur came out of the darkness and stood a few meters away from him. She was wearing a very tight black dress. She had a loving smile on her lips, and she beckoned him to follow.

"I have a lovely surprise for you, my dear," the dark beauty said to her favorite boy.

"What is it?" Smika asked, now very curious.

"Wait right here, and I will bring her to you," the queen said.

"Her?" Smika asked.

Laxur then walked away into the dark. Smika could hear the unfamiliar heartbeat coming closer. The person that came into view was new to him, a young lady roughly his age. She looked almost like the queen, with a few noticeable exceptions. She too wore a tight black dress, sleeveless with a low-cut top. She was beautiful, Smika had to admit, but who was she?

"What do you think of her, Smika?" Queen Laxur asked. "Her name is Aladynia. She is my gift to you."

"Wow. She is pretty, my queen," Smika said.

The truth was, he was not interested in this Aladynia; he wanted Laxur. But he did not want to say that to his favorite sovereign. And the idea of another person as a gift was very off putting to him.

"Thank you for saying that I am pretty, my lord," Aladynia said with youthful glee.

He was cuter than what Laxur told her, and she was already in love with him. She held out her hand to Smika, like a princess would. She wondered what they could do together.

"My queen, would she be considered a princess? She is your creation, and she was made with your flesh," Polea said as she appeared beside Laxur.

"Yes, she is a princess. Do not worry, Polea, you are the official princess. Aladynia is only a crowned princess," Laxur explained. "You are more of an Arch-Princess."

Polea noticed Smika's reaction to Aladynia, and she understood his posture. She figured that it would take time for him to warm up to her. She knew that look well. And to be honest, Polea could understand Smika's concern.

"Eventually, Smika, she will grow into a magnificent woman very similar to me. She was made from my blood. Give her time. Who knows, in that time, you two might fall madly in love," Laxur said with hope that her plan worked.

Queen Laxur was oblivious to Smika's, and Polea's, feelings about this girl. Both Polea and Smika worried about this new girl Aladynia. But they would try to get along with this new girl.

Later, Princess Polea and Smika were in Polea's bedchambers, or the dark doll house, as other Darkcons called her room. Polea loved her toys, dolls, and games. Smika and Polea usually played with her games and toys. They were natural partners in battle and in theory.

"You and I have something in common, Smika," Polea said.

"Oh? What would that be, my princess?" Smika asked.

"Aladynia. She is not what I thought she would be. I did not expect her to be labeled a princess," Polea began.

"I did not think she would be a clone of the queen." Smika looked at Polea. "You are the princess as far as I am concerned, Polea."

His words made Polea smile. He had been kind to her, even though they were not friendly at first. But now Polea trusted this young man as the best little brother a woman like her could have. He wished no harm to her, and he was always willing to help.

"Thank you, Smika. What are we going to do about her though? She was made for you, and I suspect that our queen wishes for a child," Polea suggested. "Aladynia could be a test of this need."

"I do not know. She is nice, but she does not seem to be all there," Smika said.

"She is a fully formed person with a soul."

"She actually seems to only have part of a soul. She is so fixated on one thing at a time, and she seems to only have one emotion," Polea said.

"A very one-track mind," Smika added.

"That could be a problem," Polea thought out loud.

An explosion from space rocked the whole of Z'yon. Polea made a window appear so she could look out. Smika came up behind her and had binoculars with him. He was looking into the skies to see what was happening. Polea used her new enchanted vision to see up into the skies.

In the gray skies above, Polea and Smika saw tears form. They were heavenly gateways and a lot of Utopian and Consortium ship flying out. Polea counted at least ninety-four portals.

"What is happening?" Smika asked, worried.

"We have company," Polea said. "A lot of them."

"Asora is back?" Smika said.

"Either her or someone new," Polea replied.

In the throne room Princess Aladynia ran into Queen Laxur's arms, shaking in fear. She had never been in a battle before.

"My queen! What is happening?" the girl cried.

"Some fool is attacking me," Laxur sneered.

"Who would be so foolish?" Aladynia asked.

"We are about to find out," Laxur replied.

Nine human super dreadnought starships were firing on the planet below from orbit. As they did Utopian and Consortium troop carriers were sending down wave after wave of troop landers. The dreadnoughts were disrupting Darkcon troop movements and softening the areas where their troops were going to land.

A small fleet of Darkcon warships went up to meet the attackers. This time however the Utopian and Consortium ships opened fire with new deadlier weapons. Nuclear and Anti-Matter based weapons had been mounted on the ships.

The deadly weapons laid waste to the Darkcon forces. The ionizing radiation from these weapons kept the Darkcons from using their new power to heal. The Utopian ships had to go around the radiation bubbles, while the Consortium ships could go through them.

From the bridge of one of the carriers, Princess Asora, Lord Dominus, Lady T'ula, the Historian, and Countess Marien watched the attack, and the transport ships sent down landing ships.

"How long do you plan on attacking them?" Dominus asked.

"A few hours. Does that answer your question?" Asora said snidely. "A full planetary bombardment is required. And a few strategic nuclear and anti-matter strikes will coral the Darkcons into a place of my choosing."

Dominus and Asora were still at odds because of the test near the angel's home system. Asora seemed to think that she was at war with everyone. Or that was how this appeared to Dominus. This had to end. If Asora stopped here and wins. Then she should back down. Or if she decided to continue, then Asora might have to be dealt with as well. Dominus worried that Asora was the next threat. Asora would be the most dangerous threat. Laxur while mad with power, can be exhausted. Asora has a nearly unlimited super weapons and if what he overheard was true. The Historian gave her modifications. What those modifications are and what they were for, Dominus did not know.

"You know, your sister is eventually going to come up here and stop this," Marien pointed out.

"No, she will not. Those powers have made her lazy. I and the Historian will go down there," Asora said. "I have a nasty surprise for her."

"Why do you want me down there? I hate this miserable dirt ball. The last time I was here, I got a rash," the Historian complained.

"I need you, in case something goes wrong with the weapon," Asora pointed out.

"We are also going with you, princess," T'ula said, referring to Marien and Dominus.

"Fine," Asora said, and she turned back to the window. "Have the red guard, royal guard, and Uridans ready to move."

Chapter Fifty-Eight

Escape from Z'yon

An hour passed, and the bombardment moved beyond the fortress to another part of Z'yon. A large transport ship landed outside the walls of the damaged fortress. Out came dozens of Utopians, humans, and Uridan soldiers. With them was Princess Asora, Countess Marien, Lady T'ula, Lord Dominus, and the Historian. The Princess had the modified super nuclear weapon. She had it in a specially made case, which she was holding in her left hand.

"Breach the walls!" Asora ordered the troops. The soldiers blasted down the walls with magic and firepower. Bricks and debris flew, and many dead Darkcons were found.

In the darkened throne room, Queen Laxur was trying to figure out what was happening. She could not tell what the humans and the Utopians were up to. She was also sensing other beings that she was unfamiliar with. The queen was growing frustrated, and her subjects were becoming afraid.

The doors in the throne room were locked, but Laxur could hear a battle raging outside. It went silent, and the doors seemed to unlock themselves. A feminine figure in golden armor appeared out of the darkness, holding an odd little black sphere. Princess Asora was back, and she looked mad.

"So, baby sister, you have decided to come back. I must give you points on your entrance," Laxur said politely.

"Cut the crap, Laxur. I give you one chance to surrender," Asora demanded, squeezing the sphere.

"Or what, baby sister? Are you going to throw your toy at me?" Laxur mocked the Utopian Princess.

"Actually, Asaria, I plan to nuke you and burn your empire to the ground," Asora said, holding out the sphere.

Laxur stopped laughing and looked a little shocked.

"You are lying. The humans were forced to destroy their nuclear weapons after the Great War!" Polea yelled.

"You really are a bubble-headed bimbo, Polea. No one gives up an advantage like this," Asora stated.

"And I had some help." A massive, freakish monster appeared behind Asora. "Meet the Historian."

The Historian roared at Laxur and her minions.

"What is that thing?" Dari asked, repulsed by the monstrous creature.

"He is a resident of the planet Tera. He and his Uridans have sided with me against you, and he was kind enough to modify a few old nuclear weapons for me." Asora looked at the weapon in her hand. "This one is for you."

"I have to say, I am proud of you. Who would have thought that you had this in you? But your choice of weapons is a bit odd. You do realize that if you detonate that thing, you die with me," Laxur pointed out.

"I built a transporter on one of the ships. It will pull all Utopian and human forces out before the explosion," the Historian spoke.

"It can speak?" Hyea ducked behind Laxur after the monster roared.

The succubi and incubi backed away from the Historian and his gathering Uridan. The humans and Utopians were slowly entering the room.

"Well? What are you waiting for? Restrain them!" Polea ordered the soulless creatures.

"They will get slaughtered by the Uridan, you dumb blonde," Asora said.

Countess Marien, T'ula, and Dominus appeared behind Asora.

"So you brought the family down here with you. Where is Jeia, my dear brother?" Laxur asked.

"He is here. Jeia is on one of the ships above," Marien said.

The Queen looked at T'ula, and a wicked smile grew on her lips. "Have you enjoyed the great gift that I have given you, cousin?"

"Are you mad? I have finally figured out how to get used to this form. Unless you have finally succumbed to madness," T'ula explained.

"You were lied to, T'ula, all your life. I know who your father was. Just ask my dear old mother." Laxur pointed to Marien.

"What is she talking about?" T'ula asked Marien.

The countess looked just as stumped as T'ula. Dominus, however, knew something. "T'ula, your father was Borvaen Swaye. He was Countess Marien's great-uncle. Your birth mother fell in love with him, and they conceived you," Dominus explained.

T'ula was shocked. All this time, she had a biological family that could have helped her. Marien was not even aware that her great-uncle had a wife, let alone a child. He died long ago, taking that secret to his grave.

"Enough. Queen Laxur, what is your answer?" Asora yelled in a threatening tone.

"Do not speak to me in that tone, Asora!" Laxur roared. She sent a wave of black energy at Asora; however, it just washed over her, and the Princess did not even feel it.

"It works. Well, this is more like it," Asora said with an evil grin.

She walked toward her sister, bomb in hand. Laxur sent pulses of magic at Asora, again and again. None worked, and Asora was completely unfazed by Laxur's divine magic. She had found a way to defy the goddess, queen. The Darkcons were afraid of Asora for the first time. She could kill them all and burn the empire to the ground. She would be the first Utopian monarch in history to do the job.

"Will that bomb protect Asora from Laxur?" T'ula asked the Historian.

"It will protect her from the magic, but not from Laxur directly," the Historian responded. The mad Queen was frustrated and afraid.

Her baby sister was untouchable with magic, and she did not know what other things Asora had if she were to strike physically. She had to negotiate with Asora.

"Asora, if you promise not to destroy my empire, I will stop attacking your little kingdom. Deal?" Laxur asked, hoping the ploy would work.

"No" was all Asora said.

"Why not?" Laxur asked, flummoxed.

"You are too dangerous to continue to go unchecked. Either remove the power from yourself or accept imprisonment in the Tervi star system," Asora demanded.

"You are the one who is mad. My queen would never accept such terms," Polea interjected.

"You too, bubble head!" Asora said to Polea.

"All right! You want to fight." Polea made her jade armor appear. "Then let us fight."

The blond Princess walked in front of Asora with her jade bear sword in hand. Queen Laxur was giving more power and strength to Polea, making her stronger than normal. Polea was significantly bigger than Asora now, and she was shaped similarly to Laxur.

Asora did not bother unsheathing either of her swords. She believed all she needed was the nuclear weapon in her hand.

"Back off, you oversized bimbo" —Asora pulled out a special, advanced magnum revolver with uranium-tipped bullets—"or you are going to hit the floor very hard. You being bigger does not mean a damned thing. You are slower and dumber."

Polea growled in anger, and then Asora was hit by a rock. Smika was throwing rocks at the angry Utopian Princess.

"Kid! You are going to get it if you do not stop!" Asora threatened.

"Are you threatening my acolyte?" Laxur demanded.

Then a young girl who looked like Laxur charged at Asora and slammed into her. The force knocked the bomb out of her hands, and it rolled away.

"You stupid little bitch!" Asora roared and punched the girl in the face. Then she scanned the floor for the bomb, as did the others.

Aladynia was on the floor, bleeding and crying from Asora's powerful punch. Smika ran to her side.

"Why did you do that?" Smika asked.

"I wanted to show you that I was tough too, like you," Aladynia choked.

Asora and T'ula were scrambling to find the bomb. The Historian used his special eyes to track the radiation being admitted from the weapon. He analyzed the levels; they were rising. The Princess found it as bullets and energy bolts flew all around her.

"Uh, Princess, you may not want to touch that weapon," the Historian warned.

"Why?" Asora demanded.

"The radiation levels are rising. I think the shield has been compromised and the core is leaking," the Historian advised.

"That is not good," T'ula said. She had some knowledge of nuclear devices; Countess Marien and Lady Madimoy were kind enough to give her a brief education on the subject. She knew that a rise in radiation levels was dangerous for magical beings. If they were high enough, all life will get poisoned and die horribly.

"Find that bomb at all costs!" Queen Laxur ordered with a roar.

"Oh no, you do not, sister!" Asora zapped Laxur to get her attention.

"You dare?" Laxur blasted Asora again, but the attack did nothing. Laxur noticed the coins that Asora was wearing on her necklace. Their powers had changed, and they were able to protect Asora from her magic; however, a physical attack may still work.

The Queen got off her throne and charged at her little sister. Asora saw Laxur coming at her in a fit of rage. T'ula, however, slammed herself right into Laxur's side, forcing Laxur to the ground.

"You ungrateful elf bitch!" Laxur roared. The mad queen stood back up, facing down her elf equal. T'ula made her sword appear in a sparkle of white light and pointed it at Laxur. The Queen smiled at T'ula evilly.

"You really want to fight me, cousin? You just found out that you have the honor of being a member of my family, and the first thing you do to thank me is cross swords with me?"

A massive black sword appeared in Laxur's hand. "I am honored to be a part of Princess Asora's family. You have become a shame to us," T'ula said.

Laxur pointed her sword at T'ula and zapped her with a powerful bolt of black lightning. The elf lady was blown back and crashed into Asora. Asora felt like she was being crushed by T'ula's heavy body.

"Get off of me!" Asora cried out. T'ula was shoved off by a Utopian. It was Marevin, and he came with a shotgun.

"Where did you come from, cutie?" Laxur commented to Marevin.

"From the Hydron, in orbit," Marevin replied sharply. He pointed his gun at the Queen. He shot her several times with no effect.

"You really need a better plan. If you are trying to impress my baby sister, I do not think that she is even the least bit impressed. I am not," Laxur said, and then she changed her tune.

She wanted to torment Asora, and she thought of a way to do that.

The queen whipped herself into a purple vapor and surrounded Marevin. She reformed, holding him to her body. She held Marevin's head to her chest, and she raised his face to meet hers. The queen then kissed Marevin very passionately, and at the same time, she placed a powerful love spell on him. Asora's spirits fell watching this all happen. She was about to lose her closest ally and her future husband her love.

However, instead of becoming infatuated with the queen, Marevin shot her in the chest. The spell did not work on him. Laxur, shocked by this, released him, and the young lord shot her again and again. The spell had the opposite effect on Marevin; instead of loving Laxur, he hated her and wanted to kill her.

"Die, you useless bitch!" He blasted the queen again. After he exhausted his shells, Marevin backed away to reload. He was mumbling like a crazy man as he did.

The queen was undamaged by Marevin's crazed gun strike. She

was stunned that her spell backfired.

"You are so dead, little man," Laxur threatened. She swung her sword at him, and Marevin held his gun up to block Laxur's attack. She chopped through the shotgun and punched Marevin.

Asora was impressed with Marevin. She rushed to his side to help him.

Meanwhile, the Historian was tracking the nuclear bomb. T'ula had also recovered and was back up on her feet.

"Are you well, Marevin?" Asora asked.

"Yes, my Princess," Marevin replied to her.

"He is crazy," Laxur thundered.

"We will see when I rip out your guts and strangle you with your own intestines!" Marevin roared and then charged at the mad queen.

"Wow. What have I done to you? You are completely crazy," Laxur said and dodged Marevin's knife attack. The queen grabbed the knife and magically shattered it.

Marevin reached into his jacket and pulled out a big revolver. It was loaded with eight uranium-tipped bullets. Laxur could tell that the bullets were uranium-tipped because they were glowing blue. She knew that these bullets could do some serious damage to her, and Marevin might be able to kill her in his crazed state. Laxur vanished into a cloud of mist.

Princess Polea and Smika were next to challenge Princess Asora and Marevin. The blond Princess pointed her sword at Asora, and Smika had enchanted daggers.

"You, princess, are not going to win this," Smika threatened Asora.

"Hold your tongue, boy. You have no clue what is happening," Asora barked.

"You want to bet on that?" Smika said snidely.

She pointed her sword at Polea and zapped her with a powerful blot of energy. Both Polea and Smika were struck down hard by Asora's attack. This cleared the way for the Historian to grab the nuclear weapon. He analyzed the damage and discovered that its core had been cracked.

"Princess Asora, the core and the uranium containment unit are badly damaged!" the Historian yelled out.

"How dangerous is it?" T'ula asked.

"In twenty of your minutes, the core will meltdown and explode," the Historian explained. Queen Laxur reformed and was very worried. She knew that a nuclear bomb was powerful enough to do her extreme harm.

"Give me that," Asora ordered.

"Why? If you are exposed long enough, you will suffer from radiation poisoning," the Historian warned.

"Just do it!" the princess ordered.

The Historian gave the damaged, leaking, and partly glowing bomb to Asora. It was very hot to the touch, so she placed it on a nearby table. Marevin came up to Asora with a set of tools. Asora knew a lot more about nuclear technology than he did. She took a flat screwdriver and pried off the top to reveal the inner workings of the weapon.

The mechanism inside was more complex than Asora anticipated, but she did know what everything was and what all the components did. The Princess used the tools to keep her fingers from being burned by the leaking core.

"Can you fix it?" Laxur asked, very concerned.

"Quit disturbing me, and I may be able to repair it!" Asora yelled in frustration. "Or you can come down here and repair this damned thing yourself!"

Queen Laxur backed away from her little sister. She was insulted, but she did not want Asora to fail, for once.

An explosion erupted from the other side of the room. It was enough to send Asora to the floor and the bomb was shattered. The core was now broken and unstable. Marevin pulled Asora away before the blue radiation mist got too close to her. He threw the Princess to the floor behind him and doubled back himself.

"Damn it!" Asora cursed. "We need to get out of here."

Laxur grabbed Asora by her collar and lifted her up. "You! You brought this here, and you have killed us all!"

"Put her down, witch," T'ula ordered the queen. She had her sword at Laxur's throat.

"You stupid pointed-ear fool! Do you have not a clue as to what is going on? Your kind are too stupid to understand nuclear science," Laxur stated.

"Actually, bimbo, I know exactly what nuclear technology is and how it works. In fact, I have a much better understanding than you do. Now put our sister down!" T'ula retorted.

Queen Laxur refused, and then Countess Marien stepped in. "Do as she says, Asaria, NOW!"

"I do not take orders from you," Laxur barked.

"Oh yes, you will." Marien began to chant a spell. She glowed, and in a blinding light, Asora disappeared and reappeared next to T'ula.

"What the. . ." Laxur was struck by a powerful blow behind her knees. Countess Marien kicked both of Laxur's tendons behind her kneecaps, and then she punched Laxur in the face. For once, Laxur could feel pain.

"Yield, Asaria," Marien ordered to Laxur, who was now on the ground in pain.

"Never. I am a goddess. I do not yield to anyone, especially you," Laxur stated firmly.

Meanwhile, the Historian examined the now severely damaged and critical nuclear device. "We had better leave now," the Historian ordered, and he and his Uridan ran out of the fortress.

Thousands of people flooded out of the fortress and poured into the waiting ships. The human warships pulled human and Utopian forces out as fast as possible. The Darkcons slipped into the dark, and they killed each other getting into their ships.

Countess Marien used her powers to get everyone outside. "This is not exactly a safe distance!" the Historian yelled out.

"I could not get to one of my ships from inside because of someone's intense powers!" Marien implied to Laxur.

"Hold your tongue, Mother," Laxur barked.

"Enough! Everyone get to a ship!" Asora yelled.

"They have all left. They left us all behind!" Polea looked around with dread.

Everyone else looked around and confirmed Polea's assessment.

"This is not good," the Historian said. "Oh well, win or lose."

"How can you be so calm at the prospect of your demise?" Marevin yelled out.

"Because I can be copied. My bodies have been destroyed many times. I can afford it," the Historian said, as if he was joking.

"Your compassion is overwhelming, monster," Illumin said, depressed.

"No one is going to die today," Marien proclaimed. She gathered all the powers that she had.

Her angelic power was enough to withstand the radiation. A magical bubble formed around everyone gathered around Marien.

The bubble lifted into space. Once in orbit, Queen Laxur turned to see a blinding flash of light. A powerful nuclear bomb had detonated, but it was not powerful enough to destroy the planet like Asora and the Historian had intended. The bomb was more like a normal nuclear blast.

"Great. How are we going to get home?" Marevin complained.

Asora had an idea. "Historian, is the gateway we used on Tera still working?"

"It should be. In fact, there is one in orbit of the innermost moon of Tera," the Historian pointed out.

"That is good, but where is Tera?" Laxur demanded.

"On the other side of Z'yon's orbit, you oversized bimbo!" T'ula said.

"I am not a bimbo. You will address me as you would a Queen," Laxur roared.

"I will address a Utopian queen with respect. I hold you in contempt, at best. You are no queen and not a goddess. Hell, you are not even a decent lady," T'ula said defiantly.

Countess Marien managed to guide the bubble toward the other end of Z'yon's orbit. A blacked-out planet appeared in the distance—

Tera, the planet that Marien searched for so many years. But she could not go there now.

"I and the Uridans will go down to the transwarp gateway and activate the device," the Historian said.

Marien released the Historian and the Uridan. They drifted down to a massive ringlike space station orbiting the innermost moon of Tera.

"Magnificent," Marien said at the sight.

"Stop drooling, Mother," Laxur said rudely.

"I remember telling you something similar, Laxur," Asora retorted for Marien. The queen growled in frustration.

An hour later, the giant artifact activated. A portal formed in the center.

"Is the Historian coming with us?" Marevin asked.

"I hope not," Smika complained.

"No. This is his home, and here he will remain," Asora said.

"Good riddance," Laxur said.

The portal was fully formed, and Marien guided the bubble into it. The portal dumped the bubble in orbit of Evorn, then the portal collapsed. They entered the atmosphere and floated toward the palace.

Chapter Fifty-Nine
The Price of Vengeance

On the palace grounds of Evorn, the bubble that Marien created popped, and everyone landed safely on the ground. They all landed on their feet and looked around. They were safe, at least for the moment.

"It is good to be back, I guess," Marevin said with a hint of disdain.

"Oh yes, it is. And this saved me the time to come here and raze it to the ground," Laxur thundered.

"Not if I can help it, witch!" a strong male voice roared from the distance.

Archduke Frenzen appeared with a division of royal guardsmen. He had his sword drawn and ready for a fight that he knew was coming.

"Wait!" another man yelled.

It was Puro Aga. He approached the large group of people with many priests and priestesses. They looked to have been running to catch up to the soldiers and the bubble that Marien created.

"What the hell are you doing?" Marien demanded snidely to Aga.

"Do not speak to me in such away, human," Aga roared back.

"I will talk to you however I feel like. Answer my question, damnit!" Marien barked back.

"I am here with the priesthood and the royal guard to detain Asora for the attacks on the angel's territory," Aga stated.

"What?" Asora and several others said.

"How dare you!" Frenzen snarled.

"You actually attacked the angelic empire? Wow, you are very bold baby sister. Even I would not have done that, until now anyway," Laxur said.

"You cannot be serious!" Dominus said sharply.

"Dominus, your superiors have said otherwise. They have asked me to prosecute Asora on their behalf," Aga explained.

"Oh my. This is quite a change of events. My queen, perhaps we should aid them in this," Polea suggested.

"Puro Aga, I, Queen Laxur, and my empire will help you in this matter. So, there will be a truce," the dark queen proclaimed.

"Thank you, Queen Laxur." Aga turned to Asora, who was in complete shock. "Now, princess, come with me."

Asora shook her head. She thought that it was a very bad dream. Why was Dominus not doing anything? Why was her mother so powerless? Why was Laxur siding with Aga?

"No! You will not take me!" Asora vanished in a glitter of silver and gold light.

"Find her!" Aga yelled.

Queen Laxur merely watched as everyone frantically tried to figure out what was happening. But she was also unable to feel Asora anymore. Most likely the result of those nuclear devices of Asora's.

"Shall I give the order to our forces to assist in Asora's capture?" Polea asked.

"You may," Laxur replied. "And tell them I want Asora alive and unharmed."

"I understand," Polea said.

"I still wish for her to be with us," Laxur said. "She will be found and made to see the error of her ways."

"What about the puro?" Polea asked. "That man cannot be allowed to get to Asora first."

"If he harms Asora, I will make my displeasure known," Laxur said. "Speaking of."

Queen Laxur spotted Puro Aga talking to several of his priests and priestesses. They all turned to see Laxur approaching. They prepared for a fight.

"It is cute to think that you and your corrupt rabble can fight me," Laxur almost laughed.

"What do you want?" Aga demanded.

"I want to have Asora. She will be found and returned to the palace unharmed. Am I understood?" Laxur said. Then she lends in closer. "Because if anything happens to her that I do not like. You best prepare for an early grave. And not just you." Laxur then looked at all the priests and priestesses in attendance. "All of you will die screaming and only know pure agony in your final moments. Am I understood?"

"Yes," Aga said.

"Yes, what?" Laxur demanded.

"Yes, your majesty," Aga said with disdain.

Princess Asora reappeared on the other side of Evorn. She was not powerful enough to escape the world on her own. Evorn was not populated enough for her to be caught very easily. Only thirty-five million people lived on Evorn, so most of the planet was uninhabited. This continent was, for the most part, uninhabited, except for a village or two with, at most, fifty people. It was a summer night, and she was in the only rainforest area on Evorn. Summertime meant monsoons; the rain was heavy and warm. Asora was soaked to the bone, and she was lost. Still in her armor, Asora ran as soon as she heard people coming her way.

She figured that the puro and Laxur had sent hunting parties after her. They will be everywhere now. Asora's powers still worked, and her power could be sensed. So, she had to find a place to hide that could shield her powerful magical presence.

The princess ran in the other direction, toward a mountain chain. It was too wet for her use her wings, and if there were angels after her, she could be tracked and taken down easily. She could now hear them calling her name. She stayed as quiet as she could. The rain and noises of the nature around her did a good job of masking her noises and movements.

After five minutes of running, Asora stopped near a large boulder. She had not seen nor heard the hunting parties. She dared to peak and found that they were carrying torches and running off in another direction. Away from her and to the closest village.

Asora breathed a sigh of relief for a moment. The rain was soaking her and was the only thing keeping her cool. She then noticed something odd in the foliage near her. She went in closer to examine it. As she got closer, she could hear something calling to her. It was not anything her people would use, not this was technological. The moment Asora touched the object the ground beneath her opened.

Asora fell into a hole hidden in the thick vegetation. Asora tumbled and fell several meters. She was unable to stop her fall deeper into the cavern. She was finally deposited onto a metal floor in a dimly lit room. She was dizzy but after a moment regained her wits to look around.

In pain and bloodied, Asora slowly sat up, and she did not know where she was. The beaten-up princess looked around and saw what looked like a door. She went up to the door, and it glowed and opened. Once Asora walked through, the door shut, and the other room lit up. It was an elevator. Down it went, and she could see through the glass as she descended. Asora was taken deep into the interior of Evorn, and she was amazed at what she saw: towering machines, glowing platforms, and graceful holograms. The elevator opened, and Asora slowly walked out into the giant room.

The princess was greeted by a blue glowing orb. This thing reminded her of those alien machines back on Havaina a few months back. Then the Historian's words about the UR came to her mind.

"Welcome to Tamotan Colony Command and Control. Are you the new commanding officer sent by the Central Committee of the UR?" the orb asked Asora.

It scanned her with a beam of light. It then displayed the information it gathered from the beams of light. It was a biological readout of Asora. It was in a language that no longer existed.

"I do not believe that we have been introduced. I am Asora Serafus, Princess of the Utopian Kingdom," Asora introduced herself.

"Very well. I am Emband, the main central intelligence of the Tamotan Colony. I was created in the Seanalt Laboratories in the United Republics on Tera," Emband said.

"You were created on Tera?" Asora thought for a moment. "What is the Tamotan Colony?"

"This world is called Tamotan. In fact, I am having a complete scan done to catalogue the events," Emband said.

"This world is called Evorn," Asora said.

"That is a Z'yonic term. Why would anyone from the United Republics Colonial Command allow such a primitive name?" Emband asked. "It is almost insulting."

"This world was once a UR colony? Which species?" Asora asked.

"Human, of course. The United Republics was a human dominated nation and the most advanced and most powerful nation of the empires of Tera. It was one of twenty-nine human nations, which were part of a world with two hundred other nations," Emband explained.

"So all this was built by humans? And this was once a human-dominated world?" Asora thought out loud.

"Well, the very first settlers and terraformed were humans and insectoids. They made this world habitable from its original conditions. They then placed all the plant and animal life upon it," Emband explained. "May I ask a question of you now?"

"You may," Asora said.

"You are dressed oddly and speak in a language that is not normally spoken by a UR military officer. I am detecting in your nervous system, the required command and control nanites that generals of the UR military carry to assume control. Are you the first to return after so long?" Emband asked.

The nanites that the Historian gave her. They were allowing her to communicate with this UR intelligence. He did say that she could have control of the UR's technology. She now knew that the nanites were for generals. So, she could have control over the UR's arsenal wherever it was throughout the realm. She could have a way out after all. This UR was truly forward thinking and divine.

"I can answer some of your questioned. But I need to know more about what is going on, the status of the UR systems, and a possible escape or military need," Asora said.

"Why are you asking all these odd questions? It appears..." Emband trailed off, as if in thought. "Oh no. There is a massive infection on Tamotan."

"Infection? What do you mean?" Asora asked.

"There are roughly thirty four point two million individual units in primitive dwellings, and most of the concentration of the infection is on the Yio continent," Emband said. "Mostly concentrated there will make it easier to deal with them."

"Thirty-four point two million?" Asora whispered to herself. That was roughly the same number of nonhumans on Evorn. *Is this intelligence referring to the elves, centaurs, fairies, mer-people, and the other magical creatures?* "What is the infection?" Asora asked.

"They appear to be from Z'yon. These primitives are known for causing trouble and damaging the nature of worlds. Also damaging critical infrastructure. The United Republics Central Military Command has designated them an infestation and will not allow them to leave the main star system," Emband said.

Asora was at a loss for words. The United Republics humans of ancient times seemed to be racist toward any magical creatures. Then again, it seemed to be justified. This very technology could save her. If she could convince this Emband to allow her to take command. She could decide what happens now, and not leave her fate to chance once more.

"Asora, we must activate the colonial defense systems and eradicate this infestation. I will take us to the central core. I will need you to bring the main controls online in the core to activate the defense grid," Emband said.

The two then made their way through the dimly lit rooms and chambers that Asora only caught glimpses of. She noticed more traditional mechanical drones moving about. She also could have sworn that she saw Uridan or another variant of them.

"I have a question for you," Asora said.

"Of course," Emband said.

"Are there other worlds that the UR colonized in this region of space?" Asora asked.

"Yes. This entire region is a part of the United Republics Colonial Command. The main command core world is Havaina. The defense grid was activated recently because of a scan of a nearby star system. An alien ship was detected, and the defense grid had to fend off the locals to get them out of the way of the machinery," Emband explained.

"A ship? What kind of ship?" Asora asked. "It was not an accident?"

"Unknown, but it was enough to activate the main planetary defense grid," Emband explained. "And no, it was no accident."

Princess Asora walked into another large dimly lit room. At the center was a massive hologram map of Evorn, or Tamotan as it was originally known to UR. The map showed the settlements, villages, farms, and the palace on the opposite side of the planet. The map also revealed the locations of all remaining UR technologies, buildings, other constructs, and installations.

"Here is where you can activate the primary planetary defense grid, Asora," Emband said.

"What will happen if I do activate the defense grid?" Asora asked.

"Isn't it obvious? The infestation will be eradicated in one standard hour, then the UR will be able to send replacements without interference," Emband explained.

"Eradicated? How?" the princess asked.

"A multitude of methods will be used: high-energy based weapons will generate superstorms that will cause coastal flooding, which is where most of the infestation exists. They will melt the polar ice caps, and they will generate continent-crushing super quakes," Emband said calmly. "After that for the remaining survivors the Type Four Uridan Class military attack drones will hunt them down and terminate with extreme prejudice."

This realization horrified Asora for a moment. But then again, the whole kingdom had turned on her, and the empire wanted her as a prize. This place seemed to be offering her an answer, an escape. The question was, should she use this great weapon and rid herself of these problems? If she did, more than thirty-four million people would die. She would become something far worse than her sister. Laxur thought that she was a goddess, but Asora held the fate of life itself. Not just Evorn, but the entire Realm was now in her hands.

Emband showed Asora to the control console. The console was alive with holograms and glowed blue and green. The symbols were all unfamiliar to Asora, but she had seen them before on Tera. They all then changed to appear more familiar to Asora. She figured that the nanites in her nervous system were communicating with the technology around her. This was why the UR machinery was so welcoming and obedient to her. It saw her as if she was its lord and master.

"It must be done in order to vanquish the infestation and restore Tamotan to its natural state," Emband said. "And ready for UR recolonization."

"But everyone will die," Asora whimpered.

"These parasites are below animals, according to the ecological society in the UR Committee," Emband informed Asora. "They are more destructive than a type zero civilization in the early stages of industrialization."

"No! I will not," Asora said.

"What! Why?" Emband asked, flabbergasted. "They must be destroyed."

"I value life. You may think that the Utopians are parasites, but I do not," Asora said. "Much to my surprise."

"These creatures are a threat! They are evil!" Emband started to yell. "They cannot even live without murdering or enslaving each other."

"They can be saved. I want to save them, just like I was saved." Asora began to cry.

"You have done well, Emband. She has passed my test. Thank you," another male voice echoed through the room.

"Who is there? Show yourself!" Asora demanded.

"You seem to think that you command the stars, but you are still a child with a great and terrible burden—a destiny that you were never supposed to have." A powerful old angel appeared from a golden light.

"How was my performance, Great One?" Emband's tone changed, as if he was now a different entity.

"You have done well, Emband. I was even fooled," the angel said to the hologram.

"I do enjoy a good performance," Emband said with a hint of humor.

"You look familiar," Asora said.

"I am not surprised that you do not remember me. You were only a five-day-old infant when we last saw each other. I am Talaron, Lord of all Servants of the Divine," Talaron introduced himself.

"Grandfather? Why are you here?" Asora sobbed. The old man embraced Asora and allowed her to cry into his chest. "Why is all this happening to me?"

"This was your final test, my littlest granddaughter, and you passed. Your old fate has been stripped away, and a new destiny is now awaiting you," Talaron explained. Asora looked completely confused. "You and your sister's fates were switched at young ages. Asaria was not supposed to be the abomination that she is now. That was supposed to be you, and Asaria was meant to be the princess. However, something happened, and your destinies were switched," Talaron said.

"I was supposed to be evil?" Asora began to cry more.

"Your father, in his youthful arrogance, actually disapproved of your birth. I and others however, disagreed and showed him that you were worth the life that you have and far more. You have become a redeemer of souls," Talaron said with a smile.

"I knew that my father felt disdain for me, and I felt no love from him, but I did not know that was the reason," Asora sobbed.

"Your uncle felt the same way I did, and he did what he could to make sure that you were a better person than what destiny dictated," the old angel explained.

"I remember Uncle Borvaen. He was more of a father to me than my real one was." Asora rose and investigated Talaron's eyes. "Why did you say that your people wanted me arrested?"

"What? Whoever told you that was lying. I gave no such order!" Talaron now seemed angry.

His anger made him frighten. No one crossed the lord of angels and lived to tell the tale. He knew of Asora's weapons tests and allowed it. Again, another means of testing to see who Asora was. Plus, there was another reason why he allowed Asora to carry it out. And he had not revealed that reason. But in the end Asora did him a service. Now it was his turn to help her.

"The puro, the Darkcons, the Utopian court, and the rest of the kingdom?" Asora said slowly.

Talaron growled with anger, and his fists hardened. He then remembered that he did not tell for his reasons why he allowed Asora to carry out the tests. But to have his order and words twisted was unforgivable.

"Shall I return you to the palace?" Emband asked Talaron.

"Your test is completed, Princess Asora Swaye Serafus. You are the emissary of the light and my herald. Now it is the Utopian Kingdom's turn to face the great test. You will give them this test and make them face reality. It is important that you not say anything about this. About me, what the Historian did to your nervous system. They will be faced with a choice: keep you as their leader, and their chance for survival is good. Remove you, and they are doomed to the abyss. You will either save the soul of the kingdom, or they will doom it themselves," Talaron explained.

"Thank you, Grandfather. I will do what I can," Asora said, and she kissed him on the cheek.

Talon hugged Asora one more time. Asora vanished in a sparkling glitter of gold and silver. Talon now had other work to do. For another storm was coming.

"Will she be okay?" Emband asked Talaron with worry in his electronic voice.

"She will. It will be hard for her at first. But when the second terror comes, she will have a much easier time guiding them to salvation." Talon explained. "Were you ever able to figure out where that ship came from that was over Haviana?"

"Its identity was unknown, and its design was unfamiliar. But I was able to track its course from beyond the void," Emband said.

"They will come. It is only a matter of time now," Talon said.

Princess Asora reappeared inside the throne room of the palace. She was surrounded by the elites of Utopian society and several soldiers. They were all shocked by her sudden reappearance.

"Asora? Where did you come from?" King Adium of the fairies asked as he floated up to Asora.

"I was enlightened. And I have a mission now," Asora replied.

"A mission?" Adium was confused.

"You will see, my lord," Asora said.

"Well, I will help you in any way that I can," Adium promised.

Then Asora's four ladies-in-waiting buzzed up to her with relief, and they hugged and kissed her with reverence. They so desperately missed her. Dame Sarea also came up to Asora and bowed to her. She rose back up ready for Asora to command her.

Madimoy and Jeia were next to come up to Asora. They both practically latched onto her in a powerful bear hug.

"Princess, you are well!" Madimoy hugged Asora.

"Nice to see you too," Asora replied.

"As am I," said Lady T'ula, smiling.

She missed her cousin greatly. T'ula could sense that Asora's soul and spirit seemed to have been restored. By what she did not know, but she imagined that Asora would tell her in time.

"You have guts and recklessness. I like that," the elemental demon Rakon said.

"Thank you, all of you. I should go and confront the kingdom," Asora said and walked off.

She did not walk out alone. They all followed her out of the throne room to meet the rest who hunted her.

"Maybe we should allow them to come to you," Jeia suggested.

An hour later, Puro Aga was informed that Asora had reappeared in the palace and that she was more defiant than ever. T'ula found the crown, and T'a magically protected the throne for Asora. By doing this, she had proclaimed that Asora was still the rightful ruler of the Utopian Kingdom. Marevin and Frenzen were also protecting her, making access to her difficult.

Puro Aga and his priests and priestesses confronted the defiant Princess Asora on her throne. Asora looked on with defiance. Almost begging him to attack so she could have a reason to fight.

"You have always been trouble, but not as much as this," Aga said to Asora.

"And you are a liar, and a bad one at that," Asora said.

"What are you talking about?" Aga said, now a little worried.

"I was informed that the higher powers in the angel empire did not give such orders. I have, in fact, met with the lord of angels himself. He told me that he was happy about the side effects. The test made Hailospont invulnerable to attacks from above. The angels can still get through, but no one else can. They can still live on the planet without any ill effects," Asora explained.

"I had no idea," Aga stammered.

Countess Marien and King Adium looked menacingly at the puro and the other Utopians. Queen Laxur, who had appeared during Asora's explanation, was furious. She did not like what she was hearing. But she assumed that something like this was happening anyway.

"The lord of angels himself came to you and told you this? What else did he tell you?" Queen Laxur questioned.

She had always wanted to meet the lord of angels, but Laxur knew nothing about him. She wanted to know what Asora knew about him. A meeting with the lord of all angels was an event that could never be ignored.

"This is not over, Asora. I will see you defeated," Aga threatened.

"Go ahead and try, old man. You will regret it." Asora said back.

"While then," Laxur started. "Until your fate is sealed. I will be staying here to make sure I get what I want." Laxur looked around her. "Have her locked up."

"You do not give orders here," Freemen pointed out.

"Do you want me to unleash myself upon this world again?" Laxur asked. "Do as I say, and I will not harm you."

Queen Laxur walked out as the Royal Guard put Princess Asora in chains and marched her off to one of the palace's many towers. There she would remain. And there Laxur could work her terrible purpose upon the princess.

The queen will rule, and she has won.

Chapter Sixty
Before the Storm

Deep in the endless void of space, a large craft was flying through the darkness. Beyond the black of the Great Void was indeed another part of a larger universe. A universe full of galaxies, stars, quasars, and more.

The massive spacecraft was of unknown design, and not built by anyone from the Realm. It in fact looked very much like a massive bird with wings outstretched. It had a large complex of towers on its dorsal that glowed and glittered in the darkness. The colors that dominated its hull were blacks, grey, greens, and reds. On some parts of its hull were of an alien writing.

The giant ship was traveling in normal space at a leisure pace. It did not suspect any harm would befall it. Its hull was made of nearly indestructible materials, and it was armed with only the deadliest and most formidable weaponry. It was a powerful warship of such scope and power that worlds, empires, nations, and civilizations feared.

A vast and powerful white and blue energy wave surged through the void. The very same energy that exploded from Queen Laxur when she became a goddess. Her desire to tell the entire universe of the birth of a new goddess had managed to reach beyond the Realm and into the wider universe.

This massive and powerful wave of energy struck a massive alien starship. The wave slammed into the hull like water on a wooden ship's hull. It knocked the alien vessel off its original course, and it started

Before the Storm

to tumble in space. Electrical arcs fired across its vast hull. The armor plating absorbed most of the energy, but it could not direct it. This meant that the energy was directed to several places outside and inside. The lights that shined from eh ship's various windows, and sensor technologies all went dark. The alien starship was now adrift.

Inside the ship, the lights went out and alarms blared loudly. The red emergency lighting came up. The alarm klaxons roared to alert the crew. The ship shook violently, sending machinery and people flying in every direction. Explosions tore through everything, sending waves of electrical discharges in every direction.

The artificial gravity was also damaged and caused everything inside to free float. This also had the deadly effect of shrapnel cutting through the crew members as they raced to repair and recover their ship.

The crew were in specialized armor and carried various tools to help them save their ship. They all screamed at each other in their native languages. They all fought to be heard over the arms and noises from the damage.

A breach in the hull forced out gasses, debris, and bodies. The hole was sealed by an energy field. The breach was formed from cracks in the weakest points in the hull. One crack sealed and another formed nearby.

The constant shaking also created new hull breaches and catching many unaware crew members by surprise. These unlucky souls were blown out into space. It they were lucky they were in their armor and have life support systems on. The ones who managed to regain control used magnetic boots to attach themselves to the ship's outer hull.

Meanwhile the ship's main computer was trying to reactive systems to regain control. Some were successful in stabilizing the ships orientation.

"Warning. Energy distortion has disrupted primary systems. Main power has been disabled. Multiple hull breaches detected across all decks. Federation Force One's primary core is offline. Emergency power activated," an automated voice blared over an intercom system.

Artificial gravity was restored, forcing everyone and everything to come crashing back down to the deck. Several people cried out in pain as they were crushed by either debris or the emergency gravity, which was heavier than normal. Their crew mates dug them out and hauled them to a safe location.

Hundreds of the crew were still operating in the dark. The main lighting system was damaged still, and emergency power was only to be used for the most critical of systems. Life support being one of them.

"Warning, two percent of the ship is currently uninhabitable, damaged sustained is currently at sixty two percent," the same automated voice said over the intercom.

Elsewhere inside the ship, in a dark room only lit by red light, three figures approached a lit table. Once came in by the door at the rear of the room. A second came in by a beam of red light. The third seemingly arose from eh deck below. They converged to the center of the room where a large table with controls and a complex holographic display appeared. The center of the table projected a large hologram that displayed information on astronomical, ship's information, and other things in an alien language. They came at the holo display table at the exact same time. The room was still dark with only dim red light, so they could barely see each other. The one ion the center activated the only working normal light source. It was only enough to illuminate the table. It swung around with the movement of the ship which was still tumbling through the void. The three did not seem affected by the ship's movement.

"The Tricerian Council is now in session," a male voice announced with authority.

"The energy wave that struck Federation Force One has an energy level that is too high for us to measure, but we were able to isolate an approximation of its origin," an older female voice informed.

She swiped her hand across the hologram showing astronomical data and measurements of the wave. She showed them a rough approximation of the wave. It also showed them in both real time and projected course as well as a possible origin of the wave. All based on the limited collected data they had.

"This galactic group is quarantined because of the strange energy and savage people. Our emissaries were murdered by the locals. If they have created weapons using such high energy, they are now a threat to us," another older male voice said.

"Also, the dark matter zone makes travel there difficult," the female informed.

"I doubt that those primitives have developed such powerful weapons, let alone the energy source needed to generate them. Now, Tribune, what else do we know about them?" the first male asked in an almost-threatening tone.

"Not much else," the older man said. "Other than they seem to possess unnatural capabilities that are a danger if they go beyond their confinement. We should be thankful for that dark matter zone. It's an effective barrier between the civilized multiverse and these things."

"Wasn't it rumored that some of our own are in that quarantined galactic system? The humans," the female said.

"The humans? If they still exist? This would great. They may know where Tera is. Our home," the younger male voice said with a hint of excitement. "Humans were our ancient ancestors."

"Back to the matter at hand. What do we do about this problem?" the older Tribune asked. "This was most likely an attack upon the Federation."

"I recommend observation," the female said to the Tribune. "It might have been a natural phenomenon."

"What natural phenomenon could do this?" the younger male said.

The younger male then swiped his hand across the hologram to show the older woman a series of star charts with the course of the wave. It showed data that was impossible for them to believe. This could not be natural. Or anything that they knew of to be natural.

"The amount of energy required to damage even this ship the way it did requires a series of supernovas or a long gamma burst. Neither of which struck us." The younger man said. "Our hull is made of Nuetronium for crying out loud."

"I am getting reports that the wave has accelerated in speed, spreading throughout our territory and even into our enemy's territory as well. Damaging systems and causing chaos on our worlds," the older man called the Tribune said as he activated the news feed.

It showed them images of their worlds being badly affected by the wave. Destruction on a scale that they thought should not be possible. Cities crumbling, and ships being damaged if not outright destroyed.

"Perhaps we should go there in force and investigate?" the older woman suggested.

"No, Magistrate. The primitives must be destroyed before the problem gets out of hand," the Tribune said. "If this was indeed an attack, then we, as the defenders of the natural order of the multiverse, must eliminate the threat."

"Tribune! We cannot go about the multiverse crushing any that threaten us," the Magistrate retorted. "It would be a waste of our time, resources, equipment, and manpower. We must know what we are dealing with!"

"First off we need to know what the fuck we are dealing with," the younger man snapped.

"That's just it," the magistrate said. "Our information on them is limited."

"The Feros Hegemony is a threat that we can tolerate and contend with, because we know them. This region, and the animals that inhabit the Quarantine Zone, we know virtually nothing about!" the Tribune stated forcefully.

"We need more information before we can act," the Magistrate said.

"What does the military know about them, and don't give me that classified crap." The Tribune looked at the younger man.

The man took out a glowing keycard and inserted it into the console. A red file appeared in front of him, and he opened the holographic file to reveal its contents. It showed pictures, stop images, recordings that showed what could be inside the zone.

"What you are seeing is the collected data that the military was able to obtain from eyewitnesses, explorers, and survivors." The younger man paused for a moment. "From what we can tell, there are two major factions along with a variety of smaller ones as well. The numbers of creatures that inhabit the zone are a large variety like our own." He switched the images around to show more. "As you can see from these files, many of them are violent and cruel with no purpose. As for the two major factions, as far as we can tell, there was a dispute of religious fervor. The original faction, something calling itself the Utopian Kingdom, has been the cause of most of the violence. As for the other faction, calling itself the Darkcon Empire, seems to lash out like a cornered animal."

"Fascinating," the Tribune said cynically. "More primitives and religious dumb fucks."

"So the military has been busy in the Quarantine Zone, illegally," the Magistrate pointed out, reminding him.

"We were monitoring a potential threat. That was reason enough to justify our actions," the younger man said back.

"How were the Xon able to get through the dark matter void without Legion Spheres?" The Magistrate asked.

"It's classified," the younger man also pointed out.

"Of course, it is," the older woman said rolling her eyes in annoyance.

The tribune was sifting through the data being displayed to him. She found nothing remarkable about the inhabitance of the Quarantine Zone. In fact, he hated everything about them. They were lower than animals as far as he was concerned. Then something caught his eye.

"What is this?" the Tribune asked, pointing to an image. "Are those advance electronic weapons?"

"We did find out through scans that one of two races inside was, in fact, using technology," the man said.

"What was their civilization development level?" the Magistrate asked.

"We are a four point six level, and I'll use that as a reference. Many of the factions inside the zone are barely zero point five at best. However, one of the races appears to be a strong two point seven. They even have interstellar capabilities and power generation. It appears that they don't share their advancements with the rest. A good thing for us," the younger man said. "They could be the humans we suspect still live."

"I suppose," the Tribune added. "That still does not explain the wave. Is it possible that this advanced faction generated the wave?"

"Doubtful, according to these files, the advanced race uses primitive nuclear fusion reactors or probably possesses prototype levels of antimatter-based power sources. None of which could do what that wave did," the Magistrate pointed out.

"So, that rules them out," the Tribune said. "Anyone else?"

"It would seem that technological evolution is limited to the faction that has the power systems," the younger man said.

"Then they would know who or what generated that fucking wave," the older man said. "As far as I can see this faction is the only intelligent species or civilization in the QZ."

"This is the problem," the younger man said. "Our information on them is too limited.

The older man's attention turned to another analysis of the energy wave. "That's not possible!"

"What?" the Magistrate asked.

"The wave has a biological signature in it. A life form possibly generated it," the younger man said as he saw the same data as the tribune.

"What kind of life form could do this?" the Magistrate demanded.

"Unknown, but we need to find it," the tribune said. "And kill it."

"We can send advanced tactical force into the Quarantine Zone to track down the life form," the younger man suggested. "And terminate it."

"No. We will go there in force and control the situation before the problem spreads beyond the quarantine," the older male proclaimed. "And more chaos spreads."

"Is that even necessary?" the Magistrate asked.

The tribune then pulled up another holographic data feed. This one had an official seal upon it. It was a government document meant for these three only. The tribune opened it and the other two were given a holographic copy of the same data document.

"The Assembly has contacted us, and they are authorizing whatever the Tricerian Council deems necessary to contend with the source of the wave and anything else that may potentially threaten us or anyone else," the Tribune informed his fellow councils.

"A small, advanced attack force can be deployed immediately," the younger man said.

"That will not do," the tribune said.

"Why not?" The magistrate asked.

"The Assembly has also decided that this is a big enough threat to warrant full military mobilization and action," the tribune said.

"Against type zeros?" The younger man asked annoyed at the thought. "I doubt they even have indoor plumbing. So, explain to me why I should deploy a full force against them?

"The destruction that this wave has caused is one," the tribune pointed out.

"I need time to gather information before I authorize an attack," the younger man said.

"Time is one thing you don't have," the Tribune said. "The Assembly has officially declared war upon the QZ and all that live in it."

"Then it is done," the Magistrate said.

"Well then, praetor. What are your orders as pro-counsel of the Federation?" the tribune asked.

The pro-counsel thought for a moment. He had limited information and was not going to be foolish. So, he did the one thing that made logical sense to him. He typed in a series of commands into the computer in front of him. It brought out a list of military forces across his domain. And his domain was vast indeed. He did not want to fight another war. So, this one will be quick.

"Prepare ninety legions for a full-scale invasion of the Quarantine Zone," the Praetor ordered.

"Ninety Legions? One is enough to overwhelm a galaxy. We believe that ten would suffice," the Magistrate said.

"With the limited time I've been given, the limited information is have. And the demands for blood from the Assembly. This is the most logical option," the pro-counsel said.

"I agree with the Magistrate. Ninety is overkill," the tribune said. "But war is your area of expertise after all. So, who am I to argue with such a legendary war hero. You won the final Titan War."

"What are you babbling on about?" The pro-counsel demanded.

"A war like this makes you seem too violent and could end up destroying anything useful that could exist there," the tribune said.

"You don't have the capacity to think like a soldier," the pro-counsel said.

"An unfortunate fact," the tribune replied.

"I want this crisis to be dealt with as quickly as possible. We give them no time to react, and we can then secure the zone in a short time. There may be other factors that we are not aware of. We strike hard and fast. We will stop this problem before it is beyond our control."

"What's there to expect?" The tribune demanded. "You said it yourself these are savages."

"That maybe true, but again we may not have the whole image of the battlefield that we now stand in sight of," the pro-counsel explained. "Have you ever been in a war? A battle where tactics are required to win the cycle?"

"No, we haven't," the magistrate said. "That's why you were elected."

"Since I'm being forced to fight this war. We are going to do this my way," the pro-counsel said. "Is that understood?"

"Of course. War is your domain," the magistrate said. "I will adhere to your command on this matter. As will the Yesoid."

"The Lasran will also obey your directives on all matters of this new war," the Tribune said.

"My first order will be this," the pro-counsel looked at the other two. "Tribune, Magistrate, ready the Federation for war. Muster the Legions and prepare for a multi-front attack. We will strike in one giga cycle."

"Every good," the tribune said.

"Put the whole Federation in to war mode. Mobilize the population, begin mass production of materials," the pro-counsel said.

The tribune and magistrate sent the pro-counsel's orders back to their home world. And to all the worlds of the Federation.

"Orders have been received and are being acknowledge across our territory," the magistrate said.

"Our people demand justice. The pro-counsel is legendary war hero that will lead us to victory. And we will show these savages that they cannot withstand our might," the tribune declared.

"Are you done?" The pro-counsel demanded in a very annoyed tone.

"Very much," the tribune replied.

"Never claim victory before the war beings," the pro-counsel said. "It is a very dishonorable and quite frankly a stupid thing to do."

"As you wish, pro-counsel," the tribune said.

"The Federation is now at war. We march to meet this enemy on the space of battle. And there we will decide their fate," the pro-counsel said. "Or ours."

"Very well pro-counsel, war it will be. May Korena have mercy on these poor fools," the Magistrate said.

Appendix

Glossary

Asora - (a-soar-a)
Jeia - (jay-au)
Laxur - (lux-sore)
Sysu - (sigh-Sue)
T'a - (Ta-A)
Rakon - (ra-con)
Asaria - (Au-sar-E-au)
Marien - (mar-En)
Marevin - (mar-Eve-en)
Frenzen - (fren-zen)
Dari - (dar- I)
Evorn - (E-vorn)
Havaina - (have-A-na)
Dorien - (Door-E-un)
Polea - (Pole-E-a)
Smika - (Sm-I-k-u)
Hyea - (high-a)

Nona - (No-nu)
Aga - (aug-a)
Irantanco - (I-ran-tank-O)
Z'yon - (s-I-on)
Golcon - (goal-con)
Gourni - (go-run-E)
B'nei - (ba-knee)
Friea - (free-au)
Rayne - (rain)
Madimoy - (mad-au-mow-E)
T'ula - (two-la)
Rowaton - (row-au-ton)
Darkcon - (dark-con)
Sarea - (sar-re-au)
Yane - (yay-n)
Aladynia (ala-den-yay)
Emband (M-band)

Factions

Utopian Kingdom: The main faction that is led by the main protagonist Princess Asora. This nation is a fusion of five major nation states and four smaller states. The Human Consortium or just the Consortium is one such state. A monarchy that has a king, queen, prince, or princess chosen from one of the highest noble families of the kingdom. A royal court that is made up of representatives from every noble family, house, and other powerful members of the kingdom. The capital world is Evorn. An oxygen rich world with vast oceans and large lands of mountains and fields. The Utopian Kingdom is also nation of many races. The kingdom is many millions of years old and a long-storied history.

Darkcon Empire: The secondary faction that is led by the main antagonist Queen Laxur. A unified single state under an absolute monarchy. Like its primary enemy the Utopian Kingdom the Darkcon Empire is ruled by kings, and queens. The title of emperor or empress is reserved only for the greatest of its leaders. The House of Lords is the Darkcon equivalent of the Utopian royal court. The Darkcon's are made up of Great Houses and powerful military unions. The capital world is called Dorien. A dark skied world but full of life and frequented baby super storms. The Darkcon Empire is not as old as the Utopian Kingdom but is a long-lived nation, home to many species, just like the Utopian Kingdom.

The Clan: A group of pirates and rogues that roam the realm. They were once originally Utopian citizens that found life unbearable or were cast out for various crimes or reasons. Often the clan clashed with its main opponent the deadly terrorist force the Vanguard. Often lead by a fleet captain or the council captains.

The Vanguard: The main terrorist force that wages war against primary the Utopian Kingdom but on occasion the Darkcon Empire as well. A breakaway faction from the Consortium five hundred years prior. After the end of the Great War. Lead by the Lord High General and a shadow council.

Printed in the USA
CPSIA information can be obtained
at www.ICGtesting.com
LVHW041228261023
762201LV00001B/3